ENID BLYTON'S
CIRCUS STORIES

Illustrated by Susan Hunter
and Lesley Smith

RED FOX

A Red Fox Book

Published by Random Century Children's Books
20 Vauxhall Bridge Road, London SW1V 2SA

A division of the Random Century Group

London Melbourne Sydney Auckland
Johannesburg and agencies throughout the world

Mr Galliano's Circus
First published by George Newnes 1938
Beaver edition 1979, Reprinted 1982 and 1987
Text © Darrell Waters Limited 1969
Illustrations © The Hamlyn Publishing Group 1979

Hurrah for the Circus!
First published by George Newnes 1939
Beaver edition 1980, Reprinted 1985
Text © Darrell Waters Limited 1969
Illustrations © Hutchinson Publishing Group 1980

Circus Days Again
First published by George Newnes 1942
Beaver edition 1979, Reprinted 1982 and 1987
Text © Darrell Waters Limited 1969
Illustrations © The Hamlyn Publishing Group 1979

Enid Blyton is the Registered Trade Mark of Darrell Waters Ltd

Come to the Circus
First published by George Newnes 1948
Beaver edition 1979, Reprinted 1985
Text © Darrell Waters 1969
Illustrations © Hutchinson Publishing Group 1979
Red Fox edition 1992
First published in this collected edition 1992

Printed and Bound in Great Britain by
Cox & Wyman Ltd, Reading, Berks

ISBN 0 09 914131 0

1

MR GALLIANO'S CIRCUS

Contents

1. The circus comes to town

One morning, just as Jimmy Brown was putting away his books at the end of school, he heard a shout from outside:

'Here comes the circus!'

All the children looked up from their desks in excitement. They knew that a circus was coming to their town and they hoped that the circus procession of caravans, cages and horses would go through the streets when they were out of school.

'Come on!' yelled Jimmy. 'I can hear the horses' hoofs! Goodbye, Miss White!'

All the children yelled good morning to their teacher and scampered out to see the circus procession. They were just in time. First of all came a very fine row of black horses, and on the front one rode a man dressed all in red, blowing a horn. He did look grand!

Then came a carriage that looked as if it were made of gold, and in it sat a handsome man, rather fat, and a plump woman dressed all in pink satin.

'That's the man who owns the circus!' said somebody. 'That's Mr Galliano – and that's his wife! My, don't they look fine!'

Mr Galliano kept taking off his hat and bowing to all the people and the children round about. Really, he acted just like a king. He had a very fine moustache with sharp-pointed ends that turned upwards. His top hat was shiny and black. Jimmy thought he was simply grand.

Then came some white horses, and on the first one, leading the rest, was a pretty little girl in a white, shiny frock. She had dark-brown curls, and eyes as blue as the cornflowers in the cottage gardens near by. She made a

face at Jimmy, and tried to flick him with her little whip.
She hit his wrist and made him jump.

'You're a naughty girl!' shouted Jimmy. But the little
girl only laughed and made another face. Jimmy forgot
about her when he saw the next bit of the procession.
This was a clown, dressed in red and black, with a high,
pointed hat; and he didn't walk along the road – no, he
got along by turning himself over and over on his hands
and feet, first on his hands and then on his feet, and then
on his hands again.

'That's called turning cartwheels,' said Tommy, who
was standing next to Jimmy. 'Isn't he clever at it? See,
there he goes, like a cartwheel, over and over and round
and round!'

Suddenly the clown jumped upright and took off his
hat. He turned over on to his hands again, and popped his
hat on his feet, which were now up in the air. Then the
clown walked quickly along on his hands so that his feet
looked like his head with a hat on. All the children
laughed and laughed.

Next came a long string of gaily-coloured caravans.
How Jimmy loved these! There was a red one with neat
little windows at which curtains blew in the wind. There
was a blue one and a green one. They all had small chimneys, and the smoke came out of them and streamed away
backwards.

'Oh, I wish I lived in a caravan!' said Jimmy longingly.
'How lovely it must be to live in a house that has wheels
and can go away down the lanes and through the towns,
and stand still in fields at night!'

The horses that drew the caravans were not so fine-
looking as the black and white ones that had gone in
front. Jimmy hardly had time to look at them before
there came a tremendous shout down the street:

'There's an elephant!'

And, dear me, so there was! He came along grandly,
pulling three cages behind him. He didn't feel the weight
at all, for he was as strong as twenty horses. He was a
great big creature, with a long swinging trunk, and as he

reached Jimmy he put out his trunk to the little boy as if he wanted to shake hands with him! Jimmy was pleased. He wished he had a biscuit or a bun to give the elephant.

The big animal lumbered on, dragging behind it the cages. Two of them were closed cages and nothing could be seen of the animals inside. But one was open at one side and Jimmy could see three monkeys there. They sat in a row on a perch, all dressed in warm red coats, and they looked round at the children and grown-ups watching them, with bright, inquisitive eyes.

'Look! There's another monkey – on that man's shoulder!' said Tommy. Jimmy looked to where he pointed and, sure enough, riding on the step of the monkey's cage was a funny little man, with a face almost as wrinkled as the monkey's on his shoulder. The monkey he carried cuddled closely to the man and hugged him with its tiny arms. As they passed the children the monkey took off the man's cap and waved it at the boys and girls!

'Did you see that?' shouted Jimmy in delight. 'That monkey took off the man's cap and waved it at us! Look! It's putting it back on his head now. Isn't it a dear little thing?'

At last the procession ended, and all the horses, cages, and caravans trundled into Farmer Giles's field where the circus was to be held. The children went home to dinner, full of all they had seen, longing to go and see the circus when it opened on Wednesday.

Jimmy told his mother all about it, and his father too. Jimmy's father was a carpenter, and he had been out of work for nearly a year. He was very unhappy about it, for he was a good workman, and he did not like to see Jimmy's mother going out scrubbing and washing to bring in a few shillings.

'My!' said Jimmy, finishing up his dinner, and wishing there was some more, 'how *I'd* like to go to that circus.'

'Well, you can't, Jimmy,' said his mother. 'So don't think any more about it.'

'Oh, I know that, Mum,' said Jimmy cheerfully. 'Don't you worry. I'll go and see the animals and the clown and everything in the field, even if I can't go to the circus.'

So after school each day Jimmy slipped under the rope that went all round the ring of circus vans and cages, and wandered in and out by himself. At first he had been shouted at, and once Mr Galliano himself had come along with his pointed moustaches bristling in anger, and told Jimmy to go away.

Jimmy was afraid then, and was just going when he heard a voice calling him from a caravan near by. He turned to see who it was, and saw the curly-haired little girl there.

'Hallo, boy!' she said. 'I saw you watching our procession yesterday. Are you coming to the show tomorrow night?'

'No,' said Jimmy. 'I've got no money. I say – can I just peep inside that caravan? It does look so nice!'

'Come up the ladder and have a peep if you want to,' said the little girl.

Jimmy went up the little ladder at the back of the caravan and peeped inside. There was a bed at the back, against the wooden wall of the caravan. There was a black stove on which a kettle was boiling away. There was a tiny table, a stool, and a chair. There were shelves all round holding all sorts of things, and there was a gay carpet on the floor.

'It looks *lovely*!' said Jimmy. 'I wonder why people live in houses when they can buy caravans instead.'

'Can't think!' said the little girl. Jimmy stared at her – and she made a dreadful face at him.

'You're rude,' said Jimmy. 'One day the wind will change and your face will get stuck like that.'

'I suppose that's how you got your own face,' said the little girl, with a giggle. 'I wondered how it could be so queer.'

'It isn't queer,' said Jimmy. 'And look here – just you tell me why you hit me with your whip yesterday? You hurt me.'

'I didn't mean to,' said the little girl. 'What's your name?'

'Jimmy,' said Jimmy.

'Mine's Lotta,' said the girl. 'And my father is called Laddo, and my mother is called Lal. They ride the horses in the circus and jump from one to another. I ride them too.'

'Oh,' said Jimmy, thinking Lotta was really very clever, 'I do wish I could come and see you.'

'You come this time tomorrow and I'll take you round the circus camp and show you everything,' said Lotta. 'I must go now. I've got to cook the sausages for supper. Lal will be angry if she comes back and they're not cooked.'

'Do you call your mother Lal?' said Jimmy, surprised.

' 'Course I do,' said Lotta, smiling. 'And I call my father Laddo. Everybody does. Goodbye till tomorrow.'

Jimmy ran home. He felt most excited. To think that the next day he would be taken all round the circus camp and would see everything closely! That was better than going to the circus.

2. Jimmy makes friends with the circus folk

The next day, as soon as afternoon school was over, Jimmy ran off to the circus field. A great tent had been put up. This was where the circus was to be held that night. The circus folk had been very busy all day long, getting everything ready.

Jimmy looked for Lotta. The little man who owned the monkeys came along and he glared at Jimmy.

'You go home just as quickly as ever you can,' he said. 'Go along! No boys allowed here!'

'But . . .' began Jimmy.

'What! You dare to disobey me, the great Lilliput!' said the little man, and he ran at Jimmy. Jimmy didn't know quite what was going to happen next, but a voice called out from the caravan near by:

'Lilliput! Lilliput! That's my friend! Leave him alone!'

The little man turned round and bowed. 'Your pardon,' he said. 'Any friend of yours is welcome here, of course, dear Lotta.'

'Don't be silly, Lilliput!' said Lotta, and the little girl jumped down from the caravan and ran over to Jimmy. 'This is Jimmy. And this is Lilliput, Jimmy. He has the monkeys. Where's Jemima, Lilliput?'

'Somewhere about,' said Lilliput. 'Jemima love! Jemima love! Come along!'

A small, bright-eyed monkey came running out on all-fours from under a cart. She tore over to Lilliput, leapt up to his shoulder and put her arms around his neck.

'This is Jemima,' said Lotta. 'She is the darlingest monkey in the world – isn't she, Lilliput? And the clever-est.'

'That's right,' said Lilliput. 'I bought her from a black man when I was in foreign lands, and she's just as cunning as can be. Look, Jemima – here's Nobby! Go ride him, go ride him!'

The monkey made a little chattering noise, slipped down to the ground and ran quietly over to a large brown dog who was nosing about the field. She jumped on to his back, held on to his collar and jumped up and down to make him go. Jimmy laughed and laughed.

'Come along!' said Lotta, slipping her bare brown arm through his. 'Come and see the clown.'

The clown lived in a rather dirty little caravan all by himself. He sat at the door of it, polishing some black shoes he meant to wear that night. He didn't look a bit like a clown now. He had no paint on his face, and he wore a dirty old hat. But he was very funny.

'Hallo, hallo, hallo!' he said, when he saw Jimmy coming. 'The Prince of Goodness Knows Where, as sure as I'm eating my breakfast!' He got up and bowed politely.

Jimmy laughed. 'But you're not eating your breakfast!' he said.

'Then you can't be the Prince,' said the clown. 'That just proves it – you can't be the Prince.'

'Well, I'm not,' said Jimmy. 'I'm Jimmy Brown. What's *your* name?'

'I am Sticky Stanley, the world-famous clown,' said the clown proudly, and he gave his shoes an extra rub.

'What a funny name!' said Jimmy. 'Why do you call yourself Sticky?'

'Because I stick to my job and my friends stick to me!' said Stanley. And he leapt down from his caravan, began to carol a loud song and juggle with his two shoes, his brush, and his tin of polish. He sent them all up into the air one by one and caught them very cleverly, sending them up into the air again, higher and higher.

Jimmy watched him, his eyes nearly falling out of his head. However could anyone be so clever? The clown caught them all neatly in one hand, bowed to Jimmy, and

turned two or three somersaults, landing with a thud
right inside his caravan.

'Isn't he funny?' said Lotta. 'He's always like that.
Come and see the elephant. He's a darling.'

The elephant was in a tall tent by himself, eating hay
contentedly. His leg was made fast to a strong post.

'But he doesn't really need to be tied up at all,' said
Lotta. 'He would never wander away. Would you,
Jumbo?'

'Hrrrumph!' said Jumbo, and he lifted up his trunk
and took hold of one of Lotta's curls.

'Naughty Jumbo! said Lotta, and she pushed his trunk
down again. 'Look, this is Jimmy. Say Jimmy, Jumbo.'

'Hrrrumph!' said Jumbo, and he said it so loudly that
Jimmy's cap flew off in the draught! Jumbo put down his
trunk, picked up Jimmy's cap and put it back on his head.
Jimmy was so surprised.

'Hrrrumph!' said Jumbo again, and pulled out some
more hay to eat.

'He's very clever,' said Lotta. 'He can play cricket just
as well as you can. He holds a bat with his trunk, and hits
the ball with it when his keeper, Mr Tonks, bowls to him.
Now come and see the dogs.'

Jimmy had heard the dogs long before he saw them.
There were ten of them – all terriers. They were in a very
big cage, running about and barking. They looked clean
and silky and happy. They crowded up to Jimmy when
he put his hand out to them.

'That's Darky and that's Nigger and that's Boy and
that's Judy and that's Punch and that's . . .' began Lotta.
But Jimmy couldn't see which dog was which. He just
stood there and let them all lick his hands as fast as they
could.

'I take them all out once a day,' said Lotta. 'They go
out five at a time. I have one big lead and they each have
a short lead off it, so I can keep them all together. They
do pull though!'

'What do they do in the circus?' asked Jimmy.

'Oh, all kinds of things,' said Lotta. 'They can all walk

on their hind legs, and some of them can dance round and round in time to the music. This one, Judy, can jump through hoops held as high as my head. She is very clever.'

'I like Judy,' said Jimmy, letting the little sandy-headed terrier lick his fingers. 'How do they teach the dogs their tricks, Lotta? Do they punish them if they don't do them properly?'

Lotta looked at Jimmy in horror. 'Punish them!' she said. 'That shows how little you know about real, good circus, Jimmy. Why, we all know that no animals will play or work properly for us unless we love them and are kind to them. If Mr Galliano saw anyone hitting a dog or a monkey he would send him off at once. We love our animals and feed them well, and look after them. Then they are so full of love and good spirits that they think it is fun to play and work with us.'

'I like animals too,' said Jimmy. 'I would never hurt one, Lotta, so don't look at me like that. One thing I'd like better than any other is a dog of my own – but Dad couldn't possibly buy a licence for him, so I'll never have one! How I wish I belonged to a circus!'

'I wish you belonged too,' said Lotta. 'Usually in a circus there are lots of children – but I'm the only one here and it's often lonely for me.'

'Oh, I say! Look! Who's that over there?' said Jimmy suddenly, pointing to a man who was doing the most extraordinary things on a large mat outside a caravan.

'Oh, that's Oona the acrobat,' said Lotta. 'He is just practising for tonight. Oona! Here's a friend of mine! Where's your ladder? Do go up it upside down on your hands and stand on your head on the top of it, just to show Jimmy!'

Oona was at that moment looking between his legs at them in a very peculiar manner. He grinned and stood the right way up. 'Hallo, youngster!' he said. 'So you want to see me do my tricks before you come to the circus!'

'He's not coming,' said Lotta. 'So do your best trick for him, Oona, do!'

Oona, who was a fine strong-looking young man with a mop of curly golden hair, fetched a step-ladder from his caravan. It was painted gold and looked very grand. Oona stood it firmly on the ground, turned a few somersaults on his mat first, and then walked up the ladder to the very top on his hands, waving his legs above him as he did so. When he got to the top he stood there on his head alone, and Jimmy stared as if he couldn't believe his eyes. Oona lightly twisted himself over and came down beside Jimmy on his feet.

'There!' he said; 'easy as winking! Try it yourself, young man.'

'Oh, I couldn't possibly!' said Jimmy. 'I can't even walk on my hands.'

'*That's* easy, if you like!' said Lotta, and to Jimmy's amazement the little girl flung herself lightly forward and walked a few steps on her hands.

'How I wish *I* could do that!' said Jimmy. 'My goodness! The boys at school would stare!'

'Try it,' said Lotta. 'I'll hold your legs up for you till you get your balance.'

Somehow Jimmy got on to his hands and Lotta held his feet up. 'Walk on them – walk on your hands!' she shouted. 'Go on – I've got your legs all right!'

'I can't!' gasped Jimmy. 'I can't make my hands go – my body is so heavy on them!'

Lotta began to laugh. She laughed so much that she dropped Jimmy's legs and there he was, lying sprawling in the grass, laughing too.

'You'd do for a clown, but not for an acrobat just yet,' said Oona, with a grin. 'Now off you go – I want to practise!'

'I've got to go and help Lal get into her dress for to-night,' said Lotta, as the two children went away. 'I must say goodbye, Jimmy. Come again tomorrow.'

Jimmy ran off home, his head full of elephants and monkeys and dogs and people standing on their heads and walking on their hands. If only he belonged to a circus too!

3. Jimmy learns about circus ways

Every day Jimmy ran off to the circus field to see Lotta
and to hear all her news. She was a lively little girl, kind-
hearted but often naughty, and she really could make the
most dreadful faces Jimmy had ever seen. She could
pinch hard too, and Jimmy thought that was very unfair
of her, because he didn't like to pinch back.

The circus was doing well. Every night the big tent was
crowded by people from the town, and, as it was a very
good show, many people went three or four times. Mr
Galliano wore his big top hat very much on one side of
his head, so much so that Jimmy really wondered why it
didn't fall off.

'When Galliano wears his hat on one side the circus is
taking lots of money,' said Lotta to him. 'But when you
see him wearing it straight up, then you know things are
going badly. He gets into a bad temper then, and I hide
under the caravan when I see him coming. I've never seen
his hat so much on one side before!'

Jimmy thought that circus ways were very extraordinary. Even hats seemed to share in the excitement!
He was afraid of Mr Galliano, but he couldn't help liking
him too. He was such a big handsome man, and his face
was so red and his moustache so fierce-looking. He
usually carried a whip about with him, and he cracked
this very often. It made a noise like a pistol-shot, and
Jimmy jumped whenever he heard it. Jimmy made himself a whip with a long string like Mr Galliano's, but he
couldn't make it crack though he tried for a long time.

Jimmy soon knew everybody at the circus. He knew
every single one of the dogs. He took them out with Lotta
on Saturday morning when there was no school. Lotta

had five and he had five. It was hard work keeping the dogs in order. His five kept getting tangled up, but Lotta's never did. The dogs loved Jimmy. How they barked when they saw him!

He gave them their fresh water every day. He even cleaned out their big, airy cage, and put fresh sawdust down. He liked to feel the dogs running round his legs, licking him, and yapping to him.

Jumbo, the big elephant, was taken down to the nearby stream to drink twice a day. Mr Tonks untied him and led him down. Jimmy asked if he could lead him back to his tent. Mr Tonks looked at the little boy.

'What will you do if he runs away from you?' he asked. 'Could you catch him by the tail and pull him back? Or would you pick him up and carry him?'

Jimmy laughed. 'I guess if he ran away you couldn't bring him back either, Mr Tonks!' he said. 'He won't run away, will he? He's the gentlest creature I ever saw, for all he is so big. Look how he's putting his trunk into my hand now – just as if he wanted me to lead him back.'

'Jumbo wouldn't do that if he didn't like you,' said Mr Tonks. 'Come on – step on my hand and I'll give you a leg-up, Jimmy. You shall ride on his neck!'

My word! That was a treat for Jimmy! In a trice the little boy was up on the elephant's neck. He sat cross-legged, as Mr Tonks told him to. The elephant's neck was so broad that this was quite easy. Back went Jimmy and the elephant to the tent. Then, to Jimmy's enormous surprise, the big creature put up his trunk, wound it firmly round his waist, and lifted the boy gently down to the ground himself.

'Oooh!' said Jimmy, astonished. 'Thank you, Jumbo!'

'See that!' said Mr Tonks in surprise. 'Jumbo never does that to anyone unless he really likes them. He's your friend for good now, Jimmy. You're lucky!'

After that Jimmy and Jumbo went down to the stream every day together, Jimmy always riding on the elephant's head. Jimmy saved part of his bread and cheese for Jumbo, and the elephant always looked for it

when the boy came to see him. He sometimes put his
trunk round Jimmy's neck, and it did feel funny. Like a
big snake, Jimmy thought.

There was only one man that Jimmy didn't like – and
that was a little, crooked-eyed man called Harry. Harry
never had a smile for anyone He snapped at Lotta, and
pulled her hair whenever he passed her. Once Jimmy saw
him try to hit Jemima the monkey, when she ran near him.

'I don't like Harry,' he said to Lotta. 'He has a horrid
unkind face. What does he do in the circus, Lotta?'

'He doesn't really belong to us,' said the little girl. 'He's
what we call the odd-job man – he does all the odd jobs –
puts up the benches in the ring, mends anything that goes
wrong, makes anything special we need. There's always
plenty for him to do. He's very clever with his hands –
that's why Mr Galliano keeps him on, because he can't
bear him really.'

'I saw him try to hit Jemima just now,' said Jimmy.

'I've seen him try too,' said Lotta. 'But Jemima knows
Harry all right. She hates him – do you know, she went to
his box of nails one day and stuffed her cheeks with about
fifty of his nails. He couldn't find them anywhere – and
there was Jemima running about with them in her
mouth! I saw her taking them, and I had to hide under
our caravan so that Harry shouldn't see me laughing!'

Jimmy laughed. 'Good for Jemima!' he said. 'Well, it's
a pity you have to keep Harry, Lotta. If I were Mr Galliano I'd send him away – always snapping and snarling
like a bad-tempered dog! He threw his hammer at me
yesterday.'

'Oh, he wouldn't hit you,' said Lotta. 'He's too bad a
shot for that. You keep out of his way, though, Jimmy.
However much we dislike him we've got to have him –
why, we couldn't put up the circus tents and ring without
him – and he's so clever at making special ladders and
things – and mending caravans.'

Just then Mr Galliano came up, his hat more on one
side than ever. He beamed at Jimmy. He had heard that
the little boy was marvellous with the animals, and that

always pleased Mr Galliano. He loved every creature, down to white mice, and Lotta had told Jimmy that once, when one of his horses was ill, Mr Galliano had sat up with her for four nights running and hadn't gone to sleep at all.

'Hallo, boy,' he said. 'So here you are again! You will be sorry when we move away? Yes?'

'Very sorry,' said Jimmy. 'I think a circus life is fine!'

'You do not like to live in a house? No?' said Mr Galliano, who had a very funny way of always putting yes or no at the end of his sentences.

'I'd rather live in a caravan,' said Jimmy.

'And you like my circus? Yes?' said Mr Galliano, twisting his enormous moustache into even sharper points.

'I haven't seen the *real* circus,' said Jimmy. 'I haven't the money to go into the big tent at night, Mr Galliano. But I've seen all the animals and people here in the field.'

'What! This boy hasn't seen our circus show, the best in the whole world?' cried Mr Galliano, his big black eyebrows going right up under his curly hair. 'He must come, Lotta, he must come tonight! Yes?'

'I'd love to,' said Jimmy, red with excitement. 'Thanks awfully.'

'Give this to the man at the gate,' said Mr Galliano, and he gave Jimmy a card on which was printed Mr Galliano's own name. 'I shall see you in the big tent tonight then? Yes?'

'Yes, sir,' said Jimmy, and stuffed the card into his pocket very carefully. Lotta was pleased. She squeezed Jimmy's arm. 'Now you'll see us all in the ring!' she said. 'I shall be riding too, tonight, as it's Saturday. I don't always – but Saturday is a special night. Come early!'

The little boy raced home to dinner. He was tremendously excited. All his schoolfriends had seen the circus – but he, Jimmy, had a special ticket, one of Mr Galliano's own cards – and he knew everyone there! He knew all the dogs – he had ridden Jumbo! He had cuddled Jemima the clever little monkey! Ah! He would have a glorious time tonight!

The circus began at eight o'clock and lasted for two hours. Jimmy was at the gate at a quarter past seven. He gave his card to the man there. He was one of the men who looked after Mr Galliano's many beautiful horses. He grinned at Jimmy. 'You can sit anywhere you like with that card!' he said. 'My word! Old Galliano was feeling generous this morning, wasn't he – giving free tickets to shrimps like you!'

'I'm not a shrimp,' said Jimmy, offended, for he was quite big for his age.

'Well, maybe you're a prawn then,' said the ticketman. That was just like circus-folk, Jimmy thought – they always had an answer for everything. Perhaps one day he too would be quick enough to think of funny answers – but, oh dear, by that time the circus would have gone!

The little boy went into the big tent. It was lighted by huge flares. Not many people were there yet. There were a great many benches set all round a big red ring in the middle. Mr Tonks was spreading sawdust in the middle of the ring, whistling loudly.

Jimmy chose a seat right in the very front. He whistled to Mr Tonks. Mr Tonks looked up and pretended to be surprised to see Jimmy there.

'Hallo, hallo!' he said, 'has somebody left you a fortune or what! Fancy seeing *you* here – in the best seats too – my word, you *are* throwing your money about!'

'No, I'm not,' said Jimmy. 'Mr Galliano gave me a ticket.'

The tent filled up with people. By the time eight o'clock came there wasn't an empty seat. Jimmy thought that Mr Galliano must have taken a lot of money tonight, and he wondered if his hat would keep on, he would wear it so much to one side!

There was a doorway at one end of the tent, hung with red curtains. Suddenly these were drawn aside and two trumpets blew loudly.

'Tan-tan-tara! Tan-tan-tara! Tan-tan-tara!'

The circus was going to begin! What fun!

4. Jimmy sees the circus

'Tan-tan-tara!' went the trumpets again, and into the ring cantered six beautiful black horses. They ran gracefully round the ring, nose to tail. Mr Galliano came striding into the ring, dressed in a magnificent black suit, his top hat well on one side, his long stiff moustaches turned up like wire.

He cracked his whip. The horses went a bit faster. Galliano cracked his whip twice. The horses all stopped, turned round quickly – and went cantering round the other way. It was marvellous to watch them. How everyone clapped!

Three of the horses went out. The three that were left went on cantering round the ring. They were thoroughly enjoying themselves. Mr Galliano shouted out something and a barrel-organ began to play a dance tune.

The three horses were delighted. They all loved music. Mr Galliano cracked his whip sharply. At once all three horses rose up on their hind legs and began to sway in time to the music. Their coats shone like silk. The whip cracked again. Down they went on all-fours and began to gallop round the ring. Every time the music came to a certain chord the horses turned round and galloped the other way.

Everyone clapped till they could clap no more when the horses went out, and they hadn't finished clapping when Sticky Stanley the clown came in. He did look funny. His face was painted white, but his nose and lips were red, and he had big false eyebrows that jerked up and down.

He had a broom in his hand and he began to sweep the ring – and he fell over the broom. He picked himself up, and found that his legs had got twisted round themselves, so he carefully untwisted them and then found that the broom was twisted up with them. So of course he fell over the broom again, and everyone laughed and laughed.

Stanley turned somersaults, walked on his hands, carried a sunshade with one of his feet, went round the ring walking on a great round ball, and made so many jokes that Jimmy had a pain in his side with laughing.

Then came Lal, Lotta's mother, with the ten terrier dogs. How lovely they looked, all running into the ring in excitement, their tails wagging, their barks sounding loudly in the big tent.

There were ten little stools set out in the ring, and Lal patted a nearby stool.

'Up! Up!' she said to a dog, and he neatly jumped up and sat down on his stool. Then each dog jumped up on a stool and there they all sat, their mouths open, their tongues hanging out, their tails wagging.

Lal looked grand. She was dressed in a short, fluffy frock of bright pink, and it sparkled and shone as if it were on fire. She had a bright wreath of flowers in her hair and these shone too. Jimmy thought she looked wonderful. He had only seen her before dressed in an old jersey and skirt – but now she looked like something out of fairyland!

How clever those dogs were! They played follow-my-leader in a long line, and the leader wound them in and out and in. Not a single dog made a mistake! Then they all sat up and begged, and when Lal threw them a biscuit each, they caught their biscuits one after another and barked sharply once. 'That's their thank-you!' thought Jimmy.

Lal ran to the side of the ring and fetched the big round ball that Sticky Stanley the clown had walked on so cleverly.

'Up! Up!' she cried to a dog, and it leapt up on the ball and did just as the clown had done – walked swiftly on the top of it as the ball went round! Lal threw him a biscuit for doing it so well.

Then Judy, the little brown-headed terrier, impatient to do her special trick, jumped down from her stool and ran behind Lal. Lal turned in surprise – for it was not like Judy to leave her stool before the right time.

But Judy had seen the hoops of paper that Lal had ready for her, and she wanted to do her trick and get her share of clapping. So she took hold of a hoop and ran to Lal with it. She put it down at Lal's feet and stood there wagging her tail so fast that it couldn't be seen.

Lal laughed. She picked up the hoop and held it shoulder high. 'Jump, Judy, jump then!' she cried.

Light as a feather Judy jumped through the hoop, breaking the thin paper as she did so. Then Lal picked up two paper hoops and held them high up, about two feet apart.

'Jump, Judy, jump!' she cried. And Judy, taking a short run, jumped clean through both hoops. How everyone clapped the clever little dog!

Jimmy's face was red with excitement and happiness. How wonderful the circus folk were in the things they could do, and in their love for their animals! Jimmy watched the ten dogs go happily out with Lal, a forest of wagging tails, and he knew that Lal would see that they all got a good hot meal at once. She loved them and they loved her.

The horses came in again – white ones this time – and who do you suppose came in with them? Why, Lotta! Yes, little Lotta, no longer dressed in her ragged old frock, but in a fairy's dress with long silvery wings on her back! Her dark curls were fluffed out round her head and her long legs had on silvery stockings. She wore a little silver crown on her head and carried a silver wand in her hand.

'It can't be Lotta!' said Jimmy to himself, staring hard. But it was. She waved her wand at him as she passed his seat, and – what else do you suppose she did? She made one of her dreadful faces at him!

Lotta jumped lightly up on to the back of one of the white horses. She sat there without holding on at all with

her hands, blowing kisses and waving. The horses had no
saddles and no bridles. Lotta couldn't have held on to
anything if she had wanted to.

Jimmy watched her, his heart thumping in excitement.
Whatever would she do next? She suddenly stood up on a
horse's back, and there she stayed, balancing perfectly,
whilst the horse cantered round and round the ring.

Jimmy was afraid the little girl would fall off – but
Lotta knew she wouldn't! She had ridden horses since she
was a baby. Down she went again, sitting, and then up
again, this time standing backwards, looking towards the
tail of the horse. Everyone thought she was very brave
and very clever.

Then in came Laddo, her father, dressed in a tight blue
shining suit, with glittering stars sewn all over it. He was
much cleverer than Lotta. The little girl jumped down
when her father came in, and ran to the middle of the
ring. Laddo jumped up in her place. He leapt from one
horse to another as the three of them cantered round the
ring. He stood on his hands as they went, he swung himself from side to side underneath a horse's body – really,
the things he did you would hardly believe!

Then Lotta jumped up behind him and the two of
them galloped out of the ring together, followed by a
thunderstorm of clapping and shouting. Jimmy's hands
were quite sore with clapping Lotta. He felt very proud of
her.

Jumbo came next, and he was very clever, for he certainly could play cricket extremely well. Mr Tonks
bowled a tennis ball to him and he hit it every time. Once,
to Jimmy's great delight, Jumbo hit the ball straight at
him, and by jumping up from his seat Jimmy just managed to catch the ball. And then everybody clapped *him*,
and Jumbo said, 'Hrrrumph, hrrrumph!' very loudly
indeed. Jimmy threw the ball to him and he caught it
with his trunk.

The circus went on through the evening. Sticky Stanley the clown came in a great many times and always
made everyone laugh, because he seemed to fall over

everything, even things that were not there. Lilliput and his monkeys were very clever. They helped Lilliput to set a table with cups and saucers and plates. They got chairs. They sat down at the table. They had feeders tied round their necks, and they passed one another a plate of fruit.

Jemima was the best. She peeled a banana for Lilliput and fed him with it! But then she stuffed the peel down his neck and he pretended to chase her all round the ring, and everyone laughed till they cried.

Then Jemima got into a corner and pretended to cry. When Lilliput came up she took his handkerchief out of his pocket and wiped her eyes with it. Then she leapt on to Lilliput's shoulder and spread the handkerchief over the top of his head. Jimmy laughed just as much at Jemima as he did at the clown.

Of course Oona the acrobat had a lot of clapping too, especially when he walked up his step-ladder on his hands and stood on the top on just his head! Stanley the clown came running in to try and do it, but of course he couldn't, and he fell all the way down the ladder, bumpity-bumpity-bump! Jimmy was afraid he might hurt himself, but he saw Stanley grinning all the time, so he knew he was all right.

Oona did another clever thing too – he had a wire rope put up from one post to another, and he walked on the rope, which was about as high as Mr Galliano's top hat from the ground. Jimmy hadn't known he could do that – and he wondered how Oona did it. Surely it must be very difficult to walk on a rope without falling off at all!

The circus came to an end all too soon. All the circus folk came running into the ring, shouting, bowing, jumping, and everyone clapped them and shouted too.

'Best circus that's ever come to this town!' said a big man next to Jimmy. 'Fine show. I shall come and see it next week too. That little girl on horseback was very good – one of the best!'

Jimmy saved that up to tell Lotta. He would see her tomorrow. There was no circus on Sunday. The circus

folk had a rest that day, and Lotta had said that Jimmy could spend the day with her.

'I must run straight home now,' thought Jimmy to himself. 'Mother will be waiting for me. What a lot I shall have to tell her!'

So he ran home, though he would dearly have loved to find the fairy-like Lotta with her silvery wings and talked to her.

5. A shock for Mr Galliano

It was Sunday. Jimmy remembered that he was to spend the whole day with Lotta. What fun it would be to wander about among the circus folk and see old Jumbo, and pet Jemima the clever little monkey, and have his hands licked by all the jolly little terrier dogs! Jimmy sang loudly as he got up.

He was soon in the circus field. The sun shone down. It was going to be a lovely day. But as he made his way between the caravans and the tents Jimmy was surprised to see that everyone looked gloomy.

'I wonder what the matter is?' thought Jimmy to himself. He passed the clown's caravan, and saw Sticky Stanley eating a breakfast of bacon and eggs. Stanley looked miserable. It was strange to see the clown looking like that. He was usually full of jokes and nonsense.

He saw Jimmy and called out to him: 'Hey, Jimmy, don't you let Mr Galliano see you this morning! He's forbidden any outsiders to come into the circus field.'

'Why?' asked Jimmy, in astonishment. 'He was very nice to me yesterday. He gave me a ticket for the show. What's the matter?'

'Listen to that, then!' said the clown, pointing with his fork towards the big blue caravan in which Mr Galliano lived with his wife. 'Just listen to that!'

Jimmy listened. It sounded as if about six cows were bellowing in Galliano's caravan – but it was only Mr Galliano being very angry indeed, and shouting at the top of his very big voice. Jimmy stared in the direction of the blue caravan – and as he stared, Mr Galliano came down the steps at the back.

'He's got his hat on quite straight up,' said Jimmy, at once. 'He's always had it on one side before.'

'Yes, that means bad news, all right,' said the clown. 'Hop off, Jimmy. Don't let him see you.'

Jimmy hopped off. He ran round the clown's caravan and came to the red-and-white one in which Lotta lived with Lal and Laddo, her father and mother. Lotta was sitting on the steps outside, polishing her circus shoes.

'Hallo, Jimmy,' she said. 'Come up here.'

'Lotta, what's the matter with everyone this morning?' asked Jimmy. 'You all look so gloomy, and I just heard Mr Galliano in a bad temper.'

'There's matter enough,' said Lotta, dropping her voice. 'You know Harry, our odd-job man – the carpenter who puts up the benches, does most of the packing and unpacking and all the little mending and making jobs a circus always has? Well – he ran away last night, taking nearly all the money with him that the circus took last week!'

'Oh, I say, how dreadful!' said Jimmy, shocked. 'Won't you get any money, then?'

'Not a penny,' said Lotta. 'And that's very hard, you know, because we none of us save anything. The worst of it is, Harry was so useful – we don't really know how we are going to do without him.'

'Perhaps he will be caught,' said Jimmy.

'I don't think so,' said Lotta. 'He had a good start, because he took the money when we were all asleep last night and went off about two o'clock in the morning. He may be anywhere now. I do hope we have a good week now, Jimmy – if we don't, it will be very bad for us all.'

'I hope you do too,' said Jimmy. 'I do wish I could help a bit, Lotta.'

'I suppose you don't know a good handy carpenter in your town who could come along for a week and help us, do you?' said Lal, Lotta's mother, coming to the door of the caravan. 'There are a lot of jobs that must be done before tomorrow night. Oona's ladder must be made stronger, he says. And there's a bar loose in the dogs' big cage.'

'What about my father?' said Jimmy eagerly. 'He's a carpenter, you know! He could do anything you wanted!'

'Yes, but what about his work?' said Lal. 'He can't leave that to come to us.'

'He's out of work,' said Jimmy. 'He would be glad to come. Oh, Lotta – will you come to tea with me at home this afternoon and we could find out if my father will come? I do, do hope he can.'

'We'd better tell Mr Galliano first,' said Lal. She called to her husband at the back of the caravan: 'Laddo, will you go with Jimmy and tell Galliano about his father being a carpenter?'

'Right,' said Laddo. He put down his newspaper and ran down the caravan steps with Jimmy. 'Come on, son,' he said.

Mr Galliano was with his horses, patting them and speaking gently to them. No matter how bad a temper he sometimes flew into he was never anything but gentle with his beloved horses. No one had ever seen him sharp or unkind with any animal. All his horses loved him and would do anything in the world for him.

He heard Jimmy and Laddo coming and he turned to meet them.

'What do you want?' he said, not seeming at all pleased to see Jimmy.

'Mr Galliano, sir, this boy says his father is a carpenter and could take Harry's place for the week,' said Laddo.

'Tell him to come and see me this evening, yes,' said Mr Galliano shortly, and he turned back to his horses. Laddo and Jimmy went out. Jimmy felt excited. Just suppose his father got the job to help the circus – and just suppose they kept him on! Oh, wouldn't that be wonderful!

He ran back to Lotta. 'Let's go for a walk with the dogs,' said Jimmy. 'It's such a lovely day – and everyone is so gloomy here this morning. We can get back here to dinner.'

'All right,' said Lotta, and the two ran to get the excited terriers. Soon Lotta had five of the dogs on her big lead, and Jimmy had the other five. Lotta was a little bit jealous because all the dogs seemed to want to go with Jimmy.

'I never saw anyone so good with animals as you, Jimmy,' she said. 'At least, that's not counting Mr Galliano – he can tame a wild tiger and make it purr like a cat in two days!'

The two children set off over the countryside. In a little while Lotta forgot about Harry and how he had run off with everyone's money. Soon the two were having great fun, racing with their dogs and joining in the barking with laughs and shrieks.

'Shall we let them loose for a really good run?' asked Jimmy, when they were well out in the country. 'They would love it so!'

So they let all the dogs loose, and with excited yaps the neat little terriers tore off to go rabbiting. Jimmy and Lotta sat under a tree.

'I did love the circus last night, Lotta,' said Jimmy. 'And I did think you were clever – riding on a horse standing up and never falling off!'

'Pooh,' said Lotta, making a face at him. 'That's easy. You could do it yourself.'

'I couldn't,' said Jimmy. 'I can't even walk on my hands yet, and it does look so easy when you all do it! I wish you'd teach me, Lotta.'

'All right,' said Lotta. 'But not now. I'm too hot. I wish you belonged to the circus, Jimmy. I shall be dull without you. It's nice to have someone to make faces at when I feel like it.'

'I can't think why you want to do that,' said Jimmy, surprised. 'All the same – I'd like to go with you when you go off again. But I wouldn't like to leave my mother and father behind.'

'Where are those dogs?' said Lotta suddenly. 'We mustn't lose any, you know, Jimmy. My word, we should get into trouble if we did! Hie, Judy, Judy, Nigger, Spot!'

Some of the dogs came running up and flung themselves on the two children. Jimmy counted them. 'Eight,' he said. 'Where are the others?'

They quickly put the eight dogs on the leads. Lotta looked worried. 'Whistle, Jimmy,' she said. So Jimmy whistled.

'There comes Punch!' said Lotta, and sure enough one of the missing dogs came loping over the field towards them. Jimmy whistled again and again – but the tenth dog was nowhere to be seen!

'We shall have to go,' said Lotta, looking scared. 'Whatever will Lal and Laddo say when we turn up without Darky? Come on – it's getting late. Perhaps Darky will come after us when he's finished hunting.'

They went back to the circus. No Darky came after them. Lotta was very silent. Jimmy was miserable too. What a horrid day this was after all!

'We'll put the dogs into the cage, and then we'll go and tell Lal we've lost Darky,' said Lotta. She was crying now. Lotta loved all the dogs and she couldn't help wondering if Darky had been caught in a trap. Also she knew that her mother would be very angry with her.

Jimmy opened the door of the great cage. As he did so a little dark dog crept out from under the cage itself. Jimmy gave a yell.

'Lotta! Darky's here! He must have run all the way home before us and hidden under his cage. Look!'

Lotta gave a shriek of delight and hugged Darky. 'You silly animal!' she said. 'You did give me a fright! Oh, Jimmy – I'm so happy now!'

Jimmy was glad. He squeezed Lotta's hand as they ran to the caravan for dinner. Lotta squeezed his hand back – but she was so strong that she made Jimmy yell out in pain. You never knew what that little monkey of a Lotta was going to do next! Jimmy dropped her hand in a hurry and felt half cross with her. But when he smelt the smell of frying sausages he forgot everything except that he was dreadfully hungry.

They all had their dinner sitting outside the caravan.

The sausages were lovely and so were the potatoes cooked in their jackets and eaten with butter and salt. Jimmy thought he had never had such a lovely dinner in his life. Afterwards there were oranges and chocolate to eat.

Jimmy took Lotta home to tea with him. He ran indoors with the little girl and found his mother making toast for tea. They always had toast on Sundays. It smelt good.

'Mother, this is Lotta. I've brought her home to tea because I want to ask Dad something. Where is he?'

'Out in the garden, mending the old shed,' said Mother. 'Hallo, Lotta! How's the circus going?'

'All right, thank you,' said Lotta shyly. She looked at Jimmy's mother and thought she was lovely. She was so neat and her face was so kind. Lotta had not often been inside a house, and she looked round curiously. It seemed just as strange to her to be inside a house as it was to Jimmy to be inside a caravan.

'Dad! Dad!' shouted Jimmy, running into the back garden, 'Harry, the odd-job man at the circus, has run off with the circus money – and Mr Galliano wants a new carpenter. He says will you go and see him tonight.'

'That's the first bit of luck I've had for a long time,' said Jimmy's father, delighted. 'Yes, I'll go up and see if I can get the work after tea. A week's work is better than nothing. Well, that's given me an appetite for my tea! Is the toast ready, Mother?'

Soon Lotta, Jimmy, and the two grown-ups were sitting round the tea-table. Lotta was on her very best behaviour. She didn't make a single face. She liked Jimmy's mother much too much to shock her!

After tea, Jimmy, Lotta, and Jimmy's father set off to the circus field. 'If only I can get that job!' said Jimmy's father.

'I *do* hope you do, Dad!' said Jimmy.

6. An exciting night

Jimmy, Lotta, and Jimmy's father soon got to the circus field. 'There's Mr Galliano, over there,' said Lotta, as they went through the gate.

'Right,' said Mr Brown. 'I'll go over and see him now.' He left the two children and walked over to where Mr Galliano was talking to Oona the acrobat.

'What do you want?' said Mr Galliano, seeing that Mr Brown was a stranger.

'I'm Jimmy Brown's father,' said Mr Brown. 'I'm a carpenter, sir, and I can turn my hand to anything. I'd like you to give me a chance, if you will. I'd work well for you.'

Mr Galliano looked Mr Brown up and down. He liked what he saw – a strong, kindly-faced man, with bright eager eyes just like Jimmy's.

'Come tomorrow morning,' said Mr Galliano. 'There will be plenty for you to do, yes!'

'Thank you, sir,' said Mr Brown, and he walked off, pleased. It would be fine to work at last! The two children ran to meet him. How glad Jimmy was to know that his father would belong to the circus for at least a week! What would the boys at school say when they knew that his father was with the circus all day? They would think that was fine!

Jimmy's father worked well. Mr Galliano was delighted with him. He could, as he said, turn his hand to anything. He mended five of the circus benches. He put a new wheel on to Mr Galliano's caravan. He made Oona's ladder stronger than it had ever been before. He put in two new bars where the dogs had pushed them loose in their cage. And he won Lilliput's heart by making him a proper little house for Jemima the monkey to live in – it even had a little door!

Jimmy was delighted to hear everyone praising his father. He had always loved his father and thought him the finest man in the world – and it was nice to hear people saying he was ten times better than Harry!

'His laugh is worth ten shillings a week!' said Lal. 'My, when old Brownie starts laughing, you've got to hold your sides! He's as merry as a cricket!'

Jimmy thought it was funny to hear his father called Brownie. But the circus folk hardly ever called anyone by their right name. Brownie was the name they gave to Mr Brown, and Brownie he always was, after that!

The circus did well again that week. Mr Galliano began to wear his hat on the side of his head once more. Everyone cheered up. If Galliano was merry and bright then the circus folk were happy.

Jimmy was happy too that week. He had to go to school, but every spare minute he had he was in the circus field, helping. He was always ready to give a hand to anyone. When the circus show began each night, Jimmy stood near the curtains through which the performers had to pass, and pulled or shut the curtains properly each time. He got Oona's ladder and tightrope ready for him. He took care of the dogs whilst they were waiting for their turn. He got Jumbo out of his tent too, for Mr Tonks, and took him back again when the show was over. Jumbo loved Jimmy. He blew gently down the little boy's neck to show him how much he liked him. Jimmy thought that was very funny!

When Saturday came, Mr Galliano whistled to Mr Brown – or Brownie, as he was now called – and Brownie went over to him.

'Here's your week's money,' said Mr Galliano, paying him. 'Now look here – you've done well – what about you coming along with us, yes? We can do with a man like you – always cheerful, and able to do anything that turns up.'

Mr Brown went red with pleasure. It was a long time since anyone had praised him.

'Thank you, sir,' he said. 'I'll have to talk it over with my wife. You see – I think she would be upset if I left her and Jimmy. I might not see them again for a long time.'

'Well, think over it,' said Mr Galliano. 'If you come, you can live with Stanley, the clown. He's got room in his caravan for another fellow. We go off tomorrow – so let me know quickly, yes?'

Mr Brown hurried home to dinner. He told Jimmy and Jimmy's mother all that Mr Galliano had said.

'I think I'll have to take the job,' he said. 'It's hard to leave you both, though.'

Jimmy's mother didn't know what to say. She couldn't help the tears coming into her eyes. Jimmy gave her his handkerchief.

'Oh, Tom,' said his mother, 'I shall miss you so. Don't go. I can't bear to be without you – and Jimmy will miss you so much too. We shall never know where you are, travelling about the country – and goodness knows when we shall see you again!'

'Well, we needn't tell Mr Galliano till tomorrow,' said Mr Brown. 'We'll talk about it tonight.'

Jimmy thought and thought about it. He badly wanted his father to belong to the circus – but not if he and his mother had to be left behind! No – that would never do at all! And yet they couldn't go with him. There wasn't room for them. And if his father said no to Mr Galliano, then he might be out of work again for a long time – just as he had found a job that he could do so well.

It was a puzzle to know what to do. Jimmy felt that he really, really, couldn't bear it if his father had to leave home. His mother would be so sad.

The circus gave its last show that night. It did very well, and once again there was not an empty seat in the big tent, for people came from all the towns round to see it. Somebody gave Lotta a big box of chocolates and she was very pleased. She showed them to Jimmy. 'We'll share them,' she said, emptying out half the box into a bag. 'They're lovely.'

That was just like Lotta. She was the most generous little girl that Jimmy had ever known. But Jimmy could not smile very much at her. The circus was going off the next day to a far-away town. He would have to say good-bye to everyone. He felt as if he had known the circus folk all his life, and he was sad to part with them.

'I'll come and see you tomorrow morning, Lotta, he said.

'Come early,' said Lotta. 'We'll be packing up to go, and that is a busy time. We shall start off about twelve o'clock. We've got to get to Edgingham by night.'

'Good night then,' said Jimmy, looking at Lotta hard, so as to remember for always just how she looked – she had on her fluffy circus frock, her long silver wings, her little silver crown and her silvery stockings. As he looked at her she made one of her dreadful faces!

'Don't!' said Jimmy. 'I was just thinking how nice you looked.'

'You'd better hurry home,' said Lotta. 'It looks as if a storm is coming up. Hark! That's thunder!'

Jimmy ran off. Certainly there was a storm coming. Great drops of rain fell on him as he ran through the town, and stung his face. The thunder rolled nearer. A flash of lightning lit up the sky, and Jimmy saw that it was full of enormous black clouds, hanging very low.

Jimmy's mother was glad to see him, for she had been afraid he would be caught in the storm. She bundled him into bed and he fell asleep almost at once, for he was tired.

The storm crashed on. Jimmy slept peacefully and didn't hear it. Away up in the circus field the folk there listened to the pouring rain pattering down on their cara-vans.

Crash! The thunder rolled again. The horses whinnied, half-frightened. The dogs awoke and barked. Jemima, the monkey, who always slept with Lilliput, crept nearer to him and began to cry like a child. Lilliput petted her gently.

Jumbo, the big elephant, raised his great head. What was this fearful noise that was going on around him? Jumbo was angry with it. He threw back his head and trumpeted loudly to frighten it away.

Crash! Crash! The thunder still rolled on, and one crash sounded just overhead. Jumbo, half angry, half frightened, pulled at his post. His leg was tied to it, but in a trice the big elephant had snapped the thick rope. He blundered out of the tent, looking for the one man he trusted above everything – his keeper, Mr Tonks.

But Mr Tonks was fast asleep in his caravan. Not even a storm could keep Mr Tonks awake. He snored in his caravan as if he were trying to beat the loudness of the thunder!

Jumbo grew frightened in the dark. He stood in the rain, waving his big ears to and fro and swinging his trunk backwards and forwards. Another peal of thunder broke through the night, and a flash of lightning showed the field gate to Jumbo. It was open.

The elephant, remembering that he had come in through that gate, made his way towards it. No one heard him, for the rolling of the thunder and the pattering of the rain made such a noise. Jumbo slipped through the gate like a great black shadow, and set off alone up the lane that led to the town.

No one was about except Mr Harris, the town policeman. He was sheltering from the rain in a doorway. He got a dreadful shock when he saw Jumbo lit up in a flash of lightning, coming up the street towards him. He didn't know it was only Jumbo. He fled away as fast as he could back to the police station. He was the only person who met Jumbo running away.

The storm passed. The rain stopped. The night became peaceful and everyone slept. The circus dogs lay down and Jemima the monkey stopped crying.

The morning broke peaceful and bright, though the circus field was soaking wet. Still, the May sunshine would soon dry that up.

Mr Tonks dressed himself and went straight out to

see his beloved Jumbo. When he looked into the tall tent and saw no elephant there, he went white.

'Jumbo! Where's my elephant!' he shouted, and he tore all round the field, waking everyone up. Heads peeped out of caravans and scared faces looked up and down.

'Jumbo's gone! My elephant's gone!' cried Mr Tonks, tears pouring down his cheeks. 'Where is he, where is he?'

'Well, he's not in anybody's caravan, that's certain,' said Stanley, the clown. 'Can't you see his big tracks anywhere, Tonky?'

'Yes – they lead out of the gate!' said Mr Tonks, almost off his head with shock and grief. 'What's happened to him? I'll let the police know. He must be found before anything happens to him.'

'Well, he's too big to lose for long,' said Mr Galliano, coming out of his caravan with his hat on the side of his head. 'Don't worry, Tonks. We'll soon find him.'

But somebody already knew where Jumbo had gone – and who do you suppose that was? It was Jimmy!

In the middle of the storm Jimmy awoke suddenly. He sat up in bed, looking puzzled. He had heard a funny noise outside his house. It sounded like 'Hrrrumph! Hrrrumph!' Who made a noise like that? Jumbo, of course!

'But it can't be Jumbo,' said Jimmy, in the greatest astonishment. He hopped out of bed and ran to the window. A flash of lightning lit up the little street – and quite clearly Jimmy saw Jumbo, plodding heavily up the street towards the heart of the town!

'It *is* Jumbo – and he's frightened of the storm – and has run away!' thought Jimmy. 'I must go after him!'

He dragged on his coat, put his feet into his shoes at the same time, and slipped downstairs. In a trice he was out of the house and running up the street after Jumbo. He must get him, he must! Poor old Jumbo, running away all alone, frightened of the storm!

'Jumbo, Jumbo!' called Jimmy – but Jumbo padded on and on!

7. Jimmy hunts for Jumbo

Jimmy rushed up the street, calling Jumbo. The thunder rolled round and every now and again a flash of lightning showed him the big elephant padding through the streets. Jumbo could go very fast indeed when he liked and Jimmy couldn't catch up with him. 'If only I can keep him in sight,' panted Jimmy to himself. 'Jumbo! Can't you hear me shouting to you? Jumbo! Come to Jimmy!'

Jumbo took no notice at all. He went round the corner. He lumbered up the next street and the next. He came to the market square and crossed it. Jimmy panted and puffed a good way behind him, pleased when the lightning lighted the night and showed him where Jumbo was.

Jumbo came to the better part of the town where the roads were wider, and where the houses were large, with big gardens. He padded along, his great feet making very little sound. Pad-pad-pad he went through the night, his big ears twitching and his little tail swinging. His trunk was curled up safely, for Jumbo was afraid that the thunder and lightning might harm it. Sometimes he gave a loud 'hrrumph!' and then the people sleeping in the houses near by sat up in alarm and wondered whatever the strange noise was!

The elephant left the town behind. Beyond lay the woods, sloping up a big hill. Jumbo was pleased to come to trees and grass. He plodded on right into the wood and climbed halfway up the hill. Jimmy still followed him – and then he lost him!

It happened like this – the storm suddenly died down, and the lightning stopped. Jimmy could no longer see the elephant in the flashes, and as the wood was thick it was difficult to know which way Jumbo went now that he was not going down a road. Jimmy stopped and listened. Far away he could hear something crashing through the bushes – he knew it was Jumbo, but he could not tell which way to go to find him.

'Oh dear,' said the little boy, terribly disappointed. 'I've come all this way – and I'm wet through – and I haven't found Jumbo after all!'

He stood there by himself in the dark woods, wondering what to do. And then he suddenly saw a little light shining through the trees! He stared at it in surprise.

'What can that light be from?' he wondered. He made his way towards it, feeling before him as he went, for he did not want to walk into trees. It was dark and everywhere was wet. Jimmy shivered. He wished he were back in his own warm bed!

Stumbling over bushes and roots he came at last to the light. It shone from a cottage window. The blind was not drawn and Jimmy could see inside the room. He peeped in at the window.

A man was in the room, dressed in a gamekeeper's coat and leggings. He was bending over a dog that lay in the basket. The dog was ill, and one of its legs was bandaged. The man was stroking it and saying something to it, though Jimmy could not hear a word.

'He looks a kind man,' thought the little boy. 'Perhaps he will let me come in and dry my clothes.' So Jimmy knocked gently at the window.

The gamekeeper looked up at once, in the greatest astonishment, for it was the middle of the night. He walked to the window and opened it.

'Who's there?' he said.

'It's me, Jimmy Brown,' said Jimmy, the light shining on his face. 'I came to look for Jumbo, the elephant, but I've lost him, and I'm so wet I thought perhaps you'd let me come in and dry my clothes.'

The gamekeeper stared as if he couldn't believe his ears. 'What nonsense are you talking?' he said. 'Looking for an elephant – an *elephant*! Whatever do you mean?'

'It's Jumbo, the circus elephant,' said Jimmy, and he

was going on to explain everything when the keeper told him to go to the door and come inside.

The little boy was glad to get into the cottage. The gamekeeper listened to his story in surprise. Then he felt Jimmy's coat, which he had thrown on over his pyjamas.

'I'll make a fire here,' said the man. 'You'll get a terrible chill if you keep those wet clothes on any longer. It's a mercy you found me up. My dear old dog, Flossie, got knocked down by a car this morning and I'm sitting up with her tonight to make sure she's all right. Else I should have been in bed.'

He made Jimmy take off his wet things and put on a coat and dressing-gown of his. They were much too big for Jimmy, but they were dry. The man lighted a fire on the hearth and soon there was a cheerful crackling of wood. Jimmy was pleased. The gamekeeper made a big jug of cocoa too, and the little boy sat drowsily by the fire, drinking hot cocoa and feeling suddenly very sleepy.

'I do wish I could have found Jumbo,' he said. 'I don't know how I can find him now. Mr Tonks, his keeper, will be so upset.'

'Don't you worry about finding elephants,' said the man. 'I can track a baby rabbit if I want to – and you may be sure that Jumbo will leave tracks quite plain to see! We'll go hunting for him in the morning!'

'But I must go home tonight,' began Jimmy – and then somehow his eyes closed, his head nodded, and he was fast asleep in the keeper's chair by the blazing fire!

He didn't wake up till morning. He heard the gamekeeper moving about and opened his eyes. Breakfast was on the table! There was porridge, bread and marmalade, and hot cocoa. It looked good to Jimmy.

The man had put him on a sofa in the corner, still wearing his large coat and dressing-gown. But now Jimmy's own clothes were dry and he put them on, chattering to the kind keeper all the time, and really feeling most excited. They were going to find Jumbo after breakfast!

'How is your dog Flossie?' asked Jimmy, patting the sleek head of the big spaniel in the basket.

'Better,' said the keeper. 'I think her leg will heal all right. I'll leave her in her basket this morning with some milk near by, and she'll sleep and be all right. If it hadn't been for Flossie you wouldn't have seen a light shining in my cottage last night, young man!'

'I know,' said Jimmy stroking the dog, who lifted her pretty head and gave Jimmy a feeble lick with her tongue. 'Good dog, Flossie! Get better soon! Good dog, then!'

'You're good with animals,' said the keeper, watching Jimmy. 'Flossie hates strangers – you're the first one she has ever licked.'

Soon the breakfast things were cleared away and the two of them slipped out of doors into the wet woods. The sun was shining, the birds were singing, and everywhere was golden. It was a beautiful May day.

'Look! That's where Jumbo passed last night,' said Jimmy, pointing to where some bushes were trampled down. 'We can follow his track from there.'

'Come along, then,' said the keeper. So the two of them followed Jumbo's track. It was not at all difficult, for the elephant had made a real pathway for himself through the wood.

'Look! Jumbo pulled up a whole tree there!' said Jimmy in surprise. He pointed to where a birch tree lay uprooted. Yes – Jumbo had pulled it up. How strong he was!

'Elephants can easily pull up trees,' said the keeper. 'Come on – the track goes over to the right just here.'

They went on and on through the wood, up the side of the hill – and quite suddenly they came upon Jumbo! He was lying down beneath a thick oak tree, his ears flapping to and fro, and his little eyes watching to see who was coming.

'Jumbo! Dear old Jumbo! I've found you at last!' cried Jimmy and he ran up to the big animal and stroked his long trunk. Jumbo trumpeted loudly. He was pleased to see Jimmy. He was no longer frightened, for the storm had gone – but he felt strange and queer by himself in a quiet wood, instead of in the noisy circus field, with all his friends round him. He got to his feet and ran his trunk round Jimmy lovingly.

The gamekeeper stood a little way off, looking on in surprise. He was half afraid of the enormous elephant – but Jumbo took no notice of him at all. He had got his friend Jimmy and that was all he cared!

'Jumbo, you must come back to the circus field with me,' said Jimmy, stroking Jumbo's trunk. 'Mr Tonks will be looking for you.'

'Hrrumph!' said Jumbo, when he heard Mr Tonks's name. He adored his keeper. He put his trunk round Jimmy's waist and lifted him up on to his neck. But Jimmy cried out to him to take him down again.

'Jumbo, let me down! If you take me through the trees on your back the branches will sweep me off! You are so tall, you know. Let me walk beside you through the woods and when we come to the town I'll ride.'

Jumbo understood. He lifted Jimmy down again, and then the two of them started off through the woods, down the hill towards the town. Jimmy called goodbye to the kind gamekeeper, who was staring at them in wonder, and very soon the two were out of sight.

After a while the woods came to an end and Jimmy walked beside Jumbo up a lane. Jumbo stopped and looked down at Jimmy. 'Hrrumph?' he said gently.

Jimmy understood. 'Yes, you can carry me now,' he said. 'We can go more quickly then.'

Jumbo lifted him up on to his head. Jimmy crossed his legs and sat there. Jumbo set off at a good pace down the lane and into a big road. He knew the way back quite well, although he had only been there once, the night before.

People looked up when they heard the big elephant padding along – and *how* they stared when they saw Jimmy on the elephant! They ran after him, pointing and shouting in surprise and amazement.

'It's the elephant that was lost! Look, it's the circus elephant!' they cried.

Through the market place went Jimmy, feeling tremendously proud, for really he was making a great disturbance and everyone seemed most astonished. Jumbo padded on to the circus field – and there he and Jimmy were met by the whole of the circus folk, Mr Galliano and Mr Tonks at the front, Mr Tonks yelling himself hoarse with delight to see his beloved elephant safely back again!

Jimmy had to tell his tale over and over again. Mr Tonks flung his arms round him and hugged him till Jimmy felt as if his bones were breaking. The elephant's keeper was quite mad with joy and delight. Tears poured down his cheeks as he stroked Jumbo's trunk, and the big elephant stood trumpeting in joy to see his keeper again. Everyone was excited and pleased.

And in the middle of it all, Mr Galliano, his hat well on one side, suddenly made a most surprising speech!

'Jimmy Brown!' he began. 'You are a most remarkable boy – yes? You love animals and they love you – you should live with them and care for them. Yes? Very well. We will take you and your father with us, both of you, and if your mother will come too, then we will have your whole family, and it will not be too much for us. No? You shall belong to the circus – yes, no, yes?'

Mr Galliano got quite muddled, he was so pleased and excited. As for Jimmy he was almost off his head with delight. Belong to the circus? Go off with them – and Lotta! Oh, what joy! The very thing he would like best in all the world.

'I must go and tell my mother!' he said, and he ran off home at top speed!

8. Jimmy joins the circus

Jimmy tore home to tell his mother all the adventures of the night – and to ask her if she would go with the circus. Then Dad would have a job, and he, Jimmy, would be able to help with the animals, and Mother would be with them to care for them and love them. Nobody would have to be left behind.

His mother and father were looking very worried when he got home, for they had found his bed empty that morning and hadn't known where he had gone. And what had puzzled them more than ever was to find that he had left his trousers behind! Wherever could he have gone in his pyjamas?

Jimmy soon told them all about how he had gone to find Jumbo in the middle of the night – and how he had spent the night at the gamekeeper's cottage – and they had looked for Jumbo in the morning. His parents listened in amazement.

'But listen, Mum – listen, Dad,' said Jimmy, 'I've got something much more wonderful to tell you! Mr Galliano wants *me* to go off with the circus – to help with the animals! What do you think of that? And he says you can go too, Mother – and Dad will be the odd-job man and do everything that is needed in a travelling circus!'

His mother and father stared at Jimmy as if he had gone quite mad. Then his mother began to cry, quite suddenly. She wiped her eyes with her handkerchief and said, 'I'm not really crying. I'm happy to think your father's got a good job at last – and you're quite a hero, Jimmy darling – and I can go with you both and look after you.'

'Mother, then you'll come?' shouted Jimmy, jumping

up and down in joy, and flinging his arms first round his father and then round his mother. 'We'll all be together. Oh, that will be glorious.'

'Yes – but what about a caravan?' said his father. 'We can't all share the clown's caravan, you know. That would have been all right for me – but not for you two as well.'

'We'll ask Mr Galliano about that,' said Jimmy. 'He's a wonderful man. I'll go right away now. Mother, can you pack today and come?'

'Jimmy! Of course not!' said his mother, looking round at her bits of furniture.

'Oh, Mother, you must!' said Jimmy. 'You won't want much in a caravan, really you won't. I'll get Lotta's father and mother to come along and tell you what to take.'

The excited boy rushed off to the circus field. He was singing for joy. First he must find Lotta and tell her the great news. He saw her with five of the dogs.

'Lotta, Lotta!' he yelled. 'I've got news for you! *I'm* going to join the circus too.'

Lotta was so surprised and delighted that she dropped the dogs' lead and all the dogs scampered off in different directions. The two children spent ten minutes getting them back, and then Jimmy told Lotta everything. She listened joyfully, and then gave Jimmy a big pinch.

'I can't help pinching you, I feel so glad!' she said.

'Well, it's a funny way of showing you're glad,' said poor Jimmy, rubbing his arm. 'But you're a funny girl altogether, Lotta – more like a boy – so I don't mind much – I don't mind anything today, because I'm joining the circus, the circus, the circus!'

'He's joining our circus, circus, circus!' shouted Lotta, and she threw herself over on to her hands and turned cartwheel somersaults all round the field. That made Jimmy laugh. It always looked so easy and was so dreadfully difficult when *he* tried to do it!

He went to find Mr Galliano. Mr Galliano was so pleased that Jumbo had been found and brought back safely that his hat was almost falling off, it was so much on one side. He was glad to see Jimmy again.

'You are coming with us – yes?' he cried, and banged Jimmy on the back.

'Yes, Mr Galliano,' said Jimmy, his brown eyes shining brightly. 'But we haven't a caravan, you know. How can we manage it?'

'Easy, easy!' said Mr Galliano. 'We have an old small caravan that is used for storing things in. We will take them out, and put them into an empty cage for now. Your mother can clean out the old caravan and you can all come in that! Yes? But we go today, Jimmy, we go today! Is that your father I see over there – yes?'

It was. 'Good-day, sir,' said Mr Brown, smiling at Jimmy, who was capering round in delight. 'We'll all come with you, sir.'

Mr Galliano took Mr Brown to the old caravan and told him he could have it, if he would store the things inside it in an empty cage they had. Mr Brown listened. He turned to Jimmy.

'Go back to your mother and tell her all this,' he said. 'Take Lotta with you. She may be able to help.'

'We'll not start till two hours later than usual, yes?' said Mr Galliano generously. 'That will give you and your family time to get everything ready.'

My goodness, what a day that was! Jimmy, Lotta, and Lotta's mother, Lal, went rushing off to Jimmy's home to help his mother. Lal was a great help. She looked quickly round the bare little house and said at once what was to go and what was to be sold. She found a man who would buy the things that were not wanted. She helped to take down the curtains. She said that the frying-pans must certainly all be taken – and the big kettle – and the oil-stove for cooking – and the little stool – but only one chair. The big bed could go into the caravan, for it was not a very large size, and Jimmy would have to sleep on a mattress at night, in a corner of the caravan.

It did sound exciting. Lotta said they must take their two candlesticks, and a little folding-table. The iron must be taken, for circus clothes must always be fresh and stiffly ironed. The wash-tub could hang under the cara-

van. Jimmy entered into everything, and was so thrilled
to think he would sleep on a mattress only and not on a
bed that he could hardly stop dancing around.

'Jimmy, you are more hindrance than help,' said his
mother at last. 'Go to your father and ask him if he can
bring the caravan down to the house as soon as possible,
for we can easily put the things into it here.'

Off went Jimmy and Lotta, rushing at top speed.
Neither of them could walk that day, things were too
exciting! They found Mr Brown. He had stored all the
things from the old caravan in an empty cage, and had
given it a rough clean. It was a small and rather ugly old
caravan, badly in need of paint – but to Jimmy's eyes it
was beautiful! It was a home on wheels, and what more
could a little boy want?

He went to fetch one of the circus horses to take the
caravan down to his house. Soon there was great excitement in Jimmy's street when the neighbours learnt what
was happening. 'The Browns are going off with the
circus!' people shouted to one another, and they came to
help. Lal scrubbed the floor of the old caravan for
Jimmy's mother. Lotta cleaned the windows. There were
four – two little ones at the front and one at each side.
There was a door at the back and the usual little ladder
hanging down.

The carpet was put down. It was the one out of
Jimmy's little bedroom, for the other carpets were too big
for the small caravan. No curtains fitted the windows, so
those would have to be put up later. The stove was put in
its corner. The bed was put in, but not put up. There
wasn't time for that. In went the one chair and the little
stool, the frying-pans, and the kettle and all the rest.

In the middle of it all Lotta, who had gone back to help
her own mother pack up, came flying down the road.
'Jimmy! Jimmy! We're off! Oh, do hurry! Don't get left
behind!'

The last few things were bundled into the old caravan.
Jimmy waved goodbye and ran up the steps. His father
sat on the front and clicked to the horse. His mother shut

the door of her house for the last time and ran down the path, half laughing and half crying. The neighbours kissed her and wished her luck.

'Goodbye, goodbye!' they cried. 'We'll come and see you all when next the circus comes here. Goodbye!'

The horse trotted down the street, with Lotta riding on its back, and Mr Brown holding the reins. Lotta always jumped on a horse if she could!

They came to the circus field. Everyone there was on the move. The tents were down. The cages were in order. The caravans were passing out of the big gate one by one, Jumbo pulling three of them, as usual. There was a great deal of shouting and yelling. It was all most exciting.

Jimmy's father joined the line of caravans. Jimmy leaned out of his caravan. He saw Jumbo a good way in front, plodding along steadily – good old Jumbo. He saw Lilliput with Jemima the monkey cuddling him. He caught sight of Mr Galliano shouting to someone, his hat well on one side.

Soon the field was empty. The circus was on the way to its next stopping-place. And with it were Jimmy and his mother and father, cosy in their caravan, wondering where they were going to, and what was going to happen to them.

'We've got a house on wheels, Mum,' said Jimmy happily. 'I've always wanted to live in one. We belong to the circus now. Oh, isn't it lovely?'

Jimmy's mother busied herself in putting up the bed. There was very little room left in the caravan when that was up! Jimmy had to sit on it when he looked out of the window – but usually he sat on the top step at the door, whistling a merry tune as the circus procession passed through villages and towns, enjoying all the stares and shouts he got. Ah – Jimmy felt very grand – for he was a proper circus-boy now!

9. The circus goes on the road

The first day that Jimmy travelled with the circus was really very exciting. The circus had to go slowly, for Jumbo the elephant plodded along in a very leisurely manner, and the caravans kept up with him. Sometimes the horses went on a good way in front and left old Jumbo behind with the three caravans he pulled – but then the horses had a good rest later on, so that Jumbo always caught up with them in the end.

Anyway, nobody ever minded how slow or fast the procession went along. Mr Galliano always decided how long they were to be on the road to the next town. He sent one of his men in front of him to paste up great posters in the town they were going to, telling the people there about the circus.

This time they were to be two days on the road. They were going to a very big town – the town of Bigchester – and it was a long way off. They hoped to be there on Tuesday night, and by Thursday evening everything would be ready for the circus to give its first show. Lotta told Jimmy all this as they went along. She had come to Jimmy's caravan and was sitting on the steps with him, being jolted up and down. Their caravan was being pulled by one of the ordinary horses, not one of the show horses, who were only used to pulling Mr Galliano's beautiful carriage.

'Oh, Jimmy, I *am* so glad you are coming with us!' said Lotta, her blue eyes shining like forget-me-nots. 'I shall have you to help me every day now. I wonder what jobs Mr Galliano will give you to do. You'll help with the animals, I expect.'

'Yes, that's what I'm to do,' said Jimmy proudly. 'But I

say, Lotta – won't it be funny not going to school? I've
always been, you know – and now I shan't go any more.'

'*I've* never been in my life,' said Lotta. 'I can read a
tiny bit, but I can't write.'

'Lotta!' said Jimmy, in horror. 'You can't *write*! How
dreadful!'

'It isn't dreadful,' said Lotta, going red. '*I* don't mind!
I've got nobody to write letters to, have I?'

'You want writing for other things besides that,' said
Jimmy. '*I* shall teach you to read and write properly,
Lotta. You will have to come to our caravan in the evening, and I'll show you my books and teach you lots of
things.'

'All right,' said Lotta. But she didn't look very pleased.
Lotta didn't want books – they seemed dull to her. She
made up her mind to be silly and stupid when Jimmy was
trying to teach her, so that he would soon give it up.

Lilliput waved to them from the next caravan. He too
was delighted that Jimmy was coming with them. Everyone liked the merry little boy.

'Hallo, Lilliput!' shouted Jimmy to the little fellow.
'How are Jemima and the other monkeys? Were they
frightened of the storm last night?'

'Not a bit!' yelled back Lilliput. 'Jemima got down
under the bedclothes and cuddled my feet. She always
does that if there's a noise going on outside. The others
never made a sound.'

'Oh, fancy having a monkey cuddling your feet all
night!' said Jimmy, surprised. That was the best of a
circus. The most extraordinary and amusing things happened every day. Jimmy beamed. He was very happy. He
could hear his mother in the caravan singing a little song.
She was happy too. His father had a good job with the
circus, Jimmy was going to work too, and she was going
to be with them. Everything was lovely.

Just then the caravan went over a big stone and gave
such a jolt that Jimmy fell off the steps and rolled on the
ground. Lotta laughed till she cried. 'That shows you're
not a real circus-boy,' she said. 'A real circus-boy would

never fall off caravan steps. Oh, you did look funny, Jimmy!'

Jimmy gave the cheeky little girl a push, and *she* rolled down the steps too. But almost before she reached the ground she turned a half-somersault, landed on her hands and swung over on to her feet again as lightly as a cat – and she was up on the caravan steps beside Jimmy giving him a hard pinch before he could say a word!

'Ow!' shouted Jimmy, for Lotta could give some really dreadful pinches. 'Don't!'

'Now, now, you two,' said his mother from inside the caravan. 'Those steps are not a very safe place to quarrel on. Lotta, what *have* you done to your hair? It looks dreadful. Did you brush it this morning?'

'*Brush it!*' said Lotta, in surprise. 'Of course not, Mrs Brown. I only brush it when I'm going into the circus-ring when the show is on.'

'Goodness gracious!' said Mrs Brown. 'No wonder it always looks so untidy. Now, Lotta, if you like to go and make yourself really clean and tidy, you can come and have a meal with us. I've got some sardines and a new ginger cake.'

'Oooh!' said Lotta, who was nearly always hungry, just like Jimmy. 'All right. I'll go and do what I can. It seems a waste of time, and Lal, my mother, will think it very queer when she sees me tidying up – but I'd love to have something to eat.'

She jumped to the ground and ran off to her own cara-van. Jimmy laughed.

'Oh, Mother!' he said. 'I'm sure you'll never change Lotta. She always has dirty hands and untidy hair, and she doesn't care a bit if she has any buttons on or not.'

'Well, Jimmy, don't you get it into your head that you're going to get like *that*,' said his mother firmly. 'Circus-folk are kindly, good people, but I do think they might be a bit cleaner and tidier; and Lotta's got to learn that I shall not let her come to meals here unless she sits down as clean and tidy as we do. Now, come here and wash your hands.'

Jimmy squeezed into the caravan. Really, there was hardly room to move, with the bed and the stove and the tiny folding-table. He dipped his hands into the bowl of water and washed them. He wetted his hair and brushed it. His mother was busy cutting up the ginger cake. It did look good!

Lotta soon came back. She looked quite different. Her hair shone and her face and hands were clean.

'Good girl, Lotta,' said Jimmy's mother. Lotta was pleased, she liked Jimmy's mother.

'You must sit on the steps and eat your meal there,' said Mrs Brown. 'There's no room in here. I'll give your father a sandwich and a piece of cake too, through this little front window.'

Jimmy's father was driving the horse in front. They could hear him whistling as he sat there, enjoying the May sunshine and the sweet-smelling hedges as he passed them. Jimmy's mother pushed open one of the little windows that looked out to the front of the caravan. She put out her hand and tapped Mr Brown on the shoulder. He turned round in surprise.

'Sandwiches and cake for you, Tom,' said Mrs Brown, and he took them in delight, for he too was very hungry. Soon everyone was eating hard, and there wasn't a scrap left of that ginger cake by the time Jimmy and Lotta had finished.

'Oh, I do think this is fun!' said Jimmy, looking up into the blue sky. 'Jogging along like this, nothing to worry about, no school tomorrow, holidays all the time.'

'Holidays!' said Lotta, in surprise. 'Why, Jimmy, whatever are you talking about? The only holidays we circusfolk get are the days when we travel, like this! It's hard work all the rest of the time. Yes, and you just wait till we get to Bigchester and begin to unpack everything – you'll hear Mr Galliano shouting at everyone then and, my word, you'll have to skip round and do your bit too. You don't know what hard work is yet. School is play compared to a circus life.'

The circus caravans, cages, and carriages jogged on through the long May day. The dogs yapped and barked in their cages, for they were hot and restless. Jimmy slipped along to see if they had plenty of water to drink. Such a lot of it got spilt during the jolting of the journey. He filled their big stone bowls up again, and gave them a handful of dry biscuits. They crowded round him, licking his hands and jumping up, delighted to see him. The sun shone down hotly into their big cage. Jimmy saw a blind rolled up at the top of the cage, and he pulled it down so that they might have shade. One little dog was bad-tempered with the heat and he was put into a separate cage, where he could lie quietly by himself. There were three or four of these separate cages at one end of the big caravan-cage, so that any dog could be separated from the others at times.

Usually they loved to be with one another, playing and rolling about, for they were a happy, healthy lot, very good-tempered and jolly. Jimmy peeped in at the little dog who was separated from the others and gave him some fresh water too. 'Woof!' said the dog gratefully.

'We'll give them a run when we get to our camping-ground tonight,' said Lotta. 'It will be fun to go off for a walk this evening.'

On and on went the circus caravans through the May evening. The sun was sinking now, but the days were long and full of light. Jimmy thought Jumbo must be very hot plodding all day in the sun – but Jumbo didn't seem to mind much. Once Mr Tonks stopped the caravan and took Jumbo to a stream near by. Jumbo put his long trunk into the water and then lifted it and squirted the cool water all over his dusty back. He did this a good many times till he was really cool, and then he suddenly squirted Jimmy and Lotta, who were standing near by watching him.

Lotta jumped out of the way in time, but Jimmy got soaked. How Lotta laughed!

'He often does that for a joke,' she said. 'I guessed he was going to do it. Oh, how wet you are, Jimmy!'

Jimmy laughed too, and Jumbo gave a loud snort. 'Hrrumph!'

'He's laughing too,' said Mr Tonks, his keeper. 'Come on, Jumbo – back you go.'

About eight o'clock, when the sun was low behind the trees and the shadows were very long indeed, Mr Galliano called a halt. They had come to a shady piece of woodland, and there was a brook near by for water.

At once everything was bustle and flurry. The horses were taken out of the line and allowed to graze. The caravans were turned on to the grass, and the steps of each were let right down to the ground. The dogs began to bark, for they knew that a walk was near at hand. Jemima the monkey left Lilliput and darted up a tree, where she sat chattering and laughing. The other monkeys, who were not so tame as Jemima, were safely in their big roomy cage.

Fires were made and soon delicious smells stole through the air. It was such a glorious evening that everyone ate in the open air. It was warm, and the scent of near-by hawthorn, which lay like a drift of snow over the hedges, came all round the camp, making everyone sniff in delight.

Jimmy's mother saw everybody making a fire near their caravans and she thought she would too. But she did not know the trick of making a camp-fire and soon she was quite in despair. Jimmy had gone off to help his father with some of the horses, and Mrs Brown thought she would never be able to cook her herrings.

But Lotta came skipping along to help. 'We'll get it all done by the time Jimmy and Brownie are back,' she cried. 'I'll do the fire for you, Mrs Brown.'

And by the time Jimmy and his father came back, the fire was crackling, the herrings were cooking, and it looked too lovely for words.

'Oh, I *am* going to enjoy my first evening camping out!' cried Jimmy.

10. The first night in the caravan

Jimmy thought that herrings had never tasted so nice before. It was getting dark now and the fire they were sitting round glowed red and yellow. There were two herrings for everyone, and hot cocoa and bread and butter. Jimmy ate hungrily. Everyone chattered and laughed. It was nice to be at rest again after a day of jolting and jerking.

The circus horses grazed peacefully. They were tethered by long ropes, so they could move about freely. Someone had to keep awake and watch over them all night long, for they were valuable horses. Jumbo the elephant was having a good feast, for he was hungry too. They could hear him saying, 'Hrrumph, hrrumph!' now and again, as if he were talking to himself. Mr Tonks had tethered him to a very big tree with a very strong wire rope this time – for he did not want to lose Jumbo again if a storm came.

The light of several camp-fires shone out in the piece of open woodland. Mr Galliano called one of his men to him and sent him round to each caravan.

'All fires to be out in half-an-hour's time,' said the man. Lotta explained why.

'We never leave any fire burning at night,' she said. 'A scrap of burning paper blowing out in the wind might set a wooden caravan or cage on fire. So Galliano always sets a time for every fire to be out.'

They sat around it for a little while longer, and then someone yelled for Lotta.

'Lotta! Where are you? What about those dogs? They are barking their heads off.'

'Come on, Jimmy!' said Lotta, getting up. 'We must

take the dogs for their walk before it gets too late.'

'Dear, dear!' said Mrs Brown, who didn't like these late nights for Jimmy at all. 'Must you really go, Jimmy? You ought to be in bed!'

'He can sleep in the day when we're travelling, if he's tired,' said Mr Brown. 'Circus hours are different from those of ordinary folks, Mary. Go on, Jimmy – take the dogs with Lotta. I'll put out the fire.'

The two children set off with the dogs. How pleased the animals were to stretch their legs! Lotta and Jimmy set free three of the dogs who were really obedient and would come when they were whistled – the others had to go on the big leads. They set off down a little lane that seemed to lead to a hillside.

'Isn't it lovely, Lotta!' said Jimmy, sniffing the white may as they passed it. 'And look at the moon!'

The moon was coming slowly up over the hill in front of them. The countryside was bathed in light, pale and cold and silvery. Everything could be seen quite plainly, and Lotta and Jimmy thought it was just like daytime with the colours missing.

It was a lovely walk. The two children were tired but they were glad to stretch their legs, too, for they had been riding for many hours. The dogs pulled at their lead, and the three who were free tore up and down and round about as if they were quite mad.

They did not meet anyone, for the countryside just there was quite deserted. Only a lonely farmhouse shone in the moonlight not far off. A dog there barked loudly.

'Now it's time to go back,' said Lotta. 'My goodness, I'm sleepy! Come on, Punch! Come on, Judy! Where's Darky? Whistle him, Jimmy. Your whistle is louder than mine.'

Jimmy whistled. Darky came rushing up, and they turned back. 'I'm going to try and teach *all* the dogs to come as soon as they are whistled,' said Jimmy. 'Then we can let the whole lot off the lead whenever we like, Lotta, and they will be able to have a glorious run.'

Back they went to the camp, singing loudly. Lotta

knew old circus songs, and Jimmy knew songs he had
learnt at school. First one sang, and then the other. It was
fun. The dogs seemed to like it, for they were all quiet
and good.

When they got back to the camp, all the fires were out
and everyone was getting ready to go to bed. Lilliput and
Jemima were already in their caravan, and Jimmy wondered if the little monkey was cuddling Lilliput's feet
again, or was snuggled round his neck. He thought it
must be funny to sleep with a little monkey cuddled up to
you always!

'Jimmy! What a long time you've been!' called his
mother, as the little boy helped Lotta to put the dogs into
their big cage, and fed them. 'Hurry now – it's time you
were in bed and asleep!'

'Goodnight, Lotta,' said Jimmy, as he heard Laddo,
Lotta's father, calling her. 'See you tomorrow!'

The two sped off to their different caravans. Jimmy's
mother had a bowl of cold water from the brook near by
for him to wash in. In a trice he was in his pyjamas and
was cuddling down on the little mattress on the floor of
the caravan beside his parents' bed. What fun to sleep in a
house on wheels!

'Goodnight, Jimmy,' said his mother, who was already
in bed. 'Shut the caravan door now, Tom. I know it's a
hot night – but really, I can't do as the others do yet, and
leave the door open.'

So the door was shut and all the little windows were
opened to let in the sweet air of the May night. Jimmy
threw off one of his blankets. It really was too warm to
have two! He lay there with one over him, listening to the
call of an owl in the wood, and seeing a big white star
through the side window. He heard one of the horses
whinny and a dog whine.

'I'm one of the circus-folk now,' he thought sleepily.
'I'm one of the circus-f – f – f. . . .'

And then he was fast asleep, dreaming of a long white
road he had to follow with his caravan. He slept all night
long without waking – and do you know, he didn't even

wake when his mother slipped out of bed in the morning and opened the caravan door! She had to walk right over Jimmy, and she laughed when she saw him sleeping there so peacefully.

The sun was up, and the countryside was golden. The sky was a pure blue, and everything looked new and fresh. Jimmy's mother stood looking out. She was happy. This was different from being in a town, in a dirty little street, with a tiny backyard and not a tree to be seen.

When Jimmy woke up at last there was quite a bustle going on in the camp. Everyone was having breakfast, the horses had been watered, Jumbo had been fed, the dogs had been seen to, and there was a lovely smell of frying bacon and sausages.

Jimmy sat up. 'Wherever am I?' he said to himself in astonishment, looking round the old caravan, which seemed dark compared with the bright sunshine outside. Then he remembered and gave a shout. 'Hurrah! I'm with the circus! Mother! Where are you?'

'Out here, Jimmy, cooking breakfast!' cried his mother. 'Go and wash in the brook. Your towel is on your blanket.'

Jimmy put on his things and scampered down to the brook. Oooh! The water was cold! He ran back to the caravan as hungry as a hunter, brushed his hair, and squatted down on the grass to eat a piece of bacon and a brown sausage. Lotta was having breakfast with Lal and Laddo not far away, and she waved to him.

'Sleepy-head!' she shouted.

'Lotta peeped at you four times this morning to see if you were awake, but you weren't,' said Mrs Brown. 'I wouldn't let her wake you. You're not used to circus hours yet, and I don't want you to get tired out at the beginning.'

'Oh, Mother, I shan't!' said Jimmy. 'Oh, I *am* sorry I didn't wake before. Are we going off early?'

'Yes, soon after breakfast,' said his father. 'I've got to go and help with the horses, so you must give your mother a hand, Jimmy.'

He went off, and Jimmy washed up for his mother, and did what he could. She sent him to the farm to buy six new-laid eggs and a pint of milk. When Lilliput saw him going he went with him, Jemima sitting on his shoulder as usual.

'New-laid eggs!' said Lilliput, rattling his money in his pocket. 'I'll buy some too; and you'd like one, wouldn't you, Jemima darling?'

Jemima made a chattering noise and bit Lilliput's ear gently. Then she sat on the very top of his head, and when the farmer's wife came to the door and saw the monkey there, she fled away screaming down the passage.

'It's all right!' shouted Jimmy. 'It's only a tame monkey! Please can we have some new-laid eggs and some milk. I've got a jug!'

The farmer's wife peeped round the corner of the passage. 'You take that monkey away,' she called to Lilliput. 'Nasty fierce creature!'

Lilliput grinned and put Jemima under his coat. The farmer's wife fetched six new-laid eggs and filled Jimmy's jug with milk. Then she shut the door very firmly.

Jimmy laughed and went back to the camp with Lilliput. The horses were all harnessed and ready to go. Jumbo was out in the road, flapping his big ears, with Mr Tonks beside him. Mrs Brown was standing at the door of her caravan waiting for Jimmy to come.

'Hurry, Jimmy!' she cried. 'We are just off!'

All the fires were stamped out. Every bit of rubbish had been picked up and burned before the camp was ready to go. Mr Galliano would never let any mess be left behind, for he said that made people think circus-folk were as rubbishy as their litter. And, my goodness! If anyone dared to leave papers or tins behind, what a temper Mr Galliano flew into. He was a marvellous man, kind but firm, good-hearted but hot-tempered, and everyone loved him and tried to please him.

There came the loud crack of a whip, sounded three times – the signal to go. The horses started off, and Jumbo put his best foot forward. Lilliput jumped on his caravan and waved to Jimmy. Oona the acrobat was there, and Sticky Stanley the clown was sitting in his rather dirty caravan, singing a new and funny song he had made up the day before. The circus was on the move!

Down the road they went, some of the caravans sending up smoke from their stoves through the little chimneys. Mr Galliano sat in state in his carriage, his top hot on one side. Mrs Galliano, fat and good-tempered, sat beside him. Nobody knew her very well. She kept herself to herself and waited on Mr Galliano all day long. The lovely horses drew the carriage along in great style.

'Galliano's always in his carriage dressed like that when we drive through the towns near our show-place,' said Lotta to Jimmy. 'Everyone turns out to see him and that makes them talk about the circus and they come to see it. We'll get to Bigchester about tea-time, I expect.'

Jimmy settled himself down for the day's travelling. It was exciting to see everything they passed. The circus went through little villages and big towns, through the green countryside and by big and little farms. Everyone came out to watch the procession. Mr Galliano bowed to left and right like a king, and the trumpeters on the horses in front blew loudly, 'Tan-tan-tara! Tan-tan-tara!'

People stared at Jimmy as he passed, and he felt very proud. 'I wonder what that boy does in the circus!' somebody said. 'Perhaps he walks the tightrope.'

'No, he doesn't!' yelled back naughty little Lotta. 'He just gives the elephant its bath and puts it into its cot at night!'

11. Lotta gives Jimmy a riding lesson

At about five o'clock the circus came to its next camping-place, where it was to stay for three weeks. The circus-folk had been there before, some years back, and they said that the people of Bigchester were very generous and came often to see the circus, so that Mr Galliano and everyone made a lot of money.

Jimmy was pleased to hear this. 'We shall be able to buy some paint and paint the old caravan up a bit,' he said to his father. 'And I'd like some pretty curtains at the windows, like those Mr Galliano has in his caravan.'

But Mr Brown had no time to talk when the circus reached its camping-place. The odd-job man in a circus has a hundred bits of work to do, all different, and many of them to be done all at once. Mr Brown hurried here and there and everywhere, he was shouted for by everybody, most of all by Mr Galliano, who seemed to be in twenty different places at once.

The caravans turned into a huge field. The cages were all set in one corner. The caravans were set in a wide circle together. The wagons and vans that held all the circus benches and tents and odds and ends were put in the middle. That was where the great circus tent was to be put up. Brownie, as everyone called Jimmy's father, hurried to and fro, giving a hand here and a hand there.

Mr Galliano shouted and yelled, and Jumbo the elephant lifted his trunk and trumpeted loudly as if he were trying to drown Galliano's big voice. Lotta laughed. She always kept out of the way when the circus was settling into camp, for she had found out that grown-ups were very cross when they were busy. She and Jimmy were underneath Jimmy's caravan, packing away things that need not be kept inside the small caravan – the wash-tub, a box of all kinds of things, a trunk of clothes, and an odd saucepan or two. Really, the caravan was so tiny that even a saucepan seemed in the way.

For four hours there was a bustle and noise and shout-ing. Then gradually it died down. The camp was settling in. The horses were the first to be looked after always, for they had to be kept simply perfect. They were now peace-fully eating the grass at one end of the field, under the eye of George, one of the horsemen. Jumbo was tied up to a strong post – and how Jimmy laughed to see that the post was itself tied to the front of Mr Tonks's caravan!

'Mr Tonks, Mr Tonks!' shouted the little boy, 'if Jumbo runs away again in the middle of the night, he'll drag his post off and the post will drag off your caravan, and you'll go bumping all over the place!'

'Just what I planned,' said Mr Tonks, with a grin. 'I'm not going to have Jumbo sneaking off by himself any more. No – if he goes, he takes me with him.'

A great many people from the town had come to watch the circus settling in. Jimmy felt proud as he walked about, for he could see that the boys who were watching wished very much that they belonged to the circus too. Jimmy hoped that Lotta wouldn't tell them that he bathed the elephant at night and put it to bed, as she had told the people along the road. Really, you never knew what that little monkey of a Lotta was going to say!

'We begin the circus on Thursday night,' said Mr Gal-liano to his folk. 'Everything must be ready then.'

That night Jimmy lay on his little mattress in the cara-van again, and he slept so soundly that he didn't hear Jumbo trumpeting in the night because Jemima the monkey had felt too hot in her caravan and had slipped out and played a little trick on old Jumbo. She had crept up behind him as he lay sleeping in the field, and tickled one of his big ears with a stick she had found.

Jumbo flapped his ear and slept on. Jemima ticked his ear again. Jumbo flapped it once more. Jemima went on, and at last Jumbo woke up and trumpeted loudly when

he saw the naughty little monkey sitting near by. Mr
Tonks poked his head out of his caravan door and
shouted to Jumbo to be 'quiet. Jemima slipped away,
chattering to herself in glee. She could really be a very
naughty little creature, though everyone loved her and
never seemed to mind what she did.

The next day there was a great bustle again. Banging
and hammering went on all day long. The great circus
tent was put up. It rose high into the air, and Jimmy
helped to knock in the pegs that held the ropes for it.
Then the benches were unpacked and carried to the tent.
Three of them had to be mended, and Jimmy's father
soon did that.

'Come with me into the circus-ring, Jimmy,' said Lotta
that afternoon, when the tent was up. 'I've got to practise
some more riding, Laddo says. He's got the horses ready.
You come too and watch me.'

Jimmy went with Lotta. She was not wearing her
lovely fluffy circus frock, but just her old jersey and skirt.
She kicked off her shoes when she got into the great red
ring. Laddo, her father, was there waiting, and so was
Lal, her mother. They smiled at Jimmy.

'I'll have to teach you to ride too, Jimmy,' said Laddo.
'You won't be a circus-boy till you can ride any horse
under the sun.'

Jimmy watched Laddo and Lal practising their marvellous riding. They had three white horses there and
they rode them bareback, sitting frontways and back-
ways and sideways, kneeling, standing, balancing on one
leg and then the other. It was wonderful to watch them.

'Now, Lotta!' said her father. 'Come along! Do your
tricks quickly, because we want you to learn a new one.'

Lotta leapt lightly up on to the back of a horse. She
rode round the ring once, and then jumped to her feet on
the horse's back. Up and down, up and down on the
horse's back she went as it galloped round the ring, standing there as lightly as a fairy.

Laddo took another horse and let it run side by side
with Lotta's horse. 'Jump on to his back now, Lotta!' he

said. 'Jump! Here is the place to jump – I have marked it in black.'

Jimmy saw that the broad part of the horse's back was marked with a black ring. That was where Lotta was to jump. Jimmy felt afraid. He hoped she wouldn't fall.

'Will you catch her if she falls?' he asked Laddo anxiously.

'She won't be hurt if she does fall,' said Laddo, laughing, and Lotta laughed too.

'Now, jump!' shouted Laddo, running with the second horse. Lotta jumped – and landed most beautifully cn the other horse's back, just where Laddo had marked the black ring. She kept her balance for half a moment, then lost it – and slipped gracefully down on to the horse's back, laughing.

'No, that won't do, Lotta,' said Laddo. 'Try again. You must keep your balance, and then, when you have ridden round the ring once, jump back to your own horse again.'

Lotta slithered down from the second horse and jumped lightly on to her own horse again. She stood up and waited her time. At exactly the right moment the little girl jumped and landed neatly on the second horse's back. She stood there, trying to get her balance, and this time she was quite all right. She gave a yell of delight and stood on one foot as she rode round, kicking the other in the air.

'Now back on the other horse, Lotta!' shouted her father. So back she went, very lightly, but just missed her balance again and, to Jimmy's dismay, fell from the horse.

But he needn't have been frightened. Lotta was like a cat and always fell on her feet. She landed lightly on the red plush ring itself.

Laddo was cross with her and so was Lal, her mother. 'I shall send Jimmy out if you don't work properly,' scolded Lal. 'You will spend the rest of the evening practising, Lotta, and if you can't do it properly then, you will get up at five o'clock tomorrow morning and practise again.'

Lotta sulked. She jumped on to her horse again and began practising properly. Whilst she was riding round and round, jumping to and fro, Sticky Stanley the clown came in.

'All right, Lotta; don't stop,' he said. 'I've come to practise some new somersaults. But I want to do them round the red plush ring itself, so you won't worry me.'

The clown, who didn't look at all like a clown today, because he was dressed in a yellow jersey and a dirty pair of grey flannel trousers, began to turn somersaults round the red ring. Over and over he went, and only once fell off. He fell right under the feet of one of the horses, but the horse neatly jumped over him and went on again without losing a step.

'Hey, Jimmy, you come and do a few somersaults,' said Stanley the clown. Lotta stopped the horses to give them a rest, and watched Sticky Stanley teaching poor Jimmy.

Jimmy could do one head-over-heels quite well, but he couldn't possibly do about twelve, one after another, as Stanley could. It made him giddy to do even three.

'Jimmy, you said you couldn't ride,' said Lotta. 'Come along up on my horse and see if you can.'

'But I'd fall off!' said Jimmy, in horror. 'Your horse hasn't any saddle or stirrups.'

'You must learn to ride bareback or you'll be no use on a horse,' laughed Lotta. 'Come on, up you get!'

And up Jimmy had to get. He held on to the reins for dear life, and thought that a horse was about the most slippery creature to sit on that he had ever met. He slithered first one way and then another, and at last he slid off altogether and landed with a bump on the ground.

Sticky Stanley and Lotta held on to one another and laughed till the tears ran down their faces. They thought it was the funniest sight in the world to see poor Jimmy slipping about on the solemn, cantering horse.

'Oh, Stanley, if you could only do that at the circus tomorrow night, the people would laugh till they cried,' said Lotta.

'That's an idea, Lotta!' said the clown. He looked at

Jimmy. 'Get up on the horse's back and do that again, old chap,' he said. 'If I see it once more I'll be able to do it myself.'

'No, thank you,' said Jimmy firmly, rubbing himself hard where he had been bumped.

'Go on, Jimmy, be a sport,' said Lotta.

So Jimmy changed his mind and got on Lotta's horse again. But it was just as bad as before. Jimmy simply could *not* stay on that horse. It bumped him up into the air, and then when he came down again the horse was just bumping up, and knocked his breath out of him, and he began to slide about, first this way and then the other, being bumped all the time. At last he slid right off the back of the horse over the tail, and came down with such a bump that he couldn't breathe for a minute.

Stanley and Lotta sat down on the ground and laughed again till their sides ached. 'I must do that, I simply must,' said the clown. He got up and went to Lotta's horse which galloped solemnly round and round the ring the whole time. Of course Stanley could ride very well indeed – but this time he pretended he was Jimmy, and slithered about and gave great groans and grunts, and at last fell right underneath the horse and got all tangled up with his own legs.

'Well, if I was as funny as that, no wonder you laughed at me,' said Jimmy, who had laughed so much that he couldn't stand up. 'Do that tomorrow night, Stanley.'

'Right!' said Stanley. 'I will! I'll have your horse for that, Lotta. She's careful with her feet.'

'It *will* be fun when the show opens again tomorrow!' said Jimmy. 'I *am* looking forward to it!'

12. A good time for the circus

By the next night the circus was all ready. Everyone had worked hard all Wednesday and Thursday, and now, by six o'clock, everything was spick and span, and the circus-folk were getting into their circus things.

Lotta came to Jimmy's caravan and begged Mrs Brown to iron out her fluffy skirt. 'Lal, my mother, is so busy,' she said. 'Her frock has got torn and she is mending it. Iron my frock for me, Mrs Brown, there's a dear.'

So Mrs Brown heated her iron over the stove and ironed Lotta's pretty frock. It took a long time, and whilst it was being done, Lotta washed her hair and dried it.

'Can you do that jumping trick all right now, Lotta?' asked Jimmy anxiously.

'Of course!' said Lotta. 'It's easy! You watch me to-night, Jimmy. I'll get more claps than anyone.'

When the frock was finished, the little girl ran off happily. She loved the times when the show was on. She loved the glare of lights in the big tent, the smell of the warm horses, and the shouts and whip-cracks of Mr Galliano when he went into the ring.

One by one the circus-folk slipped from their caravans and ran across to the big tent to get their animals or to find their things. Oona the acrobat placed his ladder ready and his tightrope. Sticky Stanley blew up some big balloons he was going to be silly with that night. Lilliput took his monkeys with him, and Jimmy saw that Jemima had on a new pink skirt and little bonnet. She looked as sweet as a monkey can look.

The townspeople streamed in at the gate. A man stood there blowing a trumpet – tan-tan-tara! It sounded exciting. 'Come to the circus, tan-tan-tara! Come to the circus, tan-tan-tara!'

Jimmy too had been busy. Every one of the dogs had been well brushed twice that day. They were all eager to get into the ring and do their tricks. They pawed at their cage door and yapped to be out. They had been for a good long walk that day with Jimmy and Lotta, but they wanted to stretch their legs again. Jumbo the elephant flapped his big ears to and fro and trumpeted to the people round him. He too wanted to get into the lighted ring and show what he could do!

The circus began. Jimmy stood outside the entrance that the performers used, and got things ready for them. He held the horses until it was time for them to go into the ring. He handed Oona the acrobat his ladder, and got his tightrope ready for him. He gave Lilliput the little table and chairs that his monkeys used when they had their tea-party in the middle of the ring. He was very useful indeed.

When Jumbo the elephant was plodding into the ring to play cricket with his keeper, Mr Tonks, Jimmy saw Mr Tonks making anxious signs to him.

'The ball – the ball, Jimmy!' said Mr Tonks. He had put it down somewhere and couldn't find it. Jimmy guessed that Jemima the monkey had gone off with it, and he raced off to his own caravan. Underneath it was a box, and he knew that he had an old red ball of his own there. He found it, tore back to the tent and sent it rolling into the ring just in time. Mr Tonks was pleased. Jimmy was really a most useful little boy!

After Jumbo had played cricket and had heaps of clapping and cheering, the three white horses went in, and Laddo, Lal, and Lotta rode them cleverly, standing on them, swinging from one to another and never falling once.

Jimmy watched for Lotta to do her new trick. She stood up on her own horse, a lovely little figure in a fairy-like frock, with long silver wings spreading behind her. She really did act like a fairy too, for she seemed to fly from one horse's back to another, she was so light.

Jimmy need not have worried about Lotta falling, for the little girl was as sure-footed as a goat. She jumped to and fro, always on the right spot, whilst the horses went solemnly galloping round and round the ring. People stood up in their seats and shouted loudly, for they thought Lotta was wonderful. Jimmy clapped too, from where he stood, peeping in at the entrance to the ring. How he wished he could do things like Lotta! But maybe he would be able to some day, if he practised hard.

Then in went Sticky Stanley the clown again to do his new funny trick on the horse. Jimmy watched him – he ran into the ring and jumped on to the back of Lotta's horse, which was still going round and round. The other two horses were led out by Lotta.

'Yoicks!' shouted the clown, pretending to gallop the horse – and then he began to slip off, just as Jimmy had done. First he went this way and got right again, and then he slid the other way, being bumped, bumped, bumped by the horse all the time! Oh dear, how everyone laughed! Then the clown hung round the horse's neck – then he slid back again – and at last slithered right off over the horse's tail, and landed with a bump on the ground, just as Jimmy did the day before!

Everyone laughed and shouted, and Sticky Stanley got even more clapping than he usually did. He was pleased when he ran out of the ring, doing somersaults every now and again.

He saw Jimmy standing by the ring entrance and he grinned at him. 'Hallo, youngster!' he said; 'your trick went well – didn't it? – but my word, I shall have a big bruise tonight! Here's something for you – catch!'

He threw something round and shining to Jimmy. The little boy caught it. It was a two-shilling piece. Jimmy stared in delight. He had never had so much money in his life before!

The show went off very well indeed. Mr Galliano was pleased. He wore his hat well over his right ear the next day, and Mrs Galliano bought tins of fruit salad for everyone and the biggest jug of cream that Jimmy had ever seen. It was fun eating fruit salad and cream in the field for dinner next day. You never knew what was going to happen in a circus!

Jimmy was busy all that week. He helped with the dogs, and soon Lal and Laddo left them entirely to the two children, for they loved the dogs and could be trusted to look after them well. Jimmy helped Mr Tonks with the elephant too, and learnt how to rub down the horses with George, one of the grooms. All the animals were good with Jimmy. It was really marvellous to see what he could do with them. When Darky got a bone in his throat and was in such pain that not even Mr Galliano liked to go near him, Jimmy didn't mind.

He went up to poor Darky, who was almost choking, and put his hand right down Darky's throat. He felt the bone there, gave it a sharp twist, and up it came! Darky was so grateful that he licked Jimmy's shoes till they shone.

'Good boy, Jimmy, good boy – yes?' said Mr Galliano. 'You were not afraid of being bitten – no?'

'No, sir,' said Jimmy. 'I never thought of it. Darky wouldn't bite me.'

The circus show went on until Saturday and began again on Monday. It did very well indeed, and Mr Galliano always wore his hat well on one side. He gave Mr Brown, Jimmy's father, an extra sum of money because he worked so hard and was so useful. Mr Brown ran back to his caravan with it.

'Look!' he said to Jimmy and Jimmy's mother. 'Two pounds! What about doing up the old caravan and making it look nice?'

So off went Jimmy with his father that afternoon to buy a tin of green paint and a tin of yellow paint. They meant to make their caravan really nice now. Jimmy's father mended one of the wheels which was really almost falling off, and he put the chimney on properly so that the smoke would not pour into the caravan but go streaming away outside.

In their spare time the two of them cleaned and painted the old caravan. You should have seen it! Jimmy's mother was really pleased. 'I do hope you will have some paint left over for the inside,' she said. 'It is so dark here – I can often hardly see what I'm doing. For one thing the glass in the windows is bad glass, and for another the smoke from the stove has made the walls very sooty.'

'Soon alter all that,' said Mr Brown. 'You just wait, Mary!'

By the end of the second week you wouldn't have known Jimmy's caravan. It was painted a nice bright green outside, and the wheels were green too, but the spokes were yellow. The window-sills were yellow and so was the chimney. Jimmy's father had enough money left to buy some cream-coloured paint for the inside of the caravan.

He painted it carefully, first putting all the furniture outside on the grass. 'You'll have to finish before night, Dad,' said Jimmy, 'or we'll all have to sleep in the open air.'

The inside of the caravan was very different when it was finished – so light and airy, and it looked twice as big! Jimmy's father put new glass into the windows too, and Jimmy slipped off to the town and brought some green and yellow stuff for curtains. He spent the two-shilling piece that the clown had given him.

'Lotta, will you make me these curtains for Mother?' he asked the little girl, giving her the parcel, as she sat eating a cake on the steps of her caravan.

'Make curtains!' said Lotta in surprise, and she laughed loudly. 'You must be mad, Jimmy! I can't sew.'

'Can't you *really* sew?' said Jimmy. 'I thought all girls could. You aren't very clever at some things, Lotta. You can't write, you can't read properly, and you can't sew!'

'And *you* can't fall off caravan steps without getting bumped!' cried Lotta crossly, and she pushed Jimmy off so quickly that he slipped to the ground with a bang.

Jimmy marched off without a word. He went to his

mother and gave her the parcel. 'Mother, here's a present for you,' he said. 'I wanted Lotta to make the stuff into curtains for the caravan, but she can't sew.'

His mother opened the parcel and cried out in delight. 'Oh, Jimmy! What pretty stuff – just the right colours to match the new paint on the caravan! You are a very kind little boy! Never mind about Lotta not being able to make them. I shall soon be able to make them – they won't take me more than an hour or two. And as for Lotta, I think she ought to learn a few things. I am going to teach her to read and write and sew – and in return perhaps Lal and Laddo will teach you to ride properly.'

'Oh, Mother! That's a splendid idea!' said Jimmy, pleased. 'I'll go and tell Lotta. Shall I do lessons with you too?'

'Of course,' said his mother. 'I'm not going to let you forget all you've learnt, Jimmy – and I can teach you a great deal that you ought to know.'

'I'll go and find Lotta,' said Jimmy, and off he went. But Lotta wasn't at all pleased.

'What? Do lessons!' she said, making a face. 'I've never done any and I'm not going to begin now.'

'But my mother wants to teach you, Lotta,' said Jimmy. 'I shall have to do some too.'

'You can do them by yourself,' said naughty Lotta. 'I won't come!'

'Oh yes, you will, Lotta!' said a voice behind her, and Laddo popped his head out of the caravan door. 'It's quite time you learnt about a few things besides horses and dogs. I'll teach Jimmy all I know about horses and riding, and Jimmy's mother can teach you sewing and reading and sums and things that a little girl ought to know.'

Lotta made a face and slipped down the steps. What a naughty little girl she could be when she wanted to! 'Can't catch *me*, can't catch *me*!' she yelled to Jimmy – and off she flew over the field in a trice. It wasn't a bit of good going after her – Jimmy could never catch her!

13. Poor old Punch!

The circus show went on, night after night. Jumbo played cricket and got clapped and cheered. Jemima the monkey played her tricks in the ring, and the other monkeys sat down at their little table and had their meal, with hundreds of people watching them each night. The ten little terrier dogs, neat, smart and happy, ran round the ring merrily, and Judy jumped through her hoops without once making a mistake. The circus-folk were happy.

Jimmy was happy too. He was busy all day long, for there was always something to do, and the little boy was willing to give a hand to everyone. Sometimes he was with Oona the acrobat and sometimes with Lilliput, watching him pet his monkeys. Every day he had a chat with old Jumbo the elephant, and, next to Mr Tonks his keeper, Jumbo loved Jimmy, who often brought him titbits.

Oona gave Jimmy a pair of his old soft shoes, and taught him to walk the tightrope. Once Jimmy had learnt to balance himself, he found this was quite easy.

Oona fastened the tightrope only about a foot above the ground for Jimmy, so that he would not be frightened of falling. He gave the little boy a long pole to hold in his hands, for he said that would help him to get his balance well. Jimmy stepped on the rope – and at once fell off the other side.

Lotta came to watch. She laughed loudly, and Jimmy poked her with his pole.

'Go away!' he said. 'I shall never learn anything if you watch me and laugh.'

'Don't take any notice of Lotta,' said Oona. 'She needs a good spanking sometimes. You needn't laugh at Jimmy,

Lotta – I've tried to teach *you* to walk the tightrope before now, and you've fallen off each time. If you stand there laughing any more I'll put you on the rope and let Jimmy see you fall off. Then he can laugh at *you*.'

Oona could be quite cross at times, so Lotta stopped giggling and watched Jimmy. She was rather surprised that the little boy learnt so quickly, for she had found it too difficult herself. Before the end of the morning Jimmy could walk the whole length of the tightrope without falling off – though he wobbled like a jelly, Oona said.

'We'll call you the Tightrope Jelly-walker,' Oona said, with a grin. 'Hundreds of people will come to see you.'

Jimmy jumped off the rope and put on his own boots. 'Thanks very much, Oona,' he said. 'I liked that. I'm learning to ride too. Stanley the clown thought I was so funny the first time I tried to ride, that he copied me in his turn at night, and that's why he got so much clapping this week.'

'I know,' said Oona, turning himself upside down and running about lightly on his two strong hands. 'Come on, Jimmy – what about doing a little of this?'

'I want Jimmy now,' said Lotta. 'We've got to take the dogs out.'

They went to the big cage. The dogs were lying quietly, some of them with their tongues out, for the weather was warm. One of them, Punch, did not get up and wag his tail when he saw Jimmy coming, as he usually did. Jimmy noticed it at once.

'Hallo! What's the matter with Punch?' he said. 'He doesn't seem well.'

He went into the cage and lifted up the dog's head. Punch wagged his tail feebly. His eyes were not bright, like the others'.

'Punch is ill,' said Jimmy in alarm. 'Oh, Lotta – what can be the matter with him?'

'I don't know,' said Lotta. 'Our dogs are never ill. Let's tell Lal.'

They ran off to tell Lotta's mother, and she came running to see Punch. She was alarmed, for she thought

perhaps all the dogs might catch the illness and then they
would not be able to perform at night.

'I'll fetch Mr Galliano,' she said to Jimmy. 'He knows
more about animals than anyone in the world.'

Very soon Mr Galliano came along, his top hat standing straight up on his head, for he was upset at the
thought of one of the circus animals being ill.

'Get Punch out of the big cage,' he said to Jimmy. 'Ask
your father to make him a separate kennel for himself. He
must be kept away from the other dogs.'

Jimmy lifted Punch out of the cage. The dog licked the
little boy's hand feebly. Mr Galliano took him gently on
his knee and ran his hand over him. He looked at his eyes
and his tongue and then he shook his head.

'Poor little dog – he'll be very ill,' he said. 'He's got an
illness that will turn him yellow and make him very sick.'

'Will he get better?' asked Lotta anxiously. 'He is one
of Lal's best dogs.'

'I don't think he will get better,' said Mr Galliano, his
gentle hands stroking the ill dog. 'All you can do is to
keep him warm and give him some medicine I'll let you
have. Go and ask your father to make Punch a little
kennel for himself, Jimmy.'

Jimmy sped off. He was sad. He loved all the dogs and
he didn't like to think that Punch was so ill. How could he
have got ill? He was cared for so well! He must have met
another dog when he was out and take the illness from
him.

'I shall nurse Punch myself,' thought the little boy. 'I
will make him better! I will!'

Soon Brownie, Jimmy's father, was making a little
kennel for Punch, who was now lying on a rug underneath Jimmy's caravan, his head on his paws, not even
the tiniest wag left in his tail.

'I'll nurse Punch,' said Lotta to Jimmy. 'He's my dog.'

'No,' said Jimmy. 'I'm better with animals than you
are, Lotta – you've often said so. I want to make Punch
well again. Please let me.'

'You can't,' said Lotta. 'Galliano says no dog gets better

when he goes yellow like that. Look at his tongue, Jimmy
– even that's gone yellow – and his eyes too. Poor Punch –
he's such a darling.'

'Did you get that medicine that Mr Galliano said he
had?' asked Jimmy.

Lotta pointed to a bottle on the grass. 'He's to have it
three times a day,' she said.

'I shall feed him well too,' said Jimmy.

'That's no use,' said Lotta. 'He won't want anything to
eat, and if he does eat anything he'll be sick.'

'Oh, Lotta, be quiet!' said Jimmy fiercely. 'That's not
helping me – telling me horrid things like that.'

But Lotta was quite right. Poor Punch would not eat
anything, and if Jimmy did manage to get something down
his throat, the poor little dog was sick. It was dreadful.

Jimmy thought of nothing but Punch all that day and
night and the next day. He could not think of anything to
make the dog better. He was so feeble that he could
hardly get out of his kennel. Jimmy slept beside him
during the night, on an old rug.

Oona the acrobat came to see where Jimmy was on the
third day, for the little boy had not gone to him for his
daily practice on the tightrope. When he saw Jimmy
holding Punch's head on his lap, sitting beside his caravan, he understood.

'What's the matter with the old fellow?' he asked. 'Oh,
he's turned yellow, has he – that's the jaundice. I've never
heard of but one dog getting better of that.'

'Tell me,' said Jimmy eagerly.

'Well, I once travelled with another circus,' said Oona.
'And they had three French poodles – you know, those
dogs that have their fur clipped in such a funny way that
parts of their body are bare. Well, one of them got yellow,
like this dog.'

'Yes – go on,' said Jimmy impatiently.

'Well, everyone said the dog would never get better,'
said Oona. 'But there was an old woman in the circus,
mother of one of the clowns there, and she said she could
cure him. And she did.'

'How?' cried Jimmy. 'Tell me how!'

'I don't really know,' said Oona. 'She knew a lot about herbs and roots and plants, and she used to go out early in the morning and pick those she wanted. Then she would boil them and mix them, and make wonderful medicines. It was one of her own medicines she gave the dog.'

'Do you remember what it was made of?' asked Jimmy eagerly.

'Of course not,' said Oona. 'That was years ago, when I was a lad like you.'

Jimmy almost cried with disappointment. 'Oh, if only that old woman was in *our* circus!' he said.

'I know whose circus she's with,' said Oona unexpectedly.

'*Do* you?' cried Jimmy. 'Well – write to her then, Oona, and ask her what we must give Punch. If we post the letter today, she'll get it tomorrow and we'll hear the next day – and that may be in time to save poor Punch.'

'I can't write to her,' said Oona. 'I don't know how to write. I've never learnt.'

'Good gracious!' said Jimmy. 'Mother will have to teach you as well as Lotta. Never mind, Oona – tell *me* what circus the old woman is with, and *I'll* write.'

'I don't know where the circus is,' said Oona. 'She's with Mr Bang's circus, that's all I know.'

Jimmy sighed in despair. He saw Mr Galliano passing near by and he got up and ran boldly to him.

'Mr Galliano, sir,' he said, 'please could you tell me something? Do you know where Mr Bang's circus is now?'

'Yes, at Blackpool,' said Mr Galliano, rather astonished. Jimmy shouted for joy and rushed back to Oona. 'It's at Blackpool!' he said. 'Now I'll write straight away. Mother! Mother! Have you got a piece of paper and an envelope?'

It took ages to find paper and envelope, but at last some was found, and Jimmy took a pencil from his pocket and began to write:

'Dear Mrs Bennito,' said Oona, and Jimmy wrote that

down. 'This is Oona the acrobat writing to you. Please send at once to tell us what medicine to give a dog who has gone yellow like that French poodle. Hope you are well. – Oona.'

'I haven't any money for a stamp,' said Jimmy. Oona gave him sixpence and the little boy ran off to the town to buy the stamp and post the letter. How he hoped it would get to Mrs Bennito quickly!

Jimmy went back to Punch, who was very weak, for as he wanted nothing to eat, he was going very thin indeed. Lotta was with him, crying. She had brought Punch some of her best chocolates – but of course the dog would not even sniff at them. Jimmy told her about the letter.

'Shall we have an answer today?' said Lotta, who had never had a letter in her life, and had no idea how long it took for letters to go and come.

'No,' said Jimmy. 'We can't have one till the day after next.'

'That will be too late,' said Lotta. 'Oh, darling Punch, if only you would eat something!'

Now it so happened that Blackpool was not very far from Bigchester, and Mrs Bennito got the letter that afternoon. She sent an answer at once – and the postman came with it to Mr Galliano's circus the next morning. He gave the letter to Mr Galliano, who sent it to Oona. It was a surprising thing for anyone in the circus to have a letter, except Mr Galliano himself.

Oona rushed to Jimmy with the letter. 'It's come – it's come!' he cried. 'Read it, Jimmy. I can't!'

14. The strange medicine

When Jimmy heard that the letter had come a whole day sooner than he expected, he was full of joy. He left Punch, whom he was nursing, and ran to Oona. He took the letter from him. Oona could not read, but Jimmy could.

Jimmy slit open the rather dirty envelope. The writing inside was small and difficult to read.

' "Dear Oona," ' he read – ' "This is what you must give the dog. Go out and get these things – one root of deadly nightshade – one root of – of – of – " Oh, I don't know what this is at all,' said Jimmy in dismay. 'Oona, the letter is full of the names of queer plants I don't know anything about. It's no good!'

The little boy was so disappointed that he burst into tears. He had been up all night with Punch, and was tired out. Oona put his arm across his shoulders and patted him. 'Now, now!' he said. 'Don't upset yourself so. Take the letter to Galliano. He may be able to help you. He is a wonderful man.'

Jimmy rubbed his tears away and ran to Mr Galliano's caravan. The door was shut. Jimmy rapped on it.

'Who's there?' yelled Mr Galliano. 'Go away!'

'Oh, please, Mr Galliano!' shouted Jimmy in despair. 'Please, I want your help. It's for Punch.'

Galliano opened the door. He was in a brilliant red dressing-gown with yellow braid. He looked quite strange without his top hat. Mrs Galliano, in an even brighter dressing-gown, was boiling a kettle on her stove.

Jimmy told Mr Galliano about the letter and showed it to him. Mr Galliano read it and whistled.

'Whew!' he said. 'This needs a bit of understanding.

Here, Tessa – what do you make of it? You used to be good at this sort of thing – yes?'

Mrs Galliano took the letter and read it through slowly, saying every word under her breath. Then she turned and looked at Jimmy, her kind eyes shining brightly.

'I know what all these things are,' she said in her soft slow voice. 'I knew Mrs Bennito long ago. She is a marvellous old woman.'

'Mrs Galliano, how can I get those things, please?' said Jimmy. 'Do you think they may cure poor old Punch? He is so thin and ill this morning.'

'I will come with you to the woods and find these things,' said Mrs Galliano. 'My mother was a gypsy and she knew of the magic powers there are in some roots and in many leaves and flowers. Go and tell your mother I will take you myself, and we will be back in three hours.'

Jimmy ran off. His mother gave him a basket and put into it some sandwiches and a piece of chocolate cake, for Jimmy had not had any breakfast. He patted Punch and went to wait for Mrs Galliano.

Lotta joined him. He told her what had happened. Her eyes opened wide.

'Oooh!' she said. 'Fancy Mrs Galliano going with you herself! She used to be marvellous, my mother said. She used to be the cleverest acrobat in the world, but then she got fat and gave it up. People were a bit afraid of her because her mother was a very clever gypsy, and I've heard it said that Mrs Galliano would have been a witch in the old days.'

Jimmy laughed. 'What silly things you believe, Lotta!' he said. 'Mrs Galliano is no witch – I think she's kind and clever. Here she comes.'

The caravan door opened and down the steps came Mrs Galliano, dressed in a red skirt, a black blouse, and a yellow shawl, which was wrapped round her head. The caravan steps creaked, for Mrs Galliano was indeed very big. She smiled her slow smile at Jimmy.

'Come!' she said. 'We must hurry.'

But there wasn't much hurrying, for Mrs Galliano did not walk at all fast. She seemed to know the way to the woods without asking. She stopped once by a ditch and picked a plant which smelt horrible to Jimmy. He put it into his basket.

'Have you had your breakfast, Mrs Galliano?' he asked shyly, feeling very hungry and longing to begin his sandwiches. 'I have some food here.'

'Eat it up, then, Jimmy,' said Mrs Galliano. 'I've had my breakfast.'

So, munching hard, Jimmy walked beside Mrs Galliano until they came to the woods. Her eyes darted from side to side, and she looked again and again at the letter she carried.

'Flower of woodruff,' she said, 'flower of woodruff. That is hard to find, for it is shy and small. Look for honeysuckle too, Jimmy. I need a root of that as well.'

Jimmy hunted for honeysuckle, and Mrs Galliano poked about looking for many other things. After some while the basket was empty of food and full of roots, leaves, and flowers. Mrs Galliano read the letter for the last time. 'I have everything now,' she said. 'There is one thing missing which cannot be found here – but I have found another plant that will do as well. We will go home, Jimmy.'

Jimmy went back to the circus, carrying the basket. Mrs Galliano took it from him and went up the steps of her caravan. 'I know what to do with all these things,' she said. 'The medicine will be ready in two hours' time.'

Jimmy never knew what Mrs Galliano did with the strange roots and flowers she had gathered. He heard her pounding the roots, and Lotta said that she was boiling some of the plants in a big bowl, for she had seen them. Anyway, in about two hours' time Mrs Galliano sent Lotta for Jimmy and gave him a bottle full of warm greeny-brown liquid.

'Give the dog two spoonfuls of this every half hour,' she said. 'You know how to put it in at the side of his mouth, don't you?'

'Oh yes,' said Jimmy, and he took the bottle eagerly. He went to Punch. Poor Punch – he could not even lift his head now!

Jimmy lifted up the dog's nose and put back the loose skin at one side of the mouth. There was a gap between the teeth there, and anything could be neatly and quickly poured into the dog's mouth and so down the throat. Lotta held the bottle ready and Jimmy took the filled spoon from the little girl and tipped it gently into the dog's mouth, at the side. He held Punch's head up and the liquid flowed down his throat. Jimmy gave him another spoonful.

'I hope he won't be sick and waste it all,' said Jimmy. 'Good dog, Punch. Good dog.'

The two children watched by the ill dog for half an hour and then gave him two more spoonfuls of the queer mixture. There did not seem to be any change in him.

'Let him be by himself for a while,' said Jimmy's mother. 'You can't do him any good by being with him just now. Run off and play for a little, or go and practise your riding, Jimmy.'

Jimmy went off obediently, and practised riding with Lotta. He was much better on horseback now and had learnt to grip with his knees, so that he did not slip and slide about. Lotta was quite pleased with him, though she said he would never be a marvel.

They ran back to Punch at the end of the practice – and Jimmy gave a shout of joy.

'Lotta! He's wagging the end of his tail just a tiny bit! He must feel better! Where's the medicine?'

They gave the dog two more spoonfuls of it, and he actually lifted his head up himself to take it. He tried to lick Jimmy's hand but his tongue wouldn't come out far enough. Poor old Punch – he had indeed been ill!

Bit by bit that day the dog got better. He still would not eat anything, but when Mr Galliano came over to see him that night, he nodded his head.

'He is better – yes?' he said. 'He is the first dog I have

known who got over this illness – and it is all because of you, Jimmy – yes? Tessa! Tessa! Come here!'

Mrs Galliano came over to where Punch lay in his new kennel. She stroked him softly.

'It is wonderful medicine,' she said. 'Only Mrs Bennito would know a thing like that. Here is her letter, Jimmy. Keep it safely, for you have there a cure for one of the worst illnesses animals have. He will get better now. I will send you a jar of food for him, and if you feed him with it tonight he will be much better tomorrow.'

Lotta fetched the little jar of food. She read the label on it. 'Chicken essence,' she said. 'It sounds good, Jimmy! I should think Punch will like this.'

Punch did. He licked the spoonful they gave him, and during that night he ate all that was in the jar. Gradually the yellow colour went from his eyes and tongue and skin, and he wagged his tail and gave a little yelp.

'He's better, he's better!' said Jimmy, beside himself for joy. 'Oh, Lotta! I feel so happy!'

Lal and Laddo came to see Punch. Lal had been very unhappy about him, for she had had him since he was a puppy and had trained him herself. She was very clever with animals, but not so good with them as Jimmy when they were ill. She was very grateful to the little boy.

'The next time I hear of a good little pup I will buy him for you,' she said to Jimmy. 'It is a shame that a boy like you should have no dog of his own. Thank you, Jimmy, for being so good to Punch. He would have died if it hadn't been for you.'

By the end of the week Punch was back in the show again, almost as frisky as ever! He simply adored Jimmy, and rolled over on his back in delight whenever the little boy came near. Mr Galliano was proud of Jimmy too, for he said nobody else would have bothered to take all the trouble that Jimmy had taken to find out the medicine which had cured Punch.

The next exciting thing that happened was the coming of Sammy the chimpanzee. Mr Galliano had been trying to hear of some other clever animal for his circus, and one day in walked Mr Wally and his tame chimpanzee!

Jimmy was getting used to the queer folk and ways of the circus, but he *was* surprised to see the big chimpanzee walking along through the circus field, hand in hand with its master, Mr Wally!

The chimpanzee was dressed in red trousers, blue coat, and straw hat, and it was smoking a cigarette! Jimmy stared in amazement.

'Good afternoon to you!' said Mr Wally, taking off his own straw hat and bowing himself to the ground. 'Have I the honour to be speaking to the great Mr Galliano himself?'

Jimmy knew this was a joke, so he grinned and said, 'No, and you jolly well know it! That's his caravan over there. I say! What a marvellous chimpanzee!'

'Ah, you don't know how marvellous he is!' said Mr Wally, who was a big man with a remarkably small head. 'He can ride a bicycle – he can undress himself and go to bed – he can get up in the morning and dress himself. But he won't clean his teeth.'

By this time a little crowd had gathered around Mr Wally and the chimpanzee. Mr Galliano stuck his head out of his caravan and roared loudly.

'Hie! You want to see me – yes? Then come this way, and tell your chimpanzee to wipe his feet!'

Mr Wally and the chimpanzee went up the caravan steps. 'Oh,' said Jimmy, 'I do hope Mr Galliano takes them for the circus. It *would* be fun to know a chimpanzee like that!'

'I shan't know the difference between you and the chimpanzee,' said cheeky little Lotta, grinning at Jimmy. 'You're so alike!' And then she sped away as Jimmy tore after her in a rage.

15. Mr Wally's wonderful chimpanzee

When Mr Wally came down the steps again he was smiling broadly. Mr Galliano had said he would take him and his chimpanzee into the circus. He was to go straight to the ring and show Mr Galliano what he could do.

'Come on, Jimmy,' said Lotta, appearing round a corner of the caravan. 'Let's go and watch.'

All the circus-folk went to the big tent and sat down on benches there to watch Mr Wally and his chimpanzee. Mr Wally appeared after a time, wheeling a big hand-barrow on which were a great many things covered up. These belonged to him and his chimpanzee, Sammy.

Sammy grinned at everyone and waved his hand to them. He was a young chimpanzee, high-spirited and happy, and he would do anything in the world for Mr Wally, who had had him since he was a tiny baby. Sammy had been brought up just like a child. He had had a cot of his own, he had had his own clothes, and he had even been taught to count up to five!

Mr Wally uncovered the things on his hand-barrow, and Jimmy saw that there was a cot there, taken to pieces, a little chair and folding table, and many other things. Mr Wally quickly put up the cot, and placed a mattress, pillow, and blankets in it. He set up the table with a little mirror on it, and a brush and comb, a tooth-glass and a toothbrush. He put a bowl of water on it, some soap, and a sponge.

'Surely the chimpanzee isn't going to use all those!' Jimmy said to Lotta.

She nodded. 'I expect he will,' she said. 'Chimps are very clever, you know, Jimmy. I once saw one before and he could write with a pencil. You can teach them a lot for a year or two, and after that they can't learn any more. They love learning, though – not like me!'

'Mr Wally's ready now,' said Jimmy. 'Look! I say – the chimpanzee's undressing himself!'

So he was! At a sign from his master he took off his coat, folded it neatly and laid it on the chair. He slipped off his trousers and put them on the coat. He almost forgot to take off his straw hat, but remembered it in time. On the cot was laid a pair of red pyjamas. Sammy pulled on the trousers and put on the coat.

'He's put the coat on the wrong way round!' said Lotta, giggling.

The chimpanzee heard Lotta giggle, and he waved to her. He looked down at his coat, found that he couldn't button it, and took it off again to put it the right way round. Really, it was wonderful to see him, he seemed so sensible.

He got into his cot. He covered himself up – and then he pretended to snore. That made Jimmy laugh. Mr Galliano laughed too.

'That is a new trick – yes?' he called to Mr Wally. 'I have not heard of that one.'

'Taught him that last week,' said Mr Wally proudly. 'Come on, now, Sammy – time to get up!'

Sammy sat up in bed and yawned. Lotta and Jimmy laughed in delight. What a wonderful chimpanzee! Sammy jumped out of bed and went to the little table. He took up his sponge and dipped it into the water. He sponged his face well and then, looking round for Mr Wally, he threw the sponge straight at him, full of water.

It hit Mr Wally on the nose and he gasped and spluttered. Jimmy laughed till he cried.

'Now, now, Sammy!' said Mr Wally. 'That's quite enough!'

Mr Galliano was pleased with that bit. He cocked his hat right on one side and beamed. The clever chimpanzee would be a great success in his circus.

'Get on, Sammy, get on,' said Mr Wally, seeing that Sammy was thinking of throwing the sponge at him again. Sammy took up his towel and dried himself. He even dried his feet, which he hadn't washed. That made Jimmy and Lotta laugh again.

Then he brushed his head neatly and combed it. He got up and brushed himself down with the hairbrush too. Then he began to unbutton his pyjama jacket.

'Clean your teeth, Sammy, clean your teeth,' said Mr Wally.

But that was just what Sammy wouldn't do. Although Mr Wally had tried to teach him that trick for weeks on end, the chimpanzee would never do it properly. Do you know what he did? As soon as he put the toothbrush into his mouth he bit all the bristles off! It was very expensive for Mr Wally, who had to buy a dozen brushes at a time.

Sammy bit the bristles of the brush this time too and chewed them up, though Mr Wally told him not to. Then he took off his pyjamas and dressed himself. He put on his straw hat.

'Now go to school, Sammy,' said Mr Wally. Sammy looked round and saw his satchel lying near by. He picked it up and put it over his shoulder. He went to where a little bicycle was standing, hopped on it and rode round and round the ring, waving his hand, smiling broadly, and making funny barking noises as he went.

'School time!' said Mr Wally, ringing a bell. Sammy hopped off his bicycle, took off his hat, and went and sat down on a chair.

In front of him Mr Wally put some big numbers, drawn in black on white cards.

'Now you are at school, Sammy,' he said. 'Show me number three.'

Sammy picked up the figure 3 and showed it to Mr Wally and to everyone else. Jimmy and Lotta clapped loudly. They thought that was very clever.

'Now four,' said Mr Wally. And no matter what number his master said, the chimpanzee could pick it up. But as he could not count more than five, there were only five numbers there.

'Now tell me what one and two are,' said Mr Wally.

The chimpanzee picked up the figure 3! Everyone clapped then, and Mr Galliano went into the ring.

'Fine!' he said. 'You can start tonight, Wally. Have you a cage for Sammy?'

'Yes,' said Mr Wally, pleased. 'But at night he sleeps in my caravan with me. He has a cot there. I have brought him up just like a child.'

'Won't it be fun to have a chimpanzee in the circus!' said Jimmy to Lotta, as they slipped out of the tent together to go and take the dogs for a walk. 'I hope Mr Wally will let me help him sometimes. You know, Lotta, I'd love to teach that chimpanzee to clean his teeth!'

'Pooh! You couldn't do that if Mr Wally can't!' said Lotta. But Jimmy thought he could. He went to make friends with the chimpanzee that afternoon. He was sitting in a big cage behind Wally's yellow caravan, which had come along that afternoon to join the circus. Wally was well off. He had a little car of his own, which pulled his caravan. Sometimes he unhitched the car from the caravan, put Sammy into the seat beside him and went for a drive. Then how everyone stared to see Sammy sitting in his straw hat beside the driver!

'Can I go and talk to Sammy?' Jimmy asked. Mr Wally was polishing his car. He took a look at Jimmy.

'Are you the boy that went after that elephant some weeks ago and fetched him?' he asked.

'Yes,' said Jimmy.

'Right,' said Mr Wally. 'You can go and talk to Sammy all you like. He'll love you!'

So Jimmy unbolted Sammy's cage and went in to talk to him. The chimpanzee was sitting in a corner, pulling a newspaper to bits. He loved doing that. He looked up when Jimmy came in and stared at him. He made a chattering noise. He didn't get up.

Jimmy went over to him boldly and sat down beside him. The chimpanzee gave him a piece of paper. Jimmy began to do just what Sammy was doing. He tore the paper across very solemnly. The chimpanzee was delighted. This was a game, then!

He put his arm round Jimmy's neck and bit his ear very gently. Jimmy knew that was his way of being friendly. Lilliput's monkeys did that too. He put his hand into his pocket and pulled out a small ball. He gave it to Sammy.

Sammy was thrilled. He threw the ball into the air and caught it. He threw it at Jimmy, and when Jimmy caught it and threw it back, the chimpanzee was delighted. This must be another chimpanzee come to play with him, he thought! Soon he and Jimmy were having a fine game, and Mr Wally came to watch them. He liked to see his pet chimpanzee so happy.

'Come and play with him every day, Jimmy,' said Mr Wally. 'He will love it.'

'I love it too,' said Jimmy, slipping out of the cage. 'Isn't it a fine feeling you get when animals will play with you and be friends with you, Mr Wally?'

'Ah – you have one of the greatest gifts in the world, young Jimmy,' said Mr Wally. 'One of these days you will be famous, for you will be able to do anything you like with animals, and they will love you with all their hearts.'

Jimmy went red with pleasure. Only Lotta knew how much he loved being with the animals. He was never afraid of them and they were never afraid of him. He knew what they were thinking – he knew what they were feeling. Oh, if only he had an animal of his own – one he could love and teach! How happy he would be!

He went off to have his tea. He could smell something good cooking outside his caravan. His mother looked up when he came.

'You seem to have grown these last few weeks, Jimmy,' she said. 'I believe circus life suits you.'

'Of course it does,' said Jimmy. 'Mother, I do think our caravan looks nice now, painted such pretty colours – and don't the new curtains look pretty at the windows?'

'Yes,' said his mother. 'But my word, Jimmy, I miss having rooms to move about in! If only we could have a bigger caravan – but that would cost far too much money.'

'Mother, I'll buy you one some day,' said Jimmy, putting his arm round his mother's waist and giving her a hug. 'Dad and I will make so much money at the circus that we'll be able to give you anything you like.'

'Tell Lotta that after tea I want her to come and do some lessons,' said his mother, as he ate three big brown sausages. 'You too, Jimmy.'

'All right, Mother,' said Jimmy. He liked sitting by his mother, reading to her, or writing from a book, but Lotta didn't. It was always a great business to find the little girl when lessons were anywhere about.

He ran off to find her after he had finished his meal. He saw her on the steps of her caravan, and he called to her.

'Lotta! Lotta!'

Lotta looked at him. 'Coming!' she shouted, and she ran down the steps – but she disappeared round her caravan at top speed, and when Jimmy turned round to see if she was coming she was nowhere to be seen!

Lal was peeping out of the door, laughing. 'Lotta's gone to hide!' she said. 'She guessed it was lessons this evening. Go and find her, Jimmy, and if she won't come, catch hold of her hair and bring her. She can't bear her hair pulled.'

Jimmy went off to look for Lotta, smiling all over his face. He was beginning to learn how to treat that wild little circus-girl now. In two minutes he had found Lotta and was leading her to his mother by a handful of her dark curly hair.

'Here's a new monkey, Mother,' he said. 'I found her in Lilliput's caravan, behind his bed. Lilliput said she was too bad a monkey to put with his, so I brought her along to you. See if she can be as clever as Sammy, the chimpanzee, tonight!'

16. Jimmy gets a dog of his own

The circus was doing well. When its stay at Bigchester came to an end, Mr Galliano shared out the money with his circus-folk. Everyone was pleased, especially Mr Brown, for he had earned much more than he had expected.

Even Jimmy was paid by Mr Galliano. This was a surprise to him, for he had not expected to earn any money.

'You work for me – yes?' said Mr Galliano, when he saw Jimmy's astonished face. 'You care for the animals – yes? Then you must be paid.'

Jimmy put his money away in a box and hid it in a special place under his caravan. It might come in useful some day when he himself performed in the circus. For that was what Jimmy had set his heart on now – he wanted to be a *real* circus-boy – one who went into the ring at night and did something clever to make the people laugh and cheer, just as Lotta did. She rode the horses and looked as beautiful as a fairy each night as she jumped from one horse to another. If only he could do something like that!

But Jimmy was not very good at riding. He would never be as good as Lotta.

'You have begun too late, Jimmy,' said Laddo, Lotta's father. 'I put Lotta on a horse when she was nine months old – she could ride when she was a year old. That is why she is so good now.'

Jimmy thought perhaps he might be a clever acrobat like Oona. But he was too stiff. Oona said the same thing to him as Laddo had said. 'You are too old to begin now, Jimmy. You walk the tightrope quite well – but you will never be able to do all the things I do. I began when I was one year old.'

Jimmy wondered if he could be a clown – but he felt sure he would never be able to say funny things quickly enough. Sticky Stanley always had a funny answer ready for everything – but Jimmy had to think quite a long time before he could say anything funny, and then perhaps it wasn't funny at all.

'Oh, well, never mind – at any rate I get on with the animals better than anyone else,' thought Jimmy. 'And just wait till I get a dog of my own. I'll teach it tricks that Lal has never thought of. She'll be able to take *my* dog into the ring and it will be cleverer than any of hers.'

Lal had not forgotten her promise to give Jimmy a puppy when she heard of a good one. One day she came to Jimmy and gave him an exciting piece of news.

'I have had a message from my brother, who lives in the next town we are going to,' she said. 'He always looks out for good dogs for me, and he says he has found a good little pup who will be clever at circus work. If you like to go and see him with me, I'll buy him for you if you like him.'

Jimmy was thrilled. A dog of his own at last! He beamed all over his face and thanked Lal. He longed for the circus to be on the move again so that he might see the little puppy with Lal.

Soon everything was packed up once more. Sammy the chimpanzee left before the others, for Mr Wally said his caravan was faster than the others, as it was pulled by his car. Jimmy waved to Sammy, who went off sitting beside Mr Wally in the car, wearing a new straw hat with a blue ribbon on. Jimmy had become very fond of the chimpanzee – but he hadn't managed to teach it to clean its teeth yet.

The circus was on the road again. Down the lanes went the long procession of caravans and cages and carts, with old Jumbo in the middle as usual, plodding along happily, swishing his tail and flapping his ears. He looked round for Jimmy. He loved having the little boy beside him. Sometimes he lifted Jimmy up to his head and the little boy travelled like that, much to the envy of all the other boys he met on the road.

They soon settled in the next big town. Jimmy was impatient to go and see the puppy that Lal had heard about. The next day, when the camp was more or less settled, Lal called to Brownie, Jimmy's father. He was making some new benches, for Mr Galliano expected even bigger crowds here.

'Brownie! Where's Jimmy? I want to take him into the town to see the new pup.'

'He's down at the stream with Jumbo,' said Mr Brown.

Lal sent Lotta for Jimmy. He led Jumbo back to his tent and fastened him to his post. Then he sped off to Lal.

They caught a tram to the town. Lal knew the place well and led him to her brother's. She went into a little sweetshop and called loudly:

'Benjy! Here's Lal!'

A small man with ginger whiskers came running out of the back of the shop in delight. He flung his arms round Lal and hugged her.

'Back again!' he cried. 'It's a whole year since I've seen you, Lal. Have you come to see the pup I told you about?'

'Yes,' said Lal. 'This is Jimmy, Benjy. He's with the circus. He saved a dog of mine for me when it was very ill, and I want to give him a dog of his own.'

'I'll take you now,' said Benjy. Jimmy liked the little man very much. He had the most twinkly eyes, and a mouth full of the whitest teeth Jimmy had ever seen. He fetched a cap and took Lal and Jimmy a good way away. He went into a small backyard, and showed them a kennel.

'There you are,' he said. 'In that kennel you'll see some of the finest little dogs that can be had. The mother is with them. I'd better get Mr Jiggs to let you look at them. The mother's a bit snappy with strangers.'

Mr Jiggs came out of his house at that moment – an untidy man with a long straw in his mouth that he chewed all the time he was talking.

'We've come to see your dogs, Jiggs,' said Benjy. 'This boy here wants one.'

Mr Jiggs pulled the mother dog out of her cosy kennel, and following her came four beautiful little terriers, all with wagging tails and cocked ears.

'This is the one I thought would do for you, Lal,' said Benjy, pointing to a sandy-headed dog with bright eyes.

'Yes,' said Lal, running her fingers over him. 'He's a fine fellow. He'll be as smart as paint. What do *you* think, Jimmy?'

Jimmy looked at the four dogs. They all looked up at him, wagging their short tails. The little boy looked at each one carefully. There was one sandy-headed one, two black-headed ones, and one that was half brown and half black, with a brown spot and a black spot on its back.

Jimmy looked at the little half-and-half one. Its eyes were soft and brown, and seemed to speak to Jimmy.

'Choose me!' the little dog's eyes seemed to say. 'Choose me! *I'm* your dog! Oh, choose me, Jimmy!'

The smart little sandy-headed one rubbed against his legs like a cat. The others stood back, waiting. They all seemed to know that Jimmy was choosing one of them. The little half-and-half one gave a small whine and threw herself on Jimmy. Jimmy picked her up.

'This is the one I want,' he said.

'But don't you want the smartest?' said Lal in astonishment. 'That one won't learn tricks quickly.'

'Yes, she will,' said Jimmy, cuddling her. 'I know she will. I don't know how I know, Lal – but I just know this is the dog that will learn most from me.'

'Let him have the one he wants,' said Lal to Mr Jiggs, who was still chewing his straw. 'This boy knows more about animals than all of us put together. He's a wizard with them! How much is it?'

Jimmy was so happy. The little dog was loving, and cuddled under Jimmy's jacket all the way back to the circus. Jimmy wondered what to call her.

He shouted for Lotta when he got back. She came running over to him. She had not been able to go with him because Laddo had wanted to teach her a new trick. She was longing to see the puppy.

'Oh, Jimmy!' she cried in delight as the little puppy peeped at her. 'She's sweet! Oh, I do like her brown-and-black head. It's lucky to have an animal that is half and half. What are you going to call her?'

'You name her for me, Lotta,' said Jimmy. 'I simply can't think of a single name. Tell me one that is easy to call and nice to hear.'

'I know! I know!' cried Lotta, dancing about. 'Let's call her Lucky! I'm sure she'll bring you luck, Jimmy. And it's a fine name to call – listen! LUC-ky! LUC-ky! LUC-ky!'

'Yes – that's a good name,' said Jimmy, pleased. 'Well, Lucky, how do you like your new name and your new master?'

Lucky nearly wagged her little tail off. So the two children thought she must like both her name and her master very much indeed.

'Is she to live with our dogs?' asked Lotta.

'No,' said Jimmy firmly. 'She is to be my very own dog, and I shall let her sleep on my feet at night.'

'She'll chew your blankets to bits,' said Lotta. 'Your mother will be cross.'

'No, she won't,' said Jimmy. 'Because it's too hot for me to have blankets on now, so there's none to chew. Ha, ha!'

Lotta made a face at him and gave him a pinch. Lucky licked her hand. Jimmy put her down on the grass. She tore round and round in excitement, smelling all the smells there were, and coming back to lick Jimmy's shoes every other minute. The little boy was so pleased with his pet, the first one he had ever had. He went to show her to his mother and father.

They were pleased with Lucky too. They both liked animals, though not so much as Jimmy did.

'Mother, I'm going to pay for every single scrap of food that Lucky has,' said Jimmy. 'I want her to be every bit my own dog. I shall teach her all kinds of tricks. You'll like that, won't you, Lucky?'

Lucky wagged her tail and pawed Jimmy's legs. She thought Jimmy was the nicest person she had ever seen. She was only two and a half months old, but she knew the people she liked.

Jimmy had a few very happy days getting to know his new puppy. He soon found that he had been right in choosing her, for she was really clever. She tried her hardest to understand all that Jimmy said to her.

'Lucky has a wonderful memory, Lotta,' said Jimmy, one evening. 'Once I teach her something she never seems to forget.'

'That's fine, Jimmy,' said Lotta. 'If an animal has a good memory that's half the battle. I guess Lucky will be famous when she's older.'

Lucky had a happy life. She had plenty of good food to eat, plenty of exercise, she was well brushed each day, and had so much love and petting that her little heart almost overflowed. All the circus-folk loved the merry little puppy – and Sammy the chimpanzee simply adored her. If only she would go into his cage and play with him he was perfectly happy!

She slept with Jimmy each night, and although she didn't chew the blankets, because Jimmy had none, she chewed plenty of other things. She chewed up his slippers, and his mother's old mat, and his father's pair of stockings.

But nobody really minded. She was one of the family now.

17. Lucky goes to school

Lucky the puppy grew fast. She was a smart little dog, bright-eyed and happy. She followed Jimmy as if she were his shadow.

'Lucky, you'll be going to school soon!' said Jimmy, patting her silky head. 'You'll have to learn all sorts of things and be a clever dog.'

'Wuff, wuff,' said Lucky, pretending to bite Jimmy's hand. She rolled over on her back and kicked all her legs up into the air. Lotta came over, laughing.

'Isn't she a darling?' said the little girl. 'When are you going to teach her tricks, Jimmy?'

'Right away,' said Jimmy; 'I've got a bag of biscuits. Watch me teach Lucky to sit up and beg, Lotta!'

Lotta sat down on the steps of Jimmy's caravan and watched. Jimmy sat Lucky up straight, with her back to a box and her paws in the air.

'Sit up, sit up, sit up!' he said, in a gentle, low voice. Lucky cocked her ears. She knew that voice well – when Jimmy spoke like that he wanted her to listen hard. She stayed where she was put, with her front legs in the air.

'Good little dog,' said Jimmy, and he gave Lucky a biscuit. She gobbled it down in delight.

'Do you want another biscuit?' asked Jimmy.

'Wuff, wuff, wuff!' said Lucky. She was running round the biscuit bag.

'You shall have one if you sit up, sit up, sit up!' said Jimmy. He gently put Lucky up again, so that she was begging – but this time there was no box behind her to lean on. Lucky didn't mind. She could sit up straight by herself now she knew what Jimmy meant.

She wanted to please Jimmy and she wanted a biscuit

too. So she sat up straight, waving her paws in the air.
'Now watch me teach Lucky to ask for a biscuit,' said
Jimmy to Lotta.

'Do you want a biscuit, Lucky?' said Jimmy, in his low
voice. Lucky cocked her ears. She knew the word *biscuit*
very well indeed!

'Wuff!' she said in delight.

'Then speak for it!' said Jimmy, holding out a biscuit.
'No – sit up! Sit up! Speak for the biscuit.'

'Wuff! Wuff! Wuff!' said Lucky joyfully. Jimmy threw
her the biscuit and she caught it.

'I say, Jimmy! Isn't she clever!' said Lotta. 'Fancy
learning how to beg and how to ask for a biscuit in just
one lesson.'

'Yes – she's a better pupil than you are,' said Jimmy. 'It
took you three lessons before you could say your alphabet.'

Lotta made a face. 'If you gave me biscuits each time, I
might learn it quickly, like Lucky,' she said.

'Well, it's true that Lucky has learnt this trick very

quickly,' said Jimmy. 'But I don't expect she will remember it. I shall have to teach her all over again tomorrow. I'll make her do it a few times more for biscuits and then that will be enough lessons for today for her.'

So Lucky sat up and begged a few more times and gobbled up the biscuits. Her little tail wagged hard. This was a fine way of getting biscuits!

'Now for a walk, Lucky,' said Jimmy. 'We'll take all the dogs too, Lotta. Lucky can run loose. She never goes very far away from me.'

Off they went for a long run. When they got right out on the heathery hills the two children slipped the dogs off the lead – all but two. The rest of them were now most obedient to Jimmy's long, loud whistle and would always come racing to him as soon as they heard it, no matter how many rabbits they were chasing. As for Punch, whom Jimmy had cured of a bad illness, he, like Lucky, was never far away from the boy's feet.

Jimmy and Lotta lay in the heather and talked. Jimmy was never tired of hearing all the tales of the circus-folk that Lotta could tell him.

She was talking about elephants now. 'You know, Jimmy,' she said, 'elephants have longer memories than any other animals. They never forget or forgive an unkind deed.'

'What! Do you mean to say that old Jumbo would remember that Harry, who ran off with the circus money weeks ago, was unkind to him?' said Jimmy.

'Yes, he remembers it,' said Lotta. 'And if he saw Harry again he would try to pay him out for the unkind things he did to him.'

'And does Jumbo remember the kind things that people do?' said Jimmy.

'Of course,' said Lotta. 'For instance, if you left the circus now, Jimmy, and didn't come back till you were grown-up, Jumbo would know and give you just as big a welcome as he gives you now. He never forgets a friend and he never forgets an enemy.'

'I can't understand anyone being unkind to animals,'

said Jimmy. 'They trust you so – and they all have such lovely, friendly eyes.'

'Yes, haven't they,' said Lotta looking into Lucky's soft brown eyes. 'Perhaps, Jimmy, the people that don't love animals haven't ever looked right into their eyes.'

Lucky licked Lotta's nose. 'You're just one big lick,' said Lotta, wiping her nose. 'You ought to have been called Licky, not Lucky.'

Jimmy laughed. 'You do say funny things Lotta,' he said. 'Come on – it's time to go back, Lucky! Bark for the other dogs.'

Lucky lifted up her little black-brown head and barked her small puppy-bark. The children laughed. 'Isn't she obedient,' said Jimmy, pleased. He whistled loudly. From far and near came the sound of padding paws, and soon the ten terriers, with Lucky running round them, were trotting happily back to the circus. On the way they passed a lady with a fat, puffy, wire-haired terrier.

She stood and watched the circus dogs go by. 'Poor little dogs,' she said. 'What a dreadful life they must lead in that circus! Look, Tinker-dog – how lucky you are to live with me, and not in a circus.'

Jimmy and Lotta didn't say a word when they passed the lady. But as soon as they were safely by, Lotta burst out in a rage.

'How dare she say such a thing! Can't she see how happy and well cared for all our dogs are? Can't she see their bright eyes and cocked ears and wagging tails?'

·'No, I don't suppose she can,' said Jimmy. 'Her poor dog is over fed, and looks as if he had chocolates all day long. He was fat and waddley. If she only knew it, her dog is to be pitied, not ours.'

They were soon back at the circus camp. They put the dogs into their big kennel-cage, and gave them a feed of biscuits. Lucky smelt them and wanted some too. She knew that she would have to wait till the other dogs were fed, and she wondered how to get something to eat quickly. She remembered how Jimmy had given her biscuits for begging.

Mr Tonks, the elephant's keeper, was sitting near by, eating some bread and cheese. Lucky ran up to him. She sat up on her hind legs and waved her front ones in the air.

'Wuff!' she said. 'Wuff!'

Mr Tonks laughed. 'Hey, Jimmy!' he shouted. 'Look at your pup. She's begging for my dinner.'

Lotta and Jimmy stared in surprise. Lucky still sat up, begging, wuffing loudly.

'Well! If she isn't the smartest little dog!' said Lotta. 'She's trying her trick on Tonky.'

Jimmy was pleased. Lucky was even cleverer than he had thought. What fun it was going to be to teach that bright little dogs all kinds of things! Lucky should go to school with him every day, and he would teach her patiently and gently so that in the days to come she might go into the circus-ring at night too, and do tricks to amuse the people watching.

So, day after day, Jimmy and Lucky worked together. The little dog loved her lessons. She was so bright and sometimes guessed what Jimmy meant her to do before he even showed her. In a week she could sit perfectly still with a biscuit on her nose until Jimmy said 'Paid for!' and then she would throw it up into the air and catch it. All the usual tricks that ordinary household dogs learn, Jimmy taught Lucky in a few days. Then he began to teach her others.

She walked easily on her hind legs. She carried a flag. She wheeled a little wooden pram with Lotta's doll in it and even learnt to tuck up the doll. Jimmy's father made the pram for Lucky, and it had a special handle so that her doggy paws could push it easily.

The circus-folk laughed when they saw Lucky wheeling the pram about the camp. They gave her biscuits for it, and at last Jimmy had to keep the pram away from Lucky, for whenever she wanted a biscuit she would get it out and wheel it round the caravans.

'Jimmy, that pup of yours will make your fortune one day – yes?' said Mr Galliano, laughing. 'When is she going into the ring?'

'Not yet,' said Jimmy. 'I want to teach her a few more things first. Have you seen her with Sammy the chimpanzee, Mr Galliano? They are very funny together.'

Mr Galliano went over to Sammy's big cage with Jimmy. Jimmy let the little dog in and Sammy ran to Lucky in delight. He picked up the little dog and nursed it like a baby. Then he and Lucky played catch and tore round the cage in excitement. Jimmy passed Sammy a paper hat and Sammy caught Lucky and put it on her head. Mr Galliano laughed.

'A clever little dog,' he said. 'She shall go into the ring one night with Lal – yes?'

Mr Galliano went off, his hat well on one side. He always wore it like that these days, for the circus was doing well. Huge crowds came to see Mr Wally and Sammy each night, for the clever chimpanzee amused everyone very much.

Jimmy slipped into the chimpanzee's cage and had a game with him. He picked Lucky up in his arms and whispered into the little dog's ear: 'Did you hear what Mr Galliano said? He said you could go into the ring one night and do your tricks for everyone to see. That will be a proud night for you and me, Lucky.'

Jimmy was not only teaching Lucky, but he was trying his best to teach Sammy the only trick that Mr Wally couldn't seem to teach him – he was teaching him to clean his teeth. And how did Jimmy do it? Why, he found out that Sammy simply loved the taste of aniseed, and so he rubbed the toothbrush with oil of aniseed. When Sammy smelt the aniseed and tasted it, he was thrilled, and would rub his teeth with the brush as long as ever Jimmy would let him.

Mr Wally was pleased when he found that Jimmy had taught the chimpanzee this. He gave Jimmy five shillings, and the little boy put it into the old box where he kept his savings. He had a lot of money there now.

He did not know how soon he would spend it all!

18. Mr Wally has an accident

The days went happily by. The circus was having a marvellous time, for Galliano's beautiful horses were famous, and so were Lilliput's clever little monkeys. Everyone loved Lal's dogs too. But it was Mr Wally's chimpanzee that drew the biggest crowds. There had been many clever chimpanzees before, but not one quite so human as Sammy.

Mr Wally was making a lot of money, for Mr Galliano paid him well. He bought himself a new little car to pull his caravan, and when it arrived he called all the circus folk to see it.

They stood round the little red car admiringly. Mr Wally was the only one of them who owned a car.

'Who's coming for a ride in it?' said Mr Wally. 'It's very fast – one of the best cars to be got nowadays. Now then – who's for a ride?'

But nobody seemed to want a ride. The circus-folk were used to going slowly in their caravans and nobody but Mr Wally got very excited about cars. One by one the people looking on melted away, back to their work, and only Jimmy was left.

'Would *you* like to come, Jimmy?' asked Mr Wally.

'I'd love to, Mr Wally,' said Jimmy eagerly. But just then his father called him.

'Jimmy! You've got to help me this morning. There's a job here that needs two pairs of hands.'

'Oh,' said Jimmy, in disappointment, 'I'm so sorry, Mr Wally.'

'I'll take Sammy,' said Mr Wally. 'He always likes a car ride. Go and get him for me, Jimmy.'

Jimmy fetched Sammy from his cage. He was dressed

as usual in trousers and coat and straw hat. The big chimpanzee was delighted to go out with his beloved master. He knew the car was a new one and he ran his hairy paw over the smooth paint in delight. Sammy loved bright colours, especially red.

'Get in, Sammy,' said Mr Wally, settling himself behind the steering-wheel. Sammy leapt lightly over the door and sat down beside Mr Wally in the front seat. He could open doors quite well, but it was easier to jump over them.

'Good-bye, Sammy!' said Jimmy. Sammy waved his paw. 'R-r-r-r-r-r-r!' went the engine of the car, and the little red thing set off across the bumpy circus field and out of the big gate.

Jimmy went to help his father. He worked hard all morning. He went to have a look at the chimpanzee as he was going to have his dinner – but to his surprise Sammy was not back.

'Where's Sammy?' he called to Mr Tonks, who was oiling Jumbo to make him sleek and shining.

'He hasn't come back,' said Mr Tonks. 'Mr Galliano's getting worried. Wally should have been back two hours ago.'

Just as Jimmy was sitting down outside his caravan to eat two big sausages that his mother had cooked for him, he saw a telegram-boy coming in at the gate. Jimmy's heart stood still. Was it from Mr Wally? Had there been an accident?

The boy took the telegram to Mr Galliano's caravan. Jimmy ran to him. Mr Galliano tore open the telegram and frowned.

'No answer,' he said to the boy. 'Look here!' he called to Mrs Galliano. 'Wally's had an accident with that new car of his. He's broken his leg – and Sammy's disappeared! Now what are we to do?'

Jimmy stared in dismay when he heard this. Mr Wally with a broken leg – and Sammy gone! He must have been frightened in the accident and run away. Poor old Sammy!

'Now we'll have the people scared for miles around because the chimpanzee's lost,' grumbled Mr Galliano. 'And there's Wally in hospital with a broken leg – he can't possibly go after Sammy – and what in the world shall we do when we *do* find Sammy? He can't go into the ring without his keeper.'

Jimmy felt something licking his hand. It was Lucky. An idea flashed into the little boy's head. Could Lucky find Sammy for him? He had already taught the little dog how to find all kinds of things. He had only to say, 'I've lost my handkerchief!' for Lucky to go and hunt for it till she found it. And if he said, 'I've lost my purse,' or 'I've lost my knife,' the puppy would run off to hunt at once. If it was any word she knew, Lucky would hunt till she found what was lost.

'Suppose I took her to where the accident happened,' thought Jimmy. 'And suppose I said to her, "I've lost Sammy!" Would she be clever enough to find the chimpanzee, I wonder?'

He went up the caravan steps to ask Mr Galliano. But

Mr Galliano was too worried even to listen to Jimmy. He waved to him to go away.

'I just wanted to know if I could go and . . .' began Jimmy. But Mr Galliano roared at him angrily.

'You will not go anywhere – no! Wally goes – and he does not come back, and Sammy is lost! Nobody will go anywhere today! You will stay in the camp!'

Jimmy went off, disappointed. It was no use asking Mr Galliano again. Lotta ran over to him, and he told her about Mr Wally's accident and how Sammy had run away.

'I thought if I could take Lucky to the place where the accident happened and tell her Sammy was lost, perhaps she'd find him,' said Jimmy. 'But Mr Galliano won't let me go out of the camp today – or anybody else either.'

'Pooh!' said Lotta. 'We'll go, all the same.'

Jimmy stared at the untidy little girl. 'We can't disobey Mr Galliano,' he said. 'I daren't.'

'Well, if *you're* afraid of him, *I'm* not!' said Lotta. 'I shall take Lucky myself, and see if she can't find Sammy.'

'You're not to,' said Jimmy fiercely. 'Lucky is my dog. Nobody else is to take her about but me.'

'Well, if you won't come I shall *have* to take her,' said Lotta, her eyes flashing angrily. 'You're a coward, Jimmy! You daren't do something you know is the only thing to do, because you're afraid of disobeying Mr Galliano. I don't care if he whips me. I'm going to find poor old Sammy! Think of him hiding away somewhere, scared out of his life, and perhaps being shot by somebody who is afraid of him.'

Jimmy jumped up, alarmed. 'Shot!' he said. 'Surely nobody would shoot dear old Sammy!'

' 'Course they would,' said Lotta. 'It's all very well to come and see a chimpanzee in a circus when his keeper is with him – but who wants to meet a chimpanzee down a lane or in their back garden? Nobody, outside of circus or zoo folks! Lucky! Lucky! Come with me. Goodbye, Jimmy.'

'I'm coming too,' said Jimmy. 'I'm not a coward, Lotta. I just didn't think of all that might happen. I do see that

we've got to go, even if it means disobeying Mr Galliano.
But how shall we go – and where?'

'I'll get Laddo to find out where the accident happened,' said Lotta. 'If it's a good way off, we'll go on
Beauty, my own horse. She can take us both quite easily.'

In a minute or two Lotta had found out where the
accident had happened. 'It's not very far off,' she said. 'It
happened at crossroads at Bentonville. That's six miles
away. Go and get Beauty, Jimmy, and I'll keep watch and
see that no one sees you.'

Everything went well. The circus-folk were all gathered round Galliano's caravan, whilst he told them about
Mr Wally and Sammy, and discussed with them what
they were to do in the show that night, to take the place
of Mr Wally's turn with Sammy. There was not even a
groom with the horses.

Lotta and Jimmy slipped out of a little gate at the
farther end of the field. Beauty was a strong, sleek white
horse, Lotta's very own. She easily carried the two children. Lucky, who had never been on horseback before,
was surprised to be jogged up and down, but so long as
she felt Jimmy's arm round her she did not mind anything. They went off quietly down the lane. They came
to the main road. There was a grassy edge to the road and
Beauty cantered along this happily. When the children
came to a signpost they looked at it to see the way to
Bentonville.

Lotta could not read the name, but Jimmy could, of
course. 'You'd probably have gone the wrong way, Lotta,
if you'd been silly and gone off without me,' said Jimmy,
giving the little girl a poke in the back. 'You wouldn't
have been able to read the sign properly.'

'I shall do my reading lessons better now,' said Lotta.
'It would have been dreadful if I couldn't have gone the
right way.'

Beauty began to gallop. Jimmy was quite at home on
horseback now and he enjoyed the ride. Lucky whined a
little. She thought it was all very strange indeed.

On and on they went to Bentonville and at last they got

there. They found themselves at crossroads and then they knew that they had come to the right place, for there, by the side of the road, was Mr Wally's lovely new red car, with the side wing bent and broken, and the glass splintered.

'We needn't ask anybody anything,' whispered Lotta. 'Just get down and let Lucky nose about, Jimmy. She may smell where Sammy went.'

Jimmy jumped down. Lucky wuffed in delight. It was good to be on her own four feet again. Jimmy let her run round for a while and then he called the little dog to him. He took her head in his hands and looked down into her bright eyes.

'Lucky,' he said, in the low, gentle voice that always made Lucky listen hard, 'I've lost Sammy! Sammy! I've lost Sammy! Where's Sammy! I've lost Sammy!'

Lucky cocked her ears and gave a little whine. She understood perfectly. Sammy was gone and had to be found. She could find Jimmy's handkerchief and his purse and his knife by smelling them out when they were lost – and now she must find Sammy. She nosed about to see if she could find a Sammy-smell. She ran round and about the road. No Sammy-smell there. She ran to the side. No Sammy-smell there! She ran through a hole in the hedge, on the side where the car was – and there, in the field, Lucky found a Sammy-smell! Yes – there was no doubt about it! Sammy had leapt right out of the car, over the hedge and into the field!

'Lotta! Will you wait here whilst I go after Lucky?' said Jimmy in excitement. 'She's found the right smell, I do believe – and she'll follow it till she comes to Sammy!'

'Yes, I'll wait with Beauty,' said Lotta. 'I'll take her into this field.'

Jimmy set off after Lucky. Lucky was nosing along, following the strong Sammy-smell. Jimmy was thrilled. This was his own idea! Surely Mr Galliano would not be *very* angry with him for being disobedient if only he brought back Sammy safe and sound?

And now, where *was* Sammy?

19. What happened to Sammy the chimpanzee

Lucky had picked up Sammy footprints with her clever nose – but the chimpanzee was a long way away! He had jumped right over the hedge, sprinted over the field, got into a lane that led up a hill and had gone down the other side, frightened out of his life.

Sammy had been sitting quietly in the car beside Mr Wally when the accident happened. Another car had run into theirs at the crossroads, and there had been such a loud crash that Sammy had got the shock of his life. He did not wait to see what Mr Wally was doing or saying – he just jumped and fled.

As he ran up the hill he met two woodmen walking together. When they saw the chimpanzee coming they stared as if they couldn't believe their eyes.

'Ooh! What is it?' said one.

'It's a monkey, isn't it?' said the other.

'No – an ape,' said the first man. 'My word – what's it doing here?'

Sammy stopped when he saw the two men. Into his frightened mind came the thought that perhaps these men would help him. He ambled up to them – but they tore off in terror, dropping their bags behind them.

Sammy was frightened of their shouts. He did not go after them, but he ran up to their bags. He smelt something good inside – the men's dinner! He tore open the bags and sniffed to see what the food was.

It was ham sandwiches, buns, and apples. Sammy picked up the food, ran to the hedge and crouched there. He ate everything in the bags, and most of all he liked the apples.

As he sat there a woman came up the hill. Sammy

thought she looked kind, rather like Lotta's mother, whom he knew very well. He ran out of the hedge towards her, making a funny chattering noise – his way of asking for help. He wanted to get back to Mr Wally. He felt strange with no friends around him.

The woman gave a yell and raced down the hill at top speed. She met a man and he asked her what was the matter.

'Oh, it's a chimpanzee!' she gasped.

'Nonsense!' said the man, patting her on the back. 'There are no chimpanzees here – only rabbits and foxes.'

'I tell you it *was* a chimpanzee,' said the woman. But the man still shook his head. And at that very moment Sammy appeared, trotting down the hill towards them. He thought perhaps the man might be a friend of his. As soon as the man saw him he gave a shout.

'You're right!' he said to the woman. 'It *is* a chimpanzee! Quick! Get into this house!'

They ran into a house. Poor Sammy! He was so disappointed when they disappeared and shut the door. He was lonely. He wanted Mr Wally very badly.

He went into the garden and looked around to see if he could find anyone there. The man and the woman and two other people were watching him from a window.

'I'll telephone to the police,' said the man. 'It's an escaped chimpanzee. He ought to be shot.'

'Poor thing,' said the woman. 'I believe I saw him at the circus the other night. I expect the circus-folk are looking for him.'

'Well, he can't be allowed to go roaming the country-side like this,' said the man. 'I'll tell the police to get guns and go after him.'

Sammy did not hear all this, and he would not have understood it if he had. He sniffed round the doors, tried to open them, decided that he couldn't, and went off up the hill again. He went over the top and down into a small village. There he ran into some little children. They did not know what he was and they stood and stared at him in surprise. Sammy loved children. He made his little chattering noise and held out his hand to a boy.

The little chap put his hand into the chimpanzee's.
Sammy was delighted. Here was a friend at last. He
stroked the little boy's hair. Then he began to do some of
his tricks. He was still dressed in his trousers and coat, but
he had lost his hat. He took off his clothes and pretended
to go to sleep under a bush. Then he yawned, stretched
himself and got up. He dressed himself, and then pretended to wash and clean his teeth and brush his hair.

The children crowded round him in delight. What a
clever animal! Sammy was pleased. He hugged a little
girl gently, and began to play with the children.

But it was not for long. A woman, looking out of the
window to see if her children were all right, caught sight
of Sammy and stared in astonishment and fear.

'Johnny – Ellen – come indoors at once!' she shouted.

'Oh, Mummy, but we want to play with this queer
animal!' cried Johnny.

'Come in *at once*!' shouted his mother. 'And tell the
others to go too.'

Soon the street was deserted, for all the children ran
home and left Sammy. The next thing he saw was a little
crowd of men, carrying sticks and iron bars, coming
towards him. Sammy did not know that they were
coming to hit him. He ran towards them happily, thinking he might play with them too. One of the men stopped
and took aim at Sammy. He threw an iron bar at the
chimpanzee – but Sammy dodged, held up his hand and
neatly caught it. He thought this was a new game, and he
threw the iron bar back at the men.

Luckily it did not hit anyone. The men stopped in surprise. 'It's no good throwing things at him,' said one.
'He'll only throw them back. Try to get him into a corner
and then we'll catch him all right.'

So the men spread out into a ring and gradually sur-
rounded Sammy. The chimpanzee was not taking any
notice of them for a moment. He had seen something
standing by a wall that interested him – a bicycle!
Sammy rode his own bicycle every night in the circus-

ring and he knew bicycles well. Whilst he was looking at this one, the men got nearer and nearer.

Sammy looked up. He suddenly became frightened. He did not like the look of these silent men coming nearer and nearer. How could he get away? What was he to do?

And what do you suppose he did? Why, he jumped suddenly on the bicycle, pedalled away hard and rode straight at the men. They were so startled that they got out of his way and did not stop him.

Through the crowd cycled Sammy, right down the village street and away beyond. He waved his hand to the astonished men. He was pleased with himself. He liked the new bicycle. It was bigger than his own, but he could manage it quite well. On and on he went, and soon came to another village.

But here a policeman with a gun was waiting for Sammy. Someone had telephoned from the other village and told him to be ready for Sammy. Sammy had no idea what a gun was. He pedalled straight at the blue policeman.

Bang! The gun went off. It made a sound rather like the crack of Mr Galliano's whip. Sammy was used to that – but something warned him that the gun the policeman held was not the same as the circus whip whose sound he knew so well. The chimpanzee jumped off his bicycle and ran into a garden. He crouched as he ran, for he was afraid of the gun. He came to a small shed at the back. He leapt in through a window and hid himself under some sacks. He lay there as still as could be.

And what was Jimmy doing all this time? Ah, Jimmy was getting hot and out of breath, for Lucky was dragging him on her lead across fields, down a lane up a hill and down again and into a village. There he met the parents of the children that Sammy had played with, and they told him Sammy had been there. Lucky sniffed down the village street, but lost the scent of Sammy.

'My dog can't seem to smell him any more,' said Jimmy, in despair. 'I wonder why that is.'

'Well, the chimpanzee went off on my bicycle,' said a

butcher's boy. 'So I guess that's why your dog can't smell his tracks any more. He went towards the next village. We've just telephoned there to the policeman, and he is waiting for the chimp with a gun.'

Jimmy went pale, though his cheeks were as hot as fire. Oh, surely, surely, no one would shoot dear, gentle clever old Sammy!

'Come on, Lucky, we must go as fast as we can!' cried Jimmy, and off went the two along the road to the next village. When they came there, Jimmy saw a crowd in the road.

'Have you seen the chimpanzee?' he panted.

'Yes,' said a man, pointing towards a near-by garden. 'He went there. He's hiding in a shed. The policeman is just going to undo the door and shoot him.'

'Oh, he mustn't – he mustn't!' cried Jimmy. 'He's a wonderful creature, and wouldn't harm anyone. Quick, Lucky, quick!'

They forced their way through the crowd and went round the house to the back. There were five men round a small shed. The policeman was just about to open the door and shoot into the sacks that covered Sammy. The men had looked through the window and had seen that Sammy was hiding under the heap of sacks.

'You are not to hurt our chimpanzee!' shouted Jimmy. 'He's quite harmless, and is the cleverest in the world! He is worth hundreds of pounds. Let me go to him.'

The men stared at the little boy in surprise. 'What! Go into the shed with that chimpanzee!' said the policeman.

'Of course,' said Jimmy. 'I love him, and so do all the circus-folk. He's just like a human being!'

Just then Lucky managed to squeeze herself under the door of the shed. She ran to the heap of sacks and barked happily. Here was Sammy, her friend, at last! Sammy popped his head up, picked up the little dog and cuddled her lovingly. The men looking in through the window saw this and were amazed.

Jimmy opened the door and went into the shed. 'Sammy! Sammy! Here's Jimmy come for you!' he cried.

The chimpanzee leapt up and ran to Jimmy in delight. He chattered away in joy, stroking Jimmy's head and patting his shoulder. He put his arm round the little boy and hugged him. The men who were watching were full of astonishment.

'There you are!' said Jimmy happily. 'What did I tell you? He is gentle and tame, and as clever as can be. I'll take him back to the circus with me now.'

'No, you'd better wait for a van to come,' said the policeman. But Jimmy wouldn't. He guessed that nobody would try to part him from the chimpanzee. He marched out into the road with Sammy, holding the big chimpanzee by the paw, and back the three of them went up the road – Jimmy, Sammy, and Lucky. Everyone followed them in astonishment.

'What a boy!' said the policeman. 'Never saw anyone like him in my life! Went in and took that chimp's hand as cool as you please!'

It took Jimmy and Sammy a good while to get back to Lotta. The little girl was still patiently waiting with Beauty, her horse. She was full of joy when at last she saw Jimmy coming with Sammy and Lucky.

'I was only just in time, Lotta,' said Jimmy, and he told her the story as they cantered home. Sammy sat between Lotta and Jimmy, perfectly happy and good. He held Lucky in his arms.

They rode through the circus gate. 'What do you suppose Mr Galliano will say when he sees us?' said Jimmy nervously, seeing Mr Galliano in the distance, with his top hat perfectly straight up on his head.

20. Jimmy goes into the ring

When the circus-folk saw Jimmy and Lotta riding on Beauty, the lovely white horse, with Sammy in the middle, they were amazed. Mr Galliano suddenly saw them too, and his big cigar dropped right out of his mouth.

Jimmy rode up to him. 'Please, sir,' he said, 'we disobeyed you. You said no one was to leave the camp today, but Lotta and I did, with Lucky. We felt so certain we could find Sammy and bring him back.'

'You young scamp,' said Mr Galliano, with a terrible frown – but Jimmy saw that his eyes were twinkling under his eyebrows. 'How dare you disobey the great Galliano? And you too, Lotta – you ought to know better – yes?'

'Wuff, wuff!' said Lucky, trying to get out of Sammy's arms – but the chimpanzee held her tight.

'Get down, take Sammy to his cage, give him a few bananas and come to see me in my caravan,' said Mr Galliano. The two children hurried to do as they were told. No one asked them anything, for they knew that the story must be told to Mr Galliano first.

Sammy was soon happily eating bananas in his cage. Lucky was crunching up biscuits beside him. Jimmy and Lotta hurried to Mr Galliano's caravan. Mrs Galliano was there too. She shut the door behind them.

Jimmy told his story and Mr Galliano listened.

'You have a gift for rescuing runaway animals – yes?' he said, with a laugh. 'First the elephant, and now the chimpanzee. You are a naughty boy to disobey, Jimmy, but you are a good boy, yes, to save Sammy. But we cannot let Sammy go into the ring alone. He is useless without Wally.'

A wonderful idea came into Jimmy's head. 'Please, sir, let *me* go into the ring with him,' begged the little boy earnestly. 'He will do as much for me as he does with Mr Wally. Really he will. I've played games with him and practised with him every day. And I taught him to clean his teeth, though Mr Wally couldn't. Do, do let me.'

Mr Galliano stared at Jimmy and then looked across at Mrs Galliano. She nodded her head. 'Jimmy is a good boy with animals,' she said. 'A very good boy. You let him do this, Galliano. I and his mother will make him a fine suit for tonight.'

Jimmy could have hugged Mrs Galliano. He was wild with joy. To go into the big circus-ring at last! To be there in fine clothes, under the glaring lights, with hundreds of people watching and clapping! Could anything be more exciting!

'Tell your mother to come here,' said Mr Galliano, lighting another big cigar. 'You know what to do exactly, Jimmy – yes? We will have a practice this afternoon with Sammy. Be ready in ten minutes' time.'

Whilst Mrs Galliano and Mrs Brown were cutting out red knickerbockers and a fine yellow coat with a blue waistcoat for Jimmy to wear that night, Jimmy was practising with Sammy for that night's show. He took Sammy into the ring, with all the necessary things – the cot, the chair, the table, the bowl of water, the bicycle and everything – and under Mr Galliano's sharp eye the little boy went through the whole turn just as he had so often seen Mr Wally do.

Sammy loved doing his tricks with Jimmy. He loved his master, Mr Wally, but there was something about this little boy, with his bright deep eyes and his low, gentle voice that Sammy understood and adored. He would willingly have died for Jimmy.

'Good, good, good,' said Mr Galliano, when the turn was finished. 'You are a proper circus-boy – yes.'

What a scramble it was to get Jimmy's things finished in time – and how grand he looked when he got into his red knickerbockers, his yellow coat and blue waistcoat.

He wore a round gold cap and blue stockings. He looked almost as grand as Mr Galliano himself. What a good thing he had saved up his money! When Lotta saw him she stared without saying a word.

'Well, do I look nice?' asked Jimmy impatiently.

'Oh, Jimmy! You look simply grand,' said Lotta. 'I don't feel as if I shall ever dare to make a face at you again.'

But as the cheeky little girl immediately made one of her very worst faces at him, she couldn't have meant what she said!

Jimmy felt a bit nervous when the time came for him to take Sammy into the ring. There were crowds of people there that night to see the chimpanzee, for everyone had heard of his adventures that day. Sammy was delighted to have Jimmy going into the ring with him. He did not seem to miss Mr Wally at all.

He did everything just as he should – but in the middle of it all, what do you suppose happened?

Why, Lucky escaped from her kennel and tore into the big tent to find her little master. She raced straight into the ring, barking madly. Jimmy stared in dismay.

'Go back, Lucky, go back!' he said. But Lucky was too excited to listen. She had had a thrilling day and she meant to play with Jimmy and Sammy, and not go back to her kennel.

Mr Galliano cracked his whip. That meant that Jimmy was to go on with his turn. He did hope that Lucky wouldn't spoil it! Wouldn't that be too bad, his very first night in the ring?

Sammy was just dressing himself after getting out of the cot. He was about to sit down and wash when Lucky dashed up to him. Sammy looked down at his small playmate. He lifted her up on his knee, and – whatever do you think he did?

He washed Lucky's face for her, cleaned her teeth, and brushed her hair. Oh dear, how everyone shouted and laughed! Lucky didn't like it at all and she tried to get

away, but Sammy held her tightly. Then he washed his own face, cleaned his teeth and did his hair.

When the time came for him to ride off to school, Sammy jumped nimbly on his bicycle with Lucky still tucked under one arm. How everyone cheered! They did not know that this was all Sammy's own idea – they thought the chimpanzee had been taught to play with Lucky like this.

When the turn came to an end and Jimmy went off with Sammy and Lucky, the people cheered till they were hoarse, and Jimmy had to come back three times with Sammy and bow. He was so delighted that the tears came into his eyes and he had to blink them back. Good old Sammy! Good old Lucky! They had both done their very best for him that night.

Mr Galliano was delighted with Jimmy. He told him that he could do the turn in the ring with Sammy and Lucky every night till Mr Wally was ready to come back. Then perhaps Mr Wally would let Jimmy help him.

So night after night Jimmy took Sammy into the ring and the chimpanzee grinned to hear the clapping and cheering he got – and when Lucky came dashing into the ring at exactly the right moment to be washed and brushed by Sammy, the people clapped all the more.

Jimmy's days were very full now. He had to practise a good deal with Sammy and Lucky, besides helping Lotta with the other dogs, and giving Mr Tonks a hand with Jumbo. He practised his riding too, and could now walk the tightrope just as well as Oona the acrobat could. He was teaching the clever little Lucky as many tricks as he could whilst she was young and eager, for he knew that is the best time for any animal to learn. So, from dawn to dusk Jimmy was busy, and his mother said she hardly ever saw him except at mealtimes.

Mr Wally had been pleased to hear that Sammy had been found and rescued. But he was not so pleased to hear that Sammy would go into the ring each night with Jimmy and do just as well with the little boy as he did with him, his trainer and master.

Nobody thought that Mr Wally would be jealous of Jimmy. Everyone was quite sure that when Mr Wally's leg was better he would tell Jimmy that he might help him in the ring each night with Sammy and Lucky.

But everybody was wrong. When Mr Wally came back to the cicus, limping slightly, he watched Jimmy and Sammy in the ring for one night. And then he went to Mr Galliano.

'Mr Galliano, sir,' he said, 'tomorrow night I take Sammy into the ring myself. I am quite better now.'

'That is good, yes,' said Mr Galliano. 'You will like Jimmy to help you, Wally – he is a very good boy.'

'I don't want him to help me,' said Mr Wally. 'He is a good boy with animals, but I do not want him to come into the ring with me when I take Sammy there. Sammy is mine and I trained him. No one else shall share him in the ring when I am there.'

Mr Galliano was angry. 'Jimmy did a great deal for Sammy and you should be grateful, yes,' he shouted. 'It is not much to ask that he should help you. The boy loves to go into the ring.'

'I *am* grateful to Jimmy,' said Mr Wally firmly, 'and I shall pay him well for all the time he has been taking Sammy into the ring for me. But he shall not share

Sammy in the ring now I am back. And if you tell me I must take him into the ring, Mr Galliano, then I will go away with Sammy and you will not see me again.'

Mr Wally went out of the caravan. He knew quite well he had beaten Mr Galliano. Mr Galliano could not afford to let him go just when the chimpanzee was drawing such big crowds to the circus every night. Mr Galliano sat and thought. Then he shouted for Jimmy.

He told the little boy what Mr Wally had said. Jimmy was surprised and upset. Not go into the ring any more, just when he had got used to it and loved it so! He stood and stared at Mr Galliano in dismay. 'Am I not to go into the ring *any* more?' he asked, his voice trembling a little.

'Some day perhaps, yes,' said Mr Galliano. 'But not now. There is nothing you can do except with Sammy, and Mr Wally will not have that.'

Jimmy went to his own caravan, sad and disappointed. How horrid of Mr Wally! He sat down on the big bed and thought about it. His mother found him there, his bright face looking miserable for once.

'What's the matter, Jimmy?' she said in alarm. Jimmy told her. His mother put her arm around him and squeezed him.

'Jimmy, you mustn't mind when things go wrong,' she said. 'You have been a lucky boy in many things lately. Now that an obstacle has come and you can't get what you want, don't worry about it. The best way to treat obstacles is to use them as stepping-stones. Laugh at them, tread on them, and let them lead you to something better. As for Mr Wally, don't think hardly of him. He loves Sammy, and it's quite natural that he should want him all to himself in the ring. You wouldn't like anyone to share Lucky with you, would you?'

'No, I shouldn't, Mother,' said Jimmy, feeling much better already. 'You're a darling, Mother – you say just the right things. I won't worry about this, and I won't be horrid to Mr Wally. I'll do as you say and make this obstacle into a stepping-stone to something better.'

And how did Jimmy do that? Ah, you will soon see.

21. Good old Lucky

Jimmy ran to find Lotta to tell her that Mr Wally would not let him help in the ring with Sammy any more. Lotta was angry.

'Nasty, horrid Mr Wally,' she said fiercely. 'I'll creep into his caravan tonight whilst he is in the ring and put butter into his tin of paraffin and empty his packet of tea into his cocoa-tin and. . . .'

'Lotta! You mustn't say things like that!' said Jimmy, astonished. 'You would be horrider than Mr Wally if you did that. Don't be silly.'

Lotta stared at Jimmy, surprised. 'But aren't you angry with Mr Wally too?' she asked.

'I was,' said Jimmy. 'But I'm not now. You know, Lotta, my mother says when obstacles come it is best to tread on them and use them as stepping-stones to something better. I don't know how I'm going to do it, but I shall have a try. If I can't go into the ring one way I shall find another.'

'Good for you,' said Lotta, giving Jimmy a hug. 'Look – there's Mr Wally going to feed Sammy. He's not looking at us. I expect he thinks you are angry with him.'

'Well, he won't think that long,' said Jimmy. 'Hi, Mr Wally! Can I help you to feed Sammy? I've got ten minutes to spare.'

Mr Wally turned in surprise and looked at the bright-faced little boy. He had expected him to be sulky and rude to him. For a moment he didn't know what to do.

'All right,' he said. 'You can feed him. Thanks very much. I'm busy and could do with a bit of help.'

'I'll clean out his cage too,' said Jimmy, and ran off cheerfully to get a pail and broom. Mr Wally stared after him. He had never known a boy behave like that before when something horrid had happened. 'All the same, he is *not* going into the ring with Sammy and me,' said Mr Wally to himself.

One day, when Jimmy was practising walking the tightrope under Oona's sharp eye, Lucky came up. The little dog watched her master balancing carefully on the rope, and cocked her head on one side.

'Wuff!' she said, which meant 'I'll have a try too!' And before Jimmy could say a word, Lucky gave a spring and landed with three legs on the rope. She fell off again at once, but she didn't care a bit. No – up she went again, and this time she got all four legs on, one behind the other. How funny she looked, to be sure. She stood there, swaying, and then jumped down. Oona and Jimmy stared at her in amazement. Whatever *would* Lucky do next?

'Jimmy!' said Oona suddenly. 'I believe you could teach that dog of yours to walk the tightrope. She is as clever as ten terriers rolled into one. Here, Lucky! Let's have a look at your paws.'

Lucky ran to Oona and put up a paw. She really seemed to know everything that was said to her. Even Lal said she had never met a dog like Lucky. Oona looked carefully at her hard pads.

'See, Jimmy,' he said to the little boy. 'A dog has good strong pads, divided into pieces – and if I made Lucky a thin rubber sock to wear on each foot I believe she could grasp the tightrope well, and get a fine grip. I say! A dog that walked the tightrope! Such a thing has never been heard of before.'

Jimmy listened with wide eyes and flushed cheeks. He petted Lucky and stroked her silky head. How glad he was he had chosen her and not one of the other puppies he had seen!

'I'll make the rubber socks today,' said Oona, as excited as Jimmy. 'We'll see how they work. Lucky would have to wear something – her feet are not quite right for this sort of work.'

Well, Oona kept his word. He got some thin white

rubber, and with strong gum he shaped it into socks to fit Lucky's small paws. When Lucky had them on she did not seem to mind at all. Oona had been afraid she might bite them off.

'Now bring her to the tightrope in the ring,' said Oona excitedly. 'Nobody's there just now. We'll have it all to ourselves.'

So they took Lucky to the ring, and put up the tightrope there. Jimmy ran along the rope lightly, and whistled to Lucky. 'Come up, then, come up!' he called. Lucky did not have to be told twice. Up she sprang and stood on the rope with all four feet. The rubber socks gave her a fine grip. She tried to walk a step, missed her footing and fell off. But up she went again and again – and again! Lucky loved trying new things, and her greatest joy was to try and do what her little master did. At the end of twenty minutes she had learnt to keep her balance and walk three steps.

Oona and Jimmy were too excited to say a word. They just looked at one another in glee.

'Wuff!' said Lucky, and licked Jimmy's hand. Then Jimmy found his tongue – but not to lick with. He poured out all his hopes and plans to Oona – how he would teach Lucky marvellous things, and the little dog would be famous – and he, Jimmy, would take her into the ring each night and show the people what a wonderful dog he had! Oona listened and nodded his yellow head. He was a good friend to have.

How Jimmy worked to teach Lucky! Soon the little dog could run along the tightrope as fast as Jimmy could. Then Jimmy took his mother into his secret and she made Lucky a dear little red skirt to wear, and bought her a little parasol to carry over her head – for Lucky could walk on her hind legs on the tightrope now. It was marvellous to see her. She loved her tricks and was always anxious to show off.

Jimmy worked at Lucky's other tricks too. She thought nothing of wheeling the doll's pram about and tucking up the doll. She could jump like a hare too, and could hold on to a swing-bar with her teeth and swing like that. She could dance round with Jimmy in time to music, her little hind legs twinkling in and out merrily. And then Jimmy noticed that she seemed to understand when Sammy did his tricks of counting. When Mr Wally said to the chimpanzee, 'Which is figure 4?' Lucky would go to the right figure even before Sammy picked it up himself.

'I believe she could count too – and perhaps spell,' thought Jimmy in glee. So he made some big figures and letters and began patiently to teach Lucky.

Lucky learnt easily. Soon she knew all the figures up to five, like Sammy. Then she learnt to spell her own name. This is how Jimmy taught her. He put all the letters of the alphabet out in front of Lucky, and rubbed a piece of meat on to the L. Lucky soon sniffed that out and fetched the letter. Then Jimmy rubbed the meat on to the letter U and Lucky fetched *that* out. After that she fetched out C, K, and Y. Jimmy did it all over again – and again – and soon Lucky knew that she had to fetch out the five letters.

'Wuff, wuff!' she said, her little head cocked on to one side. That meant 'I understand, Master. And I understand too that you want special letters fetched out, for some reason or other.'

In a week Lucky had learnt to fetch out the five letters of her name, bringing them in the right order – L-U-C-K-Y! When Oona first saw her doing this, he couldn't believe his eyes.

'Now she knows what I want her to do with these letters, it will be easy to teach her other words,' said Jimmy, in delight. 'And I'm teaching her to do sums, Oona. Listen, Lucky – one bone and two bones – how many?'

Lucky cocked her head one side, her bright eyes shining. She scraped with her paw on the ground three times. Then she barked three times.

'There you are,' said Jimmy. 'She can do the answer in paw-scrapes or barks – one and two make three!'

'She is a marvellous dog,' said Oona. 'I will make her a

tiny shoe for her right forefoot, Jimmy, and then when she paws the ground in her answers she will make a knocking that everyone will hear. We will stand her on a box.'

Lotta knew about Lucky, but she didn't tell anyone. Only when Lucky was quite perfectly trained was Mr Galliano to know. Then perhaps he would say he would see Lucky and Jimmy at practice in the ring. Jimmy and Lotta watched over Lucky carefully, fed her well, brushed and washed her till her coat shone, and gave her all the love that her doggy heart needed. She was the happiest dog in the show.

Jimmy would not let Lucky practise her tricks for long at a time, for Lal had told him that little and often was the best way. Any animal got tired and cross if it did the same thing too long. They were like children. But Jimmy did not need to be told of this. He knew without telling everything that was right and good for the animals in his care.

All the same he listened to Lal carefully, for he was always eager to pick up any bits of circus knowledge. He knew all kinds of things now – how to rub resin on to the horses' backs before they went into the ring at night, so that Lotta would not slip when she stood on them – how to test every rope and bolt and pin before Oona or Sticky Stanley the clown did their tricks – how to sense when any animal was not well or was going to be difficult.

Often one of the grooms would come to Jimmy for help if one of the beautiful stallion horses was restless and nervous. Then Jimmy would speak a few words in the low, gentle voice he always kept for animals, and the horse would listen and calm down. The circus-folk said that Jimmy was as good as Mr Galliano with the horses – though Mr Galliano was a marvel with animals, and had been known to go into a cage of angry fighting tigers and calm them at once with a few words.

At last Lucky was perfectly trained. She did all her tricks quickly and smoothly, and even Jimmy could not wish her to do better. Now he would ask Mr Galliano to see them in the ring.

But what a disappointment for poor Jimmy! Mr Galliano was in a bad temper that day. Someone whom he had engaged to come to his circus with five beautiful tigers had sent word to say he could not come – and Mr Galliano roared angrily in his caravan.

So, when Jimmy went timidly up the steps of the caravan and called Mr Galliano, he was met by a frowning face and an angry shout.

'Well! What do you want, boy?'

'Please, sir, I've come to ask you if you will see my dog Lucky in the ring with me?' began Jimmy nervously, for, like everyone else, he was frightened of Mr Galliano when he was angry.

'See you and your dog in the ring!' cried Mr Galliano. 'Indeed I won't! You want to waste my time – yes? Go away – and if you dare to ask me such silly things again I will send you away!'

Of course Mr Galliano did not mean all this – but Jimmy was very miserable and disappointed as he went back to his own caravan. How he wished he had not asked Mr Galliano just then – he might have listened if he had not been cross. Poor Jimmy! After he had worked so hard too!

Someone had heard that Mr Galliano had said – and that someone was Mr Wally. He remembered how good Jimmy had been when he would not let him help with Sammy in the ring. He ran over to the little boy.

'Cheer up!' he said. 'I'll see old Galliano for you tomorrow – and I'll make him see you and Lucky in the ring. You see if I don't!'

22. Lucky has a chance

Jimmy was so pleased when Mr Wally spoke kindly to him. If only he would see Mr Galliano and speak for him and Lucky, things might be all right.

'How kind you are, Mr Wally,' he said gratefully.

'Jimmy, I once did you a bad turn,' said Mr Wally, 'and instead of paying me back with rudeness and unkindness you were just the same to me as you had always been – helping me with Sammy and doing everything you could. Well, if I can do you a *good* turn now I will. You couldn't go into the ring any more with Sammy because I wouldn't let you – but I'll get you there with Lucky or my name's not Wally!'

Jimmy could have cried for joy. What his mother said was true then – if you laughed at obstacles and used them as stepping-stones they did really take you somewhere. How much better it would be for Jimmy to go into the ring with his own dog Lucky, than as helper to Mr Wally with Sammy the chimpanzee!

Mr Wally kept his word. The next day, when Mr Galliano had calmed down, and Mrs Galliano had sent all the circus-folk tins of lobster to make up for Mr Galliano's bad temper the day before, Mr Wally asked to have a word with Mr Galliano himself.

He disappeared into his caravan with the ring-master. Jimmy waited near by anxiously.

'Give Jimmy a chance,' said Mr Wally to Mr Galliano. 'I believe he has trained that dog of his till it's almost like a child, Galliano. He's longing to go into the ring again.'

'But you kept him out, Wally – yes?' said Mr Galliano. 'Then why do you speak for the boy now?'

'I speak for him because he is a good boy, one of those

few people who pay back good for evil,' said Mr Wally, going red.

Mr Galliano whistled softly. Mrs Galliano spoke to him in her slow voice from the back of the caravan.

'You should see him, Galliano. Mr Wally is right. Jimmy is a fine boy.'

'Very well, I will see him,' said Mr Galliano. 'But it will be a waste of my time, yes. I will see him in the ring with Lucky in an hour's time, Wally.'

Jimmy was overjoyed when Mr Wally came out and told him the news. How glad he was that he had taken his mother's advice and not been horrid to Mr Wally! If he had he would not have had Mr Wally's help now. He ran to get Lucky and dress her.

In an hour's time Jimmy was in the ring with Lucky. He had dressed himself in his fine circus suit. Lucky had on her quaint little skirt too. She ran about on her hind legs, wuffling in excitement. She knew quite well that something important was going to happen.

'Do your best, Lucky, old girl,' said Jimmy. 'Do your best!' Lucky licked his ear; and then Mr Galliano came in – and Mrs Galliano too. But nobody else was allowed inside the tent.

'Begin,' said Galliano – and Jimmy began. He said very little to Lucky – just a word now and again – for Lucky understand a cock of his head, a snap of his fingers, or a whisper better than a shouted command.

First Lucky did the simple things – begging and trusting and jumping and walking on her hind legs carrying a flag, a basket, or a parasol. Then she wheeled the pram and tucked up the doll. Then she walked the tightrope with Jimmy, running lightly along it on her small feet, with their thin rubber socks on. Mr Galliano had never seen a dog doing that before and neither had Mrs Galliano. They sat and stared as if they were turned to stone – could it be possible that the dog Lucky, who was no more than a puppy, had learnt all these things in a few short months?

Then came the counting. Jimmy slipped a little

wooden shoe on to Lucky's right forefoot, and stood her on a wooden stand. He cried out loudly, so that Mr and Mrs Galliano might hear. 'Lucky, listen to me! If I give you *two* bones and *three* bones, how many will you have?'

Lucky listened, her head on one side. She thought. Then she knocked with her foot – five times.

'Quite right!' cried Jimmy, throwing her a biscuit. 'Now listen again. Lucky, if I give you *three* bones and then take away *one*, how many will you have?'

Lucky knocked the answer loudly with her foot – two knocks – then she barked twice as well to show that she really *did* know the answer! Mr Galliano couldn't help giving a grunt – he was so astonished.

Then Jimmy brought out the letters of the alphabet and spread them in front of the little dog.

'Bring me the letters of your name, Lucky,' he cried – and Lucky found them and brought them to him, one by one – L-U-C-K-Y. Mrs Galliano clapped. She simply couldn't help it.

And then Jimmy made Lucky do her last trick. 'Lucky,' he said, 'can you tell me the name of the man who owns the best circus on the road?'

Lucky wagged her tail and set off to find the letters she had been taught. And what letters do you think she found? She found G-A-L-L-I-A-N-O! Galliano! Jimmy had had to put two L's and two A's into the alphabet as Galliano's name had two. Wasn't it a long word for a little dog to spell?

Mr Galliano jumped up from his seat. 'Wonderful! Amazing!' he shouted. 'This is a dog in a thousand, yes – and she shall go into the ring with you tonight, Jimmy – yes, yes, yes!'

Jimmy went red with joy and thanked Mr Galliano.

'That dog will make your fortune, yes, without doubt,' said the ring-master, and he cracked his whip which he always carried about with him.

Jimmy tore off to tell his mother and Lotta and Lal and Laddo and Oona and Mr Wally. They were all pleased and excited.

'You must have an even finer circus suit,' said Oona. 'Yes, you must have one that glitters and sparkles like mine. We will go into the town to an old dressmaker I know, Jimmy, and she will make you a magnificent suit.'

'But I haven't much money,' said Jimmy.

'You will soon have plenty,' laughed Oona. 'That dog of yours will earn more in a month than you or I could earn in a year.'

Well, from the very beginning of her life in the ring that night, Lucky was a success. Mr Galliano had not said anything about Jimmy and Lucky in his circus posters, and so no one knew that they were going to see them that night.

But when the little dog had finished her marvellous tricks, everyone stood up and cheered till they were hoarse! Jimmy had to come into the ring again and again and bow, whilst Lucky ran round and round his legs in delight. People had been astonished enough when Lucky had walked the tightrope behind Jimmy – but when they saw that the dog could count and spell, they were amazed! Mr Galliano had never known the people to cheer and clap so madly.

Everyone was pleased at the little boy's success with his dog, for they all liked Jimmy. Oona himself went to fetch Jimmy's new suit when it was done, and squeezed himself into Jimmy's caravan to see the little boy try it on. My goodness! It was like an enchanted suit. It fitted Jimmy tightly from heels to head, and even his toes glittered as he walked, for sequins had been sewn everywhere! He wore a little red velvet cloak over the glittering silver suit, and really, his mother could hardly believe it was Jimmy who stood before her.

There were only a few more days to stay in the place where the circus was then giving its show. Each night Jimmy and Lucky were cheered and clapped, and Mr Galliano seeing the seats fill up well, and the money pour into the box at the gate, tipped his hat over his right ear so much that it fell right off, and Jemima the monkey ran off with it, much to Lotta's delight.

'I suppose you'll soon be getting too grand to play with me any more, Jimmy,' she said one day, as they sat together on the steps of Lotta's caravan, eating buttered buns.

'If you say things like that, Lotta, I shall push you off the steps,' said Jimmy. 'You ought to know me better – and anyway, it isn't so much *I* that get the claps and cheers – it's Lucky.'

'You taught her, though,' said Lotta, licking the butter off her bun. 'Nobody else could have taught Lucky so well. I heard my mother say so.'

'Did she?' said Jimmy, pleased. 'Oh, Lotta – I'm so happy! First I wanted to join the circus and never thought it would happen – and it did! Then I wanted to go into the ring, and I did – and then I wanted to take Lucky into the ring, and now that's happened too.'

'Yes – you are very lucky,' said Lotta. 'And I think your dog Lucky will bring you more luck too.'

Lotta was right. Lucky brought Jimmy more good fortune. The last night that the circus was giving its show for the town, a big man sat in one of the front seats, watching. When he saw Jimmy come in, all glittering from top to toe, bringing with him his small, dancing dog, the big man sat up. This was what he had really come to see.

He watched carefully, and whistled softly to himself when he saw Lucky counting and spelling. At the end of the show he went to Jimmy's caravan.

Jimmy's mother was there, cooking some bacon and eggs for their supper. The big man spoke to her.

'Are you Jimmy's mother?' he said. 'Well, my good woman, I am Mr Alfred Cyrano, the owner of the biggest circus in the world. I want your boy to leave this circus and come to join mine. I will pay him well. He has a dog there that I could do with in my circus.'

At that moment Jimmy came up. Mr Alfred Cyrano clapped him on the shoulder. 'Hey, boy!' he said. 'That's a fine dog of yours. I'll buy her from you, and engage you to come to my circus for ten pounds a week. And I'll give you one hundred pounds for the dog.'

Jimmy couldn't say a word. Neither could his mother. One hundred pounds for Lucky – and ten pounds a week to join a bigger circus! It seemed too strange to be true. But then a thought struck Jimmy.

'If you bought Lucky, then she wouldn't be mine,' he said. 'And suppose you didn't like me after a week or two and sent me away – I would have to leave Lucky behind, wouldn't I?'

'Oh, well, if I buy the dog, she's mine,' said Mr Alfred Cyrano, lighting a cigar about twice as big as Mr Galliano ever had. Jimmy made up his mind in a flash.

'Then I say no, thank you, sir,' he said. 'I can't part with Lucky, not even for a *thousand* pounds. She's worth much more than money to me. I love her, and she loves me. And besides, it would be mean to leave Mr Galliano and all my friends here just as I am beginning to help them to make money. They took me on and were kind to me when I was just a little schoolboy and knew nothing.'

'Pah!' said Mr Alfred Cyrano; 'you are a stupid, silly boy. One day you will be sorry you did not come with the great Mr Cyrano!'

He strode off in disgust. When the news got round that Jimmy had said no to Mr Cyrano, everyone was excited. And then a message came to Jimmy to go to Mr Galliano's caravan. What *could* he want?

Jimmy did get a surprise when he found out why Mr Galliano had sent for him!

23. The wonderful caravan – and Jumbo's surprise

Jimmy set off to Mr Galliano's caravan. It was late and the little boy was tired. What did Mr Galliano want with him so late at night?

He went up the steps. Mrs Galliano opened the caravan door and he went in. It really was a lovely caravan, roomy and comfortable – much, much better than Jimmy's own. Mr Galliano was sitting at the table eating a plum pie with cream. He cut Jimmy a big slice, poured cream over it, and pushed it towards the surprised boy.

'Eat,' he said. 'I want to talk to you, Jimmy. I hear that Mr Alfred Cyrano came to ask you to sell Lucky to him and go with him to his big circus – yes?'

'Yes, he did, Mr Galliano,' said Jimmy, eating the pie hungrily. 'But I said no.'

'Why did you say no?' asked Mr Galliano, and he looked hard at Jimmy.

'Well, Mr Galliano, sir, there were two reasons,' said Jimmy, going red. 'I won't sell my dog Lucky to anyone in the world – and I'm not going to leave you, sir, either, when you've given me my first chance.'

Mrs Galliano made a gentle noise rather like the purring of a cat. Mr Galliano choked over a piece of pie. He swallowed it, cleared his throat, jumped up and gave Jimmy such a clap on the back that the little boy almost fell into his plate of pie.

'He won't leave Galliano – no?' roared Mr Galliano in delight. 'He won't sell his dog – no? He does not want money – no? He loves his dog and his friends before he loves money – yes?'

'Well, Mr Galliano, I *do* want money really,' said Jimmy. 'But not if I have to leave you or to sell Lucky to get it.'

'And what do you want money for, Jimmy?' asked Mrs Galliano in her soft slow voice, putting a cup of coffee in front of him.

'There's one very special reason I want it for,' said Jimmy. 'I want my mother to have a fine caravan like this, Mrs Galliano. She isn't really one of the circus-folk, you see, and she's been used to having plenty of room to move about in. Our caravan is so small and old and ugly, though we've made it look better since we've painted it.'

'Now listen to me, Jimmy,' said Mr Galliano, and he sat down and leaned over the table to Jimmy. 'You are a loyal and grateful boy, and I tell you those two things are hard to find in anyone. Well – I, too, can be loyal and grateful – yes? Galliano can be a good friend to those who stick to him. You shall have the caravan you want – yes, and all the things in it that you want too! You have said you will stay with me, and I know, Jimmy, that you and your little dog will bring money to the circus. Very well, then – in return I will spend money on you – yes?'

Jimmy's mouth fell open in surprise and delight. Have a caravan like Mr Galliano's – big, roomy, and beautiful? Whatever would his mother say?

'Oh, Mr Galliano – thank you!' stammered Jimmy. 'I didn't expect anything like that. I do hope I shall be worth it all to you.'

'Boys like Jimmy don't grow on every bush, do they, Tessa?' said Mr Galliano, smiling at his wife. 'You shall stay with me till you get too big for my little circus, Jimmy – yes?'

Jimmy said goodnight and fell down the steps of the caravan in a great hurry to tell his mother the grand news. What a lucky day it had been for him when he had chosen his puppy Lucky! Lotta had named her well! He bumped into Mr Tonks as he ran in the dark to his own caravan.

'Now, now, is this a new elephant or an escaped express

train?' said Mr Tonks, sitting down suddenly in the field. 'Whatever's the matter, Jimmy? Are you running a race?'

'No,' said Jimmy, and he poured out his story to Mr Tonks as they sat there in the dewy field.

'Boy, you did well to say no to Mr Cyrano,' said Mr Tonks solemnly. 'He did not want you – he wanted your dog. Two weeks after you had joined his circus he would have sent you off, without Lucky. He is not a good man.'

'Well, Mr Galliano *is*!' said Jimmy. 'And I'll never leave him as long as he wants me.'

He tore off to his own caravan, where his father and mother were sitting waiting for him, wondering whatever had happened to him.

Jimmy soon told them everything, and they sat up talking till long past midnight. 'Oh, if only I can have a really proper caravan, with plenty of room for everything, and a nicely fixed-in stove, I should be really happy,' said Mrs Brown, delighted. Jimmy's father looked proudly at his little boy. Who would have thought he could do so much?

Jimmy didn't sleep much that night. He tossed and turned, and thought of Lucky and Oona and Mr Tonks and Lotta and Mr Cyrano and everything. Most of all he thought of the new caravan he was going to get for his mother. Should he go and choose it by himself for a big surprise – or should he take his mother with him and let her choose it? Perhaps it would be best to let her choose it. He fell asleep then, and slept so late that the circus was almost ready to move off on the road again before he awoke. Lotta had fed Lucky and the other dogs. Mrs Brown would not let her wake Jimmy.

'We pass a big place that sells caravans on the way to our next show-place,' said Mr Tonks. 'It's quite near the place where we shall camp for the night.'

'I shall ask Mr Galliano if I can get it, then!' said Jimmy joyfully. So the next day, with a note from Mr Galliano in his hand, Jimmy, his mother and father all went to the caravan place. The caravans stood in a great field, ready to be bought. There were all kinds – ones to be hired for two or three weeks – ones to be lived in always, big ones, little ones, blue ones, yellow ones – ones to be pulled by horses and ones to be pulled by cars.

'I say!' said Jimmy, in surprise. 'Look at all those caravans, Mother! Whichever shall we choose?'

The man who managed the caravan place showed them a great many caravans. Mrs Brown stopped by a yellow one with blue wheels and blue chimney. 'Is this very expensive?' she asked. 'It is so large and roomy, and everything is fitted so neatly inside. Look, Jimmy, there are even taps to turn on and off, and a place to store water in so that you can get it without always running to the nearest stream! We can fill up whenever we want to, and it will last us for some time.'

The man looked at Mr Galliano's letter. 'You could have that one if you wanted to,' he said. 'It is not any more money than Mr Galliano says he will pay.'

So they chose the yellow caravan. Really, it was wonderful! There was a place for everything. There were bunks to sleep in that folded flat up against the wall to be out of the way in daytime. Mr Brown said it reminded him of a ship. There were four bunks, but Mrs Brown said it wouldn't matter, they needn't use the odd one.

There was a fine stove fitted neatly in a corner. There were cupboards all round the sides and under the bench that ran down one side. Underneath the caravan were lockers where all kinds of things could be stored. There was even a folding table, painted yellow!

'I shall hardly need to get anything to go into the caravan!' said Jimmy's mother joyfully. 'Just curtains and a clock and a carpet – things like that.'

They set off to buy these things. They bought a green carpet and green curtains, and other little things that Mrs Brown wanted. Really, their caravan would be nicer than anyone else's except Mr Galliano's!

'We'll come and fetch the caravan this evening,' said Mr Brown, putting all the things inside it. 'We'll bring a horse with us.'

But they didn't bring a horse. Mr Tonks said he would

lend them Jumbo, for the horses were tired with their long journey. So, about seven o'clock, Jumbo set off with Jimmy. Mrs Brown was busy turning the things out of the old caravan and Mr Brown had plenty of odd jobs to do. Jimmy could quite well fetch the new caravan.

He went along beside Jumbo, who was happy to be with the little boy he loved. They had to pass through a small and busy town on their way to the caravan field, and a crowd gathered to watch the big elephant pass. Jumbo was going along quite peacefully when he suddenly stopped, lifted up his trunk, and trumpeted long and loudly.

'What's the matter, Jumbo?' said Jimmy, in great surprise. But he was even more surprised when Jumbo left him and lumbered towards the crowd. The people scattered in alarm. Jumbo hurried towards a man who was standing in a doorway. He reached out his trunk and took firm hold of the man.

'Jumbo! Jumbo! What are you doing?' cried Jimmy in a fright. The man struggled, but it was no use, he could not get away from the elephant.

And then suddenly Jimmy saw who the man was. He was Harry, the bad man who had been odd-job man to the circus before Mr Brown had joined it – the man who had run off with all the circus money, and had never been found.

A policeman came running up. 'What's all this – now what's all this?' he said sternly. 'What's your elephant doing?'

'He's caught the man who stole the money from the circus,' said Jimmy. 'That's Harry in his trunk! Jumbo won't hurt him – he's just got hold of him to take him back to the circus, I expect. Elephants never forget a kindness, or an unkindness, you know – and this man was unkind to Jumbo. Now Jumbo has remembered and has got Harry.'

A crowd, with the policeman at the head, followed old Jumbo, who plodded back to the circus, holding Harry firmly. Harry was not in the least hurt, but he was very frightened at the thought of meeting Mr Galliano, whom he had robbed some months back.

Only when Jumbo was at Mr Galliano's caravan did he put Harry down – and the policeman at once took hold of his arm. Mr Galliano appeared in astonishment – and very soon Harry was marched off by the policeman, who had written down in his notebook all about the money Harry had stolen.

'What did I tell you?' said Mr Tonks to Jimmy and Lotta. 'An elephant never forgets! If Harry hadn't teased Jumbo, Jumbo would have passed him by today; but he did him a bad turn, and Jumbo remembered it and caught Harry.'

'What an exciting day!' sighed Jimmy, setting off once more with Jumbo to fetch his caravan. He got to the field at last, hitched Jumbo to his lovely yellow caravan and set off back to the camp again. It was dark when he got there, but all the circus-folk were waiting to greet him and cheer the new caravan.

'Hurray! Here comes Jimmy – my, what a fine caravan!' shouted Lotta. How excited all the circus-folk were when they saw the marvellous caravan! They had to look at everything though it was getting very late. But at last the beds were made in three of the four bunks, the door was shut, and the Brown family settled themselves to sleep in their beautiful new home. Lucky had a basket of her own, and she slept proudly on a yellow blanket to match the caravan.

'Goodnight, Lucky,' said Jimmy sleepily. 'You are Lucky by name and lucky by nature! Goodnight, best little dog in the world!'

24. The two marvellous brothers

When Jimmy awoke the next morning in the new caravan, he looked round in delight. The sun shone through
the windows and lighted up everything. All was new and
gleaming. How happy his mother would be in a home like
this! Jimmy loved living in a house on wheels. It was
most exciting.

This circus was moving off to its next show-place early
that morning. Soon the Browns were up and took their
turn at washing in the fine wash-basin. Jimmy's mother
folded back the three bunk-beds out of the way, and set
the table for breakfast, which she cooked on the bright
little stove in the corner.

'I shall love following the circus and belonging to it
now I have a fine new caravan,' said Mrs Brown happily.
'I just couldn't bear having to live in a mess and a
muddle, and being dirty and untidy, like most of the
circus-folk. I like them very much – they are generous
and kind-hearted – but, oh dear! they really are not very
clean or tidy.'

'Perhaps when they see our fine gleaming caravan they
will want one like it, and be tidy and clean too,' said
Jimmy; but Mr Brown said no, the folk were too old to
alter their ways now.

'Lotta's not too old,' said Jimmy's mother. 'She will see
our caravan and perhaps mend her ways a bit, the untidy
little thing.'

Jimmy laughed. Lotta was certainly untidy, though
she could look beautiful enough in the ring, dressed up in
her fine clothes. But he did not think that even his mother
could make Lotta wash behind her ears each morning.

The circus set off once more. Everyone was talking

about how Jumbo had caught Harry the night before, and the elephant was quite a hero. Mr Tonks was proud of him. Harry would be well punished, there was no doubt of that. Maybe he would not be unkind to an animal again.

On went the circus to its next show-place. There it settled in and once more gave its show every night. Everyone worked hard, and again the circus was a success, especially Jimmy and Lucky. How people stood up and cheered when they saw Lucky following Jimmy on the tightrope, walking on her hind legs, and carrying her little sunshade! Jimmy and Lucky had their pictures in the papers, and Mrs Brown cut them out and pinned them on the walls of the caravan.

On went the circus again, and yet again. Always it seemed to be on the move. Sometimes it stayed only three nights at a town, sometimes two or three weeks. Christmas drew near, and Mr Galliano planned an extra big circus just outside a very big town. He drew up the programme carefully.

'I must get one more turn,' he said to Mrs Galliano. 'I will get the two Marvel Brothers, yes. They sit on trapeze seats high in the air, and catch one another as they swing. It is a thing that people love, yes.'

So the two Marvel Brothers came to join the circus. They were short, strong men with beautiful straight bodies and bright, clear eyes. They brought with them a thin little dog, a black spaniel with sad brown eyes and floppy ears.

Jimmy made friends with the spaniel that same day. Its name was Lulu, and it snuggled up to Jimmy as if it had known him all his life.

'Lotta, isn't this dog thin?' said Jimmy, feeling it. 'I wonder if there's anything wrong with it.'

'Perhaps the Marvel Brothers don't feed it enough,' said Lotta. 'I'll give her some biscuits when I next feed our own dogs. I don't much like those two new circusmen, Jimmy. They smile too much.'

'Smile too much?' said Jimmy, in surprise. 'What do you mean?'

'Well, you watch them next time you see them,' said Lotta. 'They smile with their mouths and show all their lovely white teeth – but they don't smile with their eyes like you do and everyone else.'

Lotta was right. Jan and Yol, the two trapeze performers, never smiled with their eyes – but they smiled with their mouths a hundred times a day, saying wonderful things to everyone, and trying to make people think they were the most marvellous brothers in the world.

They certainly *were* marvellous. The first time Jimmy saw them swinging on their bar-swings, high up in the top of the big tent, flying from one swing to another, and catching one another in mid-air, he gazed in astonishment. He was dreadfully afraid they would fall.

'Fall!' said Jan scornfully, when Jimmy told him this one day. 'You do not know what you are talking about, boy. I have been doing these things since I was two. My father and my mother, my grandfather and my great-grandfather, were all trapeze-folk.'

The spaniel, Lulu, came up just then and sprawled over Jan's feet. He kicked it away impatiently. Jimmy went red with anger.

'Don't do that,' he said. 'You hurt the dog.'

'Well, it's my dog, isn't it?' said Jan, and he would have kicked the spaniel again if it had not gone out of his reach. Jimmy didn't say a word more. He went off to tell Lotta. She nodded her head.

'They are clever men, but not good,' she said. 'Don't let Lucky go near them, Jimmy.'

Jimmy was careful to keep Lucky away from the Marvel Brothers, for, after he had told Jan not to kick Lulu, both brothers seemed to dislike him.

Then another thing happened that made Jimmy even more careful. His father had to put up and test the big steel posts and bars from which the strong swings hung on which Jan and Yol swung each night. Mr Brown was always careful to see that these were exactly right, for he knew that if anything went wrong, Jan or Yol might fall.

One night Jan missed catching his brother as Yol came

flying through the air from his swing. Yol fell into the net below, where he bounced up and down. He was soon up again and on his swing – but Mr Galliano was angry.

'If you do that again I shall not pay you so much money,' he told the two sulky brothers. 'You know why you made that mistake? It is because you do not practise enough. You will practise every day from now – yes?'

'It wasn't our fault,' said Jan; 'the posts were not put up right. They had slipped a little. Brown had not done the job well.'

So Jimmy's father was called to Mr Galliano's caravan. But he knew quite well that he had tested every screw, every post, every bar – and Mr Galliano believed him, for he had found Brownie to be an honest and truthful man.

This made Jan and Yol dislike Jimmy even more, and they lay in wait for him behind caravans and tripped him up. The little boy was not used to people disliking him and it made him very unhappy. Also he was dreadfully afraid they might harm Lucky. He took her with him wherever he went.

Lulu the spaniel tried to go with Jimmy as much as she could. Jimmy fed her, for he knew quite well she didn't get enough food from Jan and Yol. Lulu lay on the steps of Jimmy's caravan all day long. She loved Jimmy and Lotta. But Jan and Yol were angry when they found that their dog followed the boy and girl about so much. They whipped her and shut her up in their own caravan, where she howled and scratched at the door for hours.

Jimmy and Lotta dared not let Lulu out, but they were miserable about it. The brothers' caravan was right at the end of the circus field, and nobody but the two children could hear the dog. They didn't know what to do.

'I wish they'd never come to the circus,' said Jimmy gloomily. 'They are the first people I haven't liked.'

'Oh, all circus people aren't nice,' said Lotta, laughing at Jimmy's gloomy face. 'But it's funny to meet two that don't like animals. Most circus-folk love them.'

'They've been telling everyone that my father doesn't do his work properly,' said Jimmy. 'I don't mind what

they say about *me* – but I won't have them saying things
about my father.'

'Brownie is a good sort,' said Lotta, who was very fond
of Jimmy's father. 'Cheer up, Jimmy. Let's go and take
the dogs for a walk.'

'I wish we could take Lulu too,' said Jimmy. But that
was impossible.

That night, when the Marvel Brothers went up the
steps of their caravan and opened the door, they fell
headlong over Lulu, who rushed to welcome them. Yol
hit his head against a chair and fell into a great rage.

He picked up a whip and beat poor Lulu hard. Then he
turned the dog out into the bitter frosty night and banged
the door on her. The little dog lay under the caravan,
shivering with cold. After a while she crept to Lotta's
caravan, which was the nearest, and whined. Lotta, who
always awoke at a dog's bark or whine, sat up and
listened. Lulu whined again.

In a trice the little girl was out of bed and lit a candle.
She opened the door and saw poor Lulu there, bleeding
from a cut over her eye where Yol had hit her very hard.
Lotta threw on a coat, slipped out of the caravan, and
went to wake Jimmy. The two children bathed the dog's
cut, whispered angrily about Yol and Jan, and then
Jimmy put Lucky at the foot of his own bed, and put
Lulu into Lucky's basket. She was still shivering with cold,
so he heated some milk for her and covered her up well.

In the morning Lotta and Jimmy went to Mr Galliano
with Lulu. They told him how she had come to them in
the middle of the night, cold and hurt. Mr Galliano
listened and his face grew dark.

'No one shall stay in my circus who is cruel to an
animal,' he said. 'Hey, Mr Wally! Tell Jan and Yol I
want to see them.'

Jan and Yol came, smiling and showing their strong
white teeth. Jimmy and Lotta had gone with Lulu. Mr
Galliano was standing by his caravan, whip in hand, his
top hat perfectly straight on his head.

'Here is your money,' he said to the two surprised

brothers. 'Take it and leave. I will not have anyone with
me who treats a dog as you treat yours. You will leave the
dog behind, yes.'

'But, Mr Galliano,' said Jan, forgetting to smile, 'you
can't do this. We bring hundreds of people to see your
Christmas circus. We are famous.'

'I don't care if nobody comes at all,' said Mr Galliano,
with a loud crack of his whip. 'You are clever, yes, but it is
not enough to be clever only. Leave this morning.'

The two brothers did not dare to say any more. With
dark, sulky faces they rolled away in their green caravan,
leaving Lulu behind. Jimmy and Lotta watched them go.
Everyone was glad.

'Good old Galliano!' said Lilliput, who was wearing
Jemima the monkey round his neck as usual. 'Trust him
to send off any rascals, even if he loses money in doing so.'

'He made them leave Lulu behind, and they did,' said
Jimmy. 'Lotta and I are going to share her. She isn't at all
clever, but she is a loving, gentle creature, and Lucky
loves her.'

'Jan and Yol would not dare to take Lulu with them
after Galliano had forbidden them to,' said Lilliput. 'He
could send word to every circus in the country, and no
one would take the Marvel Brothers again. I have heard
that they have been turned out of two other circuses
before this.'

'Woof!' said Lulu, and tugged at Jimmy's bootlace. 'I
am glad to be your dog now. Woof!'

25. Lotta is unhappy

The Christmas holidays were over, and the month of January was slipping away. The circus had done well all through Christmas and afterwards, and now it was on the move again. It had a long way to go to its next show-place, and Jimmy was pleased to think that his mother had such a big, comfortable caravan to live in. He was very proud of the spick-and-span home on wheels that he had been able to get for her.

Jimmy's mother kept it beautifully, too – not as most of the caravans were kept. The circus-folk were kindly generous, brave people, but they were not very clean and were dreadfully untidy. Lotta was beginning to be much cleaner and tidier, though – she was brushing her pretty hair every day and tying it back, and her face at least was clean. She was better at her lessons too, and was reading very well.

Lal was delighted. She came to see Mrs Brown one day and thanked her.

'Lotta is a different child since you and Jimmy came,' she said, pleased. 'She was such a little harum-scarum thing, and I wasn't much good at dealing with her – but now I am quite proud of her.'

'Well, you've done a lot for Jimmy too,' said Mrs Brown. 'You and Laddo have taught him to ride well, and helped him with animals – and you bought him his wonderful dog, Lucky.'

Jimmy and Lotta were always together. They sometimes quarrelled, especially when Lotta had one of her naughty days, when she made faces and pinched and punched poor Jimmy all for nothing – but they always made it up, and thought the world of one another.

'Won't it be lovely when the spring days come and we can go for walks in the early morning?' said Lotta, who loved the fresh dawns of the countryside. 'We shall be at Westsea for Easter, and that's a lovely place – we can take the dogs out for a run on the beach before breakfast each day.'

'I shall love the summer again too,' said Jimmy. 'The smell of the may as we go down the lanes – and the birds singing – and the blue sky, like forget-me-nots – lovely!'

They were sitting in Jimmy's caravan, whilst Mrs Brown did some mending. It was too cold to sit on the caravan steps now when the circus was moving. The cold wind came and nipped their legs and hands and made them shiver there. Mrs Brown would not let them get cold – so they had to come inside, and talk and play there.

It was fun to look out of the big side window and see the towns they passed. Jimmy felt quite sorry for people who lived in houses now. A home on wheels was such fun – you could go where you liked, see fresh places and new people, and then, when the time came, off you went again on rumbling wheels! Lovely!

After a whole week's travelling the circus came to its next show-place. It was February now, and the days were beginning to get longer. The birds sang madly in the early morning. Jimmy lay and listened to them. He tried to whistle as they did, and sometimes his imitation was so good that the blackbirds answered him, and the starlings sat on the chimney of the caravan and made fizzy, spluttery noises, thinking there was another starling down below.

The little boy was very happy and so was Lotta – until a dreadful thing happened.

Jimmy had noticed Lal and Laddo, Lotta's father and mother, looking rather grave and solemn the last few days, but neither he nor Lotta knew why. Sometimes they had sent Lotta out of the caravan, saying they wanted to talk over something. It was all most mysterious.

Jimmy wondered what it was all about – and then he knew. One morning he missed Lotta and couldn't find her anywhere. He hunted all round the circus field. He asked Oona and Lilliput and Mr Tonks if they had seen the little girl, but nobody had. She really seemed to have quite disappeared.

'Wherever can she be?' thought Jimmy, quite worried. And then at last he found her.

She was huddled underneath her own caravan, curled up in a big old box that stood on its side. And she was crying bitterly, with Lulu the spaniel licking her face.

Jimmy crawled under the caravan, alarmed. It was so unlike Lotta to cry. Whatever could be the matter?

'Lotta! What is it? Come out and tell me!' he begged.

But Lotta wouldn't come out, and she wouldn't stop crying. Her face was dirty and tear-stained and her eyes were swollen. Jimmy sat down beside her and put his arm round her. The little girl snuggled against him and cried hot tears all down his coat.

'Lotta, you might tell me what's the matter,' said Jimmy. 'Are you ill? Have you been punished for something?'

Lotta did not answer at first – but gradually her sobs stopped and she began to speak.

'Oh, Jimmy! Lal and Laddo are leaving the circus – and they're not taking me with them. And I've got to go to Uncle Benjy and live with him – till they come back.'

Jimmy's heart sank. It was bad enough that Lal and Laddo were leaving, but Lotta too – that was dreadful!

'I shall be so lonely and miserable,' said Lotta, her tears dripping down Jimmy's coat again. 'I like Uncle B – b – b – benjy – but I can't bear to live in a house – I want to be with the circus – and you.'

'Why aren't Lal and Laddo taking you with them?' asked Jimmy, surprised, for Lal and Laddo were fond of their clever little girl.

'Because they are going to Austria for six months, to join Lal's brother there,' said Lotta. 'He is running a circus at Budapest, Lal says – and will pay them well if they go. And they want to buy new horses out there too. But they are not allowed to take *me*.'

She began to cry again, and Jimmy hugged her hard. Poor, poor Lotta! She belonged to the circus. She had never lived in a house. She would be so miserable with Uncle Benjy – she would have to go to school there, and she wouldn't understand that a bit. She would miss her horses and Lal and Laddo – and Jimmy – dreadfully.

'When are they going?' asked Jimmy.

'After this show is finished,' said Lotta, rubbing her dirty little hand over her wet face. 'They have told Mr Galliano already. He is getting somebody else instead for Easter. They will bring their own horses, because Lal and Laddo are taking theirs with them.'

Jimmy was worried. That meant Lotta would go away very soon – in a few weeks. Whatever would he do without her? The little boy did not know what to say to comfort Lotta. As he sat curled up under the caravan with her, he heard Mr Galliano shouting:

'Jimmy! Jimmy! Where are you?'

'Here, Mr Galliano!' cried Jimmy, and he scrambled out. He ran to Mr Galliano, and saw, to his surprise, that the ring-master's top hat was on perfectly straight. What could have happened to make him put it on like that?

'Jimmy, go to your mother,' said Mr Galliano. 'She has fallen over something and has hurt her leg. Your father has gone for the doctor.'

Jimmy went pale. He loved his mother best in all the world. He sped off to the caravan, forgetting all about poor Lotta.

Mrs Brown was lying on her bed, looking ill. She smiled at Jimmy as he came up the steps.

'Don't worry, dear,' she said. 'I've only twisted my ankle. It will soon be better.'

'What a dreadful morning this is!' thought Jimmy, putting some milk in a saucepan to heat for his mother. 'First poor Lotta – and now Mother!'

The doctor soon came. He looked at Mrs Brown's leg. She had twisted it badly, and the ankle was very swollen.

'Nothing very terrible,' said the doctor cheerily, 'But

you'll have to lie up and keep that leg still for two or three
weeks, Mrs Brown.'

'Oh dear, I can't do that,' said Mrs Brown, alarmed.
'Why, who would look after Jimmy and my husband?
Who would cook their meals and see to the caravan? No –
I couldn't do that.'

'You'll have to,' said the doctor, looking grave. 'If you
don't, that foot of yours will give you great trouble.'

'I'll see that Mother rests her foot, Doctor,' said
Jimmy. 'I can do everything for her.'

'No, Jimmy, you can't,' said Mrs Brown. 'You and
Daddy are busy all day long – you won't have time to
spare to do my work too. I shall get up tomorrow.'

The doctor said no more. He went down the steps, and
Jimmy and Mr Brown thanked him for coming, and paid
him. Lotta was standing a little way off, her face still tear-
stained.

'Jimmy,' she said, running up, 'what's the matter with
your mother? Is she badly hurt?'

'No,' said Jimmy. 'It's just her foot. She's got to rest it
for two or three weeks – and she's worried because she
won't be able to cook for us and look after the caravan.
What a horrid day this is, Lotta.'

Lotta looked at Jimmy's sad face and forgot her own
troubles. 'Jimmy, don't forget what you once told me
your mother said, when troubles came,' she said. 'Tread
on them and they will be stepping-stones to lead you to
something good. Don't worry – I'll come and help each
day.'

'I don't see what good can possibly come out of a thing
like this,' said Jimmy gloomily. 'Or out of your troubles
either, Lotta.'

'Don't look like that, Jimmy,' said Lotta, who was
trying to be brave. 'I'll promise to be good over my disappointment if you'll promise not to worry too much about
your mother, and will let me help all I can.'

'You're a good friend, Lotta,' said Jimmy. 'All right –
we'll both be brave. I don't see how anything nice can
possibly come out of this – how can we use troubles like

these as stepping-stones to something better? Oh, how horrid everything is!'

Lotta ran up the caravan steps to tell Mrs Brown she would come and help each day. Mrs Brown was glad. She loved the little girl – and Lotta knew by now just how Mrs Brown liked things done. She knew that Mrs Brown liked her stove kept clean. She knew that she liked the floor washed every day. She knew just how Mrs Brown did her cooking. Oh, Lotta knew a great deal, nowadays, that she hadn't known before.

Jimmy went off to see to the dogs, and left Lotta to help his mother into bed. Lucky came to him, dancing about merrily, trying to make her little master smile. But Jimmy had no smiles that day. He could not forget that he was soon to lose his best friend – dear, naughty little Lotta.

Lotta began to forget her own troubles in helping Mrs Brown. She got her comfortably to bed and saw to her poor foot. She ran out to get something for dinner. She put it on to cook, and chattered away to Mrs Brown. She laid the tiny table beautifully, and Mrs Brown thought what a clever, handy little girl she was.

Lotta and Jimmy were plucky that day. They did not tell Mrs Brown a word about Lal and Laddo leaving. They kept their unhappiness to themselves, and smiled and talk to Mrs Brown at dinner-time to keep her happy and cheerful. She was so pleased.

'I don't know what I should do without you, Lotta!' she said.

26. Jimmy and Lotta get their reward

The days passed by. Mrs Brown's foot was slow in getting better, and she still lay in bed in the caravan, not able to walk; but she did not mind now, for Lotta spent every minute she could with her, cleaning up the caravan, washing anything Mrs Brown wanted clean, cooking the meals, and talking to Mrs Brown in her cheerful little voice.

Jimmy was proud of Lotta, for he knew how sad the little girl's heart was, as the days went by, and the time came nearer when she must leave the circus and go to live with Uncle Benjy, so far away. He wished Lotta could write better – for he was afraid she would never be able to write a proper letter to him. Six months seemed years and years – and perhaps Lal and Laddo might not come back even then.

One day three new people came to see Mr Galliano. They were the riders that Mr Galliano was going to have instead of Lal and Laddo. There were two women and one man, big strong folk, with kindly faces and ready smiles. Jimmy liked them at once. Their horses had come in a great box-like caravan, and Jimmy went to look at them. They were magnificent animals, sleek, silky, and good-tempered.

The three new riders – their names were Juanita, Pepita, and Lou – came over to their horses when they had finished talking to Mr Galliano. They looked at the little boy and smiled. Juanita pointed to Lucky, who was dancing round her.

'This is the famous dog, Lucky?' she asked, in a soft, husky voice. 'And you are Jimmy? We have heard of you.'

Jimmy went red with pride. To think that he was getting famous already! He didn't know what to say. Sticky Stanley the clown, who was near by, grinned and said:

'Oh, our Jimmy will have a circus of his own one day – won't you, Jimmy? He'll be the famous Mr Jimmiano, and wear a top hat twice as big as Mr Galliano's.'

Jimmy laughed. He patted the nearest horse. 'These *are* lovely horses,' he said. 'If you want any help with them, let me know. I always helped with Lal's and Laddo's horses each day, and so did Lotta.'

'Then you shall help with ours,' said Lou, and he smiled at the little boy. 'And Lotta too, whoever she is.'

'She's a wonderful rider,' said Jimmy shyly. 'You should just see the things she can do on horseback.'

Jimmy was pleased that the three new circus-folk were nice – but how he wished that Lal and Laddo were not going! But they were – their horses and dogs were already being packed into their travelling stables. It would not be long now before they went, and then Lotta would be put into the train and sent off to Uncle Benjy.

Mrs Brown had heard that Lal and Laddo were going, but she thought that Lotta was going with them. She was sorry to think that Jimmy would lose his little friend, but as he said nothing to her, she thought perhaps he did not mind very much after all.

'I shall miss you very much, Lotta,' she said to the little girl. 'You have been very good to me these two or three weeks. I wish you were not going away with Lal and Laddo.'

'I'm not going with them,' said Lotta her eyes filling with tears. 'They can't take me. I've got to go and live with my Uncle Benjy – in a house – and I shall hate it.'

Mrs Brown stared in surprise. 'Don't cry, dear,' she said. 'Come here and tell me all about it. You and Jimmy didn't say anything about this to me.'

'I know,' sobbed Lotta; 'we didn't want you to worry about us when you had a bad foot, and we thought that if we were brave, perhaps something good would come out of these horrid things – but nothing has. And I'm going on Saturday.'

Mrs Brown patted the unhappy little girl, and thought hard. 'Brave, kind children,' she thought. 'Here's Lotta being so kind and good to me all these days when she was unhappy, and Jimmy not saying a word.'

Then an idea came into her head. There was a fourth bunk-bed in the caravan – could she possibly keep Lotta with her and Jimmy, till Lal and Laddo came back? Lotta was a dear, useful child, and Mrs Brown loved her. She could not bear to think of her going away all by herself to her Uncle Benjy – living in a house for the first time in her life – going to school and being laughed at because she did not know her lessons very well. Mrs Brown hugged the little girl.

'Ask your mother and father if they can spare a minute to speak to me,' she said to Lotta. The little girl dried her eyes and ran off. Soon Lal and Laddo came up the steps to see Mrs Brown.

'Run off and talk to Jimmy for a few minutes,' Mrs Brown said to Lotta. The little girl went away. Mrs Brown smiled at Lal and Laddo.

'I only heard a few minutes ago that you were not taking Lotta with you,' she said. 'Now I love the child very much, and she is fond of us all. Don't send her away to her uncle's. Let *me* keep her for you till you come back. She will be happy here in our caravan with Jimmy and Brownie and me.'

Lal's face beamed. 'Oh, Mrs Brown! Would you really take our Lotta for us? We hate to send her away, but she cannot stay in the circus alone. She would be so happy with you, and you would look after her well.'

'She would be a daughter to you,' said Laddo. 'She will do more for you than she will for us. You shall have her.'

'Well, that's settled then,' said Mrs Brown, pleased. 'Now perhaps you'll find Jimmy and Lotta send them here, and I will tell them. They both deserve a bit of good luck.'

The two children came up the steps, wondering why they had been sent for. Mrs Brown smiled at them.

'I just want to tell you that something good has come out of our troubles,' she said. 'Lotta is to stay with us, Jimmy – she is not to go to her uncle's. She is to live in our caravan, and have the empty bed!'

The two children stared as if they could not believe their ears. Then they went quite mad with delight. They hugged Mrs Brown. They hugged one another. They danced round the caravan and knocked over two saucepans, a stool and a candlestick. They jumped on the bed and off again. Really, Mrs Brown couldn't help laughing at the two of them.

Lotta suddenly burst into tears, but she was laughing all the time she was crying. 'I'm not really c – c – c – crying,' she wept; 'it's only because I do feel so g – g – g – glad.'

'Well, it's a funny way of showing it,' said Mrs Brown. 'You deserve a nice surprise, both of you – you've been brave, good children, and I haven't heard a grumble from either of you.'

'Mrs Galliano says grumblers get all the bad luck going,' grinned Jimmy. 'So you won't catch *me* grumbling, Mother. Oh, I say, Lotta – you'll be able to ride the horses that Juanita, Pepita and Lou have brought with them – and maybe if you're good and patient they'll let you go in the ring with them.'

'Oh, let me go into the ring with *you* and Lucky!' begged Lotta, bouncing on the bed again. 'We could make up a fine turn together.'

'What fun we'll have these six months!' cried Jimmy, doing a noisy dance on the floor of the caravan. 'Oh, I was so down in the dumps – and now I'm up in the sky!'

'Well, you don't sound like it,' said Mrs Brown, as Jimmy danced noisily about. 'I'm sure clouds wouldn't be so noisy. Stop now, Jimmy, and go with Lotta to buy something for a nice meal.'

The children jumped down to the ground, as happy as blackbirds in spring. Jimmy ran to his special secret box where he kept his money. He took out a lot and Lotta's eyes opened wide. 'I didn't know you were so rich, Jimmy,' she said. 'What are you taking all that for?'

'Wait and see!' said Jimmy, making a face at Lotta. She made one back and they laughed. They were too happy for anything.

They went to the town and bought a fine meal, and then Jimmy went to a big draper's shop – and what do you suppose he bought? He asked to see blankets and sheets and a mattress and eiderdown!

'They are for your little bunk-bed,' said Jimmy. 'My present to you, Lotta! You shall be warm and cosy at night in our caravan.'

Lotta was excited. She had never had such lovely bed-clothes before. In fact, she had never even slept between sheets before. Most of the circus-folk had rugs or blankets, but very seldom sheets. How grand Lotta would be!

Mrs Brown laughed when she saw the two children coming home so laden. Lucky carried the basket of food in her mouth – she was a great help at shopping. They all crowded into the cosy caravan and then unpacked everything for Mrs Brown to see.

Mr Brown came in then, and had to be told the great news. He was delighted, for he too loved Lotta, and had been very pleased with the way the little girl had looked after them all whilst Mrs Brown had had a bad foot.

'We shall be a family of four now,' he said, as he sat down to his meal.

'No, five, Dad!' said Jimmy, as Lucky jumped up on his knee. 'Don't forget Lucky! You've been a great big piece of luck, haven't you, little dog?'

'Wuff!' said Lucky, neatly taking half a sausage off Jimmy's plate.

It was a very happy meal. Lotta looked round the bright, airy caravan and was glad to think it was to be her home for many months. She was glad to know she was not to leave the circus and, best of all, was not to leave Jimmy. They all began to talk excitedly.

'I'm going to help Jimmy with Lucky!'

'And Lotta's going to ask if she can go in the ring with the three new riders,' said Jimmy. 'They are such nice folk – I'm sure they will let Lotta do her turn.'

'And my foot is much better today, so I shall be able to get about and look after my large family,' said Mrs Brown.

'And I shall keep you all in order and see that you don't get too famous,' laughed Mr Brown.

'Wuff, wuff, wuff!' said Lucky, joining in.

Well, Lal and Laddo went off with their horses and dogs, glad to think that their little Lotta was left behind in the care of such kind people. The circus packed up again, for it had to go on the road to its Easter show-place, where a splendid performance was to be given. A great bustle and hurry was in the camp, and Mr Galliano cracked his whip and shouted orders for hours on end. Lotta and Jimmy loved it all. It was exciting.

And now, see, the circus is moving off once more! Here come the very fine row of black horses, with one of the grooms, dressed in red, sitting on the front horse, blowing a horn! How grand he looks!

Then comes a carriage that looks as if it is made of gold – and who is this handsome plump man and this smiling black-haired woman by his side? Why, the famous Mr Galliano and his wife, of course! See him take off his hat and bow to all the watching people and children as if he were a king! See his fine moustache with sharp-pointed ends that turn upwards, and his shiny top hat!

Now the white horses come, and with them are Juan-ita, Pepita and Lou, for these are the horses they brought with them. Pepita rides the first one proudly, looking as pretty as a picture in a blue, shiny frock. Behind comes Sticky Stanley the clown, dressed in red and black, with his high pointed hat, turning cartwheel somersaults all the way, much to the delight of the watching children.

And then a long string of gaily-coloured caravans – a red one – a blue one – a green one – and last of all a beautiful yellow one with pretty curtains flying in the breeze. On the steps, cuddling a black spaniel, sit a pair of

children – Jimmy and Lotta, for it is their caravan. How
all the children stare at the circus-boy and girl and wish
they belonged too!

And here comes the elephant, good old Jumbo, patient
and kindly as ever, pulling three heavy cages behind him.
Mr Tonks walks by his side, and sometimes Jumbo puts
his trunk round his trainer's neck as if it were an arm.
That makes everyone laugh.

Here are two open cages – one with Sammy, the chimpanzee, inside, eating a banana and throwing the peel at
anyone he sees. Mr Wally is sitting with him. In the next
cage are three monkeys, sitting in a row on a perch,
dressed in warm red coats; and riding on the step of their
cage is a little man – Lilliput, of course – with his beloved
monkey, Jemima, round his neck as usual. Ah, we know
all the circus-folk well now!

But who is this marching along on hind legs carrying a
flag, as proud as a general? Why, it is Lucky, little dog
Lucky, who knows quite well that she will get biscuits if
she shows off like this. Yes – too many biscuits.

Jimmy whistles to her. Lucky drops down on her four
feet and races off, her flag in her mouth. Good old Lucky!
You love your little master best in all the world, don't
you?

'Goodbye, goodbye!' the watching children call. 'Come
back soon! Goodbye, Galliano's circus!'

And we too must say goodbye; but if you hear of Mr
Galliano's circus coming to *your* town, go and see how
Jimmy and Lotta and Lucky are getting on.

Good luck, Mr Galliano!

2

HURRAH FOR THE CIRCUS!

Contents

1. Mr Galliano again

Tan-tan-tara! Tan-tan-tara! Tan-tan-tan-tan-tan-tara!

The noise of trumpets came down the main street of the town, and all the children rushed out of their houses, and the grown-ups went to their windows.

'What is it? What is it? It's the circus coming! Listen to the trumpets! Oh, look, here come the first lovely black horses! Oh, here comes the circus! Hurrah for the circus!'

Come along out with all the children and watch the circus coming through the town. Whose circus is it? It is Mr Galliano's famous circus – and look, there is his beautiful carriage, glittering like gold! Do you see Mr Galliano sitting in it, handsome and strong, with his enormous black moustaches curling upwards?

He takes off his top hat and bows to us! His black-haired wife smiles too, and waves her plump hand. After the glittering carriage comes a string of beautiful white horses, shining like silk, their proud heads tossing in the air!

'*Up* there, *up* there!' cries pretty Pepita, who is riding the first one, and her horse walks a few steps on his hind legs, whilst all the watching children cheer loudly. Behind Pepita come her sister and brother, Juanita and Lou, riding their horses grandly, bowing to everyone they pass. Then comes old Sticky Stanley the clown, in his comic suit of red and black, blowing a trumpet and banging a kettle for a drum, and throwing sweets to the children.

'Come and watch me at the circus!' cried Stanley. 'I'm the best bit of the circus, I am!' And then he put the

kettle on the top of his head and danced so comically
that all the children ran alongside to watch him.

Now come the caravans, the gay houses on wheels, and
how the children wish they could peep inside and see the
circus folk cooking their dinners! What fun it must be to
live in a caravan.

Now look at this glorious yellow caravan with gay curtains fluttering in the wind. Do you know who it belongs
to? Of course you do! It belongs to Jimmy, our old friend
Jimmy, who lives there with his mother and father and
Lotta. Lotta's parents are away for six months with their
horses, so Lotta is living with Mr and Mrs Brown,
Jimmy's mother and father.

There she is, peeping out of the caravan, her black
curls dancing. And there is Jimmy, sitting on the steps at
the back, and on his knee lies Lucky, his famous dog!

We get a wag from Lucky, that clever little fox-terrier,
who is as smart as paint. Lucky can walk the tight-rope,
she can count, and she can spell! Oh, Lucky is a marvellous dog, and Jimmy loves her with all his heart and is
very proud of her.

That is Mr Brown driving the caravan. Beside him sits
a plump black spaniel, Lulu, a faithful dog that Jimmy
and Lotta once saved from two cruel people. She is not
clever, but she is very loving and a splendid watch-dog.
Do you see Mrs Brown in the caravan? She is cooking
the dinner – and a good one it is, if we can judge by the
smell!

Now what a shout goes up! Here is the elephant!
Jumbo plods by, flapping his ears, and holding out his
trunk for a bun. Let's give him one! He pops it into his
big mouth at once, and Mr Tonks, his keeper, nods a
'thank you' to us. He is a kind little man, who loves his
elephant better than anything else in the world.

Jumbo is strong. He pulls three cages behind him. In
one is Sammy, the famous chimpanzee, and today he
wears an old hat belonging to Mrs Brown, and is very
proud of it. Funny old Sammy!

'What can your chimpanzee do?' yell the watching children to Mr Wally, his keeper.

'All the things that *you* can!' yells back Mr Wally. 'He can dress and undress himself – put himself to bed – ride a bicycle – clean his teeth – brush his hair! You come and watch him tomorrow night!'

Sammy puts his hat on back to front and waves to the children, smiling in his chimpanzee way. He is wishing that little dog Lucky would come and play with him, for he loves Lucky.

There is another cage behind Sammy's, and in it we see the three clever monkeys belonging to Lilliput, the little man sitting on the step. They are all dressed in red woollen coats, for the weather is still cold. They cuddle one another, and chatter to the watching children. Lilliput has his fourth monkey with him, little Jemima. She lies round his neck like a fur, whispering into his ear, and sometimes nibbling Lilliput's red hair! Funny little Jemima, she is full of tricks, and everyone loves her, though she can be very mischievous indeed when she likes!

With shouting, clapping, and cheering the circus goes by to the field where it is to camp. What a busy time it is when the circus folk set up their tents! How they shout and hunt for things they have dropped, and how quickly they settle in for a few days, making a camp of the big field, doing their washing, cooking their meals, practising their clever turns in the big red ring!

And now let us go to see our old friends, Jimmy and Lotta. We shall find them by that gay yellow caravan. Mrs Brown is calling them to come and eat. Mr Brown, who is odd-job man in the circus, has gone off to help with the tents, munching sandwiches as he goes. He is the busiest man there at these times, for everyone wants him at once! 'Brownie!' they call, 'Brownie! Give me a hand here! Brownie, where are you?'

And Mr Brown rushes from one to another with his tools, putting everything right.

It is Easter-time. The circus is at Westsea, and the field

they are camping in is quite near the sea. Jimmy and
Lotta listened to the noise of the waves as they ate their
sausages, and held their hot potatoes, cooked in their
skins.

'I've never been to the sea before!' said Jimmy. 'Oh,
Lotta, what fun we'll have here! We'll go walking on the
sands every day before breakfast!'

'Wuff!' said Lucky, licking Jimmy's hand.

'Yes, you shall come too,' said Jimmy, patting the little
dog on her soft head. 'And so shall Lulu. Mother, have
you got a sausage for Lulu? She's hungry. Lucky has had
a good meal. She mustn't have any more.'

Mrs Brown threw a sausage to Lulu – but before the
spaniel could get it, a little brown creature flashed out
from under the caravan and snatched it up. In a trice she
was away across the field, with Lulu after her.

'It's Jemima, the bad monkey!' cried Jimmy. 'Chase
her, Lulu! Get your sausage!'

The two children laughed as they watched plump Lulu
run after the artful monkey. Jemima did not want the
sausage for herself, for she did not like sausages – but she
did love teasing poor Lulu! When Lulu had run three
times round the field after her, the little monkey ran up to
the top of Jimmy's caravan and put the sausage on the
edge of the roof, where Lulu could see and smell it but
couldn't reach it!

'Jemima, you want smacking!' laughed Jimmy. Mrs
Brown took a stick and knocked down the sausage. Lulu
was quick enough at getting it this time! Two bites and a
swallow and that sausage was gone! Jemima made the
funny little chattering noise that was her laugh, and
scampered away to Lilliput's caravan. He was looking for
her, a juicy orange in his hand. She was the only one of
his four monkeys that was allowed out loose, for she was
as tame as a child.

Jimmy and Lotta finished their meal, and then they
went to give a hand where they could. Jimmy offered to
take old Jumbo down to the stream to drink water and

wash himself, whilst Mr Tonks finished putting up the big elephant's tent.

'Right you are, Jimmy,' said Mr Tonks, who knew that the little boy could be trusted with any animal in the world. 'Up, Jumbo!'

Jumbo curled his trunk gently round Jimmy and set him high up on his big broad neck. Then he set off for the stream that ran like a shining thread in the next field.

Lotta went to help Pepita and Juanita with their beautiful white horses. There was plenty of work to do with their string of sleek, shining animals, and the little girl adored every one of them, and took a great deal of trouble to keep them healthy, well-fed, and silky.

She no longer rode in the ring as she used to do when her mother and father, Lal and Laddo, kept their horses in the circus. Lal and Laddo were far away in a strange land, where they had taken their own beautiful horses and their clever dogs. Lotta missed them, and longed for the time for them to come back, when she might once more ride in the ring on her own horse.

But Jimmy went into the ring every night with little dog Lucky – and how the people cheered him when they saw the boy running into the ring, dressed in his wonderful suit that glittered like silver fire! He swung his red velvet cloak, and bowed proudly to the cheering people.

'Good old Jimmy! Good old Lucky!' shouted everyone. 'Show us what you can do!'

2. Fun for Jimmy and Lotta

It was lovely by the sea at Easter-time. Behind the circus camp rose the green hills, blazing with golden gorse.

'It smells like warm coconut,' said Lotta, sniffing. 'Isn't it lovely! I wish I could eat it!'

'You might as well eat a hedgehog!' laughed Jimmy. 'I'd like to wear a bit of gorse for a buttonhole, but it's too prickly to pick.'

Bluebells were beginning to grow in the sheltered patches here and there. Pale primroses peeped in the damp spots, and Jimmy and Lotta picked a great bunch to take back to the caravan. They were very happy.

Sometimes they walked on the hills with Lucky and Lulu, sometimes they walked by the sea, if the tide was out. They took off their shoes then, and splashed in the little waves. Lucky ran after the white edges of the waves as they came up on the sands and ran down again. She picked up a long strand of ribbon-like seaweed and tore down the beach with it streaming behind her.

'Quite mad!' said Lotta. 'Look – now she's got her nose in a pool! Whatever has she found there?'

It was a crab, very angry at being disturbed. Lucky pawed the water to try and get it, and the crab began to bury itself in the wet sand. Lucky nosed it out – and then she gave a loud bark of fright and shot backwards about ten feet, her tail down. She scraped hard at her nose.

Lotta gave a squeal of laughter. 'The crab's pinched her nose, Jimmy!'

'Poor old Lucky!' said Jimmy. 'Don't interfere with crabs, and they won't interfere with you!'

'I do miss all the dogs we used to have!' sighed Lotta,

kicking a stone along the beach. 'I wish Lal and Laddo
had left them for me to look after. I could have gone into
the ring with them then. As it is, I don't go any more. I
feel quite jealous of you, Jimmy, going in every night,
and getting such loud cheers and claps!'

'Don't be jealous, Lotta,' said Jimmy. 'Why, you have
belonged to the circus ever since you were born. I only
came last year! You're a long way ahead of me, really.
Perhaps Juanita, Pepita, and Lou will let you work with
them soon. They might let you have one of their horses
for your own, and you could ride that.'

'I'll ask them when we get back,' said Lotta, cheering
up. 'Let's go back now. Lulu! Lucky! Home!'

Lulu came racing out of the water, shaking her silky
spaniel coat. Lucky tore up, carrying a piece of seaweed
which she dropped at Jimmy's feet.

Jimmy stuck the seaweed on to a stick and gave it to
Lucky. 'Up then, Lucky!' he said. 'This is a flag now, and
you are a captain, carrying it. Up!'

Up went Lucky on her hind legs, the stick stuck in the
crook of a front leg. She strutted along behind the two
children with little steps, her tail wagging hard. Lulu
looked at her solemnly. She thought Lucky was most
extraordinary when she began to do tricks. Lulu couldn't
even beg!

Lucky showed off in front of Lulu. She put up her head
and strutted along proudly – and splash she went into a
pool of water that she didn't see!

The children laughed, and began to run. 'We'd better
hurry home now the dogs are wet,' panted Jimmy. 'We
must dry them well, for the wind is cold even though the
sun is warm!'

The two dogs had a good rub down. Jimmy was always
very careful with any animal under his care, and he knew
at once if any of them were out of sorts or unhappy.

'Look! There's old Jumbo bathing in the sea!' cried
Lotta, pointing. And sure enough, there was Jumbo solemnly wading into the water, filling his trunk and

squirting it over himself. He saw the children and his
little eyes shone.

'Hallo, Jumbo!' cried Lotta, and she danced near him.
Quickly the elephant pointed his trunk towards her and
tried to soak her with the water he had drawn up. But
Lotta was up to old Jumbo's tricks and she ran away,
laughing.

Back at the camp the children were set to work.

'Lotta, fetch me some water from the stream,' called
Mrs Brown. 'And, Jimmy, Mr Wally wants you to help
him to clean out Sammy's cage.'

'Right,' said Jimmy. 'I'll just rub down these two dogs
first!'

He got their towels and rubbed them dry. Lulu licked
his hand and went to lie down on the mat inside the
caravan. Lucky, like a little shadow, followed at Jimmy's
heels when he went across the field to Mr Wally's smart
caravan and the cage where Sammy the chimpanzee lived
in comfort.

But the cage was empty! Jimmy looked round. Where
was Mr Wally, and where was the chimpanzee? The cage
door was open and the cage was half washed out. Jimmy
shouted:

'Mr Wally! Where are you? Do you want me to help
you?'

A scared face looked out from under Mr Wally's caravan. It was one of the grooms, a man kept to help with
Mr Galliano's marvellous black horses.

'Is Mr Wally about?' he asked, in a whisper.

'I can't see him,' said Jimmy, puzzled. 'What are you
hiding for?'

The man crept out and shook himself. 'I said I'd help
Mr Wally clean the cage,' he said. 'And I left the door
unlatched. Well, that wretched chimpanzee slipped out
behind my back, threw a scrubbing-brush at me, and disappeared! Mr Wally came along, and he was so angry
when he saw the cage empty that I hid under here.'

'But where's Sammy?' asked Jimmy, alarmed.

'How should I know?' said the man sulkily. 'I'm engaged to help with the horses, I am, and I'm not going to have anything more to do with chimps.'

He went off, muttering. Jimmy caught sight of Mr Wally at the other side of the field, and he ran across to him.

'Have you got Sammy?' he called.

'No,' said Mr Wally, looking worried. 'That silly fellow must have frightened him, and he's disappeared. He'll come back all right, but I don't want any harm to come to him. Hunt around a bit, Jimmy, and call him.'

So the two of them hunted about the caravans and tents, calling to Sammy – but there wasn't a sign of him anywhere! Lucky sniffed about too, but all she did was to keep running to Jimmy's own caravan and back to Jimmy, so that wasn't much help! Jimmy's caravan was shut, for his mother had gone shopping and his father was busy. There was no one there. Lotta had not yet come back with the water.

Mrs Brown came back very soon, carrying a basket full of eggs and butter. She was surprised to see Jimmy and Wally and Lotta looking so upset, and hunting everywhere for Sammy. She went up the steps of her caravan and opened the door.

'I'll make you some tea,' she called – and then Jimmy heard her give a scream of fright. He saw his mother come tumbling down the caravan steps, almost falling to the ground in her hurry.

'Jimmy! Wally! There's a man in Jimmy's bed!' she cried. 'Come and turn him out!'

'Whatever next!' said Mr Wally, and he and Jimmy and Lotta raced to the caravan. Wally shot up the steps, and Jimmy followed.

Sure enough there was someone in Jimmy's bed! The bed-clothes were humped up in the middle, and there was a gentle sound of snoring.

Jimmy was angry. Who was this that dared to get into his own lovely bed and sleep there? He ripped off the clothes – and then he and Wally shouted with laughter!

It was Sammy the chimpanzee who was there! And he had undressed himself and put on Jimmy's own pyjamas, though they were very small for him! He had brushed his hair with a scrubbing-brush, and then curled up in Jimmy's bunk. He loved Jimmy, and when the groom had frightened him, he had slipped out of the cage and gone to find the little boy.

The caravan door had been shut, but Sammy had hopped in through the open window. He was safe!

'Mother! It's only Sammy!' said Jimmy, roaring with laughter, whilst Lotta danced round on one leg, squealing and giggling.

But Mrs Brown was not pleased. 'I put clean sheets on that bed this morning!' she said indignantly. 'You bad chimpanzee, get up at once!'

So Sammy got up, took off Jimmy's pyjamas, and solemnly dressed himself again, keeping one eye on Mrs Brown, who was really quite annoyed.

'I like chimpanzeees,' she said to Mr Wally, 'but *not* in my beds!'

'Very good, ma'am,' said Mr Wally meekly, and he went off with Sammy, whilst Jimmy and Lotta had fits of giggles all the time they were eating their tea!

'Really!' said Mrs Brown, 'you never know what's going to happen next in a circus!'

3. The circus does well

The circus went very merrily at Westsea, and Mr Galliano took the big field for one more week. Everybody was pleased, for a great deal of money was taken at the gate.

'I shall be able to get my caravan painted again,' said Stanley the clown, 'and I'll get myself a new suit too. One with a tail sewn on.'

'A *tail*!' said Lotta. 'Whatever do you want a tail for? I've never heard of a clown with a tail before.'

'That's just why I thought I'd have one,' said Sticky Stanley, with a grin. 'Think what fun you'll all have in the ring, trying to pull my tail! I'll be Sticky Stanley, the only clown in the world with a tail!'

'He sticks to his work and his friends stick to him!' said Lotta, giving the smiling little man a hug, for she was very fond of him. 'You get your tail, Stanley, and we'll do plenty of pulling!'

So Stanley bought himself a marvellous new suit, and it had a long tail like a cow's that dragged along behind him, and was always tripping him up when he turned round to go another way. Lucky thought the tail was great fun, and one night in the ring she ran after Stanley and worried his tail as if it were a rat. Stanley jumped about, and yelled, and shouted, for he really was afraid that the dog would bite it off!

Of course all the watching people thought that it was part of the show, and they laughed till they cried. So the clown thought he had better let Lucky do it again each night.

'But mind you, Jimmy, you'll have to buy me a new tail if Lucky *does* happen to bite it off one night!' said the clown. 'Or else she'll have to give me her own. I wouldn't mind a tail like Lucky's, with a fine wag in it!'

Mr Galliano paid Jimmy quite a lot of money that week, and the little boy was overjoyed. It was wonderful to think that he and his clever little dog could earn so much. He saved half of it, and bought his mother a new dress, his father a new saw, and Lotta a fine pair of shoes, which she wore to please Jimmy, though she really preferred to run barefoot.

Mr Galliano began to think of engaging some new performers for the circus. Lotta's mother and father had taken their performing terriers with them, and they would not be back for some time. The circus was doing so well that it would be a good idea to make it even better.

'What shall we have next?' he asked his wife, fat and kindly Mrs Galliano. 'We have monkeys, an elephant, a chimpanzee, Lucky the dog, and our dancing horses. We might get some performing seals, perhaps – yes?'

'Yes,' said Mrs Galliano. 'Write to Philippo and see if he will join our circus with his six performing seals. They are wonderful. They can balance long poles on their noses, they can play catch-ball, and they sit on stools and sway themselves in time to the music in a very marvellous way.'

When Jimmy and Lotta heard that perhaps the six performing seals might join the circus, they were most excited.

'I saw them once!' said Lotta. 'They are nice creatures, Jimmy, and they love doing tricks, just as the monkeys and Lucky do, and just as the horses love waltzing to the music!'

'I've never found out yet how those horses manage to dance round in time to the music,' said Jimmy seriously. 'Sometimes the music goes slow, and sometimes it goes fast – however do the horses follow it?'

'Jimmy!' cried Lotta, in surprise. 'Have you been with the circus all these months, and don't know that little trick yet?'

'What little trick?' asked Jimmy, astonished. '*Is* there a trick?'

'Of course there is!' said Lotta, laughing. 'The horses don't dance in time to the music! The music keeps in time with *them*! That's why it sometimes goes slow and sometimes fast, silly! It keeps in time with the horses, the horses don't keep in time with the music!'

'Well, I never!' said Jimmy, amazed. 'I didn't know that before.'

'I do hope those seals come,' said Lotta, dancing about. 'We'll have fun with them, Jimmy.'

But it was most disappointing, they didn't come. Mr Philippo had joined another circus, and was not free to come to Mr Galliano. The children were sorry.

'I wonder what he *will* get,' said Lotta.

'Cats, perhaps,' said Jimmy.

'Pooh, cats!' said Lotta scornfully. 'Don't you know that cats can't perform? At least, they *won't* perform – not unless they're big cats, anyway.'

'Big cats?' said Jimmy. 'What sort of big cats? Fat ones, do you mean?'

Lotta went off into peals of laughter, and rolled on the grass. 'You *are* funny, Jimmy,' she said. 'Don't you know that big cats are tigers, or panthers, or some animal of that family? They are all cats. They purr like cats too. Haven't you heard them?'

'No,' said Jimmy. 'I've never even seen a real tiger or lion, except in pictures. But I'd like to. They look such great, magnificent creatures.'

Well, Jimmy was soon to see some real big cats, for Mr Galliano heard from two people called Roma and Fric, who owned six great tigers.

He showed the letter to Mrs Galliano, and he called Mr Tonks, Jumbo's keeper, into the caravan, and Lilliput, who owned the four monkeys, and Mr Wally, who owned Sammy the chimpanzee.

'I have a letter here, yes,' said Mr Galliano. 'It is from Roma and Fric, who have six tigers. They can sit on

stools, jump through hoops, and play follow-my-leader. You have heard of them – yes?'

'I don't like trained cats, whether they are tigers, lions, leopards, or lynxes,' said Mr Wally. 'It isn't natural for cats to act.'

'They don't like it,' said Lilliput. 'They're not like monkeys, who act all the time, nor yet like Jumbo, who was bred and born in a circus.'

'It's a job to have travelling tigers,' said Mr Tonks, scratching his head. 'For one thing, we've got to have a mighty strong cage built each night in the ring before the tigers can do their turn, and that takes time.'

'Brownie can help with that – yes?' said Mr Galliano. 'We are going next to Liverpool, and Roma and Fric can join us there. Of course, people like to see performing tigers – it looks dangerous, yes!'

'I don't like trained cats, big or little,' said Mr Wally again. 'But if people want to see them, I suppose circuses have got to have them. Give me animals that enjoy learning – tigers don't! It hurts their feelings.'

Very soon the news went round the camp. Performing tigers were to join the circus at Liverpool. Lotta and Jimmy were thrilled. 'Now I shall get to know tigers too,' said Jimmy happily, for he was a boy who loved and welcomed any animal, big or small. 'I wish I knew all the animals in the world!'

'You're a funny fellow, Jimmy,' said Mr Tonks, pulling the little boy's ear gently. 'I believe you would even love performing fleas! It's wonderful how all the animals take to you.'

Jimmy went red with pride. 'I shall make friends with the tigers too,' he said.

'Don't be too sure about that,' said Mr Tonks. 'Tigers are funny things, and not to be trusted. I reckon they ought never to be in a circus. They won't make friends with anyone – not real friends, like old Jumbo there, or Sammy the chimp.'

'Well, we'll see, Tonky,' said Jimmy, and he ran off to give Lucky a bath before her turn in the circus that night.

The show at Westsea finished that weekend, and soon the circus was on the move again, travelling towards Liverpool. It poured with rain as they went, and the children sat inside their caravan, and looked out on the dreary surroundings. They did not like the look of Liverpool very much, after the freedom and beauty of Westsea.

'But never mind, Lotta!' said Jimmy, jigging in joy. 'We shall meet the tigers at Liverpool! That will be a big treat, won't it!'

4. The tigers join the circus

The circus camped before it got into Liverpool itself. The field was wet and muddy. It was hard work getting the tents up, and dragging the cages and caravans to their right place. Jumbo was very useful, but even his big feet slipped in the mud.

'The tigers aren't here yet,' said Jimmy to Lotta, in disappointment.

'No, they are coming tomorrow,' said Lotta. 'Mrs Galliano told me.'

The children were wet through when at last everything was in order that night. They went into their cosy caravan, and Mrs Brown made them take off their wet things and get into dry ones. Jimmy rubbed Lucky dry too, but Lulu the spaniel did not need to be dried, for she had kept in the caravan in her basket all the time. She loved Mrs Brown very much and liked to be near her.

Mrs Brown had a fine-smelling stew in a pan on the stove. The children sniffed hungrily. Mr Brown was pleased to smell it too when he came up the caravan steps to his supper. He took off his wet coat, washed his hands and face, and sat down at the little table. Soon everyone was enjoying the delicious stew, the chunks of pineapple that followed, and the hot cocoa.

'Ooh, isn't it cosy here,' said Jimmy. 'Who would live in a house when they could live in a caravan!'

'Well, I've never really got used to a caravan,' said Mrs Brown, pouring out the cocoa. 'It still seems funny to me not to have an upstairs and a downstairs. But I must say this is a very fine roomy caravan, Jimmy, almost as good as Mr Galliano's.'

'I love it,' said Lotta, sipping her cocoa. 'I miss my
father and mother, Lal and Laddo, but I do love living
with you and Brownie and Jimmy, Mrs Brown.'

'And we love having you, Lotta,' said Mrs Brown,
smiling at the black-haired little girl. 'You are very useful
to me in lots of ways – but you still haven't learnt that
your hair looks nicer when it is properly brushed, and that
toothbrushes are meant to be used!'

'Even Sammy the chimpanzee knows that,' said Jimmy,
grinning. 'You'd better take a lesson from him, Lotta.'

Lotta made a dreadful face at Jimmy, and gave him
such a pinch that the little boy yelled and dropped a piece
of pineapple out of his open mouth.

'And *you'd* better go and learn manners from Sammy,'
said Lotta rudely. 'Spitting out that nice pineapple!'

'I didn't!' cried Jimmy indignantly. 'You made me yell
and it fell out of my mouth. I wonder where it went.'

'Lulu ate it,' said Mrs Brown. 'Now, no more faces and
no more pinching, Lotta. You know I don't like it.'

'I've had to get in a lot of new bars and bolts,' said Mr
Brown. 'Mr Galliano wants me to make the tigers' cage as
strong as I can – the one they'll perform in, I mean.'

'Oooh, the tigers!' said Jimmy eagerly. 'I *am* longing to
see them!'

The next day, as the children were practising in the
ring with Lucky, ready for that night, they heard a
strange new sound. Lucky pricked up her ears and
listened, then put her tail down and crept between
Jimmy's legs. Lulu ran out of the big tent and tore back to
Mrs Brown for safety. Jumbo pricked his big ears at the
bellowing noise, and the four monkeys and Sammy sat
still and listened.

'The tigers!' yelled Jimmy in delight. 'I can hear them
roaring! Come on, Lotta, let's go and meet them!'

The two children rushed into the wet field. At the gate
was a great travelling-box, shut in on all sides, but with
air-holes in the roof. It was a powerful motor-van, and its
wheels churned up the mud of the field.

'It's stuck!' cried Jimmy. 'No wonder the tigers are bellowing! They can't understand what's happening! Let's go and tell Tonky, and perhaps old Jumbo will help to pull the van out of the mud. Hi, Mr Tonks! Mr Tonks!'

Mr Tonks was already undoing Jumbo's rope. Jumbo did not want to go near the van, for he disliked tigers, but he would do anything in the world for Mr Tonks. So he followed his keeper, and easily pulled the travelling cage from the deep mud.

The cage, full of roaring tigers, was hauled to its place in the field. Two people were with the cage, one a great powerful man with strange eyes, and the other a boy about Jimmy's age.

'Hallo,' said Jimmy. 'What's your name?'

'Fric,' said the boy, eyeing Jimmy carefully. 'And that's Roma over there, my uncle. I travel with him, and we manage the tigers together. What do you do?'

'I'm Jimmy, and I have a performing dog called Lucky,' said Jimmy proudly.

The boy looked interested. 'I've heard of her,' he said. 'She can walk the tight-rope and spell and count, can't she? All a trick, I suppose?'

'No, she's really very, *very* clever,' said Jimmy. 'What do your tigers do? Can I make friends with them, do you think?'

'Don't talk rubbish,' said the boy scornfully. 'Nobody makes friends with tigers. They won't let you. I advise you not to go near them. I'd like to see that dog of yours, though. I like dogs.'

Jimmy was pleased. It would be fun for him and Lotta to have another boy in the camp. They could do lots of things together. Lotta stood staring at the boy, but Fric took no notice of her.

'I've got to go and help feed the tigers now,' said Fric. 'See you later!'

He went off. Lotta made a face. 'I don't like him,' she said.

'Why, you don't even know him yet,' said Jimmy. 'He

says he likes dogs. It will be fun to have someone else to play with.'

'*I* don't want anyone else,' said Lotta sulkily. 'I don't like Fric.' She went off by herself, but Jimmy waited about by the tigers' van, wondering if he might see inside.

Soon one side was opened, and Jimmy saw the tigers. They were magnificent creatures, like enormous cats, with great white whiskers, beautiful gleaming eyes, and shining coats. They were well-fed now, and lay peacefully against one another, two in each partition of the big cage. They blinked at Jimmy in silence.

'You lovely things,' said Jimmy, looking at their great green eyes. 'I'd like to feel your furry coats!'

'Don't you have anything to do with tigers,' said a warning voice nearby. 'They are not to be trusted. A chimpanzee's all right, and so is an elephant, and even a bear knows its friends – but tigers hate this circus life and won't be friends.'

It was Mr Wally, who had come up to see the tigers too. The two gazed through the bars at the quiet creatures. One tiger got up and paced to and fro on big silent paws.

'Just like the cat we used to have at home,' said Jimmy. 'I'd like to go and pet it!'

'Aren't you afraid of those great creatures?' asked Mr Wally, in astonishment.

'No', said Jimmy. 'I'm not afraid of any animal, Mr Wally. It's not that I'm brave – it's just that I seem to understand them and their feelings, and I want them to be friends with me.'

'Well, don't try being friends with tigers, that's all!' said Wally, and he went off to his caravan, thinking that Jimmy was the strangest boy he had ever known. All the animals in the circus loved that boy – ah, he was lucky, for that was a great gift, to be friends with animals of all kinds, wild or tame! Mr Wally would like to have had Jimmy's gift of friendliness – he could manage chimpanzees, but dogs he didn't understand, and as for tigers, why, he didn't even like the feel of them in the circus!

Jimmy stayed looking at the tigers. They looked back at him. One of them began to purr gently, just like a great cat.

'You'll be friends of mine before long,' said the little boy in the low, gentle voice he kept for animals. 'You just see! I'll be feeding you soon – yes, and brushing those lovely coats of yours! You just see!'

5. Bad tempers

The six new tigers soon settled down in Mr Galliano's circus. They roared when they were hungry, but not very often at other times.

'How do you manage to tame tigers, Fric?' asked Jimmy, as he saw the small boy going to feed his six great cats one morning.

'We had all these when they were cubs,' said Fric. 'They were just like playful kittens then. It is not very difficult to train them when they are young – and the tricks they learn then they always remember when they are grown tigers. And they are afraid of me and of Roma, just as they were afraid when they were cubs. If I shout at them they cower down.'

'Afraid of you!' cried Jimmy. 'I think that's wrong, Fric. I don't think we should ever make animals afraid of us when we take them to live with us. Mr Galliano says that the finest trainers work by kindness.'

'Pooh!' said Fric scornfully; 'he doesn't know anything about tigers then. No one could be kind to tigers for long!'

Jimmy said nothing. He felt sure that Fric was wrong. The little boy looked at the slanting green eyes of the six beautiful animals. One of them began to purr as she looked at Jimmy.

'Hear that!' said Fric, astonished. 'That's Queenie, purring. She hardly ever does. She must like you, Jimmy. It's a funny thing, too, but whenever you're near their cage, they always seem to lie peaceful and quiet.'

Fric went into the tigers' cage to feed them. There was a double gate, and one was always shut if the other was open, so that no tiger could ever get out. Fric was not afraid of the tigers. He had lived all his life with Roma, his uncle, and knew all about the great animals.

With loud roars the tigers fell upon their enormous hunks of meat. They took no notice of Fric.

'Watch what happens when I shout at Queenie, and thump my fist into my hand!' shouted Fric. And before Jimmy could stop him, Fric had yelled angrily at Queenie and banged his fist into the palm of his left hand.

Queenie crouched down, her ears drooping, and her tail swinging slowly. She looked scared.

'Don't do that, Fric,' said Jimmy. 'Why should you yell at Queenie like that when she's done nothing wrong at all? That's the wrong way to treat animals!'

Fric looked cross. He threw the last piece of meat to the tigers. 'You may know all about dogs and elephants and chimpanzees,' he said sulkily, 'but you don't know a thing about tigers!'

Jimmy did not want to quarrel with Fric, for he badly wanted something – he wanted to go into the tigers' cage with Fric! Jimmy was not afraid of any animal; no, not even of a fierce tiger. But Lucky was afraid. Little dog Lucky wouldn't go near the cage, and Jimmy was glad. He did not want Lucky to slip between the bars. She would make a nice little dinner for six hungry tigers!

Roma, Fric's uncle, cleaned out the tigers' cage each day. Fric fed them. At night the great cage was moved near to the big tent or 'top' as all the circus folk called it, and a passage-way was made from the travelling cage to a strong cage that Brownie, Jimmy's father, built with Roma in the ring each night, whilst Sticky Stanley the clown and Oona the acrobat were doing clever and funny tricks to amuse the watching people.

Then the tigers walked down the passage-way and entered the cage in the ring. In this cage were set six stools – two small, two tall, and two taller still. Each tiger knew his stool, and leapt nimbly on to it, so that they sat in a row, like steps going up and down.

Both Roma and Fric went into the cage with the tigers. They were dressed alike, in red velvet suits, very tight, with short, sparkling cloaks, and both carried a long whip that they could crack as loudly as Mr Galliano could crack his.

'Aren't Roma and Fric clever with those tigers?' whispered Lotta to Jimmy. 'I don't know how they make those great beasts obey them like that! Look at Queenie jumping gracefully through that paper hoop, and breaking the paper as she goes through it!'

'And look at Basuka, on one of the high stools!' said Jimmy. 'He's going to jump through *two* hoops!'

He did – and everyone clapped the graceful jump. Basuka did not go back to his stool. He stood and glared at the people. Roma cracked his whip.

'Up, Basuka, up!' he shouted. But still Basuka stood and stared. Roma picked up a sharp-pointed iron bar and pricked Basuka with it. The big tiger growled, but jumped up to his stool at once.

'I wish Roma wouldn't do that,' said Jimly. 'I bet I could have made Basuka go back, without hurting him. It's not fair.'

Fric took up his own smaller whip then, and cracked it three times. At once one tiger after another jumped down from the stools, and ranged themselves in a circle about small Fric.

'Around you go!' shouted the boy, and cracked his whip again. At once the tigers began to pad round in a circle till the whip cracked again. Then they turned themselves the other way and went round in a ring in the opposite direction. Everyone clapped.

'Up!' roared Roma – and up went every tiger again on to the stools. The whip cracked once more. The two tigers in the middle, sitting on the tallest stools, at once stood up on their hind legs and put their front paws against each other's. Down jumped the other four tigers and went in and out of the archway made by the two middle tigers. It was extraordinary to watch.

'Fric's clever, you know, Lotta,' said Jimmy. 'And he's not a bit afraid.'

'I don't like Fric,' said Lotta obstinately. 'If he can be unkind to tigers, his own special animals, he can be unkind in other ways. I don't like him.'

'Oh, please, Lotta, don't be silly,' said Jimmy. 'We can all three have fun together. Come for a walk with us tomorrow morning, after we've done our jobs.'

'All right,' said Lotta. 'But I don't want to.'

So the next morning Jimmy called across to Fric. 'Hi, Fric! Come for a walk when you've finished this morning?'

'Right!' said Fric. So Jimmy and Lotta went to Fric's caravan when they were ready, and the boy jumped down the steps. But when he saw Lotta, he pulled a face.

'She's not going with us, is she?' he said.

'Of course,' said Jimmy, surprised. 'Why not?'

'Then I shan't come,' said Fric. 'Girls are silly. Always giggling and saying stupid things.'

'Lotta doesn't say stupid things!' cried Jimmy angrily. 'She's a fine girl. She can ride any horse you like, and she knows far more about dogs than you know about tigers!'

This was not a wise thing to say to Fric. He scowled angrily, pulled his cap over his forehead, and stalked off without a word. Jimmy called after him:

'Fric! Don't be a donkey! Come along with us. I've got some money to buy ice-creams.'

Fric stopped and turned round. He loved ice-creams – but did he love them enough to put up with Lotta's company?

'Oh, come on, Fric,' said Jimmy impatiently. 'Come, Lotta, we'll go after him.'

But now Lotta turned sulky! She swung round and stood with her back to Jimmy, and she stamped her foot in a temper. 'I'm not coming!' she said. 'If you think I'm going anywhere with that horrid boy, you're wrong. I don't like him. I won't go with him.'

'But, Lotta!' said Jimmy, 'please, please don't be silly.

You know that I want to make friends with Fric so that I can go into the tigers' cage and get to know the six tigers. He won't let me if I'm not friends with him.'

'You and your old tigers!' said Lotta, with tears of rage running down her cheeks. 'I hate you all!' And the cross little girl ran like the wind to Oona's caravan and sat watching the acrobat, who was practising steadily for that night's show.

Jimmy was upset. How silly of Lotta to behave like that! Never mind, perhaps she would forget it all by the time he came back from his walk. He would go with Fric and talk to him about tigers, and buy him ice-creams.

But Fric, too, had gone off in a temper! Poor Jimmy stood looking round dolefully, all alone.

'Hallo, hallo, hallo!' said Sticky Stanley the clown, turning cart-wheels all around Jimmy on hands and feet. 'You look like a hen left out in the rain! Come and help old Tonky rub Jumbo down with oil. He's got some cracks in his hide, and it's a big job, I can tell you, to oil *him* all over!'

'All right,' said Jimmy, cheering up, for he loved doing anything with the big kindly elephant. 'I'll come.'

So off he went with Lucky at his heels, puzzled and not very happy.

6. Jimmy and the tigers

Lotta sulked for a long time. She would not be friends with Fric, and Fric called rude things after her whenever he saw her. Jimmy was angry about it, but he could not make up his mind to quarrel with Fric, for he knew that if he did, there would be no chance of him going into the tigers' cage.

'Fric, please don't be unkind to Lotta,' he said. But Fric only laughed, and thought out another rude thing to say to Lotta when next he met her.

Jimmy bought Fric dozens of ices, scores of bars of chocolate, bags of sweets, and even a fine toy aeroplane that Fric wanted. Each time Fric promised to allow Jimmy to come with him into the big cage, but every time he broke his word.

'No,' he said. 'I'd better not today, Jimmy. If Roma got to hear of it, he'd whip me. Besides, I guess Mr Galliano would be angry if he knew.'

'Fric, I keep telling you I'll take the blame if anything happens, and Roma or Mr Galliano find out,' said Jimmy, in despair. 'Look here, you shan't have a single ice-cream or sweet till you've kept your word. I'm tired of trusting you.'

Fric was alarmed. He didn't want his supply of goodies to stop, and yet he really was scared of letting Jimmy into the cage. He knew quite well that it was not right to allow any stranger inside, for the tigers were fierce and powerful, and could certainly not be trusted with anyone they did not know. Also, he was scared of his uncle. What would Roma say if he found out?

'Wait till the tigers know you better,' he said.

'But you said that last week!' said Jimmy. 'And they know me now as well as they possibly can, seeing that they are inside the cage and I am outside. Do you know, Queenie came and rubbed her great head against my hand when I put it inside the cage-bars yesterday?'

'I don't believe that,' said Fric at once, for this was a thing that Queenie had certainly never done to Fric or to Roma either. She was the least good-tempered of the six tigers.

'All right. Come and see her do it again!' said Jimmy. So the two of them went along to the great travelling cage in which the tigers lived, two in each partition. They stared at the little boys with their green, glinting eyes. Queenie purred, got up slowly and gracefully, and came across to the bars. Jimmy put his hand inside. The great tiger pressed her head against the small hand, and purred even more loudly. Jimmy scratched her where her whiskers grew.

Fric stared, his eyes as round as pennies. 'Goodness me!' he said. 'I've never seen such a thing! Fancy old Queenie doing that! She once nearly snapped a man's hand off when he put it too near.'

'Well, *now* will you let me go inside the cage?' asked Jimmy, delighted.

'Look here, Jimmy, I'll let you in tonight, when everyone's asleep in their caravans,' promised Fric. 'You can creep up to our caravan, and put your hand inside the window. I'll leave the keys of the cage just inside, and you can take them quietly.'

'But aren't you coming too?' asked Jimmy, in surprise.

'Indeed I'm not!' said Fric. 'You can do it on your own. *I'm* not going to get into any trouble about it!'

Jimmy ran off to his dinner, his eyes bright and his cheeks glowing. Tonight! And by himself too! Oh, what a glorious adventure! He could hardly eat his dinner, he was so excited.

'Jimmy, whatever's the matter with you?' asked his

mother. 'You look as if somebody has left you a fortune! Look at him, Lotta.'

But Lotta wouldn't look. She hardly spoke to Jimmy these days, and she was so quiet that Mrs Brown was quite worried about her. Poor Lotta! She thought that Jimmy wanted Fric for a friend instead of her, and she was worried too, because she did so want to go into the ring again and ride one of the horses, and Juanita, Pepita, and Lou would not say she could. She was not at all happy.

Jimmy did not notice Lotta's unhappy face. He was much too thrilled about what would happen that night. He wondered if he should tell Lotta. Yes, he would!

'Lotta, I've got a secret to tell you,' he said after dinner, when they were rubbing down the horses together, with Lou whistling not far off.

'Is it anything to do with Fric?' asked Lotta.

'Yes, it is, partly,' said Jimmy. 'Listen, Lotta, he is—'

'I don't want to know any secret if Fric's in it,' said Lotta, in a horrid, cold voice. 'I don't like Fric, and I'm beginning not to like you either, Jimmy.'

Jimmy was most astonished. Really, what was happening to Lotta? But he could not bother himself to think about that now, for his head was full of the tigers.

That night Jimmy crept out of his own caravan very quietly, without waking his mother, father, or Lotta. Only Lucky knew, and she was tied up and could not follow. Lulu opened one eye and then went to sleep again.

Jimmy stole towards Fric's caravan. The window was open. He could hear Fric's uncle snoring inside. He stood on a wheel and put his hand inside the window. He could feel three big keys there. So Fric had kept his word this time! The little boy's heart beat fast. He carefully picked up the keys so that they did not make a single clink, and slipped down from the wheel.

He ran like a shadow to the tigers' great travelling-box. It was completely shut up. Air came in through the

ventilating holes in the roof. There was not a sound from
the cages inside.

Sammy the chimpanzee heard Jimmy's soft footsteps
and made a little noise. But for once Jimmy paid no attention to Sammy. He came to the tigers' cages, and
slipped a key into the lock. He turned the lock, opened
the door, and slipped inside. There was another door to
unlock inside, and then a gate of iron bars. Jimmy unlocked them all.

The tigers stirred and awoke. Jimmy could see two
pairs of green eyes glinting in the dark. Moonlight came
filtering in through the air-holes in the roof.

The two tigers in the first cage sniffed and growled a
little. Then Queenie, one of the two tigers, lifted her head
high and sniffed harder. Yes, this was the boy who so
often came outside the cage and talked to her in that
lovely, gentle voice. This boy had no whip, no iron bar.
This boy had a voice that was gentle like the leaves, not
fierce and harsh and frightening.

Jimmy stood inside the tigers' cage, his heart thumping
against his side. He was not afraid. Jimmy had never in
his life been afraid of any animal, and he never would be.
But he was excited, and he felt sure that the tigers would
hear his heart thumping and wonder what it was. He put
his hand over his heart to hide the thumping.

Queenie began to purr. She left her corner and silently
slunk over to Jimmy. She put her great head down beside
his right arm. Jimmy spoke to her in his special animal-
voice, strong, and low, and gentle.

'Old Queenie,' he said. 'Old Queenie, you beauty. You
great, green-eyed, graceful tiger. You love me, don't you?
And I love you. I love your grand head and your slanting
eyes, your fine whiskers and your slinky body.'

Queenie purred more loudly. The other tiger looked on
watchfully. She knew Jimmy, but she wanted Queenie to
make sure he was friendly first.

'Ruby!' said Jimmy, calling the other tiger by her
name. 'Ruby! Do you want your head rubbed, Ruby?'

But Ruby would not come near that first night. She lay

peacefully, watching with her green eyes, whilst Queenie fussed round the little boy, nearly bowling him over when she pushed him playfully with her great head.

Jimmy did not go to the other tigers that night. He slipped out of Queenie's cage after about half an hour, very pleased with his first visit. The other tigers had been restless, smelling the scent of a strange visitor, but they had soon settled down when they heard Queenie purring.

'Tomorrow!' said Jimmy excitedly to himself, 'tomorrow night I shall go again, and I will go to *all* the tigers. The big beautiful things! They will soon be my friends. How *can* Fric be unkind to them? Why, Queenie was as loving as an old fireside tabbycat tonight!'

He slid into his caravan, and didn't know that Lotta was awake, wondering where he had been! He put his head down on the pillow, and was soon fast asleep.

7. Lotta discovers Jimmy's secret

Jimmy dreamt about tigers all that night! When he awoke in the morning he remembered how Queenie had made friends with him and rubbed her great head against him, purring all the time. Jimmy looked at Lotta, and wished he could tell her, but Lotta was very sulky and quiet these days.

Lotta was wondering where Jimmy had been the night before. What had made him slip out of bed all alone? She made up her mind to watch that night and follow Jimmy.

Fric ran across to Jimmy as the little boy was practising with Lucky for the night's show. Lucky was spelling out the word 'Galliano,' fetching each letter in turn in her mouth, and putting them down in a row.

'My word!' said Fric, stopping in amazement. 'That dog is a wonder, Jimmy! How did you teach her to spell and count? Did you have her as a puppy?'

'She's not much more than a puppy now!' said Jimmy proudly. 'Yes, I taught her every trick she knows, Fric. She's a naturally clever dog, and she loves learning. I'd never teach any animal that didn't want to learn, you know. That's why I'd never teach tigers. They don't want to learn.'

'I say, Jimmy, did you go into their cage last night?' asked Fric eagerly. 'Or were you afraid?'

'Afraid!' said Jimmy scornfully. 'Of course I wasn't! Yes, I went in, but only into the first partition. Ruby didn't come to me, but Queenie did. She purred all over me and rubbed herself against me like a cat!'

Fric stared. 'It's funny,' he said at last. 'I just don't understand it. I and Roma have had those tigers from

cubs, and they know us and fear us. But you are a
stranger. Why should they be friends with you?'

Jimmy laughed, and took up a brush to brush Lucky,
though her coat already shone like satin. The little dog
stood up on her hind legs when Jimmy wanted to brush
her underneath.

'I'm going into *all* the cages tonight,' said Jimmy.
'Leave the keys near the caravan window again, Fric.'

'Well, you'll have to buy me a shilling ice-cream today
then,' said Fric greedily. So Jimmy promised, and Fric
went off to give the tigers fresh water. Roma was already
cleaning the cages out, whilst the tigers lay and watched
the big broom sweeping.

That night Jimmy once more slipped out of his caravan at midnight, and, in the pale light of the moon, took
the keys from the window of Fric's caravan, and ran
across to the tigers' big travelling cage.

Someone saw him go. Someone followed him. Lotta
slid like a shadow after Jimmy, wondering where he was
going. How she hoped he was not going off with Fric
somewhere, for the little girl hated Fric.

She was very frightened when she saw Jimmy going to
the tigers' cage, and more frightened still when she saw
him unlock the door and go inside.

'He'll be killed!' said the little girl to herself. 'I know
he's clever with animals, but tigers are different. They're
fierce and wild. He'll be killed!'

She did not dare to call out, for she was afraid of upsetting the tigers. But she slipped in at the first door and
stood outside the inner gate of the cage, trying to see what
Jimmy was doing.

By the faint light of the moon filtering in through the
air-holes, Lotta could see Jimmy and Queenie and Ruby.
And what she saw made her eyes open in astonishment!

Jimmy was tickling Queenie, the enormous tiger, who
was lying on her back like a kitten, all four paws in the
air. Ruby was pawing at Jimmy gently, asking for her
turn. The little girl had never seen tigers behaving like

that before. Usually they were sullen and fierce with human beings, but here were Queenie and Ruby playing like tame cats!

The tigers smelt her as she stood there, and turned their heads. But they knew her smell, and turned back to play with their friend Jimmy. Soon the little boy slipped into the next partition, and Lotta could no longer see him.

'He shouldn't do this, he shouldn't, he shouldn't,' said the little girl to herself. 'It's too dangerous. Suppose Jimmy stumbled over one of their paws or trod on a tail by mistake? They would turn on him, and he wouldn't have a chance of escape! Oh, what shall I do to stop him?'

She stook and waited, hoping that nothing would happen to Jimmy. 'If I tell Mrs Brown, Jimmy would never forgive me,' thought Lotta. 'And it's no use asking him not to go in, for he'd laugh at me. I know what I'll do! I'll go to Fric, and tell him I know all about this, and I'll say that if he lets Jimmy have the keys of the tigers' cage again, I'll tell Mr Galliano! He won't dare to after that! And I'll say that if he dares to tell Jimmy that I know, I'll tell his uncle.'

Jimmy was making friends with the other tigers. The big travelling-box echoed with the sound of happy purring, as all the tigers pawed at Jimmy to make him play with them, or came to him with heads down, rubbing against his side and legs. Jimmy put his arms round Basuka, the biggest tiger of all.

'You are a magnificent fellow, Basuka!' he said, in his low voice. 'I could make you do anything! But I never would, for you are too grand to do silly little tricks.'

Jimmy spent an hour in the tigers' cages, and then slipped out, happy and excited. The tigers were far more his friends than they were either Roma's or Fric's! He loved them and they loved him. Jimmy felt Queenie's warm breath on his face as he locked the inner gate. The big tiger did not want him to go. She wanted this queer, understanding boy to stay with her.

Lotta slipped like a shadow back to her caravan and was in her bunk, pretending to be asleep, when Jimmy came back. She lay awake a long time, afraid that if she did not stop Jimmy going into the tigers' cages he would one night be badly hurt.

So the next day, when Jimmy was helping Tonks to water Jumbo the elephant, Lotta hunted out Fric. The boy scowled at her, for he did not like girls.

'I want to speak to you, Fric,' said Lotta.

'Well, I don't want to speak to *you*,' said Fric rudely, and he turned his back.

'Look here, Fric,' said Lotta desperately. 'If you let Jimmy go into the tigers' cages again, I'll tell Mr Galliano, so there!'

Fric spun round in a trice and glared at the little girl. 'What do you know about it?' he demanded.

'Never mind,' said Lotta. 'But I'm not going to have Jimmy hurt by those tigers of yours, just because you're greedy for ice-creams and give him the keys each night in return for things like that! So just you look out, you horrid little boy!'

Fric rushed at Lotta and slapped her so hard that she cried out. Stanley the clown saw them fighting and he came up.

'Stop it, Fric,' he said sternly. 'Lotta, go back to your caravan.' So, before anything else could be said, the two were separated, and Lotta went sobbing back to her caravan, glad that nobody was there to see her.

But she was not there long before Jimmy came rushing up with news.

'Lotta! Lilliput is ill! He's eaten something bad, and he's got a dreadful pain. I'm going for the doctor. Look after Jemima for him, will you?'

Jimmy rushed off, and Lotta ran to Lilliput's caravan. She was very fond of the little man and his four monkeys. Jemima was his pet, and was like a mischievous child.

Lilliput was lying on his bunk inside his caravan, very white indeed. Jemima was sitting at the head of the bed,

looking doleful, for she could not understand what was wrong with her master.

'Are you ill, Lilliput?' said Lotta kindly. 'Jimmy's gone for the doctor. Does Mr Galliano know?'

Lilliput nodded feebly. At that moment heavy feet came up the steps at the back of the caravan, and Mr Galliano put his head in.

'You cannot go in the ring tonight, Lilliput – no?' he said kindly. 'You will be better soon – yes?'

Lilliput nodded. 'I'd like Lotta to take care of Jemima for a day or two,' he said. 'It's not good for her to be in here with me when I'm ill.'

'You will do so, Lotta – yes?' said Mr Galliano. The little girl picked up the small monkey and cuddled her.

'Yes,' she said. 'I'd love to look after her. She is fond of me and will be quite happy. I'll send Mrs Brown to see to you, Lilliput.'

She slipped down the steps with Jemima curled round her neck like a fur, the monkey's tiny fingers holding on to her black curls. She ran to tell Mrs Brown, who had just come back from shopping, and Mrs Brown at once hurried to Lilliput's caravan to see what she could do.

Mr Galliano arranged for Mr Wally to take Lilliput's monkeys into the ring that night, for he was just as good with monkeys as with chimpanzees, and he knew exactly what to do with them. Lotta was to care for Jemima till Lilliput was better, and only when the circus was on each night was Jemima to leave the little girl, and go into the ring with the other three monkeys to do her funny tricks.

Fric saw Lotta in the distance with something round her neck, and he wondered what it was. He went nearer to see. 'Why, she's got Lilliput's Jemima!' he said, and he wondered why. He soon found out, and then the unkind boy made up his mind to punish Lotta for what she had said to him earlier that day!

'I'll get Jemima from her!' he thought. 'And I'll hide the monkey somewhere where she can't find it. That will give her a shock! That will teach her to come and say she'll tell Mr Galliano about me!'

He could not get Jemima that day, for Lotta was near her own caravan. Nor could he tell Jimmy what Lotta had said, for the little boy was busy the whole day long. He passed Fric once, and whispered to him:

'Shan't want the keys tonight, Fric. I'll have them again tomorrow. I'm tired today, with two late nights.'

Fric nodded, and had no time to say anything more. 'Wish I could get my chance to get Jemima away from Lotta!' he thought.

His chance came the next day. And Fric took it, though afterwards he very much wished that he hadn't.

8. Oh, poor little Jemima!

Lilliput was a little better the next day, but he would not be able to go into the ring for four days, the doctor said. So Lotta was to have Jemima, his best-loved monkey, till he was well. The little girl was delighted, for Jemima was very sweet and loving.

Mrs Brown was not quite so delighted, for Jemima was the most mischievous monkey in the world! When Mrs Brown scolded her for taking down all the cups from the shelf and hiding them under the pillows, Jemima picked up some potatoes and threw them very quickly at the astonished Mrs Brown.

Lotta stopped her at once, and laughed till the tears came into her eyes. Jemima jumped on to the little girl's shoulder and nibbled her ear gently. That was one of her ways of loving anyone.

'Where's Jimmy?' asked Lotta. But Mrs Brown didn't know. Lotta wondered whether he was near the tigers' cage, so off she went, with Jemima curled round her neck, chattering nonsense into her ear.

Jimmy was not there. Lotta stood watching the great tigers, the side of whose cage was open, so that they could get the warm spring sun. And it was just then that Fric saw Lotta and Jemima, and made up his mind to take the monkey from Lotta and hide her somewhere so that the little girl would not know where to find her!

The boy crept quietly up behind Lotta. Jemima heard him and turned her head, chattering angrily, for she did not like Fric. Fric caught hold of her and dragged the monkey off Lotta's shoulder. The little girl screamed and turned round.

She saw Fric running away, holding the screaming monkey. 'Fric! Fric! Give me back Jemima!' cried the little girl. 'You wicked boy!'

But Fric only laughed. 'I'll teach you to order me about!' he yelled. But just then Jemima bit his hand as hard as she could with her sharp monkey-teeth and the boy shouted in pain. The monkey took her chance and struggled free. Frightened out of her life, she scampered round the tigers' cage, followed by Fric, who was roaring angrily.

The tigers pricked up their ears, and Queenie growled. No tiger likes disturbance and noise. Jemima scampered round again, with Fric after her. 'Come to me, Jemima, come to me!' called Lotta. But the monkey was too afraid to pay any attention to Lotta.

And then a dreadful thing happened! Fric almost caught the monkey, and in fright the little thing ran up the bars of the tigers' cage and dropped inside!

'Oh! Oh!' wailed Lotta. 'They'll kill Jemima! They'll kill her!'

Fric stopped, frightened. Jemima ran to the back of Queenie's cage. Queenie growned. Scared, Jemima ran up the dividing bars between Queenie's cage and the next. The big tigers watched her. All of them were upset now, for the shouting and running and squealing had made them restless and angry.

'Jemima, oh, Jemima, do come here to me,' sobbed poor Lotta. 'Fric, make your tigers lie down.'

But Fric could not do anything with the tigers when they were angry. He just stood and stared, with his face suddenly rather pale. He knew that Jemima was a valuable monkey and that Lilliput loved her as if she were a child.

Jemima ran about Queenie's cage, scared. She did not dare to come out whilst Fric stood outside. All the tigers were up now, and were pacing their cages, their tails swinging and their big heads down. Round and round they went, round and round, sniffing the strange monkey-smell of Jemima, disturbed and angry.

Then Queenie roared, and poor Jemima fell in fright from her place half-way up the cage-bars. In a trice Queenie put out a great paw and struck at the little monkey as she fell. Jemima tumbled with a little thud to the floor of the cage, and lay there, her brown monkey-eyes closed. She did not move.

Poor Lotta was almost mad with despair. She rubbed the tears from her cheeks and looked round for help. 'Jemima will be eaten!' she wailed. 'Oh, where's Roma? He must go into Queenie's cage and save Jemima before the tigers do anything else to her.'

Mr Galliano came up, frowning, wondering what all the fuss was about. 'Mr Galliano, look, look, poor little Jemima is in Queenie's cage, and Ruby is there too, and they've hurt her and will eat her if we don't save her!' cried the little girl. 'Get Roma, oh, please, get Roma quickly, Mr Galliano!'

Mr Galliano saw what was happening at once. He cracked his big whip like a pistol-shot, three times. This was the signal for everyone to come to him at once. From every caravan and cage, from the stables and from all corners of the field, men and women came running.

'Roma!' shouted Galliano. 'Where's Roma?'

'Here!' shouted the big, powerful tiger-tamer, and he rushed up. 'What's wrong?'

'Lilliput's monkey is in your cage,' said Mr Galliano. 'Go in and get her out before the tigers eat her.'

Roma looked at the angry tigers, pacing their cages, snarling and growling. He looked at Queenie, who was standing over the still monkey, sniffing at her.

'Go on in,' commanded Mr Galliano. 'You aren't afraid, surely!'

'Don't you go in, Uncle!' shouted Fric suddenly. 'You know what Queenie is when she's in a temper! She'll spring at you!'

'I can't go in, Mr Galliano,' said Roma. 'If it was any other tiger but Queenie, I would, but Queenie's not to be trusted.'

Just then someone staggered up – it was Lilliput, who, hearing the three cracks of Galliano's whip, had hurriedly dragged on a dressing-gown and somehow got down his caravan steps, and come to see what was the matter. When he saw his beloved monkey, Jemima, lying quite still inside the tigers' cage, he gave a loud yell.

'Jemima! My little Jemima!' he cried. 'Get her out! Roma, Fric, go and get her out! What are you waiting for? Do you want to see her eaten?'

'No one can go in whilst Queenie is like that,' said Roma sullenly.

Lilliput gazed at his much-loved monkey, and the tears ran down his white cheeks. He tied his dressing-gown girdle firmly round him and turned to Roma.

'Give me the keys,' he commanded. '*I'll* go in! I'll get Jemima. I don't care twopence for your tigers!' Roma shook his head, but Lilliput made a dart at him and snatched the keys from Roma's belt. He ran like lightning to the door of the cage. But Galliano was there like lightning too! He pulled the little man back firmly.

'No,' he said, 'no, Lilliput. Your monkey may be dear to you, yes, but you also are dear to us! We cannot have you giving yourself to the tigers, no. Go back to your caravan, yes, and we will do what we can.'

Lilliput fought against Galliano, but he was small and the ring-master was big. Whilst this was going on there came the sound of pattering footsteps and panting breath, and up ran Jimmy. He had been taking Lucky for a walk and had only just come back. When he saw the crowd around the tigers' cage he knew something was wrong, and he had run to find out.

'What's up?' he cried, and then he saw Jemima, lying quite still, with Queenie standing over her, growling and snarling.

'Oh, Jimmy, Roma won't go in; he's afraid,' cried Lotta. 'What can we do?'

'Do!' cried Jimmy at once. 'Why, *I'll* go in of course! Roma, where are the keys?'

Everyone fell silent when they heard Jimmy's clear voice shouting that he would go into the cage. Galliano turned and smiled.

'No, Jimmy,' he said. 'You may be good with dogs and chimps and elephants, but with tigers, no! You will not go in!'

'Mr Galliano, sir,' cried Jimmy, 'didn't I go and rescue Jumbo when he got lost in the storm? Didn't I find Sammy the chimpanzee when he ran away, and bring him back? Well, let me save Jemima! I'm not afraid of the tigers. They are all friends of mine.'

Then Lotta spoke. 'Jimmy has already been in the tigers' cage,' she said. 'They love him.'

Roma stared in amazement and anger. Galliano pursed up his thick lips and looked at Jimmy. 'You are a queer boy, yes!' he said. 'I do not know whether to let you or not.'

'Queenie! Queenie!' suddenly said Jimmy, turning to the big tiger. 'What a noise to make! I don't like it! Come now, come!'

When the big tiger heard the clear, low voice she loved, she raised her head and sniffed. She pressed her head against the strong bars and Jimmy pulled her whiskers gently. The great tiger purred.

'It is enough,' said Galliano. 'You may go in, Jimmy – but get the hoses out first, Oona and Stanley, and be ready to turn on the water at the first sign of danger!'

Oona and Stanley hurried to get the hose-pipes. Hosing tigers and lions with water when they became fierce was often a harmless way of making them docile and tame once more. Mr Galliano arranged for the water to be turned on should the tigers growl at Jimmy when he was in the cage. Then the boy could slip out in safety whilst the tigers were scared of the water.

'Lotta, get a net on a long handle,' ordered Jimmy, taking the keys from Lilliput, who was still sobbing. 'I'll get Queenie and Ruby to the back of the cage, and you must gently put the net over Jemima and pull her quietly out between the bars.'

'Good idea, yes!' said Mr Galliano, watching the tigers closely. The hoses were brought up and pointed at the cage in case they should be needed. Jimmy unlocked the first cage-door, shut it, and unlocked the second. He walked into the tigers' cage and looked at the two green-eyed, angry animals, whose tails were swinging slowly to and fro like a restless cat's.

'Queenie!' said Jimmy softly, standing where he was, and not making any more movement. 'Queenie! Ruby! Lovely things, aren't you! Do you want to be rubbed? Do you want to be tickled?'

Queenie looked at the boy and purred. Ruby growled softly. Jimmy went on talking. 'Come, Queenie! You must come to me. Come here. Come close. Ruby, come here. Come and smell me. I am your friend, Jimmy.'

Jimmy spoke to the tigers without stopping, always in that low, gentle voice of his that all animals seemed to love. Queenie sniffed at Jemima, and then looked at Jimmy.

'Come, Queenie, come, come,' said Jimmy, and still he made no movement. Everyone stood watching in silence. Would Jimmy really be able to save poor little Jemima?

9. Mr Galliano is angry

Jimmy still stood at the back of the tigers' cage. He did not even stretch out his hand, but his gentle voice went on and on, talking to the two tigers whilst they watched him.

'Don't you want your head to be rubbed, Queenie? Don't you want your ears stroked, Ruby? Then come to me.'

All the other tigers in the farther cages had stopped pacing round and round as soon as they heard Queenie purring. Basuka, hearing Jimmy's voice, began to purr too. All the tigers gradually became quieter. And still Jimmy's low voice went on and on and on. It seemed to Lotta that it had some sort of magic in it. Everyone had to listen. Everyone seemed to feel that they too wanted to go to Jimmy and be stroked! It was very strange.

Queenie suddenly went over to Jimmy and pressed her great head lovingly against the little boy, almost knocking him over. She purred so loudly that even Basuka's purr could not be heard! Jimmy put out his hand and rubbed Queenie's great head. Ruby turned her back on the watching people and stared unwinkingly at the small boy.

This was Lotta's chance. Cautiously the little girl lifted the long-handled net that Oona had found and pushed into her hand. Slowly, without a sound, the net was held closer and closer to the cage. It was pushed through the bars – it was placed gently over the still monkey!

Then gently the little girl pulled the net back, and Jemima came with it! Ruby turned just as the monkey was drawn out of the cage. Lotta twisted the net round quickly so that Jemima did not fall out, and in a trice

Jemima was in Lilliput's arms and he was rocking her like a baby.

Ruby was startled. She roared, and Galliano called to Jimmy, 'Out, boy! Out, quickly!'

But Jimmy laughed. He went up to the roaring tiger and looked her in the eyes. He put his arm round her neck and pressed his face against her furry cheek. The great tiger purred happily, and suddenly rolled over on to her back to be tickled like a cat!

'He could do anything with those tigers of mine!' muttered Roma to himself. 'I would like that boy. He is far, far better than Fric! Those tigers would clean his boots for him if he told them to. What a boy that is!'

Mr Galliano spoke again. 'I said, come out, Jimmy, yes!' he said. And there was something in his voice that made the little boy obey at once. He gave a parting rub to Ruby and a pat to Queenie, and then slipped out of the little cage-gate. He locked it, and unlocked the outer door. He slipped out of that, and locked it.

And then how everyone came round him and patted him and praised him. But somebody was crying! And that was Mrs Brown, Jimmy's mother, who had not dared to say a word whilst Jimmy was rescuing Jemima, but was now so glad to see Jimmy safe that she could not help crying.

'Now, now, Mrs Brown,' said Oona the acrobat, patting her shoulder. 'You should be proud of Jimmy, not cry tears all down his neck.'

'If this sort of thing is going to happen often, I declare I won't stay in the circus!' wept Mrs Brown, really upset. 'I'm not used to a circus life. I'm not used to all these scares!'

'Mother, I was quite safe!' said Jimmy. 'I could do anything with those tigers. What about Jemima? How is she?'

Lilliput had taken the little monkey back to his caravan. He had given her half a teaspoonful of brandy, and the little monkey had opened her eyes. She clutched

Lilliput with her tiny hands, and trembled, for she had
been very frightened. Lilliput talked to her and soothed
her, stroking her soft little brown head. He had forgotten
he was ill. He thought only of his beloved little monkey.

'She is not hurt – no?' said Mr Galliano, looking into
the caravan. 'Just her fright and the tumble, poor beast.
Give her some hot milk, Lilliput. She will soon forget.
How did she come to get into the tigers' cage? You can
tell me – yes?'

'Ask Lotta,' said Lilliput, not looking up. 'She said
something about that boy Fric.'

Galliano sent Sticky Stanley to fetch Lotta, Fric, and
Jimmy. All three came to his caravan, looking rather
scared, for Mr Galliano did not usually send for anyone
unless he had a scolding for them.

Mrs Galliano sat in the caravan, mending Galliano's
enormous socks. Galliano sat at the table, drumming on it
with his hand. The three children came up the steps and
stood in front of him.

'You will each tell me your tale – yes?' said Mr Galliano. 'You first, Fric. And the truth, please.'

Fric did not want to tell Mr Galliano anything, but as
he felt sure that the ring-master already knew the truth,
he thought it was better to tell it.

'I saw Lotta carrying Jemima on her shoulder,' he said
sulkily. 'I don't like Lotta, so I thought I would give her a
fright. I snatched Jemima away – and the monkey bit me,
so I had to let her go. She ran into the tigers' cage, and
when I saw that the tigers were angry I didn't dare to go
in and get her.'

'So!' said Mr Galliano, his face one big frown. 'You do
not like someone, no, so you get a little monkey into
trouble, one who had done you no harm! You are a bad
boy, yes. Now you, Lotta, speak. How is it that Fric does
not like you?'

'He doesn't like me because I knew that he let Jimmy
have the keys of the tigers' cage at night,' said Lotta, in a
low voice. 'And I said I would tell you, Mr Galliano, if he

did not stop giving Jimmy the keys, because I was so afraid the tigers might hurt Jimmy. He isn't a real circus boy, and he wouldn't know that tigers are not to be trusted.'

'So!' said Mr Galliano again, his eyebrows lifted so high that they nearly disappeared into his thick black hair. 'And now you, Jimmy? What have you to say?'

Jimmy was very red. He began to feel that it was partly his fault that Jemima had been so nearly killed. If he hadn't made Fric give him the keys, then Lotta wouldn't have been frightened about him, and wouldn't have spoken to Fric like that – and Fric wouldn't have tried to upset Lotta by snatching poor Jemima away.

'Mr Galliano, sir,' he said, 'it's quite true. I did get Fric to give me the keys. I knew Roma would never let me into the cage if I asked him. And I went in at night and made friends with all the tigers.'

'Such a thing is not allowed in any circus, no,' said Mr Galliano sternly. 'A careless boy might let all the tigers out, or, if he were not so clever as you with animals, he might be badly hurt, yes! You have saved Jemima, through your friendship with the tigers, so I will say no more but this. You will promise me, Jimmy, in the future never to enter any animal's cage unless you have my permission. That is understood – yes?'

'Yes, Mr Galliano,' said Jimmy meekly. 'May I go on making friends with the tigers, please, sir?'

'You must ask Roma,' said Mr Galliano. Then he turned to sulky Fric. 'As for you,' he said, 'you need a punishment, yes! I shall tell Roma to whip you well. Then perhaps you will think twice before you put an animal into danger – yes?'

'Yes, Mr Galliano,' said Fric, upset, because he knew that his uncle had a very heavy hand.

'Now go,' said Galliano, waving them out. 'You are more trouble than all the grown-ups put together, that is certain, yes!'

The three children went out silently. Fric ran off by

himself. Jimmy took Lotta's hand. 'Don't worry, Lotta,' he said. 'I did try to tell you my secret about going into the tigers' cage, but you wouldn't listen. Cheer up! It's all right now.'

Lotta made one of her dreadful faces, and squeezed Jimmy's arm. 'Well, you won't want to be friends with that horrid boy any more,' she said happily. 'That's one good thing! Let's go and see how Lilliput and Jemima are.'

They were quite all right. Lilliput seemed better, except that his legs felt a bit weak. Jemima was sitting on his bed, drinking milk out of her little tin mug, chattering away to Lilliput in monkey-language. She had a bruise on her back where Queenie had struck her, but it was not very bad. She was wearing a blue ribbon round her neck and was very proud of it.

'She's fine,' said Lilliput to Jimmy. 'Jimmy, I'll never be able to thank you properly for saving Jemima. You're the finest boy I know! You come to me whenever you need any help, and you'll always get it.'

'Thank you, Lilliput,' said Jimmy, petting Jemima, whilst Lotta peeled a grape for the tiny monkey. 'I don't expect I'll need any help, though!'

But that's just where Jimmy was wrong, as you will see!

10. Goodbye to the tigers

The show at Liverpool came to an end, and once again the tents were taken down, the caravans had their horses put between the shafts, and there was a great deal of noise and shouting. The tigers roared, for they hated any disturbance, and once Jimmy went into their cages with Roma to quiet them.

Roma looked at the quiet little boy, and spoke to him. 'Would you like to join me?' he asked. 'You are wonderful with the tigers, Jimmy. If anything should ever happen to your dog, Lucky, you come to me, and I will find a place for you with the tigers.'

'No, thank you, Roma,' said Jimmy at once. 'For one thing, nothing will happen to Lucky, for I am very careful of her. – and for another, I shouldn't care to train tigers. They are not the right kind of animals for tricks. They don't enjoy them. I only like teaching animals that love to learn.'

'You speak stupidly,' said Roma, offended. 'It is a grand thing to be a tiger or lion tamer.'

'Well,' said Jimmy, 'it's not the sort of grand thing I like to do. I love going into the ring with Lucky! I'd much rather go with her than with tigers.'

'It is true she is a marvellous dog,' said Roma. 'You should sell her for a lot of money, Jimmy, and buy more dogs. Then you would have a whole troupe!'

'Sell her!' said Jimmy, amazed. 'I wouldn't sell Lucky for anything. Why, I love her!'

Fric was nearby, listening. He would not speak to Jimmy nowadays, for he blamed Jimmy and Lotta for the whipping Roma had given him. He was a spiteful little boy and would dearly have loved to pay Jimmy back. But he did not see how to.

The circus moved off to its next show-place in Greenville. This was a much more countrified place than outside Liverpool, and Jimmy and Lotta were pleased. It was early summer now, and camping out was very pleasant. It was grand to wake up in the morning and hear the birds singing, the cocks at the nearby farm crowing, and the murmur of the bees in the hawthorn hedges.

'The may is like snow, all over the hedge,' said Lotta, smelling it. 'Let's bathe in the stream when we go to get the water.'

Lotta ran barefoot again, and Jimmy would have liked to, but his mother wouldn't let him. 'No,' she said firmly. 'You're not going to get into that kind of circus way, Jimmy. As for you, Lotta, run barefoot if you must, but don't forget to clean your teeth and brush your hair!'

Lotta was still not very good at keeping herself tidy enough for Mrs Brown, for she was a proper little circus girl, thinking that tidiness and prettiness were only to be kept for the ring at night. All the other circus folk thought so too, and they went about in the oddest clothes all day, except for Mr Galliano, who was always smart, and who, as his habit was, wore his top hat right on one side when the show went well!

Once he wore it so much to one side after a very good show that it fell off, and Jemima had sprung down to get it. She dashed off with it, and took it to Sammy the chimpanzee, who, very pleased indeed with such a fine hat, put it on, and walked all round the field with it! Everyone roared with laughter except Galliano himself, who was quite annoyed to see his fine top hat worn by a cheeky chimpanzee!

Once more the show opened, and the people of Greenville and all round about flocked to see it. How they laughed at the funny antics of Sticky Stanley, how they clapped the beautiful dancing horses, and stared at

Sammy the chimpanzee and marvelled at little dog Lucky!

They thought that the six tigers were marvellous too, and it made them shiver and shake when they saw Roma and Fric walk boldly into the cage in the ring. Jimmy had never been allowed to go into the ring with the tigers, though he often helped Roma.

'Soon I shall have your tigers curling round my feet like tame cats!' he said with a laugh. But Roma shook his head.

'We leave Mr Galliano's circus when this show is over,' he said. 'We are joining another circus, Jimmy. You will have to say goodbye to Queenie and Ruby and Basuka and the rest.'

Jimmy was sad. He had grown to love the green-eyed, graceful tigers. He wondered what other animals Mr Galliano would have next. He ran to ask Lotta if she knew.

'Yes,' said Lotta. 'Oona the acrobat has just told me. It's bears!'

'Bears!' said Jimmy. 'Ooooh! That will be fun!'

'Remember your promise to Mr Galliano, Jimmy,' said Oona the acrobat warningly, as he stood on his head outside his caravan, practising for that night's show.

'Yes,' said Jimmy, 'I won't forget. When will the bears come, Oona?'

'Not till we get to our next show-place,' said Oona, still balancing on his head, and working his legs above him as if he were riding a bicycle. He really could do marvellous things with his lean, wiry body! 'There will be a whole week between the end of this show and the beginning of the next, Jimmy. Quite a holiday!'

'Oh, what fun!' cried Lotta, and at once began to plan picnics and walks with Jimmy. 'I shan't be sorry to say goodbye to that horrid Fric!'

Before the tents were taken down, and before the caravans were made ready to leave Greenville, the tigers left in their great travelling-box. Jimmy had asked Roma's permission to say goodbye to each of them, before they left, and he was sad when he went into their cages for the last time.

He had left Lucky in his caravan, for Lucky was frightened of the tigers, and would not come near their cages if she could help it. Lotta and Mrs Brown were doing some washing down by the stream. Brownie was helping to pack up the cage that the tigers used in the ring.

'Goodbye, Queenie; goodbye, Ruby,' said the little boy, rubbing the great tigers' heads as they purred deafeningly into his ear. 'Goodbye, Busuka; don't forget me! Remember me when you are far away, for some day I will see you all again. Goodbye, all of you!'

There was a shout from outside. Everything was ready. Jimmy slipped out of the cage, and Roma came to lock the travelling-box carefully and shut up the open side so that the tigers could not be disturbed by anything they saw whilst on the road.

'Where's Fric?' said Jimmy. 'I must say goodbye to him.'

'I saw him over by your caravan just now,' said Roma. 'Tell him to come at once. I'm ready.'

But there was no Fric by Jimmy's caravan, and Jimmy ran back to Roma, who was just driving the heavy travelling-cage through the field-gate.

'I can't see Fric!' he called.

'He's just got in at the back!' shouted Roma. 'Goodbye!'

Fric did not peep out to wave goodbye. There was no sign of him. The engine of the powerful motor-van roared, and the tigers roared too. Down the road they went, very slowly – they were gone!

Jimmy stared after them. Goodbye to the tigers – but it would soon be welcome to the bears! How exciting it was to belong to a circus! You simply never knew what was going to come next!

He went over to Sticky Stanley and watched him practising running on his hands. Jimmy could still not walk properly on his hands. He watched Stanley turning quick somersaults, head-over-heels, heels-over-head, head-over-heels, so quickly that the little boy could hardly follow him!

'Lucky might be able to learn that!' thought Jimmy. 'I believe she could. I'll get her and make her watch old Stanley.'

He ran to his caravan and opened the door. He whistled softly. 'Lucky!' he called. 'Come along!'

But Lucky did not leap out of the door as she usually did. Only Lulu, the black spaniel, put up her sleepy head and wagged a lazy tail.

'Lucky!' called Jimmy sharply, looking quickly round the caravan. 'Lucky!'

But Lucky was not in the caravan. Jimmy ran to Mrs Brown and Lotta, who were still by the stream.

'Have you got Lucky?' he asked.

'No,' said Lotta. 'You shut her in the caravan.'

'Well, she's not there now,' said Jimmy. 'Haven't you seen her anywhere about?'

'No,' said Mrs Brown and Lotta. 'We've been busy.'

'She's somewhere about, I expect,' said Mrs Brown. 'Dogs usually are!'

Jimmy ran off. He hunted all round the circus. He asked everyone he met if they had seen Lucky. He looked under every caravan. He ran down the road and up. But there was no sign of Lucky at all. It was very strange and very worrying.

'Now, boy, now!' said Mr Galliano, when he saw Jimmy crawling out from under his gay caravan. 'What are you doing there? Do you want to see how many wheels my caravan has – yes?'

But Jimmy could not smile. 'No, sir,' he said. 'I'm looking for Lucky. She's disappeared!'

'A dog cannot disappear, no!' said Mr Galliano. 'She will turn up when it is her dinner-time, yes. That is the way of all animals – little boys too!'

So Jimmy waited and watched until it was Lucky's meal-time – but no Lucky came running up, hungry and eager. Lotta was worried too, and even Mrs Brown looked puzzled.

'I don't see how Lucky can disappear all at once like this,' she said. 'You don't think, Jimmy, that she has been stolen?'

'Oh, Mother, don't say that!' cried poor Jimmy, his heart sinking. 'Lucky, little dog Lucky, wherever can you be?'

11. Where can Lucky be?

Could Lucky really have been stolen? But who would have stolen her? There had been no strangers round the camp at all. Jimmy was almost in despair as he ran to and fro, begging for news of Lucky.

Lotta was crying. She loved Lucky, and she could not bear to see Jimmy's white, anxious face. What would Jimmy do if he could not find Lucky? He would not be able to go into the ring any more!

'It's a good thing we have a week between the end of this show and the beginning of the next,' thought the little girl, scrubbing her face dry as she saw Jimmy coming. 'Any news, Jimmy?'

'No,' said Jimmy. 'I've asked everybody, but nobody has seen Lucky.'

'Look, there is Lilliput beckoning to you,' said Lotta. Jimmy turned and saw Lilliput waving, and Jemima was beckoning, too, with her tiny finger!

Jimmy went across to Lilliput's caravan. Lilliput looked grave.

'I've been thinking, Jimmy,' he began, 'and I believe I know who has taken Lucky – if she has been stolen.'

'Who?' asked Jimmy.

'Fric!' said Lilliput. 'I remember now seeing him coming from your caravan, and he had a bag in his hand and the bag was wriggling!'

'What! Do you suppose he had poor little Lucky inside the bag?' cried Jimmy, a great rage creeping over him.

'Yes,' said Lilliput. 'And what's more, if the tigers hadn't been bellowing so, and the motor-van making such a noise, I guess I'd have heard whines coming from that bag, too!'

'Oh, Lilliput, I believe you are right,' said Jimmy, in despair. 'Fric was furious with Lotta and with me because he got a whipping from Roma – and he knew Lucky was worth a lot of money. What would he do with her?'

'Sell her, I expect,' said Lilliput. 'But it's up to us to get her back before he does. We'll go after Roma and Fric!'

'But I don't know where they've gone!' cried Jimmy.

'We can find out from Galliano,' said Lilliput. 'I'll come with you, Jimmy. You saved Jemima for me, when she was in the tigers' cage, and I told you I'd help you if ever you needed help.'

'I didn't think I'd need it so soon,' said Jimmy sadly. 'You're a good friend, Lilliput. I wouldn't know how to follow Roma and Fric, if I had to go alone, or how to make Fric own up. You'll be a great help.'

They went to tell Mr Galliano what they meant to do. The ring-master looked as black as thunder when he heard what Lilliput had to say about Fric.

'That dog is worth a lot of money, yes!' he said. 'You must get her back somehow before the show opens at Blackpool next week, for she draws a lot of people to the circus. The tigers have gone to join Mr Briggs's circus at Five-Ways, twenty miles from here. You can get there by train. Leave tonight. I think Roma will not know anything about this, for he would not do such a wicked thing, no! Fric is stupid, and only a boy. You will see that Roma understands that Fric is to be well watched in future, Lilliput – yes? He needs a very firm hand, and he does not get it, no.'

Mr Galliano was so upset about Lucky's going that his hat was perfectly straight on his head, and he looked quite queer in it. He patted Jimmy on the shoulder and pressed some money into his hand.

There was a lump in Jimmy's throat, but he did not cry. He was too anxious even to think of tears. He and Lilliput ran to Jimmy's caravan to tell Mrs Brown,

Brownie, and Lotta what they were going to do. Mrs
Brown quickly put Jimmy's pyjamas into a bag, and
kissed him goodbye.

'What about Jemima and the other three monkeys?'
asked Lotta. 'Shall I see to them for you, Lilliput?'

'I'm taking Jemima with me,' said Lilliput. 'I've never
been away from her since I had her. You see to the others
for me, Lotta, there's a good girl.'

Lotta promised, and Lilliput and Jimmy said goodbye
and ran to the station to get the next train to Five-Ways.
They just caught it, and sat without speaking whilst it
puffed along to the town of Five-Ways. Jemima had a
lovely time. She got up into the luggage rack and examined everybody's bags and baskets. The other people in
the carriage laughed loudly at her, but Jimmy was too sad
at heart even to smile at Jemima's funny ways.

Lilliput had to put her under his coat at last because
she tried to pick the flowers out of a lady's hat. The
monkey chattered a little and then went to sleep.

They got out at Five-Ways, which was a big station.
Lilliput asked the porter where Mr Briggs's circus was.
'Go down that street, keep up over the hill, and make for
the Common,' said the porter. 'The circus is camping in
the big field at the beginning of the Common. Take a
tram. It's a long way.'

So the two took a tram, and went through many dingy
streets until at last they had a sight of the Common – and
there, in a great field, was Mr Briggs's circus, with tents,
caravans, and cages, just as Mr Galliano's had.

'Now you leave this to me, Jimmy,' said Lilliput, as
they went in at the gate and made their way to the big
travelling-box of tigers they knew so well. 'There's Roma,
look! Hi, Roma!'

Roma turned, and stared in the greatest astonishment
at Lilliput and Jimmy.

'Have *you* come to join the circus too?' he cried. 'I'm
glad to see you. Hallo, Jemima! Got over your adventure
yet?'

'I want to see Fric,' said Lilliput in a grave voice.

'Why?' asked Roma at once. 'What has he done, the young scamp?'

'Roma, Jimmy's dog Lucky has disappeared,' said Lilliput. 'I saw Fric coming from the direction of Jimmy's caravan, carrying a bag – and we have an idea that he knows something about Lucky.'

'The bad boy! The tiresome lad!' cried Roma, who often had reason to find fault with Fric. 'But I haven't seen anything of Lucky on our journey here, Lilliput. Are you sure that Lucky hasn't run off somewhere, meaning to come back tonight?'

'Lucky never runs far from me,' said Jimmy. 'Where is Fric, Roma? Call him.'

'He has gone shopping into the town,' said Roma.

'Did he take a bag with him?' asked Lilliput quickly.

'I didn't see him go,' said Roma. 'Wait here for a little, and he will be back. I am going to have my supper. Will you have some too?'

Lilliput was hungry, and he sat down to share Roma's sausages, but Jimmy felt sick and could eat nothing. He sat waiting for Fric to come back. At last he saw him coming in at the gate, carrying a bag full of something. Jimmy flew over the field at once.

'What's in that bag, Fric?' he shouted. 'Give it to me!'

Fric looked astonished and frightened. 'Hallo,' he said. 'This *is* a surprise. What are you here for?'

'I guess you know all right,' said Jimmy, in a fierce voice. 'Give me that bag!'

Fric threw it to him with a laugh. Jimmy opened it with trembling hands. Inside there were potatoes and two tins of pineapple chunks. Nothing else. Jimmy dropped the bag on the ground and faced Fric.

'What have you done with Lucky?' he demanded.

'Lucky! Whatever are you talking about!' said Fric, a surprised look on his face. Just then Lilliput and Roma came up. Roma took Fric by the shoulder and spoke to him sternly.

'Fric, you will say truly whether you took Lucky or not,

and what you have done with her. Come now, speak up.'

'I don't know anything about Lucky,' said Fric sulkily,
and not another thing could any of the three get out of
him. He would say nothing but that. Lilliput looked at
Jimmy in despair. None of them believed Fric, but if he
chose to say nothing, what could they do? They had no
real proof that he had taken the little dog away.

'Turn out your pockets, Fric,' said Roma suddenly.

'No,' said Fric. 'Why should I?'

'Did you hear what I said?' roared Roma. Fric sullenly
turned out his pockets, and in them was a five-pound note!

'How did you get that?' demanded Roma at once.

'It's my savings,' said Fric, putting the note back into
his pocket. 'Can't I have savings?'

'You've sold Lucky to someone!' shouted Jimmy, and
he shook Fric till his teeth rattled in his head. 'You've
sold my little dog!'

'I haven't!' cried Fric. 'Let me go!'

Just then Mr Briggs, the owner of the circus, came up. He stared at Jimmy and Lilliput and then flipped a thumb towards the gate.

'Out!' he said. 'You don't belong here!'

There was nothing more that Lilliput and Jimmy could do. Carrying the frightened Jemima, Lilliput and the little boy went towards the field-gate, Jimmy white with anger, for he felt perfectly certain that Fric had sold Lucky to somebody in the big town.

'What can we do now, Lilliput?' Jimmy said, in a trembling voice.

'We'll take lodgings somewhere for the night,' said Lilliput, putting his arm comfortingly round the little boy. 'Tomorrow morning we will go to old Ma Lightfoot. She knows all the circus folk, and she'll be able to tell us who that spiteful Fric might have gone to with Lucky. Don't worry now, Jimmy; Lucky will be all right. Whoever has bought her will take great care of her, for she's valuable. I reckon they hope to sell her to another circus, when they see the chance.'

They looked for lodgings, and at last found a clean little house in a dirty street. The woman who took them in didn't mind Jemima a bit. She said she had once had a man lodging with her who had two young bears – and after that, well, she didn't mind anything!

'You must have something to eat, Jimmy,' said Lilliput. 'I'll get the woman to bring up a meal.'

So a lovely stew was sent up for the two of them, and although Jimmy felt sure he wouldn't be able to eat any of it, because he was so worried, he found that he could – and felt much better after it!

Lilliput was the best of friends to Jimmy that night. He wouldn't let the little boy think and worry, but told him such lovely tales of circus life that Jimmy simply *had* to listen! When they said goodnight in bed, Jemima crept in between them, and put a little paw into their hands.

'Cheer up, Jimmy,' said Lilliput. 'We'll get Lucky soon, never fear!'

12. Lotta disappears

The next morning Jimmy awoke early and lay thinking about Lucky. Where was she? Was she missing him? Did she wonder why her little master was not with her to pet her and feed her? For the first time tears came into Jimmy's eyes and he sniffed so loudly that Lilliput awoke. Jemima heard the sniff too, and awoke. She wriggled out of the bed, sat on the bed-rail and chattered at them. She looked so comical that Jimmy had to smile.

'Breakfast!' said Lilliput, smelling a good smell of bacon frying. 'Come on, Jimmy!'

After breakfast the two, with Jemima, set out to find Ma Lightfoot. She lived in a tiny house, with three parrots, two monkeys, one fox cub, three cats, and four dogs. Jimmy could hardly hear himself speak, because the parrots made so much noise. Jemima shrieked with joy when she saw the two monkeys in their cage, and at once sat on the top and chattered to them.

Ma Lightfoot was a very fat, very kindly woman, with light, piercing eyes and big gentle hands. She had been in a circus when she was young, and had trained many animals. Now she kept animals for those who wanted to board them out for a while, so hers was always an exciting house to go to. You never knew if you were going to meet a young bear in the shed, or tame white rats all over the place!

Lilliput told Ma Lightfoot all about Jimmy and Lucky, and she nodded her head.

'Yes,' she said. 'I have heard of this boy and his clever dog. He has the same gift as I have – he understands and loves, and so all animals and birds are his friends. Be quiet, Polly; be quiet, Sally!

The parrots stopped screeching, and one tried to catch Jemima's tail. Jemima threw a handful of seed at her. She screeched again, and the third one said, very solemnly, 'Pop goes the weasel!'

When the animals and birds had quietened down once more, and Jimmy had removed the fox cub from his knee, where it would keep biting off his coat buttons, Lilliput asked Ma Lightfoot what he wanted to know.

'Is there anyone in this town who would buy a stolen animal, meaning to resell it when he had a chance?' said Lilliput. Ma Lightfoot nodded her head.

'Yes,' she said. 'There's Charlie Tipps. You've heard of him, I dare say. He was turned out of all the circuses for stealing. Never could keep his hands off other people's belongings. He'd buy Lucky, hide her away, and sell her to another circus when he got the chance. You'd better go and see him. Maybe you could frighten him, and he'd give you back Lucky.'

Jimmy wanted to be off at once, so the boy, the man, and the monkey set off to the address Ma Lightfoot had given them. Jimmy was full of ideas. He was quite sure that Charlie Tipps had bought Lucky, and would be hiding her somewhere in the house.

'I shall shout "Lucky! Lucky! Lucky!" at the top of my voice as soon as the door is opened!' he said. 'And I shall whistle too – and if Lucky is anywhere about she'll answer me by barking, even if she can't get to me. And whilst you argue with Charlie, I shall slip off and look into every room of the house, Lilliput.'

'Right,' said Lilliput. 'We ought to find her if she's there!'

They came to the house. It stood by itself in a lonely street. There was a big garden with sheds here and there, for Charlie often kept animals of different sorts, and sold or exchanged them to circuses and fairs. Jimmy was certain Lucky was somewhere about.

They banged on the big knocker. Clang, clang, clang! they rang the bell too. A woman opened the door, looking surprised at all the noise. She looked even more surprised when Jimmy pushed by her, yelling 'Lucky! Lucky! Lucky!' and whistled piercingly in her ear.

'Where's Charlie Tipps?' demanded Lilliput, putting on his fiercest expression.

'He's not here,' said the woman. 'He went off early this morning in his car. I don't know where he's gone. He won't be back for two weeks. He's taken a load of animals to sell to some circuses.'

Jimmy's heart sank. Lucky must have been taken too! He rushed into every room; he went into the garden and looked into every shed. He shouted and whistled, but no little dog answered him. The boy went back to Lilliput, bitterly disappointed.

'We can't do any more here,' said Lilliput, sad to see Jimmy's unhappy face. 'Come along. We'd best go back to the circus. Our luck's right out.'

The woman banged the door after them, angry with the boy who had rushed through the house, shouting and whistling. Lilliput and Jimmy walked back to the station, not saying a work.

Everyone at Galliano's circus was sorry for Jimmy. They all loved animals and they knew what it was to give one's heart to any creature, and then to lose it. Mr Wally patted Jimmy on the back. Mr Tonks didn't know what to say, so he just shook hands. Even Mr Galliano was more upset than anyone had ever seen him, for he was proud of Lucky and very fond of Jimmy. Lotta slipped her arms round Jimmy – but to her surprise and dismay Jimmy pushed her away. 'I only want to tell you I'm sorry, Jimmy,' she said, very much hurt.

'If you hadn't gone spying on me that night I went to the tigers' cage, and got us all into that trouble over Jemima, Fric would never have tried to pay me out by stealing little dog Lucky,' said Jimmy. 'It's all your fault!'

'Oh, Jimmy, that's not fair!' said poor Lotta, bursting

into tears. But Jimmy was past being fair or kind. He was so anxious, so disappointed, and so unhappy that he just didn't care what he said or did to Lotta. His mother heard all that was said, and was sorry for both children. She called them.

'Come and have your dinner. I've something extra-special.'

But the extra-special dinner wasn't eaten. Lotta ran away to cry by herself, and Jimmy wouldn't stir from his seat on an upturned tub. He seemed to be quite a changed boy. But Brownie, his father, soon pulled him together.

'This is not the way to meet trouble, Jimmy,' he said sternly. 'The world hasn't come to an end because you have lost Lucky. Go up into the caravan and have your dinner. And don't blame others for what has been as much your fault! You know that it was wrong to borrow Roma's keys without his knowing.'

Jimmy obeyed his father, but he could not eat any dinner, he could only drink the coffee his mother had made. Lotta did not appear at all. Mr Tonks called to Jimmy to help him with Jumbo afterwards, and he managed to keep the little boy really busy until it was time for bed.

By that time Jimmy was very sorry that he had spoken so unfairly to Lotta. He knew he had been very unkind. He called to his mother.

'Where's Lotta, do you know?'

'I haven't seen her since dinner time,' said Mrs Brown. 'She didn't come in to tea. I thought perhaps you two had made up your silly quarrel, and she was with you.'

'No, I haven't seen her,' said Jimmy. 'I'll go and find her.'

But he couldn't find her, and at last he went back to the caravan. 'Has Lotta come in?' he asked. 'Is supper ready? I do feel hungry.'

'I should think you do!' said Mrs Brown. 'No dinner and no tea! I've got a nice supper for you. Lotta hasn't come back. She'll be in sometime. Maybe she's gone for a walk with Lulu.'

'Oh, if she's taken Lulu, then she's certainly gone for a walk,' said Jimmy, and he went up the steps, sniffing at the good supper Mrs Brown had cooked for him. He thought of Lucky with a pain at his heart. What was Lucky doing now? Where was she? Would she run away and come back to him? She was quite clever enough!

The Browns ate their supper. It was dark now, and still Lotta hadn't come back. Mr Brown began to get worried.

'She ought to be back now,' he said. 'I wish I knew where she had gone and I'd go and meet her. She's in our charge, and I don't like her out as late as this, all alone.'

'She's got Lulu, Dad,' said Jimmy, who was beginning to feel worried.

'Well, I'm glad to hear *that*,' said Brownie. 'She'll be company for Lotta, at any rate. Jimmy, you'd better get to bed. You look very tired.'

Mrs Brown turned back the cover of Jimmy's bunk, and then she gave a cry of surprise. Pinned on to Jimmy's pillow was a note in Lotta's babyish, scrawling hand-writing. Mrs Brown picked it up, and Jimmy and Brownie stood beside her, reading it.

'Dere Jimmy,' said the note, 'I've gon to find Lucky for you. I wont kum back till I've got her. Tell Mrs Brown not to wurry.

Lotta.'

'Good gracious!' said Mrs Brown at once. 'Whatever does the child mean? How can she find Lucky, any more than Jimmy or Lilliput could? Wherever has she gone? Oh dear, dear, what a worry – as if we hadn't enough without Lotta disappearing too!'

Jimmy was horrified. Lotta going off all by herself with Lulu to find Lucky, when she had no idea at all where the little dog could be! What would she do? Oh dear, this was even worse than Lucky's disappearance!

Off went Brownie to tell Mr Galliano. Soon everyone knew, and there was a great chattering and wakefulness in the camp. Lotta! Where was she? Nobody had seen her go. Nobody had seen Lulu. Nobody knew what to do.

And where was Lotta all this time? Ah, Jimmy would have been surprised if he had known!

13. Lotta's amazing adventure

Lotta had felt very unhappy when Jimmy had spoken to her so unkindly. She had run off crying to Lilliput's caravan, and had told the kind little monkey-man what Jimmy had said.

'Now don't fret about it,' Lilliput said, patting her on the back. 'Jimmy's dreadfully unhappy and worried himself because Lucky has been stolen. Did he tell you how we went to see Fric and Roma, and felt certain that Fric had sold Lucky to Charlie Tipps? But Charlie had gone away, we didn't know where!'

'Charlie Tipps!' said Lotta, drying her eyes. 'Why, my father, Laddo, used to know him well. He said he was a bad man, though. He once stole a white horse of ours, had it dyed black, and sold it to somebody else!'

The little girl sat thinking. If only she could get back Lucky for Jimmy! She looked at Lilliput.

'Lilliput,' she said, 'will you lend me some money?'

'Of course!' said Lilliput at once, and he took down an old brown teapot from a shelf and tipped it up. A heap of silver fell out.

'Take what you want,' said Lilliput. 'Are you needing a new dress or something?'

'No,' said Lotta, picking out some half-crowns and putting them into her pocket. 'It's a secret, Lilliput. Do you mind if I don't tell you yet?'

'Not a bit,' said kindly Lilliput. 'Hey, Jemima, the money's not for you! Put that shilling back!'

Jemima had stretched out a little arm and picked up a shilling. She had put it inside her cheek, but Lilliput made her put it back into the teapot. 'She's artful enough to go and buy herself twelve penny ice-creams!' he said. 'And then she'd be ill!'

Lotta ran back to the Browns' caravan. She picked up an old raincoat and a beret. She put on a pair of shoes. Then she called softly to Lulu, the black spaniel, and together the two slipped out of the caravan, unseen by anyone.

Lotta squeezed through the hedge at the back of the caravan, and found herself on the main road. A bus was coming, and she stopped it. In she got with Lulu, and off they went together in the rumbling bus.

'I want to go to Uptown,' Lotta told the conductor. 'How near do you go to that?'

'Well, that's a good way away,' said the conductor in surprise. 'We only go as far as Hillocks, six miles off. But you can get a bus there to Uptown, though it will take you a long time.'

It was night before the little girl reached Uptown. She had come there because she remembered that a great friend of Charlie Tipps lived there, and her father had told her that this man was very clever at altering the appearance of animals so that they looked quite different. Then they were sold again. Lotta had an idea that Charlie Tipps might take Lucky to this man.

'Where shall I sleep?' wondered the little girl, as she and Lulu got out of the bus, feeling hungry and tired. 'I can't sleep in a house. I never have in all my life! I couldn't bear it! Come, Lulu, we'll find a place somewhere.'

Lotta bought some cakes and chocolate at a little shop, and, sharing them with Lulu, she set off out of the town towards the green hills that lay on the south.

She came to a farm. She made out the shape of a big barn in the distance, and she and Lulu went into a field, crawled through the hedge, and crept quietly to the big, shadowy barn.

She pushed the door open. In the barn were stacked sacks full of something soft. 'These will do nicely for a bed, Lulu,' said Lotta. The little girl pulled some into a nice soft heap and lay down. She was very tired. She threw the old raincoat over her, and pulled Lulu close to her.

'I'm lonely, Lulu,' she whispered. 'I'll hug you, and we'll keep each other nice and warm.'

Lulu licked Lotta's nose. She was a gentle, loving dog, and it was a great comfort to Lotta to have her for company. Soon the two were fast asleep.

In the morning Lotta washed her face in a nearby stream. She did not brush or comb her hair, for she had brought neither brush nor comb with her. She shook her mop of black curls just as Lulu shook her silky black ears and coat! Then they set off back to Uptown.

'We've got to find Mr Binks, Charlie's friend,' she told Lulu. 'That was his name, I remember. But we mustn't let him see us, Lulu, for he might remember me. I went with Lal and Laddo when they went to see him about our white horse that was stolen. We must be very careful.'

Lotta asked at a post office for Mr Binks's address, for she had forgotten it. There were three Mr Binks living in the town, but as soon as she heard the address of the second one, the little girl remembered. That was the one!

She set off to find it, munching bread and chocolate. Lulu had made a good meal off threepennyworth of fresh meat at a butcher's. She trotted along happily by Lotta's feet, wondering what all the adventure was about.

At last Lotta came to a low, rambling farmhouse, which she remembered from two or three years before. There were big stables in the fields beyond, and many sheds and kennels. Lotta stood behind the hedge and gazed in. Was Lucky there? How she longed to know! But there were so many dogs barking, so many horses neighing, so many hens clucking, that it was impossible to hear if Lucky's sharp bark was among them! She watched horses being ridden round a large field. They were being trained for a circus, and they were most beautifully kept. Lotta wished she could ride one!

Suddenly an idea flashed into the little girl's head. If she dressed up as a boy, nobody would know her! She could go into the fields there, and even if Mr Binks saw her he would not remember her. She turned and ran back to the shops.

She went into a hairdresser's, and asked for all her pretty black curls to be cut short, like a boy's. The girl did not want to do it, but Lotta suddenly took a pair of scissors and began to chop off her curls herself, so the shop-girl had to finish the job properly. What a funny little thing Lotta looked when she came out!

Then she bought a shirt and a pair of blue shorts at another shop. She slipped behind a hedge on her way back to Mr Binks's house, and changed into her new clothes. When she came through the hedge into the road again, she looked exactly like a little boy!

Lotta felt rather grand. She stuck her hands into her pockets, and whistled as she went, with Lulu at her heels. The spaniel did not seem to notice that Lotta was any different. She smelt the same, and that was all that Lulu cared about!

And now Lotta went boldly into the fields around the farmhouse and examined every shed and stable to see if little dog Lucky was there. But she could not find any sign of her. 'She must be in the farmhouse somewhere,' thought Lotta.

And then a most extraordinary thing happened. A big car drew up outside the farmhouse, and out got Mr Alfred Cyrano, head of one of the biggest circuses, a man who had once offered to buy Lucky from Jimmy! Lotta knew him at once, and his great big cigar too, and she stared in amazement.

Her quick little brain set to work at once. 'He always wanted Lucky, and everyone knew it! Oh, he must have come for Lucky! So Lucky is here! He'll take her away with him. If only I could go with him! But how?'

Mr Alfred Cyrano went into the farmhouse. Lotta crept round, trying to see into the windows. At last she discovered that Cyrano and Mr Binks were at the back of the house, overlooking the fields where the horses were cantering. On the floor was a small travelling-box, big enough for a dog.

For a moment Lotta did not know what to do. Then the sound of the cantering of hoofs put an idea into her head. She would do some tricks on those horses, hoping that the two men would look out of the window and see her! Then maybe she could beg a job from Mr Cyrano, and go with him back to his circus – with Lucky! And if she didn't manage to escape somehow on the way, taking Lucky with her, she wouldn't be as clever as she thought she was!

The little girl's heart began to beat fast. She ran to a great black horse with a broad back. He had no saddle and no bridle. He shied away as Lotta came up. But the little girl swung herself up on to his back and galloped him round the field, whilst two men who were exercising the horses shouted angrily at her!

Lotta knelt on the galloping horse. She stood up! She stretched out her arms, and there she was, going lightly up and down on the galloping horse, waving to the two astonished grooms as she passed them.

From the corner of her eye she saw that Mr Binks and Mr Cyrano, hearing the shouts, had come to the window and were staring in amazement. The little girl dropped down to the horse's back, got up again, and this time stood facing backwards, looking over the horse's tail. Then she stood first on one leg and then on the other! She jumped up and down! It was marvellous!

Lotta had been a circus girl all her life, but the horse she was on was only half trained, and a stranger to her. He began to gallop so fast that Lotta had to sit down again. One of the grooms was afraid the boy – as he thought Lotta was – would be hurt. He galloped up on another horse, shouting to Lotta to let him drag her off.

But the little girl stood up again, and when the groom's horse came alongside she neatly jumped on to his own horse, just behind him, and stood there, her hand lightly on his shoulder. He brought his horse to a stop. But before he could speak to her, a loud voice shouted from the farmhouse:

'Come here, you! Who are you?'

It was Mr Cyrano, who had been watching Lotta's performance in astonishment. Lotta jumped from the groom's horse and ran up to him in her shirt and shorts.

'Who are you?' asked Cyrano again. Lotta decided to be grand.

'I am the Boy Wonder!' she said. 'Barney Beano, the Boy Wonder! I can ride any horse in the world! I'm looking for a job.'

'Well, you can ride, that's certain,' said Mr Cyrano. 'Got any luggage? You can come back with me now, if you like, and start next week.'

'I've got no luggage,' said Lotta, 'but I've got a dog. Can I bring her?'

'Yes,' said Cyrano, and he turned to go inside the house with Mr Binks. Lotta whistled to Lulu, and the two went and waited by the gate. Soon Mr Binks came to the door and beckoned. 'Take this box to the car for Mr Cyrano,' he ordered.

Lotta flew to get the box. Could Lucky be inside it? There was no sound inside, and Lotta did not dare even to whisper Lucky's name. But Lulu seemed strangely excited at the box, and sniffed all round it when it was in the car.

Mr Cyrano got in and took the wheel. Lotta was at the back with Lulu and the dog-box. Mr Binks called goodbye and the car slid down the lane.

The Boy Wonder was off to Mr Alfred Cyrano's circus! How Lotta wished that Jimmy could see where she was now!

14. Little dog Lucky!

Mr Cyrano's circus was a long way away. It was three hours before they arrived there, and Lotta was very hungry. The dog in the travelling-box had not made a sound, and even though Lotta had whispered Lucky's name, no answering whine or bark had come. It was puzzling.

When they arrived at the circus, Mr Cyrano bellowed for a man called Tiny. Tiny was simply enormous, so it made people laugh when they heard his name.

He came up. Mr Cyrano waved him to the back of the car. 'You'll find the dog I told you about in a box there,' he said. 'He's been given some sleep-medicine, so he'll have to sleep it off. He'll be all right tomorrow. Take this boy too and let him have a bunk in your caravan. He'll help with the horses and ride in the ring next week.'

Lotta went off with Tiny, who seemed quite friendly. Lulu followed at her heels. Tiny cut Lotta some bread-and-cheese sandwiches, and read the paper whilst Lotta and Lulu ate them. And then, quite suddenly, Lotta saw her own picture looking at her from the paper. What a shock she got!

She read what was printed underneath. It said:

'LOTTA, THE MISSING CIRCUS GIRL. MR AND MRS BROWN ARE VERY WORRIED ABOUT HER, BECAUSE THEY ARE IN CHARGE OF HER WHILST HER PARENTS ARE ABROAD. A REWARD IS OFFERED TO ANYONE WHO WILL BRING HER BACK.'

How glad Lotta was that she had dressed up as a boy! Nobody would know her – and she couldn't, couldn't go back till she had got little dog Lucky again! What a good thing nothing was said in the paper about Lulu!

Tiny had placed the dog-box inside an empty cage, which had its side up, so that Lotta could not see inside. So the little girl had not been able to find out if Lucky was in the box or not. She made up her mind to slip out of the caravan that night and find out. She noticed that Tiny put his cage-keys on a little shelf.

So when the camp was in darkness, and Tiny was snoring in the caravan, Lotta picked up a torch from the shelf, took the keys gently, and stole down the steps with Lulu like a black shadow. She made her way to the cage nearby and unlocked it. A little whine greeted her. Lucky had evidently awakened!

The little girl shut the door behind her, and flashed her torch in front of her, longing to see little dog Lucky, with her half-brown, half-black head, and her black spot and brown spot on her white back.

But quite a different dog looked up at her with wagging tail and friendly yelps! Lotta stared in surprise and dismay! Tears came into her eyes. Surely she hadn't gone so far in this adventure for a strange dog! Lulu ran up to the dog and sniffed her happily.

'Your head is quite black, not brown and black!' said Lotta. 'And your tail is black too. Lucky's was white! And you've got four black spots on your back instead of one brown and one black!'

The little dog jumped up at Lotta, licked her and pawed her gladly. 'You do look so like Lucky, and you act just like Lucky!' said Lotta. 'I wonder, oh, I wonder if they've dyed your dear little head and the spots on your coat and your tail to make you different! Are you Lucky?'

'Woof!' said the little dog, and she got up on her hind legs and began to do some of the tricks that Jimmy and Lotta had taught her.

Then the little girl knew for certain that it was little

dog Lucky, altered so that no one should know her. She was to be trained for Mr Cyrano's circus, and he would make a lot of money! Perhaps he didn't know – perhaps Mr Binks had made Lucky different and sold her to Mr Cyrano simply as a very clever dog, easy to train. Lotta didn't care. All she knew was that she had got Lucky back – and she was going to take her to Jimmy as soon as ever she could!

'Yes – and we'll start this very minute!' said the little girl, excited. 'Come, Lucky! Come, Lulu!'

The three slipped out of the cage and set off for the gate. It was shut. Lotta climbed over it and the dogs squeezed under. Lotta did not know which way to go, but she was quite determined to put as much road between her and Mr Cyrano's circus as she could!

For hours the three of them tramped down dark roads till Lotta was almost dropping with sleep. She found an old haystack and pulled out some hay to make a bed. She lay down against the stack with the two dogs, and slept till the sun was high in the sky!

Now she had to find out where she was. She asked at a farmhouse and found that she was at a place she had never heard of. 'I want to go to Greenville,' said Lotta. 'Is there a train that goes there?'

The farmer looked at the queer, dirty, untidy little boy with two dogs. What a little gipsy he looked!

'You walk to the station and ask,' he said. 'I've never heard of Greenville!'

So off went Lotta again, asking the way to the station – and on the way a car passed her. Who do you suppose was driving it? Mr Alfred Cyrano, looking very angry indeed, for he had heard that the Boy Wonder had run off in the night with the valuable dog he had just bought!

And Mr Cyrano saw Lotta walking along the road with the two dogs! He stopped the car and ran back, shouting angrily. But was Lotta afraid of him? Not a bit.

'If you come any nearer my dogs will bite you!' said the

little girl. 'So be careful! Show your teeth, Lulu; show
yours, Lucky!'

Both dogs bared their teeth and snarled at Mr Cyrano.
Then, as quick as lightning, the little girl ran to the hedge
and squeezed through it, running across the fields like a
hare, the two dogs beside her. Mr Cyrano knew he would
never catch them.

Lotta reached the station at last. It was quite a big one
and the little girl bought sandwiches and milk for herself
and the two hungry dogs. Then she sat down to wait for
the train to come. She was very happy. What would
Jimmy say when she walked into the camp with Lucky?
He would forgive her, she was sure, for anything she had
done that he might blame her for.

Jimmy and Mrs Brown were very worried, for they
loved Lotta and were afraid something might happen to
her, going off alone with only Lulu for company. Poor
Jimmy was more worried than anyone, for he felt it was
his fault that Lotta had gone – and he kept thinking first
of his lost dog Lucky, then of Lotta, then of Lucky, and
he felt very lonely indeed without either of his best
friends.

Towards the evening of the second day that Lotta had
been gone, Jimmy looked out of his caravan. He saw a
queer little figure coming in at the circus gate.

'Look at that boy, Mother,' said Jimmy. 'I wonder who
he is – oh, Mother, Lulu's with him! Do you think he
knows anything about Lotta?'

'There's another dog too,' said his mother, as
Lucky came bounding through the gate, delighted to be
back in her own camp again. There was a shriek from
Jimmy.

'Mother! It's Lucky – my own Lucky!'

'No, it isn't,' said Mrs Brown. 'It's not a bit like Lucky!'

But Jimmy would have known Lucky if she had been
painted blue and yellow and red! No matter whether her
head was a different colour and her spots changed, he
would know his little dog a mile away! He leapt off the

caravan steps and tore to the gate, yelling 'Lucky! Lucky! Lucky!'

Lucky yelped back in excitement and ran to meet her little master. She sprang straight into his arms and lay there, licking his face as fast as she could. Jimmy hugged her and cried, and cried and hugged her, and everyone came running up to see what was happening.

Jimmy looked up at last, and saw the strange little boy nearby, watching with a delighted grin. Jimmy stared and stared – this boy was so like Lotta; did Lotta have a brother? – could it possibly *be* Lotta?

Then the little girl made one of her dreadful faces and gave Jimmy a pinch – ah, it was Lotta all right!

'Lotta!' shouted Jimmy, and hugged her as well as he could with Lucky still in his arms. 'Lotta! You darling! You've got Lucky back. But why is your hair short? Why are you dressed like that? Where have you been? Why . . .'

Lotta laughed joyfully. She took hold of Jimmy's arm.

'I've had such an adventure!' she said. 'But I'm so hungry. Let's go into the caravan and have supper, and I'll tell you everything!'

Mr Galliano came hurrying up at that moment. He lifted Lotta up on to his shoulder and patted little dog Lucky in delight.

'And here is Lotta come back as a boy!' he shouted, his hat very much on one side. 'And here is Lucky come back as another dog, yes! You will come and have supper with me in my caravan and tell me all your news, Lotta!'

This was a great honour. Mr Brown, Mrs Brown, Lotta, Jimmy, and the two dogs all crowded into Mr Galliano's big caravan to eat a fine supper that Mrs Galliano cooked. Mrs Brown wanted Lotta to wash her hands and face, but the little girl wouldn't.

'Not just this once, please,' she begged. 'I can't wait to tell you all my adventures, Mrs Brown!'

So over a delicious supper of fried sausages, potatoes in their skins, fruit salad and cream, Lotta told her story, whilst Lucky sat on Jimmy's knee, licking Jimmy's hand whenever he raised it to his mouth.

The little girl was almost asleep as she finished her tale. Brownie carried her back to their caravan, and Jimmy and the dogs and his mother went too.

Jimmy was very happy now. He had got back Lucky, and Mr Galliano had told him that he had only to give the little dog a special kind of bath to get him back to his right colour – and he had got Lotta back safely too.

'Lotta, are you asleep?' whispered Jimmy. 'I just want to say I'm sorry for the unkind things I said to you. They weren't true and I didn't mean them. You're the finest girl in the world!'

'It's all right, Jimmy,' said Lotta sleepily. 'I don't mind a bit now that everything's all right! See you tomorrow!'

And she fell fast asleep. But Jimmy lay awake a long, long time, planning how to reward Lotta for getting back his precious dog Lucky again. What would she like best in all the world?

15. Lotta gets a fine reward!

When Lotta awoke the next morning she was very happy. She lay in her bunk, warm and cosy, thinking of all the adventures she had had that week. She saw the golden sunshine coming in through the eastern caravan window, and she sat up.

'Jimmy!' she whispered. 'Wake up! It's very early, and it's a lovely day. Let's take Lucky and Lulu for a walk!'

Jimmy awoke. His first thought was for Lucky. He had got Lucky back again! He put out his hand and felt the little dog who was lying on his feet. But what a strange Lucky she seemed, with her altered colouring! Never mind – she should have a special bath that day and wash off all the dye that had been rubbed into her silky coat.

'Come on, Jimmy!' said Lotta. So the two of them quickly dressed and opened the caravan door very quietly. The dogs leapt down after them.

'Oh, Jimmy, I do feel happy now!' cried Lotta. 'Down, Lucky! Down, Lulu! They're happy too, Jimmy. Oh, I was so miserable when Fric was here, and I was so afraid you'd get hurt going in the tigers' cage alone.'

'Let's forget it all,' said Jimmy, racing in front. 'I loved the tigers, but when I think of Fric and how unkind he was to Jemima and to Lucky, I feel as if I hate him. My mother says it's best not to hate *any*one, because you poison your own mind if you do, so I'm going to forget all about it!'

'Good idea!' said Lotta, laughing. 'Oh, what a lovely morning, Jimmy! Look at the blue sky – and those high white clouds like cotton-wool – and look at the buttercups all over the place like a carpet of gold!'

'Lotta,' said Jimmy, suddenly standing still and taking hold of one of her hands, 'I want to give you a reward for saving Lucky, but I can't think what to give you. Tell me something. Is there anything you want?'

'Nothing,' said Lotta. 'At least, there's only one thing I want, and that is to have Lal and Laddo back again, so that I can ride a horse in the ring once more. I miss my father and mother, though yours are very sweet to me, Jimmy. But I do long for a horse of my own to ride again.'

'I'll buy you one!' cried Jimmy. 'I've heaps and heaps of money now! I was going to buy some more dogs and train them for the ring, but I'll buy you a horse instead!'

'Oh, Jimmy! Oh Jimmy!' cried Lotta, her cheeks flaming red and her eyes shining like blue forget-me-nots. 'You don't really mean it?'

'I do!' said Jimmy. 'I'll never, never forget how you ran off alone to find Lucky for me. I want to give you something for that, Lotta, though I know you don't want any reward.'

'Of course I don't want a reward,' said the little girl. 'But oh, Jimmy! A horse of my own! Where shall we get it? I'd like a little black one – a pony – that I can teach tricks to, and ride in the ring by myself! Oh, do you think Mr Galliano would let me?'

The two children were so excited about the idea that they walked for miles and came back to the camp very late for breakfast. Mrs Brown scolded them, but when she heard their new plan, she forgot about their lateness and lifted up her hands in astonishment.

'What *will* you think of next!' she cried. 'Well, Jimmy dear, your money is your own to do as you like with. You had better ask Pepita and Lou their advice. But you must hurry up, because we move from here in two days, and you won't have much holiday after that, for the next show is to be a very big one. The dancing bears are coming, you know, and they draw big crowds.'

'Hey! Is Jimmy there – yes?' called Mr Galliano's voice. 'Ah, there you are, Jimmy! Come with me and bring

Lucky. Mrs Galliano has got ready his special bath, and she is waiting, yes!'

Jimmy and Lotta ran to Mrs Galliano's caravan with Lucky. Lulu followed too. A big tin bath was steaming outside Mr Galliano's caravan. It was a most peculiar colour, for the water was pale mauve with little yellow blobs floating about in it. Mrs Galliano was stirring it.

Lilliput came up to watch, with Jemima as usual round his neck. Mr Wally came up with Sammy the chimpanzee, and Tonks the elephant-man came up too. It was fun to see Lucky being bathed and brought back to her right colour again!

Sammy put his arm round Jimmy and Lotta. He loved both children. He took off his own straw hat and put it on Jimmy's head. Then he reached out to take Mr Galliano's top hat to wear himself. But Mr Wally shouted to him:

'Now, Sammy, now! You mustn't take people's hats!' So Sammy took back his own hat and tried to look good.

Lucky was put into the mauve water. She didn't like it, but Mrs Galliano held her in firmly, whilst Jimmy rubbed gently. Gradually the water became black, as all the dye slid off the dog's coat. Lotta danced round in excitement.

'It's Lucky now! She looks like herself again, dear little dog! Good old Lucky!'

Lucky tried to wuff, but yelped instead, for she did hate the mauve bath. But very soon she was out of it and was being well dried, her little brown-and-black head shining in the sun. She was herself once more! Everybody cheered and clapped Lotta and Jimmy on the back. They were proud of the two children, and especially of Lotta that day, for they had all heard of her adventures.

Suddenly there was a splash. Lulu had jumped into the bath and was looking patiently up at Jimmy. 'My turn now,' her brown eyes said. She did so like to have a fuss made of her, even if she had to have a bath as well! Jimmy laughed and lifted her out.

'*Your* black won't come off, Lulu,' he said. 'Dry her, Lotta. Isn't she funny!'

Soon two excited, half-dried dogs were racing about

the camp in the sunshine. Jimmy pulled Lotta's arm. 'Let's come and talk to Pepita and Lou,' he said. 'They're over there, exercising their horses. Let's go and ask them if they know of any pony that would do for you, Lotta.'

They went over to Lou, who was just dismounting from his beautiful white horse, Starshine. Juanita and Pepita were cantering round the field, leading a horse each as they went.

'Hallo,' said the great big Lou, his kind face breaking into a smile. 'I am glad you have your little dog back. Lotta is a good girl – she has had a queer adventure! She dressed up as a boy and rode strange horses! She should have a horse of her own!'

'Oh, Lou, that's just what we've come to talk to you about!' said Jimmy eagerly. 'I've saved a heap of money, you know, because Lucky has earned a lot for me, and I want to buy Lotta a pony of her very own that she can train and ride!'

'So!' said Lou, nodding his big head. 'Ho there, Juanita, Pepita! Come and talk to Jimmy!'

The two young women leapt down from their black horses and came over to the children, their dark heads shining as brightly as their horses' backs. They were big and kindly, slow in their talk, and gentle with their horses.

'Jimmy wants to give Lotta a black pony to train,' said Lou. 'Has our brother such a one, little sisters?'

The two dark-eyed, dark-haired young women looked at one another and spoke quickly in a language that Jimmy could not understand. Lou nodded. He turned to the children.

'Our brother keeps horses,' he said. 'Tomorrow we go to see him. You shall go too, if you like, and see if he has a pony for Lotta.'

'We will all go,' said Pepita, in her soft, husky voice. 'Be ready at nine o'clock, children.'

Lotta rushed to tell Mrs Brown. She was so excited that she fell up the caravan steps and knocked over a tub standing just inside the caravan.

'Good gracious, Lotta, anyone would think you were an escaped bear, you are so clumsy!' said Mrs Brown with a laugh. 'Pick up the tub. What's the excitement now?'

'We're going tomorrow to buy me a pony, we're going tomorrow to buy me a pony!' yelled Lotta, catching Mrs Brown round the waist and dancing all over the caravan with her.

'Now, now, Lotta,' said Mrs Brown. 'I can't dance with a full teapot in my hand, it's dangerous!'

But Lotta was too excited to listen to anything or anyone. She longed and longed for nine o'clock next day to come!

And when at last it came, what a happy party set off to the farm up on the moors, where Lou's brother kept his beautiful horses! They rode on horseback, for most of the way was on grass and heather. Lou rode his beautiful white Starshine, a most magnificent horse with a tail that reached the ground. Pepita rode a smaller horse with a little proud head that tossed all the time. Juanita had her favourite, a gentle old horse, rather fat, but clever in all the ways of the circus.

The children had borrowed two of Mr Galliano's horses for the day. Lotta had a fiery one that got up on its hind legs every now and again, and made Jimmy very nervous indeed; for Jimmy was not a good horseman and never would be, though horses all loved him. He rode the safest horse in the camp, and, even so, he felt quite scared when it began to trot!

They came to the farm, and the keen moorland air blew around them, tossing the hair of Juanita and Pepita about. But poor Lotta had hair like a boy's still, though it curled tightly and would soon grow.

'Go and look at the horses whilst I see our brother,' said Lou, and he pointed to a sloping hillside where a great many horses galloped. Jimmy and Lotta rode to the hillside, and then Lotta gave a shout.

'There's the one I want!' she cried. 'Oh, Jimmy, look, there's the one I want!'

16. The taming of Black Beauty

Jimmy looked to see which horse Lotta was pointing to. He saw a pony, jet-black all over, save for four white socks and a shining white star right in the middle of his black forehead. His eyes shone wickedly, and as the children looked at him he kicked up his heels and galloped away like the wind!

'Oh!' said Lotta, her face shining like the sun. 'Oh! He's the loveliest pony I've ever seen. Oh, Jimmy, dear Jimmy, do buy him for me!'

So when Lou came galloping across the fields with his brother – an even bigger, just as kindly man – the two had already made their choice.

'That's the one we want!' and Jimmy, and he pointed to the black pony. 'Is he very expensive?'

'He is a very good pony, yes,' said Lou's brother, Philip. 'But he is not for you. He is wild, so wild! No one can ride him. Already two people have bought him and sent him back because they cannot manage such a wild creature.'

'I want him,' said Lotta obstinately. 'Let me have him, please do. I'm not afraid of any horse! I can ride any horse that's got four legs!'

'Ah, but this one might have a hundred legs, he is so wild!' said Philip, smiling at the little girl. 'He bites, he kicks, he gallops like the wind. He has a wicked eye.'

'Yes, I saw that,' said Lotta. 'But he's the kind I like. Please let me have him.'

'It is impossible,' said Philip. 'Now you look at all my horses, little Miss Lotta, and you choose another. I go to speak to my sisters, for I do not see them often.'

The two big men galloped back to the farmhouse.

Lotta looked sulky and her eyes gleamed as wickedly as the black pony's.

'Come, Lotta, let's choose another,' said Jimmy. 'What about that brown-and-white pony over there?'

'I want that black one,' said Lotta. 'And I'm going to get him. Jimmy, make your horse-noises.'

Jimmy laughed. He could make all kinds of animal noises, and could bring dogs to him by whining, cats to him by mewing, and other animals by making strange noises that no one, not even Lotta, could make. He began making a queer noise, half like a horse's whinny and half like a gramophone running down.

The horses nearby pricked up their ears. One or two cantered close. Jimmy went on. More horses came up and nuzzled his hand. Horses always adored Jimmy.

'Go on, Jimmy, go on,' whispered Lotta. 'The black pony has heard. He's coming nearer!'

So Jimmy went on making his strange noises, and gradually the horses began to talk back to him, whinnying and nuzzling round him. The black pony came close too, its ears upright, its wicked eyes watching and gleaming.

Then Lotta did a daring thing. She suddenly leapt straight from her own horse's back on to the pony's! She caught hold of its mane. In fright and anger it reared up and stood on its hind legs. But Lotta clung to its back like a limpet to a rock.

The black pony came down on all four legs, and then streaked off like the wind, galloping round the enormous field, faster than a car! Lotta bent forward and held tight. Her knees gripped the pony's back and her hands were tangled in its thick mane. Round and round the field went the pony, snorting with fear and anger.

At last, tired out, it stood still again, and Lotta began to talk to it. She had a way with horses just as Jimmy had a way with dogs. But this pony was not easy to calm or tame. In a trice it was up on its hind legs again, trying to throw Lotta off. Then it took it into its head to lie down

and roll over, knowing that this was a sure way to make
any rider get off.

But Lotta was waiting for this. She slipped off at once,
and then, as the horse got up after rolling, the little girl
leapt straight on to his back again, and off they went
round the field like lightning!

Jimmy watched, open-mouthed. He had never seen
such a thing before. He knew that both the pony and the
little girl were trying to conquer one another. But how in
the world could Lotta stay on like that with nothing to
help her? She was a marvel! Only a girl brought up in the
circus from babyhood could do such a thing.

Others were watching too. Lou, Philip, Pepita, and
Juanita had come out to see. They said not a word, but
watched gravely. Jimmy's heart beat very fast. He hoped
nothing would happen to daring little Lotta. She looked
like a boy on the pony, with her short hair.

At last the pony stopped. It could go no farther, could
gallop no more. Foam dripped from its mouth. Its beautiful head hung down. Its legs trembled, and its eyes were
dull. It was conquered.

Lotta slipped down from its back. She put her arm
round its neck and stroked its soft nose. She spoke lovingly into its ear, and the tired pony listened. Jimmy
came up quietly. He spoke to the pony in his low, gentle
voice, and the pony nuzzled against him.

Then Philip cantered up and called to the children,
'Take the pony to the stables and rub him down.'

'Can I have him, oh, can I have him?' called Lotta.

'You have made him yours!' answered Philip. 'We have
never seen such riding, no – not in all our years in the
circus. One day you will be a wonder, little girl!'

Lotta was red with excitement and delight. She led the
pony away to the stables and she and Jimmy rubbed the
trembling little beast down.

'I was frightened for you, Lotta,' said Jimmy.

'Well, it's tit for tat then!' said Lotta, laughing. 'I was
just as frightened when you were with the tigers! Oh,

Jimmy! I'm so happy. This is just the pony I've always wanted – wild, strong, beautiful, clever! Look at his eyes! You can see he'll learn anything I want to teach him!'

Jimmy knew that the pony would be clever. He, too, liked the wilful, independent little thing, and he thought secretly that the pony was rather like Lotta herself, wild and daring and clever! He was very glad that the little girl had the one she wanted.

'I shall ride him home,' said Lotta. 'He will be fresh again by the time we've had our dinner. What shall we call him?'

Jimmy looked at the pony with its sleek black coat, four funny white feet, and the white star gleaming on its forehead. 'I once read a book called *Black Beauty*,' he said. 'Couldn't we call your pony that? He's black and he's a real beauty!'

'Oh yes!' cried Lotta. And so Black Beauty was named and became Lotta's, and the little girl could hardly bear to leave him in his stable and go to her dinner.

They all rode home afterwards, talking and laughing. Lou led the horse that Lotta had ridden, and Lotta herself rode on Black Beauty, who now had saddle and bridle and was as meek as before he had been fierce.

The little girl was very proud. This was the first horse she had ever had that was really and truly her own. She meant to train him herself, and her head was full of all kinds of things that she would teach her lovely Black Beauty. She was so happy that she sang aloud, and Jimmy was glad. He thought she looked fine riding the little pony, her hair as black as the pony's shining coat!

They rode into the camp and everyone turned out to see Black Beauty. Mr Galliano praised the pony loudly.

'You have chosen well, Lotta,' he said. 'It is a good beast, yes.'

'This girl is a wonder with horses,' said Lou. 'She should be in the ring, Mr Galliano.'

'Well, her mother and father thought it would be better for her not to go into the ring whilst they were abroad,' said Mrs Brown. 'They thought she might do something too daring if they were not there with her.'

'Oh!' cried Lotta, 'so that's why I wasn't allowed to go into the ring! Oh, it's a shame! Oh, Mr Galliano, please say I may, if I train Black Beauty properly! I will, I will, I will!'

Mr Galliano laughed. 'We will see, yes, we will see,' he said. 'It will not be long now before your parents are back, my little Lotta. Train your pony well, and maybe one day we will see you in the ring!'

Jimmy brought Lucky to make friends with Black Beauty. The little dog liked the pony at once, and Black Beauty dropped his head to sniff at the small creature that stood on its hind legs to reach his nose!

'They're friends already!' cried Jimmy, in delight. 'Oh, Lotta, what an exciting time we're having lately!'

'Yes,' said Lotta, trotting her pony over to the stables to ask Lou where she might put Black Beauty. 'Yes, we *are* having adventures lately, but Black Beauty is the nicest adventure of all! My own horse, my very, very own! I am the luckiest girl in the world – and you are a dear, Jimmy, to buy him for me. I hope he didn't cost too much money.'

'No,' said Jimmy, though the pony had cost him nearly every bit of the money he had saved. But what did that matter? Lucky and he would earn plenty more, and Lotta was happy. Black Beauty would be just as much of a success as Lucky had been – and oh, what fun if they could teach Lucky to do some tricks with Black Beauty!

'We break camp tomorrow!' said Mrs Brown that night to two tired children. 'Up early, both of you!'

'Oooh! Bears at our next camp!' said Jimmy. 'Shan't I like that! Bears, Lotta! Bears, Lucky! What fun we'll have!'

17. The bears join the circus

Next day the circus was on the move again. Once more the tents were taken down and Brownie was very busy. Soon the circus procession was on the road – cages, caravans, long strings of horses, and old Jumbo patiently pulling the three largest cages behind him.

Lotta was not in the caravan this time. Where was she? She was riding her new pony, Black Beauty, who was now perfectly obedient! How proud Lotta was as she rode on her beautiful pony! For once in a way she had brushed her short hair till it shone, and had put on her prettiest frock, for she felt that a lovely thing like Black Beauty deserved a fine rider!

Little dog Lucky was running about on her hind legs, but you may be sure that Jimmy was keeping a sharp eye on her. Since she had been stolen the little boy had hardly let her out of his sight. Lucky was already fond of Black Beauty, and for most of the journey the little dog ran on all fours by Beauty's heels, or walked on her hind legs by her nose. Sometimes the pony put down his proud little head and lightly touched the clever dog. Then Lucky gave a little yelp and tried to lick Black Beauty's nose!

'Hhrrrrrmph!' suddenly sneezed the elephant. Black Beauty was so startled that she stood straight up on her hind legs like Lucky! Lotta nearly fell off, and Jimmy shouted with laughter.

'You wait till I get you, Jimmy!' cried Lotta.

'It did look funny, Black Beauty and Lucky both up on their hind legs!' said Jimmy. 'I half thought old Jumbo would stand up too!'

They came to their next show-place at last. There was

still a day before the circus opened. Mr Galliano was expecting the bears that day, for he wanted to see them
perform in the ring before the show opened.

A large travelling-cage was already in the great field

when Mr Galliano's people arrived. Jimmy looked at it and gave a shout.

'The bears! It must be the bears! Come and see, Lotta.'

'I must see to Black Beauty first,' said Lotta, and she slipped down from the pony's smooth back. She put her arms around his neck and the pony nuzzled against her. Then the little girl led him off to have a feed and a good rub-down. She was simply delighted with her pony. She longed to teach him how to dance, and how to gallop round and round the ring whilst she did tricks on his back.

The bears were in their cage. There were five of them, three not much more than year-old cubs. They were dark brown, fat, and clumsy. Jimmy went to the bars of their cage and spoke to them.

The bears took no notice, but as the little boy went on talking, one of the cubs walked over to him with shambling feet.

'Hi there! Come away!' shouted a voice suddenly.

Jimmy turned and saw a fat man running towards him. 'Do you want to get clawed?' shouted the man.

'It's all right, Mr Volla!' said Tonks, who was nearby. 'That's Jimmy, our Boy Wonder! He went into the tigers' cage at our last show, and all they did was to purr at him like cats. Those bears will be eating out of his hand in five minutes!'

'Ah,' said Mr Volla, who had moustaches like Mr Galliano, 'so that's Jimmy. I've heard of him. He's got a marvellous dog, hasn't he?

'Yes, I have,' said Jimmy proudly. 'There she is, look!'

Lucky trotted up to Mr Volla, and then did the new trick that Jimmy had been teaching her – turning head-over-heels as fast as ever she could – over – and over – and over! Mr Volla laughed.

'I've never seen a dog do that before!' he said. 'But my bears can do it, though not so neatly as Lucky. Hup, bears, hup! Over you go!'

Mr Volla cracked a small whip he had, and all the

bears got up on their hind legs. One by one they turned head-over-heels, but they did it so comically that Jimmy laughed till he cried.

'They do it just like Stanley the clown when he wants to be very funny,' said Jimmy.

'Ah,' said Mr Volla, 'bears are the clowns of the animal world, you know. They are clumsy, and they know they're funny. They love it. You must come and watch them in the ring this afternoon when they perform for Mr Galliano. Two of them put on boxing-gloves and pretend to fight. They'll make you laugh all right!'

So that afternoon Jimmy went to watch the bears. They were real clowns, there was no doubt about it – and how they loved to fool about and be funny! They each had a stool to sit on, and one bear made it his business to wait behind one or other of the bears and take away his stool just as she was going to sit down! Of course the other bear fell flop!

'That cub, Dobby, thought of the trick himself,' said Mr Volla proudly. 'You don't have to teach him anything! He may look clumsy and slow, but his brain's as good as any clown's!'

The bears all knew their own stools. They could dance slowly and clumsily on their big hind feet, and Dobby and another bear, Susie, took paws and did a sort of clumsy polka together, which sent everyone into fits of laughter.

Then another two bears, Grizel and Tubby, had boxing-gloves put on their enormous paws, and they boxed with one another, getting some smacking blows on their noses and chests. Suddenly Grizel gave Tubby such a loud smack that Tubby sat down with a grunt and wouldn't get up again! Then all the other bears grunted loudly and clapped their paws together so that their great claws clattered.

Then Mr Volla cracked his whip again, and Dobby went to fetch a big football. Dear me, how funny those bears were with that football! They kicked it, they dribbled it, they fell over it, they hugged it! And then,

when Mr Volla cracked his whip once again, they all
solemnly took paws and danced round to the music of
'Ring-a-ring-of-roses', and when it came to the words,
'*All* fall down!' down fell every bear, plop!

Everybody clapped hard. The bears got up and bowed,
waving their big, flappy paws and winking their small
eyes. They were a great joke.

Jimmy was thrilled. Here were animals that really
liked being funny. He loved them. So did Lucky. The
little dog sitting beside Jimmy had watched the bears all
the time.

'Oh, Mr Galliano, the bears are much better than the
tigers!' cried Jimmy. 'Tigers hate doing tricks, and it's a
shame to make them. But bears just love being clowns.
Look at Dobby pretending to do a dance all by himself!'

So he was. Mr Volla had taken the other bears off, but
Dobby had turned back and come to do a little show all
by himself in the ring. His eyes twinkled. He loved showing off.

Mr Volla's whip cracked from outside the ring. Dobby
dropped down on all fours and shambled off, grunting.
Everybody clapped again.

'They are good, yes,' said Mr Galliano. 'You are right,
Jimmy. It is better to have animals that love their work.
The bears will be a great success, yes!'

And they certainly were! When the circus opened the
next night, the audience stood up in their seats and
cheered each turn. Sammy the chimpanzee; Jumbo playing cricket; Lilliput's clever monkeys; Oona the acrobat's
amazing tricks; Sticky Stanley the clown's comical ways;
Jimmy and his dog Lucky; Lou, Pepita, and Juanita and
their beautiful dancing horses – they were all cheered and
cheered again, but the bears got the biggest cheers of all!

Mr Galliano stood in the ring, dressed in his
tight-fitting red coat, his top hat well on one side, and his
moustaches very long and curling, as pleased as could be.
His whip cracked for every new turn, and only one person
in his circus was just a little bit impatient.

That was Lotta. How she longed to go into the ring with her lovely Black Beauty! If only she could hurry up and teach him to dance and to do all the things a circus pony had to learn! Then Lotta could go into the ring too!

Mr Galliano caught sight of Lotta as he strode out of the ring, and saw her longing eyes fixed on the sawdust circle.

'Cheer up!' he said. 'We shall do well here! It will be fine for everybody, yes!'

'Mr Galliano, can I go into the ring too, if I teach Black Beauty?' begged Lotta. 'You did say I could, didn't you?'

'Yes, you may,' said Mr Galliano. 'But we cannot make a new turn for you, Lotta. You will have to ask Lou if you may share a little of his turn.

Lotta was not pleased with this. She knew quite well that circus folk hate sharing their turn with anyone. Lou and his sisters liked her, but even so she did not think they would let her come in with them. They wanted all the cheers and clapping for themselves and their own horses!

Lotta told Jimmy. He nodded his head. 'Yes,' he said, 'Lou and the others are kind enough, but after all it isn't fair to ask them to let you have some of their own turn, Lotta.'

'Well, what can I do, then?' asked the little girl, almost in tears. 'What's the use of having a fine pony like Black Beauty and teaching him tricks if I can't take him into the ring?'

Jimmy thought for a while, and then he jumped up with a shout. 'I know what we'll do!' he said. 'We will teach Lucky to ride Black Beauty, and then you shall bring your pony into the ring when it's *my* turn! I don't mind sharing my turn with you, Lotta – and perhaps you could begin like that. It would be better than nothing.'

Lotta hugged Jimmy for joy. 'You are the kindest boy!' she cried. 'Oh, Jimmy, let's begin teaching Lucky tomorrow! I'm already teaching Black Beauty his tricks, and he learns like lightning!'

18. Lotta gets her chance!

The two children began teaching Lucky to ride Black
Beauty the very next day. Lucky was always eager to
learn new tricks, for she was a very clever dog and loved
to use her brains.

She knew how to balance herself on the tight-rope, so
she found it easy enough to sit on the pony's broad back,
but when Black Beauty began to trot, Lucky found it was
not so easy!

She slipped and fell to the ground, but she did not hurt
herself of course. Before Jimmy could stop Black Beauty
and put Lucky on his back again, the little dog gave a
leap and jumped up herself!

'Look at that!' said Jimmy. 'Would you believe it,
Lotta? She leapt on that trotting pony just as easily as
you do! She's holding her balance better this time, look!
She doesn't need teaching! She knows what we want her
to do and she's doing her best to learn!'

Black Beauty went cantering round and round the ring.
for Lotta had already taught her to do this at the right
pace. Lucky fell off again, and once more jumped up. She
found that by sitting on her tail she could keep her balance quite well. Before the morning had ended the little
dog could ride the pony as well as Lotta could.

'Marvellous!' said Lotta, patting the happy little dog.
'Do you know, Jimmy, I believe we could teach Lucky to
jump through a paper hoop just as I do! Once she has
really got her balance on horseback she can do that, I'm
sure.'

The two children taught Lucky and Black Beauty
together every morning, working patiently. They never

worked the animals too long, for Jimmy had long since learnt that little and often was the best way to teach, and he and Lotta always praised their animals and rewarded them.

'You know, Lotta, animals are just like people,' said Jimmy, as he was brushing Lucky one morning, and Lotta was grooming Black Beauty. 'People with brains love to learn anything and they're always trying new things. Stupid people don't want to learn and can't. Animals are the same. The clever ones long to learn, but it's no use teaching the stupid ones anything. I'm glad I was born with brains, aren't you? It must be dull to be stupid.'

'Yes,' said Lotta. 'But it must be worse to be born clever and be too lazy to use your brains. I've known some people like that, Jimmy – and some animals too.'

'Well, stupid or not, I love all animals,' said Jimmy. 'But it's more fun to be with the clever ones! Isn't is, little dog Lucky?'

Lucky licked her master's hand and yelped. She thought Jimmy was the king of the world, and she was happiest when she was trying to do what Jimmy wanted her to.

Lotta and Jimmy had a fine time with the pony and Lucky. The dog and the pony enjoyed being with one another, and worked together beautifully. Soon Lucky learnt how to leap from Black Beauty's back through a paper hoop held by Jimmy, and back on to the pony's back again! The first time she did this, Jimmy and Lotta shouted for joy. They were sure that when Mr Galliano saw the trick he would let Lotta bring her pony into the ring at last.

Lotta worked hard with Black Beauty too, teaching him to waltz as the other horses did. The little girl brought the gramophone from the caravan and Jimmy wound it up and put the records on for Black Beauty to waltz to.

Black Beauty, unlike most of the dancing horses, had a perfect sense of time. He danced slowly if the record played slowly, and quickly if it played quickly. He was very nimble on his feet, and loved the music.

He let Lotta do anything she liked with him. She had been the first to conquer him and he loved the little girl with his wild little heart, though he would not let anyone else touch him except Mr Galliano and Jimmy.

Lotta rode him at full-speed, and then, at a shout, he would stop dead! The little girl would be thrown right over his head, but she knew how to fall and, like a cat, always landed on her feet! Black Beauty would then gallop full-speed round the ring again, and Lotta would wait till he came by and leap up safely on his back.

She could ride him kneeling on one or both knees. She could ride him standing forwards or backwards. She could jump through a paper hoop held by Jimmy, and she could do something else very difficult too. This was a trick her father could do.

The trick was to lower herself under the pony's body and come up the other side safely, to sit on his back, whilst he was cantering round the ring! It was a dangerous trick, for if she slipped and fell, the pony's hoofs might cut her – but Lotta was not even afraid of that! She felt sure that Black Beauty would be clever enough not to tread on her.

She never did fall, because she was very nimble, and soon learnt to swing herself under Black Beauty's middle and up the other side. Lucky ran alongside, yelping excitedly, and sometimes Lotta would lean right down and pick Lucky up. Then they would stand up on the pony together, Lotta yelling and Lucky barking like mad.

The children always chose the early morning for their practice, because they did not want anyone else to guess what they were doing. And also, others needed the ring for practising in later on in the day. Circus folk do not need just to know their tricks – they must practise always, all the time.

At last Jimmy felt that little dog Lucky had learnt his

horseback tricks perfectly, so he went to speak to Mr Galliano.

'Lucky can ride on Black Beauty, sir, and jump through the hoops,' said the little boy. 'If you would come and watch one morning, perhaps you'd like the new turn and say we could do it one night.'

So Mr Galliano came to watch, and his eyes nearly fell out of his head when he saw Lucky's new tricks.

'That dog is human, yes!' he said. 'You will teach him to dress as a ring-master, wear a top hat, and crack a whip next! Yes! Bring Black Beauty into the ring tonight, and Lucky shall do his new trick.'

'May Lotta bring her pony into the ring, please, Mr Galliano?' said Jimmy. 'She has helped me to teach Lucky, you know, and it's her pony.'

'Very well, she may do that,' said Mr Galliano. 'Tell her to wear her circus frock.'

Jimmy flew off to tell Lotta the good news. She was to go into the ring again! Oh, what fun!

'And, Lotta, you must ride round the ring once or twice yourself, and stand up on Black Beauty, just to get a few claps!' said Jimmy. 'Maybe if the people like you, Mr Galliano will let you do more another night. Get your circus frock out and we'll see if it's clean.'

It was clean – but alas it no longer fitted Lotta, who had grown very much the last few months. The little girl was ready to cry. She knew she could not go into the ring unless she had a proper frock.

'Now, don't be a baby!' said Mrs Brown, putting on her hat and taking up her basket. 'Come along into the town with me, and we'll buy what we need for you. I can run it up with my sewing machine in no time and make you look a real little fairy!'

'Oh, Mrs Brown, you're a darling!' cried Lotta, and she put on her shoes and rushed after Mrs Brown.

Well, what a busy time Lotta, Mrs Galliano and Mrs Brown had that day, making a new frock for Lotta. They had bought gauzy stuff set with shining silver spangles, and they made the little girl a fluffy dress of this, that stood out in a short skirt like a fairy's frock. The little bodice had silver spangles on too.

Her old silver crown and wand she could use again, but new silvery stockings had to be bought. Her long silver wings were mended and repainted with silver paint – and then everything was ready, down to the silver shoes that had been bought with the stockings. They had no heels and were well-rubbed with resin so that Lotta would not slip when standing on her pony.

And now it was nearly time for the show to begin! People were already crowding in at the gate, for Mr Galliano's circus was famous. The lights were flaring in the 'big top' as the circus folk called their show tent, and Lotta was almost beside herself with excitement.

At last it was Jimmy's turn with Lucky. What a shout went up as the little boy ran into the ring, bowing to everyone, with Lucky at his heels. Jimmy looked fine in his glittering suit with its short red cloak – like a little prince, Lotta thought.

Lucky went all through her marvellous tricks, and when at last Jimmy cried, 'Spell me the name of the man who has the finest circus!' and Lucky fetched out eight letters from the pile and arranged them to spell 'Galliano', the people clapped till their hands hurt them!

This was usually Lucky's last trick – but tonight there was more to come. Lotta suddenly rode in on Black Beauty! The people stared in astonishment. Many of them had been to Galliano's circus before and they had not seen this trick.

The little girl looked lovely in her silver fairy-frock. She jumped off Black Beauty and led her to Jimmy.

'Up then, up!' cried Jimmy to Lucky, and up the little dog jumped! Off went the pony, and Lucky rode on his back in delight. Down he came when Jimmy called, and then up again whilst the pony was galloping. Everybody cheered. **The dog was even cleverer than they had thought!**

Lotta held out a paper hoop. Lucky jumped through it and landed back safely on Black Beauty. Again she jumped through another hoop. She had been so perfectly trained that she knew exactly what to do.

That was enough for the first night. Mr Galliano came into the ring to crack his whip and end the turn. Jimmy and Lucky bowed and ran out. Lotta was about to follow on Black Beauty, when somebody got up and shouted:

'Let's see the little girl have a turn! Up you go, Missie, and let's see what you can do!'

Everybody shouted and clapped. They wanted to see Lotta, too, do something, for they felt sure she could. Lotta did not dare to ride round, for she had heard Mr Galliano's whip crack and knew she must go. Mr Galliano stood wondering what to do. It was Oona's turn next. Should he give Lotta a chance, though?

'Go on, Missie,' yelled the people. Mr Galliano turned and nodded to Lotta, who was trembling with excitement.

'Get up and do what you can,' he said. And Lotta jumped on to Black Beauty's back. At last she had got her chance – at last, at last, at last!

19. Good luck for the children

Lotta knew that Black Beauty felt her excitement too. The pony was longing to show what he could do. He was a real circus animal, and loved the smell of the sawdust and the flaring lights.

Mr Galliano cracked his whip again. Lotta made a sign for music. The band struck up a merry tune, and Black Beauty pricked up his ears. Like most horses, he loved music and would not have minded practising all day long if only he had had tunes played to him!

'Round you go!' said Lotta in his ear, and the pony began to dance round and round, his hoofs keeping perfect time to the music.

The bandsmen were astonished. They were used to making the time of their music follow the dancing of the horses, but this pony followed the time of their music as if he could hear the beats properly!

So the band played in perfect time, and Black Beauty danced round and round, lifting his hoofs daintily and tossing his lovely head with its white star. The watching people thought him beautiful, but only the circus folk knew how clever it was for a horse to keep such good time with the music.

The music stopped. The drummer rolled loudly on his drum – the signal for Lotta to gallop him round and round and begin any trick she knew.

She called to Black Beauty, and he at once galloped at top speed round the ring, his hoofs making a muffled clatter on the sawdust. Lotta gave a yell, and Black Beauty stopped at once, as he had been taught. Lotta flew over his head, turned a half-somersault, and landed neatly on her feet.

But everyone had thought that she was going to be thrown and hurt, and they shouted. Even Mr Galliano was startled, but when he saw the neat way in which Lotta landed on her feet like a falling cat, he knew it was a clever trick.

The pony went galloping round the ring by himself. Lotta waited till he came round again and then deftly leapt up on to his back once more. At her next yell the pony stopped again, and once more Lotta went hurtling over his head, to fall on her feet. This time the people knew what she was doing, and they clapped loudly.

Lotta jumped back on to Black Beauty. She was enjoying herself, and so was the pony. How glad the little girl was that she had practised so hard each morning!

She knelt up on the pony's back. She stood up, a graceful little figure, bumping up and down with the pony, her
long silver wings outspread, and her silvery dress glittering like moonlight. Jimmy thought she looked lovely —
and what a clever, daring little girl she was!

Lotta stood on one foot and waved the other in the air!
Then she lightly leapt round and faced the back of the
horse. She stood on one foot again and waved to the
people, whilst all the time Black Beauty galloped solemnly round the ring.

Mr Galliano was astonished to find how well Lotta had
trained her pony in such a short time. But he was even
more astonished at Lotta's next trick of slipping right
underneath Black Beauty and coming up the other side of
him!

'Too dangerous, yes, too dangerous!' muttered Mr Galliano to himself. There wasn't a sound as the little girl did
this daring trick; but goodness, how everyone clapped
and cheered when they saw Lotta sitting safely up on the
pony once more, waving cheekily to them!

Lucky suddenly came bounding into the ring. He
wanted to do a trick with Lotta too! The little girl, who
was about to bow and gallop off, gave a shout.

She galloped near Lucky, swung right down from the
pony, and picked up the little dog! She set him on the seat
in front of her. Then she stood up again on the galloping
pony and shouted to Lucky. 'Up then, up!'

And Lucky stood up too! So there they were, the two of
them, standing cleverly on the pony as it raced round the
ring! Jimmy ran into the ring to watch.

Mr Galliano's whip cracked. Lotta must gallop out. So
out she went through the thick red curtains, waving her
hand and smiling, the prettiest little figure that anyone
could wish to see!

The people stood up and cheered her. They had not
expected to see this. She had been one of the successes of
the evening, one of the best things in a very good show.

The little girl was almost crying with joy when she

leapt off Black Beauty. She could hear the people still clapping and cheering, and she knew she had been a success.

'Oh, Jimmy, Black Beauty was wonderful tonight!' she cried. 'He did everything perfectly. He's the finest pony I have ever known.'

'And you are the best little circus rider I have ever seen!' cried Mr Wally, as he passed with Sammy the chimpanzee. 'A splendid show, Lotta! You must have practised very hard indeed.'

'She did,' said Jimmy proudly. 'She practises every single morning.'

Then up came Lou, Pepita, and Juanita, full of admiration and praise for Lotta and Black Beauty. They were not at all jealous of the little girl's success, for they were kindly folk, and Lotta had been a great help to them in looking after their string of beautiful white horses.

After the show was over, Mr Galliano sent for Jimmy and Lotta, but this time they went gladly, for they knew they had not been fetched to be scolded.

'You are not afraid to come and see me this time – no?' said Mr Galliano, smiling his big smile at them both, his top hat almost over one ear. 'You are good, hard-working children, yes! You, Lotta, may go into the ring with Jimmy each night, and work up a turn together. It is better that you two children should be together in the show. You shall be the two Wonder Children, yes!'

'Thank you, Mr Galliano!' they said, both together, their hearts full of joy. To do a turn together! This was even better than they had hoped. What fun they would have with Lucky and Beauty in the ring! What tricks they would teach that lively, clever pair!

Already Jimmy was seeing Lucky dressed like Mr Galliano, in riding breeches, red coat, top hat, and whip, riding on Black Beauty! And Lotta, too, was making pictures in her mind of all the things the four would do together!

'Won't Lal and Laddo be pleased when they come

back and find I'm in the ring too!' cried Lotta, when she got back to the Browns' caravan and told Jimmy's father and mother all about everything.

'I hope they will,' said Mrs Brown, ladling out hot soup, which the children always had after the show at night. 'You know, they said they didn't much want Lotta to go into the ring whilst they were away, as they thought the rest would do her good, and she could learn her lessons better and be taught how to be neat and clean.'

'Oh, Mrs Brown! I *have* learnt my lessons well, and I really have tried to be neat and clean!' cried Lotta. 'I know how to read and write now, and I can do quite hard sums! And now my hair is short, I'm sure I look as tidy as Jimmy!'

Mrs Brown looked at Lotta's head with its close curling mop of hair and laughed. 'You've been a very good little girl,' she said, 'and you deserve all this. Now the next thing to look forward to is your father and mother coming home. They will soon be back in the circus.'

'It will be lovely to have them again,' said Lotta. 'But oh, I shall miss living here in your nice caravan with you and Brownie and Jimmy and Lucky and Lulu, Mrs Brown.'

'Well, you must just see that you keep your own caravan pretty and nice,' said Mrs Brown. 'And you know that you can come here to us whenever you like – your little bed will always be ready for you.'

Lotta got up and gave Mrs Brown a hug. She felt so happy that night that she could have hugged anyone, even the bears!

The two children got into their bunks at last, but they couldn't go to sleep. They talked and talked about the happenings of the show that night till Mrs Brown could bear it no longer. She was tired herself and wanted to go to sleep.

'Another word from either of you and I shall get out and give you each a good spanking!' she said. And so afraid of Mrs Brown's hard hand were the two Wonder Children that not another sound was heard from either of them!

20. Things go wrong

And now, each night, Lotta and Jimmy went into the ring together, with little dog Lucky and Black Beauty the pony. The people loved to see the beautiful pony, with his four white feet and his brilliant white star on his forehead. They loved Lucky too, and Mr Galliano was pleased to see what a great success the two children were, with their well-trained animals.

The circus stayed for some time and then, as it always did, packed up and went on the road once more. It was full summer now, and the countryside was beautiful. Poppies nodded along the wayside, and Lotta picked a bunch, weaved them into a garland, and hung it round Beauty's black shining neck.

When the circus procession went through the towns now, Lotta, dressed in her shining circus frock, rode proudly on Black Beauty, and waved to the astonished children that lined the roadside to watch her pass. Sometimes Lucky rode with her, and he too waved a cheeky paw, much to everyone's delight.

And once even Jemima came to ride with Lotta and Lucky, and such a crowd came to see that a policeman had to come and push the people away so that the procession could go on! Really, it was all great fun, and the children enjoyed themselves tremendously.

One day Lotta had a letter from her mother. She could not read handwriting very well, although she could now read books, so she gave it to Jimmy to read to her.

'DEAR LOTTA' (said the letter), 'we hope to meet you at the next show place. We have written to Mr

Galliano. I hope you have been a good girl. We have not
had any letters from you for some time, so we do not
know how you are getting on. You will soon have to start
practising again, so that you may join us in the ring. We
have some fine new horses. – Love from

LAL.'

Lotta was pleased with her mother's letter. 'Oh,
Jimmy!' she said, dancing about and making Lucky
dance about too. 'Oh, Jimmy! My mother doesn't know
that I go into the ring every night! Won't she be surprised! Oh, isn't it lovely, I shall see Lal and Laddo at our
next show place!'

The children looked out for Lal and Laddo at the next
show place, but they had not yet arrived in the camp.
Lotta was longing to show her mother and father her
lovely Black Beauty. The camp settled in as usual, and
once more the 'big top' went up, and the caravans and
cages took up their places in the field.

The next day two great travelling horse-boxes drew up
outside the field and began to try to get in through the
wide gate. On the sides of the vans were painted in large
red letters, 'Lal and Laddo's Wonder Horses'. Lotta gave
such a scream of delight that Mrs Brown dropped the
spoon into the stew she was stirring.

'It's Lal and Laddo!' she shouted. 'Oh, it's my father
and mother back again!'

She flew like the wind to the field-gate and looked
anxiously for Lal and Laddo. She saw Laddo at once, and
rushed to him. She leapt into his strong arms, and he
hugged and kissed his little daughter, delighted to see her
looking so well and happy.

'My, how you've grown!' he said. 'We've missed you,
Lotta.

'Where's my mother – where's Lal?' cried Lotta.

Laddo's face grew sad. 'She's ill,' he said. 'She was
taken ill yesterday on the way here, and I have had to
leave her in hospital. But she will be better in a month or

two, Lotta, so don't worry. She had a fall when we were away, and hurt her back. She would not rest it properly, and now it is very bad again, and the doctor says she must stay in bed for five or six weeks.'

Lotta's face crumpled up and she began to cry. She had so much looked forward to her mother coming back again.

'We'll go and see her tomorrow,' promised Laddo. 'Don't fret, Lotta.'

The little girl blinked back her tears. She was dreadfully disappointed. She had looked forward so much to showing her mother her lovely new pony, and to seeing her face when she saw Lotta in the ring. And now she wouldn't be able to show her Black Beauty for ages and ages!

'Why can't Lal come to the camp and rest in our own caravan instead of in a faraway hospital?' she asked. 'I can look after her! I can do everything nicely now. Mrs Brown has taught me.'

'Well, Lotta,' said Laddo, 'I'm afraid I won't be able to join this circus now Lal is away. I must work with a partner, you know, and the only one I can get in Lal's place is Madame Fifinella and she belongs to another circus. I'm afraid I will have to go there. I just came here to see you and to tell you the news. I must see Mr Galliano too. Perhaps he can keep on Lou and his sisters.'

Lotta walked into the field with Laddo. The little girl was too horrified even to cry. Everything was going wrong – just when things had seemed so lovely too!

She hadn't got her mother, and wouldn't have her for weeks. Now even her father, Laddo, was going away to another circus. Would she have to go with him? Another circus would not allow her to have a turn all to herself. And how could she possibly bear to leave Jimmy and Lucky?

But she knew her father would want her, for he loved her and would not wish to leave her behind, now that he had come home again. She left him to go and see Mr

Galliano, and then she ran behind the Browns' caravan, sat on an upturned pail, and let the tears run down her cheeks.

Lulu the spaniel came up and licked the tears as they fell. Lotta suddenly felt as if she wanted Black Beauty to comfort her and not Lulu. She ran to the stable where he stood, and he turned his lovely head towards his little mistress. At once he knew she was unhappy and he put his long nose on to her shoulder, whinnying gently.

Jimmy found them there when he went into the stable and he stood still in astonishment. 'Lotta! Whatever's the matter?'

Lotta told him everything, between her tears, and the little boy looked more dismayed than Lotta had ever seen him. Lose Lotta! Lose Black Beauty! Not have Lal and Laddo back after all! This was dreadful.

He sat down on a tub, feeling his legs suddenly weak. Lotta wiped her eyes and looked at him. 'Can't you think of *anything* that would make things better?' she asked him in despair.

Suddenly an idea came into Jimmy's mind. He jumped up and took Lotta's hand. 'Lotta!' he said. 'I know! *I* know! Why shouldn't *you* be Laddo's partner? He doesn't know how well you've been doing in the ring! He doesn't know you've got a pony of your own! He can train you to do anything he wants done in a very short while, because you have been practising so well lately.'

'Oh, Jimmy,' cried Lotta, her eyes shining like stars at once. 'Do you really suppose he'd let me? I am sure I can do everything that Madame Fifinella can! And I don't mind how hard I have to work! But what about Lal, my mother?'

'Well, you silly, if you and Laddo are working together in our circus, you can have Lal back in your own caravan and look after her till she's better!' cried Jimmy. 'You say she only wants a good rest – well, she'll be much happier here with us, seeing you do well in the ring, than away by herself in a strange place!'

'Jimmy – oh, Jimmy, I believe you've thought of the very idea!' cried Lotta.

'Let's come and tell Mr Galliano this very minute!' said Jimmy. 'Quick, before he fixes up for Lou and Pepita and Juanita to stay on! Let's hope Laddo hasn't already fixed up with Madame Fifinella!'

Black Beauty whinnied gently. He was pleased to hear a happier sound in Lotta's voice. The little girl jumped on his back and cantered out into the open, her face still tear-stained but her eyes eager and bright. Jimmy followed her, with Lucky and Lulu at his heels.

They went to Mr Galliano's caravan. Inside they could hear Galliano's deep voice and Laddo's strong one, and they could hear the clatter of teacups as Mrs Galliano washed up.

Jimmy rapped on the open door.

'I am busy, yes,' called Mr Galliano. 'Go away for a little while.'

'But please, Mr Galliano, we must see you now!' called Jimmy; 'please let us come up.'

Mr Galliano made an impatient noise. He was not in a good temper, for he was very disappointed to hear Laddo's news. 'Come, then,' he said. 'What is it you children want?'

21. Goodbye – and good luck!

Jimmy and Lotta ran up the caravan steps. Mr Galliano glared at them.

'Why do you come disturbing me now?' he said. 'You see I am busy – yes?'

'I'm very sorry, Mr Galliano,' said Jimmy, 'but we've had such a good idea, Lotta and I. Please, sir, why can't Lotta be Laddo's partner, instead of getting Madame Fifinella and going away to another circus? She's as good as any grown-up circus rider – I heard you say so yourself to Mr Tonks the other day.'

'Your ears are too long,' grumbled Mr Galliano. Laddo looked up, astonished.

'Has Lotta been in the ring by herself then?' he asked.

'You have not heard that – no?' said Galliano. 'Ah, she is certainly a wonder, that little Lotta, though she still has much to learn. Yes, Laddo; she now has a pony of her own, the cleverest animal I have seen for years. And she and that pony perform each night in the ring with Jimmy and Lucky. It is a very good turn, yes.'

'She has worked and practised so hard, Laddo,' said Jimmy earnestly. 'She could really do all you needed if only you'd teach her what she doesn't know. She has watched Juanita and Pepita too, and she can do nearly all they can do. Couldn't you let her try for a few weeks, and then perhaps Lal will be ready to take her place again?'

'That is for Mr Galliano to say,' said Laddo, still looking very astonished to think that his small daughter had been working so hard and doing such surprising things.

Mr Galliano drummed his fingers on the table. He

turned to fat Mrs Galliano, who was still washing up, and listening.

'What do you think, Tessa?' he said. 'Will Lotta do for a few weeks?'

Mrs Galliano was fond of the two children, and she looked at Lotta. 'She would do, I think,' she said. 'It would be too much to give her such hard work for very long, but for a few weeks, yes, it would not matter. She is a clever little girl and not afraid of hard work.'

Mr Galliano always thought a lot of his wife's words. She did not talk much, but what she said was always sensible. He slapped his hand on the table and made everyone jump.

'It is settled then!' he said. 'Lotta becomes your little partner for a few weeks till Lal is well again – and you will write to tell Fifinella you do not need her after all – yes?'

'Yes, Mr Galliano,' said Laddo, surprised and delighted. 'Well, then, sir, Lal could come back to our caravan, couldn't she – and we could look after her ourselves. She would be so much happier and would get better so much more quickly if she were with the people she knows and loves.'

'Certainly, certainly, certainly!' said Mr Galliano. 'Fetch her tomorrow, yes. Tessa, things look better. We will all have strawberry ice-cream for dinner!'

That was always Mr Galliano's way. When he was pleased he would send ice-creams or bottles of ginger-beer, or whatever came into his head, to all his circus folk. He had a hot temper but a very kind heart, and all his people thought the world of him. He pushed his top hat well on one side and nodded goodbye to Laddo and the children.

Lotta and Jimmy were overjoyed. Lotta ran squealing with delight to Mrs Brown's caravan, and for the second time that morning Mrs Brown dropped the spoon into the stew. 'Lotta! I won't have you . . .' she began.

But Lotta didn't let her finish. She caught hold of Mrs

Brown by the waist and danced round the caravan with her, shouting at the top of her voice:

'Lal's coming back tomorrow! I'm going to be Laddo's partner! He's not leaving the circus!'

Mrs Brown, who had known nothing of what had happened, was quite bewildered. She pushed Lotta away and sat down, out of breath.

'Now, Lotta, behave!' she said. 'Tell me things from the beginning, you silly child. I've no idea what you are talking about.'

So Jimmy and Lotta, both talking at once, told the news. Lucky barked with excitement and Lulu whined. It was difficult to understand anything, but Mrs Brown listened patiently. In the middle of the story, Black Beauty, who had been left outside, became impatient, walked up the steps and stuck his head inside the caravan!

'Well, I never!' said Mrs Brown. 'There's that pony of yours in the caravan now, Lotta. Well, I've had dogs and monkeys, but I won't have horses. Shoo, shoo, Beauty!'

So Beauty shooed, and stood outside, whinnying for Lotta. Mrs Brown heard the rest of the story and was pleased.

'I'm glad we can have Lal back,' she said. 'Well, Lotta, you and I will be busy getting your caravan clean and tidy today, ready for Lal tomorrow, if she's coming. Jimmy, I shall have a list of shopping for you to do, for Lotta's larder will want stocking. You'd better have your dinners straight away, and then we can start.'

Dinner was lovely, for the pudding was strawberry ice-cream, of course, and really it was surprising how much those two children could eat!

Laddo's horses were now safely in the circus field. Lou and his sisters were packing up, for they were going to join another circus, after having a well-earned holiday. The children were sorry to say goodbye to them, for they were fond of the three riders and of their lovely white horses. But circus life is made up of 'Hallos' and 'Good-byes', and the children were used to it.

Lotta and Mrs Brown spent very happy, busy hours getting ready Lal's caravan. The little girl hummed as she scrubbed the floor. Lulu wondered why she was so happy and kept coming up to lick her. Lotta had to keep pushing her down the caravan steps because her paws dirtied the nice clean floor!

The mats were beaten well. Jimmy cleaned the windows. Mrs Brown sent him down to the town for some new blue cotton, and quickly made some pretty curtains herself for the windows.

The stove, which had not been used for months, was cleaned so that it shone. The little larder was washed from top to bottom, and as soon as the shelves were dry Jimmy put clean paper on each one.

'Goodness!' said Lotta, in surprise. 'Lal won't know her larder all dressed up in paper-lined shelves. We've never done that before.'

'Well, it's time you began then,' said Mrs Brown, briskly. 'You know enough now, Lotta, to be able to keep your caravan beautifully, and just see that you do, or I'll be after you with a broom!'

Lotta laughed in delight. 'You can come after me with six brooms!' she said. 'But you wouldn't catch me!'

Then off she went with Jimmy to buy all the things for her mother's larder. She skipped along very happily, and Jimmy was glad too. What a good thing he had given Lotta her lovely Black Beauty, and how lucky it was that the little girl had worked so hard!

Laddo set off to fetch Lal from the hospital. He had hired a car and put plenty of soft cushions at the back. Lotta wanted to come with him but he said no, he wanted Lal to be quite quiet in the car, and she would get too excited if Lotta were there, telling her all the news.

So the two children waited in patience – or rather, in *im*patience, for they hopped up and down, ran into the road to see if the car was coming back, hopped up and down again, chased each other, and were altogether quite mad!

Then at last the car came back and the two children set up such a yell! Everyone came running up for all the circus folk wanted to welcome back Lal, whom they loved. The car drove slowly in at the field-gate, Laddo trying not to bump over the ruts. Lal waved to everyone from the back.

'Welcome home, Lal, welcome home!' yelled everyone. 'Hurrah! Hurrah!'

How glad Lal was to come back to the circus she knew and loved so well! Laddo carried her carefully into the pretty caravan and Mrs Brown tucked her into bed. Lotta was wild with delight to have her mother back again. She hugged her at least twenty times, and told her proudly all that she was going to do. Black Beauty was allowed to come up the steps of Laddo's caravan to be seen by Lal and admired.

'He is the best pony you could have chosen,' said Lal, stroking his soft nose. Lal could stroke and fondle any horse, however wild, for like Lotta, she had a way with horses. 'He is clever, independent, and loyal. You are a lucky girl, Lotta.'

'She deserves it all, though,' said Jimmy. 'She really has worked hard, Lal, and every day she has helped Lou and the others, though she knew she could not go into the ring with them. I am sure she will be a great success with Laddo till you are better again.'

The day passed quickly, and the night came; the circus was due to open once more. People began to stream in at the gates. The lights flared in the 'big top', and Oona strewed fresh sawdust over the ring.

We will leave Jimmy and Lotta whilst they are so happy. It would be fun to follow them on their way, but all stories have to end. Soon the circus will begin once more, and shouts and laughter and the cracking of Mr Galliano's huge whip will fill the great tent.

Oona has finished spreading the sawdust. He has gone

to change into his glittering circus suit. Sticky Stanley the
clown is already in his suit, and is painting his face a
queer mixture of red and white.

Mr Wally is with Sammy the chimpanzee, dressing him
in a new coat, talking to his beloved pet as if he were a
child. Mr Tonks is rubbing down Jumbo, and he has to
climb a ladder to do that! He too is talking to his elephant
as if Jumbo were his best friend – and, indeed, he is!

Lilliput is dressing his four monkeys ready for their
nightly tea party in the ring. He is scolding Jemima because she has put four hats on, one after the other so that
Lilliput could not imagine where they were when he
looked for them to put on his monkeys' heads.

Laddo and Lotta are with their horses, giving them a
last rub-down to make them shine for the ring. Lotta is
very happy. She has on her beautiful frock and looks like
a silvery fairy as she trots to and fro. Each time she passes
Black Beauty she whispers in his ear, and he whinnies
gently, nuzzling after her as she goes.

And Jimmy is – well, where *is* Jimmy? Not in his caravan, for only Mrs Brown is there, stirring another of her
lovely stews. Brownie is busy somewhere, as he always is.
Jimmy is not with him. He is not with Lotta either, nor is
he in the ring, for that is empty, waiting for the first tan-
tan-tara of the trumpets and the crack of Galliano's whip.

We must find him and say goodbye to him. He is not
with Lilliput. Mr Tonks hasn't seen him. Mr Wally
doesn't know where he is.

What is that noise over there in the bears' cage? It
sounded like Jimmy laughing!

It *is* Jimmy, and he is playing with the five bears as if
he were a bear himself! Mr Galliano has said he may, and
Mr Volla is only too pleased to have someone who will
make his bears so happy. Lucky is dancing round, barking
in glee.

Jimmy is fighting one of the bears with a pair of
boxing-gloves on! Smack! Thud! Biff! What a game! All
the bears watch and bang their paws on the ground and

grunt with joy. How they love Jimmy, and what fun they are going to have with him!

Goodbye, Jimmy! Have a good time. Goodbye, Lucky, little dog Lucky! Maybe we'll see you again some other day!

3

CIRCUS DAYS AGAIN

Contents

1. The circus is on the road

Lumbering down the dusty lanes one warm May day went a strange procession. The country folk stared in surprise, and stopped their work to watch it pass.

'It's a circus!' said one to another. 'Look – there's an elephant! And there's a funny creature – a chimpanzee, isn't he?'

It *was* a circus! It was Mr Galliano's famous circus, on its way to its next show-place. With it was the circus boy, Jimmy, and his famous dog, Lucky. Lotta the circus girl was there, riding on her lovely pony, Black Beauty. Mr Wally was in his car with Sammy, his clever chimpanzee. Sammy was dressed properly, in coat and trousers, and he kept raising his hat most politely to all the country folk he passed. How they laughed to see him!

Lilliput, with his four monkeys, passed by. Jemima, his favourite little monkey, was curled as usual about his neck, her tiny teeth lovingly nibbling his left ear. She waved a small paw as she passed the wondering country folk.

The glorious circus horses trotted by, their proud heads held up well, their coats shining like satin. With them were Lotta's mother and father, Lal and Laddo. In a big travelling-cage behind came their performing dogs, yapping a little because of the heat of the day.

Mr Volla was in a big cage with his five clumsy bears. They were not very fond of going from place to place, and he liked to be with them to quiet them. Dobby, his favourite bear, sat with his arm round his trainer, grunting a little when the cage jolted over a rut. The side doors were open because of the warm weather, and the bears could see all that they passed. They liked that.

Sticky Stanley, the clown, got all the laughs as usual, when he walked upside down on his hands, or gambolled about, making the silliest jokes. Everyone loved old Sticky Stanley, and no matter where he was, he was always the same, merry, comical, and friendly. Oona, the acrobat, sat in his caravan watching Sticky Stanley. He was too lazy to join him just then.

The caravans and cages and horses went slowly by. There was no hurry. The circus was not opening until two nights ahead and Mr Galliano was hoping that the marvellous weather would hold out so that the circus would take a great deal of money.

'Then,' thought the ring-master, tipping his hat so much to one side that it nearly fell off, 'then I shall make my circus bigger! I shall get more clowns. I shall get more performing animals. My circus will be more famous than ever!'

A pretty yellow caravan went by. It had blue wheels and a blue chimney. It belonged to Mrs Brown, Jimmy's mother. Jimmy, his mother, and Brownie, his father, all lived in the pretty caravan together. Jimmy had bought it for his mother with the money that he and his clever dog, Lucky, had earned in the circus ring.

It was a fine caravan. It had taps to turn on over a little sink – and this was something that not even Mr Galliano's caravan had! It had four bunks that folded flat against the wall. Jimmy slept in one and loved it. It had a fine cooking stove, and gay curtains that flapped in and out of the windows in the little breeze. Mrs Brown was very proud of her caravan.

She was cooking something on the stove. The smoke went up the chimney and floated away on the hot May air. Jimmy smelt his dinner cooking and went to find out what it was. Lucky came with him, running happily on four springy paws. She was a beautiful fox-terrier, smooth-haired, small, with a half-black, half-sandy head. Her eyes were soft and brown, and she loved Jimmy better than anyone else in the world.

Next to Jimmy she loved Lotta, the circus girl – but if she had to choose between being with Lotta or being with Jimmy, it was always Jimmy she chose! Like a shadow she kept at the boy's heels, and every night slept at his feet in the bunk.

Lucky was a valuable dog. She was one of the cleverest dogs that Mr Galliano had ever seen, and it was Jimmy who had trained her. The little dog could do the most marvellous tricks, and went into the circus ring every night with Jimmy. Lotta went too, with her beautiful black pony, which Lucky could ride almost as well as the two children could! It was funny to see the small dog balancing himself cleverly on Black Beauty's back,

bumping up and down as the horse went round the ring!

'Mother, isn't it hot!' cried Jimmy, as he jumped up the steps at the back of the caravan. 'What's for dinner? It's a lovely smell.'

'Oh, Jimmy, surely you can't eat any dinner after eating four sausages for breakfast!' laughed his mother. 'I've got Irish stew here.'

'Can Lotta come and share it?' asked Jimmy eagerly. 'She's only got ham sandwiches, and she says they'll be very dry!'

Lotta's mother, Lal, was not the good cook that Mrs Brown was, and Lotta loved to come and share the delicious meals that Jimmy's mother prepared. Mrs Brown was fond of the little girl, so she nodded her head.

'Yes. Call her. She loves Irish stew.' Jimmy shouted for Lotta and she came running, her curly hair flying in the wind.

'Irish stew! Come and have some!' yelled Jimmy. Lotta was up the caravan steps with a bound. Mrs Brown turned and looked at her.

'What a dirty little grub you are!' she said. 'After all the trouble I've taken in teaching you how to be clean and tidy too. If you want any stew, go and wash your hands and do your hair. And how in the world did you manage to get that frock so dirty? Have you been sweeping the chimney or something?'

Lotta grinned and made a face. She went to turn the tap on at Mrs Brown's neat sink.

'Oh no, Lotta! You just go and wash in your own caravan in the pail there,' cried Mrs Brown. 'You're so dirty you'll make my nice clean sink black. Go along with you.'

It wasn't any use arguing with Mrs Brown, as Lotta knew. So down the steps she went again and flew to her own caravan, which was not nearly so pretty or so clean as Jimmy's. She rinsed her hands in the pail of water there, ran a wet towel over her face, brushed her flying curls, and tied a ribbon on one side. She looked to see if she had a clean dress, but each one seemed even blacker than the one she had on, so she gave that up as a bad job.

Only Lotta's beautiful, spangled circus frock was clean and fresh. However untidy and dirty the circus folk looked in their everyday clothes, they kept their ring suits and frocks very carefully indeed. The tiniest tear was always mended. The smallest spot was washed out. Nothing must spoil them when they were worn in the ring.

The two children talked about the next show-place as they ate their stew. The town they were going to was a big one.

'Mr Galliano plans to have a bigger circus if we do well

at Bigminton,' said Jimmy. 'Won't that be fun, Lotta?'

'What will he have if it's to be bigger?' asked Lotta.

'He might have another elephant – or a sea-lion. Sea-lions are marvellous at performing tricks,' said Jimmy. 'I'm almost sure he's going to have more clowns. One clown isn't nearly enough really, though Sticky Stanley is simply marvellous.'

'Well, he can't have any more horses or dogs because we've plenty of those,' said Lotta, holding out her plate for some more stew. 'Won't it be lovely to have more people in the circus. I hope they'll be nice.'

The circus procession rumbled on as the children ate their dinner. The sun shone through the windows of the blue caravan. Old Jumbo, the elephant in front, trumpeted because he wanted a drink. The dogs in the travelling cages yelped too. They wanted to run.

'Listen to them,' said Lotta. 'I hope we get to our camping place soon. They do so want to stretch their legs. Shall we take them for a walk, Jimmy, when we camp for the night?'

So, when the sun was sinking, and the circus arranged itself around a big field, the two children slipped open the door of the dogs' big cage, and let them out.

'Punch! Judy! Pincher! Toby! Come on, all of you!' cried Lotta. 'Lucky, hi, Lucky, you come too. And where's Lulu the spaniel, Jimmy? Oh, there she is! Come Lulu – we're all off for a run.'

The camp settled in whilst the children took the restless dogs for a run. Jumbo was tied to a big tree. He caressed his keeper, Mr Tonks, with his trunk, glad to be able to take a rest. Mr Tonks spoke softly to the big animal. They were the best friends in the world.

Sammy the chimpanzee sat down to a meal with Mr Wally, his master. Mr Wally talked to him as if he could understand every word – and really, it seemed as if Sammy could, for he jabbered back at Mr Wally as if he were really answering him.

The little monkey man, Lilliput, set a tub upside down,

and put some oranges and bananas on it for his four monkeys. They sat around it, peeling their bananas and chattering. Jemima peeled a large banana, bit it in half, and offered the other half to Lilliput. When another monkey snatched it from her, she flew at him and pulled off the little green coat he was wearing.

'Now, now, Jemima!' said Lilliput, peeling a banana quickly. 'Look – I'll bite this in half – and *you* shall have the other half. There.'

Jemima was pleased. She took the half-banana and ate it quickly, chattering with pleasure. Then, quick as lightning, she stuffed the peel down the neck of the other monkey. Squealing with merriment she leapt away to the top of her master's caravan. She held on to the chimney and watched the other monkey trying to get the peel from the neck of his little red coat.

The horses whinnied as Lal and Laddo rubbed them down. The five bears grunted as they ate their evening meal. Mr Volla gave them each a large piece of toffee afterwards, and it was funny to watch the bears solemnly sucking it, enjoying the sweetness.

Lotta and Jimmy came back with all the dogs, happy now after a long run. The children saw them safely into their cage, all except Lulu and Lucky, and then went to get some cocoa and biscuits from Mrs Brown.

The camp had settled in. The camp fires burned like glow-worms in the dark field. Sticky Stanley got out his guitar and sang a funny little song. But the circus folk were too tired to gather round and listen that night. One by one they went to their caravans and fell asleep.

'Isn't it fun to belong to a travelling circus!' said Jimmy sleepily to little dog Lucky, as he climbed into his bunk. 'We'll have some fun here, Lucky. Goodnight – and don't nibble my toes till the morning.'

2. Madame Prunella and her parrots

The circus opened at Bigminton after a day or two's rest. The weather kept fine, and Mr Galliano was delighted to see so many people paying their money at the gate.

'You shall have a new dress, he promised Lotta, sticking his hat on one side. 'And you, Jimmy, shall have a new ring suit that shines like the moon.'

All the circus folk liked to wear the loveliest suits and dresses that they could possibly afford, when they appeared in the ring. The shinier the better. Lotta longed to have a dress so covered with spangles that the dress itself could hardly be seen. Jimmy didn't mind so much, though he liked to feel grand when he went into the ring. But how he loved to dress up little dog Lucky.

Lucky had quite a wardrobe of coats and collars and bows. Jimmy's mother kept them all clean and mended, and laughed to see Lucky parading up and down in a grand new coat or stiff bow.

'You and Jemima the monkey and Sammy the chimpanzee are all as vain as little girls,' she said. 'As for Jemima, I wonder she doesn't carry a looking-glass about with her to see if her whiskers are straight.'

Oona the acrobat came by and called to Jimmy. 'Hi, there! Would you like to come with me and visit my cousin? She lives near here, and maybe she's going to join the circus.'

'Oooh, yes!' said Jimmy, and jumped down the steps with Lucky at his heels. 'Where's Lotta? She'd like to come too.'

Lotta was practising in the ring. She had Black Beauty there, and was galloping round and round, standing lightly on his back. When her father shouted 'Hup!' she jumped right round and stood facing the horse's tail. When he shouted again she leapt round the other way. It was marvellous to watch her.

'Lotta! Have you nearly finished?' cried Jimmy. 'Oona's going to visit his cousin, and I'm going with him.'

'I'll come too,' said Lotta, and she leapt lightly off the horse's back. She turned to her father. 'Can I go now, Laddo?' she asked. She called her mother Lal and her father Laddo, as everyone else did.

'Yes, you can go,' said Laddo. 'Leave Black Beauty. I want to trot him round with the other horses. He's a great help to them, he's so clever.'

Lotta and Jimmy ran off with Oona. They asked him about his cousin. 'Who is she? What does she do? Is she an animal-trainer?'

Oona laughed. 'Well – not exactly an *animal*-trainer. She keeps parrots.'

'Parrots!' squealed Lotta. 'Oh, I love parrots! What do hers do? Do they talk? Does she take them into the ring?'

'Of course,' said Oona. 'They talk, they recite – and they sing a song together. One of them, I forget its name, is very clever indeed. It can hold a brush in its claws and brush its crest. It can do a little dance too, whilst the music plays and the others sing.'

'Golly!' said Jimmy. 'That will be fun. I've never had anything to do with birds before. I wonder if they'll like me as much as the animals do.'

Oona looked at Jimmy and laughed. 'Oh, you'll find that all Madame Prunella's parrots will let you do what you like with them,' he said. 'You've got the secret of handling every live creature there is, Jimmy – and the parrots will be all over you.'

They caught a tram and went down into the heart of Bigminton. They came to a ramshackle little house, with a notice in the window, 'Rooms to let'. As they knocked at the door a chorus of screeches rose on the air from inside the house.

Then a deep voice spoke: 'Come in, wipe your feet, shut the door, and say how-do-you-do.'

Jimmy looked astonished. This was a funny greeting, he thought. He wasn't sure if he was going to like Madame Prunella if she spoke to them like this. Lotta saw his face and laughed.

'That's not your cousin speaking, is it?' she cried to Oona. 'It's one of the parrots, isn't it?'

'Of course,' said Oona, and he opened the door. Another voice called out in a sing-song manner:

'Here comes the sweep! Swee-ee-eep! Swee-ee-eep! Wash your face, my dear, wash your face.'

The children laughed. That was another parrot, they knew. What fun! They all went into a tiny room, and Oona kissed a small, fat little woman there. She was in a dressing-gown, sewing, and around her were about a dozen parrots, some grey and red, some the most brilliant colours imaginable.

'Good morning,' she said. 'Excuse me not getting up, but I've lost my shoes this morning, and there are pins everywhere. I upset the pin box, you see – and now I daren't leave my chair to look for my shoes in case I prick my feet.'

The children looked at the small, fat-cheeked little woman and liked her very much. Her eyes were small, and almost buried in her plump cheeks, but they shone and twinkled like blue beads. Her head was a mass of tight black curls. One parrot sat on her shoulder, singing a soft little song, and the others talked and screeched around. It was rather like being in the parrot house at the Zoo. Everyone had to shout, for they couldn't be heard unless they did.

'This is Lotta, and this is Jimmy,' cried Oona to his cousin.

'Oh, I've heard of Jimmy and his wonderful dog,

Lucky,' said Madame Prunella, smiling. 'Where is she?'

'I left her with my mother,' said Jimmy. 'I don't much like bringing her among a lot of traffic. You'll see her if you join Mr Galliano's circus. I do hope you *do*, Madame Prunella. I'd love to get to know some birds. I've only had animals so f r.'

'My parrots will never go to anyone but to me,' said Madame Prunella proudly. 'I have trained them all myself, and look after them myself – and not one will allow itself to be handled by a stranger.'

As she spoke, a large red and grey parrot lifted its crest up very high, and spoke in a deep voice. 'Eggs and bacon, ham and cheese, coffee and biscuits!' it remarked, and then, very solemnly, hopped along the edge of the bookcase where it was perched, and rubbed its great curved beak against Jimmy's cheek.

Madame Prunella stared in the greatest surprise. 'Look at Gringle!' she cried. 'Gringle! You are making love to Jimmy! You have never done that to anyone before! What's happened to you?'

'Ham and tongue, tomatoes and eggs, toffee and chocolate,' said the parrot, and stepped straight on to Jimmy's left shoulder!

Then it opened its beak and gave such a terrific screech that made Lotta jump, and gave Jimmy such a fright that he rushed to the other side of the room! The parrot flew off his shoulder, sat on the top of the curtain, and laughed exactly like a naughty boy who had played a joke.

Everyone else laughed too. 'Oh, Jimmy! You did look scared! said Lotta.

'I should think so,' said Jimmy indignantly. 'Screaming like an express train right in my ear.'

'Mushrooms and kippers,' remarked the parrot, scratching its head.

'That parrot seems to think of nothing but food,' said Jimmy.

Madame Prunella stared at Jimmy. 'Gringle has never behaved like that before,' she said. 'Jimmy, go round the

other parrots and see if they will rub their heads against
you, or talk. Mind that green and red one over there – he's
a bit bad-tempered and may tear your hand with his beak.
Go slowly.'

Jimmy was only too pleased to go round the parrots.
Lotta watched proudly. She knew better than anyone
how marvellous Jimmy was with all live creatures. She
had watched him with fierce tigers! She had seen him
with bears and monkeys. She knew how dogs and horses
all loved him. She knew that the parrots would make
friends with him at once.

And so they did. As soon as the big birds knew that
Jimmy wanted to be friendly, they crowded round him,
muttering, screeching, talking. Two perched on his
shoulders. One tried to sit on his head. The others flew
round him, making quite a wind with their big wings.

Jimmy laughed. 'I like them,' he said. 'They are clever
birds, Madame Prunella. Oh, do come and join our
circus, and let me help you with your parrots. I'd love to
know them.'

'Well, I *was* thinking of joining Mr Phillippino's
Circus,' said Madame Prunella, 'but as my cousin is with
Mr Galliano's, and *you* are here, Jimmy I'll come! I'd
like to see you handling my parrots. Maybe you could
teach them some new tricks.'

Jimmy beamed. It would be fun to have plump-
cheeked little Madame Prunella in the circus. She looked
such a comical, good-tempered little person.

But suddenly he had another glimpse of her – one that
surprised him and Lotta very much. She jumped up from
her chair to take one of her parrots – and trod on one of
the pins that lay all about the floor. She gave a screech
just like one of her parrots, held her foot and danced
angrily about, treading on yet more pins with her other
foot!

Madame Prunella was in a temper – and *such* a
temper! She screeched, she shouted, she yelled – and all
the parrots with one accord flew as far away from her as

they could! She caught hold of the tablecloth and flapped it wildly. She picked up a broom and ran at the two children as if she would sweep them from the room. They were quite frightened.

'Come away,' said Oona, grinning. 'Prunella is in one of her tantrums. She'll get out of it as quickly as she got into it – but it's safer to go when she's like this!'

The children fled down the little path to the gate. They could hear the shouting and screeching of the parrots behind them. Gringle was yelling, 'Pepper and mustard, pepper and mustard!' at the top of his voice.

'Golly! Pepper and mustard is just about right when Madame Prunella loses her temper!' said Jimmy. 'What a funny person! I like her, though she gets into tantrums – and I do like the parrots. I hope she joins the circus and comes along with us.'

A curtain was pulled aside and a window was thrown open. Madame Prunella looked out, smiling.

'Tell Galliano I'll come along tomorrow,' she called. 'About twelve o'clock!'

Like an April shower Madame Prunella's temper had passed away. Gringle was on her shoulder, rubbing against her ear. 'Sugar and spice,' he said. 'Sugar and spice.'

'We shall have some fun with Madame Prunella!' said Oona, grinning. And he was right!

3. Madame Prunella joins the show

Jimmy and Lotta told Mrs Brown all about Madame Prunella and her parrots and tantrums. Mrs Brown was amused.

'Well, if parrots join this circus, there will be even more chattering!' she said, smiling at the children who had both been talking at once. 'Jimmy, Lal has been shouting for you. He wants you to go and see to the dogs.'

It was part of Jimmy's work to help with the performing dogs, and he loved this. Every dog adored Jimmy and when he came near their cage they all pressed against the wire, some standing up on their hind legs to get near to him. Lucky, his own dog, ran at his heels, for Jimmy would never allow her to be shut up in a cage, valuable though she was.

'I say, Jimmy, it would be rather fun to tease Madame Prunella and get her into a few tempers wouldn't it?' said Lotta. 'I do think she was funny, don't you?'

'Yes,' said Jimmy, washing out all the dogs' dishes. 'We'll have a good time with her. I like her. Here, Lotta, dry these dishes. Surely you can do a bit of work too?'

'I've done my work this morning,' said Lotta lazily. 'I've groomed Black Beauty, and exercised him, and done my practice in the tent. This is your work, not mine.'

Jimmy took hold of her tiny pink ear and led her to where a clean cloth was hanging. 'I shan't stand any nonsense from *you*!' he said. 'I'll go to Mr Galliano and tell him I won't let you share my turn tonight in the ring!'

Lotta wriggled away, grinning. She and Jimmy were very good friends, though they often teased one another. She began to dry the dishes.

'Isn't it windy up here?' she said. 'You know, we're not very far from the sea, Jimmy. We might go down and bathe one afternoon.'

'I can smell the sea in the wind, said Jimmy, sniffing. 'I hope the breeze doesn't get any stronger. The tents were flapping enough already!'

Jemima the monkey sidled by. She snatched Lotta's drying cloth and tore off with it. Lotta gave a squeal of rage and ran after her. The tiny monkey was a ball of mischief, and loved to tease Lotta. She jumped on to the top of Jimmy's caravan, and twisted the cloth round the smoking chimney.

'You wait till I get you!' cried Lotta. The monkey leapt off the caravan roof and shot up a tree, where she sat grinning and chattering, looking down at the two children. The cloth waved wildly from the chimney, much to Mrs Brown's amazement when she came in from doing a bit of shopping, and there it stayed till Jimmy climbed up and fetched it down, black and smoky.

The circus opened well. Mr Wally and his wonderful chimpanzee, Sammy, amazed everyone, and they had to come back half a dozen times after their turn and bow all around the ring. Sammy loved the clapping and cheering. He took off his hat and waved it wildly, which made everyone cheer all the more.

The horses and their beautiful dancing were always loved by everyone. Lal and Laddo looked magnificent in their circus suits, as they rode their horses, glittering and shining, under the flaring circus lights. The dogs, too, were cheered, and indeed they were very clever in the way they walked, jumped, played ball, carried flags, and did all kinds of tricks. Lal and Laddo patted them and rewarded them with kind words and biscuits, and the happy little dogs wagged their tails like leaves waving in the wind!

Lotta and Jimmy, who were known as the two Wonder Children, always got long and loud cheers and claps, for little dog Lucky, and the pony Black Beauty, were mar-

vellous in their tricks. When Lucky leapt on to Black
Beauty's back, and jumped through a paper hoop, just as
Lotta had done, the cheers almost brought the roof
down! It was great fun, and both children and animals
loved it.

The children had to go to bed very late when the circus
was on, but they were used to this. Mrs Brown saw that
Jimmy went straight to bed, instead of chattering and
laughing with the other circus folk after the show, and
she had told Lal, Lotta's mother, that she would see to the
little girl too.

'Thanks,' said Lal. 'I have to see to the horses and
dogs with Laddo – so if you *will* see that Lotta is safe
in bed, instead of rushing round till midnight, I'd be
grateful!'

Madame Prunella did not join the circus for a few
days. She sent word to say that one of her parrots was ill,
but she would come before the weekend. The children
were delighted. They hung on the field gate about the
time that Madame Prunella was expected – and at last
they saw her caravan arriving. It was a very gay one
indeed!

It was bright orange, with blue wheels, and the horse
that pulled it had his mane plaited with blue and orange
ribbons, and his tail plaited too. He was an old circus
horse, and his delight at sniffing the old smells of the ring
was sweet to see. He whinnied to the other horses, and
they whinnied back.

'What talks they'll have about old times!' said Jimmy,
as he unharnessed Madame Prunella's horse and led him
to where the other horses were. 'There you are, old boy –
have a good feed, and a chat about all the circuses you
have ever been in!'

Madame Prunella was standing the perches of her
parrots outside in the sun. Each parrot was chained by
the leg to its perch, and they all screeched and squealed at
the tops of their voices. Madame Prunella scratched them
on their heads, and they chattered away happily.

'Kippers and herrings,' said Gringle solemnly to Jimmy. 'Kippers and herrings.'

'Pickles and sauce,' answered Jimmy in just as solemn a voice. Gringle put out a foot and Jimmy shook hands with him.

Gringle has certainly made friends with you,' said Madame Prunella. 'But just you mind what I say, children – no playing about with my parrots, please, or I shall have something to say to you!'

Jemima the monkey came near and the parrots set up a great screeching. Jemima grinned and chattered back. She took off her little hat and put it on a parrot's head. The parrot took it off in anger and threw it on the ground.

'You'd better tell Jemima, too, not to play about with the parrots!' grinned Jimmy. 'I say, what a row they make! I can see my mother getting headaches all the day long! I'd better move our caravan a bit farther off!'

'Boy, my parrots can be as quiet as mice in a corner!' said Madame Prunella with a gleam in her eye. She swung round on her brilliant birds. 'Hush!' she said. 'Hush! The baby is asleep!'

At once every parrot was quiet. The children looked about for the baby. They couldn't see one anywhere.

'There isn't a real baby,' said Madame Prunella. 'It's just one of our circus tricks. Whenever I say the word "baby" they have to be quiet.'

The parrot-woman had a very untidy caravan. It smelt of parrots, and it really seemed as if there was no room for anything else but a bed for her and a stove inside the caravan. All the rest of the room was taken up by cages or perches. Prunella loved her parrots so much that, like Mr Wally and his chimpanzee, she would not be parted from her pets even at night. Jimmy had often seen Sammy the chimp sleeping peacefully in his bunk opposite to Mr Wally in his caravan. He couldn't imagine how Madame Prunella could bear to sleep with twelve parrots!

'Still, I wouldn't let Lucky sleep anywhere but with me,' he thought. 'So I suppose if Madame Prunella loves her parrots as I love dogs, she feels the same.'

Madame Prunella took her parrots into the ring that night. They were an enormous success! Jimmy could hardly believe his ears at the things they could say and sing!

They all knew the nursery rhymes, of course, and they could all count and say the alphabet. Gringle could reel off the names of all kinds of food, and Pola, another grey and red parrot, could recite long poems. When they sang together it was very funny indeed, for although they knew the words well, they did not always keep good time, and the band which played the music for them, had to keep going slowly or quickly to keep time to the parrots' loud, harsh voices!

Gringle could whistle too – and his cleverest trick of all was his imitation of all kinds of noises!

'Now, Gringle, tell us how an aeroplane goes,' said Madame Prunella, who was very plump and pretty in a brilliant blue and gold skirt and bodice, with golden feathers nodding in her hair.

Gringle swelled out his throat and opened his beak – and from it there came the throbbing sound of an aeroplane! It was really marvellous.

'And now I want an ice, Gringle,' said Madame Prunella. 'Where's the ice-cream man?'

The sound of an ice-cream man's bell came jingling into the ring. Jimmy looked round in surprise – surely the ice-cream man would not be allowed in the ring! But it was only Gringle, making the exact noise of the tricycle bell!

'Now it's firework night! The fireworks are going off, Gringle!' cried Prunella – and from the clever parrot came the noises of pops and explosions, splutters and bangs – for all the world like fireworks going off on Guy Fawkes' Day! It was really most extraordinary.

Gringle could cry like a baby, howl like a wolf, and

mew like a cat. Jimmy and Lotta thought he must be the cleverest parrot in the world.

When the people cheered and yelled and clapped, the parrots went mad with joy. They danced from side to side on their perches, and screeched loudly above the applause.

'Sh! The baby's asleep!' said Prunella, and at once every parrot was quiet. They each bowed solemnly round the ring and then, fluttering round Madame Prunella, they were taken from the ring.

'Madame Prunella, we are proud to have you here,' said Mr Galliano, delighted, his hat well on one side. 'Your turn is good, very good, yes. We shall all do well at Bigminton!'

And so they did! The money poured in, and Mr Galliano went whistling round the circus camp, paying everyone well, and telling them that they were to stay another week in the windy, cliffside camp. The children were pleased. They had discovered a short way to the beach and had bathed and paddled every afternoon.

'It's fine here!' said Jimmy. 'I hope we have another good week, Lotta. I don't see why we shouldn't!'

But the next week wasn't quite what anyone expected!

4. What happened on a windy night

The second week opened well. The weather was not so good, and the wind blew even more strongly, but this did not seem to stop the Bigminton people from flocking to see Mr Galliano's famous circus. Mr Galliano bought himself a grand new circus suit, which glittered so much that it almost dazzled Lotta to look at it. 'Doesn't he look grand, standing in the middle of the ring, cracking his whip like that?' said Jimmy admiringly: 'I'll be a circus owner one day! I'll be a ring-master in top hat and top boots and a glittering suit, cracking a whip till it sounds like a pistol shot!'

'I wish this wind would stop,' said Lotta, pulling her coat closely round her shoulders. 'It's so cold when it blows. The animals don't like it either.'

Jimmy had noticed that often with the animals. They were restless and uneasy when the wind blew strongly. There were strange noises that the wind made, rattles and bangs, jiggles and whistlings, which made the animals constantly prick up their ears and turn this way and that.

The horses whinnied and stamped when the wind roared round the field. The dogs whined and growled. The monkeys sat shivering close together in Lilliput's caravan. They felt cold and frightened. Even Jumbo the elephant flapped his big ears in annoyance when the gale shrieked round his enormous head.

Lucky didn't mind the wind. She didn't mind anything so long as she was with Jimmy. But Black Beauty the pony looked around him with startled eyes when the wind flapped at his tail and sent a piece of paper rustling

against his beautiful legs. He whinnied for Lotta, and she
went to soothe him and comfort him.

'It's only the wind,' she told him. 'Don't be afraid,
Black Beauty. See how its blows my curls – *I* don't mind it!
See how it flaps my dress! It's only the wind.'

The last night of the circus came. The wind had risen
to a gale, and all the animals were nervous and restless.
Mr Galliano wondered whether he should put off the last
night, but it was difficult to put posters up in the town to
tell the people. The circus must open and do its best!

A great many people came, and soon the big top, as the
great ring tent was called, was full. The ring was strewn
with sawdust, and the band took their places. Outside the
wind roared steadily, drowning even the band at times!
All the circus folk felt they would be glad when the performance was safely over, for the horses and dogs were
nervous and disobedient! Sammy the chimpanzee was
very difficult. Just before he was due to enter the ring, he
went into a corner and took off all his clothes!

'Sammy! How tiresome you are!' cried Mr Wally.
'Jimmy, come and help me to dress him, quickly. He does
so hate the wind. He did this once before in a storm.'

Sammy was dressed, but he was so naughty that he had
to miss his turn in the ring, and go on later. Even so, he
gave a bad performance and Mr Wally was quite
ashamed of him. One of the chimpanzee's tricks was to
ride a bicycle round the ring, waving his hat to say goodbye – and then to ride out of the ring like that.

But he wouldn't ride out! He kept on and on riding
round the ring, making queer noises! He threw his hat at
Mr Wally, and nearly knocked him over when his trainer
went to get him off the bicycle! But at last Jimmy went to
help, and between them they got the naughty chimpanzee safely out of the ring and into his cage.

The wind went on howling round and round the tent.
The ropes that held down the tent creaked, and the canvas flapped and swayed. Once or twice Mr Galliano looked
uneasily at the canvas walls of the tent, and to Jimmy's

surprise he cut short two or three of the turns, and would
not let Lotta go into the ring at all. The little girl was very
angry, but she did not dare to grumble in front of Mr
Galliano.

The ring-master's hat was on quite straight – a thing
that only happened when he was worried. Lal and Laddo,
Mr Volla and Mr Wally, looked worried too. It was not
good to know that their animals were nervous and afraid.
It is only when an animal is afraid that a trainer finds it
hard to handle him.

Lucky ran round Jimmy's heels, keeping very close to
him. She knew that people were worried. When Mr Galliano brought the circus to an end, half an hour before its
time, Lotta and Jimmy went to hold torches so that the
departing people might see their way out of the windswept field.

And no sooner had they all gone than a surprising and
alarming thing happened. The gale blew down the big
tent, in which was the circus ring!

SNAP! went the ropes – and with a great flapping and
creaking the enormous tent, so carefully put up by
Jimmy's father and the other men, was lifted right up
from the ground!

Jumbo the elephant trumpeted in terror – but he was
safely tethered by a hind leg to a great tree, and he could
not run away. Mr Tonks ran to him at once.

The horses were all safely in their travelling stables, for
Lal and Laddo would not leave them out in such a gale.
The dogs, too, were safe in their cages, and the side doors
were safely closed. Sammy was with Mr Wally in his
caravan, drinking hot milk and eating a bunch of
bananas.

But Mr Volla and his five bears were walking together
across the dark, windswept field to their cage when the
great white tent rose into the air and flew flapping over
the grass. The bears saw the big white thing coming and
they were terrified. They couldn't imagine *what* it was!
Mr Volla knew it was only the tent, and he pulled quickly

at the thick rope which guided the bears. The tent missed them and flapped away – but the bears howled in fright. Two of them, Dobby and Grizel, broke the rope that held them, and ran grunting across the field.

'Help! Help!' yelled Mr Volla. 'Two of my bears have escaped. Jimmy! Brownie! Wally! Where are you! Take my bears so that I can run after the others.'

Jimmy heard him yelling and at once he and Lucky ran to help Mr Volla. Brownie, Jimmy's father, ran too, and soon they were leading three frightened bears to their cages, whilst poor Mr Volla ran wildly about the field shouting for his beloved bear cub, Dobby, and the bigger bear, Grizel.

The whole circus turned out to help. The hedges and banks and ditches were thoroughly searched, and torches flashed all about the cliff-side. Mr Volla yelled the names of his bears at the top of his voice, but they did not appear.

And then another thing happened! The big tent flapped itself round the field – and then laid itself very carefully right over the top of Madame Prunella's caravan! She was safely inside with her parrots, with all the windows shut. Her parrots, scared of the gale, were screeching loudly, and she let them screech. Other people might not like her parrots' harsh voices, but to Madame Prunella they were as sweet as the sound of larks or nightingales!

Madame Prunella did not know that the tent had draped itself over her caravan. She could hear nothing but her parrots. The birds knew that something strange had happened, and they squealed and screeched all the more.

Nobody noticed what the tent had done. Jimmy's father, who was the carpenter and handyman of the circus, noticed only that the tent had come to rest – and he quickly pegged it down where it was, meaning to see to it in the morning. He was thankful that it had not blown down when the people of Bigminton had been inside!

Nobody guessed that Prunella's caravan was hidden beneath the tent. It was quite dark, and only the big white bulge of the enormous tent could be seen dimly by the light of the torches. So there the tent was left, with Madame Prunella's caravan beneath it, till the morning.

Everyone was worried about the bears. Mr Galliano knew only too well what might happen to escaped circus animals. They would be shot without a doubt. Jimmy knew that too. He remembered how once Sammy the chimpanzee had escaped, and how he, Jimmy, had only just managed to find and save Sammy before he was killed.

He went to find Lotta. The little girl was with Black Beauty, who was trembling nervously at all the shouting and upset.

'Lotta,' said Jimmy. 'Will you come with me? I'm going to find Mr Volla's bears. Lucky can trace them for me, I'm sure – and if we manage to get on their track soon, we could bring them back before they are captured and shot by someone who doesn't know they are only harmless circus animals.

'They may be harmless in the circus, Jimmy,' said Lotta, 'but when they are away from us and frightened and lonely, they may not be so harmless! They might hurt someone! All right – I'll come. Just give me time to put Black Beauty safely into his stable.'

She slipped away. Jimmy went to the bears' cage and took Lucky to Dobby's sleeping straw.

'Smell it, Lucky, smell it,' said Jimmy, pressing his dog's sharp nose down into the straw. 'Then we'll follow! Where's Dobby? Where that cub, Dobby?'

Lucky yelped joyously. She liked Dobby, the comical clumsy bear cub. Dobby and she very often played together, and although the bear was heavy and powerful, he was always very gentle with the small dog.

Lucky sniffed eagerly, and then Jimmy took her to where the bears had escaped. Lucky put her nose to the ground and then, with a yelp, tore across the field! She had found Dobby's trail!

'Hi, Lucky! Come back!' cried Jimmy, looking round for Lotta. 'Let me put you on a lead! I can't see you or follow you if you go tearing off like that!'

Lucky came back. Lotta appeared, wearing a thick coat and scarf, for the wind was still strong and bitterly cold. She held out a woollen scarf to Jimmy.

'Come on,' she said. 'Your mother has told Galliano that she can't find you, and if Galliano roars for us, we'll have to go to him. Hurry, before we're missed!'

So through the dark, windy night the two children followed little dog Lucky. She was on a lead, and she pulled and strained at it, as her sharp, doggy nose smelt the strong scent of the smell left by Dobby and Grizel, the two escaped bears.

'I hope they haven't gone too far!' said Jimmy anxiously. 'Goodness knows where they might be by morning!'

'Well – we'll be there, too!' said brave Lotta. 'I'll walk all night if it means we can get the bears before anything happens!'

5. The hunt for the bears

The two children made their way through the dark windy night, guided by Lucky, who was pulling hard at her lead. The wind was still very strong indeed and blew the clouds to rags – but every now and again the moon shone out and the children could see where they were.

'I say, Lucky is taking us down to the seashore!' said Jimmy anxiously. 'I hope to goodness the bears haven't gone there.'

But they had, for Lucky was still following their scent. Nose to ground she smelt out the footsteps of the two bears and whined a little because she couldn't go as fast as she liked.

Down a steep, rocky cliff path went the two children – and when the moon came out for a moment, Jimmy gave a cry, and pointed to the ground.

'Look!' he said. 'Can you see the claw-marks of Dobby and Grizel? See how they hung their claws into the path to keep themselves from slipping!'

The children reached the shore. They looked around, wondering if they would see the bears anywhere. The moon swept out from the clouds at that moment, and they could see the track of footmarks going over the sand.

'Come on! They've gone that way!' cried Jimmy, pleased. 'Hurry, Lotta – we may find them round the corner of that cliff.'

They followed the footprints eagerly and went right round the point of the rocky cliff. Lucky pulled at the lead again, and the children let her drag them where she wanted to go. They could not see the foot-marks when the moon was behind the clouds, but Lucky could always smell them.

They went on round the cliff. A great wave suddenly tore up the beach and splashed Jimmy from head to foot. He looked at the dark raging sea in alarm.

'I say, Lotta! I wonder if we ought to have come all the way round that rocky cliff. If the tide's coming in, we may not be able to get back.'

'Gracious!' said Lotta, frightened. 'What sillies we are. Of course the tide is coming in. Jimmy, what shall we do – go back, do you think? The sea comes right up to the cliff here, when the tide is in. We may be cut off unless we get round that corner again quickly.'

The moon sailed out again, and the restless sea tossed beneath the silver light. Another great wave came swirling up the beach, and the children jumped up on to a rock to escape it. Jimmy looked back.

'We're cut off already,' he said, in dismay. 'Look – the tide is right round that rocky corner. We'd never get back. Our only chance is to climb the cliff here.'

'But where have the bears gone?' asked Lotta, who had almost forgotten them in the worry of the moment.

'Goodness knows,' groaned Jimmy. 'Swept off their feet and drowned, I expect. And the same thing will happen to us and Lucky if we don't get up this cliff mighty quick. Come on, Lucky – hurry! Look out, Lotta, there's an enormous wave.'

The children began to climb the rocky cliff at the back of the shore. It was slippery, and when the moon went in, it was hard to feel the best way to climb. It was slow work too, and all the time the tide came in a little more, splashing foamy fingers up the cliff, trying to catch their feet.

'I don't like the sea when it behaves like this,' said Lotta, half crying. 'I'm cold and wet and frightened. We were silly to come, Jimmy. We didn't think of the darkness and the wind.'

'Well, the wind's dying down a bit now,' said Jimmy, helping Lotta over a slippery piece of rock.

'Come on – here's a nice easy bit now.'

'Have we got to stay and shiver on this cliff all night long?' asked Lotta miserably, her teeth chattering. 'My goodness – what will everyone say?'

The wind certainly was dying down. It no longer wailed and roared around them like a mad thing. The clouds in the sky slowed down a little, and the moon shone more steadily.

'Look! There's a cave or something over there,' said Jimmy suddenly. He had spied a dark opening just above them. 'Let's see if we can get in there, Lotta. We shall at least be sheltered from the gale.'

They waited for the moon to sail out once again and then they climbed up to the cave. The opening was small, but big enough to squeeze into. It was so dark inside that the children could see nothing at all. They groped their way in, and found a rocky ledge to sit on. It was quiet and sheltered there – but how cold the two children were!

'I think we've behaved very stupidly,' said Lotta shivering. 'We just rushed off after the bears without thinking. Why in the world didn't we bring a torch? We shall both get awful colds too, sitting here all night – and then we shan't be able to go into the ring and Galliano will be angry and scold us for being stupid.'

The two sat and thought about Mr Galliano. He was very good-tempered when things went well, but both children had been in trouble before with him, and they knew that he might be angry about this. Whatever had made them come out without telling someone? Now no one would know where they were, and half the circus folk would waste the night looking for them. Worst of all, nobody would find them in the little cave halfway up the dark cliff.

Lotta shivered so much that Jimmy was anxious about her. He lifted Lucky on to her knee.

'Cuddle her,' he said. 'She's warm, Lotta. I'd give you my coat only it's so wet. I wonder if there's any dry seaweed in the cave. I'll feel around and see. We could make a kind of bed of that.'

He got up and began to stumble round the cave. It was quite big inside. Jimmy felt about but could find no seaweed – only sand on the floor and stones, and rock all around.

And then the two children suddenly heard a most peculiar noise in the cave. They listened. It sounded exactly like somebody breathing.

'Lotta! Can you hear that noise?' asked Jimmy, coming back to her. 'Do you think it's the wind – or the sound of the sea coming up into the cave?'

'No,' said Lotta, holding his hand rather tightly. 'It's in the cave. But whatever can it be? It's funny that Lucky doesn't growl or bark. She always does if there's any stranger about, or if anything's wrong.'

Lucky wagged her tail. She settled down even more comfortably on Lotta's knee. The breathing in the cave didn't seem to worry her at all.

The children listened hard. The noise went on, and on, quite regularly, as if someone was fast asleep and breathing peacefully.

'Well, I'm going to see what is making that noise,' said Jimmy, at last. 'I can't sit here and wonder any more. If there's something in this cave I'm going to find out what it is. Here, Lucky – come with me.'

'Be careful, Jimmy,' said Lotta.

Jimmy and Lucky made their way to the back of the cave. Lucky didn't bark or growl at all. Jimmy couldn't understand it.

And then he suddenly touched something warm and furry – and soft. He jumped in surprise.

A grunt came from the furry bundle at the back of the cave. Jimmy gave such a yell that Lotta fell off the ledge she was sitting on, and shook with fright.

'Lotta! Lotta! The bears are here too! It's their breathing we heard. Oh, Lotta, we've found the bears! They had the sense to find this cave too, and creep into it.'

Lotta was thrilled. She stumbled over to the corner and touched the bears. They were awake now, but did not mind the children at all. They knew their smell and they loved Jimmy and Lucky, who often played with them. Dobby, the half-grown bear cub, grunted and rubbed his head against Jimmy's arm.

'Well, that's one piece of luck, at any rate,' said Lotta. She sat down with her back to the furry bear. He was warm and soft. 'Come on, Jimmy. Let's cuddle up to the bears. They will soon make us warm. Get on to my knee, Lucky – I'll have hot-water bottles at my back then, and a hot-water bottle on my knee too.'

The children cuddled up to the sleepy bears. They were like warm fur rugs. The bears liked feeling the children there. They were company. They made the bears feel safe, for they had been very much frightened by the wind and by the flapping white tent that had flown out of the night at them.

And there in the cliff cave slept the five creatures all night long. Dobby and Grizel, the bears, grunted and twisted in their sleep. Lucky yelped once or twice as she dreamed of chasing rabbits. The children lay against one another, feeling the delicious warmth of the furry bodies behind them. The noise of the sea and the wind did not come into the cave. All was peace and quiet.

But how surprised Jimmy was when he awoke! Daylight crept in at the small cave entrance, and for a moment the boy could not imagine where he was. Then he stood up and stretched himself, stiff with the night's strange bed. The bears awoke too, and Lucky leapt off Lotta's knee and licked her hands. The little girl rubbed her eyes and stared around her.

'Gracious! Where am I?' she cried. Then she remembered, and her face fell.

'Oh, Jimmy – do you think we'll get into trouble?' she said. 'Let's hurry back with the bears quickly. Perhaps we haven't been missed.'

'No such luck,' said Jimmy, peeping out of the cave. 'I

say, look – there's a boat out. Perhaps it's looking for us. We'll get out of the cave with the bears and hail the boat. The tide is still swishing round the cliff.'

So the two children took hold of the bears' great paws, and with Lucky behind urging them on, the great animals shuffled to the cave entrance. They all squeezed out, and Jimmy hailed the boat below.

'Hi! Will you rescue us?'

The two men in the boat looked up and their eyes nearly fell out of their heads when they saw the children with *two bears*! They stared and they stared.

'We must be dreaming,' said one to the other. But when the children shouted again, they knew they were not, and they drove their boat in closer to the cliff. They didn't mind rescuing the children – but they drew the line at bears.

6. Back to the camp

'We got caught by the tide last night and couldn't get back!' yelled Jimmy to the two surprised fishermen. 'We'll be down to you in a minute.'

The bears climbed clumsily down the cliff-side, grunting when they slipped. Lucky leapt about nimbly, quite enjoying herself. Such adventures didn't usually happen to the little dog!

The children and Lucky were soon standing on a rock, whilst the boat rocked nearby. The men brought it nearer. They stared at the bears, afraid and puzzled.

'How did those bears get here?' shouted one man. 'Are they circus bears? Did they escape?'

'Yes; haven't you heard?' shouted Jimmy, his voice rising above the roar of the waves. 'They ran away last night and we tracked them here – but the tide cut us off and we couldn't get back. So we cuddled up to the bears and spent the night in a cave. Now we want to take them back to the circus.'

'I'm not having any bears in *my* boat,' said one man firmly. 'They might claw me.'

'Of course they won't, said Jimmy, who couldn't imagine anyone being afraid of bears or of any other animal either. 'Oh, do let them come – they'll only run away again if we leave them here.'

'Well, you keep the bears at your end of the boat then,' said the man at last. 'And mind you, boy, if one of those bears comes near me. I'll push him overboard!'

'He'd be difficult to push!' laughed Lotta. 'Come on, Dobby – come on, Grizel. Oh, Jimmy, it's going to be awfully difficult to get the bears in, isn't it!'

It *was* difficult, especially as the two men wouldn't help at all. They crouched back into their end of the boat and looked really scared. Dobby playfully put out a paw to one of the men.

'No, Dobby,' said Lotta, smacking the bear's paw back. 'Don't try to be funny in a boat.'

The bear sat himself down and the boat shook. Then Grizel clambered in, almost falling into the sea as he did so. Last of all, little dog Lucky leapt lightly in – and my goodness, the boat was as full as it could be!

Jimmy had to take the oars, for neither of the men would get into the middle of the boat to row. The bears were so heavy at their end that the other end of the boat was quite high up in the water.

'Never had a boat-load like this before!' grumbled one of the men. 'Whoever heard of taking bears for a row?'

Jimmy laughed as he rowed. He was glad to be going back to the circus, though he couldn't help feeling uncomfortable inside about whether Mr Galliano would be angry because he and Lotta had gone off without a word.

'Still, everyone would guess we'd gone after the bears,' said the boy to Lotta. She nodded her head. She was busy quieting the bears, who didn't much like the up-and-down movement of the boat.

'I hope they won't be seasick,' said Lotta anxiously. But the voyage was not long enough for anyone to feel seasick. The boat rounded the rocky corner of the cliff, where the waves were still splashing, and came to a sandy cove. The boat ran in, and the men jumped out. They pulled the boat up the beach, and then stood at a safe distance whilst the children tried to coax the two bears out of the boat.

But, you know, they wouldn't get out! No – the movement of the boat, strange and unusual to them, had really frightened them. They were afraid to move in case something stranger happened. It was no use pulling and tugging at them. They were far too heavy to move. They squatted down in the bottom of the boat, looking like great fat fur rugs!

'Oh, Dobby! You are a perfect nuisance!' said Jimmy, giving it up with a sigh. 'Lotta, run up to the circus field and fetch Mr Volla. I don't believe anyone but him could get these tiresome creatures out of this boat.'

'You stay here with them then, and I'll send Mr Volla as soon as I can,' said Lotta, not at all liking the idea of going back to the camp without Jimmy – but she saw that there was really nothing else to do.

She ran to the cliff path and began to climb it to the top. The bears watched her. They grunted. They were glad that Jimmy and Lucky were still with them. Lucky jumped down to the bears and tried to play with Dobby, for they were very good friends. But Dobby wouldn't play, so Lucky went and had a glorious game of chase-the-waves-and-bark-at-them till one unexpectedly ran up the beach too quickly for her, and she got her legs wet. After that she stuck closely to Jimmy's heels and growled whenever a wave came near.

Lotta climbed to the top of the cliff. She saw the circus field in the distance. It was early morning, and she did not expect people to be about. But the whole camp was up, and she could hear shouts and calls as she drew near.

She squeezed through a hole in the hedge and looked over the field. She could hear Mr Galliano's voice.

'Perhaps the caravan was blown off in the wind! This is a terrible time, yes! First the bears, then the children – and now Madame Prunella's caravan is gone!'

Lotta looked over the field in surprise. Madame Prunella's caravan gone? How strange! Where could it have gone to? Sure enough, the little girl could not see it. And at that very moment Sticky Stanley the clown saw Lotta! He gave a yell.

'Lotta! Here's Lotta! Where have you been, Lotta? We've been up all night looking for you and Jimmy!'

Everyone crowded round the dirty and untidy little

girl. Lal, her mother, came up and put her arm round her. She had been crying.

'Oh, Lotta,' she said, 'we've been so worried about you and Jimmy. We thought the storm might have blown you over the cliff, or something!'

'No, I'm quite safe,' said Lotta. 'We went after the bears, Jimmy and Lucky and I. And we found them!'

'*Found* them!' yelled Mr Volla joyfully. 'Oh, you wonderful child, Lotta – oh, you beauty! – oh, you treasure!'

Lotta laughed. Mr Volla was hugging her for joy. He had been up all night worrying about his bears, and now he was like a child because his pets had been found.

'Where are they – where are they?' he kept asking.

'And where's Jimmy?' asked Mrs Brown, who was looking pale and tired.

Lotta told her tale quickly. 'We couldn't get the bears to move out of the boat,' she finished. 'So Jimmy sent me to get Mr Volla. Can you come, Mr Volla?'

'I come at once!' cried the bear-trainer in joy. 'Oh, what a night it has been! Neither I nor my bears have slept a wink.'

'You haven't found Madame Prunella's caravan too, I suppose?' asked Sticky Stanley the clown, running alongside Lotta as she led the way to the cliff. Half the circus folk came with them, for they all loved a bit of excitement.

'Of course not!' said Lotta. 'Goodness – we would have been astonished to see Madame Prunella's caravan in that little cave along with the bears, I can tell you! How strange that she has disappeared!'

They all climbed down the steep cliff path. As soon as they came in sight of the boat, with the bears still huddled at one end, Mr Volla gave a shout of delight.

'Dobby! Grizel! Are you safe? Come to Volla!'

At the sound of their beloved trainer's voice the two bears raised their heads. When they saw Mr Volla running over the sand towards them, they scrambled heavily out of the boat and went to meet him, grunting and growling in a most comical manner.

They flung their hairy arms round their keeper, and all three danced together for joy. Jimmy began to laugh. He really couldn't help it. Then one of the bears trod heavily on Mr Volla's foot and he yelped with pain.

That made Jimmy laugh even more – and he and Lotta went back up the cliff path with everyone else, laughing and talking, telling their night-time adventures.

'Is Mr Galliano angry?' he said to Oona the acrobat. 'Has he sat up all night waiting for us?'

'We all have, young Jimmy,' said Oona. 'You can't rush off like that, you know, without being missed. You should have left word about what you were doing. Galliano is pretty down about everything this morning – the big tent is spoilt, you were missing, and Prunella and her caravan have disappeared! You know, she's a queer person – and I shouldn't be surprised if she's gone off in one of her tantrums because of the storm!'

By now they were all back in the camp. Mrs Brown came and kissed Jimmy. Galliano roared to him:

'Where have you been? Why didn't you say where you were going? Boy, I've a good mind to give you a taste of my ring whip, yes! You cannot do as you like here, no – and you take Lotta with you too. Bad, bad, very bad!'

Jimmy didn't know what to say. Everyone was afraid of Mr Galliano when he was in a temper. The boy stood there and looked pale and sulky. That didn't please Mr Galliano at all! He put his hat quite straight on his head and glared at Jimmy.

'Your tongue is gone – yes?' he roared. 'You have nothing to say to me? The bears go, you go, Lotta goes, and Madame Prunella goes! My whole circus can go for all I care!'

He cracked his whip round Jimmy's feet and the boy jumped. He had never seen Mr Galliano quite so angry and upset before, but the ring-master had been up all night and was tired and worried.

And then Lotta, who had been standing nearby, looking scared, heard a sound that made her prick up her ears at once. It was a parrot's screech! Well, Madame Prunella couldn't be so far away then!

The little girl slipped off. She ran to where the sound seemed to come from. It was somewhere near the enormous bulk of the blown-down tent, surely! The little girl stood and listened carefully. She heard a muffled voice say, 'Baked beans and tomatoes, baked beans and tomatoes,' very solemnly indeed.

'That's Gringle!' thought the little girl joyfully. 'But goodness me, wherever can he be?'

And then she suddenly knew where Madame Prunella and her caravan were! They were buried underneath the enormous canvas of the blown-down tent! No wonder they couldn't be seen. No wonder everyone thought that Madame Prunella was gone!

The little girl rushed back to Mr Galliano and pulled at his hand. She was very glad to stop him raging at Jimmy. Perhaps he would be in a better temper when he heard her news.

'Mr Galliano!' she cried. 'I've found Madame Prunella's caravan! Come quickly!'

Mr Galliano forgot his temper at once. He looked down at Lotta, surprised and delighted. 'Where is it – where is it?' he cried. 'This is good news, yes!'

'Come and see,' said Lotta, glad to see his frown disappear. 'You *will* be surprised!'

7. Prunella is found

'Come quickly and I will show you where Madame Prunella's caravan is!' cried Lotta – and everyone followed
the little girl. She ran to where the great canvas tent lay
in an enormous pile.

'The caravan is under the blown-down tent,' she cried.
'Listen – you can hear the parrots screeching!'

Sure enough the parrots *were* screeching – and someone else was too! Madame Prunella had woken up and
tried to open her caravan door, to see why the windows
were so darkened – and she found that she couldn't open
the door! The heavy weight of the tent lay all around it.
So Madame Prunella screeched too, and kicked hard at
the door.

Mr Galliano smiled. It was always funny when
Madame Prunella lost her temper.

'All right, all right, Madame Prunella,' he shouted in
his enormous voice. 'You shall be set free, yes. In a minute
or two. So be patient!'

But that was just one thing Madame Prunella could
never be! She went on kicking and hammering at the
door, and she and her parrots screeched like a hundred
express trains at once. Lotta and Jimmy couldn't help
laughing.

Then many hands began to tug at the great tent, and
presently it was moved so that Madame Prunella could
open her caravan door. It flew open and a very red and
angry little woman looked out. She had on a bright red
dressing-gown with a yellow girdle, and her shock of hair
stuck up straight just like the crest of a bird.

'She's awfully like one of her parrots,' grinned Jimmy.

Madame Prunella heard him, and she caught up the nearest thing to her hand and threw it at Jimmy angrily. It was a saucepan – but it didn't really matter what it was, because Madame Prunella could never throw straight.

The saucepan went flying through the air, and Oona the acrobat caught it neatly. He stuck it upside down on Sticky Stanley's head, and everyone laughed.

'Who shut me in? Who barred my door?' Prunella cried. Then she saw the great tent, which still lay over half of her caravan. Her eyes grew wide and surprised.

'Goodness gracious!' she said. 'So that's what happened! The big tent blew down – and I never knew!'

'There are a lot of things you don't know, Prunella,' said Oona, her cousin. 'You must have taken your parrots to your caravan last night, and gone to sleep without knowing that the tent had frightened Dobby and Grizel, two of the bears, and made them run away. You didn't know that Jimmy and Lotta disappeared, and we spent all night looking for them! You didn't know that they've turned up again with the bears, and . . .'

'Oh, what I have missed!' wailed Madame Prunella, bursting into floods of tears. She loved any excitement, and it seemed terrible to her to think she had slept through such a lot. 'How wicked of you all not to come and tell me!'

'Yes, but we didn't know where you were,' said Oona. 'We thought you had disappeared too! It was Lotta who found you just now – she heard one of your parrots screeching.'

The parrots were still screeching, all except Gringle, who kept muttering to himself, 'Bacon and eggs, bacon and eggs, bacon and eggs.' Then he raised his voice to a shout and cried, 'BACON AND EGGS!'

'The poor darling. He does want his breakfast,' said Madame Prunella, and she ran to her caravan again to feed her parrots. They were all flying loose this morning and hovered round like a brilliant cloud of colour.

Jemima the monkey was thrilled with them. She waited till one perched near her and then she made a grab for one of the bright feathers in its tail. She pulled it out and leapt away, whilst the parrot screeched and tried to claw her.

Jemima stuck the feather into the buttonhole of her little coat, chattering proudly. Everyone laughed – and then Jimmy looked at Mr Galliano. Was he going to say any more? Had he still got a scolding or a punishment for Jimmy and Lotta? But, hurrah! the ring-master was beaming again, and his top hat was well on one side once more. Good! He had forgotten about Jimmy, that was quite plain. Things were right again – the bears were safe, Madame Prunella was safe, the big tent was not really damaged!

'Come on, let's slip away to my caravan,' whispered Jimmy to Lotta. 'We're going to get off lightly this time, Lotta. Let's go and ask my mother for something to eat. I'm awfully hungry, aren't you?'

So away they went to Jimmy's caravan, and there they found Mrs Brown cooking a big meal of bacon and sausages on her neat stove.

'Mother, weren't Lotta and I lucky not to get into real trouble with Mr Galliano?' he began. And then he saw Mrs Brown's face. It was very stern indeed!

'You may think you've got off lightly with Mr Galliano,' she said sharply, 'but you've got a whole lot of trouble coming from *me*, Jimmy. How dare you go off like that with Lotta, and never think of letting me or Lal know what you were doing? We have been terribly worried all night long.'

'Well, we did bring back the bears, Mrs Brown,' said Lotta coaxingly, slipping a small paw into Mrs Brown's hand. But Mrs Brown would not take it. She was angry and hurt.

'Bears! What do I care about bears!' she cried, slapping the sausages on to a dish. 'It's you two children I care about. And to think you care so little for me that you can slip off like that and leave me to worry and worry!'

'Oh, Mother – we didn't think,' said Jimmy, upset to see his mother's white, stern face. 'We won't do such a thing again. Really we won't. We're sorry – aren't we, Lotta?'

'Yes, *very* sorry,' said Lotta, and she burst into tears, for she was tired and over-excited. Mrs Brown set down the dish of sausages and put her arms round the little girl.

'All right,' she said. 'I'll forgive you both. You're just a pair of naughty, thoughtless, independent children – but you're brave and kind too, so I won't scold you any more. Now, eat up your breakfast, both of you, and I'll make you some cocoa with plenty of sugar.'

The children were happy once more. They simply could not bear to see Mrs Brown cross or worried – now things were all right again. They ate their breakfast hungrily and Mrs Brown fussed round them like a hen with a couple of chickens.

'And now,' she said firmly, 'both you and Lotta are going to curl up in those two bunks, Jimmy, and go to sleep. You look tired out, both of you. The circus is not moving for a while and there is no show tonight – so you can be lazy for once. Get off my feet, Lucky – you've had enough breakfast! Stop pulling at my shoelaces!'

The children really were very tired, and they didn't in the least mind curling up in the cosy bunks, with Lucky and Lulu the spaniel at their feet. In half a minute they were both sound asleep, and did not even stir when Mrs Brown knocked over a pail with a great clatter on the floor.

The circus settled down once more. Dobby and Grizel joined the other bears with great delight, and there was a grunting and smacking of paws as the two adventurous bears greeted the other three.

Madame Prunella settled down too, her fright and temper forgotten. At ten o'clock the circus camp was just as usual, except that most of the grown-ups looked rather tired after their worrying night.

Mr Galliano sat in his caravan with Tessa, his fat,

smiling wife. Everyone loved gentle Mrs Galliano, and would have done anything in the world for her. She was helping Galliano to count up the money he had taken.

Galliano sat smiling, his hat cocked over his left ear, for he wore his top hat even in the caravan. The circus had done splendidly at Bigminton – and now the ring-master was planning how to make it even bigger and better!

'Tessa, we will have more clowns – yes?' he said happily. 'Two more, three more!'

'Three more,' said Mrs Galliano. 'But Sticky Stanley must be the chief clown, Galliano. He has been with us so long and is so good.'

'Yes – he shall be head clown,' said Mr Galliano. 'Ah – we shall be grand with four clowns, yes! And more animals. Now what animals shall we have? Not tigers, no! They are not happy in the ring as are the bears and the dogs and horses. We will have – we will have—'

'A performing seal!' said Mrs Galliano, who loved seals and sea-lions. 'Ah, Galliano, I remember once that my uncle had a seal that loved him so much it even wanted to have a bath with him at night. But my uncle was a big man and there was not enough room for them both in the bath – so he had a great bath made especially for him, and he carried it with him wherever he went. Then his seal could bathe with him each night. How I remember seeing that great bath always strapped to the top of his caravan!'

'Good! We will have a performing seal, yes,' said Mr Galliano. 'And what else? Lions – no. Cats – no. Then what?'

Mrs Galliano turned over a sheaf of papers and letters. She came to a picture of zebras trotting round in a ring. She showed it to Galliano.

'See, these are rare in a circus,' she said. 'Here is a picture of Zeno and his twelve trained zebras. Shall we write to him and have those? They are pretty creatures.'

'Yes,' said Galliano thoughtfully. 'Pretty – but difficult. We shall have to keep that daring young Lotta away from them or she will be trying to ride them – and zebras will not be ridden! And see, wife – here is a photograph of the amazing conjurer, Britomart. He would be marvellous to have in our circus, yes! We will write to them all!'

'And look at these performing goats,' said Mrs Galliano, opening a booklet that showed pictures of troupes of snow-white goats. But Mr Galliano shook his head.

'No – not goats. They smell too strong,' he said. 'We will have three more clowns, Britomart the great conjurer, the performing seal, and Zeno with his zebras!'

The news soon went round the camp and the children were very excited.

'Gracious!' said Lotta, skipping round happily. 'What fun we shall have! I bet I'll ride on those zebras before they've been in the circus for a week, Jimmy!'

'And I bet I'll have that seal eating out of my hand!' cried Jimmy. 'Come on – let's go and tell Madame Prunella. She hasn't heard the news yet!'

So off they ran, and soon they were talking excitedly to Madame Prunella about all the newcomers that would soon arrive. She gave them peppermints to suck, and Gringle put out a foot for one, too.

'Pickles and peppermints,' he remarked solemnly. 'Peppermints and pickles!' That clever old bird could always think of something quaint to say!

8. The circus moves on

The circus was going to leave the field at Bigminton in a few days. The children had a nice holiday, roaming about the seashore with the dogs, or riding over the countryside. Lotta rode Black Beauty, her own horse, of course – and Jimmy rode a rather quiet horse belonging to Lal. He rode quite well now, but he would never ride so well as Lotta!

She had ridden horses since she was a baby. She scared many of the folk she met on their rides by suddenly standing up straight on Black Beauty's back, just as she did in the circus. People stared in alarm and surprise, and then they smiled and said:

'Oh, that must be Lotta, the circus girl. Isn't she marvellous!'

That would please Lotta very much, and then Jimmy would tease her and say she was vain. They had great fun together, and the only thing they didn't like about their little holiday was that Mrs Brown made them both go to bed much earlier than usual.

'You will both be in bed by half past eight,' she said firmly. 'Circus hours are bad for children. I never before in my life heard of children going to bed every night at eleven o'clock and half past, till I came to join the circus. Now that there is no need to go to bed late for a few nights, you will both go early.'

This didn't please Jimmy and Lotta at all, and the first night they both disappeared about half past eight and didn't wander into the circus camp again till half past nine, very hungry indeed.

But alas for them! They were sent off to their bunks

without any supper at all – though Mrs Brown was cooking one of her most delicious stews. Jimmy saw a big tin
of pineapple chunks too, a thing he loved very much. But
not a bite did he and Lotta have!

'Bed at half past eight and a good supper – bed after
half past eight and no supper at all,' said Mrs Brown.
'You can choose which you like!'

So after that both children ate a good supper and snuggled down in their bunks nice and early. Lotta went to
her own caravan, and Jimmy slept in his with his father
and mother, Lucky, his dog, and Lulu, the old spaniel,
who loved the whole family. She had once belonged to
two men who were unkind to her – and so Jimmy took
her for his own, and she adored him.

When the circus went on the road again, the children
were happy and excited, for they knew that at the
next stopping place the new clowns and animals would
be joining them. Then what a fine circus it would
be!

'Oh, how I'll love playing with a seal!' said Jimmy,
joyfully. 'And won't it be marvellous to watch Britomart
doing his wonderful tricks, Lotta.'

'What *I'm* looking forward to is riding a zebra,' said
Lotta.

'And that is just what you won't do, no!' said a voice
nearby – and Lotta looked up to see Mr Galliano there,
his hat well on one side, and his stiff moustaches sticking
up well. 'Zebras are not horses. They are dangerous
animals. They can never be properly tamed. You will not
try any tricks, Lotta, no!'

He went on his way, swinging his great whip. Lotta
looked after him sulkily.

'Well, that's that!' said Jimmy. 'No zebras for *you*,
Lotta! I once had to promise Mr Galliano I'd never go
and play with any circus animal till I had his permission –
and you'll have to promise not to go near the zebras!'

'I didn't promise anything – and I shan't promise,' said
Lotta. 'Zebras – what are zebras! Just little striped

animals not so big as horses! I'll soon be able to do what I like with *them*!'

'Well, you jolly well be careful,' said Jimmy anxiously. He knew how daring Lotta was, and although he was no longer afraid of her hurting herself, as he had once been, he didn't want her to do anything dangerous, for he was very fond of the naughty little girl.

Lotta jumped down from the caravan steps, turned herself nimbly upside down, and walked all round Jimmy on her hands, kicking at him with her feet as she passed him. She made dreadful faces and sang as she went:

> '*Don't go near the zebras,*
> *They'll kick you all to bits,*
> *Don't go near the seal in case*
> *It frightens you to fits,*
> *Don't go near the elephant*
> *In case you make it bray.*
> *Don't go near the monkeys,*
> *They'll make you run away!*'

Jimmy roared with laughter. Lotta looked so funny walking round on her hands, her legs dangling over, and the song was so very silly. He rushed at the grinning little girl, but she leapt upright again and tore off to Sticky Stanley the clown. She hid behind him and he kept Jimmy off with a broom he was using. He laughed at the two excited children.

'My word, Lotta, I don't know why Mr Galliano wants to get any more clowns!' he said 'He could take you and Jimmy for a fine pair!'

'Stanley, what other clowns are coming?' asked Jimmy, wondering if the clown had any news. Sticky Stanley sat down on an upturned bucket and told them all he knew.

'Well, the two clowns, Twinkle and Pippi, are coming,' he said. 'They are knock-about clowns – they knock each other over, fall off everything, and have a very funny act in which they keep a fruit-shop and end up by throwing tomatoes and everything else at one another.'

'Oooh, that sounds simply gorgeous,' said Lotta, delighted. 'I'd really *love* to see people throwing tomatoes at one another.'

'Yes – it's just the sort of thing you'd like to do yourself, isn't it?' grinned Sticky Stanley, who knew what a little monkey Lotta was. 'Well, the third clown is Google. He's really funny too. He has a wonderful motorcar, and everything goes wrong with it – and in the end it blows up into a hundred different pieces! Google has a fine little dog called Squib. You'll like him. He helps Google with his nonsense.'

'Oh, this all sounds too lovely for words,' said Lotta joyfully. 'Now tell us about Britomart the conjurer.'

Stanley looked rather solemn. 'You mustn't tell this to anyone,' he said. 'But I don't like what I've heard of Britomart. Mind you, he's a remarkably clever man, and some of his tricks are so amazing that you can't help thinking he does really know a lot of magic. But I've heard he's a hard man, and unless he's given the longest time and the best turn in the ring he can be very unpleasant.'

'Well, I shan't interfere with him much!' said Jimmy. 'All I shall do will be to watch him at his tricks. I shan't want to meddle with his magic in case I find myself changed into a donkey or something all of a sudden!'

'Oh, that *would* be fun!' said Lotta. I could ride you in the ring, then. And feed you with carrots!'

'Britomart once had a circus of his own,' said Sticky Stanley, getting up and going on with his work. 'I don't know why it came to an end, but it did. And now he travels around with all kinds of shows. It's a great thing for Galliano's Circus to get Britomart. We should draw enormous crowds. You know Mr Galliano is getting a much bigger tent, don't you?'

'Is he really?' said Jimmy. 'My goodness, what fun! We'll have hundreds and hundreds of people watching us each night now, Lotta!'

When the circus had once again settled down in camp,

the children kept a watch for new arrivals. Jemima the
monkey came to sit on the gate with them, and Sammy
the chimpanzee joined them. He loved the children, and
chattered to them in his own language, slipping his hairy
paw into Jimmy's hand.

So there they all sat on the field gate – Jimmy, Lotta,
Jemima the monkey in a new green dress, and Sammy the
chimp, dressed in his usual trousers and jersey. He even
wore a tie, but as he much preferred it to hang down his
back instead of his chest, it looked a little odd. As fast as
Jimmy put the tie in its right place, Sammy put it in the
wrong place. So in the end Jimmy gave it up, and Sammy
proudly wore his nice blue tie down his back.

He had got a habit lately of slipping his paw into the
pockets of Jimmy's shorts, and taking out anything he
found there. Jimmy missed marbles and string, pennies,
sixpences, and toffee! As soon as he discovered that it was
Sammy who was the thief, he made the chimpanzee turn

out his own pockets – and then Jimmy took back all his
things!

But Sammy was so clever at taking things without the
boy knowing, that three or four times a day the chimpanzee had to turn out his pockets and give Jimmy back
his belongings! This was quite a new trick and Mrs
Brown was very shocked at it.

'That's stealing, Jimmy,' she said. 'You must punish
Sammy well if he does that.'

'Oh, no, Mother!' said Jimmy, just as shocked. 'He
doesn't know what stealing *is*. He only does it for fun. It's
just a new trick with him. I couldn't punish old Sammy
for that. He wouldn't understand. No – for a few days I
won't put anything in my pockets at all, and he'll soon get
tired of putting his hand in when he finds there's nothing
there!'

So, whilst they sat on the gate, waiting and watching
for new arrivals, Jimmy grinned to feel Sammy slipping a
paw into his pockets. 'Nothing there, Sammy old fellow!'
he said. 'Nothing there! Now you just give Lotta one paw
and I'll take the other, and you won't be able to get into
any mischief then!'

So Sammy had to sit still and quiet, a paw held by each
of the children, whilst Jemima sat first on Jimmy's shoulder, then on Lotta's, and then on Sammy's, chattering
monkey language as hard as she could go!

Then suddenly Jimmy shouted loudly, 'Hark! I hear
trotting. It's the zebras! Zeno and his zebras, hurrah!
Open the gate, Lotta, and we'll see them all trotting in!'

9. Zebras — a seal — and two little girls!

Down the country road, in the hot May sun, came a fine sight – a most strange and unusual one, that thrilled the two children and made them shout for joy.

First of all came six beautiful striped zebras, led by a groom on a small horse. The zebras trotted in a bunch together, their striped coats gleaming like satin. They looked round with big eyes that had a wild gleam in them.

Then came six more zebras – and they drew a marvellous carriage, in which sat Zeno, their trainer. Zeno was a small man, dressed in riding clothes. He had top boots on with very high heels to make him look taller. His riding coat was blue and his breeches were yellow, so he looked very gay. He held the reins of the zebras and held them tightly too. Zebras were not like horses, tame and biddable. They were difficult, wild creatures, who hated to be bridled and ridden, and hated to feel the drag of a carriage behind them. But every zebra loved Zeno, and was willing to do what he wanted, so they were a happy family, and made a marvellous picture as they trotted down the country road.

They swung in at the open field gate, and the groom jumped off his horse. He went to the noses of his zebras, and looked at his master, Zeno. Zeno got out of his carriage, which was just as brilliant as he was, for it had glittering yellow wheels, and bright blue paint every-where else. Lotta simply longed to have a ride in it.

'Where is Mr Galliano?' called Zeno in a commanding voice. He looked at the children, and Jimmy went over to him.

'There he is, sir – look,' said the boy. 'The big man with

the whip. He's seen you. Can I give you any help with
your zebras, sir?'

'Certainly not,' said Zeno. 'You don't know what you
are talking about, boy. They'll bite you as soon as look at
you.'

He strode off in his high heeled boots, a big top hat on
his rather small head. The groom stood patiently waiting
with the zebras. Lotta went softly up to him.

'May I touch a zebra?' she asked.

'Of course not,' said the man, startled. 'Do you want to
be bitten? Keep away, please. They are upset at the
change in their surroundings and I don't want them to be
handled at all. Their travelling stables are coming along
in a minute or two, and then I'll be able to give them food
and drink.'

The nearest zebra looked at Lotta out of its big startled
eyes. Lotta looked back, and made a curious noise. The
zebra pricked its ears towards her and said 'Hrrrumph!'
rather like an old man sneezing. It reached out its head to
Lotta, and the groom jerked it back.

'Get back, Zebby,' he said. 'It's no good you pretending
you want to make friends with the little girl. You only
want to bite her fingers off.'

'Oh, but he doesn't, said Lotta. 'He really doesn't.
Please let me stroke his satiny nose. He's so lovely.'

Mr Galliano caught sight of the children standing near
the zebras, as he strode over with Zeno to look at them.
He shouted at Lotta.

'Now, you bad little girl, didn't you promise not to
touch those zebras, yes! Go away at once before I come
after you. Jimmy, you can help Zeno sometime with his
zebras, for all animals are good with you, but not today
whilst they are upset at strange surroundings. Go with
Lotta.'

'Oh, if that isn't too bad!' cried Lotta indignantly, as
she and Jimmy moved away. 'To think *you* can help with
the zebras, and I can't. I can manage horses much, much
better than you, and you know it.'

'Yes, but zebras aren't horses,' said Jimmy with a grin. 'Ha ha! You won't be able to touch the zebras now you've had to promise not to.'

'Jimmy, I tell you I *haven't* promised,' cried Lotta. 'I know Mr Galliano said just now that I had – but I haven't, so there! He's made a mistake.'

'Well, you'd better tell him so then,' said Jimmy.

'I shan't,' said Lotta. They stood and watched Zeno showing his fine collection of zebras to Mr Galliano. At first they shied away from the big ring-master – but, like most horse-like creatures, they liked him, and he was able to rub one or two sleek noses before he nodded to Zeno and strode away.

Then, a few minutes later, the big travelling stables arrived – great vans, whose sides could be opened or shut. They came into the field, and the groom and Zeno were soon very busy getting the tired animals into their stalls. They had trotted a long way that day to join Galliano's Circus.

'Well, that's the first new arrival,' said Jimmy. 'Now we'll watch for the seal, Lotta. Come on. Who's bringing it, I wonder?'

The performing seal was due to arrive that afternoon too – but it was rather disappointing when it did turn up. It came in a closed van, and as it passed into the field the children heard the swish of water inside.

'It travels in a tank of water,' said Lotta. 'I never thought of that. Oh, Jimmy, we'll peep and see what it's like as soon as the van is opened. I say, look – who are those two little girls?'

Behind the van came a caravan, driven by Pierre, the owner of the seal. He was dressed in ordinary clothes, and was whistling a merry tune. He was a cheery man, with a red face and the brightest blue eyes the children had ever seen. Riding on the very top of the caravan were two little girls.

'Oh! I didn't know there would be any children,' said Lotta, pleased. 'It'll be fun to play with them, won't it?'

Jimmy wasn't so sure. He was quite content with Lotta, and he didn't want any more little girls in the circus. So he didn't say anything, but just looked at the two girls. One was about the same age as he was, and the other looked older. They grinned down at the two circus children from the top of the caravan.

'That's rather a good place to ride,' said Lotta. 'I never thought of that before.'

'It does look rather good,' said Jimmy. 'But I can't see my mother letting me ride on the top of *our* caravan.'

Pierre, the owner of the performing seal, had a thin little wife with curly red hair, as well as his two little girls. They sprang lightly down from the top of the caravan, and Mrs Pierre looked from the window.

'Jeanne! Lisa!' she called. 'Are you all right?'

The girls took no notice of their mother at all. They were bold little things, pretty with red curls like their mother. They were very dirty and untidy, and their smiles were very broad indeed.

'Hallo!' said Lisa, tossing her red curls. 'Do you belong to this circus?'

'Yes,' said Jimmy and Lotta together.

'It doesn't look much of a camp,' said Jeanne, looking round. 'We've been used to much bigger circuses than this. I call this rather a poor show.'

'Go back to a better show then,' said Jimmy, unexpectedly rude. He felt that he disliked these little girls with their red curls, bold faces, and loud voices.

'Oh, *isn't* he polite,' said Lisa, and she giggled. Her mother called her again and she took no notice at all.

'Your mother's calling you,' said Lotta.

'She can call then,' said Jeanne rudely. At that moment her father came up, and heard what she said. He gave her a slap and she squealed.

'Go and help your mother,' said Pierre, with a scowl on his red face. The two little girls went off, sulking. Pierre looked at Jimmy and Lotta and Lucky.

'You must be the two Wonder Children,' he said. 'Pleased to meet you.'

'Can we see your seal?' asked Jimmy eagerly. Pierre's wife and the girls had gone to the van and were letting down one side. Inside was an enormous tank full of water that gleamed a deep blue. In the tank swam a beautiful seal. Jimmy ran to it. The seal popped its head out of the water and looked at Jimmy with the most beautiful eyes he had ever seen. He loved the seal from that very moment.

'Oh, isn't it lovely!' cried Jimmy. 'I do love its eyes. What's its name?'

'Neptune,' said Pierre, pleased that Jimmy liked his seal. 'He's the cleverest and best seal in the world. Aren't you, Neptune?'

The seal made a strange noise and nodded its head. The children laughed. The seal seemed to laugh too, and then, diving into its tank, swam gracefully round and round, up and down, to and fro, its tail acting as a rudder to guide it.

'Would you like to feed him?' asked Pierre. 'Neptune! Dinner!'

With a gobbling noise Neptune shot up to the top of the tank. Pierre took down a bag from a nail and gave it to Jimmy.

'Throw him a fish,' he said. Jimmy opened the bag and found many fishes there. He picked one out and threw it to the watching seal. Neptune caught the fish deftly and then looked for another.

One after another he caught the fish, never missing once. 'What a marvellous cricketer he would make,' said Jimmy.

'Does he come out of his tank?' asked Lotta.

'Oh yes!' said Pierre. 'He comes into the ring with me. He and I play cricket – and he never misses a ball, as you can guess. He *is* a marvellous cricketer. He is a wonderful balancer too. He can balance a pole on the tip of his nose – and a ball on the tip of the pole!'

'Oh no!' said Jimmy, not believing this at all.

'Well, wait and see,' said Pierre, and he twinkled his bright blue eyes at them. 'Now I must see Mr Galliano and find out where I can put my caravan.'

He went off to Mr Galliano's caravan, and left Jimmy and Lotta watching the seal. It popped its head out again and made a soft noise to Jimmy. He went into the van, reached up to the top of the tank and stroked the seal's wet nose. In a trice it was right out of the tank, flapping itself round Jimmy's legs. The boy got a real surprise.

'Get back!' he cried in alarm, but the seal took no notice. It pushed itself against Jimmy's legs and nearly knocked him over. Then Jeanne and Lisa came up, and they rapped the top of the tank with a stick.

'Hup, hup!' they cried in circus language, and the seal 'hupped', and got back into the water.

'You'll get into trouble if you make my father's seal get out of the tank,' said Lisa.

'I didn't make it. It got out itself,' said Jimmy crossly.

'Crosspatch!' said Jeanne, and she pinched Jimmy. The little boy shook himself free and walked off in a huff with Lotta.

'I wish those girls hadn't come,' he said. 'I'm not going to like them one bit. Promise you won't make friends with them, Lotta.'

But that was another promise Lotta wouldn't make. She laughed at Jimmy and ran off to help Laddo with the horses. Lotta was certainly a little monkey these days.

10. The three new clowns

The circus was not going to open for two weeks, because Mr Galliano wanted all the new performers to settle down, make friends with one another, and practise their turns in the ring together.

The three new clowns were to arrive the next day, and Britomart, the conjurer, was coming the day after. Lotta and Jimmy felt too excited for words.

'Do go and chatter somewhere else,' said Mrs Brown, shooing them off the steps of her caravan. 'You are much worse than those screeching parrots.'

The parrots were excited, too, by the arrival of more animals and performers, and they screeched and chattered all day long. Madame Prunella had had to move her caravan a little farther away, for not all the circus folk would put up with such a dreadful noise!

'Swee-ee-eep!' cried one parrot mournfully. 'Swee-ee-eep!'

'Sounds as if he thinks Madame Prunella's chimneys want sweeping,' grinned Jimmy. 'Just listen to old Gringle, too!'

'Sausage and smash, sausage and smash,' said Gringle loudly.

'You've got it wrong, old boy. It's sausage and *mash*,' said Jimmy, running his fingers down the parrot's soft, feathery neck. But Gringle preferred sausage and smash, and said so, at the top of his voice.

The zebras soon settled down in the camp. Jumbo the elephant was delighted to see them. He trumpeted loudly to them whenever they passed and they whinnied back. Most of the animals liked good-tempered old Jumbo, and

Sammy the chimpanzee was so fond of him that he scrambled up on Jumbo's back whenever Mr Tonks, his keeper, was not there to stop him.

The performing seal was quite ridiculous with Jimmy. It went completely mad whenever the boy appeared, and made little snickering noises of joy. It always leapt out of the tank at once, and Jimmy had to stop it from following him all over the field.

The two girls, Jeanne and Lisa, were jealous because their seal loved Jimmy. It took no notice of either of them at all, just as they took no notice of their mother. Jimmy wondered what his mother would say if he wouldn't come when he was called, or ran off without doing his jobs, or was as rude to her as Jeanne and Lisa were to their mother.

Jimmy was rather hurt because Lotta went about so much with the two girls. She giggled with them and went to look at two beautiful dolls that someone had once given them. Jimmy felt quite left out, and he went off with Lucky to watch for the arrival of the three new clowns. He sat on the fence alone, with Lucky licking his boots every now and then. He thought it was a great pity that Jeanne and Lisa had come.

Soon a fine caravan appeared. It was painted red, and on its wooden walls were posters showing the two clowns, Twinkle and Pippi. They looked very funny with their enormous eyebrows, big red noses, wide mouths, and large ears. They grinned out of the pictures at Jimmy, and he was so busy looking at them that he nearly fell off the fence when a tousled head stuck itself out of a caravan window and yelled at him:

'Boy! Are we near the circus camp?'

It was Twinkle, one of the clowns. But he was not dressed up now, nor was his face painted like a clown's. He was just a jolly-faced man with big bulging eyes and a shock of yellow hair.

'Yes. You're there!' said Jimmy, jumping down. 'Are you Twinkle or Pippi?'

Another head stuck itself out of the window – and to Jimmy's great surprise it was exactly the same as the first one! It had a shock of yellow hair and big bulging blue eyes with a merry twinkle in them.

'Hey,' said the first head to the second head. 'This boy wants to know if I'm Twinkle or Pippi. Which am I?'

'Well, if you're Twinkle, I'm Pippi and if I'm Pippi, you're Twinkle,' said the second man solemnly. They looked at one another in such a comical manner, their eyebrows working up and down together, that Jimmy burst into roars of laughter, and Lotta came running up to see what the joke was.

Twinkle and Pippi came out of their caravan and grinned at the two children. They were exactly alike, even to the dimples in their right cheeks.

There was a roar of welcome from the circus field, and Mr Galliano came striding up. Twinkle and Pippi were old friends of his. He had known them in many circuses and shows. He shook hands with them, slapped them on the back, and took them to his own caravan to see Mrs Galliano.

'I like Twinkle and Pippi,' said Jimmy. 'We'll have some fun with them, Lotta.'

'Pooh! They are not such good clowns as *we* have often seen in other shows,' said Lisa's mocking voice. Jimmy turned away. He hated the way Lisa always mocked at everything. She had even laughed at little dog Lucky, and said that once she had seen a dog who was far cleverer than Lucky.

'And you'll see what will happen when she is three years old,' she said. 'Her brains will go! She won't be able to do so well as she does now. You wait and see!'

'Don't say such horrid, untrue things,' said Jimmy, picking Lucky up in his arms.

All four children waited to see if Google, the third clown, would come along. Sure enough he did. He drove a van, with a caravan towed behind it.

'What's in the van, I wonder?' said Lotta.

'That motor car of his that falls to bits!' guessed Jimmy. 'What fun! Do you suppose it's Google driving the van? He's got a dear little dog with him.'

It *was* Google. But Google out of the circus ring was quite a different person from Google *in* the ring! He was a sharp-faced, bad-tempered little man, and the only creature he really loved in the world was his dog Squib. He hated children and gave all four a scowl as he drove his van carefully in at the gate.

'I don't much like the look of *him*,' said Jimmy. 'He looks as if he'd like to eat us all.'

'But his dog is a dear,' said Lotta. 'Squib! Squib!'

The dog in the driving seat pricked up his ears when he heard his name called, but he did not leave his master's side. Lucky yelped to him, but he did not yelp back. He was not going to make friends with anyone until he had had a good sniff round the camp and made sure whom he would like to know! He was a very particular little dog, and so fond of his master that he even went into the ring with him and did his best to help, though he was always frightened by the *bang* that came when the motor car burst into bits!

Britomart was not coming until the next day so it was no use waiting to see any more people arrive. The children wandered round the camp, saying cheeky things to the parrots, looking admiringly at the zebras, and getting Neptune most excited by telling him that fish, fish, fish was coming for his dinner. He flapped out of his tank and flipped himself eagerly around Jimmy – and he would *not* go back into his water.

So the little boy walked off – but the seal followed him, working itself along on its flippers quite fast.

'Oh, do go back, Neptune,' said Jimmy in alarm. 'I shall get into trouble if you follow me about like this.'

The seal looked at Jimmy out of beautiful brown eyes and made little loving noises. It seemed to think that

Jimmy was the most marvellous person it had ever met, and for the first time Jimmy wished that an animal didn't like him so much!

He tried to dodge it by running round a caravan, diving under a cart, coming up the other side and jumping up the steps of his own caravan. But the seal followed him faithfully, and heaved itself up the steps of the caravan. Jimmy had shut the door – and the seal hit it hard with its nose.

'Come in!' cried Jimmy's mother, who was peeling potatoes. She had no idea there was a seal out there. Neptune hit the door such a bang with his nose that it flew open with a crash – and with many delighted noises the seal flippered itself indoors.

'Bless us all, what's this coming in!' cried Mrs Brown, in a fright. 'It's the seal! Good gracious, whatever next? Does it think it's invited to dinner, or what? Really, what with parrots and monkeys and chimpanzees playing around, I've no time for seals! Jimmy, tell it to go out. It's shaking the caravan to bits, galloping round the floor like that.'

Jimmy couldn't help laughing. The seal was doing its best to get on to his knee, it seemed. Jimmy got up and went out of the caravan. 'Come on, Neptune,' he said to the seal. 'You can't go rushing about like this. You really must stay in your tank.'

He met Pierre as he took the seal back to its tank. Pierre was cross.

'What do you mean by taking Neptune off like that?' he demanded. 'He'll come to harm, and he's very valuable.'

'I didn't take him,' said Jimmy. 'He just jumped out and followed me.'

'Lisa said you took him,' said Pierre, still very cross. The seal had gone to his side and was trying to take its master's hand in its mouth. It was a very loving, friendly creature, and nobody could help liking it.

'Well, Lisa told a story then,' said Jimmy indignantly.

'She's a naughty girl. I *didn't* take the seal. You had better make Lisa sit by the tank and guard the seal all day long. She hasn't enough to do.'

Pierre went off with Neptune, and Jimmy saw Lisa peeping round a van at him, delighted because he was angry. He ran at her and she disappeared at once.

He went to see Twinkle and Pippi. They had already made friends with Sticky Stanley and were talking eagerly about what they could all do in the ring, for they were to work together. Google was to have a turn to himself. Stanley was pleased about this, for he had not much liked the sulky look of the sharp-faced third clown.

Jimmy stayed and listened. Twinkle and Pippi were so alike to look at he still didn't know which was which – and if he asked them, they pretended not to know either, and asked one another who they were, and scratched their heads and worked their eyebrows up and down till Jimmy went into fits of laughter.

'They are twins,' said Stanley. 'No one has ever found out yet which twin is which – and I certainly don't know, and never shall know. They even have exactly the same freckles!'

Only Britomart the great conjurer was to come now – and then, the day after that, the circus was to open again, this time with all its new performers. My goodness, what a show it would be! Jimmy and Lotta could hardly wait for the night!

11. Britomart joins the circus

The conjurer did not arrive till the evening of the day before the circus was due to open again. He drove up in a most magnificent car. It was blue, with silver edgings, and the whole of the inside was blue and silver too.

Britomart was dressed in ordinary clothes, but he looked a most magnificent man, even in a dark blue suit and grey hat. He was very tall, taller than Mr Galliano, and he had even more marvellous moustaches. His eyebrows were jet black, and so bushy that they jutted out over his eyes. His eyes were strange. They were as black as his hair, but they glinted coldly, like steel, whenever he looked at anyone. He never seemed to smile, and all four children felt rather afraid of him.

He got out of his magnificent car and went to talk to Mr Galliano. He was very haughty with the ring-master, and did not even shake hands with him. As for kind Mrs Galliano, he did not even say good evening to her.

Soon a marvellous van arrived, carrying the conjurer's circus belongings. It was blue and silver, like the car, and across it was painted one word, in enormous silver letters:

BRITOMART

'Golly! Isn't he grand!' said Jimmy. 'Nobody as grand as this ever came to Galliano's circus before. He must be very rich.'

'He is,' said Lisa, who always knew everything about everybody – or pretended to, if she didn't. 'I'm surprised he came to a tuppeny-ha'penny circus like this! I can't imagine why he did!'

'For the same reason as *you* did, I suppose,' said Jimmy

crossly. 'To make some money! To hear you talk, anyone would think you owned all the circuses in the world. Hold your tongue for a little while, Miss Know-All!'

Lisa put out her tongue at Jimmy, and put out her arm to pinch him slyly. But he was ready for her and skipped out of the way.

Britomart was not going to sleep in the camp. He was going to stay at the biggest hotel in the town, and would only come out to the circus each evening, when the show began.

'Good thing too,' said Sticky Stanley. 'That man may be made of magic – but he gives me the creeps with those glinting black eyes of his!'

Everyone was very busy the next day. The enormous new tent was already up, and Brownie and the other men had seen that it was safe as could be. They did not want it to be blown off the ground, like the other one. Many new benches had been brought, and were arranged round the ring.

Even the ring itself was new, for Mr Galliano had ordered new plush sections, which, when fitted together, made a bigger ring than before.

The programme was carefully worked out. It would be longer than usual, because there were more performers, but the tickets were to cost more. Each performer was given his time and his turn, and a rehearsal was planned and carried out in the morning.

Everyone did well. Only Britomart was not there. He would never come to rehearsals, and as he was so famous, he was allowed to do as he liked. Jimmy and Lotta were in a great state of excitement. Lucky was thrilled to think that the show was beginning again, for she, like all the other animals, loved the excitement of the ring.

The first night came. The big towns near the camp knew all about the show, for Mr Galliano had sent his men to paste up enormous circus posters all over the place. So everyone knew, and hundreds of people came to see the first show. They streamed in at the big gates, where they got their tickets, and made their way to the big tent. Flaring lights lit up the inside, and big shadows danced in the roof. The band tuned up. The drummer rolled his sticks on the drum softly. Jumbo trumpeted somewhere, and some of the parrots screeched joyfully. They loved to go into the ring with Madame Prunella, they loved the clapping and shouting and cheering, just as the circus folk loved it.

The show began. The circus parade went round the ring – horses, performers, dogs, carriages, everything, bowing and waving – and then the first turn began.

It was Lal and Laddo, with their beautiful horses – and how they waltzed, how they cantered, how they stood up altogether on their hind legs, their heads magnificent with great clusters of ostrich feathers. Jimmy thought they had never done so well before.

One by one all the turns came on. Sammy and Mr Wally – Lilliput and his monkeys – Prunella and her parrots – Lotta and Black Beauty – and then Pierre and his performing seal.

That seal! It was simply marvellous! It galloped in beside Pierre, who was now perfectly wonderful in silver and gold. Neptune was cleverer than a dog! He did everything he was told. He sat on a stool. He galloped round the plush ring on his flippers. He played cricket with his master, catching the ball every time that Pierre sent it into the air.

He balanced a long pole on the very tip of his nose, and then Pierre placed a ball on top of the pole. And do you know, Neptune went round the ring with the pole on his nose, and the ball balanced safely on the tip of the pole! Jimmy couldn't imagine how he did it.

He had another trick too. Pierre brought in six bells hung on a brass rod – and what do you think Neptune did? He struck those bells with his nose, and played 'Jack and Jill went up the hill' on them! How the people cheered!

'Marvellous!' said Jimmy, as the seal galloped out of

the ring beside Pierre, trying to catch hold of his fingers as he went. 'How I do like that seal! I'd love one of my own.'

The zebras were beautiful to watch too. They trotted in, and played a kind of football match, deftly kicking the ball from one to the other.

'They look just like football players with striped jerseys on!' said Jimmy to Lotta. 'Oh, look – Zeno is going to do something else.'

So he was. The trainer got three of the zebras together, and leapt up to their backs. He put one foot on each of the outside zebras, so that he was straddled over the third one. Then, at words of command, all the other zebras took their places in front of him, and his helper threw him up the reins. And round the ring with his twelve zebras galloped Zeno, standing safely on the backs of two of them, with a third in the middle, below!

Everyone knew how difficult zebras were to tame and train, and the watching people shouted and cheered Zeno till they were hoarse. The parrots outside the ring got most excited when they heard all the noise, and they joined in the cheering too.

'Hip-pip-prah!' shouted the parrots, till Madame Prunella scolded them and made them stop. Even then Gringle kept shouting loudly, and Prunella had to take him away for a while, till he became quiet.

The clowns were an enormous success. Jimmy laughed till he cried when they built up a fine greengrocer's shop, and piled it full of fruit and vegetables, falling over one another all the time, bumping into things – and then, at the end, getting terribly angry with one another, and throwing all the fruit and vegetables about.

'Squish, squish,' went the tomatoes. 'Thud, thud,' went the turnips. 'Smack, smack,' went the oranges. Really it took quite three minutes to sweep up the ring after that ridiculous performance. Twinkle and Pippi enjoyed it just as much as the audience and they came out grinning and laughing, their hair plastered with tomatoes!

'Wouldn't you like to join us in our turn, Jimmy?'

grinned one of them. Jimmy didn't know if it was Twinkle or Pippi, for they dressed exactly alike for the ring. Stanley pretended to throw a tomato at Jimmy, and the little boy ducked, afraid of spoiling his grand circus suit.

He and Lucky were a great success too. Lucky could walk the tight-rope as cleverly as any clown, and she could spell words with letters, which always made people shout with amazement.

The thing that always astonished people more than anything else was when Jimmy asked his little dog one question – 'Which is the finest circus in the world?'

And from the mass of big black letters Lucky always picked out the one word – 'Galliano's!' That made people stand up and cheer, and Jimmy and Lucky bowed happily round the ring before they ran lightly out.

Britomart the conjurer was perhaps the most astonishing performer of all. He strode into the ring looking like a giant, for he wore big heels to his boots and a great feather in his hat, and as he was already tall, he looked enormous.

He had a strange deep voice, too, that seemed to come from his boots. He was not only a marvellous conjurer but a juggler too. He could take twelve golden balls and throw them one by one into the air, and never let them drop, keeping them circling up and down like a golden fountain. He could throw sharp knives high in the air too – three, four, five at a time – and catch them neatly by the handles, one by one, as they came down. It was astonishing to watch him.

His conjuring was wonderful as well. Jimmy and Lotta, who were watching him closely from the curtain that hung at the ring entrance, could not imagine how he did his tricks.

Britomart had a small table on which was a golden cage. The cage was empty. There was nothing in it at all. The conjurer sent his helper round the ring to show the empty cage to the people.

Then, at a deep word of command, the air was full of canaries! They fluttered out of nothing, it seemed, and flew all around the conjurer's head! At another word of command they entered the golden cage one by one – and then, strangest of all, at a third word, they completely disappeared from the cage, and it was empty once again!

'However did he do that?' cried Jimmy. 'Where have the birds gone?'

But that was not the only strange thing that the magnificent Britomart did. He took a pair of top boots and placed them in the middle of the ring, after having sent his helper round to show the watching people that the boots were empty and quite ordinary.

But dear me, were they quite ordinary? No, they were not! For as soon as Britomart placed them in the centre of the ring, and shouted a word of command, those boots began to dance! How they danced! It was simply amazing to watch them.

'They're alive!' said Lotta, half afraid. 'I never saw a thing like that before. Goodness, isn't he clever!'

Britomart certainly was. After he had juggled and conjured for twenty minutes, he bowed and strode off, followed by the loudest cheers Jimmy and Lotta had ever heard.

'And all the time he never once smiled,' said the little girl. 'What a strange and clever man he is! All the same, I hope we don't have too much to do with him, Jimmy.'

But they were going to have a lot to do with Britomart, though they didn't know it!

12. Poor Mrs Galliano!

The circus, with its new performers, was an enormous success. The third new clown, Google, was perhaps the silliest of all the turns, but he made people laugh till they cried. He was a very solemn person in the ring, and somehow this made people laugh all the more.

He had a most extraordinary car, which he drove into the ring, with his little dog Squib sitting beside him. After the car had gone once round the ring it began to make the funniest noises. Bells rang inside it, something fizzled, and a terrible clanking noise began. This all made Google look more solemn than ever. His enormous eyebrows shot up to the top of his forehead with surprise.

Squib jumped out and went under the car. Google got out too, and as he got out, the car began to give shivers and shakes, which shot Google out on to his nose. He pretended to be very angry about that. Then streams of black smoke came from the car, and Google and Squib ran to get a pail of water. Of course Google fell over and Squib got the water all over him. He barked with rage and tried to bite Google's wide clown-trousers.

Then the car ran all round the ring by itself, with Google and Squib panting after it, calling to it, and whistling as if it were a dog. Jimmy and Lotta laughed till the tears ran down their cheeks and on to their collars! They had never seen a car running away and being whistled to like a dog before.

Well, Google caught it at last, and tied it firmly to a post, so that it shouldn't run away again. He lay down flat and got underneath it. The car then ran backwards and forwards over Google, and he shouted and yelled for all he was worth. Squib pulled him out, and they both sat down solemnly to think what they could do next with the extraordinary car.

Then Google pulled all the insides out of the car and threw them down in the ring. When he had finished he got back behind the steering wheel, and hooted the horn to make Squib get out of the way. He started up the engine – and the whole car flew into bits with an enormous BANG! The wheels came off and rolled all over the ring! The back of the car fell off. The front of the car hopped away. The seats fell out. It was the funniest sight that the people had ever seen in their lives!

And there was poor old Google sitting on the ground still holding the steering-wheel, with all his car fallen to bits around him, looking sadder and more solemn than ever. No wonder the audience yelled and shouted and clapped. No wonder Squib wagged his tail happily at so much applause. Jimmy made his own hands ache with clapping, and he wished that Google would do his turn all over again.

But he didn't, of course. He and the other clowns collected the car pieces and went out, Google bowing and smiling all the time, pleased at his success.

'We're lucky, Lotta,' said Jimmy joyfully. 'We shall see Google doing that every night, as often as we like – the children in the audience are lucky if they see it once.'

The children who had paid to see the circus looked at Jimmy and Lotta in surprise and envy when *they* went into the ring each night. How marvellous to be dressed like that, and have such a wonderful dog as Lucky, and such a lovely pony as Black Beauty!

'You must be very happy,' a boy said once to Jimmy. 'What a fine life you have!'

'It's not so easy as it looks,' said Jimmy. 'Circus folk have to work hard and practise every single day! I work just as hard as you do, and harder!'

The circus show was so good that the big tent was crowded each night. The weather was fine, and many coaches and buses were run to the circus field from the distant towns. Mr Galliano was delighted. Although he had to pay the new performers a great deal of money, it didn't matter, because so many more people came to see the circus that there was always plenty of money for everyone to spend.

The new performers settled down well together, and got on splendidly – all except Google the clown and the two little girls Lisa and Jeanne. Google was certainly bad-tempered, and never made a joke outside the ring. As for Jeanne and Lisa, they were two spoilt, bad-mannered children whom nobody liked. They were always playing tricks on Jimmy, and trying to get him into trouble.

Lotta liked playing with them, and this made Jimmy cross and unhappy. Lotta had always been his very own friend, and he hated sharing her with anyone.

'Why do you go and play with those silly dolls belonging to Lisa and Jeanne?' he grumbled. 'Why don't you come with me and fly my new kite? Dolls are babyish.'

'No, they're not,' said Lotta. 'I like dolls. I've never played with them before – only with dogs and horses. You can come and play with the dolls too, if you like, Jimmy.'

'Pooh!' said Jimmy rudely. '*I'm* not a baby, if *you* are!'

This wasn't a clever thing to say to Lotta, who could be very obstinate when she liked, so off she went and played all the more with Lisa and Jeanne. Mrs Brown was sorry to see this, because she knew that the two red-haired girls were bad for Lotta. They were teaching her to be rude and cheeky, and to be disobedient too. Lal, Lotta's mother, could never manage the wilful little girl very well, but Mrs Brown could – yet now she found that Lotta was being rude to her, and disobeying her whenever she could.

Britomart the conjurer had very little to do with the circus folk. He came and went without a smile, never said good-day to anyone, and only spoke to Pierre, whom he had worked with in another circus. Everyone was rather afraid of him, and even the animals did not seem to like him, which was unusual in a circus.

Jumbo twitched his big ears restlessly when Britomart passed by. Sammy chattered angrily at him. Jemima ran away. Lucky growled.

'There's something queer about Britomart,' said Jimmy to Lotta. 'Lucky likes nearly everyone, but she doesn't like the conjurer! Black Beauty doesn't like him either. He shied at Britomart when you rode near him yesterday, Lotta.'

Zeno and his zebras were soon very much liked. He and Mr Tonks and Mr Volla made friends, and put their caravans close together. Twinkle, Pippi, and Sticky Stanley were soon very friendly, too, and they all liked Madame Prunella very much, and often sat outside her caravan with her, eating one of the wonderful curries she made. She had been in many hot countries to get her parrots, and had learned to make all kinds of queer dishes, which the three clowns loved.

Google did not make any friends, but Squib was soon a great playmate for Lucky. Those two dogs really loved one another, and played 'He' and Hide-and-seek as often as they could. Lucky even began to take part of her own dinner to share with Squib, who did not have quite such good meals as Jimmy gave to Lucky.

One morning Jimmy met Mr Galliano as he went across the field to see to the dogs with Lotta. To his great surprise Mr Galliano had his top hat on quite straight. This always meant that the ring-master was upset about something, and Jimmy wondered what it was. Jimmy was going to ask him a question, when Mr Galliano pushed the boy roughly aside.

This astonished Jimmy so much that he stood and stared. Galliano was never rough like that. The ring-master saw him staring and shouted at him.

'Have you no work to do, boy? Then you will do it at once, yes, and not stand gaping like a hungry dog!'

Jimmy scurried off, and Lotta went with him, rather frightened. 'Whatever's the matter?' she said. 'What *can* be upsetting Mr Galliano? Didn't he look angry?'

The children soon knew what the matter was. Mrs Galliano was very ill. Sticky Stanley the clown told them, and he had heard it from Madame Prunella, who had been called to Mrs Galliano in the night.

'Mr Galliano thinks the world of his wife,' said Stanley, sewing a black bobble on to his clown's suit. 'The doctor is coming soon, and until he has been and gone, you had better keep out of Galliano's way.'

So Lotta and Jimmy kept well out of the way – but Jeanne and Lisa didn't, and got well slapped for running into him round a caravan. They ran howling to their mother.

'Serves them right,' said Jimmy, pleased. 'They could do with a lot of slappings, those two. I wish I could give them a few!'

Mrs Brown went to see if she could help Mrs Galliano, who lay in the big bed in her caravan, looking white and ill. Nobody knew what was the matter with her, and everyone was very worried, for they all loved the fat and gentle Tessa.

'Do you suppose she will have to go away from the circus?' Jimmy asked. His mother, Mrs Brown, nodded her head.

'I'm rather afraid so,' she said, 'She does seem very ill, and she would not be able to stand the noise and excitement of the camp, or go on the road when it moves.'

The doctor came at last. He stayed a very long time with Mrs Galliano, Madame Prunella, and the ringmaster. When he came out of the caravan putting on his gloves, he looked rather grave. Mr Galliano followed him, the tears running down his cheeks and soaking his moustache. The two watching children were alarmed. They had never imagined that Mr Galliano could shed tears.

They did not like to see him so sad; and they ran to Jimmy's caravan. Mrs Brown went to hear the news and she soon came back and told them.

'Poor Mrs Galliano is very ill indeed,' she said. 'She has

to go to hospital and see a very famous doctor, who may be able to help her. She keeps saying that she won't leave Galliano, so goodness knows what will happen!'

'But she can't stay in that caravan if she is so ill,' said Lotta. 'Whatever will happen?'

The whole circus was worried and upset. They did not dare to talk to Galliano, who strode up and down, biting at his moustache, his hat perfectly straight. Then he went into the caravan and shut the door.

When he came out again, he called Mr Wally, Mr Tonks, and Lilliput. They went over to him, serious and quiet.

'Boys,' said the ring-master, 'I am not going to leave Mrs Galliano. I am going with her. She cannot stay here, she must go to a hospital, yes – but I cannot let her go alone.'

'We're awfully sorry about it, sir,' said Mr Tonks, looking as unhappy as poor Mr Galliano. 'But what about the circus? It must have a ring-master!'

'Yes,' said Mr Galliano. 'I have not forgotten that. You will have a ring-master – it will be Britomart!'

13. Britomart, the man without a smile

So Britomart the conjurer was to be at the head of the circus! Mr Tonks, Mr Wally, and Stanley looked at Galliano in dismay. None of them liked Britomart, though they knew he was very clever indeed, and had had a circus of his own.

'Britomart knows how to run a circus,' said Mr Galliano. 'He will do it well, yes! The show is running splendidly now, and it will go on for weeks. Perhaps by the time you are all on the road again I shall come back with Tessa – yes?'

Nobody said anything. They all felt upset at losing both Mr and Mrs Galliano, but they could not beg him to stop behind and let Mrs Galliano leave alone. The three men looked at the ground, and Mr Tonks blew his nose so loudly that it almost sounded like Jumbo's trumpeting.

Then Mr Wally spoke. 'When are you going, sir?' he asked. 'Today?'

'This morning,' said Mr Galliano. 'Tessa must go at once, the doctor says. A car is coming for her presently – I see it coming in at the gate now, yes! Now, my friends, you will all do your best for Britomart – you will promise me this – yes?'

'We'll do our best,' promised Mr Wally, Mr Tonks, and Stanley. They shook hands with their ring-master, and with serious, solemn faces watched Madame Prunella, Mrs Brown, Lal, and a nurse put Mrs Galliano comfortably in the big car. She smiled bravely at everyone. Then Mr Galliano, still wearing his riding-breeches, coat, and top hat, but without his whip, got into the car beside the driver.

All the circus folk came running, for now the news had spread like wildfire around the camp.

'Galliano's going! Galliano's going! Quick, come and say goodbye!'

They all poured out of the caravans, and rushed to wave goodbye – the grooms, Brownie, Pierre, Jeanne, Lisa, the clowns, Mr Volla, Jimmy, Lotta, Lucky, and Lulu the spaniel – what a crowd there was running beside the big car as it slowly and carefully drove out of the field, with Mr Galliano waving and trying to smile.

Then down the country road it went, still slowly, so as not to jolt Mrs Galliano. It disappeared round the corner, and everyone looked sad.

Lotta began to cry. She was very fond of Mrs Galliano. Jimmy put his arm round her. 'Cheer up, Lotta,' he said. Mrs Galliano will soon be better – and then Mr Galliano will be back, and everything will be fine again.'

There was a loud honking down the road and a great blue and silver car swept up to the field gates. It turned in, and jolted slowly over the field.

'It's Britomart!' said Lotta, drying her eyes. '*Isn't* he tall!'

The conjurer seemed even taller that morning. His jet black eyes gleamed under his bushy eyebrows, as he looked all round the field.

'Where is Mr Wally?' he called. Mr Wally came up.

'I want a meeting of all the chief performers,' said Britomart. 'Then I shall. go round the circus and see everything. I shall take the Gallianos' caravan for mine, and live in the camp, now that I am to be ring-master.'

'Certainly, sir,' said Mr Wally. Sammy came up behind his keeper, and slipped a hairy paw into his.

Take that chimpanzee and put him into his cage,' ordered Britomart. 'In my circuses performing animals are not allowed to wander about the field loose.'

'But, sir, Sammy often does,' said Mr Wally, in surprise. 'He's like a child. He plays with the children and is as good as gold. He mopes if he is shut up always.'

'I am master here now,' said Britomart in a cold sort of voice. 'Shut up the chimpanzee, please.'

Mr Wally went off with Sammy, his face as black as thunder. Mr Galliano had never ordered him about – and here was Britomart giving him orders before he had been in the camp two minutes.

'Tell two or three women to clean out Mr Galliano's caravan for me, and to stack their furniture into an empty van,' said Britomart to Brownie, who was nearby. 'I have some of my own things coming this afternoon.'

Brownie went off to tell Mrs Brown to get someone to help her to clean out the caravan. Mrs Brown hurried to find Lal, and the two women began to take out the furniture for the men to store away.

Jimmy and Lotta hated seeing everything being taken out of the caravan they knew so well. The big bed was taken to pieces, and the blankets rolled up. Even the pictures were taken down from the wall. They were only coloured posters of the many circus people that the Gallianos' knew, but they made the walls gay and bright and interesting.

Britomart went to look at the horses. He loved horses, and they stood perfectly still whilst he stroked each fine animal and spoke to it. But no horse nuzzled to him as they did to Lotta and Jimmy, Lal and Laddo.

Lotta came running back up to Black Beauty whilst Britomart was there with the horses. She jumped up on to his back and rode him away. Britomart called after her in his deep voice:

'Lotta! Where are you going?'

'For a ride over the hills,' said Lotta.

'No circus horse is to be taken for pleasure-riding,' Britomart said. 'Bring him back.'

'But he is my own horse!' cried Lotta. 'My very own. I can ride him whenever I like.'

'He may be your own but he belongs to the circus,' said Britomart. 'And whilst I am ring-master you will obey my rules and my orders, little girl. Bring that pony here.'

Lotta tossed her black curls, her face red with anger. She was about to gallop away when Jimmy, who had been listening, caught hold of the bridle.

'Don't be silly, Lotta,' he said in a low voice. 'You'll only get yourself into trouble. Take Black Beauty back. You know quite well that any ring-master has the right to make his own rules.'

Lotta struck Jimmy's hand away from the bridle, but he put it back again, and firmly led the horse to where the others stood. Lotta was so angry that she would not say a word to either Britomart or Jimmy. She slipped out of the saddle and ran to her caravan, her face still bright red. How dare anyone say she mustn't ride Black Beauty over the hills! Why, she did it every day.

'That is a spoilt girl,' said Britomart. 'She must do as she is told, or I will not let her go into the ring.'

'Good gracious!' thought Jimmy in dismay. 'Not let Lotta go into the ring – he must be mad! Whatever would Lotta say? I'd better warn her to be careful.'

He went off to find Lotta. Britomart called a meeting

of all the performers, and soon they were around him, listening to what he had to say. Only Lotta and Jimmy were not there.

Jimmy had found Lotta on the bed in her caravan, thumping at the pillow in anger, pretending that it was Britomart. The boy couldn't help smiling.

'Lotta! Don't be so silly! You'll have feathers flying all over the place.'

'I wish it was Britomart's hair I was thumping off!' said Lotta fiercely. 'I hate him! Horrid cold man without a smile.'

'Lotta, just listen to me for a moment,' said Jimmy, sitting on the bed.

'I won't,' said Lotta, and she thumped Jimmy. He pushed her away.

'You *must* listen,' he said. 'Do you know what Britomart said just now? He said if you didn't do what you were told he wouldn't let you go into the ring.'

Lotta stared at Jimmy in horror. 'Not let me go into the ring!' she cried. 'Not let me ride Black Beauty in the circus every night! How dare he say that!'

'Lotta, do be sensible,' said Jimmy. 'You know that any ring-master gives his own orders and they must be obeyed. Lal and Laddo will tell you that.'

Lotta was still in a rage. She turned sulky and wouldn't say another word. She wouldn't promise to be good, she wouldn't even say she would try. In the end Jimmy left her, feeling rather cross himself. He joined the circus folk around Britomart, who had been altering the programme of the show.

There was no doubt that Britomart was a very clever man. Most of the alterations he made were excellent. Mr Galliano was a fine ring-master, but rather free and easy, willing to let the circus folk do as they liked providing that their work was good and they were happy. Britomart only cared about whether the work was as good as it could possibly be – the happiness of the people came second or not at all.

Twinkle and Pippi found that their act was cut down. Google's was made longer. Jumbo's was cut shorter, and the performing seal was given longer. Though some of the people grumbled, most of them thought that Britomart certainly knew what he was doing.

That afternoon a van drew up with Britomart's belongings in it. Jimmy and Lotta, Jeanne and Lisa, stared in amazement. They had never seen such grand furniture for a caravan before. There was even a clock made of silver, with little black elephants running all round it. The children stared wide-eyed as the things were taken into the caravan.

'Get away,' commanded Britomart, when the children crowded too near. 'Get right away. You are not to come near this caravan. It is private. If I catch any of you near it, you will be sorry.'

Britomart looked so fierce that every child scurried away at once.

'I guess no one will be asked to call in and see Britomart in the evenings,' said Jimmy.

But he was wrong. Pierre was the only one that Britomart liked, and he invited him to his caravan many a time. Sometimes Neptune the seal went with Pierre, and it was funny to see the great creature flipping itself along beside its master.

No one else ever chatted to the new ring-master. He lived alone in the caravan, and not even Jemima the monkey dared to play a trick on him.

Lotta called him 'The man without a smile', and it was a name that suited him very well. He made a magnificent ring-master when the show opened each night, tall and commanding, and he could crack his whip even more loudly than Mr Galliano.

But nobody liked him – and how they all missed jolly Mr Galliano and his gentle wife, Tessa!

'If only they would come back,' Lotta sighed a dozen times a day. 'If only they would come back!'

14. Lotta gets into trouble

The circus stayed for a long time in the same camp, for it drew hundreds of people each night, and there was no need to move. Everything in the show went well. Britomart was really an excellent ring-master, and everything ran like clockwork.

But outside the circus things were not quite so good. For one thing, Britomart never praised anyone, and the circus folk could not get along happily without a good word. Galliano had always praised them and their animals generously, and his people loved that and worked all the harder for him. But Britomart only spoke when things went wrong, and then he found fault sharply.

Lotta was the first one to get into trouble, and it was because of the zebras. The little girl would *not* keep away from them, and they seemed to like her and welcomed her with joy whenever she slipped into their travelling-stables. Soon she was able to stroke every one of them, and Zebby even learnt to push his black nose into her hand.

Lotta never went into the stables when Zeno or his man were about, for she knew that she would be ordered out. She went secretly, not even telling Jimmy.

One day she jumped lightly on to the back of one of the zebras. It reared up in surprise, and snapped round – but when it knew it was Lotta, it stood quietly, though trembling a little.

'I believe I could ride you, Zebby,' whispered Lotta in delight. 'I believe I could! Just wait till Zeno takes you into the ring tomorrow and I'll try!'

So, the next day, when Zeno took his zebras into the

ring for their daily practice, Lotta was there. Zeno tied a
bunch of zebras together outside the ring, and took six of
them inside. Lotta ran to the bunch and loosed Zebby.

In a moment she was on his back! He reared up, and
then galloped into the ring! Lotta clung on his back, delighted.

Zeno looked up and saw her, and his eyes nearly
dropped out of his head. No one had ever ridden Zebby
before! Zebby was nervous and difficult, and sometimes
was not even taken into the ring in case he should upset
the others.

Zebby flew round the ring with Lotta on his back – and
at that very moment who should stalk in to speak to Zeno
but Britomart himself!

Lotta didn't see him. She was busy wondering if she
dared to stand up on the zebra's back as she stood on
Black Beauty – but even as she wondered this the zebra
saw Britomart standing silently at the side of the ring, and
was frightened.

It stopped suddenly – and Lotta was thrown right off
his back. She landed on her feet, like a cat, with a jerk.
Then Britomart began to roar. He had a very deep voice
that sounded as if it came from his boots, and it rang like
thunder in the ring.

'Zeno! Were you not told that no one but you and your
helper were to handle your zebras? How dare you let Lotta
ride one! It is a most dangerous thing for a child to do.'

'I'm sorry, Mr Britomart,' said Zeno, who had been as
amazed and surprised as Britomart to see one of his zebras
ridden by Lotta. 'I'd no idea she was even in the tent. But,
Mr Britomart, it's wonderful! No child has ever ridden a
zebra before. I tell you I couldn't believe my eyes!'

'Can I ride a zebra in the ring, when Zeno does his
turn?' cried Lotta, delighted at Zeno's praise. 'I can
manage any of them, really I can – but Zebby—'

'Hold your tongue!' thundered Britomart, frowning at
Lotta. 'You will certainly not ride a zebra. You are a bad
child to have tried. You might have frightened the

animal and upset all of them. Go to your caravan for the
rest of the day.'

'Oh, but—' began Lotta indignantly. She had no
chance to say another word, for Britomart took hold of
her shoulder, shook her well, and marched her to the
tent-opening. She gave a cry of rage and rushed off.

She found Jimmy and told him all about it, angry and
hurt. 'I only rode a zebra!' she cried. 'And even Zeno said
it was a wonderful thing for a child to do.'

'But you promised Mr Galliano that you wouldn't ride
the zebras,' began Jimmy. Lotta shook back her hair and
interrupted him.

'I didn't promise, I didn't promise,' she cried. 'You're
not to say I did when I didn't. If I'd promised I would
have kept my word. But I didn't, I didn't, I didn't!'

'All right, all right,' said Jimmy. 'Well, Lotta, the best
thing you can do is to keep to your caravan for the rest of
the day as Britomart said. If you disobey you will certainly be punished.'

'I'm NOT going to keep in the caravan all day!' cried
the furious little girl. 'I'm going to get Black Beauty and
ride him over the hills. That's what I'm going to do. And
Britomart can do what he likes. He may rule everyone
else in this circus, but he won't rule *me*!'

And the wild little girl ran off to get her horse, not
caring at all what anyone said. Jimmy knew that when
Lotta was in one of these moods it was no good trying to
stop her. He watched anxiously to see whether Britomart
would see her taking Black Beauty, but the conjurer was
still talking to Zeno in the big tent.

Lotta galloped off alone on Black Beauty. Jimmy wandered about, kicking a stone round the field, little dog
Lucky at his heels. The circus didn't seem the same any
more. People were not so jolly, and Britomart seemed
everywhere, with his black eyes, black moustaches, and
deep voice.

Suddenly Jimmy wondered if Britomart would go to
see if Lotta was in her caravan. It would not be like him

to give an order, and then not see if it was carried out. He would be sure to try and find out where she was.

Jimmy ran to Lotta's caravan. She lived in it with Lal and Laddo. He opened the door. There was no one there. It was an untidy, rather smelly caravan, not a bit like the spotless, tidy one his mother had. Jimmy looked round. He saw Lotta's bunk against the far end, and went over to it.

He grinned a little to himself. He took a pillow from Lal's bunk and put it in the middle of Lotta's. Then he took a saucepan and put it at the top of the pillow for a head. Then he pulled the blanket up – and the pillow and saucepan underneath looked just like some small person lying in the bunk.

'Good! thought Jimmy. 'If old Britomart takes a look in, he'll think that's Lotta in the bunk!'

He slipped out and shut the door. He waited till he saw Britomart come out of the tent. The conjurer looked for Lotta's caravan, and walked over to it. As he came up to it, Jimmy rapped on the door and cried, 'Lotta! Come out and play!'

Then he listened as if he heard someone answering him. 'Oh, do come out!' he cried, just as Britomart came up.

'Lotta has to stay in her caravan all day,' said the ringmaster sternly. 'It is no use asking her to come out.'

He opened the door and looked in. He saw what he thought was Lotta lying in the bunk at the far end, and he shut the door. He strode off, his whip under his arm. He was quite sure that Lotta had obeyed him and was in her caravan! He did not guess that the little girl was at that very minute galloping over the hills miles away!

'If only Lotta doesn't come galloping into the field in front of Britomart!' thought Jimmy.

Luckily for Lotta she didn't. She came back just as Britomart had gone off to the town in his big blue and silver car. Jimmy rushed to meet her, and hurriedly told her all that had happened.

'Britomart *really* thinks you were in your bunk all day!'
he said.

Lotta was hungry and tired, and not quite so bold as
she had been when she rode off. She slipped off Black
Beauty and began to rub him down.

'Thank you, Jimmy,' she said. 'Oh, dear, I do so wish
Galliano would come back! I know I'm going to get into
trouble with Britomart nearly every day. I just feel it in
my bones!'

'Come and have some cocoa and biscuits,' said Jimmy.
'There are some waiting for you.'

It was Madame Prunella who next got into trouble
with Britomart. He said that she must keep her parrots
quieter. They screeched all day long.

'As for that bird who yells "Butter and eggs" or "Pickles
and peppermint", he's a perfect nuisance,' said Britomart.
'You must move your caravan right to the other end of
the field.'

'It is too far for me to get water from the stream,' said
Madame Prunella obstinately, and she would not move at
all.

When Britomart saw that she had not moved even an
inch, he went angrily over to her caravan. Prunella saw
him coming, and smiled a secret smile. She knew how to
deal with angry men who shouted.

'Talk, parrots, talk,' she said in a low voice as Britomart came nearer. And at once, altogether, the parrots
talked! They not only talked, they screeched, yelled,
squealed, sang, and recited.

'Plum pudding and custard!' squealed Gringle, right in
Britomart's ear. 'Plum pudding and custard!'

'Twice one are two, twice two are three, twice three are
four!' shouted another parrot.

'Wipe your feet and put up your umbrella!' screeched a
big red and grey bird.

Britomart shouted to Madame Prunella, but the
screeching more than drowned his voice. Not a word
could be heard.

Prunella put her hand behind her ear politely, as if she were trying to do her best to hear what Britomart said. The conjurer shouted again, in his very deepest voice. But no sooner was one word out of his mouth than the whole of the parrots started off again. All the circus folk stuck their heads out of windows and doors to see whatever was the matter.

When they saw what was happening they grinned and chuckled. They knew quite well that Prunella was playing one of her favourite tricks on an unwelcome visitor. Britomart would have to go away without telling Prunella anything!

He stamped his foot and turned away angrily. The parrots screamed after him, and Gringle did a laugh exactly like Twinkle the clown's.

'Well, Prunella won *that* game!' said Oona the acrobat, with a laugh. 'It's not often anyone can win a victory over Britomart!'

15. Lotta makes new friends

When Lal and Laddo heard that Lotta had disobeyed Britomart, and had taken Black Beauty out on the hills, they were angry with her.

'You know well enough that however hard an order is, you have to obey the ring-master,' said Laddo sternly to the little girl.

'But Black Beauty is mine. I've always ridden him whenever I liked,' said the little girl sulkily.

'And as for riding the zebras, it is absolutely forbidden,' said Lal. 'You must be mad to try such a thing.'

'Zebby didn't mind. He liked me on his back,' said Lotta.

Poor Lotta! She was angry and hurt because everyone scolded her. She had always been made a fuss of, she was one of the Wonder Children – and now things were quite different. The little girl ran to tell Jeanne and Lisa all about it, and they, of course, were not at all good for her.

'You do as you like!' said naughty Lisa. 'Britomart wouldn't dare not to let you go into the ring! He knows how all the people love to watch you.'

'You're jolly lucky,' said Jeanne. 'We'd simply love to go into the ring – and we can both ride very well, you know – but we haven't any horses of our own.'

Lotta had sometimes let the two girls ride on Black Beauty, and it was quite true that they rode well. They could not do all Lotta's wonderful tricks but they were clever enough in their own way, and pretty, with their red curls and upturned noses.

Lotta went about more than ever with Jeanne and

Lisa. They encouraged her to disobey, to be sulky and rude. Mrs Brown became very angry with her.

'You are getting quite impossible, Lotta,' she said, when the little girl answered her rudely. 'I can't imagine what has happened to you. You used to be such a nice helpful child, and now you have altered so much I can hardly believe it is the same little girl.'

Lotta did not dare to be rude to Britomart, but she tried hard never to go near him, and she always ran away if he came near her. She spent a lot of her time with hot-tempered Madame Prunella, who was always pleased to tell Lotta how she had tricked Britomart by making her parrots screech so loudly that he could not make his voice heard.

'Listen, Lotta,' said Prunella to the little girl, who was sitting on the caravan steps, whilst Prunella sat in a wicker chair outside, eating an orange. 'I want you to hear something I've taught Sally, that green and red parrot over there. Sally! Say your piece!'

> *'There was a young lady of Riga,*
> *Who went for a ride on a tiger.'*

'No, no,' said Madame Prunella impatiently. 'Your *new* piece, Sally — your new piece. Come on now — Brito-mart . . .'

> *'Britomart*
> *Thinks he's smart,*
> *But he's got a stony heart!*
> *Britomart*
> *Thinks he's—'*

chanted the parrot, and then stopped suddenly as Pru-nella shook her finger at him. Britomart was coming across the field! Daring as Madame Prunella was, she was not brave enough to let Sally go on singing that song at the top of her loud parrot voice! Sally stopped singing and looked at Lotta.

'Pip-pip-pip-pip-pip!' she said solemnly.

'She's heard that on the wireless,' said Madame Prunella. 'Stop it, Sally.'

'Irish stew and Scotch eggs,' said Gringle loudly.

'Oh, he's off again,' said Prunella. 'You'd be surprised at the amount of food he knows, Lotta. Everyone has taught him something!'

Britomart had gone to see Mr Wally. Since he had told him that Sammy was not to run loose, the chimpanzee had been kept in his big cage. He was puzzled and unhappy about this. He sat huddled up in a corner and looked very miserable. Jimmy went to play with him every day, and Lucky often popped in to say how-do-you-do, but the champanzee missed wandering round the circus, in charge of either Mr Wally, Jimmy, or Lotta.

Lilliput too, had been told that Jemima the monkey must be kept on a lead or else she too must keep with the other monkeys, who had a big cage of their own in Lilliput's caravan. Jemima had been used to leaping about all over the camp, playing tricks on everyone, even on the other animals – but Britomart said she upset the zebras by sitting on their backs, and so Lilliput now had to keep her on a lead. She sat on his shoulder as he went about, and flew into tempers at times because the lead would not let her go bounding off as she pleased.

'Now, Jemima – now, Jemima,' said Lilliput to the impatient monkey one morning, as she tugged at the lead and tried to bite through it. She wanted to go and talk to the parrots, whom she loved – but Lilliput had other things to do, so she must stay with him.

Britomart came by, and Jemima chattered rudely at him. The conjurer sat down on a bench and began to tell Lilliput of a good idea he had thought of for a new trick. Lilliput listened. Britomart's ideas were usually good.

'I have a little silver and purple carriage, which I once used for a trick,' said Britomart. 'I think that it would look amusing, Lilliput, if we put two of the dogs to draw the carriage, and let your four monkeys ride in it round

the ring, when all the performers parade at the beginning
of the show. Jemima could drive the carriage – she is so
clever that you could easily teach her this.'

Lilliput thought it was a fine idea. He knew Jemima
would simply love to drive her own little carriage!

'Thank you, sir,' he said. 'That's a good idea. I'd like to
have the carriage, and I'll teach Jemima in a few days. I'll
talk to Lal and Laddo, and choose two of their sharpest
dogs.'

Jemima suddenly jumped from Lilliput's shoulder to
Britomart's, just the length of her lead. She snatched off
Britomart's hat, and jumped back to Lilliput's shoulder. She put it on to her master's head – and it went right
over it, right over his nose, and right down to his chin! He
couldn't see anything at all.

Britomart did not even smile. Jimmy, who was nearby,
laughed till he cried at the sight of Lilliput buried under
Britomart's big hat – but the conjurer merely put out his
hand, took his hat again, slapped Jemima, and stalked off,
putting his big top hat on carefully.

Lilliput told Jimmy Britomart's idea, and both of them
agreed that it was a good one.

'Could Lucky be one of the dogs?' asked Jimmy. 'And I
know the best one to choose for the other – old Punch!
He'd do anything for me. I once saved his life, you know,
and he's always been willing to learn any new tricks that
I wanted to teach him. Lotta! Lotta! Come here a
minute! I've something to tell you.'

'I'm going to play with Lisa,' said Lotta.

'Oh, do come just a minute,' begged Jimmy. 'It's something interesting, Lotta.'

Lotta left Lisa, and came over. She listened whilst
Jimmy told her of Britomart's new idea.

'I think it's silly!' she said. 'I think all Britomart's ideas
are silly. I won't help you with Punch at all.'

'Oh, Lotta!' said Jimmy, in dismay. 'You really might!
It would be so much easier if you would help me. We
could teach the dogs quickly then.'

'Well, I just shan't,' said Lotta. 'I won't do anything for horrid old Britomart.'

She ran off to join Lisa, and told her what Jimmy had said. 'You're quite right to say you won't help,' said Lisa, who didn't like Jimmy. 'Let Jimmy do it by himself.'

All the same Lotta felt rather sorry she had been so determined not to help, when she saw Jimmy and Lilliput teaching Lucky and Punch to draw the beautiful little silver and purple carriage. Once the dogs knew what they were to do, they simply *flew* round the ring, with the carriage jerking behind them.

'Hi, hi! Not so fast!' yelled Jimmy. 'You are not race-horses! Come back here, and trot slowly.'

Then the monkeys were trained to sit in the carriage – and Jemima sat up on the little driving-seat, as proud as could be, holding the reins in her tiny paws. She even clicked to the two dogs, just as she heard Lilliput click to them. Off went the tiny carriage, rumbling round the sawdust ring, the dogs trotting beautifully, Jemima driving and clicking, the other three monkeys sitting quietly on the seat together.

Jimmy laughed to see them. Britomart came in to watch. He was very pleased but he did not say so, nor did he smile or laugh.

'I don't believe he *can* smile!' whispered Jimmy to Lilliput. 'I don't think he knows how to. Wouldn't we all get a shock if he grinned at us!'

Jemima was not on a lead just then, for she had been driving round the ring. When she saw Britomart she made a little chattering noise, bounded from her seat, jumped up on to his shoulder, and once again snatched off his hat! It was all done so suddenly that Britomart hadn't time to stop her. He roared angrily at her.

Jemima darted up a steel ladder set up for Oona the acrobat, and perched the big top hat right at the top. Then she darted down again, giggling in her monkey way, and went to Lilliput's shoulder.

'Climb up and get my hat, boy,' commanded Brito-

mart. So with many chuckles that he really couldn't stop,
Jimmy climbed up and took down the big top hat, keeping
a sharp eye on Jemima in case she made a dart at it again.

Everyone was waiting anxiously for news of Mrs Galliano. At last the postman brought a letter for Mr Tonks
and he opened it eagerly. If *only* it would say that Mrs
Galliano was better and that Mr Galliano was coming
back!

Mr Tonks read the letter out loud to the circus folk,
who came gathering round to hear it.

'Dear Tonky,' said the letter, – 'This is to say that Mrs
Galliano is a little better, but it will be a long time before
she is well. When she leaves the hospital she must go
away to get really well, so I shall go with her and have a
holiday for the first time in my life. I hope the circus is
doing well, and that everyone is doing what they can to
help Britomart. I miss you all very much, yes, and I long
to be back.

'My good wishes to you all.'

'GALLIANO.'

So Galliano was not coming back for a long time!
Everyone was sad and disappointed. They said nothing
but went slowly back to their work.

'It's not Galliano's circus any more, it's Britomart's!'
said Jimmy to Lotta.

'It isn't, it isn't, it isn't!' said Lotta fiercely. 'I won't
have it called Britomart's!' And she stamped her foot so
hard that her shoe button flew off and nearly hit Jimmy
on the nose!

16. Lisa plays a trick

The circus went on doing very well, although the circus folk did not like their new ringmaster. Only Pierre, and Google the clown seemed to like him, and they talked to him, and even laughed, though Britomart did not smile with them any more than he did with the others.

Pierre's performing seal was a marvellous creature, and Jimmy and Lotta really loved it. It was so gentle and loving, and so clever that it seemed to know what trick to do before it was even taught.

Pierre had taught it to blow a tune on a whistle, and the seal loved to play the tune over and over again. It was the tune of 'Yankee-doodle went to town', and very soon all the parrots were whistling it too. Everybody got very tired of 'Yankee-doodle' and begged Pierre to teach the seal something else.

But it was Jimmy who taught Neptune to play 'God Save the King', and the seal was cheered and clapped in the ring, when he came flipping in after the last turn, and set the band going with whistling 'God Save the King' on his own whistle!

Lisa and Jeanne were jealous of Jimmy because the seal liked him much better than he liked them. This was not surprising, for the two girls were not so patient as Jimmy, though they were quite kind to Neptune. The seal tried to follow Jimmy everywhere, and he had to shut the door behind him whenever he left the big tank, or else Neptune would be out of the water and galloping after him gaily!

Once Britomart had seen the seal going after Jimmy, and had ordered him to take Neptune back at once.

'How many times in this circus do I have to say that performing animals are not to be allowed loose in the camp!' he thundered. 'Pierre! Report this boy to me if he lets your seal loose again. I tell you I will be obeyed in my circus!'

Pierre took Neptune back. 'I know he *will* try to follow you,' he said to Jimmy, 'but you mustn't let him. You must remember to ·lock the door after you, when you leave him.'

'I did *shut* the door this morning,' said Jimmy.

'That's not enough,' said Pierre. 'Neptune can get the handle in his mouth and turn it. He is as clever as twenty dogs!'

'All right, Pierre,' said Jimmy. 'I'll always remember to lock the door.'

So he did, because he had a good memory, and rarely forgot anything that he was told. Every day when he went to see Neptune, he carefully locked the door behind him after he had said goodbye.

Jeanne and Lisa were always teasing Jimmy. They jumped out at him round corners. They poured jugs of water over him as he passed by the window of their caravan. They told him that Lucky wasn't the cleverest dog in the world, and Lisa told him all about other dogs she had known, all of which could do far more marvellous things than Lucky.

'I believe you are making all these stories up!' said Jimmy impatiently. 'Everything you know of is always better, more marvellous and wonderful than anything *we* know. I'm tired of listening to you!'

He went off. Lisa made a face after him. 'Bad tempered boy,' she called. 'I suppose you think you're Britomart, stalking off with a scowl like that!'

'Let's pay him out for not believing all we say,' said Jeanne. 'Lotta! Come here! We're thinking of a trick to play on Jimmy.'

Lotta was an angry little girl these days, not friends with anyone except Madame Prunella and Jeanne and

Lisa. She nodded at Jeanne. 'All right,' she said. 'What trick shall we play on Jimmy?'

'I know!' said Lisa. 'Next time he comes to call on Neptune, and locks the door behind him, we'll unlock it again – and Neptune will go galloping after him, and maybe Britomart will see him and scold Jimmy hard.'

Lotta shook her head. 'No, that's not a joke,' she said. 'I don't think I want to do that.'

'Don't be so silly,' said Lisa impatiently. 'Of course it's a joke! We'll do it tomorrow.'

Lotta said no more, but she made up her mind she wouldn't share that trick. It was a mean trick. She didn't mind a joke, but she wasn't going to play a mean trick on Jimmy.

Next morning Jeanne, Lisa, and Lotta were sitting on top of Pierre's caravan. They had an old rug up there, and all three little girls loved to lie on it, basking in the sun, playing with the dolls. Lisa saw Jimmy coming along, with Lucky at his heels as usual.

'Here he comes,' said Lisa in a low voice. 'We'll play the trick on him that we planned yesterday.'

'I don't want to,' said Lotta at once. Lisa laughed at her.

'You're afraid to,' she said. 'Hallo, Jimmy! Come and play up here.'

'No, thanks,' said Jimmy. 'You and Jeanne pushed me off last time. If I came up I'd push *you* off, and then you'd howl the place down. I hate girls that howl.'

He went in to talk to Neptune, who was most excited at hearing Jimmy's voice. He came to the top of the tank, and rested his head there, looking at the little boy out of loving brown eyes. Jimmy talked to him.

'You've the whitest whiskers I ever saw! You've the brownest eyes in the world! You're the cleverest seal that ever lived!'

Neptune loved hearing all this. He put his big head on Jimmy's shoulder and heaved such a sigh that he nearly blew the boy's ear off!

Then Brownie, Jimmy's father, called him from the other end of the field. 'Jimmy! Come and help me to get some water, will you?'

There was a stream at the end of the field, and the circus folk got their water from it. All the horses and animals had to have their drinking troughs cleaned out and refilled every day. It was quite a job to do them all, and Jimmy and Brownie were usually very busy until they had taken water to every caravan and cage.

'Coming, Dad!' shouted Jimmy. He gave Neptune one last pat and went out of the van. He carefully turned the key in the lock and went across the field.

No sooner was he gone than Lisa slipped down the side of her caravan, ran to the van, and unlocked the door. The seal was out of the tank, butting the door with its nose, as it always did when someone left it. When it heard the key turn again, it took the handle in its mouth and twisted it to one side. The door opened!

By this time Lisa was on top of the caravan again, giggling with Jeanne. Lotta watched the seal gallop out of the doorway, and go after Jimmy. She did hope that Britomart wouldn't come along at just that moment!

Just as Jimmy was dipping the big bucket into the stream, something plopped into the water with a big splash. He turned in surprise – and there was Neptune, swimming joyfully in the water!

'I say, Dad, look! Neptune is having a fine old swim!' cried Jimmy. 'I wonder if Pierre let him out. I locked him in just now.'

The seal loved the stream. It rolled itself over and over, made funny grunting noises, and tried to catch small fish that darted by.

Just then a shout went up from Neptune's caravan.

Pierre had come along, and had found the door open and the tank empty.

'Where's Neptune?' he yelled. Lisa answered him from the top of the caravan:

'Over in the stream, playing with Jimmy.'

Pierre was so annoyed that he fired off a lot of queer-sounding words in French that Lotta couldn't understand at all. Britomart put his head out of his caravan not very far off, his black eyes almost hidden by his frowning eyebrows.

'Pierre! What is the matter?' he called in his deep voice.

'Matter enough!' shouted Pierre. 'That boy has taken my seal to swim in the stream!'

Britomart came out from his caravan, and walked over to Pierre. 'First it is Lotta who disobeys, and now it is Jimmy,' he said. 'We will see what he has to say, the disobedient rogue!'

Jimmy was astonished to see two such angry men beside him, one pouring out grumbles, the other sternly demanding why he had taken the seal.

'I didn't take him,' said Jimmy. 'I went to see him as usual, and I locked the door after me. I really did. Some-one must have unlocked it, Pierre. The next thing I knew was seeing the seal splashing about in the stream, and I thought Pierre must have let him out.'

'I think you are not telling the truth,' said Britomart in his cold voice. 'In future you will not go into the cages of any animals excepting the dogs and the horses. Is that quite clear?'

'Oh! but, sir, can't I go and play with old Sammy, and the bears, and Jemima?' said Jimmy. 'I really must. They do so love it, especially Sammy, now he's shut up.'

'You understand my orders, I think!' said Britomart. 'If you disobey I shall know how to punish you. Pierre, take the seal back.'

The three girls had watched all this from the top of the distant caravan. They did not know what was being said, but they guessed that Jimmy was getting into trouble. When Britomart came up with Pierre and the seal, Lotta slipped down the opposite side of the caravan and ran away.

Pierre waited till Britomart had gone into his own caravan and then he looked up at the two watching girls. He knew how they disliked Jimmy.

'Did you girls unlock the door after Jimmy had gone?' he asked. He did not see Jimmy nearby, carrying a pail of water. Jimmy heard the question and looked up.

'Lotta slipped down and unlocked the door, to play a trick on Jimmy,' said Lisa. This was not the truth, but the naughty little girl wanted to make trouble between Lotta and Jimmy.

Jimmy heard what she said and went very red in the face. What! Lotta played that mean trick on him! Oh, no, it couldn't be! He couldn't believe it. Lotta would surely never, never get him into trouble. He went on his way, very puzzled and upset.

'I don't believe it,' thought Jimmy stoutly. 'Lotta wouldn't do that. And yet – she's changed so much lately. She's even horrid to Mother and she used to love her. Perhaps she *did* do it – and wanted me to be punished for it. What will old Sammy do if I don't go and see him? Oh, it's too bad. Lotta's horrid and mean!'

And so, although Jimmy could hardly believe that Lotta would play such a mean trick on him, and didn't *want* to believe it either, he ended up by thinking that what Lisa said was true.

'Everything's gone wrong since dear old Mr Galliano went,' thought the boy sadly. '*You* won't change, will you, little dog Lucky? Promise me you won't!'

And Lucky said 'Wuff!' in her loudest voice, which meant, 'I'll always be the same!'

17. Prunella loses her temper

Lotta did not know that Lisa had told such an untruth about her. She was soon very puzzled because Jimmy did not seem to want to speak to her or even to look at her; as for joking with her as he used to do, or slipping his arm through hers, those were things he never did now.

'I suppose he is still cross because I play with Lisa and Jeanne,' thought Lotta, frowning. 'Well, why shouldn't I? I've never had girls to play with before and I do like their dolls. I wish Lisa and Jeanne would give me one – I've never had a doll of my very own.'

Jimmy was not at all happy. It was dreadful to think that Lotta had got him into trouble on purpose. He didn't go near her if he could help it, though when they practised together for their turn in the ring with Lucky and Black Beauty, they had to be with one another. But they did not need to practise this turn very much, for they knew it so well. So they got through it as quickly as possible, and then Lotta went as usual to play with Lisa and Jeanne, and Jimmy went to help his father.

He was not unhappy only because of Lotta. He was unhappy because he had been forbidden to go into any of the animals' cages. He couldn't play with the bears. He mustn't visit old Sammy the chimpanzee. He couldn't go near Neptune. He didn't even like to peep in at Lilliput's monkeys, who were now in their cage all day.

The only thing he could do was to go and talk with Mr Tonks, whose big elephant, Jumbo, was tied by the leg to a great tree. Jumbo was too big to go in a cage. He was out in the field and was always pleased to see Jimmy. He lifted the boy on top of his huge neck, and gently blew his hair up straight – a favourite trick of old Jumbo's.

'Cheer up, Jimmy,' said Mr Tonks, seeing the boy's dull face. 'You look as gloomy as a wet hen.'

'Well, Mr Tonks, things aren't the same since Mr Galliano went,' said Jimmy. 'You know they aren't.'

'My boy, I've seen lots of changes in my lifetime,' said little Mr Tonks. 'It doesn't do to worry about them too much. You can get used to anything.'

'But I don't want to get used to some things,' said Jimmy. 'Look at poor old Sammy, moping in his cage all day long – not even *I* am allowed to go and play with him now. It isn't good for him after being allowed free. And you know how the bears loved me to go and play with them. The cub, Dobby, cries after me when I go without playing with him.'

'Yes, that isn't good,' said Mr Tonks, lighting his pipe. 'Britomart can put on a fine circus show but he doesn't understand animals as you and I do, Jimmy – or as Mr Galliano did. You know, you don't usually find as much freedom in a circus as Mr Galliano allowed in this one – so you miss it and feel unhappy about it. Cheer up – you'll soon get used to it.'

'Well, anyway, I can come and have a talk to old Jumbo,' said Jimmy, scratching the elephant's thick skin with a laugh. 'Britomart said I wasn't to go to any animals in a cage except the dogs and horses – so as old Jumbo isn't in a cage I can still come and play with *him*!'

'Hrrrrumph!' said Jumbo, exactly as if he understood what Jimmy was saying.

'Do you like Britomart, Mr Tonks?' asked Jimmy after a bit.

Mr Tonks looked round to make sure nobody could hear him.

'No, I don't,' he said. 'Few people do – and Britomart doesn't want to be liked. He only wants to be feared. There are a few people he is nicer to than others, because they can be useful to him – Pierre, for instance, and Google the clown, who have both done him good turns in other circuses.'

'How strange not to want to be liked,' said Jimmy. 'I don't want to be afraid of Britomart, but I believe I am, Mr Tonks.'

'You don't need to be afraid of anyone, Jimmy – a clever, honest, good-natured boy like you!' said Mr Tonks, ruffling Jimmy's hair. 'You just get on with your work in your best way and don't worry about Britomart. Things will come right, don't fret.'

Jimmy went red with pleasure to hear Mr Tonks's kind words. He smiled at the little elephant man and went away, comforted. But almost at once he met Lotta running round a van. They bumped into one another, and Lotta laughed.

For a moment Jimmy wanted to laugh too. Then he remembered that Lotta had played him that mean trick and got him into trouble, and he didn't laugh. He turned away in silence.

'Jimmy!' cried Lotta. 'What's the matter? Are you cross because I play with Lisa and Jeanne? I'll come for a walk with you and the dogs this morning, if you like.'

'No, thank you,' said Jimmy. 'I expect you only say that because the two girls have gone down into the town, and you just happen to have nothing to do. I don't like girls – they play mean tricks.'

Lotta didn't know what he meant. She stared after him. '*I* don't play mean tricks!' she cried.

'Oh yes, you do,' said Jimmy, he went off with his head in the air. Lotta tossed her own head and ran off angrily. All right – Jimmy could be horrid if he liked. *She* didn't care!

She went to Madame Prunella. Prunella was putting her parrots through their usual practice. One of them was saying 'Pop goes the weasel' very solemnly.

> '*Half a pound of tuppenny rice,*
> *Half a pound of treacle,*
> *Stir it up and make it nice,*
> *POP goes the weasel!*'

At the word POP all the other parrots joined in, and

Gringle cackled with laughter too. She poked Sally, a big parrot, and whispered, 'Britomart', to her.

Sally at once began the naughty little rhyme that Prunella had taught her:

> *'Britomart*
> *Thinks he's smart,*
> *But he's got a stony heart!'*

Neither of them saw that Britomart himself was nearby. The conjurer heard what the parrot shouted, and turned when he caught his own name. The parrot repeated the rhyme at the top of her voice, and then screeched with laughter.

Britomart strode over to the caravan. Lotta was stroking the parrot and tickling it. 'Say it again, Sally,' she said. 'Say it again.'

Then she looked up and saw Britomart standing nearby, his black eyes cold and angry. Sally began the rhyme again, her crested head cocked wickedly on one side.

'Hush!' said Lotta, and she nudged Madame Prunella to make her see who was standing near. Prunella looked up – but she didn't care tuppence for Britomart. He opened his mouth and began to speak, coldly and angrily.

At a little sign from their mistress the parrots set up their screeching and squealing again, to drown the ring-master's deep voice. But this time Britomart was not to be beaten. He knew that it was no use trying to stop the parrots' noise – so he took firm hold of Madame Prunella's fat little arm, and made her come with him to where he could talk and be heard.

Prunella tried to shake off his hard fingers, but it was no use. Britomart was so strong that he could have lifted her up with one of his fingers and thumb.

'That parrot of yours will repeat his rhyme in the ring one night, Madame Prunella,' said the ring-master. 'And then, Madame, that will be the end of him.'

'How dare you take hold of me in this way!' squealed Madame Prunella, flying into a temper at once. 'Let go my arm. How dare you threaten one of my parrots!'

'That parrot will stay on its perch, and will not go into the ring, Madame Prunella,' said Britomart. 'I don't trust you. You have only to lose your temper in the ring one night to have all your parrots shouting stupid things about me. Now go back to your caravan and think over what I have said. That parrot does not go into the ring again!'

He let Prunella go, and the angry little woman shook her fist at Britomart's back, and screeched like a parrot.

'Sally's one of my best birds. She *shall* go into the ring – yes, and she shall sing many things about Britomart the conjurer.'

She went back to her parrots, tears pouring down her cheeks, her hair standing on end. Lotta was waiting, wondering what Prunella was going to do.

'Madame Prunella,' began Lotta, meaning to say that she was sorry she had made Sally begin the rhyme about Britomart without seeing if he was nearby. But Prunella would not let her say a word. When she was angry, she was angry with everyone, friend or enemy alike. She glared at the little girl, and shouted at her.

'Go away! Pestering me like this! Go away!' She picked up her broom and began to sweep at Lotta. The little girl nearly fell over. She took one look at Prunella's angry red face, and ran off at top speed.

'Sausages and SMASH!' yelled Gringle after her.

'Well, there's plenty of "smash" about,' thought Lotta, as she heard things crashing behind her, when Prunella's broom knocked over pails and boxes. 'Gringle's right! Goodness! It looks as if Madame Prunella's going to sweep up the whole circus!'

But after a time Prunella became quieter and took all her parrots into the cage. She meant to teach them something that would give Britomart a shock.

'The whole circus can be afraid of Britomart for all I care!' said Prunella. '*I'm* not afraid of him – and I'll soon show him what I can do!'

18. More trouble!

Although all these upsets and quarrels went on in the camp, the show itself was splendid every night, for Britomart was a fine ring-master. The circus folk knew that there was plenty of money coming in, and they were pleased about this. Pierre, the seal-trainer, was especially pleased, for he had not been lucky for some time.

So he chatted amiably with Britomart and praised the way he did things. Mrs Pierre kept the conjurer's caravan clean for him, and the two girls, Lisa and Jeanne, went to help too. Not that they did anything much in the way of work, but they loved to try and peep at some of the things he used in his magic tricks.

'Look!' said Lisa, one morning. 'Here's his magic wand, Jeanne! It has rolled under his chest. Let's borrow it for a bit and see if we can do tricks with it.'

The two girls smuggled it into their own caravan. But although they did their best with it, it did no tricks for them. They showed it to Lotta, and her eyes grew wide as she looked at Britomart's strange wand.

'Oooh!' she said. 'However did you dare to take that? You'd better put it back.'

'You try to do some tricks with it,' said Lisa, putting it into the little girl's hands. 'See if canaries come flying through the air, or goldfish swimming out of the ground!'

Just as Lotta was waving it in the air, Pierre came along. 'Hide it, quick!' said Jeanne. 'We shall get into trouble if our father knows we took that.'

Lotta slipped the wand down the front of her frock and went to her own caravan with it. She put it under her mattress, meaning to try and see if she could do magic tricks with it later on. She knew that it was time for her to go and practise in the ring with Jimmy.

She and Jimmy hadn't made up their quarrel. Lotta was obstinate, and Jimmy was still hurt because he thought it was Lotta who had unlocked the seal's door and let the animal out after him.

'I shan't be nice again to Lotta till she owns up about that mean trick and says she's sorry,' thought the boy to himself.

But as Lotta hadn't played the mean trick and didn't even know that Jimmy thought she had, she couldn't possibly own up to it! So things went on just as badly as before, and Lotta grew spiteful and rude, and Jimmy quiet and angry. It was all very horrid indeed.

That evening in the ring there was trouble – over Madame Prunella's parrots, of course. That angry little woman had spent two days teaching them a few new things!

She took Sally into the ring although Britomart had forbidden her to – and of course, Sally began her usual loud song of 'Britomart thinks he's smart', much to the ring-master's rage.

He cut Prunella's turn short, and ordered her out of the ring – but Prunella loosed all her parrots at once and they flew around the ring-master, screeching and squealing:

'Horrid Britomart!'

'Silly Britomart!'

'Get your moustaches cut! Get your moustaches cut!' (That was Sally, who learnt anything after hearing it two or three times!)

'Poor old Britomart – poor old Britomart!' screeched another parrot in a doleful voice.

Of course, all the people thought that this was part of the show, and they roared with laughter. How they laughed and clapped! But Britomart was not pleased at all. He cracked his whip about the ring, and gave the parrots a fright. One of the things that the ring-master hated more than anything else in the world was to be laughed at, and he was very angry indeed now.

Prunella was afraid that he might hurt one of her parrots with the whip and she called them to her. They fluttered down to her arms and shoulders and head, and grinning cheekily, she bowed to all the clapping people. Her act was cut short – but she had got more claps than usual, all the same!

Britomart followed her out of the ring. 'You will be sorry for this,' he said in a furious voice. 'I will see you tomorrow morning.'

Prunella laughed. She skipped off with her parrots and fetched her cloak. Lotta was standing nearby, waiting her turn to go into the ring with Black Beauty.

'That was fun, Madame Prunella!' she whispered. 'Weren't your parrots naughty!'

But the other circus folk looked rather grave. They felt certain that Britomart would punish Prunella in some way, and then things would be worse than ever.

Britomart had missed his black wand that evening, and had hunted everywhere for it. He called Mrs Pierre to him about it.

'Did Lisa and Jeanne help you clean my caravan today?' he asked. 'They did? Well, call them here. They may have seen my black wand.'

The two girls came, rather scared. Britomart looked at them and saw at once that they had guilty faces. They knew something about his wand.

'You found my wand this morning, didn't you?' he said. 'Bad girls! What did you do with it?'

Lisa was always quick at telling untruths to get herself out of trouble, so she answered in a hurry:

'Oh, Mr Britomart, we did find it. It was under the chest there, but Lotta snatched it from us and took it away to see if it would do tricks for her. She wouldn't give it back though we told her to.'

'So!' said Britomart, frowning, till his big black eyebrows met over his nose. 'Lotta again! Tell her to come to me.'

But Lotta had gone down into the town with her mother, and it was almost time for the show to begin when they came back. So she didn't know anything about the story that naughty Lisa had told about her. She had forgotten about the wand too – it was still under her mattress! She had meant to put it back in Britomart's caravan and had quite forgotten.

She couldn't think why the ring-master looked at her so frowningly as she did her turn on Black Beauty that night. The pony was as clever as ever, and the little girl loved to feel his shiny black body beneath her, as she stood on him, sat, and knelt – even crawling right under his body as he galloped round and round the ring!

When the show was over she ran to look for Jimmy. 'I

say, Jimmy,' she said, 'do you think poor Prunella will get into dreadful trouble tomorrow? What do you think Britomart will do? Will he send her away? Will he forbid her to go into the ring? Will he not pay her any money at all?'

Jimmy forgot that he wasn't friends with Lotta, and the two children stared at one another solemnly in the glaring lights that shone over the circus field. They both liked Madame Prunella, and did not want anything horrid to happen to her.

'I don't know what Britomart will do,' said Jimmy at last. 'Anyway, all I know is this – I certainly don't want to get into trouble with him. Mr Galliano had a temper, but Britomart is far worse. Mr Galliano got into a temper, blew up, and forgot about it at once – but Britomart remembers always. That's why he never smiles, I expect – because he is always remembering horrid things!'

'Did you see how angrily he looked at me this evening?' asked Lotta. 'I wondered what I'd done. I can't think of anything at all!'

Mrs Brown called Jimmy, and he ran off with Lucky. He too had noticed Britomart watching Lotta angrily, and he wondered why.

Jimmy and Lotta both lay awake that night and thought about Madame Prunella. They liked the excitable little woman very much, and neither of them liked to think of her in trouble. They felt sure that Britomart would send for her first thing in the morning.

And so he did. He called Pierre to him and gave him an order. 'Tell Madame Prunella I want her here in my caravan AT ONCE,' he said in his deepest voice.

'Very good, sir,' said Pierre, and went to tell Prunella.

But he couldn't find her caravan! It wasn't in its usual place. Pierre scratched his head and looked puzzled. Why had Prunella left her usual place? He looked round the enormous field, full of vans and carts and cages, and tried to see where Prunella had gone to.

He wandered round, looking for her gay caravan. He called Jimmy to him. 'Have you seen Madame Prunella's caravan this morning?' he asked.

'No,' said Jimmy, surprised. 'Why, isn't it where it usually is, over by the stream?'

'No, she's moved it,' said Pierre. 'Oh my, there's Brito-mart yelling for me. Look round for Madame Prunella, there's a good boy, and tell her she's to go to Britomart AT ONCE!'

Britomart was impatiently waiting for Pierre. 'What are you wandering all round the field for?' he said. 'Where is Madame Prunella?'

'She seems to have moved her caravan, sir,' said Pierre. 'I was just looking for it.'

Britomart made an angry noise and went down his caravan steps. He gazed round. He knew every van, cart and cage.

'I can't see her caravan,' he said at last. Then Jimmy came running up. 'Please, sir, Madame Prunella isn't in the camp at all! Her caravan is gone! There are wheel marks, new ones, going out of the gate! She must have put in her horse by herself last night, and stolen out quietly whilst we all slept.'

'Pah!' said Britomart in anger. 'How dare she leave my circus like that! She is part of the show. She has no right to do that without warning me. I shall see that she does not easily get a job in a circus again.'

He went into the caravan and slammed the door. Jimmy was upset. It was horrid to think of pretty little Madame Prunella stealing off all alone in the night like that. How they would miss her and her screeching parrots!

But just then Britomart flung open his door again. He had remembered his missing wand.

'Where's Lotta?' he called.

'In her caravan, sir,' said Jimmy in surprise. Why, do you want her?'

'Yes – I want her – and I want something else, too!' said Britomart in a grim voice. And he strode over the field to Lotta's caravan. What a shock poor Lotta was going to get!

19. Lotta is punished

Britomart rapped on the door of Lotta's caravan. Rat-tat-tat! Lotta opened the door in surprise, for not many people knocked like that. When she saw Britomart standing there, frowning, she was even more astonished.

'Lotta, you have my black wand, I think,' said the ring-master in his deep voice. Lotta stared at him in dismay. She had forgotten all about the wand. She went very red indeed.

'Where is it?' said Britomart. He pushed his way into the caravan and looked round. Lotta went to her bunk, felt under her mattress, and gave it to Britomart, trembling, for he looked angry.

'How dare you go to my caravan and steal my wand!' thundered the ring-master. 'I always said that children should never be allowed in any circus. You are a bad little girl.'

Lotta didn't know what to say. She didn't like to say that Lisa had taken the wand and lent it to her, in case she got Lisa into trouble too. She did not know that Lisa had told a bad untruth, and put the whole blame on Lotta. So the little girl stood there and said nothing at all, looking frightened and sulky.

But Jimmy, who was listening, called out in alarm, 'Mr Britomart! I'm sure Lotta didn't steal your wand. She wouldn't steal anything. She—'

'Hold your tongue, boy,' ordered the ring-master. 'I am not speaking to you, but to this naughty girl. Lotta, I will not have you in the ring for two weeks! You can stay out, and see how you like that. Lisa and Jeanne can take your place. They do not ride so well as you, but they are good enough. Perhaps that will teach you to leave other people's things alone in future.'

Britomart turned and went down the steps. He pushed Jimmy roughly aside and went to his own caravan with his wand, a tall and stern figure. Jimmy did not dare to say anything more to him. He was afraid that if he did he too might be forbidden to go into the ring.

He was dreadfully sorry for Lotta. The little girl stood in the middle of her caravan as if she was turned into stone. She did not move or say a word. Jimmy ran up the steps to her, meaning to comfort her, forgetting all about the mean trick he thought she had played on him.

But Lotta pushed him away. She pushed him right down the steps, slammed the caravan door and locked it. She even shut the windows and drew the curtains across. Jimmy was quite shut out. He heard Lotta fling herself down on her untidy bunk, and begin to sob. Poor Jimmy! It was dreadful to feel so sorry for someone and not to be able to help them. He went away after a time, and hunted for Lal, Lotta's mother.

He told her all that had happened. Lal was angry and worried.

'Poor Lotta,' she said. 'I'm sure she didn't take that wand from Britomart's caravan. I feel certain Lisa or Jeanne have had something to do with this, horrid little creatures!'

'You'd better go to Lotta,' said Jimmy anxiously. 'She's awfully unhappy. You know how proud she is of going into the ring with Black Beauty each night, and how she loves sharing my turn with Lucky. Now Lisa and Jeanne are going to ride instead. But I won't let them share my turn with little dog Lucky.'

Lal went off to try and comfort Lotta. But the miserable little girl wouldn't even unlock the door. She lay and wept till she had no tears left, thinking of the time when dear old Mr Galliano ran the circus, and everything went right. She couldn't bear Britomart. She couldn't bear Lisa and Jeanne now, either, because they were going into the ring instead of her. Oh! Oh! How she hated everyone!

'Better leave her alone to get over it,' said Mrs Brown, when Lal told her what had happened. 'You know, Lal, this may do Lotta good. She hasn't been a very nice child lately, and she has rather got into the habit of thinking that she can do just whatever she likes. She is a good little girl at heart – but she has been very naughty lately.'

'Perhaps you're right,' said Lal, thinking of the rude faces and cheeky answers that Lotta had given her. 'Maybe all the clapping and cheering she gets each night has made her vain.'

'Oh, how horrid you both are to talk of poor Lotta like that!' said Jimmy, who was very tender-hearted. 'She's terribly unhappy now, I know she is – and I don't care whether she deserves it or not, I'm sorry for her and I'd put things right if I could. I'd like to swing Britomart's whip round his great long legs!'

'Hush, Jimmy, don't talk like that,' said his mother, shocked. 'If Britomart hears you, he will forbid you to go into the ring too – and then you will not get paid and will have to go without a good many of the nice things you like so much.'

Jimmy stamped his foot and went off by himself. He was angry, miserable, and puzzled. He couldn't believe that Lotta had stolen Britomart's wand. But if she hadn't, how was it that it was in her caravan? Jimmy didn't know. He only knew that things were queer and horrid lately.

Lisa and Jeanne were excited and pleased when they heard they that were to ride in the ring instead of Lotta. They did not feel sorry for their friend. They were glad because they were going to take her place. They were hard, selfish little girls, vain and bold. They danced round in excitement when their mother fitted them for their circus dresses.

'Lisa can borrow Lotta's,' said Britomart. 'They are much of a size. Perhaps Lal has an old dress of Lotta's that she has grown out of, that would do for Jeanne.

There is no time to make new ones.'

So, much to Lotta's anger, Lisa and Jeanne put on her own dresses, the pretty, sparkling ones that made her like a fairy. Lisa and Jeanne looked lovely in them too, for they were both pretty children, with their red curls and snub noses. It made Lotta more unhappy to think of Lisa and Jeanne wearing her dresses than she felt when she thought of them taking her place in the ring that night.

'But they shan't ride Black Beauty,' she told her mother furiously. 'They shan't! If they do, I'll get on Black Beauty's back and ride away and never come back, Lal!'

'Don't be silly, Lotta,' said Lal. 'Of course no one will ride Black Beauty. He is in his stable, quite happy.'

But Black Beauty was not happy. He knew that his little mistress was sad, and he was sad too. He could not understand why she did not come to get him ready for the night's show. He stamped impatiently in his stable, but Lotta did not come.

Black Beauty whinnied, and Lotta heard him. She had refused to go out of her caravan all day, but she could not say no when Black Beauty called her. She slipped out when no one was looking and went to his stable. He rubbed his black nose against her lovingly and the little girl threw her arms round his neck.

'Oh, Black Beauty, we're not going into the ring to-night,' she sobbed. 'It's not fair that you should be punished too, because you do love showing how well you can dance and do tricks, don't you? But nobody shall ride you if *I* can't. We'll have to let that silly Lisa and stupid Jeanne take our places.'

At that moment Lisa and Jeanne came running by, dressed in Lotta's pretty clothes. They saw Lotta and called to her.

'Hallo, Lotta! So you've come out at last! Look at us – aren't we fine? We're going to do as well as we can, so that Britomart will perhaps let us be in the circus always.'

Lotta turned away without a word. She wondered how she could ever have liked Lisa and Jeanne – how she could have played with them and been so unkind to Jimmy, who had been her friend for so long. She would never, never play with them again.

Then she thought of something and turned round on Lisa. 'How did Britomart know that I had his wand?' she demanded. 'Did you tell him?'

Lisa looked at Jeanne and Jeanne looked at Lisa. They had both made up their minds what to say if Lotta asked them that question.

'What do you mean?' asked Lisa with an innocent, wide-eyed stare. 'Of course we didn't tell him. We didn't even know you had it.'

'Oh, you dreadful fibber!' cried Lotta. 'Why, you gave it to me yourself, Lisa, when you had found it under the chest!'

'We didn't find it under any chest,' said Jeanne, bounding off. '*You* found it, and you must have taken it without anyone knowing.'

Lotta stared after the two mean, untruthful girls in

amazement. For a moment she couldn't imagine what they meant. And then she guessed everything.

'They must have told Britomart that *I* took the wand from his caravan,' she cried. 'Oh, the fibbers! I'll go and tell him straight away that I didn't.'

Of she rushed to Britomart's caravan. She thumped on the door.

'Go away!' ordered Britomart, who was busy changing into his circus dress. 'I see no one now.'

'Mr Britomart! It's me, Lotta!' cried the little girl. 'I've come to tell you that Lisa told you a story about me. *She* took your wand, not me – she gave it to me to see if I could do any tricks with it, and—'

'Go away,' said Britomart. 'I do not believe you. You are a naughty girl, disobedient and sulky. Go away.'

So that wasn't any good either. Lotta went away, tears in her eyes. She met Oona the acrobat in his sparkling tights, ready for the ring. He looked solemn.

'Have you heard anything about Madame Prunella?' asked Lotta, remembering that Prunella was Oona's cousin and that the acrobat was very fond of her. Oona shook his head.

'No,' he said sadly. 'I am unhappy about Prunella. It is the first time she has ever run away from a show – and it is not good to do that. No ring-master likes to take people who have run away from shows, in case it might happen again – and that harms a circus, you know. Britomart always rubs people up the wrong way. I don't think I shall stay on with the circus when we leave here.'

'Oh, Oona, don't say that!' cried Lotta. 'The circus wouldn't be the same without you.'

Oona wasn't the only one thinking about leaving. Mr Wally was gloomily planning to take Sammy to another show if Galliano didn't come back soon. And if Mr Wally went, then Mr Tonks declared he would go too.

'Why, there won't be any of Mr Galliano's Circus left!' thought Lotta miserably. 'Whatever are we to do?'

20. What will happen to the circus?

It seemed strange without Madame Prunella, and everyone missed the noise of the screeching parrots. Nobody knew where Prunella had gone. Nobody heard from her. It was very mysterious. Britomart did not mention her name, but he altered the turns in the ring to make up for Madame Prunella's turn being missed out.

Pierre got an even longer turn, and so did Google the clown. Twinkle, Pippi, and Stanley were annoyed about this, because they thought they should have more time given to them.

Sticky Stanley asked Britomart if he and the other two might not have five minutes more. Britomart shook his head.

'Google is funnier than you three,' he said. 'You do not get so many laughs as he does – he shall have the extra time. And please do not question what I do – I am the ring-master and my word is law.'

Sharp-faced Google was pleased. A longer turn meant more money. He went across the field to talk to Pierre, who was also pleased that his own turn was to be longer. Squib, Google's dog, went at his heels.

He saw Lucky on the way and stopped to talk to him. He was very good friends with Lucky. Jimmy saw them playing together as he came up with biscuits for Lucky, and he threw one to Squib.

Google saw him and swung round. 'Don't feed my dog!' he ordered. 'You children think you can do what you like in this circus. Squib! Come here!'

Squib did not want to come, with that beautiful smell of biscuit just under his nose. He stood there wagging his tail, looking towards his master as if to say, 'Please, Master, just let me wait and have a nibble then I'll come.'

Google was always jealous if Squib liked anyone else, and he was furious because his dog would not leave Jimmy and Lucky, and come to him. He strode over to them, picked Squib up, and tried to cuff Jimmy. The boy slipped out of the way, his eyes shining with rage.

Google went off, muttering.

'That's the first time anyone has tried to cuff me in this circus,' thought Jimmy. 'Lotta's right. This isn't Mr Galliano's circus any longer. It's Britomart's – and it's getting like him – quarrelsome, selfish, hard, and horrid!'

For the first time a thought came into the boy's mind. If Mr Wally went – and Mr Tonks and Jumbo went – why shouldn't he go too? Why shouldn't he go with them, and join another circus, where perhaps there would be a nicer ring-master than Britomart? His mother and father could go with him, for any circus would be glad of Brownie's help as carpenter and handyman.

'And I guess you and I could get a job in another circus as easily as anything!' said Jimmy, stroking Lucky's soft head. 'I don't believe old Galliano will ever come back – and I'm not going to work for Britomart much longer! He has never once said how clever you are, Lucky. He looks at us as if we are worms. We won't stand it, will we?'

'Woof, woof!' said Lucky, lying on her back with all four paws in the air. She would go anywhere with Jimmy and be happy.

'You see, Lucky, even Lotta doesn't seem the same,' said Jimmy, tickling Lucky. 'We've had such fun together, she and I, and Black Beauty and you – but now she mustn't go into the ring, and she's cross and miserable and won't be friends. So perhaps it would be better to go right away, Lucky, and start all over again.'

Lisa and Jeanne came chattering by. They were very pleased at going into the ring each night. They were a great success, for although they were not nearly so clever as Lotta, they could both ride well, and looked pretty in the ring.

Lisa pulled Jimmy's hair as she passed. 'You look as if you're going to burst into tears!' she said. 'Cheer up!'

Jimmy turned his back on her. 'I suppose you think you do marvellously in the ring!' he said. 'But, my goodness, what a pair of scarecrows you look! You ought to be ashamed of yourselves, doing poor old Lotta out of her turn. I thought you were supposed to be friends of hers.'

'My word, isn't he a bear!' laughed Jeanne, and the two girls danced off happily, very pleased with themselves these days. Things were going right with them!

Jimmy went into the ring after a while to give Lucky a practice. Mr Wally was there with Sammy the chimpanzee, giving him a practice too.

Mr Wally was looking worried. Sammy was not behaving well. He was sulky. He was supposed to undress himself in the ring and put himself to bed in a cot, which he usually did very well indeed. But today he sat on the floor and moped, and although Mr Wally did his best to coax him, he hung his hairy head and would not do anything to please his master.

When he saw Jimmy coming in with Lucky he leapt to his feet and made chattering noises of joy. He ran to Jimmy and put his arms round the boy's waist, nearly lifting him off the ground with delight.

'Oh, Sammy! Dear old Sammy!' said Jimmy. 'Look, Mr Wally, he's even trying to kiss me!'

'He's so pleased to see you,' said Mr Wally. 'You know, Jimmy, he's moping terribly, now that he is not allowed to wander about with me and you as he likes. And since you've been forbidden to play with him in his cage each day he is worse than ever. Chimpanzees are like children, you know – they must have plenty to do and see, or they mope and get miserable. Now, Sammy – will you do your tricks for Jimmy?'

Oh, yes! Sammy didn't mind doing them for his

beloved friend Jimmy. The chimpanzee went through his
tricks happily, laughing when Jimmy clapped him. His
queer chimpanzee mind had not been able to understand
why his friend hadn't been to see him – and he couldn't
think why nobody took him for walks round the field
now.

Jimmy took Sammy's paw and led him back to his cage
when his practice was over. They met Britomart on the
way, and when the ring-master saw Jimmy with the
chimpanzee, he frowned.

'Didn't I say that you were not to play with the animals
any more?' he demanded. 'Mr Wally, you know my
orders, even if Jimmy doesn't!'

Mr Wally had a temper of his own. He flared up at
once. 'Mr Britomart,' he said, 'everyone in this circus
knows your orders. We can't help knowing them. You
throw them at our heads all day long. We have had more
orders from you in a few weeks than we had from Mr
Galliano in a year! But I'm not aware that either I or
Jimmy are disobeying your orders at the moment. Jimmy
is not playing with Sammy. He is merely walking back to
his cage with him.'

'That is enough from you, Mr Wally,' said the ring-
master in anger.

'No it isn't enough,' said Mr Wally. 'Not nearly
enough! My chimpanzee is moping, Mr Britomart, because of your orders. He won't do his tricks properly! If
Jimmy hadn't come into the ring this morning, Sammy
wouldn't have done a single one of his tricks. No animal
can perform if it mopes!'

'I thought your chimpanzee was not doing so well this
week,' said Mr Britomart coldly. 'I had thought I would
get someone else in his place, when we leave this camp.'

'That suits me all right,' said Mr Wally, going very red
indeed. 'In fact, that suits me fine! I'm not staying in any
circus with you, Mr Britomart. And let me tell you this –
the whole circus will break up if you go about shouting
stupid orders at us from morning to night! Why, you are

spoiling the very things you ought to use! Look at this boy, Jimmy, here – he keeps all the animals happy – they all love him – and what do you do but forbid him to play with them! Pah!'

'I shall listen to you no longer,' said Britomart, white with anger. He turned and walked off. But Mr Wally hadn't finished with him yet.

'And what about little Lotta?' he yelled. 'You go and shut her out of the ring and put in those two silly red-haired kids instead. They can't ride for toffee! They ...'

But Britomart was out of hearing. Sammy the chimpanzee suddenly began to whimper. He knew that Mr Wally was angry and he did not like it. He was frightened. Jimmy put his arm round the chimpanzee and hugged him.

'It's all right, Sammy,' he said. 'Mr Wally is just telling Mr Britomart a few things he ought to know. Good for you, Mr Wally! But, I say – you won't really go, will you?'

'I certainly will,' said Mr Wally in a most determined voice. 'And what's more, I'll take old Tonks with me, and Volla too, and Stanley and Lilliput! If anyone thinks I'm going to put up with Britomart, they're mistaken!'

And off he marched to put Sammy into his cage. Jimmy watched him with a sinking heart. It seemed as if the circus would break up before his very eyes!

'I'll have to go too,' he thought. 'I can't possibly stay here without all my friends.'

He went off, thinking hard. 'I shan't tell Lotta I'm going,' he thought. 'She won't care anyhow! So she shan't hear any of my plans from *me*!'

21. Jimmy learns the truth

Lotta was very miserable now. She hated to think of Lisa and Jeanne going in the ring to take her place each night. She would not speak to the two girls, nor would she speak to Jimmy. She just moped about the field, sometimes riding Black Beauty to give him the exercise he needed.

Jimmy did his turn with Lucky in the ring, but he would not let Lisa and Jeanne help him. The two girls begged and begged him to let them, but Jimmy shook his head.

'No,' he said, 'You are both mean and horrid. I won't have you helping me with Lucky in the ring. And if you dare to ask Britomart if you can, I'll walk right out of this circus like Madame Prunella!'

He looked so fierce that the two girls said no more. Neither of them would have dared to ask anything from Britomart, for cheeky as they were, they were just as afraid of the stern ring-master as anyone else was.

But Jeanne, the younger girl, wouldn't give up trying to make friends with Jimmy. She had suddenly decided that if only she could make Jimmy really friendly with her, he might let her, and not Lisa, go into the ring with him and Lucky. 'Then wouldn't Lisa be jealous!' she thought.

So Jeanne began to be very nice to Jimmy. She brought him a hot chocolate-cake that her mother had just made. But all that Jimmy said was— 'Hmmm! I suppose you took that when your mother's back was turned. I don't want any, thank you! I think you and Lisa are untruthful, dishonest girls.'

'Oh, Jimmy! Don't be so unkind!' said Jeanne. 'I know Lisa is horrid and unkind often – but I'm quite different. I don't tell dreadful fibs like Lisa.'

'Well, *I've* never noticed that you were any better than Lisa,' said Jimmy, polishing some horse harness so hard that his arm ached. 'Anyway, I don't like you, so go away.'

Jeanne squeezed a few tears out and sniffed dolefully. 'Well, Jimmy,' she said, 'I was very sorry that Lisa told that dreadful story the other day – you know, about letting Neptune out.'

'What do you mean?' asked Jimmy in surprise. 'What dreadful story?'

'Why, don't you remember? Lisa said that Lotta had unlocked the door of the seal's van, so that Neptune might go after you, and then you'd get into trouble,' said Jeanne. 'Well, it wasn't Lotta. Lotta said she wouldn't play a mean trick like that. But Lisa did, and then she said it was Lotta who had done it.'

Jimmy stared at Jeanne in the greatest surprise and anger. *Lisa* had played the trick – and had blamed Lotta for it! The horrid girl!

'If I could get hold of Lisa, I'd pull her red hair till she yelled the place down!' said the boy furiously. 'It was Lisa who got me into trouble over the seal, then, and not poor old Lotta – and here I've been blaming Lotta for it, and thinking horrid things about her – and they weren't a bit true! Oh, I do feel mean!'

'Yes, and Lisa got Lotta into trouble too,' said tell-tale Jeanne, thoroughly enjoying herself. 'It was Lisa who gave Lotta the wand to hide and who told Britomart that Lotta had found it and taken it.'

Jimmy simply couldn't believe his ears. He couldn't think that anyone could be so horrid. He stood and stared at Jeanne till that bold little girl began to feel uncomfortable.

'I've only told you all this, Jimmy, because I want to show you I'd like to be friends,' she said.

'You've told tales of your sister, you've shown me exactly how mean and nasty you both are – and then you say it's to show me you want to be friends,' said Jimmy at

last in a disgusted voice. 'Well, listen to me, Jeanne – you
and Lisa have made a lot of trouble and mischief, but it's
the last time you do it to me or to Lotta. I don't want to
have anything more to do with you. I don't want to speak
to you. I don't want to look at you. I won't even work in
the same circus as you! After we leave here I shall join
another circus – and I hope I never meet either you or
Lisa again!'

The angry boy turned on his heel and went away,
taking the jingling harness with him. Jeanne stared after
him, red in the face. For the first time in her life she felt
ashamed of herself. Perhaps after all it was a better thing to
tell the truth, to be honest and loyal and kind, like Jimmy.
Jeanne began to cry, and wished that she hadn't told tales.

Jimmy hung up the harness in the stable-van and went
off by himself. He wanted to think. Lucky ran silently at
her master's heels, knowing that he was worried.
Together they went off over the field, and when Jimmy
found a sweet-scented gorse-bush throwing its delicious
smell over a common, he sat down by it.

Lucky lay down by him, her head on Jimmy's knees.
Jimmy stroked the soft head. 'You know, Lucky,' he said,
'I've been unfair to poor old Lotta. I thought she had
played me that mean trick, and let Neptune out to get me
into trouble – but I might have known Lotta would never
do a thing like that, little monkey though she is.'

'Woof,' said Lucky softly. She loved Jimmy to talk to
her like this. She put out her pink tongue and licked her
master's brown hand.

'And Lotta's got into dreadful trouble all because of
Lisa, too,' said Jimmy. 'She's very unhappy. And she must
be puzzled to know why I've been so extra horrid to her.
So we've got to put things straight, Lucky. Haven't we?'

'Woof, woof!' said Lucky, quite agreeing.

'Well, the first thing we'll do, Lucky, is to go down
into the town and buy Lotta the biggest and best doll we
can find,' said Jimmy. 'She loves dolls, you know, and
she's never had one of her own. Perhaps that will make

her feel happier. And then, Lucky, we'll tell her that everything has been a silly, horrid mistake, and we'll be friends again. What do you think of that idea?'

'WOOF!' said Lucky, sitting up. It was plain that she thought it a very good idea indeed!'

'You're a marvellous dog,' said Jimmy, hugging Lucky. 'I believe you understand every single word I say! I really do. And, Lucky, we'll wait and see what Mr Galliano's next letter says, shall we – and if he is coming back soon, we'll stay here – and if he's not, we'll give Britomart notice that we are both going off to another circus. Lotta must come too. Things will soon be better, once we make up our minds to face them and see how we can beat the things we don't like!'

Lucky bounded round, her eyes shining, as she heard her master's determined voice. She knew quite well that Jimmy had made up his mind about something and was feeling happier. Then little dog Lucky was happy too!

The two went back to the camp. Jimmy looked for Lotta, but the little girl was nowhere to be seen.

'Well, never mind, I'll go down to the town now and buy that doll,' said Jimmy. 'It's funny that girls like things like dolls – but they all seem to, even Lotta. So maybe they can't help it. Come on, Lucky!'

Jimmy took some money from his money-box and went off with his dog at his heels. He couldn't help feeling much happier now that he knew it was Lisa who had got him into trouble and not Lotta. He caught a tram and was soon in the heart of the big town.

He looked about for a toyshop. He soon found one – a rather marvellous one, with all kinds of toys in it, from bears to rabbits, dolls to trains, bricks to scooters, cars to books – everything that could be thought of! Jimmy gazed in at the window.

He looked at the dolls carefully. There were all kinds. There was a baby doll dressed in long clothes whose eyes were shut, and who had tiny shining nails like a real baby. There was a cheeky looking doll dressed in a coat and a hat – but it had red hair and reminded Jimmy of Lisa and Jeanne. He couldn't possibly have *that* doll!

There were airmen-dolls, soldier-dolls, and sailor-dolls – but Jimmy didn't feel that they were the kind of dolls that Lotta would like. And then he saw the Very Doll! It was sitting in a little chair, and had a sweet smiling face, with bright blue eyes, tiny teeth, and red cheeks. Its hair was real and fell in golden curls.

Jimmy stared at the doll. He couldn't help rather liking it himself, it was such a friendly, smiling doll. It was dressed in a gay overall, and beside it were a red hat and coat, ready to put on – and a little red umbrella too!

'That's the doll for Lotta!' thought Jimmy. He looked at the price-ticket. It was very expensive – seventeen shillings and sixpence! Jimmy counted up his money. He could just buy it!

'Well, it's worth it, to make poor old Lotta a bit happy again,' thought Jimmy, going into the shop. He pointed out the doll to the shop-girl and she took it out of the window. Jimmy took it and looked at it. The doll smiled up at him and almost seemed as if it was going to laugh.

'Put it into a box, please,' said Jimmy, 'and wrap it up nicely. It's for a present.'

The girl wrapped up the doll and Jimmy paid her his money. He went out of the shop and caught the next tram back, out of the town. He walked down the country lane that led to the camp, whistling happily. It was a simply lovely feeling to carry a fine surprise like that under his arm, ready to give to someone who was miserable!

He got to the camp. 'Lotta!' he yelled. 'Lotta! Where are you?'

'She's in her caravan,' said Oona. 'I saw her going up the steps twenty minutes ago.'

Jimmy went and banged on the door. 'Lotta! Let me in. I've something to show you.'

'Don't want to see it,' said a sulky voice. But Jimmy wasn't going to take any notice of that. He flung open the caravan door and went in, beaming all over his brown face.

22. A fine old muddle!

Lotta was alone in her caravan. She was untidy and dirty, for since Britomart had forbidden her to go into the ring, she had been too sulky and unhappy to care how she looked.

She spent a good deal of time shut up in her caravan, for she didn't like to meet Lisa and Jeanne in the camp. They were unkind, and loved to tell her how well they were getting on, riding in the ring each night. She didn't like to meet Jimmy either, for he too seemed more of an enemy than a friend these days. So the sad little girl shut herself up with Lulu the spaniel and thought back to all the happy days when Mr Galliano had the circus.

'I know what I shall do,' she decided. 'I shall do what I

did once before – dress up as a boy, cut my hair short, and
run away. I shall take Black Beauty and I shall join
another circus. Yes – that's what I shall do – run away.
Nobody cares about me any more. Jimmy isn't my friend.
Mrs Brown says I am spoilt and rude. Even Lal tells me I
deserve to be punished. So I shall run away from everybody – and then perhaps they will be sorry.'

It was whilst she was thinking this that Jimmy arrived
and banged on the door. It flew open, and Lotta saw
Jimmy standing there, a broad smile on his face – the first
smile she had seen on Jimmy's face for quite a long time.

'Lotta! I've got a present for you,' cried Jimmy.

'A present? What for? It isn't my birthday,' said Lotta,
surprised.

'I know that. It's a present to make up for being horrid
to you, and thinking untrue things about you,' said
Jimmy. 'Oh, Lotta – I thought *you* had opened Neptune's door and let him out after me to get me into
trouble, and I thought it was simply horrid of you and I
wouldn't be friends at all – and now Jeanne has told me it
was Lisa who did it.'

'Oh – the mean creature!' cried Lotta in a rage. 'As if
I'd play a trick like that on you, Jimmy. You might have
known I'd never do a thing like that.'

'Yes, I might have known it,' said Jimmy. 'I'm terribly
sorry I was so horrid all for nothing, Lotta – just when
things went wrong for you too. And I've found out that it
was Lisa who got that wand, not you – and she gave it to
you and told Britomart you had stolen it. But *I* never,
never once thought that, Lotta. Really I didn't.'

'I should just hope you didn't,' cried Lotta, her eyes
flashing. 'Good gracious! To think that awful Lisa said
things like that about me. I'll pull her hair out. I'll pinch
her hard. I'll—'

'Well before you do all that, just take a look at this,'
said Jimmy, afraid that Lotta would fly out of the caravan to find Lisa that very minute. He pushed the big
parcel into Lotta's hands. The little girl looked at it, and

then began to tug eagerly at the string. Like all the circus folk, she really loved a present.

The string came off. The paper slid to the floor. Lotta took off the lid of the box – and the blue-eyed, golden-haired doll smiled up at her in its friendly, loving way.

'*Jimmy!* A real doll of my own – and the loveliest, darlingest one too!' squealed Lotta in the greatest delight. 'Jimmy, how did you think of such a present? Oh, Jimmy, I do love it. It's the most beautiful doll I ever saw – much, *much* nicer than Lisa's or Jeanne's. And oh, look at its overall – and its little red coat and hat – and gracious goodness, it's got an umbrella too!'

Jimmy stood and grinned all over his face at Lotta's delight. He had never felt so pleased in all his life as when he saw Lotta's face at that moment. Lotta was his friend, and she had been unhappy, and now she was happy again. Jimmy felt warm and happy too.

Lotta lifted the lovely doll out of the box and hugged her. She swung her to and fro and the doll opened and shut her long-lashed eyes. Lotta looked at her lovingly, and wondered what to call her.

'You give her a name, Jimmy,' she said.

'Lisa,' said Jimmy at once, with a grin.

Lotta squealed and made a face. 'Don't be silly. I wouldn't give the name of a horrid girl to a lovely doll like this. I'll call her Rosemary Josephine Annabella – there, dolly, three beautiful names for you!'

Lotta put the doll back into its box and looked at Jimmy. She flung her arms round his neck and hugged him. 'You've made me feel happy again,' she said. 'Let's be friends again, Jimmy. I'm awfully sorry I was horrid to you when I went to play with Lisa and Jeanne. I can't think how I behaved like that now.'

'Well, we'll forgive one another and begin all over again,' said Jimmy. 'You know, Lotta, it's not been all our fault really – things have gone so badly since Mr Galliano went away and Britomart seems to have upset everything and everybody. Did you know that half the circus folk are leaving after this show is ended?'

'No,' said Lotta, startled. 'I haven't talked to anybody, really, these last few days. Do you mean they're leaving Galliano's Circus – not coming back? I know Oona was thinking of it, but I didn't know all the others were too.'

'Well, Mr Wally's going,' said Jimmy, and he told Lotta about the quarrel between Britomart and Mr Wally. 'And Mr Volla's going – and Tonks – yes, and I'm going too, Lotta!'

'*Jimmy!*' cried Lotta in dismay, clutching at his arm. 'Don't say that! I couldn't stay here without you – oh, just think of having to live with Lisa and Jeanne always!'

'You needn't,' said Jimmy. 'You and Lal and Laddo must leave too. See, Lotta? We'll all leave together. We'll go and join another circus, and have a fine time, just as we always used to have.'

'But suppose Mr Galliano comes back?' asked Lotta. 'He'd be very unhappy to find his circus split up.'

'Well, we'll wait and see what his next letter says,' promised Jimmy. 'I won't tell Britomart I'm going until after we've heard from Mr Galliano. Then we'll know what to do.'

So it was left like that, and the children waited impatiently for more news of Galliano. Lotta was much happier now. She loved her doll, and spent hours dressing and undressing it. She was very sweet to Jimmy, and tried her best to be good and helpful to Mrs Brown and Lal. They were pleased, and thought that the old nice little Lotta had come back once more.

Britomart at last had another letter from Mr Galliano. The news went round the camp at once, for the postman gave the letter to Sticky Stanley to deliver to Britomart and the clown knew the writing at once. Everyone gathered in a crowd outside Britomart's caravan to hear the news. Soon the ring-master appeared with the letter in his hand, his face as stern as ever.

'You seem to know that I have a letter from Mr Galliano,' he said, glancing round at everyone. 'You will wish to hear what he says. I will read it to you.'

He unfolded the letter and read it.

'DEAR BRITOMART, AND DEAR FRIENDS ALL, – You will be happy to know that Mrs Galliano is much better now, and in six months' time she will be as well as ever she was. She has to go for a long holiday now, in the south of France – and as the show is going so well under the direction of your new ring-master, I shall take a holiday and go with her. So I shall not be back with you for some time. I will write again as soon as I have news. I send my best wishes to you all, and hope that the show will go on doing as splendidly as ever.

'GALLIANO.'

Google and Pierre were pleased, for they were the favourites of Britomart. But no one else looked pleased except Lisa and Jeanne. With whisperings and mutterings the rest of the circus folk went back to their caravans, sad at heart. Galliano wasn't coming back for half a year. They couldn't work for Britomart so long. It was impossible. The circus must break up.

That day Mr Volla went to Britomart and warned him that he and his bears would leave the circus when the run was finished. Lilliput said the same. Mr Tonks said the same too, but very sadly, for he had been with Mr Galliano's Circus for many years. Oona the acrobat said he was going, and Sticky Stanley the clown.

And Jimmy marched up the caravan steps too, and told the ring-master that he and Lucky would find a new circus as soon as they left the show-place they were in. Jimmy's heart beat fast as he said this, for Britomart was angry and white.

'Go then,' he said to Jimmy. 'There are many dogs as clever as yours. We shall not miss you!'

Jimmy went to find Lotta. He told her that he had warned Britomart that he and Lucky would soon be looking for another circus. He had already spoken about it to his mother and father, and they were quite willing to leave, and to go seeking a happier circus in their pretty blue and yellow caravan. They had plenty of money for a holiday first.

Lotta flew to find Lal and Laddo. 'Lal! Laddo! Everyone's leaving Britomart's circus. Have you told him we will go too? I won't stay! I won't!'

Lal and Laddo looked grave. Laddo shook his head. 'We can't go, Lotta,' he said. 'We signed a paper to promise Britomart that we would stay with him for at least a year. We shall have to stay.'

'Laddo!' cried Lotta in horror. 'You don't mean we'll *have* to stay! You can't mean that! Why, everyone's going – even Jimmy! I can't be left behind if Jimmy's going!'

'You'll have to stay behind,' said Lal. 'The others only promised to stay till the end of this show, but Britomart made us promise to stay for a year. We promised for you, Lotta. So you'll have to make the best of it.'

'Oh! Oh!' wailed Lotta. 'Everything's going wrong again! Oh, Lal! Let me go with Mrs Brown and Jimmy, and you stay on here.'

'Of course not, Lotta,' said Laddo. 'Don't be such a baby. We have to earn our living – and we are staying on with Britomart to earn it. He pays us well and though we don't like him, it can't be helped. It's time you grew up a little and knew that you have often to do things you don't like.'

Lotta fled away, sobbing. She found Jimmy and poured out her woes to him. Jimmy was horrified. 'Oh, goodness, Lotta – I'd never, never have said I'd go if I'd thought you'd have to stay. I'll go and tell Britomart that I'll stay on!'

But that wasn't any good. Britomart was sharp and short with Jimmy. 'Once you give me your notice and say you want to go, that finishes it,' said Britomart in his cold, deep voice.

'Now here's a fine old muddle,' thought Jimmy in dismay. 'How in the world are we going to get out of it? *I* don't know.'

23. Lotta disappears!

The show was going to come to an end in a week's time. The circus had had a marvellous run but it was now time to move on. As the circus folk had made a great deal of money, most of them meant to have a holiday before joining another circus. But nobody felt very happy even about their holiday.

'It's so horrid to split up like this, just when we had such a good show together,' said Lilliput, stroking Jemima, who was round his neck as usual – though on a lead now.

'But we can most of us meet in another circus,' said Jimmy hopefully.

Lilliput shook his head. 'Some of us may,' he said, 'but it rather depends on who is already in a circus, you know. For instance, *you* might be taken on with Mr Phillippino's show, Jimmy, because he has no performing dogs at all at present, and he'd be glad to have you – but I wouldn't be taken on there because there is already a trainer with seven monkeys. Phillippino's wouldn't want two lots of monkeys.'

'I see,' said Jimmy, his heart sinking. 'Oh, Lilliput – I shall so hate to say goodbye to any of my friends. As for leaving Lotta behind, I can't bear to think of it.'

'Well, you'll have to, old son,' said Lilliput sadly. 'That's the worst of the circus world – there are such a lot of goodbyes; but never mind, we usually meet again in the end.'

'I never want to meet Lisa and Jeanne again,' said Jimmy fiercely. 'And they'll probably be the very ones I *shall* meet!'

Lilliput laughed. 'Cheer up! Those youngsters will get themselves into trouble one day. I can see it coming.'

When Lotta's two weeks were up, Britomart sent a message to Lal to say that Lotta might ride in the ring again that night. There was now hardly one more week left of the show, and he wanted the clever little girl to do her turn.

'Lal, what about Lisa and Jeanne?' asked Lotta. 'They won't be riding in the ring, will they, if I do?'

'Yes,' said Lal. 'Their mother has made them frocks of their own and Britomart says they may share your turn. They have done very well, Lotta. I don't like either of them, but they are quite clever with horses.'

'If they are going to share my turn, I won't go into the ring,' said Lotta, sticking out her round little chin in a determined manner.

'You'll have to if Britomart says you are to,' said Lal. 'Don't be silly, Lotta. You are acting like a baby. It is your own fault that you were punished, after all.'

'Well, it just wasn't!' said Lotta. 'It was Lisa's fault. I didn't tell you before – but everything has been Lisa's fault, really it has, Lal. And it is a dreadful feeling to think I'll have to stay on with Britomart's circus, and see that horrid Lisa every day!'

Lotta was nearly in tears. Lal was very sorry for the little girl, but she couldn't see that things could be altered. Lal knew very well that it was impossible to have everything as one liked it – sometimes things went well and sometimes they went badly. Well, people just had to put up with whatever happened, and show a brave face and laugh, that was all!

'Mrs Brown has washed and ironed your circus frock,' she said. 'Lisa had made it dirty. It is ready for you to put on tonight. You can go and dress in Jimmy's caravan, Mrs Brown says, and she will see that your dress is all right. Now dry your eyes and be cheerful, for goodness' sake!'

Mrs Brown had ironed Lotta's pretty, shining frock,

and it looked beautiful. It was on a hanger at the end of Mrs Brown's spotless caravan, waiting for Lotta to put on that evening.

'Lotta will love riding Black Beauty in the ring again,' thought Mrs Brown. 'It's a pity that the child has had such a bad time lately – but I really think she is nicer now, so perhaps she has learnt a few lessons. How I shall miss her when we leave!'

Jimmy was helping Laddo with the dogs. Lal was with her beloved horses. Mrs Brown looked at the clock and hoped that Lotta wouldn't come in too late to change. 'I want to give her hair a good brush, and see that she gets a really good wash,' said Mrs Brown. 'She doesn't look as if she has washed properly for days, the little monkey!'

The hands of the clock moved on slowly. Lotta was late! Mrs Brown looked out of her caravan to find the little girl.

'Lotta!' she called. 'Lotta! Hurry up! It's getting late!'

But Lotta didn't answer. She wasn't anywhere nearby, so Mrs Brown hurried over to Jimmy.

'Jimmy! For goodness' sake find Lotta and tell her she really must come now. I want to get her clean and tidy, and see that her frock is all right. Hurry now – she must be somewhere over at the other end of the field.'

'Right, Mother,' said Jimmy, who had nearly finished his job. He put down the last dish of fresh water in the dogs' big cage and ran off to get Lotta.

'I guess she's hiding away so that she doesn't have to go into the ring with Lisa and Jeanne,' thought the boy, who understood fierce little Lotta very well indeed. 'I don't blame her! I'd just hate to share my turn with those horrid girls.'

He called Lotta. There was no answer. He looked under all the caravans, but no Lotta was there. He even stood on tiptoe and looked on top of the vans, for since Lisa and Jeanne had come, Lotta had often climbed to the roofs with the two girls.

At last Jimmy gave it up. He went back to his caravan, and called to his mother.

'Mother! I can't find Lotta. I'm afraid she's hiding. I've looked everywhere.'

'The naughty little girl!' said Mrs Brown, vexed. 'Really, she thinks she can do exactly as she likes! Here I've got everything ready for her – and she'll be very late.'

'Mother, I don't think Lotta means to go into the ring with Lisa and Jeanne,' said Jimmy. 'I think she's hidden herself away so that she shan't.'

'Well, she will get into serious trouble with Britomart then,' said Mrs Brown anxiously. 'Look – here are Lisa and Jeanne – perhaps they know where Lotta is.'

But they didn't. They were surprised to hear that Lotta was not to be found. Lisa nudged Jeanne with her elbow and whispered something to her. Jimmy couldn't hear what it was.

The two girls ran off to Britomart's caravan. Jimmy watched them. 'Nasty tell-tales!' he said. 'Look, Mother – they've gone to tell Britomart that Lotta's hiding. How they do love to get people into trouble!'

But they had gone to say something else as well! Lisa knocked on Britomart's door, and he called out in his deep voice, 'Come in!'

Lisa opened the door timidly. Britomart glared at her. 'Oh – it's you. Have you got a message from your father?'

'No, Mr Britomart,' said Lisa. 'We've just come to say that Lotta won't go into the ring with us tonight. She's hiding!'

'I will not have such disobedience!' Britomart growled. 'Her father shall whip her for this.'

'I know how you could punish her,' said Lisa boldly. 'She loves her pony, Black Beauty, and she won't let anyone else ride him. But *I* could ride him, Mr Britomart! And when Lotta hears that someone else has taken her own pony into the ring, she will be sorry that she disobeyed you.'

Britomart looked at the red-haired Lisa and her sly

little face. 'Very well,' he said shortly. 'Get her pony and
ride it. It will teach her to come to her senses.'

Lisa and Jeanne flew off, afraid that Britomart would
change his mind. To ride Black Beauty in the ring! This
was something that the little girls had always longed to do.

They ran to tell Jimmy. He was astonished to see them
running back so quickly, looking so excited.

'Jimmy! Get Black Beauty out for us! Britomart says
we can ride him in the ring tonight, as Lotta won't.'

'You horrid little tell-tales,' said Jimmy. 'No – I won't
get Black Beauty for you! Get him yourself – and I hope
he bites you!'

Jimmy slammed the caravan door in a rage. Lisa and
Jeanne rushed off to the stables, pretty little figures in
their bunchy dresses sewn with glittering sequins. Nobody
would have guessed that they could be such horrid little
girls.

They flung open the door of the stable-van and went to
Black Beauty's stall.

It was empty! No Black Beauty was there! 'Where is
he?' said Lisa in dismay. 'He must be in one of the other
stalls.'

The two girls hurriedly ran down the stable-vans and
looked for Black Beauty. But only the other circus horses
were there, sleek and satiny, looking in surprise at the two
excited children.

'He's *not* here,' said Jeanne. 'Then where is he?'

'With Lotta, of course,' said Lisa angrily.

'But where's Lotta?' said Jeanne.

'Goodness knows!' said Lisa. 'Not hiding in the camp,
anyway. *She* could hide herself, but she couldn't hide a
big creature like Black Beauty. She's gone off somewhere
on him. Goodness – Britomart will be angry, won't he?
He forbade Lotta to ride the pony by herself out of the
camp.'

The girls rushed to tell everyone. Jimmy was worried
at once, and so were Lal and Mrs Brown. Lotta was such
a monkey – goodness knows where she would go or when

she would come back! And what would happen to her when she did come back? Some horrid punishment again, Jimmy was sure.

'She'll come back tonight, after the show,' said Mrs Brown, comforting him. 'Don't worry, Jimmy. She's just taken Black Beauty away so that Lisa and Jeanne can't ride him in the ring. I expect she guessed that they might try to.'

'Yes – that's it,' said Jimmy, feeling better. He had forgotten how once before Lotta had run away, dressed as a boy – and he didn't want to think she might have done that again. So he hoped and hoped that Lotta would be in the field waiting for him when the show was over that evening.

But Lotta wasn't. She didn't come back at all that night. Everyone was cross and worried about it. What would the mad little girl do next? It was really too bad to behave like that.

'She's taken her new doll with her,' said Lal, appearing at the door of her caravan. 'Now why did she do that? Oh dear, wherever is the child?'

And where *was* Lotta? Why had she gone, and what was she doing? Ah, she had made her own plans – and very strange plans they were, too!

24. Lotta's big adventure

Lotta had been very upset and angry to think that she must stay behind with Lal and Laddo, and work under Britomart for at least half a year more.

'Jimmy will be gone, and little dog Lucky – and kind Mrs Brown – and Mr Wally and Sammy – and Mr Volla and the bears – and dear old Tonky and Jumbo – and Oona. Oh, I can't bear it!'

The little girl was lying under her caravan with Lulu the spaniel, who licked her every now and again, sad that Lotta was unhappy. Lotta took a stick and dug it into the ground. She drew some letters – and they were the ones that little dog Lucky used to spell out so cleverly every day – G-A-L-L-I-A-N-O.

'Oh, Mr Galliano, if only you knew what is happening to your famous circus, you would try to come back quickly!' said Lotta. 'You'd stick your top hat straight up on your head, look fierce, and tell Britomart he's no good. Oh, if only you would come back!'

Lotta dug her stick hard into the ground, wishing that she was sticking it into Britomart! Then a thought came into her head.

'I wonder what Galliano would do if he heard that we are most of us going to leave his circus,' she said to herself. 'I wonder if anyone has told him. I know Britomart wouldn't, because he would be sure that Galliano would be angry and disappointed. I guess he's only told him the good things and not the bad.'

Lotta began to think about going into the ring that night with Lisa and Jeanne. She was quite determined not to – but she knew that Britomart would be very angry

indeed if she disobeyed again. 'I think I shall take Black
Beauty and ride away until the show is over tonight,'
thought the little girl. 'If I say I won't go into the ring,
Britomart is quite horrid enough to say that those two
red-haired creatures can have my pony to ride. And I
won't have that! I'll ride away, far away – and perhaps I
shall come to where Galliano is with Mrs Galliano.'

Now no sooner had she said that to herself than Lotta
sat up straight in excitement, banging her head hard
against the underneath of the caravan. But she didn't
even feel the bump.

'Gracious! Why didn't I think of that before! I'll *go* to
Galliano and tell him all that's happened – and maybe he
will turn Britomart out of the circus and put Mr Wally or
somebody in his place. Oh, goody, goody! That *is* an
idea!'

Lotta was so excited that Lulu became excited too and
barked.

'Sh!' said Lotta. 'I don't want anyone to know where
I am. We'll wait here till there's not many people about,
Lulu, and then I'll slip out and get Black Beauty and
darling Rosemary, of course. I shan't leave *her* behind
for Lisa to get.'

Lotta wondered where Mr Galliano was staying. She
knew that Mrs Galliano was out of hospital now, and that
they were both staying somewhere whilst Mrs Galliano
got better. How could she find out? She did not dare to
ask Britomart, and she was sure that no one else knew, for
the circus folk rarely wrote letters. Some of them could
not even read or write.

'I'll get into Britomart's caravan and find the letter
from Mr Galliano,' thought Lotta. 'I hope he doesn't
carry it about in his pocket. Lulu, we can see Britomart's
caravan from here. We'll watch and see if he goes out.'

Britomart did go out, and it wasn't long before Lotta
was creeping out from under her caravan. No one was
about except Mr Tonks, and he was rubbing Jumbo with
oil, and paid no attention to Lotta. The little girl ran

quickly over to Britomart's caravan. She was up the steps
in a trice, and shut the door. She looked around. Where
would Britomart keep his letters?

It was easy to see. There was a small desk at the back of
the caravan – and on it were spread a few letters and bills.
In a trice Lotta spied Galliano's last letter, slipped it
down the front of her frock, and ran from the caravan.
Nobody saw her. Nobody knew what she had done. Lotta
squeezed under her caravan again and looked at the
letter. How glad she was that she had taken lessons from
kind Mrs Brown and knew how to read.

She read the address at the top of the letter: 'British
Hotel, Langley Holme, Devon.' Lotta had no idea where
Devon was, but she didn't care. She could always ask. She
stuffed the letter back and slipped out again. This time
she found a small bag and put into it some bread, some
cheese, biscuits, chocolate – and her doll! That was all.

Then she watched to see when she could get Black
Beauty out without being seen. She had a very good
chance, quite unexpectedly. Two of the zebras, who were
being exercised at the other end of the field, were suddenly frightened by a cow that poked its head over the
hedge. One escaped from Zeno, and he yelled for help,
for a frightened zebra is dangerous.

Everyone ran to catch the zebra, or to see what was
happening. Jimmy went too – and so Lotta could not tell
him what she was going to do.

She was sorry about that. She did not want to slip away
without seeing Jimmy – and besides, she thought he could
tell Lal and Laddo of her plans. She dared not tell her
father and mother herself, in case they forbade her to go,
and fierce little Lotta was quite determined to do what
she had made up her mind to do.

She got Black Beauty out easily. She slipped on to his
back, whispered into his ear, and cantered quickly to the
nearest hedge. She did not dare to go out of the big field
gate, for she was certain to be seen if she did. So she set
Black Beauty at the high hedge, and the horse rose

beautifully into the air, cleared the hedge, and galloped over the next field. Lotta was safe!

Lotta rode on all that afternoon. She had stopped a party of school-children and asked them which was the way to Devon. They stared at the bright-eyed little girl on her beautiful horse, and thought she was marvellous. One boy got out his school atlas from his bag.

'Look,' he said, 'I'll show you exactly where you are now, and you will see that Devon is the next county to this. This is Dorset.'

He opened the atlas, and showed her the map of England. Lotta had learned just a little geography from Mrs Brown, and she looked closely at the map.

'What a lucky thing for me that Devon is the next county, and not somewhere right at the top of the map,' she said. 'Does your map show a place called Langley Holme, boy?'

'No,' said the boy, looking at it. 'It doesn't. Whereabouts is it?'

'I wouldn't be asking if I knew,' said Lotta. 'Oh dear – how am I to know if Langley Holme is at the top of Devon or at the bottom.'

'It's on the south coast, near a big port called Plymouth,' said a little girl shyly. 'My auntie used to live there. That's how I know. Show her Plymouth on the map, John.'

Plymouth was easy to see. 'That's good,' said Lotta, pleased. 'It's on the sea-coast, isn't it? I must just look out for sign-posts marked Plymouth, and go steadily on till I get there. Then I can ask for Langley Holme.'

She galloped off, and the school-children looked after her admiringly.

Lotta rode on steadily, delighted to see 'Plymouth' on a sign-post at the next cross-roads. She made up her mind to give Black Beauty a good long rest about seven o'clock, and a feed and water, and then to ride on all the night. 'Then if people start looking for me, trying to get me back before I've seen Mr Galliano, they won't be able to –

because I'll have nearly got there tomorrow,' she said to her doll Rosemary, who was sitting just in front of Lotta, smiling away as if she was really enjoying her strange ride.

At seven o'clock Lotta and Black Beauty took their rest. Black Beauty was a strong horse and was not at all tired. He was longing to gallop on and on with his little mistress sitting sturdily on his back. He could not understand why Lotta and he were going so far, but he didn't care. He would take Lotta to the end of of the world if she wanted him to!

At nine o'clock they were off again, the doll sitting in front of Lotta once more. The moon rose after a while, and it was easy for Lotta to read the sign-posts. Many people stared in wonder at the curly-haired girl riding on so steadily, but she was gone before they could even shout to ask where she was going.

All night long the little girl rode on. When dawn came she was so tired that she could no longer sit on Black Beauty's back. She saw an old rick standing in a field and slipped off her horse. She gave him a drink and a rub, and then told him to eat the grass. She cuddled up against the rick, shut her eyes, and at once fell fast asleep.

Nobody saw her there, and nobody saw Black Beauty, who soon came to lie down near his sleeping mistress. It was noon when Lotta awoke and stretched herself. She remembered where she was, and leapt to her feet. She rinsed her face in a little stream and shook back her curls. She finished up all the food she had brought with her, and leapt on to Black Beauty's back again. The horse whinnied with joy. So he and Lotta were to go galloping on once more!

Plymouth was farther than Lotta thought, but gradually the miles shown on each sign-post grew less and less – and at last, towards evening, another name appeared on a sign-post. Lotta squealed with joy.

'Langley Holme, two miles. Oh, Black Beauty, we are nearly there! We don't even have to go to Plymouth. It's

before we come to Plymouth. Come on – we'll soon see
dear old Mr Galliano and Mrs Galliano too! You've
never seen them, Rosemary – but you'll love them.'

She galloped on, very tired now, but much happier;
and soon she came to a quiet little seaside place, with a
pretty sandy beach where people bathed. On a little hill
nearby stood a big hotel, with golden letters across it:
'British Hotel'.

'Just the place we're looking for,' said Lotta happily.
She rode down the street that led to the sea, turned up
along the promenade, and went on towards the big hotel.
A great many people sat on a verandah outside, drinking, and eating ices. How they stared when the dirty,
untidy little girl rode up, her horse's hooves sounding
loudly in the street!

Lotta gazed along the row of surprised people, looking
for Mr Galliano. Everyone stared at her. Whatever did
this strange little girl want? What was she doing here,
stopping outside the hotel, staring at everyone? The hall-
porter came out and spoke sharply to her.

'Go away! Don't stare like that, little girl.'

'Is Mr Galliano here?' asked Lotta. 'I want Mr Galliano.'

'I certainly shan't tell any of our guests that *you* want
him,' said the rude porter. 'Now, go away.'

Lotta stared at him, her lips beginning to tremble, for
she was very tired and anxious. And then, just as she was
turning Black Beauty round, she heard an enormous
shout.

'LOTTA! MY LITTLE LOTTA! What are you doing
here?' And out of the hotel rushed dear old Galliano, his
eyes nearly falling out of his head in surprise!

25. Lotta gets her way

Lotta gave a squeal of joy. Yes – it was Mr Galliano, though he looked quite different dressed in white flannels and a shirt, instead of his usual riding-breeches, top-boots, and top hat. He was fatter, too, but his jolly face was just the same and his moustaches stuck up stiffly as they always did.

'LOTTA!' he yelled. 'Is it really Lotta?'

'Yes,' said Lotta, and she slipped down from Black Beauty. She was so tired that her legs would not stand under her. Mr Galliano picked her up in his arms, nodded to the porter to take Black Beauty, and carried the little girl into the hotel. Everyone stared in amazement, but neither Lotta nor Galliano cared. Let them stare!

Galliano took Lotta into his own sitting-room, and there sat Mrs Galliano, much thinner and paler, but with her same gentle smile. How amazed she was to see Lotta in Galliano's arms!

'Lotta!' she cried. 'How did you come here? Is anyone with you?'

'Only Black Beauty and Rosemary,' said Lotta, setting her doll down beside Mrs Galliano. She looked happily round, and settled herself comfortably on Galliano's knee. She flung her arms round his neck and hugged him. She took Mrs Galliano's hand and squeezed it. Tears came into her eyes and fell down her cheeks, but she smiled all the time because she was so happy to be with the Gallianos once more.

Mrs Galliano pressed a bell nearby, and ordered hot milk and biscuits for Lotta from the waiter. 'Eat and drink before you tell your story,' she said. 'There is plenty of time.'

So Lotta ate and drank – but she told her story at once, with her mouth full, for she could not wait.

'Oh, Mr Galliano, your circus is all breaking up,' she said. 'Mr Wally's going, and Mr Volla, and Tonky, and Oona, and Jimmy, and—'

'But why?' cried Galliano in astonishment. 'Nobody told me this. Each time I hear from Britomart he tells me how marvellously the show has been going, and what a lot of money comes in, yes! What is the matter then?'

'Oh, the show has gone well,' said Lotta, 'but, Mr Galliano, we do hate Britomart so. Do you know that he has never once smiled since you left?'

'Well, I can't see that that matters much,' said Galliano, puzzled. 'Something more must have happened besides that, yes!'

So Lotta told how stern Britomart had been, how he had forbidden Jimmy to play with the animals, how Sammy was moping, how Mr Wally had quarrelled with the ring-master, and how she, Lotta, had been forbidden to go into the ring for something that was not her fault.

'And oh, Mr Galliano, everyone is so angry and miserable and nobody will stay with Britomart – except Lal and Laddo, who signed a paper to say they would stay with the circus for a year. And that means I have to stay too. And I just couldn't stay without Jimmy and Lucky, so I came to find you and tell you. Mr Galliano, dear Mr Galliano, can't you do something?'

Then Mrs Galliano spoke in her slow, soft voice. 'My little Lotta, there is only one thing for Galliano to do. He must go back. He cannot see his famous circus split up so that there is nothing for him to return to when I am better.'

'But, Tessa, you are not better yet – and I promised you that I would stay until you too were well enough to come back to the circus, yes!' said Mr Galliano, rubbing his right ear in a very worried manner. 'I cannot break my promise, no.'

'You want to make me happy, Galliano, don't you?' went on Mrs Galliano. 'Well, I shall only be happy if you go back and become ring-master again in your own circus. I will not go to the South of France. I will stay here in this peaceful place, where I have my friends around me. And in six months' time I too will come back. I am so much better already! If you stay here with me, and let your circus go to pieces, I shall be so sad that I shall fall ill again. And you would not like that, Galliano.'

'No – no, indeed, I should not like that,' said the ring-master, gazing at his wife anxiously. 'Well, Tessa, you are always right, yes. I know that. Never have you given me bad advice, no, never. So I will go back to Galliano's Circus, and it shall be mine once more! And Britomart must go!'

Lotta gave such a squeal that Mrs Galliano jumped. The little girl flung herself on Mrs Galliano and pressed her cheek to hers. 'Oh, Mrs Galliano, you dear, kind, unselfish person! Can you really spare Mr Galliano to come back to us? We do want him so much. Oh, how glad I am I came and told you everything!'

'Now, now, you must leave me some breath, child!' said Mrs Galliano, laughing. 'Yes, of course Galliano must go back. Why, if he does not return soon to his circus he will be so fat with sitting about that he will not be able to get into his riding-breeches and coat any more! A fat ring-master is a poor sight.'

Lotta was so excited and glad that she could not keep still. 'I want to ride straight back and tell the others,' she cried. 'Where's Black Beauty? I'll start now and tell everyone else. Oh, how glad they will be!'

'No, no, Lotta, you can't do that,' said Mrs Galliano. 'You are tired out. You must stay here for the night. You will like to see this hotel. It has a fine big bath with taps that run hot and cold water, and a towel-rail that keeps your towels warm and dry. And—'

But Lotta would not listen. 'I'm not tired,' she cried, 'I'm not, I'm not! Oh, do let me get Black Beauty and go back again! I know the way.'

'My dear child, even if you are not tired out, Black Beauty is,' said Galliano. 'You don't want to ruin him by over-riding, do you? He will be no use if you do.'

'Oh no, I don't!' said Lotta at once. 'Yes – he must be tired, the darling. I'll go and see to him. Come on, Rosemary.'

'No, Lotta,' said Mrs Galliano. 'There are men to see to Black Beauty, and he will be quite happy. You are to come to my room and go to bed. I will have a little bed put by our big one, and you will love to sleep there.'

Lotta really was so tired that she could hardly walk to the big bedroom, whose windows looked out over the calm blue sea. She had a bath in a marvellous green bath, and dried herself with a big soft towel from the hot towel-rail. Then she ate some ice-cream pudding, curled up in the dear little bed beside Mrs Galliano's, and fell fast asleep in a trice. The doll lay beside her, its long-lashed eyes closed, just like Lotta's.

The two Gallianos looked down on the little girl, and then looked across at one another. 'She is a wild little thing,' said Mrs Galliano, 'but how full of courage she is! It is good that she came to tell you all that has happened, Galliano. You have been fretting for your circus, I know – and now it is clear that you must go back.'

Mr Galliano sent a telegram to Lal to say that Lotta was safe with them. Lal could not believe her eyes when she read that Lotta was in Langley Holme with the Gallianos!

'But how did she get there– how did she know the way – why did she run away to them – how did she know where they were?' she kept saying to everyone a hundred times. But nobody knew the answers. Only Jimmy smiled a little secret smile to himself.

'Lotta could do anything in the world if she once made up her mind to do it,' he thought proudly. 'There's no stopping that little monkey if she means to do something. I'm often cross with her, and would like to shake her, but she's a dear, brave girl and I'm proud of her. *I* know why she went to the Gallianos – to tell them about Britomart. I wonder if they'll be able to do anything. My word – Britomart looks as black as thunder now he knows where Lotta is!'

And Britomart certainly did look black! His great eyebrows met together as he frowned over the telegram that Lal showed him. He almost threw it back at Lal.

'I won't have that child of yours in any circus of mine,' he said.

'But you can't send Lotta to another circus when we are with *your* show!' said Lal. 'If you mean that, Mr Britomart, we can't come with you. We can't desert Lotta.'

'Pah!' said Britomart, and stalked off, fuming.

The show was ending. Mr Tonks was trying to find another circus to take old Jumbo to. Mr Wally was waiting to see if Tonks was lucky – then maybe he would go with him. Bit by bit the circus folk were packing their things, ready to go on the road again. They had been so long in camp that they felt quite strange to be on the move once more. Things were strapped on the tops of vans, and swung underneath. Lilliput looked sad, for he did not think he could go with Tonks and Mr Wally. Zeno had decided to stay with Britomart, for he was well paid and the ring-master did not interfere with him very much.

Nobody had heard anything more from Mr Galliano and Lotta. But nobody worried about the little girl now, for they knew she was safe, and they were sure she would not come back for some time.

And then, one evening, there came a rumbling down the road that led to the camp. A car was coming – a taxi-cab. Jimmy looked at it in surprise, for taxis seldom came to the circus field. Who could it be?

He soon knew, for Lucky began a most terrific barking

and flew to meet the taxi. Lucky's sharp ears had heard a voice she knew – Lotta's!

And sure enough, there was Lotta hanging out of the window, yelling and shouting to Jimmy! 'I'm back! I'm back! I've still got Rosemary – but Black Beauty is coming by horse-van in a train. Mr Galliano said it was too far for him to be ridden back. And oh, Jimmy – Mr Galliano's here too!'

Jimmy gave an enormous yell and rushed to open the taxi-cab door, and out stepped dear old Galliano in his riding-breeches, top-boots, and top hat – looking a little fat, it is true, but just the same as ever, smiling and jolly, his stiff moustaches standing straight out on each side of his mouth.

And then such a shout went up in the camp as the news was flashed from mouth to mouth!

'Galliano! Good old Galliano! He's back again! Welcome, Galliano! My goodness, we're glad to see you!'

What a welcome for their old ring-master! Mr Galliano was so excited and pleased that tears came into his eyes, and he wiped them away with an enormous red-spotted handkerchief. He gazed round at the tents, the carts, and the caravans, and took a deep breath.

'It's good to be back again, yes,' he said. 'Very, very good!'

26. Good old Galliano!

Mr Galliano shook hands with everyone and Mr Wally let out Sammy, the chimpanzee, because even Sammy knew that the old ring-master was back, and wanted to shake him by the hand too. So it was a very happy family that gathered round Mr Galliano and fired questions at him.

'How is Mrs Galliano? Is she coming too? How did Lotta find you? Have you come back to stay?'

'Where is Britomart?' asked Galliano, looking towards his old caravan.

'Gone down to the town,' said Mr Tonks. 'Mr Galliano, sir, have you heard about how we are going to split up and part? We can't work for Britomart; we've tried, but it's no use.'

'I'm coming back to you,' said Galliano, sticking his hat right on one side of his head. 'Yes – I am coming back to you! There shall be two circuses – one that will go with Britomart, and the other that shall stay with me and be Galliano's! Tessa is well enough for me to leave her now, and she wants me to come back, yes!'

'Hurrah!' yelled everyone, and went quite mad. Lisa and Jeanne stood in surprise, staring at Mr Galliano, wondering what was going to happen. They were not at all pleased to see Lotta back again, and with Mr Galliano too! The little girl had not said a single word to them, but looked at them with such scorn that they felt really uncomfortable.

'And now I want to have a word with each of you,' said Mr Galliano. 'You, Tonks; you, Wally; you, Lilliput, Oona, Volla, Stanley. Let us go to your caravan, Wally.'

In Mr Wally's comfortable caravan Mr Galliano heard all that his friends had to say about the circus, and he frowned and nodded.

'Yes – it is time I came back,' he said. 'I thought that Britomart would do well with you all – but I see I was wrong, yes. Yet he has had circuses before, and should know how to treat his people.'

'Mr Galliano, sir, Britomart has always made the same mistakes,' said Oona. 'I have heard much of him before. He cannot make friends with the circus folk, and although he is a good ring-master, and has plenty of fine ideas, sooner or later people will not work for him.'

'You see, sir, you are one of us,' said Tonks. 'You laugh and joke with us, you are kind, you help us when things go wrong. It is true that you are angry at times – but only when you have a right to be, and then it is soon over. We all love you and Mrs Galliano, sir – and – well – that's the secret of working happily together.'

Mr Galliano cocked his hat even further on one side and beamed all over his broad face.

'That's the nicest speech I have ever had made to me, yes!' he said. 'And I too will make one back to you! I and Tessa are proud of you all – you are like children to us, and we are father and mother to our large circus family. We must see that you are happy, yes, and then we are happy too. But Britomart – poor Britomart – he cannot know what happiness is.'

'Well, he always looks either angry or fierce,' said Mr Wally, who did not feel any pity for the harsh ring-master at all. 'He deserves to be unhappy for the way he treats us all.'

When Britomart came back, he was surprised to find Mr Galliano waiting for him. The old ring-master was not unjust or scornful, but he did tell Britomart a few truths that he thought he should know.

'Britomart, my circus is going to pieces under your hand, yes!' he said. 'This I cannot allow, for I have built it up myself, and it is my pride and joy. You may handle the show well when it is in the ring, but you cannot handle my circus folk. Britomart, a little kindness and praise would have kept these folk happy, yes – but all you gave them was harsh words and punishments.'

'Galliano, you have spoilt the people in this circus,' said Britomart in his usual cold, deep voice, his black eyes flashing. 'They are disobedient, rude, and quarrelsome. No man can manage a camp like this.'

'I have managed it for years,' said Galliano, 'and I am going to manage it again, yes.'

'Everyone is leaving, except Zeno, some of the clowns, and Pierre,' said Britomart.

'No one is leaving – except those you say!' said Mr Galliano, putting his hat on straight and looking stern. 'Britomart, take your share of the money and what performers will go with you. Make your own circus, if you can – you will not keep it long until you learn that only one thing rules a camp, and that is kindness, yes!'

Mr Galliano left the caravan, his hat still straight on his head. Britomart was left alone. He stared after the old ring-master, and a sad look came into his big black eyes. He knew himself to be a cleverer man than Galliano – but he was impatient and scornful where Mr Galliano was kind and understanding. He was a lonely and unhappy man – but it was his own fault.

'If I get another chance, I'll try Galliano's ideas,' he thought. 'Look at the circus folk out there, crowding round him – they never gave me those smiles and handshakes and claps on the back. They'll all stay with him – and I shall be left with Pierre and one or two others. I shan't try to make a new circus – I shall go off again on my own, and be Britomart the conjurer.'

So that evening Britomart packed his things, cleared Galliano's caravan for him, and drove off in his magnificent blue and silver car. He said goodbye to no one, for he was a disappointed and rather ashamed man. No one waved to him. No one wished him luck. He was gone, and nobody cared. Poor Britomart – the worst enemy he had was himself.

What an evening that was in the camp! It happened to be the last evening of the show, and Galliano, of course, was to be ring-master.

'We'll make it the best show we've ever given,' cried Sticky Stanley in delight, turning six somersaults at once. 'And, Lotta, you'll be able to have your turn again!'

Galliano forbade Lisa and Jeanne to go into the ring – much to Jimmy's delight and Lotta's. Now that he knew how those two unpleasant children had got Jimmy and Lotta into trouble, Galliano had no time for them, and ordered them out of his way whenever they came near to beg him to let them go into the ring that last splendid evening.

'You have a lesson to learn, yes!' he shouted at red-haired Lisa. 'I will treat you as Britomart treated Lotta – you will both go to your caravan and STAY THERE! And if I see you out of it, I will chase you with my big whip, yes.'

Of course everyone knew that Galliano would do nothing of the sort, but Lisa and Jeanne were very much afraid he might. So they scuttled off to their caravan, crying bitterly, and Lotta and Jimmy watched them go.

'Well, it isn't kind to be glad when people are unhappy,' said Jimmy, 'but really, Lotta, those two deserve a bit of trouble now.'

'I hope they get lots,' said Lotta fiercely. Then she laughed. 'Oh, Jimmy – I'm so happy now, that I can't even feel really fierce about Lisa and Jeanne! I just don't care about them any more. In fact, I'm so happy that I might even go and show them my lovely new doll! They've never seen her yet.'

'Don't you do anything of the sort,' said Jimmy. 'Why, you might find yourself feeling so happy you'd *give* Rosemary to Lisa!'

'Oh!' said Lotta with a squeal. 'You know I'd never do that. Come on, Jimmy – it's time we got ready for the show. We shall do our turn together again. I shall ride dear old Black Beauty in the ring, and hear the claps and shouts. And it will be Mr Galliano standing in the middle, cracking his whip, instead of stern old Britomart!'

Lotta danced off to put on her sparkling circus frock. The little girl was so happy that her eyes shone like stars. It was Galliano's Circus again – Jimmy was staying on with Lucky – things would be the same as they used to be. And it was she, Lotta, who had found Mr Galliano and got him back! No wonder Lotta felt proud and excited and happy.

An hour before the circus began, a caravan came up the lane to the field. It was bright orange with blue wheels – and Jimmy knew it at once.

'Lotta! Lotta! Quick! Here's Madame Prunella come back again – hark at her parrots all screeching!'

And sure enough it was! Somehow Prunella had heard the news that Britomart was gone and Galliano was back, and she too had come to join in the last night of the show. Oh, what fun! How the plump little woman hugged and kissed everyone, and how the parrots screeched and squealed!

'Fried fish and chips, fried fish and chips!' yelled Gringle in excitement, and the children laughed in delight. 'Good old Gringle! We *have* missed you!'

It was a splendid show that night, for everyone was happy and determined to do their best for Galliano. He stood in the middle of the ring, his hat well on one side, his sunburnt face very happy indeed. The only things that made him feel uncomfortable were his clothes! They really were much too tight for him now.

The people clapped and shouted and cheered till they were hoarse. They stamped their feet at the end of the show, and waved their hats and handkerchiefs.

'Best circus we've ever seen!' they said to one another. 'Quite the best!'

It was late before everyone went to bed that night. How they talked! How they sang and laughed in the camp, till the dogs got restless and whined, and Lucky fell fast asleep in her master's arms.

Galliano sent them all off to their caravans at last. They stumbled up the steps, yawning, but very happy. The circus was not to split up after all! They were all to go on the road as usual.

All? Well, not quite all. Google did not want to stay, for he said there were too many children in the camp for his liking. And Pierre was not going with the circus either, for Galliano had heard from Mrs Brown that Lisa and Jeanne would be better away. Also Pierre had been friendly with Britomart, so that no one really felt that they wanted him to stay.

Jimmy was sorry that Neptune was to go, for he liked the clever seal. But never mind, Madame Prunella was back again with her flock of wonderful parrots. Zeno was staying, and Twinkle and Pippi, so the circus was very big still, and had plenty of performers.

'Goodnight, Jimmy,' said Lotta, going to her caravan. 'Isn't everything lovely now?'

'Yes – and all because you were such a fierce little girl and wouldn't put up with the horrid things that were happening,' said Jimmy. 'Good for you, Lotta! I'm proud of you!'

The two children were soon fast asleep. Lulu the spaniel lay on Lotta's feet, and Rosemary the doll was beside her. Little dog Lucky was on Jimmy's toes, and they all dreamed happily of the good days to come.

'Good old Galliano!' said Jimmy in his sleep. 'I'm so glad you're back again, Galliano – good old Galliano!'

4

COME TO THE CIRCUS

Contents

1. A New Home For Fenella

'Fenella! Where are you?' called Aunt Janet's voice. 'Come here a minute. I've got something to tell you.'

Fenella put down her sewing and went to see what her aunt wanted. She was ten years old, small for her age, with a little pointed face, green eyes and a shock of wavy red hair. She had no father or mother, and had lived all her life with her Aunt Janet.

Her aunt was peeling potatoes in the kitchen. She looked up as Fenella came in. 'Help me with these,' she said. 'Fenella, I've got some news for you.'

'What is it, Aunt Janet?' asked Fenella, suddenly feeling that the news wasn't going to be very good.

'Well, Fenella – I'm going to be married,' said Aunt Janet. 'And I'm going out to Canada.'

'Oh, Aunt Janet!' said Fenella. 'To Canada! That's a long way, isn't it – far across the sea? Shall we like that?'

'*I* shall,' said Aunt Janet. 'I've been there before. But you're not going, Fenella. I'm going to marry Mr White – you've seen him here sometimes – and he wants us to go and work on his uncle's farm in Canada. But we're afraid we must leave you behind.'

'Leave me behind – here, all alone!' cried Fenella in alarm. 'But what shall I do? I'm only ten.'

'Oh, you won't be left here, in this house,' said Aunt Janet. 'You're going to your Uncle Ursie's. He and Auntie Lou will look after you now. I've told Auntie Lou how good you are at sewing, and she wants somebody she can train to help her with the circus dresses.'

'Am I to go and live at the circus?' cried Fenella, and her eyes filled with tears. 'I can't. I can't. You know I'm afraid of animals. And there are bears there, and elephants, and chimpanzees. I know, because Uncle Ursie told me so when he came here to tea with Auntie Lou.'

'Oh, you'll soon learn to like animals,' said Aunt Janet, emptying the dirty potato water out of the bowl. 'Anyway, there's no help for it, I'm afraid. You've got to go somewhere – and Harry – that's Mr White I'm going to marry – he doesn't want to take you out to Canada with us.'

'Nobody wants me!' wailed Fenella, suddenly. 'My father and mother are dead, and you don't want me, and I know Uncle and Aunt won't want me either.'

'Now, don't be silly,' said Aunt Janet, briskly. 'Uncle Ursie is very, very fond of his bears, and he'll be fond of you, too. As for Auntie Lou, she's got a sharp tongue, but if you are a good girl and help her, she'll soon take to you. I'll miss you, Fenella – you're a good, quiet little thing – but what Harry says has got to be done.'

Fenella went back to her sewing. But she couldn't see to stitch any more, because the tears would keep coming into her eyes and dropping on the dress she was making. It wasn't much of a home, with Aunt Janet – just a little cottage, rather tumbledown, with a yard behind it – but at least it was somewhere she knew and felt safe in. And although Aunt Janet made no fuss of her, and sometimes grumbled because she had to bother with her, still, she was kind in her way.

But the circus! That was quite a new world – a frightening world to Fenella, who ran away if she saw even a gentle old sheep, and screamed if a dog jumped up at her. Whatever in the world would she do in a place where elephants and bears, monkeys and dogs roamed about all the time? She couldn't go there. She couldn't.

She thought of Uncle Ursie and Auntie Lou. Auntie Lou had screwed-up hair, a screwed-up face, and a screwed-up mouth. Her tongue was sharp, and she had very little patience with anyone, not even with her slow-going, placid husband, Uncle Ursie, who looked after the bears, and was really rather like a bear himself, clumsy, lazy and a little stupid.

Fenella thought of the three elephants, and the two hairy chimpanzees that Uncle Ursie had told her about. She had never been to his circus, so she could only imagine everything – and it seemed very frightening indeed.

'There'll be monkeys about – and I shall keep meeting the elephants – and, oh dear, Uncle Ursie will expect me to like his awful bears! I don't want to go. Oh, why can't Aunt Janet take me to Canada with her? I don't want to go there either, but I'd rather go across the sea to a far-away land than go and live in the circus. I shall just HATE it. I know I shall.'

Poor Fenella! Her whole world seemed to be turning upside down. Aunt Janet began to pack her things. She sold most of the furniture in her little cottage. Strangers always seemed to be coming in and looking round at this and that.

Then the day came for Aunt Janet to be married. She had bought some pretty blue stuff for Fenella to make herself a bridesmaid's dress. Fenella was a marvel with her needle. She could make anything! She knew how to use a sewing-machine, too, and was really a clever little girl. She made her blue dress carefully, but she didn't want to wear it!

'I don't want to see Aunt Janet married. I don't want to say good-bye to her. I don't want to leave here! Oh, why did all this happen?' poor Fenella said over and over again to herself.

But Aunt Janet *was* married, and Fenella did wear her

blue frock, which everyone said looked lovely. Then
Aunt Janet kissed her good-bye, and drove away with
Uncle Harry, waving till she was out of sight.

Uncle Ursie and Auntie Lou hadn't come to the
wedding, because the circus was rather far away just
then, and was about to put on a show. Fenella was to be
put on the train, in the care of the guard, and was to go
off to the town where the circus was, all by herself. She
was full of dread about this.

'But it will be quite an adventure for you, Fenella!'
big, burly Uncle Harry had said.

'I don't like adventures,' Fenella had answered. And
she didn't. She was afraid of them. She didn't like
strangers. She didn't like anything she didn't know. She
was a scared little mouse, as Aunt Janet had often said.

And now she was to go and live in the middle of a big
circus. It was a world of its own, with tall, shouting Mr
Carl Crack, the ringmaster, as its king. Fenella had heard
about him from Aunt Janet, and she felt afraid of him
already. Mr Carl Crack! She pictured him with a big
whip, cracking it if anyone disobeyed him. Oh dear! She
would hide away in a corner if ever she saw him.

Mrs Toms, her next door neighboor, came up to her,
smiling kindly. The wedding was over. The guests had
gone, Fenella stared forlornly round.

'Well, Fenella, dear, you come along with me now, as
your auntie said, and we'll get you out of that pretty
frock and into your brown one. Then off we'll go to the
station to catch that train. And in no time at all you'll
be off to the circus – my, what a lucky girl you are!'

Fenella didn't say anything. She went home with Mrs
Toms. Mrs Toms had five children, all rough and loud-
voiced. They crowded round Fenella and told her how
lucky she was to be going to live in a circus.

'Wish *I* could!' said Sam, the eldest. 'My word, I'd
ride all the horses, and the elephants, too!'

'And I'd make friends with the chimpanzees and teach them all kinds of things,' said Lucy, a big curly-haired girl with a wide smile. 'I'd love to have one for a pet. You'll have a lovely time, Fenny.'

'I shan't,' said Fenella. 'I shall hate it. I don't want to go a bit. I wish one of you could go in my place, and I could stay here.'

'Oh, you'll soon get used to it, and you'll wonder why you didn't want to go,' said Mrs Toms, briskly. 'Now, are you ready? Sam, take Fenny's bag. That's right. Who wants to come and see her off?'

Everyone did, though Fenella would really rather have gone alone with kind Mrs Toms. Her children were so *very* rough and noisy. The shy little girl hated walking to the station with such a crowd of shouting children round her. But they meant it kindly, and were sorry for her.

'Come along quickly – the train's just coming in!' cried Mrs Toms. 'Here's your ticket, Fenny. Let us on to the platform, please, Inspector, we're just seeing this child off!'

Fenella was pushed into a carriage. Mrs Toms hurried to ask the guard to keep an eye on her during the journey. The children all crowded round Fenella, and Lucy gave her a hug.

'Write to us! Tell us about the elephants and what their names are!'

'Be sure to tell us if you like the bears your uncle has!'

'Do make friends with the chimpanzees and tell us what they're like!'

'Good-bye, Fenny! Cheer up! Good-bye!'

'Good-bye! You're off!'

The train steamed slowly out of the station. Fenella waved till she could see the Toms family no more. Then she sat back on her seat, feeling sad and forlorn. She had left her only friends behind. Aunt Janet was off to

Canada. And here was she, Fenella, going to an uncle
and aunt she hardly knew, and who she felt sure didn't
really want her – to a place full of roaring, growling,
barking animals.

There were two old ladies in the carriage, but they
took no notice of the little girl at all. Once or twice the
guard came in to see if she was all right. She had a packet
of sandwiches with her, and when the guard told her it
was one o'clock she ate them. Then she fell asleep, whilst
the train rocked over the rails at sixty miles an hour.

When she awoke, the guard was in her carriage again.
'Wake up, Missy! You're there! This is Middleham,
where you've got to get out.'

Half asleep, Fenella got hold of her bag, and scrambled

out of the train. She stood on the platform and watched it go off. Then she turned to go out of the station. Aunt Janet had told her what to do next. She had to give up her ticket and then ask where the bus started that went to Upper Middleham, where Mr Carl Crack's circus was.

A porter told her. 'There it is, Missy – over there in the corner of the station yard. Hop in. It will be going in a minute or two.'

She got in. 'I want to go to Mr Carl Crack's circus,' she told the conductor. He gave her a ticket and took a penny from her. 'I'll tell you when to get out,' he said.

The bus lumbered through the countryside, and at last climbed a hill, and then slowed down on the slope the other side. 'Here you are!' called the conductor. 'This is the circus field.'

Fenella got out. She stood looking down on the circus field, her heart sinking. There was the circus, the place she was to live in.

Gay caravans stood everywhere, with smoke coming from some of their chimneys. Tents were here and there. Travelling vans were pulled up at one end of the field. A very, very big tent stood in the middle, a flag waving from the top. Painted on the tent were four enormous words.

'MR CARL CRACK'S CIRCUS'

Fenella had arrived. Now her new life was to begin!

2. Mr Carl Crack's Circus

Fenella put her bag down on the ground and climbed a gate nearby. She sat on it and looked at the big circus field. What a lot seemed to be going on!

Men and women walked about busily. Horses were being cantered at one end of the field. Fenella could hear the men shouting to them.

Then she saw an enormous elephant lumbering along, waving his trunk. Beside him walked a very small man indeed. Fenella felt scared. She made up her mind she would keep as far away from the elephants as she possibly could. What big ears they had! And what funny little eyes.

Not far off was a small woman with something round her shoulders. At first Fenella thought it was a fur. Then, to her great astonishment, she saw that it was two tiny monkeys, each clinging tightly to their owner. The little girl shivered. How could anyone have monkeys round their necks?

Then a pack of barking dogs was suddenly set free from a big travelling cage, and to Fenella's horror they came tearing over the field towards her. But they swerved away as they came near and went over to the big elephant. They ran in and out of his legs without fear, and the big creature was very careful where he put his feet down.

As she sat there, a man came over towards her. Fenella looked hard at him, and then saw that he was her uncle.

She hardly knew him because he looked very different from when she had seen him last.

He had come to tea with Aunt Janet, his sister, looking very smart and clean and neat in a well-brushed Sunday suit, and a bowler hat.

Now he was dressed in a very old, very dirty pair of flannel trousers, and a brightly striped jersey; his hair was long, and standing up all over the place. He had little eyes, and a big nose and mouth. Fenella couldn't help thinking he looked a bit like a bear, for he was fat and clumsy. But he looked quite kind.

'So you've arrived, Fenella!' he said. 'Come along and see your aunt. We've been expecting you for the last half-hour. Had a good journey?'

Fenella nodded. She didn't like the look of Uncle Ursie today. He looked so dirty and plump and clumsy. He grinned widely at her and his little eyes almost disappeared. He held out a very dirty hand.

'Come along. Don't be shy. My, what a neat, prim-looking little thing you are! Like your Aunt Lou. Never a thing out of place with her. Too tidy altogether for my liking!'

Uncle Ursie was very talkative. Fenella didn't really need to say a word. He pulled the little girl along over the big field, carrying her heavy bag for her.

They passed a man doing the most extraordinary things. As they came by, he suddenly bent himself right backwards till his head went between his legs and came out at the other side. His face grinned at Fenella from between his knees. She was frightened.

'Don't you worry about old Wriggle,' said Uncle Ursie. 'He's one of our acrobats. Regular contortionist he is. He can do anything with that rubbery body of his. He'll pull it inside out one of these days.'

They came to a neat red caravan with blue wheels. 'Here we are!' said Uncle Ursie proudly. 'Do you like it?

Pretty, isn't it? The blue wheels were your aunt's idea, and the blue chimney, too. Hey, Lou, are you there?'

Aunt Lou appeared at the door of the caravan. It was at the back. Fenella looked up at her. She saw a small neat woman, dressed in a dark blue cotton frock with red spots and a red belt. Her hair was screwed up in a tight bun at the back, and her eyes and mouth looked tight, too. She gave Fenella a thin kind of smile.

'Oh, there you are! I've kept dinner for you. Come on in and eat it.'

Fenella went up the steps of the caravan. She looked round. Inside it was a room full of furniture. On one side was a broad seat, that Fenella saw would be a bed at night. On the other side, folded up out of the way, was a narrow bunk. That would be for Fenella.

'Do you live in this caravan?' she asked. 'Don't you ever live in a house?'

Aunt Lou gave a snort. 'In a house! What do you take us for? I wouldn't live in a house, not if you gave me a hundred pounds! How could you live with a circus if you have a house with roots in the ground! No, no – you want a house on wheels, so that you can go where you like. Now, here's your dinner.'

Fenella was just going to say that she had had some sandwiches, when she smelt the good smell of the dinner. She decided to eat it and sat down. It was certainly very good.

'Your aunt's a good cook,' said Uncle Ursie, watching Fenella eat. 'And you won't find a cleaner caravan than ours! No, nor a more comfortable one. I'll say that for your Aunt Lou, she's a worker, she is – and a wonder with her needle, too!'

'Stop your talk,' said Aunt Lou. 'Get along and do some work, Ursie. Leave Fenella to me.'

Uncle Ursie clambered down the steps to the ground, and the whole caravan shook as he went.

'Big and clumsy as a bear,' said Aunt Lou, in a sharp voice. 'Now you eat all that up – and there's some fine peaches in syrup for you, too.'

'It's kind of you, Aunt Lou,' said Fenella, timidly. She was afraid of her sharp-faced aunt.

'Well, I expect something in return,' said Aunt Lou. 'You're clever with your needle, aren't you? Well, I shall expect you to help me with the sewing. I've too much for one pair of hands to do.'

'What sewing?' asked Fenella.

'I sew for all the circus folk,' said Aunt Lou. 'There's always plenty of dresses to be made, and you wouldn't believe how careless people are with their things. Mending, mending, mending! You just look at that!'

Fenella looked at the corner where her aunt pointed. Piled there was a heap of gaily-coloured skirts and coats, stockings and jerseys. Fenella leaned forward and picked up a very small coat indeed. She looked at it curiously.

'Whose is this?' she said. 'It looks as if it would only fit a doll! I've got a doll called Rosebud. It would just about fit her!'

'Oh, that belongs to one of Mrs Connie's monkeys,' said Aunt Lou, in such a disagreeable voice that Fenella looked at her in surprise. 'I don't know why I've got to sew for monkeys, the dirty little creatures! But that Mrs Connie, she says she doesn't even know how to thread a needle, the lazy creature – so Mr Crack has told me to dress-make for the monkeys, too. Bah!'

Fenella couldn't help thinking it would be lovely to make little coats and dresses for monkeys, even though she knew she would be afraid to fit one on. She went on with her dinner, enjoying the peaches in their sweet juice.

'Well, I'll help you with the sewing, Aunt Lou,' she said. 'I'd like to. I love sewing. And I can use a sewing-machine, too.'

'Well, that's a thing you'll have to do without,' said

Aunt Lou. 'A sewing-machine, indeed! We're not mil-
lionaires. Now, have you finished? Well, you go and tell
your uncle I want him to go and buy some sausages, or
he won't have any supper tonight.'

Fenella didn't at all want to go out alone in the big
circus field, with so many strange people ambling about,
and animals appearing round any tent. But she didn't like
to say so, because Aunt Lou wasn't the sort of person who
would like that at all.

So the little girl went timidly down the caravan steps
and looked about for her uncle. She saw him not far off
and went across the grass to him.

CRACK! A loud noise, like a pistol-shot, made her
jump almost out of her skin. Something touched her
lightly and she drew back, wondering what it was.

Then a loud voice roared at her. 'Get out of the way,
ninny! What are you doing over here? Nobody's allowed
in my part of the field. Serves you right if you got licked
by my whip!'

Fenella turned and saw an enormous man, burly and
big-headed, with a grey top-hat on his head, standing
not far off with a whip in his hand. He had a big nose,
and great brown eyes, topped by the thickest, shaggiest
eyebrows that Fenella had ever seen. It was the eyebrows
that frightened her most.

The voice went on roaring at her. 'Who are you? No
one is allowed in this field unless they belong to the circus.
Clear out! Mind the dogs don't bite you! Mind the bears
don't eat you! I won't have children wandering about my
camp!'

Fenella was so very frightened that she ran away at
top speed. She didn't stop till she got to the field gate.
She climbed over it and ran down the lane, then into
another field. She lay down under a gorse bush, panting.

'It must have been the great Mr Carl Crack himself!'
she thought. 'Oh, dear. I never saw that he was standing

there and cracking his whip. It almost touched me. What a terrifying person he is! I daren't live in his circus. I daren't, I daren't. I shall run away. I shall go to the next town and go and live with a dressmaker there, and earn money by helping her. I'll never, never go and live in Mr Crack's circus. Why, he looked as if he could eat me!'

Fenella was tired and scared. She began to cry softly. Then she heard a curious sound and sat up. It came from the other side of the thick gorse bush.

It was the sound of birds singing and whistling. It went on and on. Birds flew down from trees to the other side of the bush. The whistling changed to a curious chirruping and at once a dozen nearby sparrows chirruped back.

Fenella dried her eyes. She crept softly round the bush, and peeped. She saw a most curious sight.

On the grass, sitting up straight, was a boy of about twelve. It was he who was whistling so like the birds. Round him, some on branches, some on the ground, were all kinds of wild birds, enchanted by his calls.

But, most extraordinary of all, was a big bird squatting beside him. It was a large white goose! Fenella could hardly believe her eyes.

Suddnly the goose saw her and crackled loudly. All the birds flew away. The boy turned and saw her.

'Hallo!' he said. 'Who are you? I'm Willie Winkie the Whistler. And this is my pet goose, Cackles. Come and talk to me. Why have you been crying? You come along and tell me, Green-Eyes. We'll soon put things right for you!'

3. The Boy And The Goose

Fenella stared at the boy without saying a word. He had pale gold hair, so fair that it was almost white. His face was completely covered with freckles, and he had a dimple in each cheek that went in and out when he smiled. He was smiling now.

'Come on, silly,' he said, and held out his hand. 'You're not frightened of old Cackles, are you? She's a darling. Shake hands, Cackles.'

To Fenella's great surprise the large goose stood up and, balancing herself awkwardly on one leg, held out the other foot to Fenella. It was a large, webbed foot, and the little girl didn't want to touch it.

'Oh go on,' said the boy. 'Don't be mean. Cackles will be awfully hurt if you don't shake hands. I tell you, she's the friendliest goose in the world. Aren't you, Cackles?'

'Cackle,' said the goose, agreeing. She still held out her paw, and Fenella at last took it and gave it a feeble shake. It felt cold and clammy. The goose sat down again and put her big, yellow beak on the boy's shoulder.

'Now, you tell me why you've been crying,' said Willie. 'Anyone been unkind to you?'

'Yes,' said Fenella, tears coming to her eyes again. 'Mr Carl Crack has. He shouted at me and told me to clear out, and he was so angry that I ran away. I shall never go back.'

'I say! Are you Ursie's niece?' said Willie, sitting up

straighter. 'I heard you were coming, but I thought you'd be a lot bigger. How old are you?'

'Ten,' said Fenella. 'I used to live with my Aunt Janet, but she's married and gone to Canada. I haven't got a father or mother. They died when I was little. So I've got to come and live with Uncle Ursie and Aunt Lou. And I don't like them. I don't like anybody I've seen at the circus. And I am so scared of all the animals, too. I'm going to run away!'

'No, you're not,' said Willie, and he put an arm round her. 'Wipe your eyes, silly. You'll love living with us after a bit. Fancy wanting to live an ordinary life, in a house, when you can live in a circus, with animals all round you, and have a house on wheels that can take you away wherever you like!'

'I'd rather not,' said Fenella. 'I'd rather run away.'

'But you'd only be brought back,' said Willie. 'You would, really. And then everyone would be very cross with you, which would be a pity. I tell you there are lots of nice people in Mr Crack's circus. I'm one of them! And my mother is another. I haven't got a father, so I look after my mother and she looks after me! And Cackles looks after us both. Don't you, Cackles?'

'Cackle,' said the goose, and made a little hissing noise in Willie's ear.

'Don't,' said Willie. 'You tickle. Move up a bit, Cackles. You're leaning too hard on me.'

Cackles moved up. Fenella watched in surprise. 'Does she understand everything you say?' she asked.

'Everything!' said Willie, with a grin. 'I had her when she was a gosling — that's a baby goose in case you don't know — and I found her half dead down a lane. Goodness knows how she got there, poor mite. I took her to Mum, and we warmed her and fed her — and here she is, simply enormous, the Cleverest Goose in the World! I take her in the ring with me when we give a show.'

'Do you really?' said Fenella, opening her eyes wide in wonder. 'But what can she do?'

'Oh, she's a marvel!' said Willie. 'She wears a red shawl and a cute little bonnet, and she carries a shopping basket under her wing. And I'm the shopkeeper, and she buys what she wants from me. I tell you, we bring the house down, me and Cackles!'

'I'd like to see you in the circus-ring with Cackles,' said Fenella.

'Well, it's no good you running away then, or you won't,' said Willie. 'You stay with us and you'll soon get to know us and like us.'

'But I'm so afraid of Mr Crack now,' said Fenella, remembering that enormous voice of his.

'You don't need to be,' said Willie. 'He's the kindest fellow really – but he's hot-tempered, and maybe he didn't see you and was afraid he'd hurt you with his whip-cracking – so he roared at you to get out of the way. If he'd known you were Ursie's niece and had come to live at the circus, he'd have been kinder. But a whole lot of town kids are always wandering about the field, scaring the monkeys and sometimes opening cage doors. He gets wild with them.'

'Oh,' said Fenella. Then she remembered something. 'Willie, what were you doing when I heard you whistling? I saw a lot of birds round you.'

'Well, I told you I was Willie Winkie the Whistler, didn't I?' said the boy. 'Want to see what I can do? All right then – watch.'

Fenella sat absolutely still. Cackles took her head from the boy's shoulder and curled it under her wing. She sat still, too. Then Willie began to whistle like a blackbird.

'Phooee, phoo, phe-dee-de, phoolee dooee,' he whistled, sounding like a flute. Fenella gazed at him in amazement. How could he sing like a bird? Nobody would know it wasn't a bird singing! A nearby black-

bird answered the whistling boy and flew nearer. Willie
fluted back, and the bird drew nearer still. Then the boy
changed his song and imitated the chaffinch's merry
rattle. One answered him and soon two or three came
round.

Willie whistled like a great-tit. 'Pee-ter-pee-ter-pee-ter,
pee!' he whistled. And three great-tits answered and came
flying down.

Soon there was a ring of birds round the boy, who,
except for his mouth, did not move at all. Fenella kept
as still as a mouse, fascinated. The goose did not stir a
single feather.

Robins came when Willie imitated their rich, creamy
little song. Thrushes came, and a wagtail, too, calling its
musical 'chissik, chissik', in answer to Willie. Fenella had
never seen birds so close in her life. One of them actually
hopped on to Willie's foot. Then a robin flew to the top
of his head and carolled loudly.

Cackles uncurled her long neck and hissed. The robin
flew off in alarm. So did the other birds.

'Oh, Cackles! You shouldn't mind if a robin perches
on my head!' said Willie, laughing. He stroked the soft
feathers of the goose, who hissed softly and pecked
lovingly at his hand.

'She's jealous if any bird comes too near,' said Willie.
'Well, what did you think of all that?'

Fenella looked at Willie with shining eyes. 'I think
you're wondeful,' she said. 'Oh, Willie – how do you do
it?'

'Little secret of mine!' said Willie, and he laughed.
'Like to see it?'

'Oh, *yes*!' said Fenella. Willie put his hand into his
mouth, and then took out what looked like a cherrystone
with a hole in it. 'That's my secret, he said.

'But – what does *that* do?' asked Fenella, puzzled.

'I fix it in between two of my teeth,' said Willie. 'And

it helps me to make all those whistling noises. My father used to imitate birds, too. He had a lot of these stones and things. I found them and practised with them. It's in our family. My great-uncle was a famous bird-whistler, too.'

Fenella couldn't understand how a little cherry-stone with a hole in it could possibly help Willie to make all those bird-noises. He popped the stone back into his mouth, and did a few trills. It was marvellous.

Cackles stood up and began to peck at the grass hungrily. That made Fenella suddenly remember something. 'Oh dear! I've just remembered! Aunt Lou told me to tell Uncle Ursie to buy some sausages for his supper tonight – and I forgot.'

'Well, we'll go and fetch them,' said Willie. 'Come on. That will put your aunt in a good temper! Hey, Cackles, coming?'

Cackles came with them. Fenella was afraid that the dogs they met might snap at her, but Cackles was not afraid of any dog in the world. One peck from that big beak and the biggest dog would fly howling down the street!

The three of them, much stared at, arrived in the little town of Upper Middleham. Willie bought some sausages. Then he bought a bar of chocolate for Fenella. She was very pleased.

'You *are* kind!' she said. 'I don't think I'm going to run away after all. It won't be so bad if you're there. I'd like to be friends with you and Cackles.'

'Cackle,' said the goose, and pressed against the little girl.

'There you are!' said Willie. 'She says she'll be friends with you, too! We'll have some fun, Fenny. I'll take you round the circus and introduce you to everyone. You needn't be afraid if *I'm* there! Even the elephants eat out of my hand.'

Fenella thought that Willie Winkie was the most

wonderful boy she had ever met. What twinkling eyes he had! What a lot of freckles – and what funny little dimples! She had never seen a boy with dimples before, but they suited Willie. She wished she had one, too, that went in and out when she smiled, like Willie's. But she hadn't.

They went back to the circus. Fenella felt nervous when they went in at the gate. Suppose she met Mr Crack again, with his enormous whip. She would want to run away!

They did meet him. He came swinging round the corner, humming loudly. leading a most beautiful black horse. 'Hallo, Willie Winkie!' he said, 'How's old Cackles? And who's this young lady with red hair and green eyes?'

Fenella trembled. Surely he would know she was the little girl he had roared at not so long before.

'This is Fenella, Ursie's niece, who's come to live at the circus,' said Willie. 'She's to help Lou, you know, with the sewing.'

'Oh, so you're Fenella!' said Mr Crack, and he fished in his pocket. He brought out a bag of sticky sweets. 'Here you are then, girl. Sweets for you, and don't you give any to that greedy goose. And mind now, if anyone scares you, or shouts at you, you just come to me, Mr Carl Crack – and I'll crack my whip at them and scare them into fits! Ho ho ho, that's what I'll do!'

He stood towering over Fenella, his face one big kind smile. The little girl couldn't help smiling back as she took the sweets. He didn't seem a bit like the man who had roared at her a few hours back.

Willie took her hand. 'What did I tell you?' he said. 'You don't need to be scared of Mr Crack – unless you do wrong. But you're a good little girl, I can see. Come along and meet my mother. We're going to have a fine time together, you and Cackles and I!'

4. Circus Folk

Willie took Fenella to his caravan to meet his mother.
'This is my Mum,' he said. Fenella looked at his mother.
She was thin and worn-looking, with untidy brown hair
with a good deal of grey in it, and she looked untidy in
her dress, too. She needed a button on her blouse, and a
hook on her skirt. Both were done up with big safety
pins.

But she had dimples just like Willie's, and such a lovely
smile that Fenella liked her at once.

'Well, so you're Fenella,' she said, and she gave the
little girl a kiss. Fenella was not used to being kissed, and
it warmed her heart. 'I've heard about you from your
Aunt Lou. You've come to help her, haven't you? She'll
keep you at it all right!'

'Got anything to eat, Mum?' asked Willie. 'I bet
Fenella's hungry!'

'There's some buns in the cupboard there, and some
strawberry jam somewhere,' said Willie's mother.

'What's your mother's name?' whispered Fenella.

'Aggie,' said Willie, giving Fenella a bun.

'I can't call her Aggie,' said Fenella, shocked.

'Well, everyone does,' said Willie. 'You can call her
Aunt Aggie, if you're so particular.'

So Fenella called her Aunt Aggie, and she seemed quite
pleased.

'Nice manners you've got,' she said to Fenella. 'And
what pretty neat clothes you're wearing, too. Clever with

your needle, aren't you? Wish I was. But I'm not. Can't even get myself to sew a button on! And as for Willie there, well, if he wants anything mending, he does it himself.'

'I'll do it for him,' said Fenella, eagerly. 'I'd like to. And I'll sew a button on your blouse for you, Aunt Aggie, and a hook on your skirt.'

'There's no call to point out I've got safety pins where buttons ought to be!' said Aunt Aggie, looking suddenly offended. Fenella went red. But Willie nudged her and grinned.

'It's all right. Don't worry. Mum's never annoyed for long.'

He was right. Before two minutes had gone by Willie's mother was rattling on about the circus, and how it was to open the next night, and what a good show they hoped to have.

'And my Willie here, he always gets the most claps, him and his old goose,' she said.

'I don't, Mum!' said Willie, but his mother would have it that he did. The two of them finished their buns and jam, and then, with Cackles waddling beside them, Willie took Fenella round the camp to show her everything.

It was an astonishing walk for the little girl. She half-wondered if she was dreaming when she saw so many strange sights.

There were the three elephants, Dolly, Dick and Domo, in the charge of a little man not much taller than Fenella herself.

'This is Mr Tiny,' said Willie, and the little man bowed gravely to Fenella. He was dressed all in white, with white boots and a white hat. 'Just trying my things on for tomorrow night,' he explained to Fenella. 'Your aunt has made me some new ones. Do you like them?'

He swung himself round and round to show Fenella. 'Fine, aren't they?' he said.

'You look lovely!' Fenella said, and the small man beamed. Beside his enormous elephants he looked tinier than ever. Fenella kept well away from the tremendous creatures.

'You needn't be afraid of them,' said Mr Tiny. 'They won't hurt you. Harmless as me, they are!'

He went up to Dolly, the smallest of the elephants. 'Hup!' he said. 'Hup!'

And Dolly put down her trunk, wound it gently round the waist of the little man, and set him on the top of her big head. Fenella was startled.

'Hup!' said Willie, too. 'Hup!' And Dick, the next elephant, did exactly the same, winding his trunk round Willie's waist, and lifting the boy high up on his head.

'You say "Hup!" to Domo!' called Mr Tiny. 'And he'll lift you up, too.'

But Fenella backed away quickly. What! Be lifted up by an elephant's trunk and set on his head! She couldn't imagine anything she would hate more. Mr Tiny and Willie laughed at her horrified face. Willie slid cleverly down to the ground.

'Come on! We'll see Mr Holla. He's teaching his chimps to play cricket this year. It's funny to watch them.'

'I'm afraid to go near the chimpanzees,' said Fenella, pulling back.

'Don't be silly! You'll love them,' said Willie. 'See that one grinning at us? He's called Grin, and he's the wickedest, comicalest chimp you ever saw. There's the other, looking hurt and solemn. He's always like that. He's called Bearit. Grin and Bearit. Look out for Grin. He'll have the sweets out of your pocket if you're not careful.'

Grin was like his name, one big grin. He showed very white teeth, and Fenella couldn't help feeling afraid of him. But he put out a gentle, hairy paw and stroked

her arm softly, making a funny, loving little noise as he did so.

'He likes you!' said Willie. 'He doesn't do that to many people, I can tell you. Here's their trainer, Mr Holla. How are you getting on teaching your chimps cricket, Mr Holla?'

Mr Holla was a jolly-looking man, with long, powerful arms like his chimpanzees. They adored him. They liked nothing better than to put their hairy arms round his neck and hug him. Each chimpanzee was dressed carefully. Grin wore a pair of red shorts and a yellow jersey. Bearit wore a pair of yellow shorts and a red jersey.

'They've got caps, too,' said Mr Holla to Fenella. 'But they were naughty with them yesterday, so I've taken them away for a punishment today.'

'Oh. What did they do?' asked Fenella curiously.

'They wear caps,' said Mr Holla. 'And Grin climbed up on top of your aunt's caravan yesterday and put his red cap on her chimney, and Bearit put his on Aggie's chimney. So both their stoves smoked and they were angry. And now today I won't let either of the chimps wear their caps, so maybe they won't do that again. They're full of tricks.'

Grin had sidled up to Fenella. Somehow she couldn't help liking him. He looked so comical in his shorts and jersey, and he stroked her arm as if he thought she was the nicest little girl in the world.

Then he suddenly bounded off at top speed, with Bearit after him. He leapt up on to the top of Mr Holla's van, which was nearby, and began to look at something he held.

'It's my sweets!' said Fenella indignantly. 'He's taken them out of my pocket. And all the time he was stroking my arm and pretending to be friendly.'

'Well, you won't see your sweets again,' said Mr Holla. 'They won't come down till they've eaten them all. Rascals they are. Worse than a dozen children!'

Mr Holla went into his caravan and came out with an orange. 'Here you are,' he said. 'You have that instead of your sweets. And don't be too cross with Grin and Bearit. Come and make friends with them some time. They love children.'

A pack of dogs suddenly came rushing over to Willie. Fenella shrank behind him, but the dogs took no notice of her.

'Here are all the performing dogs!' said Willie to
Fenella. 'I help with them. This is Tric. This is Fanny.
This is Corker. This is Bouncer. Will you get down,
Buster! Stop it now! And leave my shoelace alone,
Scamp. Aren't they lovely, Fenella?'

They were all so merry and full of fun that Fenella
couldn't help liking them. Most of them were terriers, but
there were two poodles and one mongrel.

'He's about the cleverest of the lot,' said Willie, patting
him. 'Hup, Pickles, hup.'

And up went Pickles on his hind legs at once, and then
threw himself light-heartedly over and over in the air,
somersaulting time after time. Fenella stared in wonder
at him. But when Willie began to make a fuss of him, all
the other dogs were jealous and came rubbing against
Willie for some affection, too.

'Don't they love you!' said Fenella, and began to
think it must be very nice to be so much loved by animals
as Willie was. She held out her hand to one of the poodles,
feeling very brave, meaning him to come and sniff at it,
and perhaps lick it.

But the poodle very gravely put up his paw, too, and
shook hands. Fenella laughed. 'Oh, they're so clever. Who
teaches them? Do they like being taught?'

'We only teach the clever ones,' said Willie, 'and they
love it, of course – just as clever children enjoy their
lessons. We never whip them – only reward them when
they have done well. Now let's go and look at Mrs
Connie's monkeys.'

He sent the dogs off and walked with Fenella to the
other side of the field, where there were two caravans,
both painted a bright green, with yellow wheels. Across
each was painted 'MRS CONNIE AND HER MAR-
VELLOUS MONKEYS.'

Outside one of the caravans a tea-party was going on.
Seven monkeys sat at a table, each on a small chair. Each

had a banana in his or her hand, and they watched a tiny, wizened woman, looking rather like a monkey herself, who sat at the head of the table. She was talking to them.

'Now Millie, now Minnie, now Mollie, remember your manners. Peel your banana neatly like this. That's right. Only peel it half-way, remember, Jimmy! You've taken your peel right off! Naughty, naughty!'

Jimmy looked like a bad child caught doing something wrong. He whimpered and tried to put the peel back on his banana. The others had half-peeled theirs and were patiently waiting for Mrs Connie to let them bite a bit off the top. Fenella saw that each monkey had its own tiny mug with its name painted on it. How lovely!

Mrs Connie suddenly saw them. 'Hallo, Willie. Who's this? A friend of yours?'

'It's Fenella, who's come to live with her Aunt Lou,' said Willie. A scowl came over Mrs Connie's face.

'That Lou! Mean, selfish woman! She makes such a fuss when she has to sew something for my monkeys. Well, girl, I hope you're not as mean as your aunt, that's all. If you are, I'll have nothing to do with you. Nothing! Jimmy! Behave yourself! You've thrown your skin on the floor. Pick it up at once!'

Jimmy picked it up. Then, when the next monkey wasn't looking, he took a neat bite off the top of its banana. The monkey howled loudly and chattered to Mrs. Connie.

Fenella laughed and laughed. Mrs Connie looked pleased. 'Comical, aren't they?' she said. 'Good as gold, really.'

Fenella thought they looked sweet. Some were dressed in tiny skirts, others in tiny shorts. Willie pulled at her hand.

'Come on. There's lots more to see. Let Mrs Connie get on with her tea-party. Well, do you like us all?'

'Oh, I *do*,' said Fenella, her face glowing. 'I do, Willie. I'm *so* glad I didn't run away!'

5.   Uncle Ursie's Bears

Just as Fenella and Willie were leaving Mrs Connie and her troupe of monkeys, Uncle Ursie saw them, and came up.

'Well, Fenella,' he said, 'making friends with everyone? Hallo, Cackles.'

'Cackle,' said the goose, and dug his beak affectionately into Uncle Ursie's boot.

'Hey, don't do that,' said Uncle Ursie, and pushed the goose off. She hissed, and dug her beak into his leg.

'Too affectionate, that goose of yours,' said Uncle Ursie, rubbing his leg. 'Seen my bears yet, Fenny? What, not seen them! Come along then. Finest animals in the show!'

He took them to a big van, one side of which had been folded back. Bars were all along the open side, and at one end was a door. Uncle Ursie opened it and went inside.

A big brown bear stood up as he came in. Fenella had seen so many animals now that she actually didn't feel afraid. 'Come and make friends with Fenny,' said Uncle Ursie to the big bear.

'His name is Clump,' said Willie. 'He won't hurt you. Your uncle has had him since he was a baby. Hallo, Clump.'

Clump grunted right down in the middle of himself. Fenella wasn't sure what she ought to do, so she put out her hand. But the bear put both his arms round her and gave her a hug. She gasped.

'Haven't you heard of a bear-hug?' asked Uncle Ursie, with a grin all over his face. 'Clump, stand on your head.'

Clump rolled over and then, to Fenella's surprise, stood on his head. Then he turned three slow somersaults, and ended up sitting beside Uncle Ursie. He at once put his arms round Uncle Ursie's knees and hugged them.

'Stop it,' said Uncle Ursie. 'You'll crack my knee-joints. Now then – where's Bobbo?'

Bobbo was asleep in the straw at the very back of the cage. He awoke and yawned. Fenella stared at him, and her heart went out to the little fat brown bear. He was only a baby!

She forgot that she was ever afraid of animals. She held out her arms for the dear little bear. Uncle Ursie picked him up, and gave him to her. He cuddled into her arms and stared up at her out of small, brown eyes. He yawned again.

'Oh, you're a pet!' said Fenella. 'Uncle Ursie, I want to play with him every day. Oh, he's so cuddlesome and soft I'd like to take him to bed with me at night!'

'Ho! And I wonder what your aunt would say to *that*!' said Uncle Ursie. 'A bear in your bed, indeed. Bobbo! Do you hear that? This little girl wants to make you a pet and take you to bed.'

'Ooof,' said Bobbo, and rubbed his blunt nose with one of his paws. Fenella really loved him. He was such a baby.

'Does he go into the ring and do anything at all?' she asked Uncle Ursie.

'He goes into the ring all right, but he doesn't do anything yet. He's too young,' said her uncle. 'He will watch Clump, and do what he does later on. He's a comical little fellow. Maybe he'll be a kind of bear-clown. Some bears are just naturally comical you know. Willie, take that goose of yours out of the cage. One blow of Clump's paw and that will be the end of her.'

'Oh, Cackles can look after herself all right,' said Willie. 'We had a tiger here once, and she gave him a peck, because he lashed out with his tail and hit her by mistake!'

It was getting dark now, and Uncle Ursie came out of the cage with the others. Fenella had to put down the baby bear. He grunted softly as if he didn't want her to leave him.

Uncle Ursie locked the cage. 'Come along,' he said to Fenella. 'Supper-time. Then bed for you! You must be tired with your long day.'

'She hasn't seen the horses yet, or Fric and Frac, the riders, or Malvina — and she hasn't seen Groggy, our old clown — or the others, Ricky and Rocky, and Micko and Tricks,' said Willie. 'And there's Wriggle, too, she hasn't seen.'

'Yes, I've seen *him*,' said Fenella. 'He put his head between his knees and looked out at me from there. I didn't like it.'

Willie laughed. 'Oh, you'll have to get used to old Wriggle. He's got a body made of rubber. Wait till you see him tread on his head!'

'He couldn't!' said Fenella. 'You're making that up. Oh, I wish I could see the clowns.'

'They don't look any different from me or Willie here,' said her uncle. 'Not in ordinary dress, I mean. And they're not very funny out of the ring, either. Except old Groggy. You wait till tomorrow evening, Fenella, and you'll see them in the ring, all dressed up in their clown clothes. Then they'll look like clowns – and act like them, too. You'll be doubled up with laughter. Come along now, or your aunt will be shouting for us. Get along, Willie, and take that goose with you. The sight of her drives Lou mad, ever since she climbed into the caravan and ate all the salad she had got ready for our dinner.'

'Cackle,' said the goose, and walked away as if she was offended.

'Good night, Fenella,' said Willie. 'See you tomorow. And don't you run away in the night, or I shall be very cross!'

Fenella laughed. No, she wasn't going to run away now. She began to feel excited at the thought of sleeping in a caravan. She had never done that before. It would be fun.

She went up the steps into the brightly-lit caravan, followed by Uncle Ursie, who was sniffing loudly.

'Sausages, I declare! My, I'm hungry, too! And onions with them – and tomatoes. We're in luck.'

At Auntie Janet's Fenella had never had any supper except a piece of bread and butter. But things were different at the circus. The circus folk liked good meals and plenty of them. There was always a cooking-pot smelling delicious at the back of somebody's caravan, or the smell of frying sausages or bacon. There was tinned fruit at nearly every meal — peaches or apricots, pears or pineapple.

Such things had been a Sunday treat at Auntie Janet's. The circus folk had to depend a good deal on tinned stuff, and they bought the tins by the dozen. Fenella was thrilled to see a tin of apricots open on the shelf – and goodness, was that a jug of cream?

It was. The little girl found that she was hungry and she sat down to her plate of sausages, onions and tomatoes with a good appetite. Whatever would Auntie Janet say if she saw her eating a supper like that?

She was very sleepy afterwards, but her aunt made her help with the washing-up. Fenella took a look at the corner where all the gay clothes had been, waiting to be mended. Her aunt saw her look.

'All done,' she said. 'Whilst you were out gadding this afternoon. There will be no more for a bit. Everything's ready for the circus to open to-morrow – but afterwards there'll be plenty to do again – rents and tears, buttons off, new dresses to make. You'll have to start work then.'

'I'll be glad to help you, Aunt Lou,' said Fenella.

'Well, we can't afford to keep you here with us, unless you do your bit,' said Aunt Lou. 'We're not rich folk, you know. Everybody has to turn to and help in a circus. We're like one big family. You be a good girl and I'll be glad to have you. You be lazy and you'll get the sharp side of my tongue – and Uncle Ursie can tell you how sharp that is!'

Uncle Ursie grunted. 'Sharp! It would go clean through a battleship that tongue of yours, once it gets going. You used to be such a sweet-tempered girl, Lou. Don't you be too hard on the youngster. She's all we've got, now Janet's gone away. She seems a nice enough kid.'

'She might be worse,' said Aunt Lou, and her voice was not quite so sharp. 'She'll have to have some schooling, too, Ursie. Maybe we'd better ask Presto to teach her lessons, when he's got time. She's only ten.'

'I can read and write and do sums,' said Fenella. 'And I know a lot of geography and history.'

'Do you now?' said Uncle Ursie, in admiration. 'Well, that's more than some of us know here in this circus. There's two or three can't even write their own names. Yes, I'll ask Presto to teach Fenella when he can. He's a good-hearted chap, and clever as paint.'

'Who's Presto?' asked Fenella, with curiosity, for she hadn't heard of him yet.

'Presto? Oh, he's the juggler and conjurer,' said Uncle Ursie. 'Marvellous fellow. You'll have to be careful to do what he says, or he may use a bit of magic and turn you into a chimp!'

'Now don't tell such stories,' said Aunt Lou. 'Fenella won't want to learn from him if you say things like that. Maybe if she goes to lessons with him, that young limb of a Willie will go, too. He's not had any more schooling than a fly! I doubt if he can read properly yet.'

Fenella was astonished to think that Willie might not be able to read. How dreadful! She had been able to read since she was five. She thought about Presto. Fancy having lessons from a conjurer! That really *would* be exciting. He might do tricks for her, if she worked well. Living in a circus camp was going to be very exciting indeed.

'Get into your bunk, Fenella,' said her aunt, letting down the little narrow shelf, and piling bedclothes on it. 'Go and rinse your face and hands in the stream outside. The light from the caravan will show you where it is.'

Fenella washed herself in the cold stream. She went back into the caravan, found her brush and comb and brushed her hair well. Aunt Lou watched her.

'You've nice hair,' she said. 'I had a little girl once with hair like yours. It used to shine like that when I brushed it.'

'What happened to your little girl?' asked Fenella. 'Did she die?'

'Yes,' said Aunt Lou. 'She fell ill, and I couldn't get a doctor in time. Now you get into bed, quick! You won't wake up till goodness knows when if you stay up any later. Hurry!'

She didn't offer to kiss Fenella. The little girl climbed into her bunk sleepily. 'Good night, Aunt Lou,' she said.

'Good night,' said Aunt Lou, in her sharp voice, and threaded a needle to do some darning of her own. Fenella shut her eyes.

She heard the shouting of some of the circus folk outside. She heard the whinny of a horse, and the barking of two or three of the dogs. Then she heard the loud cackle of the goose, not far off.

'Willie's taking her round the field with him,' she thought sleepily. 'I like Cackles. And I like Willie and Willie's mother – and oh, that darling little baby bear, Bobbo! I love him!' And then she was fast asleep, and dreaming that she was wheeling Bobbo in her dolls' pram, with Cackles walking beside her!

6. The First Morning

Fenella slept soundly that first night in her aunt's
caravan. She was so tired that she did not wake up until
both her aunt and uncle were up and about, and having
their breakfast. The smell of frying bacon awoke her.

She turned over in her little bunk and tried to think
where she was. She looked up at the ceiling and saw all
kinds of things hung there, and was astonished. Aunt
Janet's ceiling had never had anything hung on it at all.

But, of course – this wasn't Aunt Janet's bedroom!
This was Uncle Ursie's red caravan! She was in Mr Carl
Crack's circus! She was one of the circus folk now. Fenella
felt her heart jump in excitement, and she sat up at once.
Where did that smell of bacon come from? It was really
a very nice smell indeed.

There was no one in the caravan. Fenella jumped out
of her narrow little bunk and went to the open door at
the back. She looked out on to the circus field, which was
busy and crowded and full of noise. Circus folk got up
early, and did many jobs before they had their breakfast.
Horses, sleek and satiny, were already being cantered
round the field by Fric and Frac the riders, and by a
lovely girl, dressed in riding breeches, Malvina.

Fenella stood there in her nightdress, drinking in the
sunny air and the lively scene. Her aunt, just below on
the ground, saw her.

'So you're awake at last!' she said. 'Come along down
and have your breakfast, quick!'

'What! In my nightdress? Oh, I *couldn't*!' said
Fenella, quite shocked. She disappeared into the caravan
to dress.

'Well, if you're so fussy, let your breakfast get cold,'
said Aunt Lou.

'Now, now,' said Uncle Ursie. 'The child has been
nicely brought up by Janet. You let her keep her nice
ways and good manners, Lou. Wouldn't you have wanted
our own little girl to be like that?'

Aunt Lou said nothing. She put some bacon on a plate
for Fenella, and covered it up to keep it warm. Very soon
the little girl jumped down the steps. Uncle Ursie put his
big clumsy arm round her.

'Well, it's nice to see you looking so perky and pleased
with yourself. Now, you tuck into that bacon and then
you can come and help me with the bears.'

'She's got to help wash up and clean the caravan first,'
said Aunt Lou, in her sharp voice.

'Oh, of course I will,' said Fenella at once. She knew
already that she must do what Aunt Lou said before she
did anything that Uncle Ursie suggested. If she didn't
they would neither of them ever hear the end of it! Oh,
dear – Aunt Lou was such a cross kind of person. What a
pity!

Fenella watched the life of the circus going on round
her as she ate. The dogs came tearing by, and Willie
was with them. Behind waddled Cackles as usual. Where
Willie went she was sure to go. The dogs kept well
out of her way. They knew her sharp beak only too
well.

'Hallo, Fenny! Sleep well?' called Willie. 'Hey,
Bouncer, will you come here! Tric, what are you doing?
Drop that, Buster, drop it! You get plenty of good food
without picking up any old rubbish!'

Horses whinnied by the stream, where they were being
watered. Dolly, Dick and Domo suddenly trumpeted,

making a tremendous noise, that made Fenella upset her
tea in fright.

'Haven't you ever heard an elephant's voice before?'
said Uncle Ursie, mopping the tea off her frock with a
big, red handkerchief. 'You'll soon get used to it. They
want their breakfast, you see. A cartful of hay they'll eat,
all in a twinkling!'

'They use their trunks just like hands,' said Fenella,
forgetting to eat her bread and marmalade. 'Look – they
put their food into their mouths with their trunks. Uncle,
are their trunks very, very long noses?'

'Looks like it!' said Uncle Ursie. 'They must have
grown longer and longer, because elephants like to reach
up to pull down leaves from tall trees. Ho, ho! If my nose
was much bigger than it is, I'd use it for a hand, too!'

'It *is* rather big, isn't it?' said Fenella, looking at her
uncle's large nose. He wasn't a bit offended. He put up
his hand and felt it.

'Yes, it's big enough – it's a snout like old Clump's, your
aunt says. Don't you, Lou?'

'Let the child eat her breakfast,' said Aunt Lou. 'We're
late as it is.'

Fenella quickly finished her bread and marmalade. The
early summer sunshine shone down on the camp, and in
the distance the fields were golden with buttercups.
From somewhere nearby came the sweet, rich scent of
may-blossom. Fenella sniffed it eagerly. However could
she have thought it would be dreadful to live in a circus?
Why, it was the most exciting thing in the world!
And already she was not nearly so much afraid of the
animals.

She thought of Bobbo the baby bear. She would hurry
up and help her aunt with the washing-up and cleaning,
and then perhaps Uncle Ursie would let her play with the
little bear. He was such a darling.

She helped Aunt Lou neatly and quickly. 'I must say

your Aunt Janet has brought you up well,' said Aunt
Lou, in a nicer voice than she had used to Fenella so far.
'I can see you'll be quite a help to me, for all you're only
ten.'

'I mean to be, Aunt Lou,' said Fenella. 'It's so kind of
you and Uncle Ursie to take me in, when I've got nobody
else. Now can I go and see the bears?'

'Yes, off you go,' said Aunt Lou. 'But remember,
Fenella, that today is a very busy one for us circus folk
because we're giving our first show here this evening, and
you'd best not get in anyone's way. Most of all keep out
of Mr Carl Crack's way. He's always in a temper the first
day the show opens.'

'Oh,' said Fenella, rather alarmed. She made up her
mind to run and hide if she saw Mr Crack anywhere. She
didn't want him to shout at her again, or crack that
enormous whip round her feet.

The little girl made her way to where her uncle was
cleaning out Clump's cage. The big bear was sitting
outside on the grass, watching Uncle Ursie. He was
chained to a tree-stump.

'Where's Bobbo?' asked Fenella.

'Oh, Willie's taken him for a walk,' said Uncle Ursie.
'Now just you bring me that clean straw over there, will
you. No, not that, child, it's the dirty straw! We can't
give old Clump dirty bedding. That's right.'

Fenella looked round for Willie. She saw him at the
other end of the big field, with Bobbo and Cackles. She
sped off, nearly falling over Bouncer and Buster, two of
the dogs, who were having a race all by themselves.

A small man in shorts and jersey was blowing up
enormous balloons outside a caravan. They were beautiful ones, very big, and very gay. On each of them was
printed a name. Fenella tried to see what it was.

'Mr Groggy,' was what she read. Yes, there it was on
each balloon. 'Mr Groggy.' So this small man in the funny

little shorts must be Mr Groggy, the chief clown. He
didn't look a bit like one.

He saw Fenella staring at him and he looked up and
winked at her. Then he screwed up his face in a most
remarkable manner, and made a loud popping noise like
a lot of balloons going bang. Fenella looked at him in
alarm.

'That's what my balloons will do tonight in the ring,'
said Groggy, making his face look like itself again. 'They'll
go popping off. What a pity, what a pity!'

He got up to get some more balloons, and came back
to his chair. He sat down and the chair doubled itself up
under him. Groggy found himself on the ground. He got
up and pulled his chair straight.

'Now don't you do that again!' he said to the offending
chair. 'Pretending you're too weak to bear my weight!'
He sat down on it again, and once more the chair gave
way and Groggy found himself on the ground. Fenella
gave a squeal of laughter.

'That chair!' said Groggy, and he shook his fist at it.
He straightened it again, and pretended to sit down on it
suddenly. The chair remained as it was. Then the clown
sat down again – and once more the chair buckled up and
there was the clown sprawling on the grass!

Fenella laughed and laughed. Mr Wriggle the acrobat
came up, grinning. 'Hallo! Is old Groggy showing you
what that chair of his can do? Like to see me tread on
my head, Fenella?'

'No thank you,' said Fenella hastily, looking at Mr
Wriggle's long, lean body. 'I'm just going.'

'Well, have one of my balloons before you go,'
said Mr Groggy, and he handed her a big blue one.
He sat down on his chair and again it sent him to the
ground. Laughing to herself, Fenella ran over to join
Willie.

'Oh, you've got Bobbo with you!' she said. 'Let me

carry him. Do let me! He's like a toy bear, so soft and cuddly.'

'Well, let him walk a bit first,' said Willie. 'He always enjoys his morning walk. He likes seeing all the other animals. We always let the animals mix together as much as we can, so that they know one another and get used to their different smells. Bobbo loves to amble round.'

Fenella walked round the field with Willie. Bobbo, on a lead, followed clumsily, his fat little body waddling along as slowly as Cackles. The goose liked Bobbo. She hissed softly as they went. 'She's talking to him,' said Willie. 'Telling him this and that, like I tell you!'

'Everyone seems awfully busy this morning,' said Fenella, skipping out of the way of two men hurrying along with a big bench. 'Oh dear – what are all these men doing with those benches?'

'Getting ready for the show tonight,' said Willie. 'The big top's up. We've got to get the ring ready now and the seats for the people.'

'What's the big top?' asked Fenella.

'The circus tent, of course, where the ring is,' said Willie. 'Come over and peep inside. Don't tell me you've never been to a circus! My, my – what an ignorant little girl you are!'

Fenella had never been taken to a circus in her life. She peeped inside the 'big top' as Willie called the great centre tent. She saw a red ring in the middle of it, which two men were strewing with sawdust. Around the ring other men were setting dozens of wooden benches.

'Can I see the show tonight?' asked Fenella, in excitement. 'Will Aunt Lou let me?'

'See the show! I should just think so,' said Willie. 'And mind you clap me and Cackles as loud as ever you can! My word, you'll enjoy yourself tonight!'

7. Getting Ready For The Show

Everyone was busy and excited that day. Even the animals seemed to know that the circus was giving a grand show that evening. The elephants trumpeted dozens of times, the horses whinnied and neighed, the dogs barked, Cackles hissed and cackled, the bears grunted, and the monkeys chattered in little high voices. As for the chimpanzees, they were quite mad, and Mr Holla had to speak to them very sternly indeed.

'What have they done?' asked Fenella, seeing Grin and Bearit putting their hands over their faces like children who have been scolded.

'Grin found a bucket of water and threw it all over Bearit,' said Mr Holla. 'Soaked him through. Then Bearit got the empty bucket and tried to put it on Grin's head. And all the time Aggie was looking for her bucket of water. She *was* cross. So was I, when I saw Bearit's clothes dripping wet!'

Fenella laughed. The chimps took a look at her through their fingers, for their hands still covered their faces. Then Grin made a chattering noise and took her hand. She didn't mind at all.

'He likes you,' said Mr Holla. 'He wants you to go for a little walk with him. I saw you with Bobbo in your arms this morning. Do you like him?'

'Oh, he's a darling,' said Fenella. 'And I like Clump, too – he's so fat and clumsy.'

'Chimps are much better than bears,' said Mr Holla,

half-jealously. 'Got more brains in their feet than bears have in their big heads. You watch what Grin and Bearit do in the ring tonight! You'll be surprised.'

Fenella watched everything and everyone that day, rather shy, but very thrilled to be part of the camp. She kept out of Mr Crack's way. Indeed, everyone did if they possibly could, for he was strung up to such a pitch of excitement that he almost lost his voice through shouting orders all over the field. His whip cracked, his top-hat flew off twice in the wind, and he stamped about in his enormous boots like a giant!

'Don't you be afraid of him!' said Uncle Ursie, when he saw Fenella skip out of the way and hide under a caravan when Mr Crack came roaring by. 'He's always like that on show-days. Can't help it. He'll be all right afterwards.'

Aunt Lou was now doing a few last-minute jobs that had turned up unexpectedly – a button to sew on to Malvina's beautiful costume – a tear to mend in Mr Groggy's clown's dress – black bobble to put on Micko's hat. Fenella offered to help, but her aunt shook her head.

'No,' she said, her needle flying in and out, 'I can do these few things. You go and watch the circus getting ready. Look at the gate over there – the people are already lining up to get in. They know that Mr Carl Crack's circus is a fine one to see!'

'It's the best in the world!' said Fenella, making up her mind that it really must be. She watched the circus folk parading about, looking suddenly very different now that they had got on their beautiful, gay circus clothes. How grand they looked – and how very lovely Malvina was. She was one of the trick-riders, and when she came by Fenella looked in wonder at the glittering stars in her hair, and the smaller ones sewn on to her lovely dress.

The clowns were all dressed up now, too. Mr Groggy looked extremely funny, for he had put on a false nose that was longer and bigger than even Uncle Ursie's. He had put big white rings all round his eyes, and painted his mouth red, making it most enormous. He carried his bunch of big balloons, and also his peculiar chair.

The other clowns were ready, too, and Mr Wriggle the acrobat was in a tight-fitting suit of shining gold. He saw Fenella and winked at her. 'I wish you'd watch me tread on my head,' he said in a pleading voice. 'Look, I just do this – and . . .'

To Fenella's alarm he twisted himself over backwards and his head appeared under his left arm. She stared in horror.

'No, don't tread on your head. Don't do anything like that,' she begged Mr Wriggle. 'I don't like it.'

'Well, well, well! How do you like *this* then?' cried Mr Wriggle, in a gay voice, and threw himself over on to his hands. He walked on them very fast indeed, his legs waving in the air.

'Oh, that's very clever,' said Fenella. '*I'd* like to do that! Oh, here's Willie – and Cackles. Willie, you look FINE! And oh, doesn't Cackles look sweet?'

The goose looked like Mother Goose in the nursery rhyme books. She had on a dear little bonnet with a feather in it, and wore a red shawl. Under her wing she carried a shopping basket. She cackled as if she was very pleased with herself. Indeed, she was, because there was nothing she enjoyed better than dressing up with Willie and waddling after him in the ring.

Willie looked very grand indeed. He had on a shining white suit, with a cloak edged with bright red. His round, white hat had a red feather in it, very long and wavy. He looked quite a different boy.

'You look like a prince,' said Fenella, admiringly. 'Oh, Cackles – how *do* you carry your basket so nicely?'

'I clip it to her wing – look, there's the clip,' said Willie, showing Fenella a big white clip that fastened the basket under Cackle's wing. 'I say – here's your uncle. He wants you for something.'

Fenella hardly knew her uncle at first when she saw him. He, too, had put on his grand circus clothes, and looked quite different. He wore Russian dress, with big top-boots, a red coat with a belt, red breeches tucked into his boots, and a tall, round black fur cap. His big nose seemed to suit him now. He smiled at Fenella.

'Well, how do like us when we're properly dressed? Hold Bobbo for me for a minute, will you? He's getting so excited that he won't be able to do a thing when he gets into the ring.'

Fenella held her arms out gladly for the little bear, who was whimpering with excitement. He sensed all the pre-parations, and felt all the eagerness of the hurrying circus folk, and it was too much for his baby mind. He cuddled against Fenella gladly.

'You're a darling,' she said. 'Don't shiver so, Bobbo. It's very warm tonight!'

'He's shivering with excitement, not cold,' said Willie. 'Some of the dogs get like that. They love all the thrill of the show. Bouncer gets so excited sometimes that he shivers from head to foot. But he's quite all right as soon as he gets into the ring.'

Mrs Connie passed by with her monkeys, and Fenella didn't know her! No wonder, for she had left off her old draggled skirt and shawl, and had dressed herself in a frilly skirt, short to her knees, and a gay little blue coat. She wore a bright golden wig, and was talking gaily to her little troupe of monkeys. Each of them was in his or her circus dress, and looked very smart indeed.

'Is that really Mrs Connie?' said Fenella in amazement. 'But she looks *young* now! And she looked awfully old before.'

'Doesn't matter what you look like in the daytime, in

the camp,' said Uncle Ursie, 'but at night, when the show
is on, we must all be young and gay and strong. Look at
the people pouring in now. We shall take a lot of money
tonight. Mr Crack will be pleased tomorrow.'

'Where shall I sit?' asked Fenella. 'In the front row
of the seats? Oh, I do hope I can, then I shall see everything.'

'In the *seats*! Don't be so silly,' said Willie. 'Fancy one
of us in a *seat*! You'll be behind the curtains with us of
course, Fenny. You'll see us all go in, in our turn. You
belong to the circus now, you know.'

A bell rang. All the circus folk still outside the big top
hurried towards it. It was almost time for the show to
begin. Hundreds of people were now in the great tent,
waiting eagerly. The smell of animals rose on the air, and
Fenella wrinkled up her nose. She would soon get used
to that smell, and not even notice it. The town children,
waiting impatiently on the benches in the big tent, smelt
it too, and began to clap loudly, for they wanted the show
to begin.

Fenella went behind the great red curtains that hung at
one end of the tent, through which the performers appeared to do their turns. In the space beyond the curtains
were the circus folk, the horses and other animals, all
getting into order, and waiting impatiently for Mr Crack
to give the signal.

'We all parade round first,' Willie told her. 'Fric, Frac
and Malvina go with a string of horses, and then Mr
Crack, in his golden carriage, drawn by Malvina's own
six snow-white Ponies. Then all of us, one after another.'

Mr Crack's voice rose above the noise. 'Fric! Lead the
parade.'

And then, with a great blare of trumpets, Mr Carl
Crack's Stupendous Circus began. The big red curtains
were swung aside, and through them cantered some of
the magnificent circus horses, shining like satin, their

proud heads tossing great plumes as they went.

Fric and Frac were dressed as Red Indians with great feathered head-dresses. Their faces were painted in brilliant colours, and they looked very grand and rather frightening. The children in the audience clapped and shouted wildly when they saw them. They thought they were real Red Indians. Fric and Frac gave some blood-curdling yells as they rode round, guiding the string of horses.

Then came the six snow-white ponies, the foremost one ridden by the beautiful Malvina. They drew a shining coach in which sat a most resplendent Mr Crack, bowing this way and that as everyone cheered him.

His carriage stopped. He got out, a big impressive figure, his whip in his hand. He took off his grey top-hat and bowed. He called out in a tremendous voice :

'Ladies and gentlemen – welcome to Mr Carl Crack's Grand Circus. On with the SHOW !'

And then, tumbling over and over, came the clowns and Mr Wriggle the acrobat, Mrs Connie and her monkeys, Mr Holla and his two chimpanzees, looking very fine in circus clothes. Mr Tiny and the three elephants, Uncle Ursie and the bears, Willie and Cackles – the whole string of circus performers, dressed in their finest clothes, bowing and smiling, yelling delightedly at all the shouts and claps and stamps of applause.

Yes, the circus had begun – and to a little girl peering through the curtains, her heart beating fast, it was the most exciting moment of her life. Yesterday she had been a small girl all alone – now she was one of this big circus family. She belonged to them all and they belonged to her. What fun, thought Fenella, oh, what fun !

8. Fenella Sees The Circus

The circus was very fine indeed. After the parade, when everyone had walked or ridden round the ring, bowing and smiling, the show really began.

First came the horses, cantering beautifully one after the other, round and round the ring. They went in time to the music, and they obeyed Malvina's slightest word or nod. They turned themselves round and round, they waltzed, they made themselves form patterns, and they knelt on one knee and bowed their heads when they had finished.

The band played all the time, and Fenella couldn't imagine how the horses kept time – but they all loved music, and had been specially chosen because of their liking for it. The little girl clapped and shouted as loudly as anyone as the lovely horses cantered out of the ring, with Malvina standing on the back of the biggest.

Then one by one the other turns went on. The three elephants were an enormous success, for Mr Tiny had taught them how to play tennis. He and Domo played against Dicky and Dolly. They had a net stretched across the ring, and they played quite properly with a tennis ball and rackets.

'Oh, Domo is very, very good!' said Fenella, watching him hit the ball hard with his racket, which he held firmly in his trunk. 'Oh good, Domo! Well hit!'

Dolly hit the ball such a smack that it went right up to the ceiling and down again. It bounced high and

Dicky lunged out with his racket in his trunk. 'Smack.' The ball flew into the delighted audience, and a small boy caught the ball and flung it back.

When the game was over Domo curled his trunk round his beloved Mr Tiny and put him gently on his great grey head. Mr Tiny stood there, dressed in white from top to toe, a small, bowing figure. Everyone cheered wildly. Then out lumbered the big elephants, their trunks swaying to and fro.

'We're next,' said a voice in Fenella's ear. She turned and saw Mrs Connie, looking amazing in her bright golden wig. Her monkeys were riding in a small carriage! Two monkeys were the horses, the driver was a monkey with a whip, and the other four monkeys sat in the carriage as passengers. They looked really amusing, and were clearly enjoying the fun immensely.

The driver-monkey was so excited that he quite forgot himself as he drove into the ring, and stood up and did a little dance, cracking his whip round his head. The passenger-monkeys knew he shouldn't do that, and one of them tried to pull him down.

'Be good now, be good!' hissed Mrs Connie. 'Jimmy, stop dancing and sit down.'

They had a tea party in the ring and behaved most beautifully. Then, after that, in went the clowns, shouting and falling over each other, playing all kinds of ridiculous tricks, and popping poor Mr Groggy's beautiful balloons whenever they could creep up behind him without being seen.

In despair he handed the rest of them to some of the children in the audience, who, of course, were simply delighted. 'Look,' they said to one another, 'the balloons have got the clown's name on – Mr Groggy – we've got some of his own balloons!'

Then turning cartwheels and somersaults over and over again the clowns rushed out shouting, to make room for

Mr Wriggle the acrobat. A tightrope made of strong wire
had been stretched across the ring whilst the clowns had
been playing about, and Mr Wriggle walked this lightly
and easily. Fenella thought he was wonderful.

'*I* couldn't walk on a wire like that!' she said to Willie,
who was nearby. 'I should fall off. Oh, what's he doing
now?'

Mr Wriggle was now swinging to and fro on a little
silver swing high up in the roof of the big tent.

'Suppose he falls?' said Fenella to Willie. 'Will that
net underneath catch him?'

'Yes. But he never falls – unless he means to!' said
Willie, with a grin. 'Sometimes he thinks he'll give the
people a fright, and he pretends to be in difficulties,
almost falling but not quite – and then he gives a frightful
yell and lets himself drop. My word, it gives the people a
scare, I can tell you!'

'Look at him holding by one foot and swinging!' cried
Fenella. 'Oh, I don't think I can watch him. I shan't!'

She turned away and looked behind her. There she
saw an adorable little house, complete with a front path
and a gate! On the gate was painted 'Mother Goose's
Cottage'.

'Oh!' cried Fenella, 'I haven't seen that before. Willie,
is that what Cackles uses in the ring?'

'Yes,' said Willie. 'That's her house. Isn't it, Cackles?
She stays in it till I call her out. I do a lot of bird imitating
first, you know, before Cackles joins me.'

'When do you go into the ring?' asked Fenella,
eagerly. 'Soon? I'm longing to see you. Are you nervous,
Willie?'

'Nobody's ever nervous!' said Willie, scornfully. 'We've
lived all our lives in the circus. Most of us were born in
one. Why should we be nervous? Hallo – it's my time to
go on.'

Out came Mr Wriggle, bowing as he came backwards

through the curtains. Into the ring went Mr Crack, with his big whip, to announce Willie.

'And now, ladies and gentlemen, we present to you Willie Winkie the Wonderful Whistler. He will imitate for you all the birds of the air, and will introduce to you Cackles, the trained goose, the only goose in the world who goes shopping!'

He cracked his whip. The trumpets shrilled out and in ran Willie, looking beautiful in his shining suit and red-bordered cloak. Uncle Ursie carried in the little Mother Goose Cottage, helped by Fric and Frac. They set it down carefully, hearing a warning hiss from inside. Cackles was already there, behind the little front door, waiting for the time to appear.

Willie was really wonderful. He whistled and fluted, and it seemed as if the circus tent must be full of calling birds. He put his hands to his mouth and blew through his thumbs, making a hooting noise just like an owl. From somewhere outside the tent an owl answered him.

The audience were so quiet that everyone heard the answering owl. Then Willie sang like a nightingale in the night. It seemed impossible that a boy could make such natural bird-sounds. When he bowed low, to right and left, everyone clapped madly. 'Encore!' they cried. 'Encore!'

Willie waited for silence. Then he made other bird noises. He clucked like a hen. He crowed like a cock, he gobbled like a turkey, he quacked like a duck.

The children roared with laughter. And then Willie cackled like a goose! That was Cackles' signal to come out. Before the surprised and delighted eyes of hundreds of watching children and their parents, the little front door of the small cottage opened, and out walked Cackles herself!

She had her bonnet on nice and straight, and her shawl

was very neat. Under her wing she carried her shopping basket.

She walked down the little front path and with her beak she opened the catch of the gate. Out she went into the ring.

And now Willie was behind a little stall on which were set butter, eggs, lettuces and other things. Willie had taken off his feathered hat and put on a shopkeeper's white cap. He had tied an apron round his waist – he was a shopkeeper!

Cackles walked solemnly up to him.

'Cackle, cackle, cackle,' she said.

'A pound of butter, Madam? Certainly!' said Willie, and handed her a packet of butter. The big goose took it in her beak and put it carefully into her basket.

'Cackle, cackle,' she said again.

'An egg? Yes, Madam. New-laid today!' said Willie, and handed her an egg. The goose was very careful with it. She put that into her basket, too.

'Cackle, cackle, cackle,' she said to Willie.

'A nice fresh lettuce? Here you are, Madam. That will be two shillings altogether,' said Willie. The goose took a purse out of her basket with her beak and handed it to Willie. He took the money from it and gave it back to Cackles, who put both purse and lettuce carefully into her shopping basket.

'Cackle,' said Cackles, and walked away.

'Good day, Madam,' said Willie. Cackles walked solemnly to her little front gate. She bowed her head gracefully to left and right, undid the gate, shut it, and walked up the little path. She undid the front door, walked in, and slammed it shut.

Then what a clapping there was! What a shouting and stamping! Willie bowed dozens of times, delighted, and then ran off. Cackles came out of her little house and waddled after him, cackling loudly.

'Oh, Willie, Willie, you were marvellous! And so was Cackles!' cried Fenella, still clapping hard as the two of them came through the curtains. 'Oh, wasn't Cackles wonderful? I'd no idea she could do all that.'

'I taught her myself,' said Willie proudly.

'Isn't he fine?' said Willie's mother, who had been watching Willie through the curtains, too. She looked drab and plain in her ordinary clothes, beside all the glittering gaily-dressed circus performers. Her lovely smile lighted up her face as she looked proudly at Willie. Fenella smiled, too. Willie was her friend, and she was very, very proud to have somebody so clever for a friend.

The clowns went on again, Mr Groggy with a fresh supply of balloons. Then Fric and Frac went on to do some trick-riding with their horses. Then came the performing dogs, yelping madly with joy. The two poodles and the mongrel were the cleverest. One poodle could turn somersaults in a most remarkable manner.

'But once he starts he's difficult to stop!' said Willie. 'He gets sort of wound up. Ah, he's stopped now. Now they're going to play football. Hark at the yells!'

Every dog got a big biscuit as a reward, and carrying them jealously in their mouths, they tore off through the red curtains to eat their tit-bits in some safe corner. Fenella sighed with excitement. She hadn't known that such a world as this existed. And to think she would be able to see all this again and again and again.

The two chimpanzees were a great success, and so was Presto the juggler and conjurer. Uncle Ursie and his bears got as many claps as anyone. There was not a poor turn in the whole circus. Everyone put up a good show and when the circus folk and their animals paraded themselves once more round the ring, to bring the performance to an end, the audience stood up and cheered so loudly that Fenella had to put her fingers in her ears!

'How they've all enjoyed it!' she said to little Bobbo the bear, who was half-asleep in her arms. 'But who do you think enjoyed it most of all, Bobbo? I did! I really, really did!'

9. The Next Day

The circus show was over. The people who had come to
see it were streaming over the field towards the gate, to
catch buses that stood there waiting.

'Wonderful!' they said. 'Best show we've ever seen!
We'll come again. My, weren't those elephants good?'

The three elephants were taken by Mr Tiny to sleep
under a big tree. It was hot that night, so they would be
glad to sleep out of doors. Domo trumpeted and that
started all the rest of the excited circus animals making
their various noises, too. They were like children, easily
excited by one another, eager to join in everything that
went on.

The chimpanzees were taken off to Mr Holla's big
caravan. Fenella followed curiously, wanting to see where
they slept. She peeped inside Mr Holla's caravan, and saw
two bunks there, one on each side, both made ready for
sleeping in, with sheets, blankets and pillows.

'I sleep in this bunk,' said Mr Holla. 'And Grin and
Bearit sleep together in the other. They curl up in each
other's arms. Grin snores sometimes, but otherwise they
are very good at night.'

'Who dresses them in the morning?' asked Fenella.

'They dress themselves,' said Mr Holla. 'I've had them
since they were babies, you know, and I've taught them
just like you teach children. They even clean their teeth.'

'Oh, *do* they?' said Fenella, amazed. 'I *would* like to
see them do that.'

'Grin! Where's your toothbrush?' said Mr Holla. Grin pounced on a small toothbrush and waved it at Mr Holla, showing his teeth in his usual wide grin.

'Use it,' commanded Mr Holla, and Grin rubbed the brush over his teeth.

'Isn't he clever?' said Fenella. Grin was pleased with her praise and at once began to brush his hair, or rather the fur on his head. But as he did it with his toothbrush it didn't make much difference to it!

'You don't brush your hair with your toothbrush, Grin,' said Mr Holla in disgust.

'Fenella! Where are you?' suddenly called Aunt Lou's voice. 'Now where has that child gone?'

'I'm here, Aunt Lou,' cried Fenella. 'Oh, don't say I've got to go to bed. I do feel so excited.'

'We're all going to have a meal first,' said Aunt Lou. 'Then you must certainly go.'

It was fun having that meal, so late at night. Each caravan had its own camp-fire burning brightly outside, whilst soup heated over the flames, or a frying-pan sizzled with bacon or sausages. Fenella was too excited to eat anything except some pineapple and custard. She sat on the step of her uncle's caravan, and watched the little camp-fires burning here and there in the dark blue of the night.

Someone began to play a banjo. 'That's Micky or Tricks, I expect,' said Uncle Ursie. The tune was jerky and jolly, and one or two of the circus folk began to sing it in low voices. Fenella yawned. She would have liked to sit there the whole night and watch the fires and hear the twanging of the jolly banjo, but her eyes were shutting all by themselves.

'Get into your bunk quickly,' said Aunt Lou, giving her a push. 'Go along now. You're not used to these late hours. You'll have to go to bed early when we go on the road to our next show-place.'

'Oh, do we go to other places?' asked Fenella. 'I hadn't thought of that. Goodness, how exciting it will be to move off to somewhere else. How long are we staying here?'

'Two more weeks,' said Uncle Ursie. 'This is a good place for a circus. There are plenty of biggish towns nearby that will send people to see us. But we must move on in two weeks. Go into the caravan now. Fenny. You're yawning your head off.'

Fenny went up the steps. She thought she would never be able to go to sleep because her mind kept seeing again and again all the things that happened in the ring. But no sooner was her head tucked into her pillow than she was fast asleep. She did not stir or wake till late in the morning – so late that Aunt Lou had cleared away the breakfast, washed up, and cleaned the caravan!

Fenella looked round the spotless caravan. Uncle Ursie was whistling just outside. Fenella called to him.

'Uncle Ursie! Am I very late waking up?'

'Well, it's nearly dinner-time, Fenella!' said Uncle Ursie, with a chuckle. 'But never you mind. It's good for youngsters to sleep all they can. Makes them grow. Your aunt said if you wanted anything to eat, there's some cake in the cupboard there, and she's left you some egg sandwiches as well. There's some milk there too.'

'Uncle Ursie, have you done the bears?' asked Fenella, dressing quickly. 'I wanted to help you with Bobbo again.'

'Yes, I've done them,' said Uncle Ursie. 'But you can take Bobbo for his walk, if you like, when you've had something to eat. Keep him away from the chimps though, because they'll tease him.'

Fenella ate some breakfast, sitting on the steps of the red caravan. There was the usual noise and bustle in the camp. Willie was nowhere to be seen.

'He's gone to the hills with the dogs, taking them for a really good long walk,' said Uncle Ursie. 'He's a good boy, Willie is – always giving a hand with something.'

'Oh – I do wish I hadn't waked up so late,' said Fenella. 'I'd have liked to go with Willie and the dogs.'

'You can go plenty of other times,' said Uncle Ursie. 'Are you ready to get Bobbo? Come along then, we'll get him.'

Bobbo was delighted to see Fenella, and waddled over to her, making little grunting noises. Uncle Ursie was very pleased.

'You see if you can't teach Bobbo to do a few tricks for you,' he said. 'He's going to be a very clever little fellow.'

'Oh, I couldn't teach him anything!' said Fenella. 'I wouldn't know how to. But I love him. I never, never thought I'd love a real live bear – but this one's like a toy one, so cuddly and sweet.'

She carried Bobbo back to the caravan with her. She set him down for a moment and then went into the van and fetched out Rosebud, her best doll. She showed her to Bobbo.

Bobbo looked solemnly at the doll. He didn't understand what it was. But somebody else did! There came an excited little chattering noise, and down from the roof of the next caravan bounded Millie, one of Mrs Connie's monkeys. She sat herself on Fenella's knee and put out a little brown paw to Rosebud, touching her gently.

Fenella was startled to have the monkey jump on to her knee. She didn't know whether to be afraid or not. The monkey looked up at her with dark brown eyes, and made its little chattering noise again. Then it patted Rosebud on the cheek.

'Your paw is just like a tiny brown hand,' said Fenella, and took it into her hand. She opened the funny little fingers. Millie stared at her – but it was the doll that the monkey had come to see.

Rosebud wore a blue bonnet with little pink roses stitched on each side, over the ears. Millie the monkey pulled the string and the bonnet came undone. In a trice

the monkey had whipped it off, and had leapt in one
bound to the top of the caravan.

'Chitter-chitter-chatter!' said Millie, and put the bonnet on her own head!

'Oh!' cried Fenella, 'you naughty little thing! Give me
back Rosebud's bonnet at once!'

But Millie took no notice. She had never had such a
pretty bonnet in her life! She took it off and looked at
it. Then she put it on again, this time back to front. She
looked very quaint and comical. Fenella couldn't help
laughing. She went into the caravan with Rosebud and
Bobbo, who had to be helped up the steps, because he was
so round and fat. Fenella put Rosebud into her bunk and
covered her up.

Millie the monkey, wondering where Rosebud had
gone, let herself carefully down the side of the caravan
and peered in at the open window. How she liked that
doll! She waited till Fenella had gone out again, and
then she swung herself in through the window, still with
the doll's bonnet on her head.

She went over to the bunk, and turned back the cover,
looking at Rosebud. The doll had her eyes shut now,
because she was lying down. Millie touched her eyelashes
gently. Then she began to chatter to the doll.

Fenella was outside, looking for the naughty monkey.
She saw her aunt coming up with a big shopping basket,
and went to meet her. 'I'll take that for you,' she said.
'Look at Bobbo, Aunt Lou. He's made such friends with
me.'

Her aunt went into the red caravan and Fenella followed her with the basket. Bobbo tried to clamber up the
steps after them.

Aunt Lou gave a scream. 'Look at that monkey – with
your doll's bonnet on, Fenella! Now what did you let that
tiresome creature in here for? I won't have animals in my
caravan. I'm not like Mr Holla, wanting to have them

sleeping inside with me, nor yet like Mrs Connie, wearing them round her neck, the silly creature!'

'Oh, Aunt Lou – I didn't know that the monkey was . . .' began Fenella, surprised.

Millie leapt to the top of the cupboard, knocking over a jug that was stood there. It fell and broke. Aunt Lou gave an angry cry. 'Look at that! I've told Mrs Connie time and again she ought to keep her monkeys with her. Letting them loose like this – and you inviting them into my caravan and dressing them up in your doll's clothes. You're a naughty girl.'

'But Aunt Lou!' began poor Fenella again, almost in tears, 'I didn't—'

'You take that monkey back to Mrs Connie and tell her if I catch it loose again I'll not make a single thing more for any of her troupe!' cried Aunt Lou. 'You tell her that!'

'Oh, I couldn't say that,' said Fenella, crying. Her aunt gave her an impatient push. 'Do you want a slap?' she said. 'Do as you're told. Ah – now I've got you, you wicked little monkey! Here, Fenella, take it, and mind you deliver my message, or I'll lose my temper!'

Aunt Lou had lost her temper already, it seemed to poor Fenella. She took the chattering monkey and made her way out of the caravan, tears running down her cheek. How could she give a rude message to Mrs Connie? Her Aunt Lou oughtn't to make her say things like that!

10. Aunt Lou In A Temper

Fenella, with the monkey in her arms, and the little bear Bobbo behind her, made her way to Mrs Connie's caravans. Mrs Connie herself lived in one, and her monkeys had the other.

Mrs Connie was busy doing some washing. She didn't look a bit nice, as she had done in the ring the night before. Her bright golden wig was put carefully away in its box, the frilly skirt and little blue coat were hanging in the caravan. Mrs Connie looked the little old wizened woman that she was.

She looked up at Connie with brown eyes very like Millie the monkey's. 'Hallo,' she said, 'where has that little monkey been? Not in mischief, I hope.'

'Well – he came into my aunt's caravan,' said Fenella. 'He saw my doll Rosebud there, you see – and – and – well . . .'

'And that sour-faced, sharp-tongued aunt of yours lost her temper with you and the monkey, I suppose, and packed you off with Millie?' said Mrs Connie, guessing quite right.

'Yes,' said Fenella. 'She – she doesn't seem to like your monkeys very much, Mrs Connie.'

'I suppose she sent me a rude message?' said Mrs Connie, rinsing her soapy clothes out over the grass. 'Oh, go on – you can tell me what it is. I'm used to her rude ways. All because she doesn't like using her needle to dress my little ones!'

'She just said – that if you didn't keep your monkeys with you she wouldn't make any more clothes for them,' said Fenella, going red.

'Ho, she did, did she? Well, you go back and tell her that if she will sew herself a nice new face, with a bit of a smile on it, and put a cheerful, kindly tongue into her mouth instead of the one she's got, I'll keep my monkeys under lock and key with pleasure!' said Mrs Connie, losing her temper very suddenly, in a way she had.

'Oh – I couldn't possibly say that,' said Fenella, in alarm. Taking rude messages from one person to another was dreadful. Whatever would Aunt Lou say to Mrs Connie's message!

Mrs Connie looked Fenella up and down with scorn. 'I expect you're like your aunt – turning up your nose at this and that – nagging and scolding. How your poor uncle stands that tongue of hers is more than I can make out. He must be a poor worm!'

Aunt Lou suddenly appeared round the side of the caravan. She had heard what Mrs Connie said, and her mouth looked more screwed-up than ever.

'Not one more thing do I make for those smelly monkeys of yours, Mrs Connie!' she burst out. 'Not one! And you can go to Mr Carl Crack a dozen times, if you like, and complain. I'm not making anything more for them!'

'Smelly! They're not smelly!' cried Mrs Connie, in a rage. 'Don't they get bathed every week, and brushed twice a day! Ho, you don't know what you're talking about. Smelly, indeed! What about Ursie's bears?'

Fenella began to cry. She wasn't used to upsets like this. Mr Holla, who was nearby, strolled up with a smile on his face. He patted Fenella on the shoulder.

'Now don't you get upset,' he said kindly. 'They're always at it, these two, hammer and tongs. You go off to

Willie – look, he's back again with the dogs – and take
Bobbo with you. He likes the dogs.'

Fenella wiped her eyes and went off. Oh, dear! Why
did Aunt Lou have such a bad temper? Would she really
not make any more things for the monkeys? Surely if Mrs
Connie complained to Mr Carl Crack, he would fly into a
fearful rage too, and crack his whip all over the place!

She ran to meet Willie. The dogs greeted her joyously,
jumping up at Bobbo and trying to lick him. He screwed
himself up in Fenella's arms, and looked with surprised
eyes at the noisy little creatures below him.

Mr Crack appeared from a very grand caravan. It was
not a horse-drawn one like the others, but one that could
be pulled by a car. Behind the van was Mr Crack's
magnificent car. Willie had already shown it to Fenella.

The little girl turned to run when she saw him, for
she was still scared of him. But he put out a big hand and
pulled her to him. He was smiling all over his big face.
His shaggy eyebrows did not look so fierce as usual.

'Now what do you want to run away from me for?' he
asked, putting his hand into his pocket. 'You're Fenella,
aren't you? That's a nice name. And here's something nice for you, because I can see you're a good little
girl.'

He put a bag of big, round peppermints into her hand.
Fenella thanked him shyly. She didn't know what to think
of the broad, giant-like man, roaring like a lion one
minute, and kindly as a big dog the next. He gave her a
bear-like hug.

'I like little girls. You come and tell me if anything
goes wrong with you, and I'll put it right. That's what
they all do in this circus. Nobody's really afraid of Mr
Carl Crack! Are they, Willie Winkie?'

'Well, sir,' said Willie, hesitating, because he knew that
he himself felt very scared of Mr Carl Crack when he was
in a temper. And many a time he had skipped out of the

way of that big, curling whip, which could give a nasty nip when Mr Crack liked!

But Mr Crack was in a very good temper that morning, and nothing could make him do anything but smile. The show had been a marvellous success last night, and much money had been taken. It looked as if the next nights would be as good. So Mr Crack had left his whip behind him in his lovely caravan, and was going about with smiles all over his face.

Fenella and Willie went off with the bag of peppermints. 'I shan't let those chimps near me till I've finished these sweets this time,' she told Willie. 'Have one? Oh, look, Willie, Bobbo wants one, too!'

'He likes anything sweet,' said Willie. 'No, don't waste them on the dogs, Fenny. They'll only spit them out. And don't give any to Cackles in case she chokes.'

Fenella told him about the quarrel between her aunt and Mrs Connie. 'Oh, don't you worry about that,' said Willie. 'They're always squabbling, those two. The only thing is – Mrs Connie gets over her temper quickly, but your aunt doesn't. I'm afraid she'll give you the rough side of her tongue all day. You come and have dinner with me and my mother if she's too bad. Aggie understands.'

'It sounds funny to me, you calling your mother Aggie,' said Fenella.

'Well, Mum then,' said Willie. 'Come on, let's put the dogs away, and we'll go and watch the elephants having a bathe in the stream.'

Dicky, Dolly and Domo were very funny when they had their bathe. It wasn't really a bathe because the stream was small and the elephants enormous. What they did was to put their trunks down into the water, and take in as much as they could – and then up went their trunks and they squirted the cool water all over their backs!

'Oh! I never knew elephants could do *that* before!' said Fenella in delight. Then she gave a squeal, because

Domo had turned towards her, and was squirting water all over her! She ran behind a tree, shaking the drops from her dress, and laughing.

The elephants had a fine time. They seemed to enjoy paddling in the stream, and they squirted water over themselves till they were thoroughly wet. Then Mr Tiny led them back to their tree. Domo, seeing Bobbo the bear wandering under his feet, put his trunk down, picked the tiny bear up gently and set him on his head!

Bobbo gave a frightened grunt and Fenella gave a scream. 'Oh, he'll fall, he'll fall! Mr Tiny, quick, make him take Bobbo down. He'll fall!'

But Bobbo didn't fall, because the big, gentle elephant held him on safely with his trunk all the time. He looked at Fenella out of his wise elephant eyes, and seemed

to say. 'What! Did you really think I would let Bobbo
fall?

Fenella went back to her aunt's caravan when it was
dinner-time. She peeped inside. Aunt Lou looked very
grim indeed.

'Oh, so you're back again, are you?' she said in her
sharpest voice. 'Playing about all morning, and then
coming back to see what I've got for your dinner. You'll
start work tomorrow, my girl. Wasting your time like
this!'

'Aunt Lou, I—' began Fenella. But Aunt Lou would
never let anyone get a single word in, once she had started
scolding.

'And don't you go near Mrs Connie or her monkeys,'
she went on. 'She's a mean, disagreeable, lazy woman.
And I mean what I said – I'll not make a single thing
more for those monkeys of hers, not one! Let her thread
a needle herself for a change, and set to work. Do her
good!'

'Aunt Lou, may I go and have dinner with Willie?'
asked Fenella timidly, trying to get a few words in.

'Oh, go if you want to,' said Aunt Lou in a sour voice.
'But you come back this afternoon and do a bit of washing
for me.'

'Oh yes, aunt,' said Fenella and escaped thankfully
down the steps. She ran across the field to where Willie's
caravan stood. Cackles was outside, squatting on the
grass. Willie poked his head out of his caravan window.

'Come to have dinner with us?' he asked. 'I thought
you would! I know old Lou when she's in one of her
moods. Come on in.'

Fenella had a good meal with Aunt Aggie and Willie.
'Shall I help to wash up?' she said afterwards.

'Oh, no,' said Aunt Aggie. 'Willie will take the things
down to the stream and rinse them for me. If you want to
do something, Fenella, you could sew some buttons on his

shirt for me! 'Tisn't that I can't do it – but I just seem to put it off and off. You do it, there's a good girl.'

'Of course I will!' said Fenella, and went to work with a will. Willie took a tray of dishes out to the stream and rinsed them clean. Cackles went with him, pecking at the bits left on the plates. Willie whistled like a blackbird as he worked, and two blackbirds flew down beside him in wonder.

'Clever boy, isn't he, my Willie?' said Aunt Aggie to Fenella. 'Just like his father! Have you finished putting those buttons on? Oh, and you've mended that hole, too. My, you're a neat one with a needle! Your Aunt Lou will be glad of your help, I know.'

'I think I'll go now, Aunt Aggie,' said Fenella, getting up. 'Thank you for my nice dinner. I've got to do something for Aunt Lou now, so I'd better go.'

She sped over to her own caravan. Aunt Lou was sitting outside, sewing. 'So here you are!' she said, in a nicer voice. 'Well, go and get that bit of washing from the caravan, and do it for me. And tomorrow, as I said, Fenella – you'll start work properly, and no mistake about it!'

11. Willie Doesn't Want Lessons

The bustle and excitement of the evening's show began
all over again about tea-time. The circus folk once more
shed their drab, rather dirty old clothes, and put on their
finery. Such sparkling dresses, such shining suits, such
sweeping feathers and gay colours! Nobody would ever
think they were the same people who had wandered here
and there over the camping field in the daytime.

Fenella watched them all coming from their caravans,
and wished that she, too, had a beautiful dress to wear in
the ring. She began to plan one for herself. Then she shook
herself. 'How silly I am!' she thought. 'I shall never go
into the ring like Willie. So I shall never need a gay
glittering frock. But oh, how nice it would be to look like
a princess every evening!'

Mrs Connie appeared in her golden wig and frilly skirt.
Her monkeys were all dressed in their pretty, gay ring
costumes. Fenella wondered if her aunt had made them.
Certainly she had made them beautifully, if so. Fenella
began to think of other frocks and suits for the little
monkeys. A little red soldier suit for Jimmy would be
lovely!

Mrs Connie waved to Fenella, but the little girl didn't
dare to smile and wave back, because her Aunt Lou was
nearby. She felt sure she would get a hard slap if she did!

Then once again the show began, and Fenella stood behind the big, red curtains, hearing the people shout and
clap, watching the performers doing their clever turns.

Presto the juggler and conjurer was very skilful indeed. He could juggle with twelve balls at once, keeping them going up and down in the air, catching them and throwing them up again, never missing once. His conjuring was marvellous, too, and Fenella couldn't imagine how he could take so many yards and yards of coloured ribbon out of his mouth!

She looked at him shyly as he came out. This was the man who was to teach her and Jimmy. Did he look cross or impatient? She knew she would be afraid of him if so, because Fenella could not bear loud voices or cross looks.

Presto did not look cross or impatient. He looked rather sad. He had never smiled once in the ring, even when the cheering people had yelled 'Encore! encore!' at the tops of their voices. He stalked through the curtains, solemnly, his long, black cloak, lined with bright scarlet, sweeping behind him. He was a tall, thin man, with piercing dark eyes. and hair as black as night. He wore in the ring the tall, pointed hat, set with brilliant stars, that enchanters or wizards are supposed to wear.

'He looks a bit frightening,' whispered Fenella to Willie, who was standing beside her with Cackles. 'I wish we hadn't got to learn lessons with him, Willie.'

Willie had heard about this idea from his mother and he wasn't at all pleased. He wrinkled up his freckled nose in dismay.

'Fancy having to waste time learning *lessons*! I've never been to school. Have you, Fenella?'

'Oh yes, of course I have,' said Fenella. 'I thought everyone had to go to school. How did you learn anything if you didn't go, Willie?'

'Oh, Mum taught me a bit – but she doesn't know much herself, really,' said Willie. 'And once we had a nice tightrope walker called Anna, and she helped me a lot. We can't very well go to school properly, us circus children, because we're always moving on from place to place, you see.'

'Can you read?' asked Fenella. Willie went rather red.

'Course I can,' he said. 'Don't be silly.'

A loud burst of clapping told them that Uncle Ursie was coming out with his bears. Through the red curtains he came, bowing low, with Clump and Bobbo. Bobbo saw Fenella and went to her at once, getting a hard peck from Cackles because he pushed against her! But Bobbo didn't mind. His fur was much too thick to feel anything like that!

'Fancy being able to see all this every evening!' sighed Fenella in delight. 'I shall never, never get tired of it, Willie.'

'Oh, it will seem quite ordinary to you after a time,' said Willie laughing. 'It's all so new, isn't it? You wait till you've been with the circus for a month or two – why, you won't even bother to come and peep through these red curtains then! You'll go to bed early, and sleep soundly in your caravan, whilst we're doing the show.'

'I shan't!' said Fenella, indignantly. 'I shall always, always want to see you all doing your turns – especially you and Cackles, Willie, and Uncle Ursie and the bears. I do think Clump is clever the way he turns head over heels.'

'Did you notice one of the dogs in the ring tonight?' said Willie. 'He wouldn't stop turning somersaults, he was so excited. And even when we all played football he went on turning head-over-heels without stopping. He always does that when he's excited.'

Fenella was glad to tumble into bed again that night. 'Work tomorrow!' she thought. 'Lessons with Presto. Or do I call him Mr Presto? Is that his real name, I wonder? All the circus people seem to have such queer names. And I shall have to start on some sewing with Aunt Lou, too – mostly mending, I suppose. But there will be new dresses to make after this show, I expect. I shall like that. I wish I could make a suit for Bobbo. Oh, wouldn't he be sweet all dressed up! But perhaps he wouldn't like it. The monkeys love it, so do the chimps.'

She fell asleep. She didn't wake up quite so late the next day, as she had done the morning before, and was actually in time to have some breakfast.

'Have you spoken to Presto about the children?' asked Aunt Lou, as Uncle Ursie got up to go to his beloved bears.

'Yes. He's quite willing. He's got books and pencils, he says,' said Uncle Ursie. 'Fenella and Willie are to go at ten o'clock this morning.'

'Uncle Ursie! Is he kind?' asked Fenella, anxiously. 'He looks so sort of – well, solemn and sad you know.'

'I've never seen him smile, now I come to think of it,' said Uncle Ursie, rubbing his big nose, trying to remember a smile of Presto's. 'No, not even when Grin got hold of Mrs Connie's golden wig and put it on his own head. We all laughed fit to kill ourselves – but Presto just looked as solemn as ever.'

'He's very clever,' said Aunt Lou. 'He can speak Latin and Greek. He's a gentlemanly fellow, too – not really one of us. He's a good teacher, though, Fenella, so you learn all you can from him. And see that Willie goes regularly, if you can. It's really time that boy could read properly.'

'He says he can,' said Fenella in surprise. 'And he's so very, very clever, I'm sure he'll be better at everything, and beat me easily.'

'Well, you'll see,' said Aunt Lou. 'Now you've just got time to help me clean the caravan, Fenella, then you go over to Presto's caravan. And this afternoon I want you to help me with the mending. It seems as if everyone in the show last night tore a hole in their clothes or ripped a button off!'

Fenella went to find Willie just before ten o'clock. He

was giving Cackles a paddle in the stream. She loved that.

'Oh, Willie, it's time to come to Presto,' said Fenella anxiously. She hated being late for anything.

'I'm not coming,' said Willie.

Fenella stared at him in dismay. 'Why not?' she asked. 'Oh, Willie – I can't go alone!'

'I don't want to come,' said Willie, not looking at Fenella at all. 'Waste of time, that's what it would be. Can't I earn my own living, and help to keep my mother, too? Don't we get on all right without lessons? I'm not coming.'

Fenella's eyes filled with tears. She was very disappointed. Lessons without Willie wouldn't be any fun at all.

'Willie, I don't want to go without you,' she said in a very small voice. 'Do come.'

'Why do you bother to go yourself?' said Willie, sounding rather scornful. He splashed Cackles all over with water, and the goose cackled in delight.

'Well, you know I've got to,' said Fenella. 'Aunt Lou would scold like anything if I didn't. I daresay she'd slap me, too. And anyway, Willie, lessons are fun. I like reading and doing sums. And I like writing too. And I do love hearing about other countries and other people.'

'Well, you go then,' said Willie, and he still didn't look at Fenella. She couldn't think why Willie was like this; it puzzled her.

'Look at me, Willie,' she said suddenly. 'Why don't you look at me when you speak, as you usually do?'

Willie glanced up at her and then looked away again. But he saw the disappointed face of the little girl and the tears shining in her eyes. He grunted.

Fenella stood for a moment longer, and then, as Willie still went on splashing the goose, she turned to go.

'Well, good-bye then,' she said, still in a small voice. 'I shan't enjoy lessons a bit without you.'

She walked across the field to Presto's caravan. It was a black one, painted with silver and gold stars, moons and suns. At the door sat a big black cat, sunning itself. It always went into the ring with Presto and sat there solemnly, whilst he performed. Then it stalked out with him.

Fenella felt rather miserable. She didn't want to have lessons all alone with the solemn conjurer. She looked at the shut door of the caravan, and the cat sitting silently on the step. Should she knock? Would the cat mind her stepping over it? It looked as solemn as Presto himself!

She stood there for a moment, not quite knowing what to do. Then she heard footsteps behind her, and a hand slipped through her arm.

'I'm coming, Fenny,' said Willie's voice. 'I hate to see you going off all alone! I'm coming, too!'

'Oh *Willie*!' said Fenella in delight, her face beaming. 'Thank you! Now I feel quite different. Why have you changed your mind?'

Willie didn't tell her. His kind heart couldn't bear to see the little girl go off alone, looking so disappointed and sad. The boy grinned at her and knocked loudly at Presto's door, making the cat jump in fright and leap down the steps.

'Here we go!' said Willie. 'And let's hope I please Presto, because I don't want to be turned into a cat like old Cinders there!'

'Come in!' said a quiet, low voice. They opened the door and went in. Now for lessons with the conjurer! Fenella wondered if they would enjoy them. She did hope so!

12. At School With The Conjurer

Presto the conjurer was not dressed in his long, black, red-lined cloak now, nor was he wearing the tall pointed hat Fenella had seen him in the evening before. He sat at a table, dressed in a dark blue jersey and dark blue trousers, looking a little like a fisherman. His piercing eyes looked at both children, and Fenella felt sure he could see what she was thinking!

'Good morning,' he said. 'I am glad you have come. You are Fenella, are you not?'

His voice and way of speaking were not a bit like the voices of the other circus folk. He did not smile, but neither did he look cross. He just looked serious and solemn.

'Yes. I'm Fenella,' said the little girl shyly. 'It's kind of you to say you'll teach us, Mr Presto.'

'Can you read?' asked the conjurer. He pushed a book over to her, and flipped open a page. 'Read me a little of this, if you can.'

Fenella looked at it. It was very easy! She read out clearly from the page. 'The cat saw a rat and it ran under a mat. The cat could not get the rat. The dog came up and—'

'Oh, that's too easy for you, I can see,' said Presto. 'Try this one.'

He gave her another book. Fenella read from it at once. 'The princess was lost in the wood. She looked all round, but the big dark trees shut out the sunlight, and she did not know which way to go. Suddenly—'

'Why, you can read as well as I can!' said Presto, sounding as if he was smiling. But he wasn't. He looked just as solemn as ever. 'That is very good. You are the first circus child I have known who has been able to read without stumbling at your age.'

'Well, I'm not really a circus child,' explained Fenella. 'Not till a few days ago, anyway. I lived with my aunt in a house and I went to school. I was top of my form sometimes, Mr Presto.'

'And now Willie,' said Presto, handing Willie the first book he had given to Fenella. Willie took the book. Fenella saw that a wave of red was creeping over his face and even his neck. What *could* be the matter?

Willie cleared his throat. 'The cat,' he began, 'er, the cat saw a rat ...'

'Wait,' said Presto. 'That is what Fenella read. I have turned the page since then. Now the tale is about a dog.'

'Oh,' said Willie. He glued his eyes to the page. 'The dog,' he began, and stopped. Fenella peeped at where he was reading. 'The dog ran,' she helped him.

'The dog ran – to – the – er, er to the, er – p—' stammered Willie. Fenella stared at him in surprise. Could it be that the wonderful, marvellous Willie Winkie the Whistler couldn't read even such little short words? Willie wouldn't look at Fenella.

'Oh, Willie! You *can't* read – and you said you could!' said Fenella.

'I thought I could,' mumbled Willie. Presto took the book from his hands.

'You will soon be able to,' he said. 'If you come to me each day, Willie, you will learn much. You are a clever boy, as we all know. You will learn easily.'

Willie cheered up a little. He took a quick look at Fenella to see if she was scornful of him. But she wasn't. She squeezed his arm.

'Oh, Willie. I shall be able to help you. Perhaps Aunt

Lou would let me come to your caravan in the evenings with a book and we'll read it together. Oh, I'm glad I can do something better than you can, Willie, because now I shan't feel so small and silly. You see, everyone in this circus seems to be able to do something really wonderful, except me – even Cackles your goose. I can't help feeling glad that I can read better than you!'

Willie gave her his old cheerful grin. So long as Fenella didn't despise him for having so little learning, that was all right! Willie couldn't bear to be looked down on. The little girl smiled back.

'I'll soon read better than you can!' said Willie. 'Shan't I, Presto?'

'We will see,' said Presto. 'Fenella, let me see how well you can write, whilst I help Willie a little with his reading.'

Fenella settled down at the table with a pencil and an exercise book. She liked lessons. She meant to show Presto what beautiful writing she could do. She wrote carefully whilst Willie stammered through an easy page of reading.

Cinders, the big black cat, sauntered in and sat down on the table beside Fenella. The cat had the brightest green eyes that Fenella had ever seen. 'Is he magic?' asked the little girl. 'He looks as if he is.'

'Then perhaps he is,' said Presto. 'We will draw a chalk ring round him, when we have finished lessons this morning – that is if you are a good girl – and we will say a few magic words, and see what happens.'

Fenella felt excited. This was better than lessons at school. She had never had a magic cat sitting beside her there, waiting to have a chalk ring drawn round him. She bent to her writing again, listening to Willie's voice.

Presto was a good teacher. He was very patient, and he did not scold at all. Fenella looked at his solemn face, and she liked him. She liked the nice clean look he had, and his neat clothes, and she liked his quiet, well-spoken voice. He didn't seem like a circus performer at all.

Willie's writing was even worse than his reading. His arithmetic was queer. He could do any sum in his head, quickly and well – but he couldn't work out one that Presto set down on paper, not even the very easiest!

'Yes, my boy, you have a good and quick brain, and I tell you this – if you use it well and train it, you will go far,' said Presto, in his serious voice. 'But if you do not train it, it will not be of much use or pleasure to you. Only you can choose.'

Willie was tired of lessons. He didn't like being cooped up in the caravan, when he could be out in the hills with dogs, or racing over the field with the horses. He looked at Presto, and felt that it would be a great bore to go on and on with lessons.

'Well. I'll try,' he said at last. 'But lots of the circus folk get on quite well without much book-learning, Presto.'

'They would get on even better with it,' said Presto. 'Now, Fenella, you have been a good girl, and you have written me out a fine page of writing – we will see if Cinders is a magic cat or not!'

Presto put Cinders down from the table, and then moved it across to the end of the caravan. He took up the rug below, showing a black-painted, highly-polished floor.

He made a curious noise with his tongue and Cinders strolled into the middle of the floor and sat down, curling his tail round him. He looked up at his master with his queer green eyes.

Presto drew a chalk circle round him. Then he chanted a queer string of words that Fenella thought must be magic. She listened half-fearfully. Willie watched with a smile on his face. He had seen many of Presto's wonderful tricks before.

The cat miaowed loudly three times. Then Presto spoke softly to him.

'Cinders, my cat, have you a present for the good little girl? Tell me, have you a present?'

'Miaow!' said Cinders loudly, and looked at Fenella.

'Well, come from the magic ring then, and let us see what you have got for Fenella,' said Presto. The cat got up and walked out of the ring, its long black tail waving in the air. Where it had been sitting was a little white hankerchief, folded very small.

'There is your present, Fenella,' said Presto. 'Take it!'

'How did it get there?' asked Fenella, in wonder. 'It wasn't there before Cinders went and sat down. It's magic!'

She picked up the little handkerchief and opened it. In

one corner was embroidered a tiny black cat with green
eyes, just like Cinders!

'Oh, it's lovely!' said Fenella, pleased. 'Is it really for
me? Oh, thank you, Mr Presto. Thank you, Cinders.'

Willie grinned to hear Fenella thanking Cinders, who
was now sitting with his back to them all, as if he was
tired of being with them. Presto did not smile, but his
eyes looked in a kindly way at Fenella.

'Come tomorrow,' he said. 'It is a pleasure to teach a
good little girl like you.'

The children left the caravan together. 'His face doesn't
smile at all, but his voice often does,' said Fenella. 'Oh,
isn't it a fine hanky? The best I've ever had. Willie, didn't
you like having lessons with Mr Presto?'

'No, I didn't,' said Willie. 'My, I'm stiff with sitting so
long! I'm going up in the hills with the dogs. Coming,
Fenny?'

But Fenella couldn't because it was almost dinner-time,
and she didn't want to get into trouble with Aunt Lou.
'Isn't it your dinner-time, too?' she asked Willie.

'Oh, Mum doesn't mind what time we have our meals,'
said Willie. 'Hallo, Cackles! Did you miss me? Maybe
tomorrow I'll take you to lessons, too. Then you'll learn a
lot!'

Fenella laughed and sped off to her aunt's caravan.
She had enjoyed her morning, and she had the lovely little
hanky to show her aunt that she really had pleased
Presto. And this afternoon she would be able to work on
some of the lovely circus clothes and get them ready for
the night. Then she would be able to peep through those
curtains again and watch the show. She would never get
tired of that, never, whatever Willie said!

13.   The Days Go On

Soon a whole week had gone by. Fenella felt as if she had lived in the circus camp for months. She began to get used to the different life, and she liked it.

She helped her aunt with the caravan in the morning, and at ten o'clock she went with Willie to Presto's caravan. He took Cackles the goose on the second day, and as soon as Cinders saw her, he spat and hissed.

To his great surprise Cackles hissed back, even more loudly. Cinders arched his back and made his tail three times its usual size. The goose cackled loudly and Cinders leapt back in fright. He had never seen the goose so closely before, for Cinders was a home-cat and hardly ever left the caravan.

Then Cackles put her head neatly under her wing, meaning to settle down and go to sleep, whilst Willie did whatever he wanted to do in this strange caravan. Cinders was amazed to see the goose's head disappear.

'Aha! The goose can also do magic, Cinders,' said Presto, in what Fenella called his 'smiling voice.' 'Willie, if you want your goose to come to lessons, she must wait outside for you. I cannot have Cinders spitting and hissing like damp wood on a fire all the time!'

So Cackles had to wait outside. She squatted down on the top step in the sun, much to Cinders' annoyance, for that was his own favourite place. But nothing would shift the big, heavy goose once she had taken up her place. Cinders did not like the look of that quick beak, either!

In the afternoons Fenella settled down with her aunt to do the circus mending. There always seemed plenty to do. Aunt Lou grumbled because she said the circus folk were so careless with their clothes.

'If they had to sew up their holes themselves, and stitch back the ripped frills, they'd be more careful,' she said, threading her needle. 'And look at this skirt of Mrs Connie's. I believe she tears it on purpose! This is the third day she's sent it in for mending.'

'I'll do it, Aunt Lou,' said Fenella, knowing that her aunt would go on grumbling all the time, if she had to spend an hour or two on Mrs Connie's clothes. The monkey woman had not dared to send in any of her monkeys' clothes since her quarrel with Aunt Lou. One or two of them were beginning to look rather ragged, but Fenella didn't like to offer to mend them herself. She was afraid of making another upset between the two.

At tea-time they stopped work and Fenella watched the circus folk getting ready as usual for their evening show. There was always such a bustle then, and the little girl was surprised to see how often the circus folk lost or forgot something they needed for the ring that night.

'Where's my balancing stick?' Mr Wriggle would moan. 'I put it down somewhere. I can't walk the tight-rope without it. Anybody seen it?'

'Oh – that must have been what Grin or Bearit was carrying!' Fenella would say. 'I wondered what it was. Oh dear, Mr Wriggle, I hope those chimps haven't broken it!'

'They've hidden it in Mr Holla's caravan, I expect,' Mr Wriggle would say. 'That's where they always hide their treasures. Thanks, Fenella. I say – you wouldn't like to see me tread on my head, would you?'

'Oh *no*, thank you, Mr Wriggle,' Fenella would say. 'I should hate it. Please don't keep asking me that.'

But Wriggle always did ask her. She had never seen

him tread on his head yet, and she hoped she never would.
She thought he was very, very clever the way he wriggled
his rubbery body into all sorts of queer positions, but she
didn't like it. He was a most remarkable acrobat, and
great friends with everyone.

Wriggle wasn't the only one who was always losing
things. Mrs Connie lost things regularly, and so did
Aggie, Willie's mother. Fenella got quite good at finding
what was lost, and everyone agreed that the little girl
was very useful. Aunt Lou began to feel rather proud
of her.

She didn't say so, though. She was still as sharp-tongued
as ever, and if Fenella sewed a wrong button on, or made
a frill a little crooked, she would fly out at her in a great
rage. Uncle Ursie used to look quite troubled when he
heard Aunt Lou scolding the little girl.

'Now, you turn that tongue of yours on me instead,' he
would say. 'I don't mind it, Lou. I'm used to it. All you
say runs off my back like water off Cackles' feathers. But
Fenella isn't used to it. She's a good little thing and you
shouldn't scold her like that.'

'It's good for children to get a good scolding now and
again,' Aunt Lou would say. 'And don't you interfere
with me, Ursie, or you'll be sorry!'

On Saturdays two shows were given, one in the afternoon, and one in the evening. So there were no lessons
that day, and any sewing and mending that had to be
done was done in the mornings. The circus folk were tired
on Saturday night. Tempers were sometimes short then.
Fenella heard Micko and Tricks, two of the clowns,
quarrelling in loud voices, and she was alarmed.

'I'll leave!' shouted Micko. 'I won't work with you
again, Tricks! Getting all the laughs for yourself, and behaving as if you hadn't got a partner. I'll go off to
Nicky's show, and leave you by yourself!'

'Oh dear! Will he really do that?' Fenella asked Uncle

Ursie. 'Micko's so fond of Tricks. They've been together for years, haven't they?'

'They'll have made it up by tomorrow night,' said Uncle Ursie, comfortingly. 'There's plenty of hot tempers in a circus like this, but they simmer down usually. If they don't, Mr Crack comes along, and he soon settles things, I can tell you!'

And sure enough, by the next night, after a quiet, peaceful Sunday, with church bells ringing from the villages around, Micko and Tricks were as good friends as ever, and Fenella, to her joy, saw them walking round the camp, arm in arm as usual. She really couldn't bear anyone to quarrel.

'I shall never quarrel with you, Willie,' she said to him. 'And you'll never quarrel with me, will you?'

'I shouldn't think so,' said Willie. 'But you never know! Things blow up suddenly, you know.'

'Well – it takes two to make a quarrel – and you can quarrel all you like with me, but I shan't quarrel back!' said Fenella. 'Willie, when do we move on? It will be fun to feel our caravan moving along on its wheels. I've never been in one that went along the road.'

'We'll be on the road in a week's time,' said Willie. 'And I believe we're going to a seaside place, Fenella. You'll like that. We can take the dogs for their run on the sands each day – or up on to the cliffs. And maybe we'll bathe. I can't swim though. Can you?'

'Yes,' said Fenella, happy to think that here was one more thing she could do that Willie couldn't. 'I'll teach you. It's easy. Cackles can swim with us!'

The days flew past. Nothing much happened those last few days except that Grin disgraced himself by escaping from the camp, going to a nearby house, and picking every single flower in the garden there. He came back delighted with himself, carrying a most enormous bunch of all kinds of flowers.

Mr Crack was not pleased. He roared at poor Mr Holla. 'Look after your chimps better than that! Are we to have the police here, because of them? You will pay to the lady of that house whatever she asks you for the flowers.'

Grin was sternly punished. His cap was taken away, and he hated that, for he was always very proud of wearing a cap. He was made to stay in his cage the whole of one day, instead of going about the camp with Willie or Mr Holla or anyone who would take him. Everyone was forbidden to speak to him for that day.

Fenella was very sorry for him. She felt sure Grin hadn't meant to be naughty. She had seen the flowers and liked them, so he had picked them. But Grin did know better than that! He had done it out of mischief, and Mr Holla knew he must punish him.

The last show in that district was a great success. Everyone did better than usual. Mr Groggy gave away twice as many balloons. Mrs Connie's monkeys threw bars of chocolate to the cheering children on the benches. Millie bit hers in half before she threw it, and kept a bit for herself. Mrs Connie found it stuffed into Millie's little hat that night!

Dicky, Domo and Dolly hit balls out to the audience, and Mr Tiny yelled that any boy or girl who caught one could keep it. Altogether it was an exciting and glorious evening, and Mr Crack was in such a good temper that he didn't stop smiling once the whole evening. In fact, Presto was the only one who neither smiled nor laughed, but Fenella thought that even he had a twinkle in his eye.

'Why don't you smile?' she asked him, when he came to stand by her, to listen to the cheering that followed the elephants' fine performance. 'You never smile, Mr Presto. *Can't* you?'

Presto said nothing. Willie pulled at Fenella's sleeve.

'Don't ask him that,' he whispered. 'Something dreadful once happened to him, and he vowed he would never smile again. So he never will!'

Fenella felt sorry she had said anything. She crept away, looking back at the tall, solemn figure in the great black cloak and pointed hat. There were times when Fenella really did think Presto was an enchanter out of Fairyland. He looked so very striking with his deep dark eyes and his jet-black hair.

The circus had done very well indeed in those two weeks. Mr Crack made a most generous share-out, and everyone received a good amount of money. Even Aunt Lou was pleased, and she gave Fenella a shilling for herself.

'Oh, thank you!' said Fenella. And then Uncle Ursie gave her two shillings! Fenella felt that she was rich. She would buy ice creams for herself and Willie. And did Cackles like them, too? She knew Grin and Bearit did, and as for little Bobbo, he would lick a dozen up if he could.

'Tomorrow we pack up and go off,' said Uncle Ursie to Fenella. 'That's a job, I can tell you! The animals don't like it, either. They'll make a fine old noise. You can take charge of Bobbo, if you like. He's so fond of you now he'll do anything for you, and you will be able to keep him quiet and happy.'

'Oh, I will,' promised Fenella happily. She looked forward to the move. It might be a tiresome job for the circus folk – but it would be all new to Fenella.

'Our caravan will roll away on its wheels,' she told Rosebud, her doll, in bed that night. 'How will you like that? A house that moves by itself, and goes for miles and miles. Won't it be exciting!'

14. The Circus Goes On The Road

The next day the circus folk were busier than Fenella had yet seen them. The big top, the great circus tent, had to be taken down. All the benches had to be stored neatly on big lorries. The various circus properties such as steel posts for the tightrope wire, the tennis net the elephants used for their game, odd tables and chairs, had to be packed into another lorry.

The camp was due to set off at a certain time. All the vans, carts, cars and lorries were to start one after another. The lorries would go on in front, Mr Crack's lovely car-drawn caravan would follow, and then all the horse-drawn caravans and carts.

'What about the elephants?' asked Fenella, watching Uncle Ursie sliding shut the side of the bears' cage. 'Do they go in a travelling cage, too? I haven't seen one big enough for them.'

'Oh, no. They walk,' said Uncle Ursie. 'They are rather slow, so they'll start last, and catch us up at night.'

Grin and Bearit were shut up in Mr Holla's caravan. The door was locked, and the windows were fastened, so that the chimps were safe. Fenella saw their hairy faces peeping out of the window, looking rather dismal.

The monkeys were all in their own little caravan. The dogs were in their travelling cage, restless and rather bad-tempered at being shut up, after their long time of freedom. The lovely circus horses were to be ridden in a long string by Fric, Frac and Malvina.

'Who's going to drive Mr Crack's lovely golden carriage?' asked Fenella. 'We're going to take that too, aren't we?'

'Of course!' said Uncle Ursie. 'Maybe Willie will drive it. He did last time. Malvina says it bores her to do a thing like that when she can take the string of horses along with Fric and Frac!'

'Oh – is Willie *really* going to drive the golden carriage?' cried Fenella. 'Uncle Ursie, do you think he would let me drive it with him?'

'I didn't know you *could* drive!' said Uncle Ursie. He was putting the old brown horse that belonged to him and Aunt Lou, into the shafts of their red caravan. 'Hey, get up there. Anyone would think you'd never been between shafts before, Dobbin!'

'I *can't* drive,' said Fenella. 'I really meant – would Willie let me sit with him? Oh, I would so love that! You don't suppose I could sit in that carriage, do you?'

'I don't see why not,' said Uncle Ursie. 'Why, would it make you feel very grand, Fenny?'

'Oh yes – I'd feel like a princess!' cried Fenella. Then her face fell. 'But do you think Aunt Lou would mind, Uncle Ursie? She has been rather cross today.'

'Oh, nobody likes moving day,' said Uncle Ursie. 'There you are, Dobbin, you're in at last. Now don't you go galloping off till I'm ready!'

Fenella smiled. Dobbin didn't look as if he could gallop two steps! He was the fattest barrel of a horse Fenella had ever seen. She liked him. He had big brown eyes, and he nuzzled into her shoulder when she went near. Fenella was often very surprised at herself nowadays. She did things she would never have dreamt of doing three weeks before. Why, she would never go within yards of a horse before she came to the circus! Now she spoke to every one of them, and had learnt to caress them in the same affectionate way as all the circus folk.

Fenella sat on the steps of her caravan and watched the busy scene in the field. The lorries were moving off through the gate, heavily laden, each covered up in tarpaulin sheets to keep everything safe and dry. Then went Mr Carl Crack's car, driven by himself, his fine caravan bumping heavily over the ruts in the field.

He raised his top-hat as he went out of the gate. 'See you later!' he roared to everyone, and they waved back. Then down the narrow lane went his caravan, drawn by the powerful car.

Dicky, Dolly and Domo, the three elephants, were waiting patiently under the tree for the time to come when they could walk out of the gate, too. Domo trumpeted loudly. Mr Tiny patted him on the trunk.

'Now don't be so impatient. You know we go last of all. We'll be there in good time.'

Then the brightly-coloured caravans began to move out of the field gate, one by one, drawn by the caravan horses – quite different creatures from the proud, shining circus horses. Dobbin and Clover, Daisy and Brownie, Star and Grumps, all the ordinary horses, now came into their own, and hauled along the caravans, walking slowly and peacefully.

'When do the circus horses go?' asked Fenella, watching everything, and waiting impatiently for her caravan's turn to come.

'They're going a different way, over the commons and through the woods,' said Uncle Ursie. 'Better for them than hard roads. There they go now. Malvina's on the leading horse. What that girl can't do with horses isn't worth doing! They say she was put on a horse before she was two months old!'

Malvina, looking as spruce and smart as ever, sat lightly on the beautiful leading horse. She was one of the few circus folk who looked as lovely out of the ring as in it. She and Fric and Frac spent most of the time with their beloved horses, and Fenella had had hardly a word with them at all. They were always so busy.

More caravans passed out of the gate. There went the two caravans belonging to Mrs Connie. Fenella could hear all the monkeys chattering together excitedly in one of them. Mrs Connie, looking more like a monkey than ever, drove the first caravan. Micko drove the monkeys' van, with Tricks whistling beside him.

Mr Groggy's van went. Presto's striking black one slid out of the gate, too, drawn by a jet-black horse. Presto drove the caravan himself, looking as solemn as ever, and beside him, solemn and serious, too, sat Cinders the black cat.

'I'm sure Cinders is a witch-cat,' thought Fenella, watching. 'Oh, there go the chimps. Poor Grin and Bearit, they don't like being locked up.'

Then came Fenella's turn. The travelling cage of the bears was driven by Uncle Ursie, and the red caravan by Aunt Lou. A little white pony pulled the bears' van, trotting quickly along, tossing its white mane.

'He used to belong to Malvina's string of snow-white ponies,' said Uncle Ursie. 'But he's too old now for the ring. So I bought him from Malvina for the bears' van. He's glad to stay with the circus. He'd be very lonely without all the people he knows.'

Fenella climbed into the red caravan. She wanted to feel the very first movement it made. Aunt Lou clicked to Dobbin. He took a step forward and pulled the cart. Fenella felt it moving – then it ran bumpily along on its four wheels. They were off !

'Our house is rumbling away on its journey !' said Fenella to herself in delight. 'It feels lovely. Bumpity-bump, shakity-shake, there it goes over the field where we have stayed so long. Oh, I do like it better than a house with its roots in the ground. It's fun to have a house that moves ! Go on, Dobbin, go on !'

They passed the little golden carriage into which Willie was now putting the six snow-white ponies. Fenella yelled to him as she passed.

'Willie, we're going! Do, do catch us up. And Willie, could I sit with you and Cackles sometime, please?'

'Goodness, child, don't yell in my ear like that,' said Aunt Lou. Fenella dropped off the caravan and ran to Willie.

'Willie, did you hear me? Can I come with you part of the time?'

'Course you can,' said Willie. 'There'll be room on the driving seat for both you and Cackles, too. And maybe you'd like to ride in the golden carriage whenever we pass through a town or village. That will make everyone stare!'

'Oh, Willie, could I?' said Fenella in delight. 'I did just wonder if I could. Do keep close behind us if you can, for I'm sure Aunt Lou won't let me out of her sight if she can help it.'

'Fenella! FENELLA!' yelled Uncle Ursie's deep voice. 'Come along. We're waiting.'

'Coming!' called Fenella, and raced across the field to the gate. She clambered up beside Uncle Ursie, in front of the bears' van, for she saw that Aunt Lou had rather an impatient look on her face, and she did not want to drive with her.

Off they went. Out of the gate and down the lane, right to the bottom of the hill and up another one. The wind blew freshly, and the sun shone down warmly. Buttercup fields spread golden on every side. Fenella felt very happy indeed.

Aunt Lou called her. 'Fenella! I haven't had time to tidy up the caravan this morning. You go in and do it, there's a good girl.'

Fenella skipped down from beside Uncle Ursie and ran a few steps in front. She climbed up into the red caravan, and began to tidy it. It was queer to stand in it whilst it rumbled and jolted about, but it was fun. Fenella noticed that Aunt Lou had put away everything that might fall and break.

'I've done it, Aunt Lou,' she said, and climbed up beside her aunt. 'Isn't this lovely? I do like going on a journey like this, don't you?'

'Well, I've done it so many times that I don't really notice it,' said Aunt Lou. But all the same she seemed to like the peaceful jogtrot of the horse, and looked round at the buttercup fields with pleasure.

'My little girl used to like those,' she said, with a nod of her head. Fenella wanted to ask her about her little girl, but she didn't like to. So she said nothing. Dobbin jogged on and on, and after some time Fenella began to feel hungry. Suddenly her aunt put the reins into her hands.

'You drive now, Fenella,' she said. 'I'll go and get something for us to eat.'

'Oh, Aunt Lou! I can't drive Dobbin!' cried Fenella in fright. But Aunt Lou had jumped down and was going to the door of the caravan. Fenella *had* to drive! She stared ahead in fright, clutching the reins.

But Dobbin didn't need any driving. He knew that all he had to do was to follow the van in front, and to go at the same slow pace. It didn't matter to him whether Aunt Lou held the reins, or Fenny. In fact it didn't really matter whether *anyone* held the reins. Dobbin would go on for miles all by himself!

So in a few minutes Fenella got over her fright and began to enjoy herself. She was driving a caravan! Whatever would her Aunt Janet say if she saw her – and all the children she had once known at school, too!

'I feel important!' said Fenella to herself. 'I really do. I belong to a circus. I'm driving a real live horse in a caravan! I wish Rosebud was beside me. Aunt Lou! *Please* could I have Rosebud? Do let me!'

And for once in a way Aunt Lou smiled and gave Rosebud to Fenella through one of the little front windows. There they sat, side by side, Fenella and Rosebud, enjoying themselves immensely. What a lovely journey!

15. Fenella In Trouble

Presently a shout came from the front of the long line of horses and caravans. It was passed along from one to another.

'We're stopping on the common! We're stopping on the common!'

When the procession came to the big open common, the caravans were all drawn up to the side. The horses were taken out for a rest and a feed, and were set free. They were all too well-trained to wander away, but kept near the circus folk, cropping the grass peacefully.

May trees were still out, and the scent of them filled the air as Fenella sat down on the dry, wiry grass with Willie, Cackles, Aunt Aggie, Aunt Lou and Uncle Ursie. There were sardine sandwiches, egg sandwiches, sausage rolls and two kinds of cake. There was a bag of oranges, too, so the two children had a good feast.

Cackles pulled at the grass around, but did not seem to like it very much. She came to share Willie's sandwiches. Willie offered her a lettuce and she took it greedily, tearing it to bits with her strong yellow beak.

'She loves lettuce,' said Willie to Fenella.

'Does she like ice-cream?' asked Fenella, remembering the three shillings she had.

'No,' said Willie. 'Good thing, too. She'd gobble down about a dozen if she did!'

'Bobbo likes them,' said Fenella. 'Uncle Ursie said so.

I'm going to buy ice creams for us, Willie, next time I see an ice-cream man!'

They lazed on the sunny grass, enjoying their rest. Some of the horses lay down. The animals in the caravans cried to be let out. They could never understand why they had to be shut up during the journeys from place to place.

Fenella thought of Bobbo. She was sure she could hear him whimpering. 'Uncle Ursie! Please, please do go and get Bobbo,' she begged. 'I'm sure he's unhappy. I want to give him an ice-cream, and I expect an ice-cream man will come along soon.'

'Too lazy to move!' said Uncle Ursie, sleepily. He was lying on his back on the grass, his eyes shut. Aunt Lou was talking to Willie's mother. Fenella didn't like to bother Uncle Ursie any more about Bobbo. What a pity! She heard the bell of an ice-cream man, and jumped up. 'Six sixpenny ice-creams, please,' she said, and the man took six from his ice-cold barrel.

Fenella gave one to Willie. He was thrilled. 'Just what I wanted,' he said. 'Thanks, Fenny.'

'One for you, Aunt Aggie,' said Fenella, 'and one for you Aunt Lou.'

The two women looked up, surprised. 'Well, if that isn't generous of you, Fenella!' said Aunt Aggie. 'Thank you. Spending your money on us like that! I declare that's just like your own little Carol used to do, Lou. Soon as she had a penny, off she'd go and spend it on someone.'

'Yes,' said Aunt Lou, and she looked pleased, too. 'That's nice of you, Fenella. But remember that you must save money as well as spend it!'

'Oh yes, Aunt,' said Fenella hastily, hoping that Aunt Lou wouldn't ask her how much money she had left out of her three shillings. She would have to say none at all!

'Uncle Ursie! Here's an ice-cream for you,' said Fenella, and pommelled him. 'Do wake up, or it will be melted. And Uncle Ursie, please can I go and give this one to Bobbo? I bought it for him.'

'Good gracious! One for Bobbo!' said Uncle Ursie, opening his eyes. 'Well, here's the key of the cage. Go and give the ice-cream to him.'

Fenella took the key and went back to where the bears' caravan was drawn up to the side of the road. She slid the key into the lock and turned it. She opened the door and went in. Bobbo was in a corner, rolled up in a ball, whimpering to himself. Fenella picked him up.

'Dear little bear!' she said. 'I've got an ice-cream for you. Come and have it!'

She took him out of the caravan, and went over to Willie. Then she fed Bobbo with the ice-cream and he made little grunting noises of delight. Fenella and Willie ate their ice-creams, too, whilst Cackles looked on. Bobbo made himself into a mess, but licked it all off with his red tongue.

Nobody noticed that Fenella had left the door of the bears' van open. Nobody saw Clump come to the opening and look out. Nobody knew that he had crept out from the van and gone into the bushes. He was so very, very quiet!

But suddenly, from over the common, came a scream. Then another and another. Everyone sat up in fright. What was the matter?

'Help! Help!' came the voice, and then it screamed again. 'Save us, save us!'

Uncle Ursie, Willie, Micko and Tricks raced over the common to where the voice came from. Fenella could still hear it. 'Oh, help, help, help!'

In a little hollow were two ladies having a picnic. They had just laid themselves down to have a little sleep, when they heard the crackling of twigs.

When they looked up, what did they see but a big, brown bear looking down at them! No wonder they screamed. A bear! A bear on the common they walked over each day! Could it be true?

Clump looked at the two scared women. When they screamed, he was frightened and growled. That scared them all the more. They clutched one another in fright.

Clump decided to try and please these noisy women. So he solemnly turned head-over-heels three times and then sat and looked at them, holding a paw as if to say: 'There you are! I did it for you! Do be friends!'

It was just then that Uncle Ursie and the others came into the little hollow. They saw Clump there and the two frightened women. Uncle Ursie spoke sternly to Clump.

'Clump! How dare you wander off like this? Come here!'

Clump came obediently to Uncle Ursie. He pushed his

head against him, trying to make his master understand that he hadn't meant to do any harm. Uncle Ursie spoke calmly to the two women.

'Don't be afraid. He is quite harmless. May I ask you to accept two tickets for our circus? Then you will see the bear perform.'

'It ought to be reported to the police,' said one of the women angrily.

'You would only get the poor bear into trouble,' said Uncle Ursie. 'I'm very sorry, Madam. Pray do take the tickets to make up for your fright. Perhaps you have children who would like to use them, if you don't want to.'

His politeness had a very good effect on the two women. They smiled and took the tickets. 'Well, we did have a fright!' said one to the other. 'Quite an adventure!'

Uncle Ursie took Clump quickly back to the caravan. He looked cross. 'What was all the screaming about?' asked Aunt Lou.

'Clump got out and wandered loose,' said Uncle Ursie. He didn't say anything about the unlocked door. But Fenella knew at once that it was her fault. She went very red indeed. She got up with Bobbo in her arms and went over to Uncle Ursie.

'Uncle! It was my fault that Clump got out. How *could* I have been so careless as to leave the door open! Oh, Uncle, please forgive me. I won't do it again.'

'You might have got poor Clump into serious trouble,' said Uncle Ursie severely, but he didn't look quite so cross. 'If you have anything to do with animals in a circus you must be very careful about open doors. I shouldn't have given you the key. Now, give me Bobbo. He must go back again into the van.'

When Aunt Lou knew what had happened she scolded Fenella, too. The little girl was very much upset, and cried. Willie was sorry for her.

'Cheer up,' he said. 'We all do silly things sometimes. You come along now and get into the golden carriage! That will cheer you up!'

'Oh *can* I, Willie?' said Fenella, drying her eyes and smiling a watery smile. 'I'd love that. I'll bring Rosebud, too.'

'We're passing through two or three villages soon,' said Willie, taking her to where the carriage was. He put the little white ponies in, and then climbed up to the driver's seat. 'Now, you get in, Fenella, and we'll drive off before your aunt can stop us!'

Fenella got into the little golden carriage, and sat down. She put Rosebud beside her. Cackles flew up by Willie. The boy clicked, and the ponies trotted off, drawing the golden carriage behind them.

Fenella sat in it like a little princess, feeling very grand indeed. The carriage passed Uncle Ursie and Aunt Lou. They stared in surprise. Aunt Lou was just about to shout to Fenella to come back, when Uncle Ursie put his hand on her arm.

'Let her be,' he said. 'She's had a good scolding this afternoon. But she was a generous girl with her ice-creams for everybody, wasn't she – so let her have her little treat.'

And Aunt Lou closed her mouth again and did not call to Fenella after all. Away went the little girl in the carriage, full of delight. When they came to a village all the children there came out to see the circus procession – and how they stared to see Fenella in the golden carriage!

'Look at her! She's like Cinderella!' shouted a boy. 'Cinderella had a golden carriage, didn't she? My, isn't she grand!'

'Hey, look at the goose!' yelled another child. 'Is it a live one?'

'Cackle, cackle, cackle!' said the goose, and everyone knew she was alive all right!

What fun it was riding in the golden carriage, or sitting

squashed in between Willie and Cackles on the driving seat ! Fenella thought she had never had such a happy day before.

She was very tired when the procession halted for the night. Again they came to a common, and drew up all the vans and carts there, letting the horses loose.

Night came down, and the stars shone out. On the common camp-fires began to gleam as the circus folk lighted them to cook a meal. Soon the smell of frying bacon mingled with the smell of may. Fenella cuddled against her Uncle Ursie, almost too tired to eat anything, but enjoying the starry night, and the queerness of camping out in a strange place she didn't know.

She fell asleep leaning against her uncle. He lifted her up, and her doll, too. 'I'll just pop her into her bunk as she is,' he said to Aunt Lou. 'She's tired out !'

Then, after a time, the camp-fires died down, and one by one the circus folk went into their caravans to sleep, calling good-night to one another. Their animals slept, too.

'Good night,' said Willie to Cackles. 'Sleep well ! Happy dreams, Cackles – and don't wake me too early tomorrow !'

16. Camping By The Sea

When Fenella woke up the next morning, the first thing she heard was the trumpeting of the three elephants. She sat up in her bunk and looked out of the little window above her head. She saw Mr Holla on the common nearby with Grin and Bearit, and behind him were Mr Tiny and the elephants.

'Oh, the elephants caught us up all right then,' thought Fenella, pleased. 'They hadn't arrived when I fell asleep last night. I don't even remember going to bed.'

She was up and about very quickly. Willie took her to the nearest stream, and she washed herself in the clear, cool water.

'We always have to camp near water,' Willie told her, 'because of the animals. They want plenty to drink. Look at Fric and Frac and Malvina setting off already. They joined us in the night, too – did you hear them? Now they are going off a different way again, over those green hills you can see over there. They probably won't touch a road at all! I went with them once and helped with the horses when Fric strained his side. We had a fine time.'

Once more the long line of caravans moved off, when the circus folk had had their breakfast. It was a lovely day again. Fenella sat beside Uncle Ursie, chattering happily. He listened to her, pleased.

'You're good company, little Fenny,' he said. 'Your tongue is never still now, but I like to hear you talking away. And my, how brown you're getting! Quite one of us, now, you look.'

Fenella was indeed getting brown. All the circus folk were as brown as berries, for most of their life was passed out of doors.

'I haven't got as many freckles as Willie, though!' said Fenella. 'His face is covered with them. He's got two dimples, like Aunt Aggie's, that go in and out. Did you know, Uncle Ursie?'

'Well, I can't say I ever noticed that,' said Uncle Ursie, smiling. He clicked to the little white pony, and it trotted a little faster to catch up with Aunt Lou's caravan. 'Let me take the reins,' said Fenella. 'I'd like to. I can drive now, Uncle Ursie.'

'Well, you get Willie to let you drive Malvina's six ponies!' said Uncle Ursie. 'They need a bit more driving than old Snowy here.'

'Oh no! One horse is quite enough for me,' said Fenella. Uncle Ursie handed her the reins, and she took them proudly. 'See, Rosebud,' she said to her doll, who was sitting beside her as usual. 'See how well I drive!'

'Rosebud could drive Snowy just as well as you!' said Uncle Ursie, teasingly. 'Here, you look!'

He took the reins from Fenella and twisted them round Rosebud's small arms. Snowy trotted along as if he hadn't noticed anything at all!

'Rosebud's clever, isn't she?' said Uncle Ursie, laughing at Fenella's face. He gave the reins back to the little girl. Snowy trotted on and on. In front stretched the line of caravans, and behind, too. Sometimes, when they climbed a hill, Fenella could see the whole lot, one behind the other.

'Shall we get there tonight, wherever we're going?' asked Fenella. 'I wouldn't mind if it took us weeks, Uncle Ursie. I like this.'

'Oh, we'll be there this afternoon, I expect,' said her

uncle. 'Clump and Bobbo will be glad. They wouldn't like to go on the road for long. They hate being shut up. So do all the animals.'

'Oh, yes. I forgot about them,' said Fenella. She peered back through the small window that looked into the bears' van. 'Poor Bobbo. He can't understand it. He keeps curled up in a ball, and whimpers. Clump's walking up and down and growling, Uncle.'

The caravans stopped at dinner-time again for a meal, but not for long. Then on they went, and suddenly, from the top of a hill, Fenella saw something blue that spread out flat before her, about a mile away. She gave a cry.

'Oh, the sea! Willie, Willie, look can you see the blue water? It's the sea!'

She went to sit beside Willie and Cackles. 'Soon be there now,' said Willie, and he pointed to where a big, sloping field lay on a cliff overlooking the sea. 'That's where we're camping. A bit windy, but that will be nice this hot weather. There'll be a little path down the cliff to the sea, I expect. What fun the dogs will have on the sands!'

'Bobbo will like it, too,' said Fenella. 'So shall I!'

By tea-time the circus caravans were up on the high field. The wind blew strongly. 'Have to see that the big top is put up very carefully,' said Uncle Ursie to Willie. 'A bit more of a wind and the tent would fly over into the sea!'

Mr Carl Crack's caravan was already in the field, and so were the big lorries laden with the circus properties. As the caravans streamed into the gateway of the field, there came the sound of horses' hooves, and Fenella gave a shout.

'Hurrah! Here are the horses, too! Now we only want the three elephants, and we'll all be together again.'

Aunt Lou had done a bit of shopping at the last town

they had come through. Her larder was now well-stocked, and she had bought more cottons and buttons, and some gay cloth. She showed the cloth to Fenella.

'This is for Mr Holla. He wants a new suit for the ring. You can help me to make it.'

'Oh, I should like to,' said Fenella. 'And how I should like to make a suit for little Bobbo, too, Aunt Lou. He's so sweet and funny – really like a little bear-clown. I'd like to make him a tiny clown suit, and a pointed hat like Groggy's, with black bobbles on it.'

The circus folk began to settle down in their new camp. The caravans were pulled together to shelter each other from the strong wind. The field sloped down almost to sea-level at one corner, and here there ran a bubbling brook, which joined the sea, running over the sand. Mr Holla took his elephants down to it as soon as they arrived. They were hot and dusty, and they enjoyed squirting themselves with the cool, clear water.

Grin and Bearit went too near them, and were squirted, too. But they liked that, and danced round the great elephants, getting wetter and wetter till Mr Holla yelled to them to come away.

By the time that night came, the camp was quite settled in. The big top was not yet up, nor were the lorries unpacked. They would have to wait till the next day. It was enough that all the horses had been settled in, fed and watered, that the animals were now happy and comfortable, and the circus folk at peace after their two day's journey.

The smell of cooking arose, as Aunt Aggie, Mr Tiny, Malvina, Aunt Lou and Mr Grogy all began to fry bacon, sausages and tomatoes at the same time, on fires built cleverly of twigs, criss-crossed over one another. Fenella sniffed with pleasure.

'Oh, how lovely! And are those tinned pears and cream for us, Aunt Lou? You do get nice meals.'

'Ah, you wait till we get a rainy week or two, and nobody comes to our shows, so that money is short!' said Aunt Lou. 'Then you won't get nice meals! You'll have to make do with bread and margarine then. But whilst we've got the money we feed well.'

'Do the animals have to go short of food, too, when money doesn't come in?' asked Fenella, thinking that it would be dreadful if Bobbo went hungry.

'Good gracious no, child! Whoever goes hungry the animals don't. You may be sure of that. Your uncle would rather starve than see Clump or Bobbo hungry. And Willie would go without food for days to feed Cackles and those dogs.'

'And I'd go without this nice supper if I thought Bobbo was hungry,' said Fenella, seriously. Uncle Ursie heard her, and was touched. He gave Fenella a hug.

'Why, if you're not a proper little circus kid already, Fenny! That's the way to talk! Did you hear that, Lou? That's the kind of thing our Carol would have said, isn't it now?'

Aunt Lou said nothing to that, but pursed up her lips a little. Fenella couldn't tell if she was angry or sad. But she wasn't angry, it was clear, because she gave Fenella the kind of sausage she liked best of all, rather burnt, and burst a little at one side.

'Oh, thank you, Aunt Lou,' said Fenella. 'That's how I like sausages best! I *am* hungry! I was never so hungry in my life before as I have been since I've come to live with you.'

'You'll grow as fat as Bobbo!' said Aunt Lou, in an unexpectedly pleasant voice. 'Never mind if you do. You could do with a bit more fat on you. Your legs are too skinny.'

Fenella went to find Willie after she had had her supper and helped to do the washing-up. Willie was putting the dogs back into their big travelling cage, after having taken

them for a short run. Cackles was nearby as usual, hissing
if any dog came too near.

'I'll get Bobbo for a minute!' said Fenella and ran to
ask Uncle Ursie if she could have him. He nodded. 'But
no leaving the door open now, Fenny!'

Fenella took Bobbo over to Willie and Cackles. The
goose was quite used to the fat little bear now, and liked
him. Bobbo went up to her, stood up on his hind legs and
waved a clumsy paw.

'Oh, look! Bobbo is standing up all by himself!' said
Fenella, pleased. 'And he's waving a paw at Cackles.
Isn't he funny? Oh – down he goes with a bump. He
always looks so *very* astonished when he sits down
suddenly like that, doesn't he, Willie?'

'Cackle, cackle,' said Cackles, and pulled gently at one
of Bobbo's hind paws with her beak.

'She's telling him to get up!' said Fenella. They played
with the bear and the goose till it got too dark to see.
Then Fenella heard her aunt calling and ran off with
Bobbo in her arms.

'I shall like to go to bed tonight, hearing the sound of
the sea all the time,' she said to Aunt Lou. 'It's a lovely
noise. And I like this wind, too, too. It's got a nice sea-
weedy smell. Can I go and paddle tomorrow, Aunt Lou?'

'If you do your lessons, and help me nicely with the
sewing,' said Aunt Lou. 'Brush your hair well tonight. It's
all tangled with the wind.'

Soon Fenella was ready to climb into her bunk. She
stood on the steps of the caravan in her nightie. The wind
blew round her legs and she liked it. 'Good night, Uncle
Ursie! Good night, Aunt Lou! Won't it be nice to wake
up and see the blue sea tomorrow? Good night!'

17. Willie And Fenella

Fenella awoke to the sound of the sea the next day. She lay in her bunk and listened to it. She had only once before been to the seaside, and she felt very happy to think that she was going to be near it for some time.

'Perhaps Bobbo will like to paddle and bathe with me,' she thought. 'And I'm sure Grin and Bearit will. We shall have a lovely time!'

After breakfast she asked her aunt if she was to go to Presto for her usual lessons. 'Of course,' said Aunt Lou. 'It's nearly ten o'clock. Take the book he gave you to write in and go.'

'Can I take Bobbo, too?' asked Fenella. 'Willie always takes Cackles.'

'Certainly not,' said her aunt. 'Go along now. Find Willie.'

Willie was just about to let the dogs out and take them on the seashore. 'Willie! Aren't you going to lessons?' cried Fenella, running up.

'What! The first day we're here?' said Willie. 'Presto won't expect us.'

'Oh, yes, I do,' said the conjurer's voice, and Presto walked round the caravan. 'I might give Fenella here a holiday, Willie, but not you! You have a lot to learn – more than Fenella has.'

Willie didn't like that. He put on a sulky look that Fenella had only seen once or twice before.

'I can't come today. I've got to take the dogs out.'

'You can do that when you have finished with me,' said Presto, his voice going rather cold and stern. 'I do not arrange to give up my time for nothing, Willie. You will come now.'

Fenella stared anxiously at Willie. He still looked sulky. But he, too, had heard that warning note in Presto's voice. He slammed the door of the dogs' cage shut, almost nipping Bouncer's nose.

He followed Fenella to Presto's black caravan, still looking sulky. On the way they met Mr Crack, striding over the field to look at the horses. He nodded to Presto.

'Got your two pupils, Presto? That's good! I hope they are getting on well. They are lucky to get this schooling from you!'

Willie scowled. Mr Crack raised his shaggy eyebrows. 'Well, Willie, what's up? Don't you like lessons?'

'Got the dogs to take out,' said Willie, still looking down on the ground.

'Now, see here, Willie,' said Mr Crack, 'you take your chance of schooling! Do you think I'd ever be head of a circus like this if I'd never had any schooling? I'll have to send you away from the circus to a proper school, if you're not careful. It's the law of this land that every child should be taught its lessons.'

Fenella was scared. She didn't want Willie to be sent away to school. 'He'll come, Mr Crack,' she said earnestly. 'He's always come before. He's getting on very well.'

'Well, my orders are that these two children go to you five mornings a week,' said Mr Crack to Presto. 'Hear that, Willie? Now take that scowl off your face and go!'

Mr Crack strode off looking rather annoyed. Sulking made him angry. 'A sulky animal or a sulky human being will never do anything worthwhile!' he always said. 'If I get hold of an animal that goes into the sulks, I never bother with it again. It's no use to me.'

Willie was not very nice that morning. Fenella tried to

talk to him and cheer him up, but he was still in the
sulks. Presto was patient with him. Fenella tried to make
up for Willie's behaviour by working extra well – but that
didn't please Willie either.

'Sucking up to him!' he whispered to Fenella crossly.
'Just because you know I'm doing badly, you try to suck
up to him and do extra well!'

'You're horrid, Willie!' said Fenella, almost in tears,
for she couldn't bear Willie, her cheerful friend, to be
like this.

Presto took no more notice of Willie, but set him some
writing to do, and began to teach Fenella geography
from a big globe he brought from a corner. She learnt
quickly and well and he was pleased with her.

'I'm awfully thirsty,' said Fenella, when lessons had
finished. 'I really must get a drink!'

'Here is one,' said Presto, and gave her a jug and a
cup. 'Pour it out for yourself.'

She began to pour from the jug – and then she almost
dropped the cup! 'Oh!' she cried. 'I've poured two tiny
goldfish into the cup from the jug. But they weren't in the
jug, Mr Presto, or I'd have seen them. How did they get
into the cup?'

'Dear, dear!' said Presto, and poured the water from
the cup back into the jug. Fenella peered into it. There
were no goldfish to be seen.

'Now pour it out again,' said Presto. 'I hope this time
the water will be clear!'

But it wasn't! The goldfish appeared again in the cup,
although Fenella was quite certain they were not in the
jug when she poured out the water. She stared at Presto
in wonder.

'You really are magic!' she said. 'What shall I do? I
can't drink the goldfish.'

'You will have to go and get a drink from your aunt,
I'm afraid,' said Presto, in a regretful voice. 'I'm so sorry.

It does sometimes happen to me that goldfish appear in my drinking water.'

Fenella went off puzzled. Willie followed. He looked more cheerful now that lessons were over.

'Isn't Presto clever?' said Fenella. 'Last time we had lessons he kept making my rubber disappear, and I kept finding that I was sitting on it. This time there are gold-fish in his drinking water. Oh, Willie – I think we're lucky to have lessons with a conjurer. Don't you?'

'No,' said Willie, going gloomy again. 'Lessons with anyone are awful. I shall never learn to read.'

'Willie, do let me help you,' begged Fenella. 'You always say you've got things to do when I come to see you in the evenings with our books.'

'Well, I'll see,' said Willie. 'What's the time? Hurrah! Presto must have let us off early. We've got time to take the dogs down to the shore. Come on!'

The dogs went nearly mad with joy at being taken down to the fine stretch of sand by the sea. They tore down the little path that wound down the cliff-side, almost knocking over Mrs Connie who had been down for a paddle.

The children left Cackles and Bobbo behind. They meant to take them down to the sea after tea. Fenella jumped the last bit of the path down, and landed on the firm golden sand She stared round.

'Oh, Willie! It's lovely! Look at the shiny shells every-where in the sand. And do see the tiny, lacy waves curling over at the edge. Quick, let's take off our shoes!'

They were soon paddling, shouting merrily to one another. Willie had quite forgotten his sulks. The dogs raced one another, and some of them splashed boldly into the sea, barking bravely at the waves.

'Aren't the dogs enjoying themselves?' said Willie. 'Hey, Pickles! Fetch this stick. Let's see if you can swim.'

'Yes, of course he can,' said Fenella, watching the little

dog swimming after the floating stick. 'Oh, Willie, I want a swim, too. Let's bathe tomorrow. No, let's bathe after tea! Have you got a bathing suit?'

'No, but Micko has,' said Willie. 'He'll lend me it. What about you?'

'I haven't got one either, but I'm sure I can quickly make one this afternoon, if Aunt Lou will let me,' said Fenella joyfully. 'Oh, look at Bouncer – he's sniffing at that crab. There, I knew he'd get a pinch! Come away, Bouncer, or you'll get another!'

That afternoon Fenella sat down to help her aunt with the usual pile of sewing. They were busy on Mr Holla's new suit. It was to be made of the gay, red cloth that Aunt Lou had bought in the town.

Aunt Lou cut it out cleverly from a pattern. She began to tack it together. 'You can sew up these seams,' she said.

'Oh, I do wish we had a sewing-machine,' said Fenella. 'We could do all this so much more quickly then.'

'I've never had one,' said Aunt Lou. 'And it's not likely you will, either, Fenella, so just get on with the seams as quickly as you can.'

When they were almost finished, and the suit was ready for Mr Holla to try on, Fenella remembered to ask about a bathing dress for herself.

'Aunt Lou, I do want to bathe this evening after tea. I can swim, you know. Willie can't, so I'll teach him. Is there a bit of stuff I can have for a bathing dress?'

'No, I've nothing that will do,' said Aunt Lou. 'Nothing at all.'

She saw the little girl's disappointed face, and rose suddenly. She went to a little trunk at the back of the caravan and opened it. She delved down into it, felt about for a moment and then brought up a beautiful little bathing suit in pure white, with a shiny belt of bright red.

'You can have this,' said Aunt Lou, and gave it to

Fenella. 'You've been a good girl to help me so well this afternoon.'

She did not wait to be thanked but went out of the caravan at once. Fenella stared at the little suit in delight. It would just fit her! How kind of Aunt Lou.

She sat and thought for a minute. Whose was this little suit? Uncle Ursie came into the caravan to get his pipe and saw Fenella sitting there. 'You hurry up and get out of doors,' he said. 'It's lovely out. Had your tea?'

'Yes, we had it whilst we were sewing,' said Fenella. Uncle Ursie went out. Fenella undressed quickly and put on the bathing dress. It fitted her perfectly. She ran down the steps to find Willie.

Uncle Ursie was outside, smoking. He looked up – and then his face wrinkled up in astonishment. He stared at Fenella. 'Where did you get that suit?' he asked at last.

'Aunt Lou gave it to me,' said Fenella. 'Why do you look so surprised, Uncle?'

'Well – that suit was our little Carol's,' said Uncle Ursie. 'Why, Fenny – your aunt must be fond of you to lend you that! But don't you let her see you in it, or she may be sorry she's lent it you, and want it back.'

'Then I'll go and bathe *now*,' said Fenella, anxious to keep the lovely little suit. 'Willie! Come along quickly! I'll get Bobbo, and we'll go down to the sea.'

18. A Lot Of Fun – But Jimmy Is Naughty

Willie, Fenella, Bobbo, and Cackles made their way down the little cliff path. Bobbo had to be helped.

'He might roll all the way down if he fell, he's so fat,' said Fenella anxiously.

'He wouldn't hurt himself,' said Willie. 'His fur is so thick! Come on, Cackles. Don't be so slow.'

Cackles suddenly spread her great white wings and flew down to the shore. Willie grinned. 'Good for Cackles! She got out of scrambling down over these rocks, and I don't wonder!'

Soon they were all dancing about in the waves at the edge of the water. Willie had borrowed Micko's bathing trunks. His body seemed very white indeed, compared with his brown face, neck and arms. Fenella laughed at him and splashed him. He splashed her back and she squealed.

Cackles paddled solemnly, too, occasionally giving a cackle of joy. Then she suddenly waded in much deeper, and launched herself like a battleship, gliding off beautifully.

'She's using her great feet like paddles to get along with,' cried Fenella, following her. 'Come out deeper, Willie. Do!'

But neither Willie nor Bobbo would go out very far. Bobbo was not really sure if he liked this curious water, that seemed to run after him, and then run away from him – and then, as soon as he went cautiously near it again, ran after him once more. Willie, who couldn't swim, was afraid of getting out of his depth.

So Fenella swam after Cackles the goose. 'Oh, Cackles, isn't it lovely?' she cried. 'I'd like a ride on your back. Cackles, will you let me? You're big enought to carry me.'

But Cackles didn't understand, or didn't want Fenella to ride her. She kept slipping away when Fenella tried to hold her. Willie yelled with laughter.

'I'll buy you an ice cream, Fenny, if you can ride Cackles!'

But Fenella couldn't win that ice cream! Just when she thought she really had got on to Cackles' broad white back, the goose dived under the water, and down went Fenella, too, gasping and spluttering. Willie lay down in the water and laughed, kicking his legs up into the air, much to the interest of Bobbo, who couldn't imagine what Willie was doing. He came cautiously nearer to see. Then he sat down with a bump beside Willie, lay down himself, and kicked, too, grunting happily, and splashing Willie. Willie sat up.

'Fenny, look at Bobbo! Isn't he a clown? Really, he'd bring the house down if he went in the ring and did this sort of thing! We really ought to teach him a few tricks.'

Bobbo rolled over and over in the water. He was enjoying himself very much. Then he gave another grunt and sat up. He looked up the shore and grunted again.

The children looked, too. A small figure was skipping down towards them, dressed in tiny shorts and a little coat and hat.

'Oh, it's one of Mrs Connie's monkeys!' said Fenella. 'He must have seen us from the cliff and come to join us.'

'It's Jimmy,' said Willie. 'Hey, Jimmy! Do you want to paddle?'

Jimmy didn't only want to paddle. He wanted to bathe like the others. With joyful chattering he began to tear off his clothes. Away went his shorts in the wind, and away went his jacket! His cap went sailing away on the strong breeze, too.

'Jimmy! You mustn't do that!' cried Willie. 'Oh, look, Fenny, the wind has taken all Jimmy's clothes and blown them out to sea. Can you get them?'

'I'll try,' said Fenella and began to swim after them. But she couldn't get them. They soon became soaked with water and vanished.

Fenella swam back to Willie out of breath. 'Will Mrs Connie be cross?' she asked. 'It wasn't really our fault. Oh, do look at Jimmy. He's splashing Bobbo. Aren't they funny together?'

Willie was shivering. He hadn't kept himself warm with swimming as Fenella had. 'Come on out,' said Fenella. 'You'll get a chill. Brrrrrr! I wish we'd brought towels down with us. Anyway, the climb up the cliff will soon warm us.'

'Come on, Cackles,' yelled Willie. The goose had seen that the others were ready to go, and was already swimming towards them. She waddled out of the water, shaking hundreds of silvery drops over the children. Then Bobbo got up and shook himself, too. Jimmy leapt about like a mad thing, and wouldn't be caught.

'We'll have to leave him if he won't come,' said Willie, shivering more than ever. 'Come along, Fenny.'

But as soon as they all started up the steep cliff path Jimmy came, too, scampering behind them, sometimes on all fours, sometimes on his hind legs, chattering loudly.

'Shall I tell Mrs Connie about Jimmy's lost clothes, or will you?' asked Fenella.

'I will,' said Willie kindly. 'I know you'd be scared of telling her. Anyway, she can't eat us for it! It really wasn't our fault. Jimmy simply tore them off and threw them away!'

Willie went off to dry himself and dress. He said he would find Mrs Connie as soon as he got his clothes on.

Fenella ran to her own caravan and was soon dry, and dressed, with an extra coat on till she felt really warm.

Aunt Lou and Uncle Ursie were talking to Fric and Frac at the other end of the field. Aunt Lou had Mr Holla's new suit over her arm. She had been fitting it on Mr Holla, and he was very pleased with it. Now it had only small alterations to be done, and buttons and braid to be sewn on.

Fenella skipped over to them. She looked at the tall, straight Fric and Frac, two brothers who came from Russia, and who were really wonderful horsemen. She thought she liked them best in their Red Indian costumes, even though they did look very fierce then.

Willie went to find Mrs Connie as soon as he was dressed, but she was not in her caravan. He peeped inside the monkeys' caravan. They were all there but Jimmy. Where could that little rascal be? Well, he would have to wait till Mrs Connie came back before he could explain what had happened to Jimmy's clothes.

Jimmy the monkey was feeling scared. He was so used to wearing clothes that he felt queer without them now. The wind blew and he wished he had his little coat on. He went and sat on the top of Aunt Lou's caravan, hugging the chimney, which was warm. He saw Fenella slip in, in her bathing costume. He saw her slip out again and go over to the other end of the field.

Jimmy slid down the side of the red caravan and peeped in at the window. On a shelf he saw Rosebud lying, smiling her stiff doll-like smile. Jimmy looked at her for a long time. He couldn't understand that doll. She looked alive, but she never spoke or moved.

But she had beautiful clothes! Jimmy took a quick look round and then disappeared inside the window. He went over to Rosebud. He tugged at her coat, but it wouldn't come off because it was done up with hooks and eyes, and Jimmy was only used to buttons.

Then he saw a small trunk beside Rosebud. In it, neatly packed, was all the doll's wardrobe – coats, dresses, petticoats, vests, everything that Fenella had made for her herself. The monkey shook out each little garment and looked at it, chattering to himself in a low voice.

He found a red silk frock. It was very beautiful and soft, and Jimmy loved red. He pulled it about and then slipped it over his head. He pulled it down straight, and felt pleased. Now he was dressed again. He was grand!

He found a white coat edged with fur, Jimmy knew how to put his little arms in to sleeves, for Mrs Connie had taught him that. He soon had the coat on. It was back to front, but Jimmy didn't mind that! He capered about the caravan, feeling very pleased with himself.

He went back to the trunk again. He saw some red shoes there, and he pulled them out. He fitted them on his little hind paws, and did up the buttons. These took him a long time, but he was a very persevering little monkey indeed. At last the buttons were done up. Now for a hat!

Rosebud's best hat was wrapped up in tissue paper. Jimmy tore off the wrapping. Ah, what a hat! It was made of straw, with bright red roses all round it, and a blue ribbon floating down the back. Rosebud looked really sweet in it when she wore it. Fenella had made it for her on her last birthday.

Jimmy put it on. He didn't know which was back and which was front, so he just jammed it on anyhow, and the blue ribbon hung down over his right ear.

The monkey heard a noise outside and crouched down in a corner. It was Uncle Ursie passing. Jimmy waited till he was gone, then scampered out of the caravan. He looked a very peculiar sight, rather like an ugly doll come alive, all dressed up!

Mr Holla saw him first. 'Hey!' he cried, seeing Jimmy sitting on the top of a caravan. 'Who's that?'

Willie and Fenella ran up. 'It's one of Mrs Connie's monkeys,' said Willie. 'How she has dressed him up! I've never seen one in that costume before!'

Fenella gave a loud squeal. 'Oh! It must be Jimmy. The bad, bad monkey! He's got at Rosebud's trunk of clothes, and he's dressed himself up in her best things. Oh, oh, Willie, get him before he spoils them all!'

But Jimmy knew very well that his lovely new clothes would be taken away from him if he was caught, so he led everyone a very fine dance indeed. He bounded about, chattering and squealing. In the end Grin caught him – and spanked him, too, much to Jimmy's dismay.

Fenella was almost crying. 'Oh, Rosebud's beautiful clothes! Oh, Aunt Lou, he's torn the frock – and the hat is spoilt!'

Mrs Connie arrived just then. When she heard what Jimmy had done she threw back her head and laughed. 'Ah, that Jimmy! He is the naughtiest and cleverest monkey in the world! What has he done with his own clothes?'

Fenella was cross. Mrs Connie shouldn't have laughed like that. 'He came down to bathe with Willie and me, and he took off all his clothes and threw them away into the water,' she said.

Mrs Connie stopped laughing. This was serious. 'What! He has no clothes! Then what will he do when we give our next show? He must have clothes for that!'

Aunt Lou looked grim. 'Well, it's no use coming to *me* for them, Mrs Connie. I'm not making any more clothes for your monkeys. I can tell you that! You shouldn't leave your creatures loose when you go out.'

'I didn't! That Jimmy must have squeezed himself out through the chimney!' said Mrs Connie. 'What am I to do? He must have clothes, he must!'

19. Willie And Fenella Make A Plan

The circus folk told the story of mischievous Jimmy over and over again, and everyone laughed. 'That Jimmy! He is as clever as a whole bagful of monkeys!' they said.

Aunt Lou kept her word about not making new clothes for Jimmy. 'No,' she said, when Mrs Connie came to her about it. 'I'm not paid to dress your monkeys, as I've told you before – and why should I work my fingers to the bone, sewing clothes for animals, when all they do is to throw them off into the sea!'

'He didn't know what he was doing,' pleaded Mrs Connie. 'You know what monkeys are. Lou, make him a new suit. He can't go into the ring undressed. Some of the others want new things, too.'

'They can want then,' said Aunt Lou grimly. 'Or you can for once in a way put a thimble on your finger and take a needle and thread, and do a bit of work yourself!'

'You're a hard one!' said Mrs Connie. 'Yes, you are! Hard on your old Ursie, and hard on Fenny here. Not a bit of softness or affection for anyone. You listen to me, Fenny – when you've had enough of that hard old aunt of yours, you come to me, see! I'll let you live in my caravan with me, and you can help to look after my precious monkeys.'

'I shouldn't let Fenella go even if she wanted to,' said Aunt Lou, angrily. 'She's in our charge. Now go away and look after those awful monkeys of yours a bit better.'

Fenella was sorry for Mrs Connie. She had quite for-

given Jimmy for taking Rosebud's clothes. She knew that
the monkey hadn't really meant to be naughty. She spoke
to her aunt.

'Will Mrs Connie go to Mr Crack, Aunt Lou? Will she
tell him you won't make things for the monkeys? You
make them for Grin and Bearit, and for Cackles the
goose.'

'She can go if she likes,' said Aunt Lou. 'But I'm not
obeying even Mr Carl Crack if I don't want to. He can
turn me and your uncle out of his circus if he likes. I
shan't change my mind about those monkeys.'

'Oh, Aunt *Lou*! Could he really turn you out?' said
Fenella in horror. 'Make you and Uncle Ursie – and me,
too – go away from the camp and not come back? What
would we do?'

'Why – would you mind so much?' asked Uncle Ursie,
who had just come into the caravan. 'You've not been
with us more than two or three weeks!'

'Oh, Uncle Ursie – I'd hate to leave!' cried Fenella.
'I love this caravan – and the bears – and everyone –
especially Willie and Cackles. Oh, please, Aunt Lou, do
make dresses for the monkeys. I'm sure Mrs Connie will
go to Mr Crack and he'll say you are to; and if you won't,
we'll be turned out.'

'It's true that Mr Crack will not have anyone going
against his orders,' said Uncle Ursie. 'There's been one or
two who have – and they've been yelled at and turned out
of the camp in a few hours.'

Mrs Connie did go to Mr Crack. He frowned as he
heard her complaint. ' 'Tisn't just this time, Mr Crack
sir – it's many a time she's complained about dressing my
monkey's. She and I, sir, we can't live in the same circus
much longer. I'll go. I'll go somewhere where there's
people who'll think more of me, and dress my monkeys
as befits them, the little clever creatures.'

Mr Crack didn't like Aunt Lou. He thought her a bad-

tempered, scold of a woman. Few people had a good word
to say of her.

'She used to be nicer,' he said to Mrs Connie. 'Perhaps
that was before you joined us, Connie. She changed when
she lost Carol. That was her little girl, you know – the
cleverest little thing you ever saw! She had a mane of
red hair like Fenella's.'

'What happened to her?' asked Mrs Connie.

'Well, Carol was a fine swimmer,' said Mr Crack. 'In
those days Ursie used to have performing seals, too, and
Carol used to go into their tank with them, and do all
kinds of tricks. Clever as paint, she was! She could even
stand up and ride on a seal's back – and that's a slippery
trick to do if you like!'

'My, she must have been clever,' said Mrs Connie.

'Well, Carol got a chill one day,' said Mr Crack, 'and
instead of keeping her warm in bed and fussing her a bit,
Lou let her go to the show as usual, and swim in the seal's
tank. The water was cold. The child fell very ill afterwards, and she died. People blamed Lou very much for it,
and she changed after that, grew bad-tempered, and
never let anyone mention Carol's name.'

'Poor Lou!' said Mrs Connie. 'What happened to the
seals?'

'She made Ursie sell them, so now he's only got his
bears,' said Mr Crack. 'I'm fond of Ursie, and if it wasn't
for him, and the fact that Lou is a wonder at making
show clothes, I'd have got rid of her long ago. Well,
Connie, I'll give orders that she's to dress Jimmy from
head to foot. If she doesn't, out they go!'

Mrs Connie was now half sorry that she had come to
Mr Crack with her complaint. She hadn't heard all Lou's
story before. She, too, liked Ursie. 'Well,' she began,
'maybe I can get my sister in to help with the monkeys'
clothes, Mr Crack.'

Mr Crack frowned till his shaggy eyebrows hid his eyes

completely. 'I've said what's to be done,' he told Mrs Connie. 'I never change my mind. You know that.'

He walked over to the red caravan the next day. Uncle Ursie was there, and Fenella. Aunt Lou had gone by bus to get something she wanted in the town.

'Morning, Ursie,' said Mr Crack. 'Where's Lou? Tell her when she comes back that my orders are that she dresses those monkey as usual – and she's to make a new outfit for Jimmy, top to toe!'

Uncle Ursie looked very troubled. 'Yes, Mr Crack, sir, I'll tell her. But you know what Lou is – so obstinate when she's made up her mind about anything. I doubt if she will do as you say.'

'I, too, am obstinate!' suddenly roared Mr Crack, and made Fenella almost jump out of her skin. 'If she disobeys me – out she goes and you with her!'

Fenella began to tremble. She did so hate people to roar and bellow and lose their tempers. She felt quite certain that Aunt Lou would refuse to do what she was ordered.

And so she did. 'I'm not changing my mind,' she said to Uncle Ursie, when he told her what Mr Crack had said, and she looked grimmer than ever. Her lips almost disappeared, she screwed her mouth up so tightly. 'He can turn us out if he wants to.'

Fenella was very unhappy that day. She didn't pay much attention to her lessons and Presto scolded her for the first time. Willie looked at the gloomy little girl in surprise. 'What's up?' he whispered.

'No whispering,' said Presto. 'Pay attention to your work. I am not pleased with either of you this morning.'

The two children were impatient to be out of the black caravan. It was not a very nice day, cloudy, and still very windy. When Presto said they might go, they ran to a big lorry full of benches, and squeezed underneath it, finding shelter from the wind. 'Now you tell me what's the matter,' said Willie. 'I've never seen you look so gloomy before!'

Fenella told him. 'So it looks as if we might be turned out of the camp in a few days,' she said, tears in her eyes. 'And I don't want to go, Willie. I don't want never to see you and Cackles again.'

Willie gave her a squeeze. He thought for a few moments. Then he turned to Fenny. 'Could *you* make a new suit for Jimmy, top to toe?' he asked.

'Why yes, I suppose so,' said Fenella in surprise. 'But why?'

'Well, silly, that's a way out of the difficulty, isn't it?' said Willie. 'All you need to do is to make the new suit without anyone seeing you – pack it up neatly – and leave it in Mrs Connie's caravan sometime, with Jimmy's name on it. She'll find it, think your aunt has made it, report it to Mr Crack – he'll be pleased, and nothing more will be said!'

'Oh,' said Fenella, blinking away her tears. 'What an idea, Willie! Do you really think it would work? It couldn't be wrong to do that, could it?'

'Well, it's going to please a whole lot of people,' said Willie. 'It'll please Mrs Connie – it'll please Mr Crack – and Jimmy the monkey! It'll please your aunt and uncle when Mr Crack doesn't turn them out – and it'll certainly please me, too!'

'Oh, and me as well!' said Fenella. Her eyes shone. 'I could easily make a suit for Jimmy – a little red soldier suit, Willie. But where will I get the stuff for it? And where can I make it so that no one will see me?'

'My mum's got plenty of old stuff you can use,' said Willie. 'She was once an acrobat, you know, and had pretty dresses like Malvina and the others. She's kept them all. I'm sure she'd let you have one to cut up.'

Fenella simply couldn't imagine the thin, worn Aunt Aggie dressed in beautiful clothes and performing in the ring as an acrobat. 'Where shall I make Jimmy's suit?' she said. 'I mustn't let Aunt Lou or Mrs Connie see me.'

'You can come to our caravan in the evenings,' said Willie. 'You were going to bring books and help me to read, weren't you? Well, everyone will think that's what we're doing – studying together. And I really will do some work, Fenny, see? Just to please you. We'll have to let Mum into the secret but you needn't mind that. She'll never give us away.'

Fenella felt pleased and relieved. Surely, if Mrs Connie found a beautifully-made little suit for Jimmy in her caravan, everything would be all right?

A seagull swooped down over the cliff and called loudly, 'Eee-ooo, eee-ooo!' Willie immediately imitated it.

'Eeee-ooo, eeee-ooo!' he called. The gull heard him and flew down to the ground. Willie went on calling and calling, and one by one more gulls dropped down to the ground in surprise. They thought that surely one of their number must be in distress, under the caravan.

'Eee-oo, eee-oo, eeeeoooo!' they called, and began to circle round and swoop down by the dozen. Willie and Fenella laughed to see them!

The circus folk wondered at the enormous collection of gulls that had suddenly appeared. Then Mr Holla caught sight of Willie under the caravan.

'Ho, it's you!' he said. 'You must imitate gulls in our next show, Willie! You will bring them into the tent, and everyone will clap! That will be a good trick to play.'

Willie and Fenella crawled out, laughing. The gulls flew away. Cackles waddled up, looking indignant. She had not liked so many big birds about in *her* field.

'Oh, Cackles! We've got a secret!' said Fenella. 'But we're not going to tell it even to *you*!'

20. Fenella Sets To Work – Where Is Bobbo?

That evening Fenella went to Aunt Aggie's caravan with two reading books. Her Aunt Lou saw her go. 'Are you going to help Willie with his reading?' she said. 'That's good of you, Fenella. If they ask you to stay to supper, you can, because your uncle and I are going out.'

Fenella was pleased. She was sure that Willie's mother would ask her to stay. She was quite a favourite with her. Now she would have a really long time to start on Jimmy's new suit!

Willie had told his mother all about their secret. She listened in silence. 'Well, Willie,' she said, 'I like old Lou, for all her sharp tongue. She's a sad woman under her grimness and scolding. She loved that girl of hers very much and blamed herself for her illness. She'd be miserable away from Mr Crack's circus. She's been with it for years and years. I'll find some stuff for little Fenny to sew up, and if Mrs Connie takes the suit and says nothing, well, that's all to the good. Lou won't have to go, and we'll have little Fenny with us still. I'm really fond of that red-haired child.'

Fenella came in smiling. 'Willie, I've brought your books,' she said. 'Has he told you our secret, Aunt Aggie? Are you going to help me? Oh, good! Now, Willie, you're to sit down and read out loud to me, whilst I get on with my job!'

'All right, Aunt Lou-Fenella,' said Willie with a grin and everyone laughed. Aunt Aggie pulled some bright red

silk out of a box. 'This was once a skirt of mine,' she said.
'I wore it when I worked with three acrobats, and it
was so pretty I've never had the heart to part with it. It's
getting on for twenty years old, that skirt – but maybe it's
still good enough for you to use, Fenny!'

Fenny fingered the thick red silk. 'Oh, it's lovely!' she
said. 'Thank you, Aunt Aggie. Can I really cut it up?'

'Well, *I'll* never use it again!' said Aunt Aggie with a
sigh. 'I'm spry enough for my age, but I'd never be able
to work in the ring again. You have it, my dear.'

Fenella set to work. She glanced at Willie. 'Go on!'
she said. 'Begin your reading! You don't want to be
bottom of my class, do you?'

Willie grinned and began to read, very haltingly. But
he was certainly beginning to get better. Fenella corrected
his mistakes, as she busily began cutting out. Aunt Aggie
watched her in admiration.

'How you can cut out that little coat – and listen to
Willie reading at the same time and put him right when
he goes wrong – beats me! I'll have to get you to teach me
to read, too, Fenny.'

Fenella stopped her work in amazement. She stared at
Aunt Aggie. 'Can't *you* read?' she said. 'Goodness! Of
course I'll teach you, if you like.'

'You're a clever little girl,' said Aunt Aggie; and the
praise was sweet to Fenella, for she got very little of it
from her Aunt Lou.

She knew Jimmy's measurements because she had seen
her doll's clothes on him. She cut out trousers and coat,
and then asked Aunt Aggie if she had cardboard she
could use to make him a round, red, pill-box hat, such
as soldiers used to wear.

'I could cover it with red,' she said. 'And, oh, Aunt
Aggie, is that gold braid I can see in that box? May I
use that, too? I can make his soldier suit look awfully
smart with that!'

Fenella got on very well indeed that evening. She enjoyed the time very much. It was fun to hear Willie reading and making mistakes she could put right. It was exciting making such a fine little soldier suit for Jimmy. It was nice to have supper with two people she liked, sitting on the caravan steps with Cackles just below to rest her feet on.

'I wish I lived with you and your mother,' she said to Willie. And she thought to herself that she would soon tidy up and clean the dirty caravan, mend all Willie's clothes, and his mother's, too, and make new curtains to take the place of the ragged ones at the window.

'I must go now,' she said at last. 'I've had a lovely evening, really lovely. The suit has just got to have the gold braid on it, that's all, and the buttons, if you can find me some, Aunt Aggie. Little brass ones, if you can find any. I'll cover the hat tomorrow, too, if I've got time.'

Bobbo whimpered as Fenella went by his cage. She hadn't taken him with her that evening, and he missed her. She looked into the big cage. 'Bobbo!' she said, 'Are you lonely? I'll go and ask Uncle Ursie if I can play with you for a bit.'

She went to the red caravan. There was no one there.

Of course – Aunt Lou and Uncle Ursie were out. She saw the key of the bears' caravan hanging up on its nail. She took it down.

'I'm sure Uncle Ursie wouldn't mind if I took Bobbo into the caravan to play with him for a bit,' thought Fenella. 'I'll be careful to lock the door after me, so that Clump can't get out.'

She took the key and went to the cage. It was almost dark now, and she couldn't see where Bobbo was. But he could see Fenella all right! He was waiting at the door for her eagerly, a little soft, round barrel of a bear, whimpering for his friend. Clump took no notice. He had had a good meal, and was sleepy.

Fenella took Bobbo out, and locked the cage door carefully. Then she lifted Bobbo into her arms and walked with him to the caravan. 'You're growing,' she said. 'You're getting heavy, Bobbo. Don't grow too fast, or I won't be able to lift you. Now, here we are. We'll play a game, shall we?'

But it was almost too dark to play. Fenella looked at the oil lamp that stood on its shelf. Should she light it? She never had, and she was rather afraid of it. She didn't like the big 'plop' it made when it was lighted.

'I won't light it,' she said to the bear. 'You can just sit in my lap and I'll tell you a story.'

Bobbo didn't care what they did so long as he was with his friend, Fenella. She sat him on her knee, cuddled him, and began to tell him the story of the Three Bears. She thought that would be a very good tale for him.

When she had finished she felt hungry. It must be getting late! She went to the little larder and opened it. She felt about on the shelf. There was some bread and butter there, and a jar of honey. Good! Bobbo would like that, too.

She had put Bobbo down on her bunk when she went to fetch the food. When she went over to him, he had fallen fast asleep! 'Oh, I wish I could see what you look like, asleep in my bunk!' said Fenella. She clambered up beside him, and ate the bread and honey. Then, feeling tired, she cuddled down beside the warm, soft little bear.

'I must take you back and go to bed, Bobbo,' she said sleepily. 'I – really – must!'

But in half a second Fenella was asleep, too! She was very tired, and she slept as soundly as the little bear, cuddled up close to her.

Aunt Lou and Uncle Ursie came back by the last bus. They walked through the field gate and made their way to their caravan. 'I'll just see if the bears are all right,' said Uncle Ursie. He always went to look at them last thing, before he went to bed. He put his hand inside the dark caravan and felt about for his keys.

He took the one belonging to the bears' cage and went over to it. He unlocked the door and went in. He switched on his torch and spoke softly to the bears.

'Clump! Bobbo! Are you all right?'

Clump answered him with a grunt. He was curled up in his favourite corner. Uncle Ursie kicked the straw from the heap in the other corner, expecting to see Bobbo curled up there. But he wasn't, of course.

Uncle Ursie looked round the cage in alarm. Where was Bobbo? He wasn't anywhere to be seen! He wasn't in the cage at all!

Uncle Ursie, puzzled and upset, locked the cage door and went to Aunt Lou. 'Bobbo's not there,' he said. 'He's gone! Someone must have taken him! Or do you think he can possibly have squeezed through the bars?'

'Oh, Ursie!' said Aunt Lou. 'No, surely he couldn't have done that. He's too fat. Besides, he would have got out before now if he *could* have squeezed through the bars!'

The caravan was still dark. Aunt Lou hadn't lighted the lamp for fear of waking Fenella. She had felt for the little girl in the bunk, but had not touched furry Bobbo.

'I'd better rouse the camp,' said Uncle Ursie. 'Bobbo's too valuable to lose like this. Besides, he'll be terrified. I'll get Holla and Tiny. Wriggle will help to search, too.'

He set off to the caravans belonging to the three men. They were all in their bunks and asleep. They got up at once when they heard Ursie's news, and pulled on their trousers and jerseys.

'We haven't seen him wandering about,' said Holla. 'He *must* be in his cage, Ursie. Maybe he's curled up with Clump. It's impossible for him to get out.'

'Well – we'll have another look if you like,' said Uncle

Ursie, and they went back to Clump's cage. But no, it was quite certain there was no Bobbo in with him.

'We'd better separate and go round the camp to search,' said Holla. But just then there came a low call from the red caravan. It was Aunt Lou.

'Come here a minute!' she said. They all came up the steps. 'Come right in,' she said, and switched a bright torch on to Fenella's bunk. The four men stared.

For there, lying tightly curled up together, their arms round one another, were Fenella and the lost bear! They were both sound asleep.

Mr Holla chuckled. 'Well, well! That little Fenella of yours is a caution! You ought to get her to do something with that young bear, Ursie. She might come into the ring one day with him, if she makes anything of him. They're a pair, I must say!'

Aunt Lou looked rather cross. 'I'm sorry Ursie has had to wake you all up,' she said. 'Fenella's most tiresome to do this. I'll scold her in the morning.'

'No, don't,' said Wriggle hastily. 'She meant no harm. I don't mind being waked up, when I see that sight – Fenny and the bear!'

The men went back to their caravans, all chuckling at Fenella and the bear. Ursie tried to pacify Aunt Lou. He took the sleeping bear gently away from Fenella and put him in his cage with Clump. Fenella didn't stir.

'Now don't you get cross with her tomorrow,' said Uncle Ursie when he came back. 'She's a good little thing really. You give her a few smiles, Lou, instead of harsh words. I might have guessed where Bobbo was! I will another time!'

21. Lessons For Willie, Fenella And Bobbo!

The next morning, rather to Uncle Ursie's surprise, Aunt Lou did not scold Fenella very hard for what had happened the night before.

Fenella was sorry when she heard how upset Uncle Ursie had been, and how he had waked up Mr Holla, Mr Tiny and Mr Wriggle to help him look for the bear.

'And all the time he was curled up with me, fast asleep,' said Fenella. 'Oh, Uncle Ursie, I must have fallen asleep without meaning to. I'm so sorry.'

'It's not good to do things that cause trouble to other people,' said Aunt Lou; but that was about all she said. Fenella went to say she was sorry to Mr Holla and the others.

'Oh, don't mind about *that*,' said Mr Holla. 'I never mind being waked up in the middle of the night!'

Mr Tiny had taken his elephants down to the sea for a bathe, so she couldn't speak to him. But she found Mr Wriggle in his caravan.

'I'm sorry you were waked up last night all because of me,' she told him. Wriggle said he didn't mind at all, he rather liked it.

'It was nice of you to come and say you're sorry,' he said. 'Not many people do that, you know. As a reward I'll tread on my head for you.'

'Oh *no*, thank you all the same,' said Fenella hurriedly. 'Mr Wriggle, you know I don't want to see you do that. Oh, please don't!'

Mr Wriggle was doing such alarming wriggles and bends and twists that Fenella really did think he would end in treading on his own head. She ran off quickly to find Willie.

'Come along to Presto,' she said. 'It's time. Willie, did you hear about me and Bobbo last night?'

'Course I did,' said Willie. 'I guess you got the rough side of your aunt's tongue this morning.'

'No, she didn't say much,' said Fenella. 'Come on, Cackles – lessons!'

Lessons went well that day. Willie's practice in reading the night before seemed to have helped him. Presto was pleased. 'You shall give Willie a present,' he said to Fenella. 'You have something in your pocket for him.'

Fenella put her hand in her pocket. She brought out a tiny china goose, just like Cackles!

'Oh, look, Willie!' she said. 'A tiny china goose! And it's for *you*! Mr Presto, you *are* magic! There was nothing but my hanky in there just now!'

'And what is this that Willie has behind his ear?' said the conjurer. 'Aha! A tiny wooden bear!'

Willie felt something behind his ear and put up his hand. Sure enough there was a little wooden bear there! Willie grinned. He handed the bear to Fenella, who was delighted with it.

'Oh, is this for me? Thank you, Mr Presto! Oh, I do think I'm lucky to have lessons from a conjurer!'

Presto almost smiled, but not quite. He took up their two rubbers, two rulers, two pencils and two pens. Deftly he threw them up into the air so that they circled one by one over his head, and caught them as they came down, sending them up again time after time.

'I wish I could do that,' said Fenella. 'I do really. I wish you'd put juggling and conjuring on to our lesson timetable, Mr Presto.'

'Ah, those things would take years to teach to you,'

said Presto, putting everything neatly back on the table again. 'You must begin when you are two!'

'Oh, dear – it's too late for me to begin then,' said Fenella. 'But Bobbo isn't two yet. I could teach him things, couldn't I, Mr Presto?'

'When a young animal loves and trusts anyone as much as that little Bobbo loves and trusts you, Fenella, you can teach him anything!' said Presto. 'He is intelligent, that little bear. He imitates well. You should make him yours, Fenella, and teach him. Then maybe one day you could go into the ring with him, and he will bring pleasure and delight to many boys and girls!'

Fenella's eyes shone. 'Oh, Mr Presto! You don't really mean I could ever go into the ring! Willie, did you hear that? Let's teach Bobbo together. After all, you taught Cackles, didn't you, Willie?'

The two children went out into the sunshine. Cackles was pleased to see them. As usual she had been sitting patiently on the steps waiting for them. Cinders had quite given up trying to stop her. One day when he had refused to move from his favourite seat on the top step Cackles had simply squatted down on him. He had been buried under a cascade of warm feathers, and was frightened almost out of one of his nine lives!

'I'm going to get Bobbo,' said Fenella. 'I think I'll begin teaching him this very day, Willie. What shall I teach him?'

'He's such a little clown,' said Willie. 'Teach him clownish tricks. Give him a balloon and see what he does with it.'

Fenella sped off to ask Mr Groggy for one of his lovely big balloons. He gave her three, all ready blown up.

'Let's take Bobbo into the ring and practise with him there,' said Willie, peeping into the big tent, which was now up and flapping in the strong breeze. 'There's nobody here at the moment.'

They took Bobbo into the big ring. He knew it well, of course. Fenella showed him one of the balloons. He remembered how Mr Groggy so often turned head-over-heels when he carried his balloons. The little bear tried to stand on his head to go head-over-heels, and fell over with a flop. He sat down looking comical, and then stretched out a paw for the balloon.

It bounced away from him. Bobbo got up and followed it. He hadn't enough sense to hold the string, he tried to pick up the balloon itself.

But his paws were not made for picking up balloons. The children roared to see him going after the big balloon, which bounced away every time he pawed it. But suddenly one of Bobbo's claws pierced the rubber and the balloon burst with a loud pop.

Bobbo was amazed and horrified. Where had the lovely balloon gone? Whimpering loudly he ran to Fenella to be comforted, holding out his paws.

'You know, Fenny, we've only got to let him play about like this each day, and give him things like balloons – and perhaps an old doll of yours – and so on – and Bobbo will teach himself!' said Willie. 'He's so funny. Oh, Fenny – could you make him that clown's suit you were speaking of? He'd look lovely in that, and he really does act like a clown.'

Cackles came into the ring. She looked for her house, but it wasn't there. She went through the red curtains to find it. Bobbo followed her. Cackles found her house, opened the gate, walked up the cardboard path and went in at the front door.

She shut it loudly. Bobbo was surprised. He, too, walked in at the gate and up the path. He pushed at the door, but it was latched shut. He lifted his paw and banged loudly.

'He's knocking at the door! Oh, Cackles, let him in!' cried Fenella in delight. But Cackles wouldn't. This was *her* house, wasn't it? Bears could keep out of it!

But suddenly she opened the door and gave Bobbo a peck that surprised him very much. Then she slammed the door shut again. The children yelled with laughter.

Fenny! We've only got to let these two do things like this, and they'll bring the house down!' cried Willie. 'Why shouldn't you come into the ring with me and Cackles? It would be fun! I could go in and do my bird imitations first – and then you could come in with Bobbo – and he could go and bang at Cackles' front door – and she won't let him in; we could make quite a play of it!'

'Willie! Would you let me come in with you when you do your turn, would you really?' cried Fenella. 'Oh, I'd love that. I'd never dare to go in alone with Bobbo. Never. But if I could go when you're there. I wouldn't mind a bit.'

'Of course you could,' said Willie. 'My word, we'd make quite a stir, Fenny. Fenella and her pet bear, Bobbo, Willie Winkie and his pet goose, Cackles! That would look fine on the posters, wouldn't it?'

'Do you suppose I could have a very pretty dress?' said Fenella. 'A sort of fairy dress?'

'Have what you like,' said Willie. 'Look like a princess, or a fairy – or Marigold in the tale of the Three Bears!'

'I'd rather be a fairy, I think, with wings,' said Fenella. 'I wish Presto had enough magic to make wings fly. Oh, Willie, I do feel excited.'

'Well – it's easy to make plans,' said Willie. 'But it's difficult to get things going. Don't hope too much, because Mr Crack may think it's a silly idea, and your uncle and aunt may refuse to let you go into the ring, anyhow. And Bobbo may not be so good as we think him.'

But it wasn't a bit of good Willie pouring cold water on their plans. Fenella was absolutely sure everything would happen just as she wished it.

'I shall make a clown suit for Bobbo at once,' she said.

'Aunt Lou will give me the stuff, I'm sure. If not, your mother will! Oh, Willie, shall I earn some money, like you, if I do go into the ring?'

'I expect so,' said Willie. 'Why, what do you want money for?'

'I want to buy Aunt Lou a sewing-machine,' said Fenella. 'Then she can sew six times as quickly as she does now, and she won't mind making clothes for the animals as well as the circus folk.'

'You're rather a dear, Fenny,' said Willie, smiling at the eager little girl. 'Giving everybody ice creams as soon as you get a few shillings – and wanting to buy a sewing-machine for that bad-tempered aunt of yours if you earn any money!'

'Look at Bobbo now!' said Fenella. 'He's got another balloon. Oh, Willie, he's standing on it. Don't, Bobbo, it'll burst. I'll find you one of the dogs' footballs. You can stand on that.'

Bobbo did. He could balance very well. He not only stood on the big ball but by moving his hind paws a little to and fro he made the ball move, with himself on top of it!

'Just like Micko does!' said Willie. 'Bobbo, you're a born clown, and a clever one! Come along now, and you, too, Cackles. We shan't get any dinner at all if we stay here much longer! We've had a jolly good morning, Fenny, haven't we?'

22. The Little Soldier Suit

The circus was to have a short holiday before giving its next show. Mr Crack's performers had been working very hard, and some of them were tired. Also, Mr Crack wanted the clowns to think of some new tricks, and these had to be practised.

Each performer could book the ring for a certain time each day for any practice he wanted. In the mornings Fric, Frac and Malvina were there with their horses. After them came the clowns, thinking out new jokes and new tricks. Mr Groggy was very clever at this.

Willie had to ask for a time for himself and Fenella. He went to Mr Crack, who asked why he wanted the time. Surely Cackles the goose knew her part too well to need more time to rehearse?

'Well, sir, we've got an idea we could work up a turn with little Bobbo the bear and Fenella,' explained Willie. 'He just adores Fenny, you know.'

'That won't be any good,' said Mr Crack, who was not in a very good temper that day. 'Fenella hasn't been with the circus more than a few weeks. You ought to know that it takes years to make a performer, Willie! I'd never let Fenella go into the ring!'

'But, sir,' began Willie, 'we could—'

Mr Crack cut him short. 'Have the time for practice if you like! But it will be wasted, because I can tell you now, Fenella will not be allowed to go into the ring. She will not be good enough for that. And Bobbo isn't old enough.'

'Yes, but . . .' tried Willie again, and Mr Crack drew his shaggy brows over his deep-set eyes warningly. He was about to yell! He reached out for his famous whip.

Willie didn't stop to finish. He fled! He didn't want that whip curling round his legs. That was what usually happened when anyone argued with Mr Crack. He went to find Fenella, feeling disappointed.

Fenella listened, and her mouth went down at the corners. 'Oh! I do think he might let us try. How horrid of him!'

'Well, he says we can have the time to practise, though it will be wasted because he won't let you or Bobbo go into the ring,' said Willie. 'Do you still want to try and work up a turn with Bobbo and me and Cackles?'

'I won't give up!' said Fenella. 'We got the idea, and it's a good one. Let's go on with it even though Mr Crack is horrid about it. And I shall make Bobbo his clown suit, too, so there!'

Willie laughed. 'You're a funny one!' he said. 'So scared sometimes, and so determined at other times. All right, we'll try out our idea, even though it comes to nothing. Ask your uncle if we can have Bobbo each day.'

Uncle Ursie didn't mind at all. He said it was good for the little bear to play about in the ring and learn all he could whilst he was young.

'It is the only time really to learn anything, when you are young,' he said. 'It is the same for children as for animals. You can't teach an old dog new tricks, but you can teach a young one all the tricks in the world – if he will only learn them! Some animals are like Fenny – they have eager minds and love learning anything. Others are slow and hate learning. It is of no use to teach them.'

'Bobbo is so clever,' said Fenella. 'Once he has found out how to do something, he does it again and again, Uncle. You should see him trying to balance himself on the dogs' football!'

'Oh, can he do that?' said Uncle Ursie in surprise. 'There are some bears who are remarkably clever at such a trick. I have a much bigger ball you can use with Bobbo if you like. One that will be easier for him to walk on.'

He rummaged about under the red caravan, and found an old box. He took out a big ball, gaily coloured in red, yellow and blue. It was firm and strong.

'Oh!' said Fenella, pleased, 'that will do beautifully for Bobbo. Uncle Ursie, what an exciting box! What is this? And, oh, look at these dear little balls!'

'That's a balancing pole one of my performing seals used to have,' said Uncle Ursie, picking it up. 'He was called Flippers, Fenny, and he was one of the cleverest animals I ever had to do with. He could balance this pole on the end of his nose, and a ball on top of that! These were the balls he used to play with.'

'Oh, I *do* wish you had your seals now,' said Fenella. 'I should love them.'

'Yes, and they'd love you,' said Uncle Ursie. 'Flippers was so loving that he would follow me all over the camp, if I let him out of his tank, flopping about after me like a great dog. He'd kiss me, too.'

'Did Carol, your little girl, like him?' asked Fenella.

'She was a marvel with Flippers and the others,' said Uncle Ursie, remembering. 'The things she could do! You know, Fenny, though you're not really one of the circus folk, you fit in so well that you might have been with us for years – and you do remind me of our little Carol, the way you get on with the animals – especially my bears.'

'I know I can't make up to you for your own little girl,' said Fenny shyly. 'But I'll try to make up just a bit. It's so kind of you to let me live with you, Uncle Ursie. I didn't want to come at first, you know, but now I'm glad I did. I was dreadfully disappointed when I heard I wasn't to go to Canada with my Aunt Janet.'

'Were you really?' said Uncle Ursie. 'Now don't you

tell your Aunt Lou I said you reminded me of Carol. She wouldn't like it.'

'Oh, I won't,' said Fenella. 'Can I really have this big ball for Bobbo, Uncle? He'll love it.'

Bobbo certainly did love that big ball. He seemed to know what it was for immediately he saw it. He ran to it, grunting, and whilst Fenny held it for him he clambered up on it, got his balance, and began to walk it round the ring, very earnest and very pleased.

He fell off with a bump. He sat up looking most surprised, grunting. He got up and went after the ball again. He wasn't going to give up. This was fun. Cackles the goose watched him, and when she saw Willie and Fenella laughing and calling out praise to Bobbo, she wanted to do something, too.

So she waited till Bobbo was once more on the ball, and then she went and pecked him from behind. He fell off at once in surprise, and Cackles hissed in delight. The children roared with laughter.

'Who would ever have thought that a baby bear and goose would act together?' said Willie. 'Fenny, you *must* make that clown suit for Bobbo as soon as ever you've finished Jimmy's red soldier suit.'

Fenella went to work on the red soldier suit again that evening. She sat in Aunt Aggie's caravan, sewing away, whilst Willie once more read out to her from a book. He was really finding it easier to read now, and he began to realise that if only he would set to work and do a little hard practice in reading he would soon be able to read as well as Fenella.

'That's a really beautiful suit,' said Aunt Aggie, admiringly. As good as anything Lou could make. How grand Jimmy will look in it! Though I must say it's more than that mischievous little monkey deserves. Did you know that he had taught Grin and Bearit to throw things over the cliff, and watch them sail away in the wind?'

'Oh, no! Has he really?' cried Fenella. 'Isn't he *naughty*, Aunt Aggie? Though I'm sure that Grin and Bearit could quite well have thought of such a mischievous thing themselves.'

'Mr Holla caught the three of them throwing pails and brushes over the cliff,' said Aunt Aggie. 'Fric and Frac were very angry about it, because they are what they use for the horses. Mr Holla made Grin and Bearit go down and fetch every single thing. And as fast as they brought them up Jimmy threw them over the cliff again. Nobody could catch him. I must say I think Mrs Connie ought to keep him locked up.'

'He pines if he's locked up,' said Fenella. 'She says he would die if she kept him in his cage all day.'

'Maybe he would,' said Aunt Aggie. 'You never know with monkeys.'

'Did Mr Holla punish Grin and Bearit?' asked Willie.

'Of course,' said Aunt Aggie. 'He took away those dolls they like to play with – their toys – and shut them up in his caravan. I heard them yowling like children.'

'Oh, it's such fun to live in a circus camp,' said Fenella, her needle flying in and out. 'All kinds of things happen every day – things that never never could happen to ordinary people. I'm sure I would never have had a baby bear for a pet if I'd lived all my life long with Aunt Janet. And I wouldn't have wanted one either. Now I can't imagine what it would be like to be without Bobbo.'

'That little suit is going to make Jimmy look too smart for words!' said Willie. 'Is it finished yet?'

'Yes. I'm just putting a bit of braid round his red hat, and the whole thing's done,' said Fenella happily. 'There! I'll wrap it up now, and we'll leave it in Mrs Connie's caravan when we know she's out, Willie. Then I'll set to work tomorrow on Bobbo's clown suit. Perhaps Aunt Lou will find me some stuff. I can't keep asking you for things, Aunt Aggie.'

'Oh, you're welcome,' said Aunt Aggie. 'And you're such a help to Willie, too, in his lessons. You come to me if there's anything you want.'

That evening Willie and Fenella took a parcel across to Mrs Connie's caravan. She was out, but the door was open. Jimmy was inside, playing with the saucepans on the shelf. He skipped out as soon as he saw Willie and Fenella.

'He just *won't* be caught!' said Fenella. 'I'll leave the parcel on Mrs Connie's bunk. There! It's got Jimmy's name on it, so she'll know who it's for. We'd better shut the door and the windows, Willie, or that monkey of a Jimmy will take off the paper, and dress himself up in the suit and spoil it.'

They went out and shut the door behind them. They wondered very much what Mrs Connie would say when she found the suit.

'I hope it doesn't make any trouble,' said Fenella anxiously. 'I mean – suppose she thanks Aunt Lou for it – and Aunt Lou thinks I shouldn't have done it – and . . .'

'Oh, don't meet trouble half-way,' said Willie. 'Come on, let's take Cackles and Bobbo down to the sea for a bathe. It's so awfully hot. Get your bathing suit and I'll borrow Micko's again. We'll have a lovely time splashing about!'

23. A Surprise – And A Shock

A great many things happened the next day. It seemed quite an ordinary day at first. Fenella woke up, had her breakfast, chattered to her aunt, and then began to tidy the caravan.

'You get on with it whilst I go and measure Malvina for her new riding coat,' said Aunt Lou. 'I'll be back in half an hour. Then it will be time for you to go to Presto for your morning lessons.'

She went off. Fenella began to sweep the caravan floor. Uncle Ursie was outside, polishing up the big bright chain he put round Clump when he led him into the ring. Clump was very tame and would not hurt anyone, but many people were afraid if they saw that the bear had no chain on him.

Suddenly Mr Crack called to Uncle Ursie.

'Hey, Ursie! Here's a letter for you! The postman has just been.'

The postman came to the camp each morning and delivered all his circus letters to Mr Crack, who sorted them out and gave them to the various circus folk – whenever they had a letter, which wasn't very often.

Uncle Ursie was surprised. He took the letter and went back to the caravan with it. He opened it and read it slowly. Then he gave a shout.

'Hey, Fenny! Who do you think this is from? It's from your Aunt Janet! She's in Canada now and very happy – and she's sent you some money she had for you, and forgot to arrange about. She sends you her love, too, and says you must write to her, because she misses you very much.'

'Oh, does she say that?' said Fenny, coming down the caravan steps looking pleased. 'What money has she sent, Uncle Ursie? How nice of her.'

'It's a lot of money. It's twenty pounds,' said Uncle Ursie. 'I'd better put it in the savings bank for you, Fenny.'

'No, you have it, Uncle Ursie, because I'm sure I cost you a lot of money to feed,' said Fenella. 'I have such a big appetite now!'

'I wouldn't take a penny,' said Uncle Ursie. 'Not a penny. It's a pleasure to have a little girl like you. And besides, look how hard you work at your sewing, Fenny – you earn your keep and more with your needle! No, the money is yours to do as you like with. Maybe you'll want to spend it some day.'

A wonderful idea came into Fenella's mind. She would buy a sewing-machine for Aunt Lou! That would be a very good return for the kindness she and Uncle Ursie had shown her by taking her to live with them when they really couldn't have wanted her.

'Uncle Ursie – I want some now,' she said suddenly. 'I want very badly to buy something. Could I have some now?'

'What do you want to buy all of a sudden?' asked Uncle Ursie, amused.

'I can't tell you yet,' said Fenella. 'But, uncle, I really do promise you that it's something you and Aunt Lou will be very, very pleased about when you know what it is. You can trust me, can't you?'

'Oh, I can trust you all right,' said Uncle Ursie. 'And, after all, it's your own money. But you can't possibly have it all. How much do you want?'

Fenella wondered how much a sewing-machine would

cost. She hadn't any idea at all. Could she get one for five pounds? Or would it be more? She would have to ask Aunt Aggie or Mrs Connie. They might know.

'I don't quite know how much I would want,' said Fenella. 'Could you give me five pounds, do you think, Uncle Ursie?'

'That's a terrible lot of money,' said Uncle Ursie, 'But, yes – you can have it, if you really promise me I shall not be cross at the way it's spent.'

He counted out five one-pound notes and gave them to Fenella. She was thrilled. 'Now I can buy that sewing-machine!' she thought. 'And Aunt Lou will be able to do her work twice as quickly and three times as well! She will be pleased. I can easily show her how to work it.'

'I'll put the money into Rosebud's trunk,' she told Uncle Ursie. 'I'll keep it there till I go to spend it. Oh, what a surprise, Uncle Ursie! How kind of Aunt Janet to send me the money. I'll write to her this very day. I expect Mr Presto will let me write a letter in lesson-time. I'll go and fetch Willie now and tell him.'

She ran off, longing to tell her news. But Willie was nowhere to be seen. She passed Mrs Connie on the way and wondered if the monkey woman had tried on Jimmy's new suit yet. Mrs Connie's face was all smiles. She beckoned to Fenella.

'Would you like to see something?' she asked. 'Come and look!' She led the way to her caravan. Sitting on the table, as proud as punch, was Jimmy. He was dressed in his red soldier suit, and it fitted him perfectly! He looked really marvellous! His little round red hat was set on one side of his head, and kept in place by the chin-strap.

'Now isn't that perfect?' said Mrs Connie happily. 'I've never seen Jimmy look so grand. It's the finest suit he's ever had. And I've told him I'll take it away from him and let one of the other wear it, if he isn't good. Aha, he'll be good all right now – won't you Jimmy?'

Jimmy certainly looked a good, well-behaved little monkey that morning. He loved fine clothes, and knew that he looked smart. He chattered a little and then, standing up, he walked up and down the table, showing himself off.

'I'd never have thought it of Lou,' said Mrs Connie. 'Making Jimmy such a fine suit, after the words we had, and the way she vowed she'd not make Jimmy a thing. It's really kind of her, and I'm going to tell her so.'

'Oh, don't say a word to her,' said Fenella, alarmed. 'Just don't say anything about it, Mrs Connie. She – she doesn't expect you to.'

'Maybe not! But she's going to get a word of thanks from me whether she wants it or not!' said Mrs Connie. 'And I've made her a cake, too, see, Fenny – One of chocolate, with a banana filling – just what she likes. You'll be having it for tea, I expect.'

Fenella was even more alarmed. This would never do. She didn't want Mrs Connie to make such a fuss about the suit, because after all, her aunt hadn't made it, and it would be just as well if nothing was said about it at all. Fenella began to wish she hadn't made the suit. But surely Aunt Lou wouldn't be angry with her about it? She had only done it for the best.

She looked at the clock in Mrs Connie's caravan. 'Oh, dear – is that right?' she asked. 'It's past ten o'clock. I really must go, Mrs Connie. But do please not say anything to Aunt Lou about the suit!'

Mrs Connie was puzzled. Didn't Fenella want her aunt to get the words of thanks due to her? Of *course*, she must go and tell Lou how much she liked the suit. If Lou could turn out to be so kind and generous, Mrs Connie was going to be the same! There was that lovely chocolate cake to take, too. That would please Lou!

Fenella sped off. Wherever was Willie? He couldn't be in Mr Presto's caravan, because he always waited for her.

She ran to the dogs' cage. They were not there. She called to Mr Wriggle, who was nearby.

'Have you seen Willie? I can't find him.'

'He went off with the dogs,' said Wriggle. 'I expect he forgot all about lessons! Not too keen on them, is he? I say – can you stay a moment? I'd like you to see me tread on—'

'Oh, no, thank you!' cried Fenella and ran off. Willie *must* be somewhere about! But no, he wasn't. The dogs were gone and so was Willie. She ran round to Aunt Aggie's caravan to ask her if Willie would be back soon, and bumped into Mr Crack, who was striding along in his big top boots.

'No, now!' he said. 'What a hurricane! What are you in such a hurry for?'

'I'm looking for Willie,' said Fenella.

'Aha! It's lesson-time, I suppose,' said Mr Crack, and he looked at his enormous gold watch. 'A quarter past ten. Isn't ten o'clock your time? Surely you aren't keeping Mr Presto waiting?'

'Well,' said Fenella, not liking to say that she had been hunting for Willie, 'well, you see, er – yes, I'm afraid I *am* a bit late this morning, Mr Crack. I'll go right away now.'

'Where *is* Willie?' suddenly roared Mr Crack after her. Fenella was struck dumb. She never could say a word when people roared at her. She stared at Mr Crack in fright. Thank goodness he hadn't got that cracking whip with him.

'Have you lost your tongue?' said Mr Crack, losing his temper. 'I asked you – where *is* Willie?'

'Gone to the shore with the dogs,' said Wriggle, strolling up, and taking pity on Fenella's fright. 'He will be back soon, I expect.'

'Tell him to come to me as soon as he gets back,' commanded Mr Crack, and strode off scowling.

'Oh, dear,' said Fenella, looking in dismay at Wriggle. 'Now Willie will get into trouble. Oh, what will Mr Crack say to him?'

'He'll give him a hiding, I expect,' said Wriggle. 'Well, young Willie ought to have sense enough to obey orders. You'd better go now, or you'll get into trouble, too.'

Fenella ran off, very troubled. Presto was waiting impatiently in his caravan. He frowned when he saw Fenella.

'Twenty minutes late!' he said. 'I thought you had better manners, Fenella. I am ashamed of you, and you make me feel cross. Where is Willie?'

'I don't know,' said poor Fenella. 'I'm sorry I'm late, Mr Presto.'

'If it happens again, you will get no more lessons from me,' said Presto. 'Not one. I will have nothing to do with ungrateful people.'

This was dreadful. Fenella tried to settle down to her writing, but she couldn't help thinking and thinking about Willie. In half an hour's time he came in. Fenella looked up at him. He glared at her furiously.

'Beast!' he said. 'Telling tales of me! Making me go to Mr Crack. I suppose you're glad I got a hiding from him! I'll never speak to you again.'

'Oh, Willie!' said Fenella and burst into sobs. 'I didn't tell tales of you! At least—'

'That is enough,' said Presto coldly. 'You deserved all you got, Willie, and you know it. Stop crying, Fenella. If you told tales of Willie you deserve to be miserable. If you didn't, then you can explain to Willie afterwards. I will have no more disturbance in here this morning!'

It was a dreadful morning. What with Willie's scowls and Fenella's tears and Presto's coldness the time seemed twice as long as usual. Oh, dear – whatever could Fenny do to put things right with Willie?

24. Things Go Wrong

Lessons were over at last. There were no presents for good children that day! Fenella tried to take Willie's arm. 'Oh, Willie! I didn't tell tales. I met Mr Crack when I was looking for you, and I just *said* I was looking for you, but it wasn't tales, really it wasn't.'

'Ho! that's what *you* think, you mean little thing!' said Willie. 'Anyway, it cost me a hiding, and I've been yelled at by Mr Crack till I'm almost deaf. I didn't mean to be late. One of the dogs ran off and I had to go and look for him. You might have guessed that – but you're so mean you'd thought you'd go and tell tales of me.'

Fenella began to cry. 'Willie, you must believe me. I'm not mean like that. Willie, don't push me off like that, you're horrid.'

'So are you,' said Willie. 'I tell you, I don't want to speak to you again. Keep away from me and Cackles.'

'Willie, we're not quarrelling, are we?' said Fenella, scared. 'We always said we'd never quarrel. It takes two to make a quarrel. I *won't* quarrel!'

'I don't care what you do,' said Willie, and walked off. Fenella went slowly to the red caravan, feeling very unhappy. She thought she would tell her Aunt Lou and perhaps get a little comfort.

But no! The day had gone wrong, and it went on and on going wrong, in the way some days have. In the caravan was a very angry Aunt Lou indeed. When

Fenella came in, she took the little girl by the shoulders and gave her a hard shake.

'What do you mean by sucking up to Mrs Connie and making that suit for Jimmy behind my back? You sly little thing – never saying a word to me about it – letting her think I'd made it. As if I'd go back on my word! I said I wouldn't, and I meant it. You're a bad, deceitful girl. I told Mrs Connie a few things this morning, and she went out of here smiling on the other side of her face, I can tell you!'

Fenella listened in horror. She could hardly say a word, but at last she got a few out. 'Oh, Aunt Lou – she only meant to be nice to you – and that cake . . .'

'Ho, that cake! I threw it out to the gulls!' said Aunt Lou, and she looked so hard and unkind that Fenella turned away in despair.

The little girl went to the door, but Aunt Lou called her back. 'I've not finished with you yet! What about this money your uncle had for you? You're not going to spend that five pounds, let me tell you! Such waste! And what were you going to spend it on, I'd like to know?'

'It was a secret,' said Fenella. 'I was sure you and Uncle would be pleased when you knew what it was. Do wait and see, Aunt Lou, before you make up your mind I was going to waste it.'

'Well, you won't have it,' said Aunt Lou. 'However foolish your uncle is, I'm *not*. You can't have any of that money to spend till you're much older.'

Fenella went down the steps. What horrid things were happening. Willie angry with her, Presto angry, Mr Crack angry, and Aunt Lou furious! And now no doubt Mrs Connie would be, too.

But surprisingly enough Mrs Connie wasn't. She saw Fenella creeping away by herself, and she was really upset when she saw how sad the little girl looked. She ran to her.

'Don't you look like that, my lovey! It's that sharp-tongued aunt of yours, I suppose. Why didn't you tell me it was your own kind little heart and clever fingers that made that suit for Jimmy? Silly child! If you'd told me that I'd not have said a word.'

'Everyone's so angry with me,' sobbed Fenella. 'Even Willie!'

'You come into my caravan and talk to me,' said Mrs Connie. 'Things go wrong sometimes, but they soon clear up if we face them properly. You come along with me.'

The little monkey woman had the kindest heart in the world. She made a fuss of Fenny. She gave her a big slice of gingerbread with peel in it, and put a glass of sweet lemonade before her.

'To think you made that beautiful little suit!' she said. 'Well, well! You're a marvel. It fits Jimmy like a glove. It was like you, Fenny, to think of a thing like that and never say a word. Your aunt will get over it, never you fear. As for Willie, he'll get over his sulks, too. He's a nice boy, but he's too big for his boots sometimes. A hiding won't hurt him.'

'But he thinks it's all because of *me*,' said Fenella. She took a bite of the cake. It was delicious. She sipped the lemonade and began to feel better. It was nice to have someone fussing her like this.

She began to tell Mrs Connie everything. The little monkey woman listened patiently. Grin came to the door of the caravan and she waved him away. He always turned up when cake was about. Fenny didn't even see him. She went on talking, and felt better and better as she poured out everything to Mrs Connie.

She told her about the money and how she wanted to buy a sewing-machine for Aunt Lou, and how her aunt had vowed she wouldn't let her have it. She told her about Mr Presto and how he had said she was ungrateful, and had been so cross too.

'What shall I do?' she asked. 'How can I make Willie believe me? And do you think Aunt Aggie will be cross as well, and not help me with stuff to make Bobbo a little clown suit? I did want to start this evening.'

'Oh, Aggie will be all right,' said Mrs Connie, making up her mind to run across and tell her how unhappy Fenella was, and that she really hadn't meant to get Willie into trouble. 'Don't you worry about that. If I were you I'd keep away from Lou till she's got her temper back again. She'll be all right soon. You go across to Aggie's and sew there. And if Willie's there, just talk to him as if nothing had happened. He can't keep it up for long.'

'All right,' said Fenella, feeling more cheerful. 'And I'll go tomorrow and see if I can buy that sewing-machine for Aunt Lou.'

Mrs Connie looked in amazement at Fenella. 'What! You'd do that even after she's scolded you like this! You're a forgiving child, Fenny. I wish you were mine!'

'It might make Aunt Lou feel happier if she knew I wanted to give her something,' said Fenella. 'I don't *feel* as if I want to, really, at this very moment, Mrs Connie – I feel that she's horrid and mean. But I know that things would be so much easier if she had a sewing-machine – she wouldn't need to work so hard, and she'd love it.'

Aunt Lou didn't bother about where Fenella was. She was so annoyed with her for making the little suit for Jimmy, and not saying anything about it. Uncle Ursie did not make things any better when he stuck up for Fenny.

'She only did it out of the kindness of her heart, so that you wouldn't have to, and so that Mr Crack wouldn't turn us all out for your defiance,' he said. 'I wonder you can't see that, Lou. Would you have said the same if our little Carol had done it? No – you'd have thought she was a clever, kind little kid, you know you would. You've changed, Lou. Carol wouldn't know you for her mother if she was alive now.'

Aunt Lou was horrified to hear such a thing from kindly old Ursie. She took a look at herself in the glass. She saw her grim face, the hard, thin-lipped mouth and the cross-looking eyes. No, Carol wouldn't know her now!

'Fenny's so like Carol,' said Ursie. 'She's like her in looks, with that mane of red hair, and she's like her in ways. Look at the way she gets on with the animals, and yet she was never in a circus before. Mark my words, Lou, you won't keep that child long if you treat her harshly. She'll be writing to her aunt in Canada to take her away, and I don't blame her. But I should miss her now.'

Aunt Lou began to feel most uncomfortable. There was

a lot of truth in Ursie's words. Then her temper rose again and she spoke spitefully to him.

'You're a soft old man, that's what you are! And Fenny's not so simple and sweet as you think she is!'

Uncle Ursie went out, cross and unhappy. People like Lou made so much trouble in the world! What a pity.

Fenella stayed with Mrs Connie till tea-time, for she really did not dare to go and see if her aunt wanted her to help with any sewing. After that she went across to Aunt Aggie's caravan. Mrs Connie had already been to see her and had explained things. Aunt Aggie, knowing Willie's way of sulking at times, nodded her head.

'Don't you worry, Connie. I'll make Fenny welcome. I'm sure the child really didn't tell tales of Willie. She's not that sort. You send her here. If Willie's in the sulks, he can stay out.'

So Fenella came timidly to Aunt Aggie's caravan and was made very welcome. 'I'm going to be hard at work,' announced Fenella. 'That is, if you'll give me some more stuff to sew, Aunt Aggie. I want to make something for Mr Presto, to show him that really and truly I *am* grateful for all he has taught me. And I'm going to make a new bonnet for Cackles to show Willie I'm sorry for making him unhappy. And I'd like to start the little clown suit for Bobbo.'

Willie was not there. He came in once, saw Fenella, and went out again, scowling. Nobody took any notice of him. Fenella found some gold stars in one of Aunt Aggie's boxes and was thrilled. 'May I have these? I want to make a little black mat for Cinders to sit on, when Mr Presto draws a chalk circle round her to do some magic. And if I sew some stars on, it will match Mr Presto's cloak and caravan!'

The little mat was soon finished. It looked very grand with its pattern of gold stars. Aunt Aggie admired it very much.

'You're clever, Fenny! And it took you no time at all to make it! Whatever will you do next!'

'I'm turning this old straw hat of Rosebud's into a bonnet for Cackles,' said Fenella, pleased at Aunt Aggie's admiration. 'That won't take me long either. It's going to have little red ribbons hanging down the back. Cackles will look sweet in it!'

It was tried on Cackles an hour later when it was finished. Cackles certainly looked beautiful, and rather fancied herself. She waddled across the floor of the caravan showing off her new bonnet.

'Look, Willie!' said Aunt Aggie, as Willie appeared suddenly. 'What do you think of Cackles' new bonnet?'

Willie gave it a glance. He thought it was very fine indeed. But he wasn't going to say so! 'It's all right,' he said ungraciously, and disappeared again.

Then Fenella had an hour left to start Bobbo's clown suit. Aunt Aggie had given her some fine white stuff that had once been a cloak. It was just the thing. Fenella began to cut out the suit, frowning, as she tried to think out exactly how it should go.

She was sorry when she had to stop. 'Well, you ought to feel better now,' said Aunt Aggie, and gave her an unexpected goodnight kiss. 'You've been doing things for other people all the evening. There's nothing like that for making things come right!'

25. Has Fenella Run Away?

The next day Fenella remembered that she meant to go and buy her aunt a sewing-machine. Aunt Lou had been a little nicer to her, but not much. Uncle Ursie had been exactly the same as usual. Willie still avoided her, and would not say a word.

She went to her lessons at ten o'clock. Willie was there before her! He wasn't going to risk being tackled by Mr Crack again.

'Ah, nice and early this morning, I am pleased to see!' said Presto. Fenella gave him a little parcel.

'You're always giving *me* presents. So now I've made *you* one,' she said. 'At least, it's for Cinders. I just wanted you to know I *am* grateful for all the time you spend on me.'

Presto opened the parcel. When he saw the beautiful little mat, embroidered with its gold stars, he was touched and pleased. 'Now that is very kind of you, Fenella,' he said. 'You do not sulk or bear malice when people scold you. I am proud of you. Here, Cinders, sit on this and be proud to have such a fine mat of your own. We will take it into the ring with us when next we go!'

Willie did not look pleased. 'Sucking up again,' he muttered under his breath.

'I'm not,' said Fenella indignantly. 'Didn't I make Cackles a new bonnet last night? Well, I wasn't sucking up to *you*, was I? I just wanted to show you I was sorry you'd been in a row.'

Willie said no more. He had really been very pleased with the little bonnet, but he always found it difficult to come out of his sulks once he had got them badly. Aunt Lou and Uncle Ursie were going to be busy that afternoon. 'I've got to go and see to all Mr Crack's clothes in his caravan, and look them over,' she said to Ursie. 'I'll be back for tea, though.'

'I'm going to take Clump and Bobbo down to the shore,' said Uncle Ursie. 'It's so hot. What are *you* doing, Fenny? Coming with me?'

'Well, no, if you don't mind,' said Fenella. 'I've got something important to do.'

'All right,' said Uncle Ursie, thinking perhaps she was going off with Willie and the dogs. 'See you at tea-time.'

'Yes, I'll be here,' said Fenella. 'I'll put the kettle on to boil ready for you.'

Aunt Lou took her work-basket and went. Uncle Ursie fetched the bears and disappeared down the cliff path. As soon as they had gone Fenny went to her doll's trunk. Where was that five pounds?

It wasn't there! It was gone! Fenella kept on feeling through all the clothes, but no, the money was not there. She guessed then that Aunt Lou must have taken it. She stood in the caravan, her face red, tears starting in her eyes. Then she blinked them back. It was silly to keep wanting to cry when things went wrong, Willie hadn't cried even when he had been whipped by Mr Crack the day before.

She thought hard. 'Aunt Lou didn't know what I wanted the money for, else she surely would have let me use it. Well, I'll go and ask Mrs Connie to lend me some, and I'll pay her back when I get Uncle Ursie to give me more money. Oh, dear—I do wish Aunt Lou had *told* me she was going to take it away. But I suppose she did it because *I* didn't tell her about making that suit for Jimmy.

She went to Mrs Connie's caravan and told her she

needed the money. 'Uncle Ursie has gone down to the shore, or I'd ask him,' she said. 'Could *you* lend me some, please, Mrs Connie? You know that I'll pay you back this evening when I get it from Uncle Ursie.'

Most circus folk are generous and eager to help one another. Mrs Connie didn't hesitate for a moment. Fenny wanted the money – and she wanted it for a kindly deed, too. Then she should have it! Lou had taken that money out of the doll's trunk, had she? Then she, Mrs Connie, would be all the more pleased to let Fenny have the same amount! She counted out four pounds in pound and ten shilling notes, and a pound in silver coins.

'There you are,' she said. 'You take the bus at the gate, and you get out at the ninth stop. That's the town of Merring-on-Sea. There's some fine big shops there. You'll have to ask them to *send* the machine, you know. It will be too heavy to carry. I only hope it won't cost more than five pounds!'

Fenella set off. She saw Willie in the distance and waved to him. But he didn't wave back, and she felt sad. She caught the bus and was soon trundling away through the countryside.

Tea-time came. Aunt Lou came across from Mr Crack's caravan after a hard afternoon's work. She frowned when she saw there was no kettle boiling. She had been hoping that Fenella would have had the kettle ready and bread and butter cut. If she had, Aunt Lou was quite prepared to be better-tempered!

Uncle Ursie came up from the shore with two wet and happy bears. They had all had a lovely time. Uncle Ursie was never so happy as when he was with his bears. He had been with bears and seals all his life, and to him they were like his children.

'Where's Fenny?' he said. 'I suppose she's not back yet. I was hoping to tell her all about Bobbo's antics this afternoon. He's a real comic.'

Fenella didn't come after tea. She hadn't arrived by six o'clock. Uncle Ursie went across to Willie. 'Have you seen Fenny?' he asked.

'Not since she caught the bus at two o'clock this afternoon,' said Willie. 'Why, isn't she back? Where did she go?'

It was news to Uncle Ursie that Fenella had gone off by bus. He was puzzled. He went to Aunt Lou and told her.

'Where can the child have gone?' he said. I hope she'll come back soon.'

But seven o'clock came and no Fenella. Uncle Ursie couldn't sit still. 'You don't think she's run off, do you, Lou?' he said. 'She's been very unhappy, you know. It would be dreadful if we lost Fenny, as well as Carol.'

Aunt Lou began to be alarmed, too. She wished she

hadn't scolded Fenny so hard. After all, the child hadn't done any harm – she had only tried to put things right without telling her. She went across to Mrs Connie.

'Have you seen Fenella?' she asked gruffly, for she hadn't spoken to Mrs Connie since she had quarrelled with her the day before.

Mrs Connie saw that Lou was anxious and she was pleased. She wasn't going to tell her where Fenny had gone, or why! No, let her think the child had run away! That would do Lou good to think she had driven a child away by her harshness!

'Fenny came and borrowed five pounds from me,' said Mrs Connie. 'Then off she went.'

'Good gracious! Five pounds!' said Aunt Lou, remembering guiltily the money she had removed from the doll's trunk. 'Oh, Connie – has the child run away? Has she taken the five pounds to try and get out to Canada! Maybe a child would think it wouldn't cost more than that.'

'Lou, if Fenny ran away I wouldn't blame her,' said Mrs Connie. 'You had one dear little girl, and you lost her – and here you have another sent to you, and you treat her unkindly, and she runs away. What's the matter with you? You need a change of heart. Ursie will run away from you one day, too!'

Aunt Lou turned away miserably. She felt quite sure now that Fenny had run away. The police would find her, no doubt – and everyone would know Fenny had run away because she, her Aunt Lou, had treated her badly. She had shut her heart to Fenny. Fenny wasn't Carol, but she was like her, and Aunt Lou wouldn't have anyone in her heart but Carol. She was wrong, very wrong. She had lost her chance of having another child growing up and loving her.

When nine o'clock came everyone in the camp was alarmed. They all knew now that Fenny had gone by the two o'clock bus and hadn't come back. Mrs Connie also began to think, as everyone else did, that Fenny had run away. 'She just made the buying of that sewing-machine an excuse,' she said to herself. 'She'd have been back long ago if she'd just gone for that. Poor Ursie, he does look bad. He was fond of that little niece of his.'

Presto wanted to take Mr Crack's car and go off and look for Fenny. Mr Crack wanted to telephone the police. But the circus folk always kept away from the police if they could, so nobody thought much of that idea.

Aunt Aggie was crying. 'I wanted her to come and sew with me this evening,' she said. 'I waited for her. She was making a clown suit for Bobbo.'

'She brought me a lovely little mat for Cinders,' said Presto. 'She was a kind child. Mr Crack, we must do *something* to find her!'

Mr Holla and Mr Tiny said they would go out and look for her. Everyone wanted to do something. Willie was simply horrified to think that Fenny really might have run away.

He went to his mother. 'Mum, I didn't even wave to Fenny when she went to catch the bus. And I haven't spoken to her all day. If I'd been decent she wouldn't have gone, I'm sure. If only she'll come back safe and sound I'll make it up to her.'

Aggie wiped her tears. 'Yes, you've done your share in making her unhappy,' she said. 'But, mark my words, she won't come back.'

This made Willie feel more wretched than ever. He was thoroughly ashamed of himself now, and wanted to make things up to Fenny and see her smile at him. Cackles knew he was unhappy and pressed herself against him.

Uncle Ursie went to Aunt Lou in the caravan. She was sitting at the table doing nothing. Uncle Ursie spoke to her.

'Lou! If Fenny has really run away, and is found and

brought back, ought we to make her stay if she doesn't want to? You don't want the child, do you? If you'd rather she didn't come back to us again, I can arrange it. I'm fond of the child myself, but if you don't want her, and she doesn't want to live with us, I'll see she goes somewhere else where maybe she'll be happy.'

To Uncle Ursie's immense amazement Aunt Lou burst into tears, a thing he had not seen her do for years. 'I do want her!' sobbed Aunt Lou. 'I wouldn't take to her because she wasn't Carol. But now I'll love her because she's Fenny. Suppose something's happened to her, Ursie! I'll blame myself all my life long, just like I blamed myself for Carol. If only she comes back safe and sound I'll soon show her I want her. I've been cruel and hard – but if Fenny comes back I'll be different.'

'Poor Lou,' said Uncle Ursie, and put his arms round her. 'Don't take on so. You just show the child we want her, when she comes back. Then she'll be as right as rain.'

'But where *is* she?' said Aunt Lou anxiously. And that is what all the circus folk were saying. 'Where *is* Fenny?'

26. Bravo, Fenny!

Just as Mr Crack was getting into his car to go out and search for Fenny with Presto, a shout went up from someone at the gate.

'Here she is!'

And sure enough, there she was – a very tired, limping little Fenny, scared of the dark, and very much afraid of being scolded by everyone. Mr Crack ran to her and swept her off her feet.

'Here she is, bless her! Where have you been, you scamp! You've given us a real scare!'

'Fenny! I'm so glad you've come back!' That was Willie. He tried to hug her, but could only reach her legs, as she was on Mr Crack's shoulder. 'Oh, Fenny, I've been so worried about you.'

Then Uncle Ursie and Aunt Lou came running up, too. 'Give her to me,' commanded Aunt Lou, and Mr Crack put her down. To Fenny's great surprise and pleasure Aunt Lou put her arms round her and hugged her. She pressed her cheek against Fenny's and wouldn't let her go.

'You shouldn't run away,' she kept saying. 'You shouldn't. You shouldn't. But, thanks be, you've come back!'

Uncle Ursie hugged her, too. Fenny felt more and more surprised and pleased. She had been expecting plenty of scoldings, not all this petting and kindness. Everyone crowded round, trying to get in a word or a pat.

'I couldn't do without my good little pupil!' said Presto's deep voice, and Fenny looked up at him and smiled. He smiled back, a sudden and delightful smile that made his whole face look different.

'Mr Presto! You've smiled!' cried Fenella. 'You did, you did. And you vowed you never would. Please smile again.'

Aunt Aggie, Mrs Connie, Wriggle and all the others came to make sure that Fenny was really back again. It was most astonishing to see how the little girl had made her way into their hearts during the short time she had been with them. Aunt Lou couldn't help feeling proud to see what affection they had for her.

She was carried back to the red caravan by Ursie. Mr Crack came with them. He wanted to find out what had happened to Fenella.

'I didn't run away,' said Fenella, surprised that anyone should think she had. 'Why should I? I like being with the circus. I just went to buy Aunt Lou a sewing-machine with some money I got yesterday.'

There was a dead silence. Aunt Lou swallowed a lump that had suddenly come into her throat. Fenny went on. 'I borrowed some money from Mrs Connie and I went. There wasn't a sewing-machine shop in the first town, so I went on to the next and found one there.'

'And did they sell you a sewing-machine?' said Mr Crack, very much interested in Fenny's story.

'No, they wouldn't, because I hadn't enough money and because they said I was only a child,' said Fenella. 'I was awfully disappointed. But they gave me this paper, look, Aunt Lou. And if you'll fill it in and send it to them, with the money, they will send you a lovely machine. I saw it. I shall love using it, too!'

Aunt Lou couldn't say a word.

'You're too good to be true, Fenny,' said Uncle Ursie. 'Here's your Aunt Lou been scolding you for all she was worth – and all you do is to go out and buy her a sewing-machine. I never knew such a kid. Lou, the next three times she's naughty, we won't scold her at all, will we?'

'No,' said Aunt Lou, her face looking younger and softer than it had for years.

'Won't you really?' said Fenny in delight. 'Oh, then I'll do some things I've longed to do. I'll take Bobbo to bed with me one night and let him sleep there all night through!'

Everyone laughed. 'Well, what happened next?' asked Mr Crack.

'I went down to the seashore at that town,' said Fenny, 'and I stayed too late to catch the bus back here. I didn't know it went so early. So I had to walk all the way back. That's all. I thought you'd be very cross with me for being late.'

'All's well that end's well,' said Mr Crack, opening the door of the caravan. 'Go to sleep now, Fenella, for you must be tired out.'

Fenella was soon in bed. Aunt Lou bent down and kissed her. Fenella was so surprised that she didn't kiss her back. Then she put her arms round Aunt Lou's neck.

'You're nice,' she said sleepily. 'Always be nice, Aunt Lou. I love you when you're nice.'

Fenella soon forgot about her adventure, but the circus folk didn't. Willie didn't let Fenny out of his sight after that. Mr Presto, once he had remembered how to produce a smile, found that he had plenty, and it was nice to use them.

'Why didn't you smile before?' asked Fenella one morning. 'I do want to know.'

'It's something I want to forget,' said Presto, 'and if I tell you I shan't forget it, shall I? I shall forget it soon, if you keep making me smile. Now what about a spot of magic this morning? Shall we have Cinders in, and see what happens?'

It was Aunt Lou that made things so much nicer for
Fenny. She still had a sharp tongue if things didn't go
right, but she showed Fenny that she was fond of her,
and she accepted the sewing-machine with so much
pleasure that Fenny laughed to see her aunt's delight.

'I never saw such a clever machine!' she said. 'Never!
Do you mean to tell me it does all those different stitches?
Well, I never did! Let's use it this very afternoon.'

'We can go on with the clown suit I'm making for
Bobbo,' said Fenella. 'We could finish it between us. Can
we, Aunt Lou? Then we'll try it on him. He'll look so
sweet.'

He did! The little white clown suit with its black
bobbles fitted him well, and the clown hat that went with
it gave him a most comical look. He capered about
clumsily and everyone clapped him. He sat down suddenly and looked round in surprise. Then he clapped his
paws together solemnly.

'Can we go into the ring one night?' begged Fenella of
Uncle Ursie. 'Willie and I have been practising with
Bobbo every day now. The circus opens again tomorrow.
Can't I just *try*, Uncle Ursie!'

'Mr Crack has to decide that,' said Uncle Ursie. 'You
ask him to see your turn with Willie, Cackles and Bobbo,
and hear what he says. I think it's very good myself.
Maybe he'll let you try.'

'And can I have a very, very pretty frock?' asked
Fenella. 'We could make one, couldn't we, Aunt Lou?'

'Yes. I could make you a lovely one,' said Aunt Lou.
'I've got some frilly stuff for a skirt. And you could have
a little cloak edged with red like Willie's if you like.'

'Oh, I'd like wings edged with red instead!' said
Fenny. 'I've always wanted to have a fairy's dress. Uncle
Ursie, *please* ask Mr Crack if he'll see our turn.'

Mr Crack said he would. He turned up in the ring that
afternoon. Willie, Fenny, Bobbo, Cackles and Uncle

Ursie were there waiting for him. Aunt Lou was watching
from the seats. Mr Crack joined her and nodded his head
for Willie to come in with Cackles.

He watched with great interest and a good deal of
astonishment from beginning to end of the carefully re-
hearsed turn. Willie was as good as ever with his bird
imitations, and with Cackles – but this time there was
Bobbo as well, in his little clown suit, waddling here and
there, balancing himself on his big ball, going after
balloons, following Cackles into her house and banging
at the door !

And there was Fenny, too, guiding him and helping
him, rather nervous, but determined to show Bobbo off
to the very best advantage.

'Very good indeed,' said Mr Crack at last, and Aunt
Lou began to clap. 'Willie, I have a mind to let you and
Fenny try this turn together. If it goes flat, Fenny can step
out. If it's a success, she can stay in. Bobbo is very good –
a natural little bear-clown. You get them sometimes like
that. Fenny is a marvel with him. A very good little show.'

Fenny almost ran to him and hugged him. But he was
the great Mr Crack, and she was still rather scared of him,
so she didn't. She just stood and beamed. Willie squeezed
her arm.

'We'll bring the house down !' he whispered. 'Now
you'll have to get busy with that new dress of yours,
Fenny.'

Soon the camp was busy once more with its prepara-
tions for the next show. Its short holiday was over. Now
to work again !

The circus folk were glad. They liked the excitement of
dressing up, the glare of the lights in the big top at night,
the shouts and cries, the cheers and clapping. It was their
life and they could not be happy for long without it.

And now Fenella, too, felt the same excitement. Her
fingers trembled as she put on the beautiful little fairy

dress Aunt Lou had made for her. Uncle Ursie dressed Bobbo, who was just as excited as Fenny herself. He tried to turn head-over heels with his hat on.

'*Not* with your hat on, Bobbo,' said Uncle Ursie. 'Take it off first. How many more times am I to tell you that?'

The great evening had come. Hundreds of people streamed in at the gate, eager to see the wonderful show. Drums sounded and trumpets blew to welcome them. The ring was strewn with clean, fresh sawdust. Everything was ready – and the show began.

Shall we peep in? Here we are in the middle of the show. What is going on? A boy stands in the centre of the ring, whistling and fluting like a dozen birds. Then he quacks like a duck – he cries like a seagull – and the seagulls outside answer him and swoop down to the tent.

And now here is a little girl coming in. How pretty she

looks with her red hair fluffed round her excited face. Her frilly skirt bounces up and down and she has white wings edged with bright red.

'She's a fairy!' whisper all the watching children around. 'She's a fairy. And, oh, look – is that a tiny clown?'

Yes, it is. It's Bobbo, of course, proud to wear his beautiful clown suit, eager to get claps and cheers from all these watching people. How comical he is! And look at that goose coming out of the little house to do her shopping!

Everyone roars with laughter. Cackles does her shopping – and Bobbo follows behind, trying to get her basket from her.

'Look out, Cackles, he nearly had it! Aha, serve him right, you pecked him very neatly. But he doesn't care! He's off after that big ball.'

So the four of them gave their first turn, and when at last Cackles goes to her house and slams the door, and Bobbo follows and knocks loudly, there is such a howl of laughter that even Mr Crack, peering with delight through the red curtains, is surprised.

Bravo, Fenny! Bravo, Bobbo!' he shouts as they come out together, Bobbo's paw in Fenny's hand. 'Well done, Willie, well done, Cackles! A very fine performance.'

And we must clap, too, and shout loudly. Bravo, Fenny! Bravo! You deserve your success, and so does little Bobbo. You're just at the beginning of things now. What will you do in the future?

Well, that's another story. I must tell it to you some day!

Other great reads from **Red Fox**

Further Red Fox titles that you might enjoy reading are listed on the following pages. They are available in bookshops or they can be ordered directly from us.

   If you would like to order books, please send this form and the money due to:

ARROW BOOKS, BOOKSERVICE BY POST, PO BOX 29, DOUGLAS, ISLE OF MAN, BRITISH ISLES. Please enclose a cheque or postal order made out to Arrow Books Ltd for the amount due, plus 30p per book for postage and packing to a maximum of £3.00, both for orders within the UK. For customers outside the UK, please allow 35p per book.

NAME _____

ADDRESS _____

_____

Please print clearly.

Whilst every effort is made to keep prices low, it is sometimes necessary to increase cover prices at short notice. If you are ordering books by post, to save delay it is advisable to phone to confirm the correct price. The number to ring is THE SALES DEPARTMENT 071 (if outside London) 973 9700.

Other great reads from **Red Fox**

Animal stories from Enid Blyton

If you like reading stories about animals, you'll love Enid Blyton's animal books.

THE BIRTHDAY KITTEN

Terry and Tessie want a pet for their birthday – but when the big day comes, they're disappointed.

ISBN 0 09 924100 5   £1.99

THE BIRTHDAY KITTEN and
THE BOY WHO WANTED A DOG

A great value two-books-in-one containing two stories about children and their lovable pets.

ISBN 0 09 977930 7   £2.50

HEDGEROW TALES

Go on a journey through the woodlands and fields and meet the fascinating animals who live there.

ISBN 0 09 980880 3   £2.50

MORE HEDGEROW TALES

A second set of animal stories packed with accurate details.

ISBN 0 09 980880 3   £2.50

Other great reads from **Red Fox**

Magical books from Enid Blyton

Enter the world of fairyland with the magical stories of Enid Blyton – and enjoy tales of goblins, pixies, fairies and all sorts of strange and wonderful things.

UP THE FARAWAY TREE

If you climb to the top of the Faraway Tree, you can reach all sorts of wonderful places . . .

ISBN 0 09 942720 6   £2.50

THE GOBLIN AEROPLANE AND OTHER STORIES

Jill and Robert are working outside when they are whisked away on a strange adventure . . .

ISBN 0 09 973590 3   £2.50

HOLIDAY STORIES

A lovely collection of stories with some magical characters.

ISBN 0 09 987850 X   £1.99

THE LITTLE GREEN IMP AND OTHER STORIES

An enchanting collection of stories about some very special people – including the mischievous green imp.

ISBN 0 09 938940 1   £1.50

RUN-ABOUT'S HOLIDAY

Run-About is Robin and Betty's magical friend – and life is never dull when he's around!

ISBN 0 09 926040 9   £1.50

THE FIRST GREEN GOBLIN STORYBOOK

When three goblins team up offering to help *anyone* do *anything* life becomes full of adventures for them . . .

ISBN 0 09 993700 X   £2.99

THE ENID BLYTON NEWSLETTER

Would you like to receive The Enid Blyton Newsletter? It has lots of news about Enid Blyton books, videos, plays, etc. There are also puzzles and a page for your letters. It is published three times a year and is free for children who live in the United Kingdom and Ireland.

If you would like to receive it for a year, please write to: The Enid Blyton Newsletter, PO Box 357, London, WC2N 6QB, sending your name and address. (UK and Ireland only)